Fiona Walker lives in Worcestershire with her partner and two children, plus an assortment of horses and dogs. Visit Fiona's website at www.fionawalker.com.

THE SUMMER WEDDING

Fiona Walker

sphere

SPHERE

First published in Great Britain in 2013 by Sphere
Reprinted 2013 (twice)

A CIP catalogue record for this book
is available from the British Library.

ISBN 978-0-7515-4794-8

Typeset in Plantin by M Rules
Printed and bound in Great Britain by
Clays Ltd, St Ives plc

Papers used by Sphere are from well-managed forests
and other responsible sources.

MIX
Paper from
responsible sources
FSC® C104740

Sphere
An imprint of
Little, Brown Book Group
100 Victoria Embankment
London EC4Y 0DY

An Hachette UK Company
www.hachette.co.uk

www.littlebrown.co.uk

Twenty years ago, I cryptically dedicated my first novel, *French Relations*, to those I love most. This dedication is for the Saint alone, with love beyond words and (tape) measure. Thank you for being my rock, my sage and the best person to giggle with in the world. *Dulcius ex asperis*.

Chapter 1

1991

It was the first day of the autumn term at Old Gate College, the furthest scholarly outpost of the University of London, its walled campus a leafpit of learning that nestled between the pristine golf courses and boutique villages of commuter Surrey.

A new intake of undergraduates was congregating in the great hall of the historic Founders Hall to pay residence fees, some still clinging to the parents who had driven them there, others queuing alone and casting around for friendly faces.

Melanie Holden – known to her friends as 'Laney', from Kent, reading English Literature and Drama, likes Ionesco and Curly-Wurlys, has a cuddly dinosaur called Eric – was trying to radiate confidence, but was way out of her comfort zone, her intimidation compounded when she spotted that term's man bait in a parallel queue. The girl was exquisitely pretty, flicking her burnished curls as she laughed alongside a handsome olive-skinned hunk who looked like a polo player; they could have stepped out of a Ralph Lauren aftershave ad. They made a great deal of noise, giggling and flirting, radiating glamour and talking horses. The girl had a curious accent which Laney couldn't immediately place, possibly South African.

Then a smooth, clipped voice said in her ear, 'She has more eyes following her across the room than a porter in an ocular prosthetics warehouse.'

The oblique joke, delivered with deadpan cool, made her laugh, and she turned to find a handsome stranger, like a highwayman in

1

long leather boots, a floor-length coat and red spotted neckerchief, beside her. The startling light grey eyes were framed with lashes so tangled and dark he just had to be wearing mascara.

They now took a leisurely tour of her body. 'Great dungarees.'

'Actually, it's a playsuit, but thank you.'

'Does that mean you play dirty?'

'It's dry-clean-only, but I'm not.' She grinned. Tall, buxom and fresh-faced, Laney had always preferred icons to fashion trends and, after several seasons of channelling Toyah, she'd recently begun styling herself on *The New Avengers'* Purdey. In truth, the pudding-basin haircut was more Victoria Wood than Joanna Lumley, polo-necks emphasised her wide shoulders and big chest, and cat-suits made her look like Super Mario, but she certainly stood out as individual, and the highwayman's attention was all hers: he couldn't take his eyes off her.

'I must warn you that I'm desperately in love with you already,' he confessed as the queue shuffled forward. 'Your embonpoint is breathtaking. Simon de Montmorency.' He held out a long, thin hand tipped with silver-painted nails.

'Laney Holden.' She shook it, admiring the silk cuffs and the signet ring featuring an S with a crown above it. She had no idea what an 'embonpoint' was, but it sounded wonderfully sophisticated.

'Do you think you could love me too, Laney?' he wondered.

'Oh yes, absolutely.'

'Marvellous. We can be one another's first campus *futuito*.' The glitter in his eye made it clear that *futuito* wasn't an ice-cream flavour. 'What's your room like?'

'I share with a chain-smoking historian called Birgitta.'

'Then we'll go to mine. I have a charming westerly aspect on the fourth floor with Grace Jones posters and a cafetière. If you show me a good time, I'll rustle you up some Arabica afterwards.'

She'd never met anyone like Simon de Montmorency; he had to be the son of mad aristocrats, she decided, and almost certainly gay. As the queue shortened, he kept her in stitches, those pewter eyes focused on her. He was funny, irreverent and fearless, part With-nail, part Noël Coward. Excited to have her first gay friend – an all-girls boarding school in Sussex had limited her opportunities to be a fag hag, which she felt was a thespian rite of passage – she was honoured to be singled out, and disappointed when they had to stop play-flirting to tackle paperwork.

She got appalling giggles when she noticed that the name on his halls of residence bill was Sean Pegg.

'It was printed before I put in my Deed Poll application.' He flicked his curtains of hair out of his eyes.

'Why change your name?'

'Sean was a boring little squirt from Croydon,' he whispered. 'You mustn't tell a soul he ever lived. I was a square Pegg, but now I intend to fill a round Holden.' He reached a warm hand to her cheek and steered her into a short, sweet, smiling kiss. 'Come for a drink. I'm so hopelessly bewitched by you, I'm afraid I'll fluff my seduction without a few tequila chasers for panache.'

'I *love* your coat!' gurgled a voice behind them. It was the man bait, gazing up at Simon with eyes as green as lime cordial. 'You look like a highwayman.'

I thought that. Laney glowered inwardly.

Amid shrieks of delight that they were all studying Drama, the babe was introducing herself as Mia Wilde. Her polo player was now gazing at Laney, his eyes like two Galaxy Minstrels. If Simon was quirkily handsome, this boy was beautiful.

'I'm Leo Devonshire.' He kissed Laney's cheeks. He smelled lovely, of lemony aftershave and expensive shampoo. She guessed being a millionaire's son meant having carte blanche with one's black AmEx at Penhaligon's.

'We're off to get trolleyed,' Mia was saying to Simon, in an accent Laney now realised was more Preston than Pretoria. 'Would you two like to come?'

'We'd be delighted!'

Laney felt a stab of disappointment, but then Simon breathed in

3

her ear, 'Forgive me . . . I have no cash and they look minted. We'll lose them after they've bankrolled a few Jose Cuervos.'

Nevertheless, she noticed his eyes were drawn to Mia's bottom as it disappeared across the room. She could hardly blame him. It was as pert as two scoops on a double cornet, watched by at least half the eyes in the room, the other half fixing on the polo player's high-goal haunches. They were the ultimate rich playthings, Laney decided.

Within minutes her preconceptions about the snaky-haired spoiled brat and her olive-skinned partner were blown sky high as they all stretched out on the sunny grass of the Founders quad drinking pints from the Fall Inn.

Mia Wilde was from Lancashire tenant-farmer stock and had battled to pursue her acting dream instead of taking the veterinary route her parents had preferred for the first family member to make it to university.

'The only theatre they want me to perform in has padded walls with a winch to hold horses upside-down – "Four legs good, five acts bad" is the Wilde motto.'

Huge rows over her choice of course had even led her to leave home a year before. 'I lost my full grant because Dad wouldn't sign the forms, so I deferred my place here and went to live with my boyfriend in London, waitressing to earn the money to study. It took almost a year, but they relented in the end.' She grinned, swigging her Guinness. 'Never work with children and animals, isn't that what they say? I love them both to bits – Dom and me will have loads of pony-mad kids after we've collected a few Olivier Awards for the mantelpiece.'

Laney was shocked: her own daydreams of becoming the next great comedy actress, marrying Alan Rickman and bearing his babies were kept firmly hidden beneath wisecracking cool.

'You have a boyfriend in London?' Leo watched her with eyes as dark as the Guinness, clearly more than a little in love already.

'He's in Yorkshire at the moment.' She stared into her pint, a shadow crossing her exquisite face. 'Dom says I keep men on tight leads, which is his excuse for getting pissed in Leeds when I'm not around.' She looked up at him with that wicked smile. 'He'll be wildly jealous I'm hanging out with such a stud muffin.' She clinked her glass with Leo's. 'I'm made up we're all on the same course – me and Leo only just met in the queue too. He recognised my pendant as an eggbutt and I knew we'd be mates.'

'What's an eggbutt?' Simon's eyebrows shot up. 'Sounds like a sex toy for chickens.'

'It's a horse bit,' explained Laney, who had gone through a pony-mad phase.

'You're in the gang.' Mia grinned. 'Leo's parents were trick riders in a circus. Isn't that amazing?'

'You made that up.' Simon snorted.

Although he looked like a polo player, Leo Devonshire turned out to be a soft-spoken, self-effacing eighteen-year-old from Reading with a passion for musical theatre. His parents had indeed toured together in a circus, although his Russian father now sold pension plans and the family home was a thirties semi in Caversham where his Spanish mother ran a dog-grooming parlour. 'They came to Britain in the sixties with a clapped-out Barreiros lorry and six stallions, and now they have a Vauxhall Cavalier and two Shih Tzus. Mamá wanted me to go to La Complu, the university in Madrid, but when I explained that getting a place here is harder than breeding a perlino horse, they understood.'

'Devonshire's not a very Russian name,' Simon pointed out.

'Dad changed it for their double-act. He's Dmitri Kazak by birth.'

'You must make the most of that *Dr Zhivago* heritage. It's great for chat shows – look at Peter Ustinov. I adore that man. We're distantly related on my mother's side, I believe.'

'So you have Russian blood too?' Mia asked excitedly.

'De Montmorency blood has been mixed by the centrifuge of war and passion through seven continents over many centuries,' Simon said grandly.

Laney tried not to giggle. Wildly jealous that modest Leo could lay claim to being the son of liberty horsemen, Simon kept very quiet about Sean Pegg's upbringing in Croydon, hinting instead at an orphaned childhood, forfeited nobility, penury, scholarships and a de Montmorency curse: 'I too had to fight to get here,' he said. 'The Sorbonne were furious I turned them down, but I hate Paris. It's full of emaciated women carrying dogs around in handbags.'

Laney felt breathless as he rattled out anecdotes and witty one-liners with the speed of his beloved Ustinov. 'The de Montmorency family motto is *"Merda taurorum animas conturbit"*. We all die young and impoverished but, my goodness, we spring-load our short mortal coils to the full. *Corripe cervisiam!*' He raised his pint.

'What does that mean?' asked Mia.

'Seize the beer!' He downed it in one, giving Laney a long, hungry look that both confused and excited her. She couldn't fathom him at all, especially when he leaned forward to whisper in Latin, *'Frequentasne hunc locum?'*

She raised an eyebrow and his eyes didn't leave hers, the pupils so large and dark that the pale irises were just silver linings. She could suddenly hear her heartbeat thudding in her ears and felt a twinge deep in her groin, the same unfamiliar, exquisite pull she'd experienced necking a rugby hunk at her cousin's eighteenth.

'It means "Do you come here often?"' Leo translated kindly. 'I did A-level Latin. And I think your family motto is bullshit, Simon.'

Simon laughed delightedly. *'Et tu, Kazak?'* He turned back to Laney, silver linings glinting. 'Don't tell me you're the unacknowledged daughter of a Calcutta slum nun who walled you up in a cave like Antigone and begged you not to come here?'

Laney was almost too embarrassed to admit that she'd divided her cosseted childhood years between a picture-postcard Kentish oast-house and a Blytonesque boarding school, and that her parents, both GPs who indulged in am-dram in their spare time, had encouraged her to study theatre arts. Her biggest struggle in life thus far had been shutting her suitcase to go on holiday.

Her new friends were clearly astonished that somebody as boringly middle-class had been accepted on to the famously edgy Old Gate Drama course.

'You're too posh for us, Holden!' they joked, then insisted on pronouncing 'Laney' in cut-glass tones for the rest of the afternoon.

Eventually they moved on to the Students' Union, where a freshers' disco was revving up, the girls diving straight into the loos to salvage laughter-washed mascara.

'Are you and Si an item?' Mia asked, borrowing Laney's ultra-fashionable matte-brown lipstick.

'Steady on! We only met five minutes before I met you.'

'He *seriously* fancies you.'

'But isn't he gay?'

'About as gay as you are, I'd say.' She turned with a swish of long hair, purring seductively in Madonna tones, 'Wanna get it on, Laaaaney?'

Laney giggled and returned to her mascara, but her belly was now squirming deliciously at the thought of her wild highwayman wanting to take her to his bed for *futuito* ... whatever that was. 'What about you and Leo? Do you fancy him?'

'He's sweet, but I'm totally mad about Dom.'

'Your boyfriend in Yorkshire?'

'He's called Dominic Masters. He's a professional actor,' she boasted, pretty face lighting up. 'We met at the National Youth Theatre and I played Cressida to his Troilus. He's Yorkshire born and bred – we're the Wars of the Roses, us.' She fished around in her crocheted bag, drawing out a photograph of a craggy youth with intense blue eyes. His face was powerful, with high cheekbones and white-blond hair. He probably played drug pushers and murderers in *The Bill*, Laney decided.

'How long have you been together?'

'Four years – I was fifteen when we met and he was about to turn five.'

Laney was horrified.

'Dom's birthday's February the twenty-ninth.' Mia chortled. 'He'll be six next year, but he's twenty-three really. He graduated from RADA this year,' she explained proudly. 'He had three job offers straight off – one a movie role – but he took the season at Agitprop Theatre in Leeds to stay close to his roots. He's fierce on politics. When he won the Bancroft Gold Medal for best actor in his year, he reckoned they'd only awarded it to him because he's a miner's son, so he gave it to another actor he thought deserved it more. Dom won it on merit, but that's the way he is. He's a bloody-minded sod.' She smiled fondly, but the shadow crossed her face again. 'I'm going to miss him something rotten.'

'I bet he misses you just as much.' Laney patted her arm reassuringly.

She smiled wryly. 'He's a method actor. Right now he's too busy being a druid in a Howard Brenton play to notice I'm gone.'

'Then we'll build a stone circle round your room in halls to lure him here.'

'You're so lovely. I hope we'll be mates, you and me.'

'Me and Mia.' Laney hoped so too.

'That's sound. You and Mia, Laney, are going to be best mates.'

'Of course we will,' Laney agreed happily, wondering if it would test the new friendship to ask her to say the thing about Simon fancying her again.

But Mia was already rattling on, wired from first-day nerves and too much Guinness. 'I can't tell you how terrified I've been about coming here. I wanted to flunk it and stay with Dom, but he's so proud of me getting this place. He told me to act the part when I arrived. I'm all right when I'm acting, it's being myself I'm lousy at – the oldest dressing-room cliché,' she said. 'And I promised myself I wouldn't drink too much, flirt with anybody or talk about him, and that's all I've done. I'm normally not this daft ... Well, not always ... I know I can be a soppy cow – my friends back home say all I do is bang on about him – but they're still just into horses and they don't get how a lad can change your life. He's my world, you know?'

Something about the way she said it told Laney that this ravishing chatterbox stud magnet really was madly in love, the sort of love she'd yet to experience. She studied the photograph of the fierce-eyed, belligerent militant and hoped he wouldn't call Leo out.

He certainly wouldn't have wanted to see the suggestive way that Mia and Leo were soon grinding their hips together to Happy Mondays and the Shaman, their exclusivity clear for all to see, heedless of other hopeful male undergraduates showing off their dance moves as they tried to attract Mia's attention.

By contrast, Laney and Simon bopped about like a pair of lady pensioners in nylon frocks trying a jitterbug at a tea dance and wary of electric shocks if they touched. They'd both stopped drinking anything more than water, and Laney couldn't remember when she'd last eaten, but she wasn't remotely hungry. Simon still couldn't take his eyes off her. That ticklish feeling in her groin was back, the gorgeous pull of lust, teasing like a finger on a drink can, eager to release the fizz.

She guessed Simon was biding his time, waiting for the perfect song, and she was determined to match his poise despite an urge to shimmy seductively closer with comedy aplomb. He had the smooth patter and Byronic mini-series looks, whereas she was more Joan Sims than Joan Collins, but the mirth in those pale grey eyes was giving her knock-out doses of confidence as her excitement mounted. At last she'd met somebody who got off on laughter too; they could share the joke of their overwhelming mutual attraction.

When Right Said Fred announced that they were too sexy for their shirts, Simon's pale eyes rolled in frustration. Beside them, Leo and Mia were miming a strange, shirt-removing theatrical interpretation. Laney and Simon edged away, their eyes entangled. Just as she was about to gesture that she was going to get another drink, a dancer knocked her against him. His arms closed around her and, before she knew what was happening, she felt his lips against hers. At that moment, Laney wouldn't have been surprised if they had started to crackle with blue strobes of electric charge, like two sci-fi characters in a space transporter. Simon was a Don Juan of kissing, confident, unhurried, unstoppable, oblivious to everything around him. She kissed him back, blown away by the head-rush. She'd never imagined her body could respond like this, a great coil of lust rising from her solar plexus, circling around Simon, pulling his torso against hers, catching her breath in his mouth and guiding her tongue towards his.

Oh God, I'm snogging to Right Said Fred, she thought vaguely, but it no longer mattered. She couldn't hear the music over her racing blood. The finger was tug-tug-tugging at her ring-pull.

Simon tore himself away, his eyes almost all pupils, the silver linings a glittering eclipse, the whites bright in the ultraviolet disco lights, glowing along with his smiling teeth.

'I think we should go back to my room, don't you?' he mouthed.

Simon's room was a romantic little garret up in the eaves of the fourth floor of Founders, with bare-board floors and peephole casement windows, making Laney think of *La Bohème*. He didn't turn on the main light, just lit the gas fire so the room glowed orange. Despite the heat and her reddening cheeks, Laney couldn't stop her teeth chattering.

'There's something I should tell you,' she blustered before they started kissing again and she lost the power of speech. 'I'm a bit inexperienced.'

He cupped her burning face in his hands. 'Me too.'

Yet when his lips moved against hers, she knew he had to have diplomas and degrees in love-making compared to her. He seemed to know exactly what to do to turn her on, every finger he laid on her making nerve endings leap with unfamiliar, greedy ecstasy.

'I'm a virgin,' she gulped, pulling away.

'We're none of us far off that.' He started to unbutton her play-suit, breath catching as he discovered her pink satin bra.

'Big puppies,' she said before she could stop herself, then wanted to die of embarrassment. What had happened to her brain? She sounded like an eager dog breeder welcoming a litter of Newfoundlands.

'You. Are. Beautiful,' Simon breathed, his eyes reaching up for hers again, mouth following to her lips.

Her face still flamed, ring-pull twanging below, but her gargantuan bra was a monster of underwiring and heavy elastic scaffolding. She'd always longed to be a small-breasted totty, like Mia, who could get away with thin-strap lace teddies, but her boobs were huge. Her mother had marched her into M&S for regular fittings since she was thirteen, refusing to give in to tearful pleading for anything fashionable.

Yet Simon seemed delighted with her mammoth satiny orbs and their sturdy truss, which he was exploring for hooks.

Eager to get in on the act, she reached for his shirt buttons.

'There's something I must tell you too,' he breathed. 'I'm a total fake, but I never fake orgasms and neither must you. Do you promise?'

Laney suddenly had the unbuttoning skills of a toddler. His breath on her neck and his fingers against her back were making the ring-pull tighten in her groin; she was certain an all-consuming climax was only moments away.

'We'll work out how to do this.' He kissed his way from one side of her throat to the other, still searching for the bra fastening while edging her towards his cassette deck. 'We are going to be so good, you and me. We'll have a double first in Foreplay soon. But tonight I am a selfish bastard and I want to get this bloody lovely bra off and get naked and naughty. I hope you feel the same way.'

'I do,' she breathed – and then, realising this sounded embarrassingly like a marriage vow, added enthusiastically, 'Let's shag!' which sounded far worse, but thankfully he'd just pressed Play on his stereo and Bowie growled, 'Let's dance!', which covered her shame.

Together, they hauled her bra hurriedly over her head.

'Oh, Laney.' His eyes glowed as her breasts spilled free, buoyant and pink-nippled, resting on a creamy curve of midriff. 'Laaaaaney. I am so in love with you.'

As Bowie put on his red shoes and danced the blues, the conversation stopped and all sorts of gasping, panting, laughing and groaning sound effects started up, from which Laney could barely identify her own voice, just as the sticky, slippery confusion of kisses, tongue, buttons, arms, zips and legs became a glorious muddle of excitement and disrobing. Opening a condom was a new-found land, as was the amazing upstanding member protruding from Simon that he rolled it on to. The fizz that was now foaming around the ring-pull in her belly was rapidly reaching maximum pressure. She'd never seen an erection close to, and knowing that this one, so beautifully long, smooth and sheathed, was all for her was overwhelming: it looked far too big to fit into her, yet the infinite possibilities it bestowed brought a total thrill.

I'm a sensible middle-class girl from Kent about to lose my cherry on my first night at university, she reminded herself as Simon kissed his way joyfully up her body and angled for entry. I should be so ashamed.

But looking up at him, her hands on his chest, she had no doubt whatsoever that she wanted this to happen as much as he did. Another wave of excitement shuddered through her. Across the room, the gas fire puttered furiously and Bowie was replaced by Grace Jones singing 'Slave to the Rhythm'.

Simon's face was more compelling than ever as it hovered above hers, the grey eyes glittering, his laughing cavalier mouth suddenly serious as he tipped his head to touch her lips with his and breathe a warning: 'This might hurt, my beautiful girl.'

At first, as he began to part the curtains on the Holden stage debut, Laney panicked that he would never get past Security, that she was a freak of nature who was too uptight to perform despite the slippery wetness that was trying to lap Simon in like a moon tide. But when he pushed through the door, she almost burst into laughter, blinded by sensation, biting her lip to stop herself talking nonsense because she had no idea what her lines were and didn't trust herself to improvise. It felt strange and amazing being so full of Simon in body as well as mind.

As they bucked and plunged, Laney wasn't sure how much of her 'Oh, oh, oh' was actually 'Ow, ow, ow' because pain, pleasure and newness were mixed so tightly that it was impossible to separate them, a crescendo of such closeness and intensity that she thought they'd never be able to peel their bodies apart.

Yet no sooner had she begun to get her head around the fact that he was inside her than he murmured, 'I can't hold on … you are just too gorgeous … forgive me, gorgeous Laney! I love you!'

Which were the first words Laney heard when waking up in Simon's bed on her first full day at university. 'I love you, gorgeous Laney. You are a splendiferous shag. Can we do it again all day?'

'Are you bisexual, Demon?'

He closed one eye, and she felt her breath catch. Questioning a guy's sexuality the morning after the night before was right up there in the Melanie Holden Anthology of Shame, alongside sitting on the family hamster, cheating to get Brownies badges and tearfully demanding to be taken home at 2 a.m. on her first sleepover.

But then she heard a soft laugh. '*Demon?*'

'De Montmorency … De Mon … Demon,' she explained, blushing deeply.

'I like that.' He stretched across the pillow to kiss her long and hard, breaking away just as she was becoming cross-eyed with lust. 'And I love you. I first fell in love with you at the group interview with that awful crimped, crazy-colour hair and a kilt that showed off your great legs. You were so funny and sexy I thought I'd collapse a lung laughing and never sleep again.'

'You were there?' She gazed at him in wonder. She was certain she would have remembered someone as theatrical and beddable as her highwayman at the first nerve-racking Old Gate workshop – held to select the best candidates to go forward for interview.

'Sean Pegg was there.' He didn't blink. 'You won't remember him. But you'll never forget me.' Smiling, he started to kiss her again and, to her wriggling consternation, he kissed ever lower.

'I'm not clean,' she complained.

'We're together now. We can be as dirty as we like,' he insisted, burying his lips and tongue between her legs.

'They say the worst thing about oral sex is the view, don't they?' she groaned, writhing with shame and pleasure.

'It's breathtaking, trust me' – he raised his head briefly, grey eyes amused – 'but I was always taught not to speak with my mouth full, so stop cracking jokes and tell me what feels good.'

'That does,' she assured him, as he resumed licking and kissing his way around her erogenous zones, although she couldn't resist wisecracking between compliments: 'Cunnilingus and fellatio sound like characters from *commedia dell'arte*, don't you think? Ooooh, yes . . . up a bit . . . We had a beagle once that gave tongue when it found a scent, but my mother got muddled up and said to a neighbour, "He's always giving head on walks—"'

He reached up to cover her mouth just as the lapping waves of pleasure reached a point where she was hanging from her upturned boat, ready to let go.

'Is this coming?' she asked, lips moving against his fingers, one of which inadvertently slid up her left nostril.

'I think it's the giggles,' he said, eyes bright, 'but it's damned close. God, you are beautiful.' He licked the swollen clitoris again, his tongue a soft, caressing beat.

Years of fiddling at home had led Laney to many an orgasm, but this was no longer a private shame: it was a shared delight, a landmark moment that made happiness reverberate around her body like a loose firework as she came laughing, a burst of weightless pleasure.

'Never leave me.' He kissed his way up to her mouth, his tongue salted with her own body.

'Why me?' she had to ask.

'If it takes me until the day I die, I'll make you realise how perfect you are,' he breathed against her breastbone. 'Besides, you have by far the best tits of any girl on campus.' She smiled down as he cupped one and kissed its pink nipple. 'You unleashed the demon in me, Laney. I am reincarnated.'

His cock was already hard against her thigh once more. Laney reached down to stroke it with her fingers, amazed at its satiny smoothness. 'Third-leg Pegg left at least one lovely legacy.' She started humming 'Jake the Peg'.

The warm lips were removed from her breast and her fingers were left clutching thin air as he rolled away, muttering, 'Sean Pegg is dead, OK? He pegged out.'

Aware that she'd upset him, Laney edged after him to press kisses to his bare shoulder, but on finding a tiny tattoo there bearing the same crested S monogram as his ring, she couldn't let the subject drop. 'How do your parents feel about that?'

'We'll need a clairvoyant to find that out,' he said, after a pause. 'They're dead too.'

Appalled, she wrapped her arms around him. 'How long?'

'Four years. Mum had cancer – she died within three months of diagnosis. Not long afterwards my father had a heart attack. He was dead by the time the ambulance arrived ... We'd been watching *Casualty*, which I always thought ironic.' For once there was no glib joke. 'I'd rather not talk about it. They're all dead now, including Sean. The Peggs have pegged it. You are my brave new world,' he started to kiss the little moles on her chest, 'and we've just landed here together.'

Laney was overwhelmed by such compassion and desire that she couldn't immediately speak. Then, without warning, those silver-lined eyes snapped up and watched her face as his hand slipped between her legs. 'Stick with me, baby, and we'll achieve brave new world domination.'

She gasped, her slippery, eager welcome taking even her by surprise as it drew his fingers straight in. Then she laughed, reaching for another condom. 'Let's be brazen Huxleys.'

Soon known to all as 'Demon', Simon cut a flamboyant dash even in a Drama Department already full of talented eccentrics. At his side, Laney blossomed, making friends easily with her warmth and humour, her obvious love for Simon silencing all the cynics who claimed that a relationship started on the first day of university could never last, although they still muttered behind their hands that the formidable duo wouldn't make it into a second term, particularly when it became obvious that they both had serious commitment problems. This was nothing to do with their relationship, which was strong, honest and close, but they overcommitted to absolutely everything else. They auditioned or volunteered backstage for every Drama Department studio production, became active members of campus arts clubs and debating societies, went clubbing with friends at least once a week, caught the best of London's stand-up and theatre, and were soon nominated unofficial social secretaries because they were so good at organising get-togethers.

Simon was one of those frustrating individuals who could party and screw all night, spill into an exam half cut and still achieve the highest mark of his year. And he charmed absolutely everybody, from tutors to fellow undergraduates; doors opened and adoring audiences formed everywhere as he breezed through tutorials and workshops. He never seemed to need much sleep, and his ability to knock back vast amounts of alcohol, dope and sugary black coffee to keep going far outweighed Laney's wimpy limits. Her addiction to the things he could do to her body, however, was so great that she couldn't keep away even when she desperately needed rest. Laney was studying English as well as Drama, which meant more lectures, tutorials and essays. Having a boyfriend meant lots of delicious overnight love-making. As a result, she hardly slept; the weight dropped off and her physical self-confidence soared. Mia and Leo worried she was going to burn out.

'You've got to calm down, chuck,' Mia advised, with the serenity of one whose long-distance relationship meant she was totally up to date with her work and could give her all to a spell-binding performance as Stella in *A Streetcar Named Desire* each evening, a role that had already marked her out as a huge talent.

'It'll look good on my CV,' Laney defended her Pro Plus- and caffeine-fuelled lifestyle.

'Staying up all night smoking dope with Demon?' tutted Leo, who made it no secret that he disapproved of Simon's debauched lifestyle.

'Well, I am taking *joint* honours . . .'

Making love with Simon was the learning curve to which she dedicated every night. They were both improving fast, and while she still giggled a great deal, she also climaxed with regularity, intensity and delight as Simon hung on longer, relaxing into the warm welcome of her body. He had no inhibitions and an amazing imagination – she teasingly nicknamed him Budgie because he especially loved mirrors and toys – and was happy to play for hours upon end, which made for an exciting voyage of discovery as they tried every position, exploring different angles and depths, penetration sensations that left Laney reeling and weak-legged, her body coursing with aftershocks from being brimful of Simon, orgasm and love. She grew ever more bold and daring, overwhelmed by the emotion she'd always believed frightened men off, but which Simon lapped up. He was incredibly tender, for all his foppish wit, and told her constantly that she was the epitome of perfection. Yet he refused to be drawn any more on the subject of losing his parents so young, insisting that Sean's years of counselling had been enough.

'This is the best therapy I could hope for,' he insisted each time he took her to his bed, and Laney's heart and body unfolded amid the creased sheets.

Unlike Simon, Laney had always had to study very hard to achieve good academic marks. As a result of spreading her time thin and her legs wide, her first-term grades were mediocre at best, even though Mia lent her her notes and provided helpful crammers over tea in her room. 'I know your relationship is now officially on the Old Gate Chemistry curriculum under "exothermic reactions", Laney chuck, but you're here to read Drama,' she warned. 'We could all tell Simon had his hand up your skirt in this morning's Jacobean Tragedy lecture, and that sneezing fit you had was definitely phoney.'

Laney blushed crimson. 'People knew?'

'Of course they did. You know how many girls on our course envy you Simon's five-finger exercises? There's a waiting list.'

In fact, the only queue longer than the one waiting for Demon to be single again was the queue waiting for Mia Wilde to dump her macho northern boyfriend.

Chapter 2

With her exquisite face and petite figure, amazing bronze hair and deep green eyes, Mia Wilde had quickly become the source of a huge number of undergraduate crushes. She soon had more gentleman callers than an 0898 number, more dinner dates than a restaurant critic, and never had to buy her own Guinness.

'I don't know why you always say yes,' grumbled Leo, who resented the interruption to their cosy alliance of evenings spent reading and swotting together.

'I like studying people,' Mia explained simply. She'd always found human behaviour fascinating, constantly alert to habits and idiosyncrasies she could use in her acting, and loved nothing more than to talk theatre, politics, literature and even farming, her knowledge and interest making her beguiling company. Vivacious, attentive and flirtatious when drunk, Mia was accused of giving out mixed messages to her band of male admirers, but she genuinely saw them all as 'mates'. Her love was for her soulmate, Dominic Masters. Mia's wannabe campus beaux sulked like mad whenever his battered Triumph motorbike was parked in a bay outside Founders Hall, which was rare because he lived two hundred miles away. His acting commitments afforded little time off, not even allowing him to watch Mia captivating her audience in the Tennessee Williams.

'It's like he's deliberately avoiding her world here,' Leo confided to Laney. 'The only time he's been around I was at home for the weekend, and you and Demon were off at some rave.'

Laney's first encounter with the legendary boyfriend was not good. She'd trotted to Mia's room late one night with HobNobs, mildly pissed and in need of advice over a petty row with Simon, but Dominic Masters had opened the door wearing nothing but Mia's pink bathrobe. He'd looked every bit as frightening as he had in the photograph, and a great deal sexier. Testosterone rose off him like fumes from a smelting plant, and it was pretty clear what he'd just been doing. Simon would have laughed, but he looked furious.

'You must be Dom!' she said brightly. 'I'm Laney. Is Mia around?'

'It's almost midnight.' Dom's voice was both furious and fabulous, a deep Yorkshire purr that came from the very base of his throat. No dialect coach could have created that: it was innate.

'Is something wrong, chuck?' Mia called from the bed, in which she was wearing nothing but a Paisley quilt and an orgasmic flush.

'No! Just thought you might be free for a chat, but—'

'We're trying to get some sleep.' He closed the door with a bang.

'I didn't know he was going to be here!' she grumbled to Mia the following day after Dom had set off for Leeds.

'Neither did I.' Mia shuddered with delight, having barely got out of bed in twelve hours.

Laney secretly thought Dominic Masters had been born to play Heathcliff, as antisocially fierce and instinctive as Mia was loyal, wilful and joyful. After that, she made one or two attempts to draw friends and lover together when he visited, but it was never an easy fit. A committed method actor, Dom lived so deep within his roles he was impossible to read. The others found him intimidating: dedicated to his profession, he seemed so much more grown-up than them.

Dominic might have had few birthdays, but he was no longer the truant who had been expelled from two schools before his talent proved a ticket to freedom from the bleak prospects offered in a Yorkshire colliery town. Now he was being tipped as the next Sean Bean, and smouldered with aloof self-confidence and misanthropy. He seemed to resent Mia's new friends' camp, high-jinks camaraderie and showed no desire to join in raucous pub crawls or cosy tea-and-toast parties.

The close-knit gang resigned themselves to the fact that their bubbly, sensitive friend preferred to keep them all at arm's length when Dom was around. The couple rarely left her room, which she insisted was her choice: 'I want to keep him all to myself. If I could wear his cock inside me all day, I would.'

Laney tried to hide how shocked she was at Mia's earthy confession. She and Simon might behave like randy stoats in private – and occasionally get carried away in lectures – but she never discussed the intimate details, even with Mia. It felt too sacred. Yet Mia, who worshipped Dom, was open and unapologetic about her desire for him. 'When we were first together, he insisted we wait until I was sixteen before we slept together . . . By then, I just had to close my eyes, think of him, touch myself and come. I still do. He's hung like a Holstein bull.' She winked naughtily.

Theirs was an extraordinary bond that went far beyond sex: they shared hours of calls each week and exchanged long letters, and Mia pined after each all-too-brief visit, crying on Laney's shoulder as she struggled to stick with the course that separated them.

'You have to,' Laney urged. 'You're so bright and work so hard, and everyone's saying you're the best actress the department's ever seen. Dom's obviously really proud of you.'

'He says I'm too clever for him,' she sniffed, 'but he knows more about theatre than anyone here. He's obsessed with it. And his acting is out of this world.' To prove her point, she insisted all her friends trek to Leeds by train to watch him preview in Agitprop's new adaptation of Emile Zola's *Germinal,* in which he scorched the stage as the idealist miner and activist Etienne. Only Leo remained unimpressed: 'Give me *Les Mis* any day – at least it has a few good tunes.'

None of Mia's university friends was more disparaging about the brooding Dominic than Leo, who saw him as wholly unworthy of Mia's open-hearted *joie de vivre*. Leo was an inseparable part of the Old Gate Campus foursome, he and Mia the Tom and Barbara to Laney and Simon's Margot and Jerry, a pair of joyful self-dramatists with a pragmatic edge and plenty of get-up-and-go. Leo doted on Mia, his beautiful, kind-hearted muse for whom he cooked, made clothes and even famously procured a horse – hiring it from a local stables with money earned from his weekend job so that she could enjoy a few hours in the saddle. She stood up for him against the sneering rugger buggers who plagued his corridor with late-night revelling, cheered him through bouts of homesickness, spent hours wandering London galleries companionably at his side and sang hits from his favourite musicals with him. A sincere, hard-working perfectionist, Leo had an enviably level head and rarely got angry, but Dom's unannounced visits tested his patience: Mia would cancel their planned nights out at the drop of a motorcycle helmet.

'He is incredibly selfish,' he grumbled to Laney after yet another aborted theatre trip. 'He has almost no time off over Christmas and is expecting Mia to spend her holiday chasing him around the country on tour.'

'Long-distance relationships rarely last through university,' she reassured him, without conviction. 'They'll probably split up over Christmas . . . as indeed might Simon and I.' He'd accepted an invitation to spend Christmas with her family, but was already kicking up a stink about the separate bedrooms and smoking ban.

When the Old Gate students returned from the festive break, Mia was more loved-up than ever, wafting around a snow-caked campus with fresh-faced happiness.

'Don't tell me Santa gave you a pony?' Leo asked miserably.

'Dom took me to see Ned's Atomic Dustbin at Brixton Academy – I love that band.' Her boyfriend's musical taste was a long way from the old Broadway shows Leo adored, and while Mia insisted she loved both, she clearly found hard-core rock far sexier, along with pretty rocks. 'He gave me this.' She flashed a silver ring with a huge green stone on the middle finger of her right hand. 'Green opal – it's for energy.'

'We should club together to get Laney one,' he sighed.

Laney had returned from her Christmas holiday exhausted from frantically copulating with Simon in the garden shed behind the family veggie patch at every opportunity, and the furious arguments in the oast-house kitchen because the Holdens had refused to let her go to an illegal rave in Wiltshire with him for New Year.

The term kicked off with auditions for the big spring departmental production, *The House of Bernarda Alba*, and Mia read for the part of Adela with such spell-binding conviction that nobody was in doubt she would be cast in the central role, the youngest of five sisters oppressed by their power-crazed mother. The play was being directed by Professor Andrew Crutchley (or Prof. Crotch as most students called him), who had adapted his own translation of

Lorca's work, eager to explore the themes of sexual repression, lust and female beauty with his all-female cast.

The title role went to Laney, whose initial euphoria at being given such a meaty part was soon overshadowed by the realisation that Prof. Crotch was angling his interpretation entirely around Adela, with Bernarda featuring as little more than a comedy grotesque. His translation pared her part to almost nothing, and when rehearsals began she wasn't even called for the first fortnight.

By week four, Laney's lines had halved again and Mia's rehearsal calls had doubled, although she seemed grateful to throw herself into the role, increasingly on edge because Dom kept cancelling visits: any free time he had during the final run in Leeds was spent visiting directors and auditioning for new roles.

'His agent's got lots lined up for after the Agitprop season,' she explained – before skipping a Lorca rehearsal to sneak up to London and meet him after a group casting.

She returned late that night even more troubled, rushing to Laney's room for a heart-to-heart only to find she and Simon were out partying. Instead she trailed across the building to visit Leo, who made toast on his gas fire and spread it thickly with his mother's home-made marmalade, which contained oranges from her family's farm in Spain.

'Dom wanted to see *Death and the Maiden* while he was in town,' she told him shakily. 'It was amazing, but I needed to talk about the future, not sit in return seats three rows apart at the Royal Court. Then we . . . ' She blushed.

'What?'

She shook her head, knowing that the sort of information she could have shared with Laney tonight was not for Leo's ears. He wouldn't want to know that she and Dom had been so desperate for one another that she'd insisted they enact a naughty loo-cubicle fantasy during the interval, only to find it a disinfectant-scented anti-climax. The rush, tension and a split condom had kept her usual ecstatic response infuriatingly on the brim, and it still bubbled hungrily now, along with a churning anxiety like indigestion.

She licked jammy toast crumbs from her lips and studied Leo's beauty, wishing he was Dom, but they were oil and water: Leo was all softness, so calm, tactile and kind – most girls' dream boyfriend, although she had never had any predatory signals from him as she did from other guys; either Leo was biding his time or he wasn't interested in taking her to bed. Most importantly, Mia sensed he understood that she loved Dom in a way that entertained no rivals, and for all his disapproval, he'd never do anything to threaten her happiness. Right now, she needed to talk too badly to care that she was trying to keep her burning oil alight in icy water.

'I'm frightened he's going to outgrow me,' she blurted.

'Like a pony?'

'If you like.' She chewed a nail. Leo moved her hand away gently, having battled all the past term to stop her biting her nails. It was a sign that a big worrier hid behind the joking, flirty performer. 'I'm so scared of losing him,' she went on. 'I hate us being so far apart. He's such a workaholic, he gets lost in it.'

'And you deserve a Mia-holic.' Leo sighed, fetching a bottle of Christmas brandy from his book cupboard and pouring slugs into espresso cups. 'I'm merely a humble trainee in holism and tortured genius, but I can offer you some advice: dump him now and you'll spare yourself the heartache of growing out of *him* when you get a Hollywood break and he's still looking back in anger in the provinces.' He was gratified that she got the joke, laughing in mock outrage.

'Nobody else could get away with saying that, you bastard!'

It wasn't the warm, supportive confessional with Laney that she'd craved, but in many ways the pep talk served Mia better. Afterwards, she vowed to stay positive and give her all to rehearsing the Lorca play, pouring her passion into the role and her love into long, heartfelt letters, which Dominic rewarded with postcards from every destination he visited in search of work, each one saying, 'I love you' and 'Wish you were here' in his distinctive, spiky hand.

'Hardly Catullus,' Leo said bitchily, but he made no more pleas for her to end the relationship. Mia lined the postcards up on her mantelpiece in order of preference, the London landmarks leading the way.

Even when Dom bailed out of a promised visit on Valentine's Day to attend a recall in the Midlands, she remained optimistic. 'It's something big, he says. He's not allowed to talk about it.'

'Don't tell me they're bringing *Crossroads* back?' Laney suggested. She thought Dominic's small, apologetic Valentine's card, featuring a Picasso sketch of a horse, very shabby compared to Simon's vast hand-made one to her, or indeed to the tens of cards Mia's admirers had crammed in her pigeonhole, many of which she had yet to open. 'He'd better be here to support you in the Lorca with the biggest bunch of roses this side of Covent Garden.'

'It's the last week of *Arturo Ui*. He's got performances every evening,' Mia admitted.

'Can't he throw a sickie? He has an understudy, doesn't he?'

'That would be totally unprofessional,' Mia said, but it was obvious she was desperate for him to see her in the role everyone thought was likely to win her a professional career. 'I'll talk to him when I go up to his birthday party. That's on his day off,' she added, before Laney could mutter about hypocrisy. 'I'll be staying over.'

'Poor you.' Laney shuddered, recalling mention of the unheated flat Dom shared with his fellow cast. 'Lots of intense actors and politicos banging on about the recession.'

'Actually, the party's at his dad's house.' Mia had a very soft spot for Dom's racing-mad father, a retired miner who suffered from emphysema. Increasingly house-bound by his illness, he doted on her and the regular cheery postcards she sent from college featuring horses and little bits of news.

'Surely Dom could come down for a rehearsal?' Laney had

already block-booked tickets for friends and family. 'Does he even know you have this part?'

'Of course,' Mia scoffed. 'I talk to him about it all the time on the phone, and he's really helped me get into the role. He's hugely proud, but this *Arturo Ui* run is exhausting.'

'No more exhausting than you running from Prof. Crotch's wandering hands. Is it true he's asked you to go naked in the final act?'

'He thinks the part demands it.'

'What does he know? My part demands lines, but he's cut most of those.'

'I said no.'

'That's about all I say in the entire play.'

Unusually for an Old Gate Drama academic, Professor Andrew Crutchley liked things of tradition and beauty. Despite its heavy sexual symbolism, his *House of Bernarda Alba* was set to be among the tamest of recent departmental productions. At the next rehearsal, Prof. Crotch compromised on Adela's nudity, suggesting Mia wear a transparent negligé. He also told Laney that she would be wearing a fat-suit 'to demonstrate Bernarda's character is a physical as well as a psychological grotesque'.

'It's Mia I feel sorry for,' she complained to Simon. 'Prof. Crotch is such a lech and he's taking total advantage of her to stage his own fantasy.'

'You are my eternal fantasy and I will lech after you in a fat-suit like mad,' Simon growled. 'You've lost too much weight. I love every inch of you and hate to see such magnificence scaled down.'

Simon was designing the set, but when Laney asked if he was inviting anyone to see the show, he gave her his charming smile. 'You know the answer to that.' He fobbed off those fellow undergraduates who were agog to see the de Montmorency clan in the flesh with a dismissive drawl: 'I've banned them.' Only Laney knew the truth about his parents, and he remained tight-lipped on the subject even with her.

In the six months since he'd arrived at Old Gate College, Simon might have done a brilliant job at convincing his fellow Drama students of the de Montmorency birthright, a mysterious past, unfashionably right-wing opinions and erudite wit, but they remained unconvinced about his sexuality and many assumed he would come out sooner or later, despite his almost symbiotic attachment to Laney, whom some unkindly dismissed as a mother figure. His flamboyance confused people.

The Lorca set was being constructed in the cavernous workshops alongside the theatre, and Simon had long since replaced his highwayman's leather with a Russian officer's woollen greatcoat and wolf-fur trapper hat stolen from the costume store. They were the only things capable of keeping out the cold in the old metal hangar where he worked to bring his amazing creation to life. His designs marked him out as a rare talent, being brilliantly engineered as well as beautiful. The design for the Lorca set was dominated by a ten-foot-tall, intricately carved crucifix which, with Daliésque ingenuity, came apart throughout the play into chairs, table, pews and bed. To cheer himself on through the late nights, Simon had painted I LOVE LANEY on the back of every backcloth and stage flat, to which some wag soon added a B and an R to make BLARNEY.

'They can think what they like,' he muttered, but the rumour that his relationship was less than genuine had intensified since his inclusion on Prof. Crotch's Lorca crew. The professor was well known within the department for liking things played straight, with the notable exception of his male cast and crew. Notoriously eager to claim *droit de seigneur* with his female leads, he always went to great lengths to ensure that very few heterosexual men were ever involved in his plays, believing that his own sex appeal would take a boost if he cleared the field of potential rivals. To be branded one of Prof. Crotch's gay hussars didn't bother Simon in the slightest.

Leo was also on the design team, costumier angel to the demonic set designer, but far from bringing the two of them closer, it created discord between them. Simon liked to test Leo's limits when he called on him in the costume room. Having noticed a startling similarity between Leo and the young Lorca in a photograph, he nicknamed him Federico and teased him mercilessly.

'Apparently Salvador Dalí did some of Lorca's set designs, and the poet was rumoured to be madly in love with him, but Dalí would have none of Federico's backstage passes. He was a front-entrance man. I bloody love Dalí.'

'Actually, he had a huge phobia of female genitalia,' Leo pointed out drily. 'He also preferred to watch his wife screwing other men than partaking; it's called Candaulism.'

'Surely that's watching one's wife screw candles,' Simon joked feebly, irritated that Leo, who spoke fluent Spanish, was always far better read than he was on any given subject.

'Prof. Crotch will have Mia screwing a candle live on stage if she's not careful,' Leo said darkly. 'He's *such* a creep around her. He wants Adela in a transparent nightdress for most of the last act so I've promised Mia I'll cover as much as I can with embroidery. She's worried Dom-ineering will kick off if he sees her flashing her nips onstage.' His quiet scorn for pervy Prof. Crotch was only exceeded by his distrust of Dominic Masters. 'I can't believe she's bunking off for two days to go to his birthday party in the last week of rehearsal.'

'Well, he does only get to host one every four years.'

'Like the Olympics and general elections,' sighed Leo, who found politics and sport equally tiresome. 'As long as he doesn't keep her up all night listening to Dusty Bin.'

'Ned's Atomic Dustbin.' Simon smiled.

'Have you heard it? Horrible racket.'

'"I know I'm a sucker, but live your life again with me!"'

Leo glared at him. 'I appreciate the overture, Simon. But now's really not the—'

'It's what Domineering wrote in Mia's Valentine's card – or words to that effect,' Simon told him. 'Laney told me. I forget the exact quote, but it's from a Dusty Bin song. Mia keeps it in her bag and reads it twenty times a day.'

'How romantic,' Leo sneered, and they both flicked up the *3-2-1* finger gesture.

When Laney bustled in to find them collapsing with laughter in a rare moment of connection, she narrowed her eyes suspiciously, not immune to the gay-romance rumours currently circulating around the department. While Simon played to the gallery and Leo ignored them, she couldn't help but take them personally.

'You're here to try on your fat-suit, I take it?' Leo wiped his eyes and reached for the hideous, bulging Babygro he'd covered with glued-on shoulder pads and American-tan tights.

'Jesus.' Simon shuddered. 'I thought that was the dead body for the first funeral scene.'

'I'll try it on another time, thanks.' Laney smiled stiffly.

Chapter 3

Mia spent the first part of the coach journey up the M1 listening to the cassette she'd bought at the Ned's Atomic Dustbin gig, singing along to 'Terminally Groovy', which Dom said made him think of her every time he heard its raucous mantra about a gorgeous woman who couldn't be let go. Eventually, hushed several times by her fellow passengers, she swapped the tape in her Walkman to a compilation Leo had made for her. It was altogether mellower stuff, featuring lots of show songs on one side and on the reverse his favourite Aztec Camera tracks, along with Sinead O'Connor, Texas, Deacon Blue and a double-act called Shakespeare's Sister whose song 'Stay' Mia adored. Now it made her think of Dom.

She closed her eyes and kissed the green opal on her finger. She'd bought Dom a ring for his birthday in return, blowing almost her entire term's food budget on an amazing silver eye ring from the Great Frog, which Simon had assured her was the height of biker street cred. She'd had it inscribed inside and she hoped he'd get the joke. He could be notoriously difficult to read but, once ignited, his sense of humour was the most rewarding of high-grade fixes. She felt a tiny twitch of guilt that she was missing rehearsals to travel up to Yorkshire for his sixth birthday, but her heart was rolling too fast to let it catch.

'Staaaaaaaaaaaaaaay wiiiiiiith meeeeeeeeeeeeee!'

A finger tapped her on the shoulder and she realised she'd been singing again. She pulled out her earphones and reached across the aisle to pick up a copy of the *Mirror*, abandoned by a passenger who'd got off at Sheffield. It had a feature about leap-year proposals that kept her entertained for the last few miles as she pitied poor women reduced to going down on bended knee to long-term boyfriends who had never got around to it after twenty years or more. She and Dom had been together just four years, but she struggled to remember a time without him and the familiar ache of longing that went with loving him. She'd been feeling sexy as hell in recent days, a late period making her hormones go into overdrive. She could feel it building in the pit of her stomach now, heartbeat and sex drive cogged together so that the faster one drummed, the faster the other revolved.

He was waiting at the coach stop, leaning against his bike, reading a Faber play script. Mia's heart raced like a bilge pump in a storm at the sight of him. He'd been growing his pale hair for his most recent role and it was blowing in the wind.

'Happy birthday, baby!'

Her feet barely touched the ground as she leapt from the coach straight into his arms, lips already against his and body white hot with delight. When his tongue slipped inside her mouth, she deliberately caught it between her teeth, curling her own tongue around it. His kisses deepened and she threaded her hands round his neck, pulling him closer, body concave against his.

'Steady!' He laughed, pulling gently away and reaching for the helmets. 'This is Barnsley bus station, not the moors. God, I've missed you.'

'Then let's go there,' she demanded, the pulse between her legs multiplying tenfold at the thought of racing to Thurlestone Moor to get down and dirty before they got trapped in the family's front room with the best bone-china mugs and a fruitcake. She was Adela, wanting Pepe's body fused with hers. 'Let's go to the moors.' They'd make love in the heather and then she'd give him the ring and ask him to come to her show.

But Dom, who was currently playing invidious control freak Arturo Ui on stage eight times a week, apparently had no intention of following the forces of nature.

'Too far, too bloody cold.' He shot her a regretful look and clambered aboard as she shrugged on backpack and helmet.

Mia's Old Gate friends might refer to her boyfriend as 'Domineering' to wind her up, but she'd always seen herself as the sex maniac of the relationship. Dom had lost his mother when he was very young and his attitude to women remained complicated. He was by turns neglectful and unbelievably devoted; he approached love-making with the same meticulous intensity as he did acting, with the same spell-binding effect. He had far more self-discipline than she did, taking his work so seriously that he never got drunk during a run and always got enough sleep. He claimed it was a throwback to his bad-boy years, when he'd been permanently out of control, and Mia knew he was terrified of slipping back into that red mist. His ambition to succeed in the theatre had given him an equilibrium his childhood had lacked. But the hooligan was never far from the surface, and Mia secretly loved it when impatience got the better of them and her beloved control freak ravished her, the ultimate sexual improvisation. The theatre-loo tryst might not have lived up to its heart-thundering, clothes-ripping opening scene, but it had done nothing to diminish her raging desire to be ravished again.

As they ate up the miles between the town and Dinfield, she

clung to Dom from the pillion seat, heart seeming to slam right through her coat and his leathers into the hard muscle of his back. She swallowed excitedly when the engine slowed as they drew alongside the big wooded nature reserve known as The Rakes and swung into the parking area. Bouncing over the ruts, Dom sneaked the bike around the few dog walkers' cars, past the barriers and into the woods, roaring up an avenue, back tyre slipping on the pine needles as he turned on to a narrower, darker track and sped towards the most isolated corner, which they both knew well.

There they dragged off their helmets and abandoned the bike to slip into a little wooden storm shelter, not caring that it was so cold they could see their breath clouding and mingling before their tongues entwined again. Mia hiked up her short wool skirt and kicked off her trendy cable-knitted tights as he kissed her neck, reaching beneath her woollen jacket, thumbs finding her nipples through her sweater, still hardened by the wind chill and tightening to pips of pleasure as he circled them.

She was unbuckling his leathers now, racing in to find hot, familiar skin twitching against her cold fingers.

'Warm your hands up first!' he laughed, breathing on his own fingers before pulling her knickers aside and finding a warm, slippery salutation waiting there.

'Oh, *Mia culpa!*' he growled, an old shared joke, his greatest weakness being his unstoppable desire for her.

'*Salus mea, lux mea, vita mea,*' she breathed, her Latin much improved from her short acquaintance with Leo, who acted as translator when Simon wooed Laney with Catullus and Horace.

'Now you're showing off, with your clever university talk,' he grumbled, fingertips teasing her clitoris.

'You're the one showing off,' she gasped. 'You turn me on like a switch.'

Before she could reach further inside his leathers, he took her by surprise and slipped two fingers inside her, his thumb still trigger-light on her clitoris.

She laughed into his mouth, as she felt his other hand slip firmly behind her buttocks. 'You devil!'

She could feel him gently lifting her until she was on the balls of her feet, his fingers still inside her, wrapping around her pubic bone, their tips starting to stroke.

'You know what this does to me,' she gasped, head slamming against his chest, breath thickening, her hands reaching up and gripping instinctively around his neck as he found her weak spot with practised ease.

'Hold on tight.' He lifted her higher, making her squeal at the sensation of being suspended on his amazing, deft fingers and that teasing thumb.

Two minutes was her record and today she knew that she was going to beat it. The first shockwaves were already lapping down to touch his fingers before coursing out through her pelvis.

Now more slippery than ever and positively rippling with blissful trails of sensation, she needed to feel him inside her and to give him a share of the depth-charges detonating there. Moving her deeper into the shelter, he propped one foot up on the bench seat and unzipped the flies of his leathers. Then he reached into his pocket.

'We don't need one.' She wriggled higher, feeling his erection against her, knowing they could have each other skin-on-skin for once. 'I'm due on. We're safe. Birthday treat.'

Both hands supporting her weight beneath her buttocks now, he lifted her higher then lowered her on to him, his eyes on hers, breath quickening as she drew him up within her and dared him deeper and faster, taking her melting, freefall pleasure all over again as he powered his way to a loud, irrepressible finale.

Mia wrapped herself tightly around him as he came.

'I love you!' she breathed, a little dragon's puff of steam in the cold floating into his ear. She wanted to give him the engraved ring straight away, but she'd abandoned her rucksack by the bike. 'I have a surprise for you.' She clambered down to terra firma, weak-legged.

'Me too.' He kept his arms tightly around her. '"I am giddy",' he laughed, still breathing hard, forehead against her neck, pale hair tickling her chin as his voice spoke meltingly low; '"expectation whirls me round".' Looking into her eyes with his bold blue gaze, his face wreathed with smiles, he kissed her long and hard on the mouth. 'I was going to wait to tell you at the same time as Dad and Alison, but I can't wait. I've just been offered a season with the RSC. They want me to play Troilus.'

'Dom!' she shrieked. 'Why didn't you say anything before?'

'Didn't want to jinx it. I only found out yesterday.'

'Omigod, you're in the Royal Shakespeare Company!' she whooped. 'That's so bloody fantastic I'll even forgive you being a secretive sod and blowing me out on Valentine's Day. That was the recall, wasn't it?'

'I felt bad about that.' He hung his head. '"To be wise and love exceeds man's might."'

'It's our play,' she breathed, battling to stop her pride distilling towards sadness that she wouldn't be his Cressida this time. 'At least you don't have to learn any lines.'

'Happen I'd know them now even if I hadn't played the role, I had to go back that many times to read the part. I couldn't say anything in case I didn't get it. You're the first person I've told. Wait until you hear the rest of the cast.'

Mia listened open-mouthed as he recited names as familiar to her as Heinz and Bird's Eye. That year's Stratford repertory company read like a *Who's Who* of theatre and film, and among them was a very famous theatrical impresario's daughter who had been cast as Cressida. It was dynastic stuff.

A faraway expression crossed Dom's face when he talked about her, as star-struck by acting pedigrees as his father was by flat-racing sires. 'She's an amazing actress. None of your raw talent, but her emotional range is bloody fantastic. I'm really looking forward to working with her. She pushed hard for me to get the role.'

'How nice of her,' Mia said, aware that jealousy was pricking her happiness balloon. He was *her* Troilus and she was his Cressida. She didn't want him exploring the role with another actress. What if he fell in love with her as he had with Mia? Would she be better in the role than Mia had been?

'I acted my balls off to get this break,' Dominic was saying. 'There were rumours Toby Stephens was the front runner. The director was pretty jumpy about hiring an unknown, although it helped that I know the script and that Julia and me read so well together.'

'Well done! I'm so proud of you my heart's bursting,' she said brightly, jealousy making her brittle and over-bubbly. She could feel hot semen trickling down her legs and realised she had nothing to wipe herself with. Their woodland coupling suddenly felt no more romantic than their last rushed union, which at least had come with tissues and hot water on tap.

Turning away to rezip his leathers, he was too euphoric to notice her darkening mood. 'It's a bloody intense rehearsal schedule,' he said, pale brows creased. 'If you think Agitprop worked us hard, they're nothing on this. I'll be in two other shows in the repertory as well as *Troilus*. We'll not get to see much of each other.'

'We're used to that,' she said lightly, determined not to reveal her escalating terror, but her teeth were chattering as she forced a smile, and panic rose in her throat. She was losing him just as she'd always feared she would, watching him move on to bigger and better things while she was still a student.

'You have the best arse in the world.' He watched as she bent over to put on her tights. 'Please don't tell me that pervert director's still hassling you to get your kit off?'

'No, it's fine.' She pulled them up, feeling far too uneasy to ask him about coming to see her play Adela. What interest would he have in a bunch of students playing Lorca when he had a lead role at the RSC next season?

'You said you had a surprise for me.' He turned her round as she straightened up, burying another kiss in her mouth of such sweet intensity she longed for it to restart her frozen, fearful heart, like a kiss of life, but all too soon the cold air bit at her lips again.

'It can wait.' She buttoned her coat, eager to curl round him on the bike and race to the companionable warmth of his father's house.

'Happy birthday, cock!' Dom's sister Alison greeted him at the door of the family's little terrace, baby bulge covered with icing sugar. Three years older, she had softer features against the same white-blond hair, making her look like a pregnant cherub. 'Our dad's been fretting you're both late. Hello, Mia, duck. You look frozzed too. Have a drink to warm you up.' She reached for the teabag caddy.

'Family-size Scotch, thanks.'

Sucking in her lips, Alison caught her brother's eye, clearly convinced that Mia was being led astray by all those boho university types. 'She looks peaky, doesn't she, Dom?'

'Looks more beautiful than ever to me.' He reached out to catch her hand, but Mia was already rushing through to greet his father, who hugged her.

'You all right, duck? You look peaky.'

'*Twin Peak*ies, that's me.' She cupped his face and kissed it. 'And I'm all the better for seeing you. It's been too long since Christmas.'

He patted her hands beneath his, beaming. 'They keep you right busy at that college, don't they? I hear you're putting on *The House of Eliott*. Our Alison loves that.'

'Actually it's *The House of Bernarda Alba*.' She smiled.

'I'd come and see it, but Alison's baby's due that week – did I hear you ask for whisky?' He heaved himself up and went to the sideboard to fish out the bottle of Johnnie Walker he'd got for Christmas and only brought out for special guests. 'Dominic reckons the director's a right barmpot, but says you could act the role blindfold.'

'Dom said that?' She'd thought her little college role had hardly registered with him, yet he'd told his father the dates.

'He reckons you're for superstardom.' He turned back with her

36

drink. His eyes were the same petrol blue as his son's and Mia had no doubt of their explosive power in their day. 'I've told him he must make an honest woman of you before you slip his grip.'

She took a large, warming gulp, turning as the birthday boy came into the room at last, sporting an I AM 6 badge that his sister had pressed upon him. As always he seemed uncomfortable in his childhood home, a domesticated fox who had broken out into the wild.

'Isn't that right, Dom?' his father ribbed. 'We Yorkshire men like us wives young. You don't want to let this one get away.' It was a favourite tease of his, and Dom rolled his eyes. But today's news had made Mia more sensitive than usual.

'I think that should be the other way around,' she said, the heat of the Scotch emboldening her. 'It is a leap year, after all. Girls are allowed to propose today.'

'Ha!' Dom's father laughed uproariously, exploding into wheezy, coughing cackles while his son raised an eyebrow.

'Yorkshire men are old-fashioned,' he said quietly, perching on a sofa arm and taking her hand, blue eyes still glittering from their antics in the woods. 'We like to do the proposing.'

Mia's heart slammed against her ribs as he straightened the green opal ring, his expression impossible to read. The doorbell ringing made her jump so much her drink spilled.

'Get that, will you, Dom?' Alison called from the kitchen, where she was piping sugary curtains on a huge square cake shaped like a stage.

For the next hour, members of the Masters family trooped in with birthday greetings. Soon Dom's sweater was covered with more I AM 6 badges as uncles, aunts and cousins from neighbouring Dinfield terraces wished him many happy returns and asked him when he was going to be on the telly.

When he announced his news about the RSC season, they assumed the same polite congratulatory stance as they would if he'd told them it was a season at Butlin's. Excitement mounted when he mentioned his co-star, whom a surprising number of male

Dinfield residents had seen in a small-budget British art movie called *The Persistence of Memory*.

'It has a supermodel in it who gets her kit off,' explained a cousin who worked in Blockbuster. 'Manager brought it in by mistake, thinking it was sci-fi, but word got round that it was mucky and we had the video out on loan non-stop last year. Story's a bit crap, mind, all about some artist wi' a limp dick – that O'Shaughnessy bloke's in it, and Helena Bon-whatnot. Your Julia got her kit off too, Dom. Fit lass. I'll loan it ya.'

'Her father's a successful director so I'm amazed she needs to take her clothes off to further her career,' Mia said hotly as she headed to the dresser to help herself to more Johnnie Walker, where she was waylaid by Dom's aunt, wanting to share the news of her terrier's surprise litter.

'I know how much you love animals, duck. Maybe you'd like first pick?'

'We're not allowed pets on campus,' she said regretfully, wishing that she could have a dog's loyal, adoring company through the long terms away from Dom; she missed her family's little pack desperately.

'I won't offer one to Dominic,' the aunt confided in an undertone. 'It don't seem right when he's just got that job with the RSPCA – all those poor strays.'

The family stayed hours, cramming their mouths with Alison's home-made cake, tea and keg beer as though the three were a gourmet trinity. Dom said little, watching Mia charm them all.

Social as ever, already tight, Mia started to enjoy herself. She was always a headline act in Dinfield, where Dom's cousins paid court, refilling her glass and recounting hair-raising stories of his delinquency. When a few of the hard-core revellers marched him to the pub at the end of the street to buy a celebratory round, she joined in their raucous renditions of 'Happy Birthday', standing on a chair and singing Marilyn Monroe descant with mock-burlesque dance moves, to cheers of delight.

Dom looked increasingly disapproving, but Mia was on a roll, needing the attention, wanting him to see her at her most captivating. Had Leo been there, she knew he would have taken up position at the piano and accompanied her through more Marilyn hits – her 'Diamonds Are a Girl's Best Friend' was Drama-party legend, along with 'I Wanna Be Loved By You'. For all his humility, Leo was a classic showman, whereas Dom kept his feelings hidden deeper than the disused mine shafts around Dinfield. Mia was vaguely aware in her increasingly drunken bubble that her juvenile exhibitionism, an attempt to rouse him, was having the opposite effect. She wondered what it would take to get the hooligan to come out and party.

A pint of Guinness and a Baileys later, she was back at the house with the last stragglers, cracking a bottle of Piat d'Or brought by the dog-loving aunt ('the posh stuff'), when she remembered that she hadn't yet given Dom his birthday present. He was talking quietly to his father, brows lowered, and his expression darkened when she tripped across the room, landing unsteadily at his feet.

'"I'm terminally groovy. Don't pass up on me, baby!"' she said brightly, which silenced everybody in the room. Dom's blue eyes widened.

Fumbling in her bag, she pulled out the ring box. The wrapping paper was ripped and looked awful, so she tugged it off and opened the box to pick out the ring. Inside, the inscription was the Ned's Atomic Dustbin song line he'd quoted in his Valentine's card about living life again with her, minus 'sucker', which she and the jeweller had agreed was a bit crude.

Dom's dad gasped. 'Bloody hell, lad, she's going to do it, tha knows.'

Remembering her leap-year threat earlier, Mia fought giggles as an air of expectation filled the room. Mischief coursed through her, along with a much sharper, colder blade of fear, the same blade that had been paring away at her confidence since his RSC news, telling her that she was losing him. Well, she wouldn't lose him if they were man and wife, she thought squiffily.

'Will you marry me?' she blurted.

There are moments in life when someone sobers up unnaturally quickly. This was one of them. Mia was three-Alka-Seltzers-and-an-ice-bath sober in seconds, but by then it was too late.

'*MIA'S PROPOSED!*' shrieked Alison, followed by an even more expectant hush as they awaited Dom's answer.

He gaped at her, his blue eyes so wide and stormy that she half expected to see a whirlpool eddying from one to the other. Beside him, his father was having great difficulty breathing, tears of happiness in his own faded blue eyes.

There was an agonising pause, longer than anything she had counted down in a Pinter workshop. In a panic, Mia forced a smile and started humming 'Terminally Groovy', but gave up because her throat was full of ashes. Dom's eyes hadn't left hers, but neither had any muscle moved in his face, and Mia knew she had embarrassed him deeply. She wanted to sing 'STAY!' at the top of her voice and beg for forgiveness, but the ashes were shifting fast as a volcano of shame rose in her. Perhaps she hadn't sobered up as quickly as she'd thought.

A moment later, she was violently sick on the Masters' patterned carpet.

Chapter 4

That Mia made it through the final rehearsals and first performances of the Lorca production was largely down to Laney and Leo staying up on late-night soggy-shoulder vigils, taking breaks only to bulk-buy phone cards for Mia to feed into the payphones in the halls of residence while conducting long, strained conversations with the man she thought she'd just frightened away.

'I humiliated myself in front of his whole family!' she wailed at

Laney after another stilted call, during which Dom had barely said a word and The Proposal was not mentioned.

'So just tell him you were pissed and it was a mistake.'

'It wasn't a mistake, though, was it? Just the timing. I want to spend the rest of my life with him. I know I'm only nineteen, but why wait? I love him so much. It's only ever going to be him!'

'But why hurry?' Laney countered. 'You both have great careers ahead of you. Concentrate on those first. Share some life together. Marry when you're ready to enjoy it. I'm sure that's what Dom thinks.'

To her surprise, Mia shook her head emphatically, turning the green opal ring round and round on her finger. 'Dom said Yorkshire men are old-fashioned and like to do the proposing. And his dad said, "We like us wives young."'

Laney was astounded. The macho northerner had blindsided them all yet again.

'That's good, isn't it?' Mia said shakily, then her face crumpled. 'Julia is only twenty-two. That's still two years younger than Dom. If he marries her, he'll be a part of one of the oldest acting families in England.'

'Whoa, let's calm down about the Julia thing.' Laney was all too accustomed to Mia's jealousy about the RSC co-star. 'Dom didn't give you an answer, did he?'

She shook her head, eyes downcast. 'We didn't have much time to talk about that, what with the alcohol poisoning and me having to get back here to rehearse. All he said was that he agreed with the ring inscription. Do you think he was just being kind?'

'I don't think of him as kind.'

'Then you don't know him at all!'

Mia gave Leo even shorter shrift when he dared to suggest that Dominic was being heartless by refusing to talk about it. 'His mother died when he was tiny, so he's never found it easy to open up. He's better at showing how he feels than talking about it. I have to give him a chance to show me what he wants.'

All week Mia veered between despair and hope, clinging to the conviction that Dom might just roar up on his bike at any moment to demonstrate his Yorkshire machismo and propose to her, which Laney and Leo thought was crazy, although Simon infuriated them by buying into the romantic optimism.

'Dominic must know he's mad to turn her down,' he said, on one of the few nights Laney left Mia's room to share his bed. 'She's an astoundingly good actress, a total fox and a cheap date. The girl gets drunk on cherryade. He's a lucky man. *You* need more pints than Eric Bristow to get going these days.'

She bristled. 'Our poor little vixen isn't eating or sleeping, keeps being sick and leaves ten messages a day at Agitprop and his digs. She has to calm down. It's making her ill.'

'It helps her get into the role. You could try being a bit more obsessed about me,' he suggested hopefully. 'Tie me up, get a riding crop out, tell me you'll die if I leave you, that sort of thing.'

'Are you're planning to leave *me* then?' she asked in a panic.

'Of course not. And Dom-ineering will never leave Mia. He's as wrapped up in her as I am in you. It's one of the only things we have in common. We're like swans: we mate for life.'

Knowing Simon's fondness for self-aggrandisement, Laney dismissed the boast. But then Dominic left a message for Mia saying he'd arranged for his understudy to take over for one night at Agitprop so that he could see her in the Lorca show. It was unheard-of for workaholic method actor Dominic to skip a single performance. Mia now believed more than ever that if she wowed him with her performance as Adela, all would be well and questions would be popped along with the last-night champagne corks.

Racing through her final costume change, Mia strained her ears for her cue, but it was impossible to hear the crackling Tannoy over the laughter in the dressing room as Simon danced around singing 'Viva España!'. Swigging from a half-bottle of vodka, he was threatening to dress as a bullfighter and wander on stage for the curtain call as a last-night prank.

Spare safety pins tucked in his teeth, Leo stepped in behind Mia to help her adjust the lacy nightdress.

'Is that Poncia's line about crossing the ocean?' she asked anxiously.

'You've got loads of time, don't worry,' Leo soothed, straightening her shoulder straps and pressing his warm thumbs to her tense muscles to loosen them. 'Bernarda's only just finished quizzing her. You're bound to get talent-spotted tonight. I heard there are casting agents in.'

She smiled gratefully into the mirror, green eyes huge, and he reached up a hand to tousle her hair, enthralled as always by the snaking spirals the colour of driftwood that framed her face.

'I only care what Dom thinks of it,' she breathed, and Leo felt a quiver go right through her.

He raised an eyebrow. 'He'll think more of you if we powder that shiny forehead and reapply your lippy. Come on, pucker up.' He reached for the make-up box.

It was the final performance. Dom would be in the audience, and Mia trembled so much that Leo had to wipe lipstick smears away with a tissue.

Now they checked the decency of the hateful see-through nightie that Prof. Crotch had deemed vital to show Adela's naked vulnerability in the scenes leading up to her death. There wasn't much of it, although Leo had tried his best to cover her modesty with embroidery and lace trims.

Just as he'd arranged the lace for maximum coverage, the dressing-room door burst open and Laney thundered in to change, sweating heavily in her fat-suit. 'God, they love me tonight! I can just hear RADA begging me to do a postgrad diploma. Roll on curtain call and party. Stage is all yours now, treasure.' She blew a kiss over her shoulder at Mia, grateful that her nightly humiliation as mute matriarch in a fat-suit was on a five-minute break, then kissed Simon and grabbed the vodka bottle. 'Knock 'em dead.'

'I think you'll find this is an *ensemble* piece, Melanie,' hissed the postgraduate student playing María Josefa, as she stalked up to the props table to collect the lamb that her character cradled onstage, and which Prof. Crotch insisted was a symbol of defiled innocence.

Laney poked her tongue out at her behind her back.

For all her bravado, it had been a disastrous run for Laney. With her title role cut to its bones, and increasingly frustrated that Mia just had to walk on stage with her huge green eyes full of un-spoken emotion to enthral the audience, she'd overacted and played for laughs all week, turning Bernarda into a Les Dawson drag act. Laney knew she was sharing the stage with a very rare talent, but that didn't make it any easier to take the constant com-parison. Mia's overwrought emotions just enhanced her presence. She seemed hardly aware of the effect she was having, yet her per-formance moved everybody to tears. Last night, the audience had been in shreds.

Vibrating with nervous excitement now, Mia adjusted the embroidered circles to cover her nipples and waved away the vodka Laney was proffering. 'Have you spotted Dom yet?'

'Must be sitting right at the back. Didn't he come backstage during the interval?'

'I told him not to when we spoke on the phone last night. My nerves couldn't take it.' She started towards the dressing-room door, transforming into Adela with every step, her huge eyes glit-tering with fervour as she determined to steal out of her mother's house and meet lover Pepe el Romano in secret.

Laney and Simon exchanged knowing glances and shared another vodka-fuelled kiss.

Leo claimed the Smirnoff while they were distracted and took a sip. 'Dom-ineering's not even here, is he?'

Laney shook her head. 'Don't think so.'

'Knew the bastard would let her down.' His face darkened.

'Well, she *did* rather freak him out last week,' drawled Simon.

'She was drunk. They've talked it through on the phone. He promised to be here.'

'If he's out there, I'll spot him from the wings.' Simon picked up Mia's discarded lipstick and applied it, smacking his handsome, curling lips and smirking at his reflection. He suited make-up absurdly well. 'Kiss me, Federico,' he pouted at Leo over his shoulder. 'You must join me on stage at the curtain call. You'll be Lorca's ghost complaining about Crotch's damnable liberties with your creation. Give you a chance to use your Spanish.'

Leo was determined not to let Simon sabotage the last night. 'Come up to the prod box to watch the last act,' he entreated.

'You just want to canoodle with me, Federico, you cad!' Simon lifted a fan from the props table to prod at him before snapping it open and holding it coyly up to his nose.

'In your dreams,' Leo said huffily, snatching back the fan and carefully refolding it. 'You make a lousy drag act.'

'Don't be so cruel. I weel call myself Consuela Dominguez, or Con Dom to *mis amigos*.' He put on a Spanish accent, which sounded more Speedy Gonzales than José Carreras. 'I ham just poor, misunderstood *señorita*. Men use me once and throw me away.'

Despite himself, Leo laughed. For all the outward disdain, he was secretly flattered by the comparison to Lorca, who'd been dazzling as a young man, with his huge dark eyes and raven-wing brows. Having a latter-day Dalí as a friend was growing on him too, and he couldn't help admiring someone so fearless, although Simon's artifice irritated him, as did the way he played up to the 'budding romance' that cast and crew had been gossiping about throughout the run. Leo ignored it, his attention on Mia. Tonight he was appalled that Dom had let her down. 'She's out there acting her heart out and he couldn't even be bothered to turn up,' he lamented. 'He knows how much it means to her to get a role this big in her first year.'

'She watched every show he was in at drama school,' Laney agreed, 'getting the coach down to London between A levels, sharing his rotten digs, cooking and cleaning for him.'

'I told you he's mad to turn her down,' Simon said lightly. 'Laney won't even do her own washing, let alone mine.'

'I just don't wash my dirty linen in public. That's why I take it home every fortnight.' Roughing up her bobbed hair, Laney looked at her pale-faced reflection, transformed from soft school-girl to cutting-edge student in just six months. Dyeing her hair black to play Bernarda made her look more street cred, and the puppy fat had dropped off. Despite much adjustment from Leo, the fat-suit looked ridiculous with her slim neck and face poking out. Far from embracing her trendy new image, Simon complained that as well as her curves he missed the cosy domesticity with which she'd clucked around him in their first term.

'When I asked for a leap-year proposal,' he was grumbling to Leo now, 'Laney told me to take a running jump. If you ask me, Dominic Masters is an ungrateful bastard.'

'Why marry at all?' she snapped. 'Mia's not yet twenty. With her looks and talent, her future multi-millionaire husband's probably still married to his first wife.'

'Her parents married at twenty, his were even younger,' Leo pointed out. 'She thinks it'll make her feel safe.'

'My mother didn't marry until she was nearly forty,' drawled Simon, 'and she always said the shame and fear almost finished her off, but it was sixty Rothmans a day which finally did that.' Catching Laney's eye, his own flashed a warning, the truth out of bounds. 'Better to marry while you're young and pretty like us, darling.'

'But this is the nineties!'

'Exactly.' Simon held the vodka bottle like a bouquet and feigned walking up an aisle. 'Marriage is very rock-and-roll right now. If Amanda de Cadenet can do it with a Durannie at nineteen, Mia can. You know what a trendy young thing she is. Kurt and Courtney did it on a beach last month, Patsy Kensit has just made a marriage of Simple Minds. How about it, Holden? You, me, a Las Vegas chapel . . . ' He stopped in front of her, blinking coyly.

Laney laughed. 'Are you proposing to me, Demon? Because the answer is no.'

He shrugged. 'You're right. Leo would make the best wife of all of us. Will you marry me, Federico?'

'Hardly, darling,' Leo said witheringly, then shocked the others by adding, 'but I wouldn't have turned Mia down.'

Chapter 5

Having briefly appeared on stage to fetch a glass of water – her character's excuse when caught creeping through the house to get outside to meet her lover – Mia waited in the wings for her next cue. Her eyes scoured the audience through the gauze side-drops, which Simon had painted with red Moorish fretwork to represent heat and passion. She couldn't see Dom anywhere. His wild mop of white-blond hair usually made him stand out, even in a dark auditorium, but all was in shadow.

She gnawed at her lips anxiously. He had to be out there. She was putting on her best performance yet for him. She could still hear his deep voice resounding in her head: 'Yorkshire men are old-fashioned. We like to do the proposing.'

Hailstones were hammering down on the theatre roof as the gales that had been pounding the UK all day elbowed frozen thunderclouds around. It was asking a lot for an audience to suspend disbelief and feel the Andalucían heat, but the cast were giving it their all. The postgrad playing María Josefa was dancing around onstage, dead lamb held aloft as she sang to it between the high kicks and groin thrusts that Prof. Crotch had choreographed to depict decaying sexuality.

Mia gazed out at the dark seating again, scanning two hundred silhouettes for a familiar outline. His decision to come tonight had made her sick with hope.

She'd been sick a lot that week, a daily encounter with bile at breakfast. Always nerve-ridden during a production run – although the churning fear disappeared the moment she stepped onstage – Mia was familiar with the race to the loos to vomit that always accompanied her half-hour call, but this week had been worse than ever. Unlike most of her fellow cast members, Mia would never drink during a performance, but her after-show chats with Laney or Leo had involved the occasional bourbon and Coke, and she had suffered appallingly in the mornings, stomach heaving, head pounding. Some days, like today, the nausea stayed with her from dawn until dusk. She hadn't eaten properly all week and weight was dropping off her.

That morning when she'd gone in desperation to the campus sick bay for beta blockers, the nurse had asked if she could be pregnant. Now the memory of the condom splitting at the Royal Court and then their skin-on-skin tryst in the woods was ringing sirens in her head and an unopened pregnancy test was burning a hole in her bag in the dressing room. She hadn't dared confide her fears to anybody, not even Laney.

She closed her eyes tight, breathing slowly. She would see Dom again tonight. She was not pregnant. All would be well. He felt the same way about her as she did for him. 'We like us wives young.' Like Pepe el Romero preferring vibrant young Adela over her sister Angustias, whom he must marry to unite their estates. Then Mia felt another sword-tip of panic at her breastbone. What if Dom preferred the gifted young daughter of the famous stage director to her?

She was so absorbed that she missed her cue to cross the stage and exit into the garden so that Adela could meet her lover. In the wings opposite, the actress playing her vengeful sister Martirio was waving her arms frantically. Several members of the audience coughed as they stared at an empty stage. From another exit, the postgrad was twirling the lamb so fast to attract Mia's attention that its head flew off and hit a light.

Mia jumped in horrified recognition, raced onstage and forgot to adjust her embroidery, which thrilled at least half of the audience and meant Prof. Crotch instantly forgave the late entrance as her breasts spilled from the flimsy fabric and flashed their nipples lusciously.

The prof. was less forgiving later that night when Mia tipped half a can of Guinness into his crotch at the after-show party.

'She's really quite drunk now, isn't she?' observed Simon as he and Laney paused outside the packed green room with armfuls of red velvet drapes, their own inebriation held in check by the need to finish the strike, the task of dismantling the set, which all cast and crew were honour-bound to complete, but which in reality always fell to stage management, the techies and the set designer.

'You know Mia.' Laney sighed. 'It only takes two thimblefuls of hooch and she's out of control.'

The cast was in riotous party mode, crammed on to ancient sofas and rickety chairs, breaking into four-packs of beer and half-bottles of spirits. Camel Light smoke infused the air, with a faint tang of pot.

Now Mia flounced out of the green room and reeled unsteadily along the corridor to seek comfort with Leo in the costume room, where he was predictably eschewing the scrum to share flutes of Kir Royale with props designer Agnes as they packed away mantillas and fans.

'Straight to Captain Leotard and his Wrestling Conscience,' grumbled Simon, who was in a very bad mood because, having got within metres of the stage dressed as a bullfighter just as the curtain call began, he'd been brought down in the wings by Leo, who had lain on top of him until the audience left, thus ensuring his prank was foiled.

'He did it for the sake of the play,' Laney muttered, trotting alongside him to the storeroom to pack the drapes away on the overloaded shelves.

The stage-side Roman wrestling moment meant gossip was now rifer than ever that the boys were involved in a pink love triangle and had been enjoying a little behind-the-scenes canoodling.

Secretly terrified that the gay rumours had the ring of truth about them, Laney had done nothing to dispel the story, joking instead to the dressing room at large that Simon was all bull and no fight, her 'Tory-adore' who couldn't resist Leo because of his resemblance to Michael Portillo. As a result she was in hot water with Simon, who claimed the de Montmorency mystique had been dented and that her sarcasm smacked of lovelessness. 'You of all people should know I'm not fucking gay!' he'd raged.

She was helping him with the strike by way of apology, but they were still scrapping and he remained indignant that his grand finale had been scuppered. 'I really think Leo bloody enjoyed it. I swear he had a stiffy by the end,' Simon growled.

'And did you?'

'Of course not!'

'Maybe I can change that,' she purred, kicking the door shut and curling her arms around him in the dark. 'It was for your own good, my darling Demon. This way the audience will remember your beautiful set as well as Mia's stunning performance . . .'

She waited for him to compliment her performance too, but he said nothing, just laid a finger on his lips. Then she heard Mia's raised voice in the adjacent room and Leo's soothing tones as he sought to calm her down.

' . . . put his hand up my top, the bastard! Then he had the *nerve* to tell me how delighted he was that my boyfriend wasn't in the audience! He's lucky I didn't nut him.'

'Just soaked his nuts.'

'Waste of good stout, mate. Here, give me that blackcurrant stuff.'

'It's crème de cassis – it's quite strong.'

'Good! I am going to get mullered. You can only stop me drinking when I say, "What boyfriend?"'

'I'm sure there's a perfectly good reason that Dom hasn't—'

'Don't make excuses for him, Leo! I know you hate him. Right now I hate him too. Be grateful. You're always telling me to forsake my Dominican faith. Tonight, chuck, I'm going to get incredibly pissed and seduce somebody to cheer myself up.' She broadened her accent to pure Bet Lynch.

'Crotch clearly didn't make the grade,' whispered Simon. 'Maybe Leo'll get lucky at last.'

Laney bit her lip: she knew how headstrong Mia became when drunk, from proposing to boyfriends to dancing on tables. Dom's non-appearance had derailed her, anger and disappointment blotting out daydreams of romantic reunions and backstage betrothals. Her performance tonight had been spell-binding, but the one person she'd wanted to see it hadn't turned up, and now she was on a path to self-destruction.

On the other side of the wall, Leo seemed equally perturbed. 'You *wouldn't*!'

'Just watch me. Serves him bloody right.' She was slurring badly. 'I shall take a man to my bed for one night only and make him pleasure me until dawn.'

'Count me out.' Leo laughed nervously. 'I need my eight hours.'

'Eight inches more like,' Mia teased, too squiffy to care that she was crossing an invisible line. 'You *loved* holding Demon down earlier, admit it.'

Laney bit her lip harder. She burrowed lovingly in Simon's trousers and found, to her alarm, that he had already sprung to attention with rigid enthusiasm.

'I was admiring the matador's costume,' Leo said airily. 'The stitchwork's incredible.'

'Shame nobody in the audience saw it, you bastard,' hissed Simon, then groaned as Laney gripped tighter. 'Steady on – don't break it.'

They both jumped as the lights came on and Brendan, who was head of technical effects, came in with a rolled stage gauze, pipe sticking through his beard, like an ancient prospector. 'Don't mind me, kids. I've seen it all in here, trust me. Just remember this is a safe-sex area – "Don't be a fool, cover the tool."' He chuckled, depositing the gauze on a shelf and leaving in a cloud of St Bruno Ready Rubbed.

Still in Laney's grip, Simon's enthusiasm was rapidly subsiding, as was her confidence. Laney was a resilient, loyal sort, but Simon was her first serious boyfriend, and the rumours about his sexuality had frightened her more than she dared admit.

Right now she badly needed to feel his ardour, but when she made a last effort to tease and tug him back into life, he just wilted further in her hand. He pulled a fresh half-bottle of Smirnoff from one inside pocket of his leather coat and one of Southern Comfort from the other.

'Let's go next door and get pissed in the sartorial salon,' he suggested. 'It sounds as though Mia needs a slow comfortable screw. I'm sure the "blackcurrant stuff" will suffice as a sloe-gin substitute.'

She zipped up his trousers irritably. 'What about the strike?'

'We're now on it. We'll picket the wig stands. Even I can be a union man, as long as it's Equity. Are you coming out too, Holden?' He marched from storeroom to corridor.

Laney followed him. 'Coming out' wasn't a phrase that filled her with confidence tonight.

'Fill me up, Demon, darling!'

'Are you referring to your glass, Wilde child?'

'Let's start there and who knows where we'll get . . .'

Laney had never seen Mia so wired, wanton or wilful, and Simon was encouraging her as they played drinking games, tried on costumes, fooled around with truth-or-dare and continually raided Agnes's discarded bag for cigarettes. They were like two naughty children on a sugar rush.

Unable to curb the debauchery in his costume room, Leo was working his way through a bottle of peach schnapps as he exchanged increasingly cross-eyed, long-suffering looks with Laney, who had no idea what to do. Far from camping it up, Simon now appeared to be on a mission to prove his heterosexuality by flirting with the prettiest girl in the class, and Mia was a willing accomplice.

Agnes had long since departed to join in the dancing in the studio theatre, where an ad hoc disco always struck up at after-show parties. Laney could hear the KLF booming out from the big warehouse space, their leafy Surrey campus's answer to Brixton's Fridge.

Simon and Mia were still trying on costumes, laughing uproariously as Simon donned a Roman centurion's helmet and breastplate that made him look like an armoured cockatoo.

'C'mon, Laney!' Mia urged as she reeled around in a wimple and a corset over her party hot-pants. 'You'd look choice in some of this.'

Laney tried to join in the fun with a mob cap, Venetian mask and fur stole, but it was not a good look. When department heart-throb Adam Oakes put his head around the door to check out the rival party, he let out a cry of horror. Then he spotted the kinky nun and the gladiator and his eyes almost popped out of his head.

'This is obviously where it's at,' he drawled, closing the door behind him and producing a spliff.

Second-year Adam was a department legend because he had once modelled for Gap, looked like Morten Harket from A-ha and was rumoured to have slept with a leading cast member of *Howard's Way*, although he refused to name names (opinion was split between the pretty blonde daughter and Kate O'Mara). Prof. Crotch hadn't let him near the Lorca production team, but he'd come to see the last night and stayed on for the party. It was pretty obvious his sights were set on one cast member.

'You were sensational,' he told Mia, settling in the small space between her and Leo and lighting the spliff. Adam and Mia had starred together in last term's *Streetcar Named Desire* and, while she'd shown no desire to ride on his tram then, she clearly had very little sense of direction tonight. 'You absolutely stole the show.'

Laney was feeling increasingly disheartened that nobody had mentioned her own performance. Even her parents, who had come the previous evening, had managed no more than 'You were jolly brave.' When the spliff came her way, she had a few puffs in the hope that it would make her laugh.

Mia took a very long drag, covered her mouth and made a dash for the loo.

Laney groaned, following her. 'I bet we have to carry her back to her room.'

'I can do that,' offered Simon, pulling off his helmet and thrusting it under one arm as he caught her up.

Adam shot into the corridor after them, spliff still in hand. 'I'll help you put her to bed.'

'We'll *all* do it,' Leo insisted.

While the male trio waited by the swing door like expectant fathers, Laney stomped into the Ladies and stood by the cubicle in which Mia was retching.

'You OK?'

'Be fine in a minute! Can you fetch my bag from the dressing room? I need a . . . tampon.'

Grumbling under her breath, Laney battled past the men in the corridor, fetched Mia's bag and took it back to thrust beneath the door.

There was a lot of rustling, then the sound of peeing.

A long pause ensued.

'Have you passed out in there?' Laney asked.

'Just gathering my thoughts.'

The pause dragged on, followed by a sharp intake of breath and more rustling. Laney didn't like to interfere in the private menstrual practices of friends but it did seem a very long wait for a change of tampon.

'Let's go back to halls,' she yawned, increasingly light-headed from the pot and now racked with tiredness. All the nights she'd stayed up with Mia that week were taking their toll.

'I'm going to bloody dance my arse off.' Mia burst out of the cubicle and marched to the basins to splash cold water on her face and rinse her mouth. Having just ejected several slow screws and a Kir Royale, she was back on her seduction course, green eyes glittering dangerously. 'Have you got any gum?'

Laney felt in her pocket and handed over two wraps of Juicy Fruit.

'Thanks. Shall I let Adam Oakes knob me, d'you reckon? I hear he stays the distance longer than Desert Orchid.'

'Absolutely not. Half the college would know by breakfast. He's *so* indiscreet. Besides, aren't you on your period?'

'False alarm!' There was something unnaturally shrill about Mia's voice and the frantic way she was washing her hands as though auditioning for Lady Macbeth. Looking at her, Laney wondered if she'd taken something. She didn't know a lot about drugs, but Mia could have had something stashed in her handbag. She was chewing the gum frantically.

'You need to go to bed alone,' she told her.

'I get frightened alone.' Mia pushed back her amazing hair and looked at her reflection, pinching her cheeks and rolling her lips to add colour. 'You're lucky – you can have Simon in your bed every night.'

'Not much lately,' Laney muttered.

But Mia wasn't listening. 'My bastard boyfriend can't be arsed to come here tonight, let alone dignify my proposal with an answer. All he can think about right now is *Troilus and* bloody *Cressida*. "From false to false, among false maids in love".' She dashed away the tears welling in her eyes, blotted the running mascara with her thumbs, then washed her hands again.

Laney knew Mia needed saving from herself, yet she was reluctant to offer to sit up with her for another night. These vigils were ruining her love life and she badly needed to recapture the lost spark.

Mia was wearing the soap down to nothing beneath the taps. 'Simon says she looks like Isabella Rossellini and has massive boobs – "damned choice", I think he said.'

'Who?' Laney demanded.

'Julia – the actress playing Cressida. She starred in a movie about Dalí that Simon's watched. He says it's rubbish, but there's lots of gratuitous nudity and you get to see Niall O'Shaughnessy's willy. Apparently it's very long and hooked, and if you freeze-frame it at the right moment, it looks exactly like Gonzo's nose.'

'I had no idea he'd studied it that closely.' Laney swallowed uncomfortably.

'I'll show him!' Mia cried drunkenly.

'Show him what?' Laney was struggling to follow the thread, the dope she'd just smoked taking hold as images of the blue Muppet twirled disturbingly in her head, along with Simon's flaccid reaction to her storeroom seduction. Without warning, she found tears in her eyes.

Mia might be wired and slaughtered, but her hug radar never failed, and Laney was soon enveloped in a tight if somewhat lurching cuddle. 'Hey, chuck, less of the waterworks. What's up?'

'It's the r-rumours ab-bout Simon and L-Leo.'

'They're bollocks, trust me. There's no way Demon wants to bowl from the pavilion end. He's only interested in *you*.'

'His maiden leg-over.' Laney sniffed shakily, unconvinced. 'He once told me he wouldn't say no to group sex with the Bangles. Isn't the drummer a transsexual?'

'They're all girls, Laney. He prefers Nefertiti to King Tut, so keep your chin up and walk like an Egyptian.' Mia lurched back to the mirrors to tease out her wild curls. 'If you believed all the rumours in this department, you wouldn't find a straight man here tonight, and we know that's a lie. Adam Oakes is incredibly good-looking, isn't he?'

'You mustn't sleep with him,' Laney warned.

'I bet he's fantastic. Half the cast of *Howard's Way* can't be wrong.' A wicked smile spread across her face.

'Have you taken drugs?' Laney demanded beadily, then felt stupid as she remembered they'd both tooted on the spliff.

Mia was already reeling towards the door. 'Not a truth drug, that's for sure.' She laughed hollowly. 'If Dom doesn't want to make an honest woman of me, what the hell?' She cannoned into the doorframe as she breezed out, and Laney realised that she was totally out of control.

The studio theatre, stripped of its stage set, had turned into a temporary nightclub, its dance floor lit by a few low, purple-gelled Fresnel lenses and a flashing rope that the techies had rigged up. With the seating still in place, along with the white tape on the stage floor marking place points for furniture, it was as though the play was still being performed but having undergone a dramatic scene change. Laney had an unpleasant feeling the final act was just beginning.

Simon hailed her from the front row, where he was sitting with Leo like Statler and Waldorf in *The Muppet Show*, both now extremely drunk. 'There you are!' He offered her the last of the Southern Comfort, which she ignored, watching Mia and Adam already writhing on the dance floor to Madonna's 'Justify My Love' in a way that suggested they were going to continue the performance late into the night with the aid of a sprung mattress and without the need for clothes.

'We have to stop her doing something she regrets,' Laney said, aware that she sounded as pious as Mary Whitehouse. Adam was a terrifically sexy dancer and a fast operator, his lips on Mia's neck, hands pinning her hips to his.

'They make a beautiful couple,' sighed Simon. His Roman

helmet was now hugged to his chest, his chin resting on the feathered plume. 'Shame to break it up.'

Leo, who had polished off the last of the vodka from the costume room, now reached across for the remaining Southern Comfort. 'A demonic act.'

'As opposed to a Dominic act?' Simon sniggered.

'Don't bring that bastard into it.' Leo took another draught of Southern Comfort and winced. 'He has a lot to answer for. This performance is all for him, but he's still not here to see it.' He sighed, closing his eyes.

'At this rate we'll have to carry Leo back to his room too,' Laney predicted, now swigging a can of cola in a bid to sober up.

'I'll do it,' Simon offered nobly, slotting the helmet on Leo's head then searching his capacious pockets for more alcohol. 'You'll never lift him.'

'*I'm* looking after Leo!' she insisted, holding the cola can away from him before he could empty the two Malibu miniatures he'd found into it. 'You can take Mia.'

He glanced reluctantly at the stage, where the sexiest girl and boy on campus were putting on a white-hot floor show. 'What if Adam puts up a fight?'

She eyed the canoodling couple. 'Use your fists if you must.'

'I'd rather not.' He admired his long bony fingers, the nails of which were currently Tory blue in the lead-up to the election. 'These beautiful draughtsmen are our future, Laney baby. I couldn't possibly use them to fist Adam.'

It was a typical throwaway Simon joke, playing the fine line between camp and coarse.

But tonight Laney was too paranoid from the dope and dismayed by his flippancy to laugh. All the jibes about Simon being gay had finally conspired to tip her over the edge. They hadn't made love in days. Before she knew what she was saying, she lashed out: 'Why don't you just admit you wish I had a Y chromosome, Y-fronts and K-Y Jelly?'

Simon looked baffled. 'What are you talking about?'

Her outburst coincided with a lull on the dance floor as the tech crew in the prod box replaced Madonna with Gloria Estefan, to a series of groans and catcalls. Coming off the stage in protest, the sweaty cast and crew eyed the front-row argument with interest.

Tears springing to her eyes, she howled, 'Why not just admit you're gay, Demon?'

Simon's eyes widened with amazement.

'I've always known!' Laney wailed. 'I guessed you were bent from the start but I just loved being with you too much to care. I love you to bits, but I know I'm the wrong sex.'

'What the fuck are you talking about, Laney?' He laughed incredulously.

'There's no point denying it!'

'Of course there is!' Simon was annoyed now. 'I'm a straight-forward straight bloke. If you want me to prove it to you, I'll do it.'

'I told you, there's no *point*!' Tears were pouring down her face. 'You should be proud of who you are. I'm so proud of you.' In the background the party-goers, except Adam and Mia, who were locked together, oblivious to all around them, were watching the argument unfold amid much nudging and 'Told you so's.

'There *is* a bloody point!' Simon bellowed. He strode towards her, brushed past her and marched out on to the dance floor, where he threw a punch at Adam Oakes's perfect cleft chin, decking him with one blow. Then he hoisted Mia over his shoulders to carry her out of the auditorium. After an initial squawk of fury, she giggled and began kicking him.

Shock enfolded Laney like a protective layer of bubble wrap, muting her crashing heart. With her fellow students gaping at her, she felt as though that evening's audience was lined up around the stage: Bernarda was honour-bound to keep up a show of bravery for them. With self-righteous aplomb, she lifted her chin and marched across the dance floor, where Adam was crawling around screaming that he'd lost a veneer and a tinted contact lens.

Laney sat him down beside Leo in the front row and handed him back his porcelain tooth front. 'I couldn't find the contact lens, I'm afraid.' Her voice sounded unnaturally clipped.

Still wearing the Roman helmet at a jaunty angle, Leo peered drunkenly across at Adam and his damaged tooth. 'Demon's got a hell of a right hook.'

To Laney's alarm, Adam started to cry. 'I must look like Shane MacGowan!'

'I'll take you to the sick bay in a minute,' she offered in her strange fifties radio announcer voice. 'They'd better check you're not concussed. Maybe a dentist can do something about the tooth.'

'Get a gold one like Madonna,' Leo suggested, pulling off the helmet and regarding it groggily, as though contemplating Simon's infinite jest. 'Sorry about Demon. He's a dickhead; a very straight dickhead.'

'More's the pity,' sighed Adam, his missing tooth giving him a lisp.

Laney looked at him sharply.

'I've fancied him since the first day of term,' he admitted, 'but he's totally besotted with you, Laney.'

Beside her, Leo giggled. She elbowed him sharply in the ribs to shut him up. 'But you've slept with dozens of women, including one from *Howard's Way*. How can you fancy Simon?'

'"What is straight?"' he started quoting from *A Streetcar Named Desire*. '"A line can be straight, or a street, but the human heart, oh, no, it's curved like a road through mountains."'

Leo swallowed his laughter, dark eyes wide and wise as he looked from Adam to Laney, trying to sober up. 'I think Demon is more of a tunnel-through-the-mountains man.'

The skin on Laney's face seemed to ice over as she saw the enormity of her mistake. She'd publicly accused the man she loved of denying his true sexuality and ignored his shocked protests, swept away by her sense of betrayal and self-justification. Oh, God, he'd

60

even offered to prove it to her. How far would he go now to do that?

'Oh, shitty shit!' She ran towards the exit in search of a tall, manly student with a chip – and a drunken Mia – on his shoulder.

Watching her go, Adam started to laugh. 'I think I just came out,' he lisped, standing up and turning back to Leo. 'I'm going to bum a fag. Care to join me?'

'Not bloody likely!'

Adam raised a handsome eyebrow. 'I'm just talking about smoking a cigarette, Leo, but I've always found you hugely attractive . . .'

Leo picked up a small pearly oval from the seat beside him, handing it over as he stood up unsteadily. 'The only thing you're going to pull tonight is the tooth fairy, Adam. I'm going to check on Mia.'

Chapter 6

Laney had never felt anger like it. Until tonight she'd imagined she was immune to the sort of blistering heartache Mia had talked about, but now she felt it burn through her veins and blaze so hot in her lungs she was amazed fireballs didn't roll from her nostrils as she ran towards Founders Hall, feet echoing beneath the archway into the main quad.

As she passed the row of payphones in the cloisters, one was ringing mournfully, but she ignored it. Behind her, she could hear a bunch of drunken revellers pick up the call, rowdily offering to take a message.

On the third floor, R.E.M. was playing so loudly from Mia's room, the floorboards in the corridor outside shook. 'Mia? Mia! Simon! It's Laney.'

The music droned on, but she was certain she could hear Mia's earthy giggle, with the snorting top-note she always saved for particularly dirty jokes. She froze as she heard one of Simon's distinctive whoops, which she recognised from their most electrifying sexual adventures. Her heart felt as though it was splitting open in her chest.

'Mia! Simon! Let me in!' She hammered on the door. 'Fire! Rape! Free puppies!' She kicked the door hard, making the notepad attached to it fall off its Blu-tack. Beyond the door, R.E.M. blasted on unabated.

'Oh God, this is all my fault.' Laney slumped against the wall, listening to Michael Stype losing his religion. She knew how he felt. Reaching for the fallen notepad, she looked at it tearfully: *Dom called 3.30. Says 'break a leg'.*

She covered her ears as more giggles and whoops penetrated the booming soundtrack.

She was furious with Simon for 'proving himself' with her best friend. She was livid with Mia for betraying their friendship. Most of all, she was angry with idiotic, disbelieving Melanie Holden for imagining that her amazing six-month romance had had to be secretly flawed because everything she did turned bad. She'd got a title role in a departmental production and ended up in a fat-suit with no lines; she'd got a gorgeous boyfriend and dared him to prove he wasn't gay. She wanted to drop down from the West Wing roof and abseil through the window to break some furniture and scream at both of them for not answering the door; she wanted to hurt them like they were hurting her.

A shadow fell across her and she looked up hopefully, eyes swimming, desperate for it to be Simon, but it was one of the drunks from the cloisters.

'Meshage for Dominic Mastersh,' he slurred. 'Hish dad shaysh the babyshbeenborn and he'll call back intenminush.'

Too choked to speak, Laney thrust the pad at him to write it down, but the messenger was already lurching away, singing along as R.E.M. was replaced by Ned's Atomic Dustbin.

Realising he had been looking for Dom, Laney resumed her door-hammering, praying that it was him in there and not Simon. But the giggles and laughter had fallen silent and there was no response.

Eventually she trailed to the phones and waited in a freezing draught for one of them to ring. Eventually one sprang to life. 'Acorn Antiques,' she answered. 'I'm afraid Miss Babs is indisposed having her embonpoint reupholstered in Old Gold Dralon. May I help?'

'I'm trying to contact Dominic Masters,' came a broad Yorkshire rasp. 'I'm on a hospital payphone, so this has to be quick.'

Laney was battling not to cry. 'I'm not sure he's here.'

'You know him then?'

'I'm a friend of Mia's,' she said, adding silently, Or I was until tonight.

'Am I glad to talk to you! The last lad I spoke to was proper kaylied. Be sure to tell Dominic his sister's had the baby. Say our Alison's fine. It was touch and go. Nipper had to come out t'cat flap in t'end, but mother and baby are right as rain. Dominic's an uncle.'

It was slowly dawning on her that Dom must be here. 'Are you sure he was coming here tonight, Mr Masters?'

''Appen I am, lass.' He chuckled. 'Tell Dominic it's a bonny little girl. Five pound one. Name of Adele, like our Mia suggested. Alison couldn't be doing with Cressida. Tell him he's to come home and meet his niece as soon as he's got his answer. And he must bring our Mia along for a double celebration.'

'Double celebration?'

But, with a series of beeps and clanks that indicated a coin being rejected as credit ran out, the line went dead.

She pounded back up the stairs to the third floor and almost fell over Leo sitting with his back propped against Mia's door, Shakespeare's Sister singing 'Stay' at top volume behind him. He had the spiral notepad in his hands, which he made a fumbling attempt to pocket when he saw Laney, but he was so clumsy with drunken tiredness that she reclaimed it easily. A new message had been added in the last few minutes. On a fresh page, in Simon's distinctive, looping hand, was *DO NOT DISTURB*.

Sobbing, Laney fled.

Laney's chain-smoking roommate had invited her boyfriend to stay over that night. Trying to ignore the giggling and fumbling beneath the duvet that was taking place on the opposite side of the room, she lay awake cuddling Eric the dinosaur until the dawn light stole across the ceiling. That was when she heard a light tap on the door.

She was out of the room like a shot, ready to strangle Simon with the corridor fire hose, but it was Mia, still wearing the clothes she'd had on the night before, her hair scraped back off her green-tinged face. She looked about twelve.

Laney stared at her in silence, too upset to speak.

'Can we talk?' Mia's voice was so hoarse it was barely audible, although whether from penitence or simply the result of smoking, laughing and fornicating all night was impossible to tell.

'Not in here.' She closed the door on the exhibitionist roommate. 'We'll go to yours.'

Mia looked away guiltily. 'Simon's still asleep. I've tried violence and cold water but he won't even open one eye.'

'He'll be like that for hours.' Laney turned to march towards the stairs. 'Let's have breakfast.' She always needed food in a crisis, and never more so than now.

The echoing emptiness of the Founders Hall refectory early on a wet Sunday morning in March afforded them a curious privacy.

Having loaded her plate with a greasy fry-up, Laney derived a cruel pleasure from the fact that Mia took one look at it and had to rush to the loos to be sick.

When she came back, sliding into the seat opposite, she announced shakily, 'Last night did *not* happen.'

'It did.' Laney prodded her tomato with her fork. 'You were together *all* night. You both heard me knocking.'

'We couldn't hear anything over the music.' Mia was making slow progress through a slice of dry toast.

Laney pushed her plate aside, food uneaten.

'You have to trust us,' Mia pleaded. 'Please don't split up over this. He'd be lost without you. Like I'll be lost without Dom.' Her face crumpled.

Laney looked away to hide her own tears. 'His father phoned last night, when you were listening to music with *my* boyfriend.'

The bloodshot green eyes blinked. 'He called here?'

'He obviously thinks Dom's with you. He was very excited about the baby.'

Mia laid down her toast, deathly pale. 'The baby?'

'Dom's an uncle. You should pass on your congratulations.'

'Think I might just have to be sick again first.' She bolted.

Laney looked at her plate. She formed the sausages into a wonky smile in a face with mushroom eyes, tomato cheeks and a hash-brown nose, capped with scrambled-egg hair, which she decided reminded her of Dom's. She laid the bacon over the top and turned it into Simon, with his foppish curtains of dark hair.

Incandescent with rage again, she picked up the plate and carried it out of the refectory and across the quad to the West Wing, rattling up two floors in the birdcage lift before marching to Mia's room. Finding the door unlocked, she stormed inside and up-ended the contents over the familiar body that was sprawled on the Paisley duvet on the floor.

'Breakfast in bed, darling!'

Simon didn't even stir.

Heading to the sink, she filled the two chipped mugs balanced there and tipped cold water over him.

He opened one eye.

'Is it still raining?' he mumbled, blinking water away.

Laney gritted her teeth. 'What *exactly* happened in here last night?'

'Is this one of those lateral-thinking puzzles, like the unopened parachute?' He sat up slowly, and she saw that he was still pretty much fully dressed – he'd discarded his coat and his shirt buttons were undone, revealing the leather bootlaces around his neck from which hung a succession of amulets. She had to fight an urge to grab them and twist the truth out of him.

He was looking around him in total bewilderment. 'Isn't this Mia's room?'

'Don't try that I-can't-remember-a-thing trick with me!'

He regarded her groggily. 'The last thing I remember is mixing cocktails in the costume room,' he said.

Laney growled ominously. 'It'll come back.'

Returning to her room twenty minutes later to find Laney still furiously cross-examining Simon, Mia did an about-turn and raced across the quad to Leo's corridor. He answered the door in quaintly old-fashioned striped pyjamas, blinking sleep and hangover from his eyes, teeth chattering. Lighting his gas fire with shaking hands, he beckoned her into his narrow bed to keep warm until the room lost its chill.

'Dom's dad thinks he set out from Leeds after lunch yesterday.' Mia curled around him. She was shaking all over, her wet cheeks like ice through the cotton PJs. 'He should be here.'

Leo hugged her tightly. 'If that's the case, he'll turn up. His bike's probably broken down again. I bet he rang and nobody picked up – you know how many people here ignore the payphones ringing or can't be bothered to pass on messages.'

She snuggled closer, too wretched to believe him. 'I think he changed his mind. He's outgrown me, like I said. I thought you'd be glad.'

Her chin was on his shoulder so he had to crane his neck to look at her face. 'You know how I feel.'

Those green eyes fixed on his. 'Jealous?'

'Exactly.' He kissed her nose.

She looked into his kind dark eyes, astonished by the affection in them. In the six months they had been close friends, he'd never tried to do more than hold her hand.

'Do you want to make love to me?' she asked.

Smiling, he traced her lips with a forefinger. 'Loving you is enough.'

'I've really goofed up with Laney.'

'They'll kiss and make up,' he assured her. 'Laney's very forgiving.'

'I'll never forgive you, you thoughtless bastard!' Shouting felt great, assuaging her guilt and anger in one. 'You bastard!' Laney repeated. She'd never shouted at anyone like this before. 'Fucking bastard!'

Simon's silver eyes, paler than ever, were shot through with the red of too much drink, dope and regret. 'I don't remember anything.'

'I heard laughter! I was outside that door half the night. Can you imagine how humiliated I was?' In the back of her mind, she worried that Simon might suddenly remember she had accused him of being gay. But for now venting her spleen was too satisfying to stop.

'What's more, you drink too much, flirt too much and take me for granted! You'd better clean up your fucking act.' She had never sworn so much. She added a few more 'bastard's under her breath for good measure.

Simon looked up at her through his lashes, the picture of contrition. Then, without warning, he grabbed her wrist and towed her to the bathroom block at the far end of the wing, where he located a free shower cubicle and hustled her inside.

'What are you doing?' she shrieked as he turned on a lukewarm deluge. They were both still fully dressed and soon soaked through.

'Cleaning up my act, and your mouth.' He started to kiss her throat, pulling off her top.

Laney was about to protest that sex was the last thing on her mind, but she could already feel his excitement hard against her belly, and an unexpected mule-kick of lust stopped her lips. This was the moment she'd wanted so badly last night in the prop cupboard, an instinctive, fast and relentless proof of desire. Within seconds, she was hoisted around him and he was filling her up, fingers digging into her buttocks, tongue deep in her mouth, cock punching up inside her. It felt angry and feral and delicious. She was almost mortified to find herself coming so quickly, appalled that her body was abandoning its inhibitions totally on this of all days, so that their first joint orgasm exploded inside her as they let out loud, almost mournful groans, repeating each other's name, voices loaded with love and regret. And as the high washed over her, her anger was rinsed away.

'I could do this all day.' Simon found her lips with his, his heat still pulsing out inside her.

Laney smiled into his mouth, determined that he would.

When Mia returned to the West Wing, the birdcage lift was out of order and she had to pause every few steps on the three flights of stairs to hold back the nausea. Halfway along the corridor she spotted her Divinity-student neighbour, waiting malevolently to harangue her about last night's loud music.

'I'm going to complain to the porter,' she snarled. 'This place gets worse every day. Apparently the lift's now out of action because some couple has commandeered it for a love-in, John-and-Yoko-style.'

The notepad was hanging back on its pin by Mia's room number, with a new message written on it in Laney's large, round hand. *You're right – last night did NOT happen xx*

Mia ripped it off and clutched it to her lips with relief.

'I expect an apology at least!' her neighbour snarled.

Tears in her eyes, Mia held up the note by way of explanation, then slipped into her room. There, she dashed to the window that looked out across the playing fields to the main entrance gates, willing a motorcycle to come through them.

Chapter 7

Dominic Masters did not appear in the last three performances of Agitprop's Brecht run. Nor did he turn up for the first read-through in Stratford. Nothing had been heard from him since the afternoon he'd called Mia's halls of residence to wish her luck for her final performance in the Lorca. The last person to have spoken to him before he disappeared seemed to have been the fellow student who had posted the note on Mia's door.

Mia tried desperately to track down whoever it was, leaving flyers all over campus asking for their help, but no one came forward.

Dom's father was convinced he'd been heading for Surrey to propose to Mia. 'We had words after your visit. He said you were too young and clever to be stuck with a bad-tempered sod like him, and I told him he was a fool to let you go. Then he asked for his mother's ring and left promising to make things right.' But Dom had said nothing to his flatmates about where he was going the day he'd disappeared; his fellow actors at Agitprop Theatre knew he was ducking out of a show, but hadn't been told why.

Feeding cards and coins into the payphones in the glass-walled quad corridor, Mia rang hospitals, the police, Centrepoint, old National Youth Theatre friends, even the RSC to track down new co-star Julia. Every avenue led to a dead-end. She travelled back and forth to Barnsley on the coach, but her guilt and helplessness just grew with each visit to his old home. Dom's father's health quickly worsened with the stress, his breathing so bad that he needed constant oxygen. Alison, usually super-practical, had her hands full, juggling an invalid parent and visits to the paediatric unit at the hospital with Adele, who wasn't putting on weight as she should.

It was Mia who made the decision to report Dom as a missing person, but given his age and the scarcity of details surrounding his disappearance, his case wasn't a priority: a man in his twenties going AWOL somewhere between Yorkshire and Surrey after a lovers' tiff was not seen as a serious concern.

Yet it made Mia's life almost unbearable. Her university friends kept her going. Laney coaxed her to eat something each day, mopped her tears and reassured her that she wasn't to blame; but it was Leo who kept her sane, taking the night shifts during which Mia talked non-stop, her clever head running through every scenario, unable to sleep at all. Leo had never hidden his dislike of Dom, but he could see her need for information to get her past the shock and fear. Together they wrote letters and phoned radio stations, sent out posters and press packs, but no useful information came back, just vague sightings and communications from cranks.

Mia stared out of her window across the playing fields a great deal in the month after Dom disappeared, watching as the thickening pelt of grass deepened from lime to emerald, spring bulbs burst forth in ecclesiastical purple and gold, and rainbows capped the rugby posts when April showers collided with spring sun. Her customary colourful optimism, meanwhile, seemed to turn grey.

'She's like the French Lieutenant's Woman.' Laney sighed as she helped Simon pack up his chaos ready to vacate halls for the Easter holidays, which they were planning to spend together. 'The rugby team think their luck's in, having Mia Wilde gazing out at the touchline. They're laying bets as to which of them she fancies.'

'Actresses always need props and wings.' Simon stooped to pick up a textbook that had strayed from the pile Laney was lobbing into a box. It was Lorca's collected works, and he studied the photograph of the playwright on the cover. 'Leo really does look terribly like Federico García Lorca.'

'"Ay, the pain it costs me to love you as I love you!"' she quoted Leo's favourite Lorca poem.

Simon looked at her, silver eyes gleaming. 'I would take any amount of pain for you – oof!' He groaned as she dropped a pile of set-design source books into his lap.

'These were due back at the library six weeks ago.'

'My criminal activities know no bounds.' He scattered the books and pulled her on top of him, reaching up beneath her skirt. 'Make love to me, darling, before they throw me in jail.'

Simon had been adoring and repentant ever since The Night That Never Happened. As though determined to cast a spell to hang on to the magic he and Laney shared, his latest purchase from London's Camden Lock had been a multi-coloured wizard's coat, which he matched with thigh-hugging 501s and sixteen-hole Dr Martens with tartan ribbons for laces. With the charm of a hypnotist, he'd set about wooing her into forgetting the pain. He still had no recollections of the night that now haunted her, ransacked her dreams and threatened the fragile truce between them.

The only time it was possible to forget it was when they were making love, like now, the passionate playfulness they shared excluding all else, each gasp, groan, play-bite, laugh and shudder a shared language of intimacy and reconciliation.

Afterwards, she glanced at the alarm clock now resting on top of a box of cassettes and remembered she'd promised to be somewhere ten minutes earlier. 'I'll take these books back.' She removed a guide to Moorish architecture from beneath her knee and kissed him perfunctorily.

'What about the fines?'

'Loving you costs me . . .'

Little secrets and lies have started creeping in, she thought, as she hurried across the lower quad to scale the stone stairs into the West Wing and up to the third floor. She wasn't sure why she hadn't told Simon that she'd agreed to meet Mia that afternoon but suspected it was because he might want to come along too.

Laney knew she policed Simon over-zealously around Mia these days, although her natural inclination to keep Mia at a much greater distance had been thwarted by the devastation that had ripped through her friend's life since Dom's disappearance. He'd still made no contact, and Mia was rapidly falling apart.

In the weeks leading up to the Easter break, she had shrunk before their eyes, skin grey, beautiful tresses turning to lank dreadlocks. She'd stopped attending lectures and tutorials and failed to complete her essays. Earlier that week, Prof. Crotch, vengeful after the Guinness dousing, had suggested she swap to a less demanding course, or take the term off and resit the year.

But, as Laney was about to discover, Mia would need far longer than an academic term to sort herself out, having already unwittingly embarked on a new term of forty weeks.

'I'm pregnant,' she announced shakily as soon as Laney closed the door. Having lost so much weight, she looked younger than ever. 'I thought the first test was wrong – I was a bit tipsy when I did it. But I've weed on another stick since then, and seen Matron. It's a done deal.'

The room was like a furnace. Mia's appetite had clearly returned and she'd been working her way through her last half-loaf of Mother's Pride, toasted on the gas fire and smothered in Nutella. She stared at a burned slice with tears pouring down her face.

Despite the heat, Laney felt as if a slab of ice had struck her a body blow. She wanted to ask straight out if it could be Simon's, but the words choked her. Instead she managed to mumble, 'Whose is it?'

Staring into the glowing gas fire, Mia crumbled a toast crust in her fingers and whispered, 'Mine. Me and my idiotic, immaculate preconceptions.'

Laney inferred that there were grounds for doubt. 'What are you going to do?'

Two more slices of Mother's Pride were slotted into the improvised wire-coat-hanger toaster. 'Keep it, of course. Don't even think about arguing. It's not up for debate. I am having this baby.'

Almost suffocating, Laney went to open the window. That night had not happened, she reminded herself firmly. This baby was not Simon's. He was nothing to do with it. Mia was a pregnant student whose boyfriend had disappeared. Her life was in crisis.

She stared across the playing fields at the horse chestnuts in the distance, their candles starting to gleam from the dark foliage. 'You could be a very great actress, Mia.' She knew that two casting agents had sent incredibly positive letters to Mia after the Lorca production, suggesting she give them a call. Both had been cast aside because they had contained no news of Dom.

'I *will* be a very great actress,' Mia said determinedly, 'and a very great mother, Laney. I'll go through with this with or without you, but your support would make a world of difference. I want you to be godmother.'

Laney shifted uncomfortably. 'You know I'd be lousy, summoning the devil for fun on his eighteenth, that sort of thing.'

On cue, thick smoke filled the room. Laney turned, and saw that the Mother's Pride was flaming merrily in the gas-fire toaster. She raced across and hooked it into the little washbasin with a knife, dousing it with water.

Mia was crying again, so she crouched to wrap an arm around her. 'Of course I'll support you, whatever you do, you clot. I'm incredibly touched I'm the first person you told.'

'Leo already knows.'

'Is he going to be godfather?'

'He's offered to be father.'

Laney's jaw dropped. 'Did I miss something?'

The big green eyes looked up imploringly. 'I'm from eight generations of Lancashire farmers, remember. A child needs a dad. Leo couldn't agree more – he says he wants to look after me and this child more than anything, and his mother will be over the moon.'

'But he's ...' The words died in her throat. She thought she knew Leo better than most. She adored him for his wit, sensitivity and intense loyalty to his close friends, the way he clucked around them, teased them, styled them and supported them. He could magic amazing meals from student junk food, recite Lorca and Antonio Machado in Spanish, play exquisite guitar, loved to paint and sketch and was incredibly entertaining. In many ways, although he was the youngest and quietest, he parented them all. She knew he had a special empathy with Mia – they could spend hours talking horses, which they both loved and had grown up around, and they made each other laugh like no others – but as a father figure to an unborn child, he seemed cast from entirely the wrong mould.

'He's my best friend,' said Mia, simply. 'My best *boy* friend,' she added, squeezing Laney's arm. 'And I can hardly marry you.'

Laney groaned. 'Please don't tell me you're getting *married*?'

'How could I refuse? He's making my dress – our dresses.'

'He's wearing a dress too?'

'Yours, you daft cow. You're chief bridesmaid.' She forced a bright smile. 'You and Mia ...' She led her in their friendship catchphrase, first coined within hours of meeting one another and often repeated.

'Me and Mia,' Laney obliged hollowly.

'We'll put on a great show.'

Laney knew that she should argue, but a small voice in her head was stalling her, telling her that this way Mia's baby would have a father and it wasn't Simon. She had a duty to speak up for everyone's sake, most of all Leo's. She couldn't understand what he would get out of it when Mia was in love with another man.

'What about Dom?' she asked carefully.

Mia's face adopted the expression it wore when any mention was made of The Night That Didn't Happen, a perfect mask of detachment, the actress within able to subvert her feelings despite the tears still drying on her cheeks.

'He's out of my life now.' Her voice was brittle with the effort of feigning indifference. 'Trust me, I'm looking forward to the future with my baby, whose father is very much *in* my life.' She gave

Laney a hard look, making her panic again that Simon's name would be mentioned.

To her shame, she kept her thoughts against the marriage quiet. No doubt two sets of parents would get involved over Easter, second thoughts would abound and it would all look totally different in three weeks' time. 'When's the big day?' she asked, humouring Mia.

'A fortnight. Gretna Green. You'll be back by then. I checked. Leo's talking to Simon now – we want him to be best man.'

'You're eloping?'

'Isn't it exciting?' She laughed, sounding more like the wilful, idealistic Mia.

Laney's eyes widened. 'Life isn't a Lorca play, Mia. *Blood Wedding* ended very badly.'

'This isn't going to be a blood wedding, or a white one for that matter,' Mia insisted. 'It's going to be a bloody good marriage. Just you watch.'

Chapter 8

2012

Undressing her lover with the aid of a pair of pliers and a can of WD-40 was becoming familiar practice to Iris. His grand guard was warped from lance strikes and his bevor battered from falls; the buckles on his cuirass straps had rusted and his pauldrons were so bent from multiple blows to the arms and shoulders that they resembled car bumpers in a demolition derby. Removing his chain-mail standard over his head was like lifting a shoal of heavy metal fish.

I've got myself a real-life knight in shining armour! Iris announced to all her friends via text the day that she accepted Dougie Everett's marriage proposal.

Removing a suit of armour from a stunt man took a straight face as well as engineering prowess. There was always a moment when Dougie was stripped to his doublet and hose that Iris fought uncontrollable giggles, especially if he was still wearing the quilted bonnet tied under his chin like an Australian surf guard's patrol cap. The doublet was part straitjacket, part bad eighties pop video, and the hose were covered with buckles like a punk's drainpipe bondage trousers. But any laughter died when they were unlaced and she drew aside the linen shirt to reveal a tanned, muscular torso covered with bruises as blue as his eyes. He was her hero, an old-fashioned caballero of seduction. The two men – boys, really – that she had slept with before him bore no comparison, their couplings sweating and nervous occasions of self-discovery. Dougie was a maestro, as sexually bold as a young medieval king with his mistress. And removing armour certainly beat loosening a tie or unzipping a hoodie. What followed was unbridled pleasure.

In the weeks they'd been together, Iris had found herself on whole new learning and pleasure curves, as well as spread-eagled on beds, sofas, tables and hay bales as Dougie manoeuvred her around hotel rooms and horseboxes as boldly and skilfully as he rode, until she was supple, obedient and joyful to his touch. Making love with him was intense, vivid and devoted. Dougie may have ridden a lot of horses – and women – but when he found a good one he kept them for life, and while the news of his engagement broke many hearts, he had no intention of breaking his marriage vows.

The announcement that Iris Devonshire was marrying playboy Dougie Everett received a mixed reaction. It was a provocative match, and some even called it a cynical publicity stunt – the daughter of a well-known actor getting engaged at just nineteen to a notorious hell-raiser amid a flurry of tabloid interest. On the surface, her beau was many young women's fantasy figure, a dashing stunt rider with the face of a laughing cavalier, renowned for his charm and daring.

One didn't have to scratch the surface of his armour very deeply, however, to see the base metal beneath the silver plate. Well known as a blue-blooded bruiser, Dougie Everett was a society playboy, bred in the purple from old establishment stock and now living in the pink. At twenty-eight, his colourful past was well documented. Kinder souls blamed Dougie's waywardness on his father's public disgrace at a time when he was most vulnerable: he was the son of the outspoken Tory peer and former cabinet minister Vaughan Everett, once Thatcher's young golden boy, exposed in the noughties as a serial philanderer who had accepted more cash for questions than a quiz-show host.

Fed up with loyally appearing at the gate for photo shoots holding her disgraced husband's hand, Dougie's mother had eventually run off with her fitness trainer, after which the teenage Dougie had gone increasingly off the rails, always in trouble at boarding school, bombing most of his exams, and later being thrown out of Officer Training Corps in a notorious drugs scandal. The would-be cavalry officer then played fast and loose with London's social set before unexpectedly settling upon his forte as a daredevil horseman, re-enacting jousting tournaments at stately homes, showing off courtly skills at county fairs and standing in for actors in film and television. He now ran his own team of horses from a rented yard in Buckinghamshire.

It was when he'd got a job working on the fourth of the hugely successful Ptolemy Finch fantasy-adventure movies that he'd met Iris, daughter of legendary heartthrob Leo Devonshire, who'd followed in her famous father's screen-acting footsteps at a young age to play the role of Purple, sidekick to boy-hero Ptolemy. While her co-star, Con O'Mara, needed Dougie to double in all the horse-riding scenes, Iris was an accomplished rider who did her own stunt work. She had soon developed a fierce crush on charming, fearless Dougie, and riding off into the sunset together now was a dream come true.

Despite the cynical rumours that he was only marrying her to further his acting ambitions, Iris loved Dougie deeply. He was her battle-worn soldier, misunderstood and maligned but as brave and loyal as Sir Galahad. His affection-starved upbringing made it hard for him to demonstrate his emotions, but when he did – particularly when they were making love – his vulnerability could move her to tears. He also made her cry with laughter on a daily basis.

When news of the forthcoming nuptials broke, Iris's mother Mia was publicly as sanguine as ever, but privately far less reticent, alternating between hysteria, fury and desperation that her daughter was about to 'throw away' her life. Renowned for her charity work and her great beauty, Mia had lived vicariously through both husband and daughter, supporting them unswervingly through every high and low. That one now lived an entirely separate life in LA and the other wanted to abandon her ambitions so young devastated her.

But it was as though a rainbow had burst through the clouds above Iris's rainy life. She had become increasingly studious in recent years, to the degree that, until she met Dougie, she had been poised to turn her back on her early acting success and return to full-time education, longing to lead a normal life away from the media glare.

Accustomed to press interest throughout childhood because of her father's fame, she could never have anticipated the degree to which her entire life would become public property when she was cast as Purple. She had spent most of her teens synonymous with a pointy-eared, half-alien temptress. As each film was made, Ptolemy's loyal sidekick's costumes had got smaller and tighter in inverse proportion to the actress who played her growing up. By the fourth, *Ptolemy Finch and the Emerald Falcon*, she'd been reduced to wearing little more than a sculpted bikini in most scenes, including the fight sequences and the dramatic horse charge. That was when she'd first encountered Dougie and fallen for the handsome, laughing daredevil straight away. Her crush had raged unreciprocated until the London première, when he had presented Iris with a huge emerald pendant in front of the crowds in Leicester Square and kissed her in the most romantic of brave-hearted, audacious gestures. Their love affair had taken off like a rocket.

Just three months later, Iris was sporting a huge ruby on her ring finger. She no longer intended to take up her place at Durham University away from the press spotlight. She was going to ride all over the world with Dougie, and the spotlight could do what the hell it liked as long as it didn't frighten the horses.

Her refusal to sign her contract for the sixth and final Ptolemy movie had caused huge consternation among the producers and film-goers. With the fifth now in the can and a release date set for the following year, pre-production of *Ptolemy Finch and the Raven's Curse* had ground to a halt. The surrounding publicity pointed the blame firmly at Dougie's dusty riding boots, although Iris had decided to resign as the world's favourite pointy-eared eye candy months before she'd met him. Dougie had tried to persuade her to finish the series, but public opinion had already cast him as a baddie, stealing England's finest young jewel, and there had even been a death threat against Purple's real-life fiancé.

Iris's close friends knew how unhappy she had been in recent years and how demoralising she found playing Purple and the celebrity that came with the role. Although often reported as nervy and neurotic, she possessed an impulsive optimism that made her hard to derail once she'd set upon a course. She was also fiercely stubborn. Nobody dared suggest that what she was doing was wrong. Nor could they deny how charming and good-looking Dougie was, or how madly in love the couple seemed, and his social circle brought huge fun to parties and outings. The ad hoc engagement bash, staged at a sprawling Cotswolds manor belonging to one of Dougie's relatives, had gone on for three days.

*

Of all Iris's friends, Chloe Benson had known her the longest. Growing up just a few fields apart, on the leafy slopes where the banks of the Thames swept up towards the Chiltern Hills, the girls had met through a mutual passion for ponies and remained close, united by a love of all things four-legged and a hatred of public scrutiny. Both had famous fathers and had grown up familiar with bullying and false friendship.

Chloe was one of the very few who knew just how strongly Iris shared her father's distaste for fame. At fourteen, Iris had confessed that finding out she'd won the role of Purple was the worst day of her life. When, four years later, she'd excitedly announced that she had a place at Durham to read English, Chloe had been thrilled for her. The girls had last seen each other very briefly at Christmas because Chloe had been working towards her degree in veterinary science at a farm placement over most of the holiday, and Iris had talked of nothing but her delight at the prospect of student life. They'd excitedly pinned down their long-standing plan to travel together to a five-week slot the following summer. The girls had already plotted a route along the Mediterranean coast, much of it on horseback.

Down-to-earth pragmatist Chloe did not make friends easily. Straight-talking and stubbornly antisocial, she was always buried in a book or playing with a computer when she wasn't tending something four-legged; she would quite happily pass several days without speaking to a soul. Her self-possession had never fazed Iris, whose own mother also far preferred animals to humans and who adored Chloe for her fierce independence, her kindness, and the fact that she found celebrity a totally false god.

Chloe's father was comedy legend Oscar Benson, which inevitably led to the assumption that she should be wildly funny, which she wasn't, although she shared his rubbery face, expressive eyes and solid frame. She also shared his hair, the trademark bedsprings halo that made him unmistakable and her deeply self-conscious. Growing up as Oscar's daughter meant she knew how contrary public and private faces could be, the hapless, cuddly funnyman that the public loved at odds with the cold, money-obsessed businessman he was at home.

His two marriages had been cool-headed investments. Chloe's mother had been heiress to a Brighton entertainment magnate, who had helped launch Oscar's early stand-up career; she'd later invested a great deal of her inheritance in her husband's film-industry interests. Although he had found fame as a stand-up comic in the nineties, Oscar was better known as a film-industry insider now, but he'd never stopped craving the celebrity that had slipped away from him and looking for ways to buy it back. Growing up, Chloe had been acutely embarrassed that her father would often bellow, 'Do you know who I *am*?' to bemused strangers.

Thanks to his second marriage, however, it was a phrase Oscar no longer needed to use. Laney had come with no personal wealth or notoriety, but he'd spotted her talent as a screenwriter, and recognised that the cheapest way to invest was to marry her, a move that had recently netted him the biggest box-office comedy hit of the decade and rejuvenated his performing career. Currently based in LA, where he had a sequel in development, Oscar was lapping up his new-found cachet as the British Eddie Murphy.

By contrast, Iris's father Leo seemed to have fallen upon fame as nobly as a knight upon his sword. Having made his name in feel-good romances, he was now playing the title role in the long-running US network television series *Chancellor*. An ever-popular chat-show guest, renowned for his anecdotes and self-deprecating wit, Leo had often been quoted as saying he'd never intended to be an actor, having always dreamed of a career as a costume designer, just as his daughter secretly longed to be an academic – or so Chloe had thought until Iris announced that she was getting married instead.

Chloe was sitting an anatomy paper when Iris's text came through. Emerging from the exam, she read the message in a daze, the last of her Pro-Plus-and-energy-drink cocktail fading away and rendering her too blunt with tiredness to absorb her friend's news. She messaged back a promise to call soon.

Her first year as an undergraduate in Nottingham had been so intense that she'd spared little thought for Iris in recent weeks, although she had seen *Ptolemy Finch and the Emerald Falcon* and sent her a text saying how much she'd enjoyed it, especially her incredibly brave riding. Despite their long-standing closeness, the two girls had few friends in common, their trips home to Oxfordshire rarely coinciding in the past year. Chloe never read red-tops or gossip magazines, and while she loved Twitter and Facebook with near-geeky compulsion, she was no dedicated follower of trends, preferring quirky science, oddball comedians and her small circle of acquaintances to celebrity scandal. In a recent phone call, her mother had passed on the news that Iris had a bit of a romance going on, but Chloe was too frantic juggling course modules to take it in.

It was only when Iris messaged her again that evening, asking her to be a bridesmaid for a summer solstice wedding, that Chloe took in the scale of what was happening: this engagement was going all the way up the aisle at breakneck speed.

Her first reaction was to feel aggrieved. She'd worked hard all year, missing out on Christmas and Easter holidays to fulfil placements with dairy cattle and then sheep. She sent a curt reply: she wasn't sure she'd be available now that her summer travel plans needed rearranging. She then agreed her third student placement to follow straight on from the end of the summer term, knowing the date coincided with the ceremony.

Warm-hearted as ever, Iris wrote a long apologetic email straight away, explaining how much she loved Dougie and begging Chloe to reconsider. You are my oldest friend. To not have you at my wedding would be like missing a limb. I know we'd planned our travels together around then, darling Chlo, but we WILL do that another time, I promise. Please say you'll be there. XXX

Chloe replied: Am doing animal husbandry EMS in poultry farm throughout. Self-justification still burned at her core, filling her nostrils with an unpleasant smell that had a tang of jealousy.

Iris was immediately on the case: Of course your studies are the priority; I admire you so much for it. You are amazing to be so dedicated. And if I can't claim you as a bridesmaid, I would really like a hen night. You can't possibly refuse to be a part of that. We'll choose the date to suit you. Animal husbandry and feathers galore ... XXX

Grudgingly, Chloe let herself be talked into it: Iris needed her old friends on side right now – a moment's Googling showed that her parents' disapproval had gone viral.

Iris had inherited her mother's desire to spread happiness and good will, and in particular to her father. 'Please be happy for me,' she implored when they finally spoke on the phone after a week's terse exchange of text messages. 'I absolutely adore him.'

'Adore him, yes,' Leo said, his soft voice crackling on a bad line. 'Just don't marry him. You're way too young.'

'You and Mum were the same age as me when you married.'

'That was a lifetime ago.'

'*My* lifetime, not yours,' she breathed unhappily. 'Please be here to give me away.'

'Darling, you know that's impossible. I'm working all the—'

'You're just too bloody frightened of giving yourself away, you mean!' She rang off.

In floods of tears, she rode her little Italian scooter incredibly badly on the ten miles of dual carriageway between home and Dougie's stable yard, where she drew comfort from the familiar smells as she leaned across a wooden rail to watch him ride. Completely focused upon his task, Dougie was repeatedly galloping a hot-headed Friesian stallion up to a circular disc attached to a wooden T and spearing it squarely with the weighted lance beneath his arm.

He reined left and rode up to her as soon as he saw her, navy eyes squinting against a lowering sun that dyed his blond hair the colour of ripe papaya. 'What did he say?'

'He's not even bothering to come over from the States.'

'Oh, poor darling!' Spearing the lance tip into the grass along-side, he leapt from the big black horse and threw the reins over its handle before gathering her into his arms. 'I'm sure we can talk him round. He hasn't even met me yet.'

'Forget it. I know him. He has no intention of changing his mind. He'll plead filming commitments, but that's bullshit. If he has enough time to talk to Mum on Skype for hours on end, he has enough time to pop home and give his daughter away. They were talking most of last night.'

'At least they've agreed we can host the wedding at Wootton. That's huge progress.'

Wootton was the Devonshire family's riverside home just outside Morley-on-Thames, a white-tiered Palladian confection perfect for a fairy-tale wedding.

'It's only so they can control it all,' she complained. 'I haven't told you about the conditions.'

His arms tightened around her. 'What conditions?'

'Must be unplugged – no cameras, phones or tablets. Absolutely no press interviews or photo shoots before, during or after. No rock bands or fireworks. No stunts. Guest list capped at a hundred.'

'No press. Christ!'

'The only condition I agree with,' Iris pointed out. 'But the guest-list cap is ridiculous – so many friends will miss out.'

'They're trying to control you, Riz darling.' Smelling of mints, aftershave and hot horse, he drew her into a long, breathless kiss. 'We're in charge now, remember?' he said when they finally came up for air. 'The future Mr and Mrs Everett. I do the cherishing, and you love, honour and obey. It'll be a very traditional marriage, not like your parents'.'

'I just want them to be happy for me.'

They kissed even longer this time before he pulled away. 'This is going to be our special day. Let me speak with your father.'

'You'll never get hold of him,' she predicted gloomily.

'I'll fly to LA. If you tell him I'm on my way, he can hardly refuse to see me.'

'You'd do that?'

His deep blue eyes glittered into hers from beneath their long, sooty lashes. 'As soon as he meets me, he'll see what's best for his daughter. I'll have him eating out of my hand as well as offering to give away yours, Riz.' He cupped her face in his hands. 'Even if he really can't get off set, he can give us his blessing.'

'I'll come with you!' Her face lit up.

He shook his head. 'Turn your back and your mother will erect a medieval obstacle course of rolling boulders and boiling oil to make me run the gauntlet along the aisle. We need you here to make sure the wedding goes ahead the way *we* want it.'

She giggled. 'We're keeping the ceremony really simple, though, aren't we?'

Unhooking the reins from the lance, he swung easily back into the saddle and reached down to help her up in front of him.

'Just you, me and the horizon, Riz baby.' He kicked the stallion's sides so that he sprang straight into full tilt and charged across the turf.

Chapter 9

Hurtling around the streets of downtown Nairobi on the back of a motorbike taxi, Griff Donne felt as though he was moving under water, the incessant rain thundering down and tyres whooshing through muddy rivers. Weaving in and out of the brightly coloured *matatus*, with music blaring, horns beeping, voices shouting, his driver never once took his hand off the throttle.

When they arrived at the address Griff had been given, he thrust a few shillings at the man and dived inside. If he'd expected a sleazy back-street drinking den full of street-walking *malayas* and their pimps swilling illegally brewed *changaa*, he couldn't have got it more wrong. The mix in the packed, rowdy bar was easygoing and laughter-fuelled; yellow Tusker labels and white smiles flashed through the dark room where drinkers crowded around bleached-wood tables and waitresses threaded past, trays aloft. On a small stage a five-piece band played *benga* loudly enough to make the floorboards jump.

Peeling off his sodden leather jacket and slicking aside dripping hair, Griff searched the tables, praying he hadn't missed his moment again. His eye was caught by the glint of white-blond hair in a corner and he felt the adrenalin kick in. A month of flying around Kenya chasing false leads to dead-ends had finally paid off. Here was the gold at the end of the rainbow.

As he fought his way across the room, Dominic Masters looked up and those extraordinary blue eyes narrowed.

'How many TIMES?' he bellowed. 'I told you the answer is no.'

At either side of him two huge-shouldered Kenyans whom Griff recognised from the Mara River Camp crew stood up protectively as he approached, but Dominic held up his hand to still them.

'*Sawa*.' To Griff's surprise, he broke into a rare smile and gestured towards a free chair. 'As you clearly need to dry off, Griff, you can join us for a beer. Sit.'

From the vivid scars on his handsome, creased face to the knot in the elbow of his shirt where his forearm should have been, Dominic Masters looked every inch the unapologetic action hero that Griff had been battling to befriend, but tonight he had clearly imbibed enough to be unusually mellow. Griff settled into an empty chair as Dominic signalled for a waitress.

'A Coke for Ngara – and Leboo will have a Stoney.' Dominic indicated the cheeky Kikuyu man and the tall, surly Masai, members of the four-man team who helped inflate each balloon that Dominic piloted, then chased it around the Masai Mara before packing it away again.

'Cheers.' He raised his Tusker Malt to his lips as soon as it arrived.

The Kikuyu said something to Dominic that Griff didn't understand. He spoke a smattering of Swahili, but this was a Bantu language. The blond Yorkshireman laughed and raised his bottle. 'He says you're a very good tracker to find us here and that I should give you a job.'

Ngara gave him a toothy smile. Griff had always liked him best among Dominic's support team. By contrast, Leboo gazed past him at the act on stage.

'We fly back to the Mara tomorrow,' Dominic said in the rich voice that Griff knew television viewers would love. 'You should have stayed put in camp and waited for me to return to tell you my answer is still no.' He chuckled, eyeing the younger man over the lip of his bottle.

'What brought you to Nairobi?' Griff knew from previous conversations that Dominic hated the noise and pollution of big cities.

'Hospital. They want to fit me with a bionic arm.'

'You've never had a prosthetic?'

'I've always got by well enough. But then I flew a guest at the camp last year who works with US soldiers who lost limbs in Iraq and Afghanistan, and he kept on at me to see what could be done. He put me in touch with a specialist here in Kenya and I promised to come. Now I've fulfilled that promise, I can go home.'

Griff noticed Leboo's big eyes swivel to look at his boss, dark with disapproval, but he said nothing.

'Leboo and Ngara had never seen the capital city,' Dominic went on, 'so I brought them along for the ride. Now, like me, they can't wait to leave.' He signalled for more beer. 'You like Nairobi, Griff?'

'I prefer the savannah.'

'Maybe Ngara's right. I should offer you a job. You'd make a great co-pilot.'

Dominic Masters was a legend among safari balloonists and Griff longed to document him. Rugged, bloody-minded and brilliant at tracking game, he was known throughout the East African savannahs as the Cloud Man, and intrepid tourists had sought him out over the last decade to pilot them on the flight of their lives, first in the Serengeti and now at the luxurious eco-camp on the banks of the Mara. Well known for his white-blond hair, scarred face and broad Yorkshire accent, Dominic 'Cloud Man' Masters sounded like an intrepid character from a *Boys' Own* comic, especially when one knew the danger he courted in trying to conserve the wildlife he tracked from the air.

For several weeks Griff had based himself in the Mara, trying to persuade Cloud Man to take part in a television documentary. He had grasped every opportunity that came his way to shadow him in the balloon, watching him track, learning quickly and sharing the adrenalin rush as he began to understand his work and the immense skill it involved. Dominic Masters was a fascinating subject, his energy and dedication unparalleled, with a surprising flip-side in the joyful entertainment he gave visitors. Despite the crippling tourism slump, Mara River Camp remained fully booked in high season, and this had a great deal to do with the man who flew the eight-person basket within inches of the wildlife. He was a spectacular pilot and a spell-binding tour-guide, his descriptions packed with knowledge, passion and wit. Griff was convinced that the man and his work would make mesmerising television.

It was the voluntary work Dominic did to fight poachers that made him truly irresistible. Since the post-election decline in tourism in Kenya, poaching had become a huge problem again, its perpetrators flooding across the Tanzanian borders armed with AK-47s, machetes and snares. Dominic patrolled the Mara triangle in a small, camouflaged balloon, and radioed in any suspicious sightings to the NGO rangers. It was an extraordinarily brave act, given how vulnerable to attack he was, suspended in a basket just a few hundred feet above bandit camps using a specially adapted second burner that reduced the sound to a minimum. He'd been shot at many times. Griff had heard that it was during one such encounter he had lost his arm and acquired the livid scars that distorted the skin on one side of his face, running from one cobalt blue eye to his jaw. To the right, Dominic Masters was enviably handsome; to the left, he elicited fear and pity in equal measure. In Griff, he inspired intense curiosity. As heroes went, Dominic was close to Griff's idea of perfection.

But Dominic had never bought into the idea of a documentary. In fact, he had become increasingly resistant to the idea the more Griff pushed it. A fortnight earlier, when the rains had arrived and the balloons were packed away, he had told the Welshman to go away and stop wasting his time. Griff had been chasing his tail ever since.

Griff's tenacity lay behind his success as a television adventurer. Told that Masters had a beach house just outside Mombasa where he liked to hang out off-season, he'd flown straight there in pursuit, but found the modest weatherboard shack shuttered up, its padlock rusted. A neighbour had told him that Cloud Man no longer came here, put off by the Western tourists, the *mnazi* joints and the sex trade. A wild-goose chase had led Griff to Tanzania, then across the Serengeti to Lake Victoria and north to Homa Bay, chasing false leads. Everybody knew Cloud Man, it seemed, but he'd always just moved on, and Griff had become increasingly convinced that he was being laid a false trail. He'd been about to fly back to the UK and start digging in Yorkshire when one of the Mara River Camp receptionists, who had a bit of a crush on him, called with the information that Cloud Man was in Nairobi.

Now that he had found him, Griff knew he had just one shot at securing the man's cooperation. Mellow on Tusker, high at the prospect of returning to the Mara, this was the Cloud Man with his guard at its most relaxed.

'I have a new proposal,' he pitched straight in. 'If you agree to make this documentary, you don't have to appear on camera. We can shoot it in a way that means you are never seen. I can front it all, but I need your voice.'

Dominic raised an eyebrow. 'My voice?'

Griff pulled his smartphone from his pocket and switched on the digital sound recorder. 'Let me interview you,' he entreated. 'Share your knowledge with viewers. I'll shoot all the footage as though they're your passengers, both in the big balloon and the scout balloon. They see through our eyes. It's just me with a camera and sound mike. You've seen the tapes I gave you so you know my style. It's low-key and intimate.' Griff knew his footage was impressive. In the past two years, he'd travelled extensively in South America and Central Africa in search of lost tribes and rare wildlife. His informal hand-camera style was exhilarating to watch and had drawn much critical acclaim.

Having no television of his own and little interest in home news, Dominic had no idea that Griff was currently suspended from work pending an internal investigation, his contract and career in jeopardy. Griff's loyal crew on *Undercover Safari* refused to point fingers of blame, but the senior executives knew who had been responsible for taking them so deep into Sudan in search of illegal big-game-hunting parties that their kidnap had been inevitable, the subsequent ransom making British headlines. Griff was convinced he'd be back in harness as soon as he had Cloud Man as a subject.

'I haven't watched the tapes yet,' said Dominic, with crushing bluntness. But then he eyed him curiously. 'You just want my voice, you say?'

'It has the most amazing timbre. What part of Yorkshire are you from?'

'Remind me why I should work with you, Griff, apart from the fact you are clearly a very good tracker.'

Which was when it occurred to Griff that loading Cloud Man with DVDs, books and press releases had been the wrong tactic. Dominic had no interest in Griff's career as an adventurer, his military background, the SBS survival training, his gruelling expeditions and the chance encounter that had led to an award-winning career in television. He watched things as they happened; he was as reactive as the game he studied. He needed stampeding.

'This is the best opportunity you will ever get to publicise the need for more funds to fight poaching in the Mara,' he said. 'If you turn me down, you're turning down a lifeline.' For both of us, he added silently, then went for broke: 'Say no and you might as well take an automatic rifle and shoot the animals yourself.'

Dominic regarded him silently for some time. Then he said, 'I'd want to remain completely anonymous. You'd refer to me only as "Cloud Man"?'

Griff couldn't hide the elation in his face as he registered the change of heart. 'Done.' He held out his left hand to shake. 'A Donne deal.'

There was a long pause and Griff's hand wavered halfway across the table for what seemed like an eternity.

To his consternation, Dominic looked away. 'I'll think about it.'

'What's there to think about?' His palm slapped on to the tabletop. When Dominic said nothing, he raged on: 'Surely the Conservancy is the most important thing? Think of the impact! You couldn't buy this sort of publicity.'

Dominic studied him thoughtfully, intense blue eyes unblinking. 'You are the television hero, my friend. Learn to fly a balloon and maybe we'll make your film.'

Griff knew he was being played well. Nothing could have appealed more than the idea of becoming a cloud man himself. 'You'll teach me?'

'You must qualify as a pilot first.'

'How long does that take?'

'A year, maybe.' His eyes creased with amusement at Griff's shocked expression. 'That would get you off my back for a bit, huh?'

Sitting back in his chair with a sigh, Griff half-heartedly pursued the idea. 'How did you become a professional balloonist?'

'I trained in South Africa,' Dominic said unhelpfully, before leaning away from the table to call a waitress.

'A bottle of Scotch, more Coke and soda,' he told her, then turned back to Griff. 'The local whisky is pretty rough, but it can make mute men talk.'

Griff perked up. He might finally be getting somewhere.

When the drinks came, the young Kenyans realised that their boss wanted to speak alone with the filmmaker and drifted away.

'Near Barnsley,' Dominic said as he poured two Scotches, and it was a moment before Griff registered that he was answering the question he'd been asked earlier. 'Little town called Dinfield. You won't've heard of it.'

'It featured a lot in the news during the miners' strike,' Griff recalled. 'Didn't the police beat back several hundred men in the picket line and claim they were rioting? Later they were forced to apologise and pay compensation.'

'How d'you know that? You can't've been born then.' Dominic looked surprised. 'Is that what they teach you public-school lads in history lessons these days?'

'I'm from the valleys. My father was a coal miner like his father before him. They stayed out the whole year. The strike was talked about more in my house than any world war, although by the time I was born Da had a window-cleaning round and Tadcu – that's my grandad – was on the dole.'

'So why d'you talk like a toff?'

'I still sounded more Captain Cat than Captain Oates when I came out of the forces, but television producers like their stars to be understood by Wisconsin housewives. They'd love your Yorkshire accent,' he added hastily. 'It's got just enough African dust in it to add spice without losing its authenticity. It's good you've kept it, and stuck to your roots.'

Dominic laughed. 'I gave everything up when I came here, especially politics. When I'm rich I live like a rich man, when I'm poor I live like a pauper. I treat everyone I meet the same, regardless of their wealth or background. And that includes you, toff or Taff.'

Griff raised his glass. The whisky – a local concoction called

Hunters Pride – was having a remarkable effect on Dominic, who had started to talk about his memories of the miners' strike: 'I was with the pickets most days. Dad was always mad at me for bunking off school, but there wasn't much he could do once I turned up, and his union brothers loved me. They called me their mascot.'

The little phone counted up the minutes of recording time as the fabulously sonorous voice talked on, as entertaining as always but this time with a whole new script.

Across the room, his two workmates kept a close, wary eye as Dominic laughed and joked about his childhood; they knew such displays of loquacity were rare, and inevitably ended in violent eruptions.

For a man who had given up politics when he came to Africa, Dominic Masters liked to talk about them a hell of a lot, Griff reflected half an hour later, as his phone ran ever shorter on memory and battery life.

The level of the whisky bottle had also plummeted. Griff, who had no great capacity for alcohol, was struggling to pronounce 'Scargill' without slurring. Yet Dominic, who was utterly lucid, had given nothing more revealing away than his recollections of union men; his father was clearly a local hero in Dinfield.

'Is your dad still involved with the union?' Griff asked, trying to steer Dominic back to more personal memories.

'You'd have to ask him that.'

'How did you lose your arm?' Griff blinked hard to focus on that extraordinary face.

'Bike accident.'

'Here?'

Dominic shook his head and topped up his glass. The rain still pounded down outside, audible now that the band had stopped playing.

'How long ago?'

'Almost a lifetime.'

'Were you a balloonist then?'

'No. I told you I learned in the Cape. I'd been working in a vine-yard for an Afrikaans family, driving a delivery truck. They were branching into tourism and my English was better than anybody else's, so they paid and I flew the guests.'

'Wise move. You have the voice.'

He chuckled, adopting his thickest Yorkshire brogue: 'See all, 'ear all, say nowt. Eat all, sup all, pay nowt. An' if th'ivver does owt for nowt, allus do it for thissen.'

It was starting to occur to Griff that the whisky was a cunning trick to anaesthetise him; Dominic might be talking more and enjoying the *craic*, but his audience would never remember a word in the morning. He pushed his glass to one side, now too tired to be subtle. 'So if I Google "Dominic Masters from Dinfield" what will I get?'

He looked across the table sharply. 'I've no idea.'

Having Googled 'Dominic Masters' a lot in recent weeks, Griff doubted he would get any more than he had already, which was mostly LinkedIn connections to a sales manager in Basingstoke and a few others who shared the name. As he'd left the UK in the nineties, he was under the internet radar. The Mara River Camp website was lavish, with plenty of breathtaking balloon shots, but Cloud Man's real name was nowhere on it and his reputation entirely word-of-mouth.

Yet Dominic was jumpy at the prospect of an internet trail, making Griff suspect he was hiding something.

He noticed that his phone had switched itself off, plucked it up and jabbed at the power button. The battery had just a bar left. Almost howling with frustration, Griff set it back on the table. 'Is it the fear that somebody's looking for you that keeps you lying low, or are you more afraid that nobody is?'

Dominic closed one eye as he absorbed this. To Griff's relief, he laughed. 'Both, I guess. You really don't want to know.'

'I really do,' Griff assured him, eyeing the little phone groggily and saying a silent prayer that it kept going. 'You want me to fly a balloon to get shot at. You tell me why, one miner's son to another.'

Dominic laughed so uproariously that he had to mop his eyes. Watching him, Griff blinked in horror. For a moment it had looked as though he had three eyes. Then he realised that the third was the chunky ring Dominic wore.

'When I regained consciousness after the crash, I could still feel the fingers in my right hand,' Dominic said. 'A doctor said something about trans-radial amputation, but I was too spaced out to understand. I was trussed up and pegged out, unable to move anything but my fingers. I thought my girlfriend was beside me . . . I could feel her hair against my fingertips, her breath on my palm as she kissed it.

'The doctors insisted there were no fingers or hand there; my lower arm was gone. They kept repeating the same information: "You have been involved in a serious road traffic accident. You have lost your right hand and forearm. You also have severe facial injuries. You have extensive body burns. Please try not to move." I thought I was dreaming. I just kept flexing the fingers of my right hand.

'I could only hear medical staff talking to me when they stood to my left – I was totally deaf on the right – but I took in enough to piece together the basics: high-speed crash on the M1, sixty per cent burns, half my face seared away, right arm amputated at the elbow. The accident had happened somewhere near Nottingham, but I'd been transferred to a specialist unit in the south-east. There'd been no other casualties. Any personal belongings that could identify me had been destroyed in the fire. I found out later it was joyriders who took me out – they probably never even saw me or had a clue what was going on until they went from eighty in the fast lane to zero on the central reservation with me and a Triumph Bonneville trapped under their stolen Astra. They'd run off long before it all went up in flames. Unfortunately I was still there.

'The hospital staff kept asking me who I was, but speaking hurt like hell. My face felt like it had been encased in burning glue. They asked my name again and again. They even offered me an interpreter, thinking I didn't understand English – one nurse did a lot of parlez-vous-anglais and sprechen-sie-deutsch, I remember. That's when I realised they really had no way of tracing me. I'd bought the bike from a bloke in a pub in Wakefield and never got around to registering it. Nobody could link it to me. So I stayed quiet.'

Griff was confused. 'Why not tell them who you were?'

'I needed time to think, to form a plan before I started to speak again. I knew as soon as they told me how badly injured I was that I mustn't burden my loved ones. I wasn't about to expose them to the sight of me reduced to a burned, truncated mess. My dad had been ill a long time and could hardly look after himself. My sister was about to have a baby. My girlfriend—' He looked away sharply to compose himself. 'My girlfriend had her whole life ahead of her. I was determined they shouldn't find out where I was.'

He spoke pithily and without sentiment.

'The medics put the fact I wasn't speaking down to post-traumatic amnesia, so the nurses nicknamed me Golden Boy, which got shortened to Goldie, like the *Blue Peter* dog.' He laughed drily. 'It was Olympic year and the Games were on everyone's minds – they all hummed "Barcelona" as they changed beds and hung around the ward televisions. I was a model patient. I did every exercise, applied every cream, took every drug prescribed and completed every arduous, repetitive drill – but it was bloody-mindedness, really.' The smile faded. 'Getting rid of the masks and splints so I could walk free was all I cared about. I was told I'd never regain hearing in my right ear, but when my eye reopened and I could see a world to my right, I wept with joy and so did all the ward staff. It was like being in the third act of a bloody Chekhov play.'

Griff could well imagine the nurses' reaction to those intense blue eyes looking at them. 'When did you start to speak?'

'When the support worker explained that I was unlikely to be eligible for compensation,' he explained. 'My bike was uninsured and the lads from the stolen car had never been traced, so any court claim could take months and go nowhere. Once I was out of hospital, I'd be relying on state help, and she needed to know who the hell I was to set that up. The ward staff had already started a collection for me – enough to buy a ferry ticket, I figured – so I told her who I was and that all I needed was my passport. We argued a lot, but I talked her round in the end. She broke a lot of rules sorting it, but she did me proud and never gave me away. I let the nurses think my only family was overseas and that's where I was heading when I'd healed enough. Their collection grew bigger – clothes, a backpack, a Walkman. A pair of walking boots came from one of the consultants, all scrunched up in the *Daily Telegraph*. That's where I read an announcement from the "Wilde family of Downhurst, Lancashire" that their only daughter, my girlfriend, had just got married.'

Griff was no longer aware of low battery life, his own or his gadgetry's. He felt plugged into the mains.

It was such a simple story. He'd imagined blackmail, murder or smuggling. Instead he had a love story about pride and sacrifice. Unwilling to be a burden to those he loved after an accident had wiped out a burgeoning stage career, Dominic had determined to put as much distance between himself and his home as he could and never look back.

'I knew I had to walk away and let them all live their lives in peace, but I was so angry when I read that Mia had married, I couldn't think straight. It was her birthday coming up and I got her a card, but I found my left hand and my screwed-up head were pretty much illiterate as a pair. In the end I sweated tears to write a couple of sentences legibly. The day I left hospital, I asked a nurse to address the envelope and post it. Since then, not a single day has passed when I wouldn't have retraced my steps to snatch it back and never let it be sent.'

'What did you write?'

He studied the chunky ring on his finger. 'You wouldn't understand.'

'Try me.'

'I told her to live her life again and forget I ever existed. God knows how much it must have upset her. She didn't deserve it. It was her twentieth birthday.' He sighed. 'This year she turns forty.'

Griff noticed the way his scarred face contorted with pain as he spoke of her. 'Surely she deserves to know what happened to you?'

The blue eyes hardened. 'She got the card. She knows I'm alive.' He kept all sentiment out of his voice, rigidly self-controlled now.

'She probably thought it was a suicide note.'

'Then she'll already be free.'

'No, she fucking won't!' Griff exploded, drunkenness making him lose his rag.

Dominic made no comment, simply pushing the bottle aside. 'Mia always said I lived so deep within my roles she thought I might never emerge. This time, I won't. I've been rehearsing enough years to play the part. She was always the instinctive actor; I've had to work much harder.'

'So she's an actress?'

'She could never have been anything else.'

Griff racked his memory for actresses he'd heard of with the name Mia, but unless Dominic had followed in the footsteps of Sinatra, Previn and Woody Allen, he guessed her success had to be quite modest. 'What is she doing now?'

'Why would I want to know?'

He rocked back in his chair. 'You let her go because you thought she'd be better off without you. Surely you still want to keep track of her?'

'She's not a lioness I reintroduced into the wild. Acting was her life. That's what she'll be doing.'

'Who did she marry?'

'Leonardo Mikhail Eduardo Devonshire,' the deep, gravelly voice intoned, like a judge passing sentence.

'Leo Devonshire?' Griff snorted disbelievingly.

'They met at university. He wanted to be a costume designer. She was his "muse".'

His jaw dropped. 'You were in love with one half of Leomia?'

'They're a double-act?' He looked confused.

'You really have no idea?' Griff was uncertain how much was genuine, how much drunkenness and how much he was being fed a line. He was a fan of *Chancellor* and caught up with each series in a great box-set binge whenever he had a long enough break to do so. The lead character was complex and renegade and delivered some of the best lines being written in drama right now. Leo Devonshire was a sublime actor, as subtle as he was engaging. His marriage was British celebrity royalty, with Mia a model queen and the ravishing Iris Devonshire its fairy-tale princess.

Griff loved to read British newspapers online and, while celebrity trivia was not his bag, he had followed the Leveson Inquiry and seen enough stories surrounding Leomia and the Devonshires' long-distance marriage to pick up the insinuation that the real queen in the family was not beautiful Mia. Griff's younger sister Ceinlys was a huge fan of the couple and argued vociferously that all the rumours were rubbish, but now he had a missing twist to the tale sitting in front of him, and his clever head was racing just as fast as his old-fashioned romantic heart was pounding.

'Surely it's only fair to put the record straight?' he suggested now. 'It wouldn't be too hard to get a message to Mia just to let her know that you're still alive and well and—'

'No!' Dominic bellowed. Ngara and Leboo hurried towards him. He held up his hand to them and fixed Griff with a deter-mined stare. 'You leave her out of it. This conversation stops here and is now forgotten.' The bluest of eyes fixed him for a long time. 'I will agree to help you make your film on the condition that you fly the balloon. Then you will be a cloud man too, and I will be your voice. Go to South Africa to get your licence.'

Griff wanted to argue that it would take far too long to do that, that the famous annual migration and river crossing he wanted to film would have passed, his career would be even more stagnant by the time he'd mastered aviation law and meteorology. But he knew better than to cross Dominic again. As it was, he'd got far further tonight than he'd dreamed possible.

He picked up his phone and pocketed it. 'My lips are sealed, I swear.' My heart and hard drive are another matter, he added in his head.

Exhausted, Griff collapsed into his hotel bed fully dressed, but when he closed his eyes, sleep eluded him. He saw Leo Devonshire's handsome face, laughing with Letterman, joking with Morgan, relaying a great anecdote to Jay Leno, teaching Ellen knitting stitches and swapping shoes with Conan. He was the ultimate dapper Disney prince and had voiced several animations in his earlier years, when his physical perfection had matched that of the artists' creations.

Griff imagined Dominic in hospital all those years ago, battling to come to terms with his injuries, certain that he was doing the right thing in sparing the woman he loved a lifetime in a supporting role. Now, if only he knew it, she was apparently doing just that.

He could not assume to know the inner workings of the Devonshires' marriage from the little information he'd gleaned in newspapers, yet a great sense of injustice was welling in his chest. It was the same righteousness that had forced five-year-old Griff to confront the playground bullies who'd hung a puppy from a tree by its collar to beat it. Twenty years later, it still sent Griff into danger, whether deep into Sudan in search of poachers or recklessly into a marriage to deliver a message from an ex-lover.

He sat up and snapped open his battered laptop to Google 'Mia Devonshire'. Twenty minutes later, he was booking himself on a flight to the UK.

Chapter 10

'Are you Simon de Montmorency's wife?'

'That's right. My name's Laney.'

'I just love your husband!'

'That's a coincidence. So do I.'

'Shame we haven't seen as much of him in Burley-on-Thames as we hoped to when you two first arrived. I suppose he's always busy, being such a big star?'

'Very.'

'I recognised you straight away. I've seen your photograph in the magazines, attending premières and so forth with him.'

'Oh yes?'

'You should take no notice what they say, you know. The pressure on women to stay thin is ridiculous. You're . . . normal, especially with all those children. How many do you two have?'

'Simon has five, but—'

'There you go! I gained a stone with each of mine too. It's so lovely to know not all celebrities are married to stick-insects, especially a dish like Simon. Gives us all hope!'

'With Simon's reputation, I should think there's always hope. Now, if you'll excuse me, I really must pay for this.'

'Of course . . . oh, you've dropped it. Let me . . . I say! You must be a glutton for punishment!'

As Laney drove through Wootton's water meadows, she spotted Mia and Iris hacking along the riverbank, their Iberian hot-bloods high-stepping in front of the dense wall of willow-herb and loose-strife. Both women raised their arms.

Laney hooted the car horn cheerfully. It was only as she turned right beneath the trees in the direction of the boathouse that she glanced into the rear-view mirror and realised they hadn't been waving. Instead, they were conducting an animated argument, gesticulating at each other. Laney remembered that during her first year as an undergraduate the famous acting coach Verity Lang had visited Old Gate College and homed straight in on Mia, as every professional did. 'You are an exquisite actress,' she'd told the young Mia, 'but you will never become one of the greats unless you learn to control your hands. You are not directing traffic.'

Today Mia was trying to bring a party bus with no brakes under control before it crashed. With less than a week to go until her wedding to Dougie Everett, Iris was showing no signs of entertaining second thoughts.

In the past month, Mia had spent hours confiding in Laney, lamenting her daughter's decision to marry so young, convinced that Dougie would bring only heartbreak. A notorious playboy and freeloader, he'd come into conflict with his future mother-in-law from the start by referring to her as 'darling Milfy' and extolling his love of fox-hunting despite her well-known opposition to blood sports. Mia had begged her daughter to take more time, but headstrong Iris was determined to have her big midsummer day. Thus Mia had reluctantly agreed to host the ceremony at Wootton rather than lose control of the event completely.

Only Laney knew how bitterly Mia now regretted that decision. The press coverage was already huge, and speculation rife as to whether Iris's father would even turn up. Mia had already confided in Laney that Leo wouldn't be at the ceremony because he couldn't get out of his filming commitments in America at such short notice, but his absence would do nothing to quash the ever-present rumours that their marriage was over in all but name.

Laney parked beneath the lilac tree and breathed in its sherbet sweetness as she ducked beneath its mauve chandeliers and made her way along the path to the boathouse. Originally converted as a studio for Leo, the wonky little wooden outhouse was as romantic and humble as the grand Palladian house it belonged to was iced with artifice and pomp.

Laney was immensely grateful to Mia and Leo for letting her use it as an office while her own home remained in perpetual building-site chaos. There was something magically Kenneth Grahame about it, flanked by its willows and looking out across the Thames. Steps led up to a large open-plan room with a balcony, and a small wet-room to the rear. Laney had done little to personalise it in the few weeks she'd used it, simply moving the desk to the french windows to overlook the Thames, throwing them open on warm days like today. Leo's paintings still covered the walls, often featuring the Spanish horses he and his wife adored, bold, semi-abstract and cheering.

Laney missed Leo. When she'd moved to LA with her second husband Oscar, they had made great efforts to see one another, and he had been her shoulder to cry on as the short marriage had fallen painfully apart, but he was working harder than ever these days. They all were.

Her phone lit up as it received a picture text from Simon, who had clearly just woken up and found her side of the bed occupied by the dogs: Thought you'd forgotten the Immac again ... come back and fornicate.

She stifled a resentful huff – he rarely got to spend a day at home after all, let alone enjoy a lie-in. Then she laughed as another picture arrived of their builder, Fred, peering through the bedroom window from the scaffolding, a metal tape measure in one hand. We'll show him the dimensions of my extension ...

She took a photograph of her laptop screen with the words I HAVE A DEADLINE in large type on it and sent it to him.

'You have to try talking to Iris again!' Half an hour later Mia marched into the boathouse, still wearing her riding gear. 'She respects your opinion, Laney.'

Laney saved her work, trying not to think of her deadline. Mia was already filling the kettle in the little kitchenette, making lots of clanks and crashes because she was angry. 'She won't listen to a word I say.'

'You were just the same at that age,' Laney reminded her. 'And remember what happened when I told you not to marry Leo?'

'I took your advice very much to heart.'

'You married him. And then you barely spoke to me for almost a year.' The Devonshires had taken a twelve-month leave of absence from Old Gate before returning to complete their degrees.

'We were living in rural Spain. Nobody used the internet or had a mobile phone then. I did write.'

'One postcard telling me Iris had been born, and then three months later a christening invitation.'

'Exactly! You're Iris's godmother. You *have* to speak to her – it's your moral duty. Why can I only find instant? You must have freshly ground decaffeinated.'

'Is that my moral duty too?'

Nothing much had changed in twenty years, Laney reflected. Mia still appeared unannounced at any hour, in need of immediate advice and coffee made to her exact specifications. Today's deadline was a killer, and Laney had briefed her friend accordingly, but she'd forgotten as always. In her more suspicious moments, Laney wondered whether Mia had offered her the Wootton boathouse as an office purely to have a counsellor conveniently close to hand, but she knew that was ungrateful. It was impossible to get any peace in her own home just a few miles away. The boathouse was a haven by comparison, and she secretly adored Mia's visits, just as she adored Mia.

'I've met Dougie less than half a dozen times,' Mia lamented, 'and on every occasion he's got drunk, bribed the dogs and flirted with me outrageously.'

'Sounds like Simon,' Laney said as another picture text came through, showing the Bloody Mary he was currently laying claim to at home as he no doubt chatted up the au pair and played Dr Doolittle with choc drops and a Labrador to each side.

'Don't say anything, but he even tried to stick his tongue down my throat at Easter,' Mia confided.

'Simon?' Laney bleated.

'No! Dougie. He was very drunk, although that's no excuse – it was the first time he came to stay at Wootton. Leo was away in LA, of course, and poor Iris had a terrible cold and went to bed early. One minute Dougie was helping me clear away supper, the next he was all over me, calling me Milfy and saying he'd fancied me since he was a teenager. He only stopped when one of the dogs bit him. I kept quiet about it at the time, but that was before they got engaged. Perhaps I should tell Iris now, while I still have the chance to make her think about what she's doing?'

'Absolutely not. It's just your word against his, and Iris will believe him.'

'Why they can't wait a bit longer is beyond me,' Mia went on. 'It's bad enough being asked to watch my daughter make the mistake of her life, but now that I've been forced to reschedule the Wootton Gala, I've discovered my flamenco ensemble is booked solid for the rest of summer. The only day they can do is my birthday.'

'The big four-*olé*,' Laney joked, suddenly seeing something positive to grasp at. 'Something to look forward to!'

Every year, Mia hosted a themed garden party to raise funds for the Devonshire Foundation, the charity she and Leo had set up to help causes close to their hearts. Now in its fifth year, the Wootton Gala had a reputation for raising gargantuan sums, and was known to some as the WAGala because Mia always galvanised a troupe of helpers made up of the wives, girlfriends, partners and families of celebrities to host and perform each year. Tickets starting at two hundred pounds a pop were offered to a carefully compiled guest list, and always sold out within days.

This year's party had been postponed to make way for the

wedding. If it was moved to share the celebratory birthday slot in late July, Laney saw it as a terrific excuse to make it the best party ever, something special to cheer up Mia and unite the family again. The Spanish fiesta theme was close to all the Devonshires' hearts, and Leo couldn't fail to show his support for his wife's landmark birthday as well as raising funds.

'You have to hold the gala on your fortieth,' she insisted. 'It's kismet.'

'The best ten years of a woman's life are between thirty-nine and forty,' Mia muttered. 'Kismet would be Iris leaving the cunning stunt man to stand all alone at the altar.'

She was doing her waspish act. Laney knew her well enough to see through it, one of her friend's oldest guises, born of the movie heroines they'd admired as students, icons like Dietrich, Davis and both Hepburns. It was one of the acts Leo loved most.

'Has Leo tried talking to Iris again?' Laney asked.

'Daily.' She stirred her coffee so violently that half of it slopped out of the mug. 'She won't take his calls. He's desperate to fly home, but they're filming back-to-back episodes all this month.'

'Surely the studio would release him for his daughter's wedding?'

'*If* there's a wedding,' she snapped. 'And no, they won't. You know American networks. You have to give six months' warning if you need a pee these days.'

Having worked on an American sitcom-writing team, Laney knew exactly how impossible it was to have a personal life on studio time.

Mia was stalking around the space now, straightening piles of books and print-outs, gathering up a bag spilling notepads and pens, clearing away old newspapers folded to half-finished crosswords. 'How's the new script treatment going?' she asked Laney. 'And why haven't you brought the dogs to work with you today?'

'They distract me,' Laney replied pointedly.

'You need dogs for company.' Mia perched on the battered

106

leather sofa, drawing a cushion into her lap and cuddling it in the absence of a conveniently warm four-legged friend. 'It's not fair leaving your poor boys cooped up in the house for hours on end.'

Mia was only happy in a room that had more animal legs than furniture ones. Given a house as big as Wootton, that was a lot of fur. She collected stray cats and abandoned dogs like some women collect shoes. Her fields were inhabited by ageing ponies, donkeys, sheep and goats as well as the Spanish horses she bred, and her garden teemed with rehomed peacocks, fan-tailed doves and ornamental bantams. Even the huge yews that stood sentry alongside the carriage circle were animal-shaped, a feat that had taken gardener Franco years of patient pruning. They were among the few of Wootton's menagerie that could be described as well trained. The three vast Spanish mastiffs that guarded the well-fenced perimeters were notorious sexual and social miscreants.

'The dogs are very happy today,' said Laney. 'Simon's at home and is hell-bent on getting out the whistle and striding across the garden in plus-fours to see if they remember anything from gundog boot camp.'

To celebrate moving out of Central London to the Home Counties when they remarried, the de Montmorencys – or Demons as they were commonly known – had acquired two black Labrador puppies that Simon had christened Kensington and Chelsea ('When we leave, they'll say, "There goes the neighbourhood"'). He'd then spent a fortune sending them away to school to ensure they would behave impeccably on shoots, a pastime he was eager to embrace in order to live up to his Deed Poll name now that he was embarking on country life. Over the years he'd added a great deal of detail to Simon de Montmorency's outlandish back story, combining the plots of *Out of Africa* and *White Mischief* with his favourite Wilbur Smith novel. His privileged childhood in colonial Africa now contained at least one political uprising, a sexual scandal and a lot of spurious detail about the fall in coffee prices. He'd long ago been exposed by the gutter press as Sean Pegg of

Croydon, but nobody minded that he'd stuck with his de Montmorency persona. Simon was adored and accepted wherever he went, the ultimate English eccentric, now destined to be a peacock amid country-set pheasants. His 'gun dogs' had already become delinquent family pets.

'Simon really should get himself a shotgun to go with the dogs and complete the look,' Laney went on, 'but he's probably afraid I'll hold it to his head if I catch him with his trousers down again. As I keep reminding him, the dogs are the ones who do the picking up.'

'I saw he'd tweeted about that this morning,' Mia said vaguely, a new convert to social media, which she followed to keep tabs on Iris and her friends.

'That I'd shoot him if I caught him with his trousers down?' gasped Laney.

'That he was planning to work on Ken and Chelsea's retrieving . . . although he might have mentioned teaching them to retrieve his wife from her writing tower.'

Simon was a huge hit on Twitter, which suited his epigrammatic one-liners perfectly, delighting an ever-expanding legion of followers. He regularly referred to Mrs Demon in his tweets, and had urged his witty wife to get involved, but Laney – who'd once been humiliated on Twitter – was reluctant to conduct any of their marriage in public. Already burdened with managing his website traffic and Facebook page, she refused to follow him, worried that the private stream of picture messages just for her would stop if they began communicating after @s.

'We can all see how tightly belted Simon's trousers are these days,' Mia was saying. 'You have to trust him, Laney. He's obviously trying his hardest.'

Laney rolled her eyes. The Demons had admittedly enjoyed a very jolly meal in the Plump Poussin last night, where they'd managed to lay off the high-grade sarcasm and third bottle of wine, later making love instead of arguing, but she remained uptight. 'He doesn't appreciate that I can't just drop everything when he comes home to play lord of the good manners. This deadline is really on top of me.' She turned back to her computer screen with a loaded sigh.

But Mia was oblivious to the hint, and quickly distracted as she spotted the pharmacy bag on the kitchen surface. 'What's *this*? How many times have I told you to go to a professional?'

Laney swallowed anxiously, certain that she'd hidden the pregnancy test in her laptop bag. It was bad enough that the woman in the village chemist had seen the box, let alone Mia. She didn't want to reveal how pathetic she was in buying one just a few hours after her first attempt at conception this cycle, but she couldn't help herself. She must have spent hundreds on Clear Blue in the past year – she should bulk-buy them at discount and stockpile. Yet it was part of the secret ritual, celebrating each sexual encounter during her fertile days with the 'treat' of a test. In a good month, she'd have three or four little boxes stashed away.

But the box Mia was holding up wasn't a pregnancy test, it was the Lush 'n' Lovely hair dye purchased at the same time. 'Please tell me you're not going to use this?'

'I can't idle away a morning at Daniel Galvin to cover up a few grey hairs,' Laney scoffed.

'This is not suitable for blondes as light as you.' Mia was studying the packaging. 'It's called Autumn Glow. I guarantee your hair will go pink.'

'Rubbish. I've dyed far more often in the sink than on stage. I was a redhead for almost a year at college, remember? And I went blue-black for Bernarda Alba.'

'Along with every bathroom on your floor of the halls of residence.' Mia held the box further away to read the back with lowered brows. 'Hair's much less forgiving after forty. My colourist is doing this wonderful thing for older blondes, putting in dark roots to hide grey growth.'

'Why would I want to look like I have roots? I'm natural. And I'm not forty yet.'

'It takes years off.'

'I'll stick with my method, thanks.' Laney returned her attention to her laptop and started typing random nonsense to cover her embarrassment. She didn't like to admit that she couldn't afford the sort of money Mia spent at a salon each month. Simon had to pay a tax bill soon that was roughly three times what they had in the bank, and the builders still hadn't received their last interim payment. She had to meet today's deadline so that she could chase the finished script with an invoice. As soon as that was done, she would return to ghosting Simon's latest travel memoir, along with his light-hearted Christmas book, then write the script for a catering-industry awards ceremony he was compèring.

Laney was ashamed that she hadn't had time to comb her hair and was wearing a creased sundress on its third day. Mia's burnished curls always shone as though every strand had been hand-polished, her flawless skin glowed and her body was still as slender and firm as it had been when she married. Even today, make-up-free, with her hair scraped back and green eyes turbulent, she looked no more than thirty. However much Laney knew her own job satisfaction came from looking into a screen rather than out from it, she still envied Mia her beauty and the instant admiration it brought.

She thought of the woman in the chemist, demanding to know if she was Simon's wife, then putting in requests for him to help out with charity events and fêtes. She'd been enjoying life at the hub of a bustling village community until Simon's over-zealous press-cuttings service had forwarded the link to an anonymous blog called the Burley Hornet, which reported:

The Rubenesque Mrs Simon de Montmorency, new chatelaine of Red Gables, shows a lack of humility and a clumsy deportment unbecoming of a television celebrity's wife. Twice married to the Big Dish of the Small Screen, Mrs Demon wears a permanent scowl when out and about in Burley, moves like an elephant seal and has remarkably stubbly legs.

Simon had laughed when she'd shown it to him, telling her to take no notice of jealous slander. Laney pretended not to give a jot, but she now shaved her legs obsessively and walked everywhere as though she had a book balanced on her head, with a beaming smile plastered to her lips. She knew she should be accustomed to negative press, but it cut closer to the bone to have such bile coming from her neighbours. She felt like an unsightly cabbage that had gone to seed in Britain's Best Kept Village.

'You will speak to Iris today, won't you?' Mia pleaded. 'She's around all day. The hen party isn't kicking off until late afternoon.'

Laney glanced at the clock in the corner of her screen. 'I'll try. Where are they going?'

'Punting and then a fancy-dress supper at the rowing club. Haven't you read your invitation?'

Laney was sure she hadn't received one. 'Iris doesn't want an old bag like me there.'

'Of course she does! Even Abuelita's going to be there.'

'Your mother-in-law's going to the hen night?' Laney tried to envisage Leo's tiny, crooked Spanish mother Jacinta, or Abuelita as she was known to the family, a hair's breadth from her eightieth birthday, doing the conga on her mobility scooter while wearing a pink wig and an IRIS'S HEN NIGHT T-shirt.

'Isn't it a hoot? Iris was insistent she must have her "Lito" there. I was uninvited this morning for calling Dougie a prat, so you must be there to spy for me. Chloe Benson's organised it.'

'That'll be why I'm not invited.' In the three years Laney had been married to Chloe's father, the teenager had refused to look her in the eye, let alone talk to her. Then, when Oscar had famously told Laney via Twitter that he was filing for a divorce ('You will take away nothing from this marriage apart from the fifty pounds you've gained'), his daughter had victoriously retweeted until it had gone viral.

'You've both put that behind you now.' Mia wouldn't be deflected. 'Chloe refused point-blank to be bridesmaid and, what with Leo not coming to give his daughter away, Iris will be terribly lonely going up the aisle.' Her big green eyes welled. 'We have to stop her.'

Laney doubted anything she could say or do would change Iris's mind. Mia had created such an idyllic *Cider with Rosie* childhood for her daughter that it was inevitable the apple cart would career off course when somebody came between them – and Dougie Everett appeared to have broken every wheel and ripped up the entire orchard. The more Mia railed against the match, the more Iris pulled away, yet their need for one another was still clear.

'She insists she'll ride Scully up the aisle,' Mia said now. The Andalucían dressage horse Escultor XVI – known as Scully – was Mia's top stud stallion, sixteen hands of pure white, highly trained power that was worth as much as a new Ferrari and looked like a unicorn that had dropped its horn. 'She knows that means I'll have to stay calm on the day. He's so sensitive and clever – he picks up on my moods like a collie.'

'Perhaps you can train him to trot past Dougie and swim across the Thames before Iris has had a chance to get off.' Typing as she spoke, Laney realised that what she was saying had appeared on the screen.

'The thought has occurred to me,' Mia giggled, sounding more her old self, 'although I was thinking more along the lines of Scully performing a capriole to send the bridegroom into orbit.'

'Is that the move where they jump in the air and kick back?'

'When they were war horses, it was used to kick away the enemy. Abuelita could train them to do it in her day.'

'I could use a move like that around Burley-on-Thames.' Laney turned to face her friend. 'As soon as this wedding is over, you can concentrate on your display of Spanish horses at the Wootton Gala.'

Smiling valiantly, Mia nodded. 'You're right, Laney chuck. And you will be my stable jockey. You can't say no. It'll be a great way to show you off to everyone.'

'My horse-riding days are long gone,' Laney gulped, trying to imagine herself in full, flouncy fiesta dress sitting out a capriole. The Burley Hornet would have a field day.

'But you'll write the cabaret sketches, won't you?' Mia insisted. 'Lots of lovely girlfriends have volunteered to perform this year, so they need top-class material.' She reeled off a list of names guaranteed to make any self-respecting gossip columnist weep with joy at the prospect of covering the glitziest annual fund-raising garden party in the Home Counties. 'They'll all think your writing is *so* funny, and of course they adore Simon.'

Since moving to the area, Laney had come to appreciate that the Thames-side social scene had a strict entry code that made no allowances for stubbly legs, multi-tasking or a stressful job, although a celebrity husband was a low-level credit. In order to fit in, one should also have a plethora of well-groomed children, along with lots of money and free time. Despite lacking these qualifications, Laney had thus far been granted an honorary access-all-areas pass by virtue of her friendship with Mia, the true queen of the scene.

'We make so much money for the charities,' she enthused. 'They're relying on us. How wonderful to have a *bona fide* Hollywood scriptwriter in the team!'

'Only one of my scripts ever went into production, and that was because I was married to the star and executive producer in Oscar. I didn't even get a credit.'

'I always credit you for it. *And* it was the third most successful film of its year. Besides, you co-wrote *Eden Place* for a decade. Round here, that carries as much weight as any box-office record.'

The long-running British soap opera had given Laney her step on the career ladder, enabling her to generate a regular income while Simon was breaking into showbusiness. She didn't like to admit how much she still missed the security and camaraderie of that job, and the fun they'd had during their early years of marriage.

Nowadays her bread and butter was from radio drama, a creatively stimulating yet relentless freelance slog that just about covered the household bills and patched the Demons' regular financial shortfalls when Simon's ex-wives sprang surprises or he overlooked a tax bill or simply blew the house-restoration budget again. Laney's occasional film or television script commissions boosted the coffers, along with her regular appearances on the radio panel show *Quick Wits*. but she had to chase every opportunity right now to keep the roof over their heads, quite literally given the thousands of antique red clay tiles that had just been painstakingly removed from their house in order to replace rotten joists.

Another picture text arrived from Simon. He'd finished his liquid breakfast and clearly just tried out the newly refitted shower in the master en suite, where she'd reluctantly allowed him to cover the walls with a découpage of nude sketches he'd done of her when they were first together as students.

'What's that?' Mia peered over her shoulder.

'Simon's latest extension.' She held it away and admired it, tempted to abandon any hope of working and head home for a siesta. The au pair would be at her language school for the next few hours: they could have the house to themselves. Then she remembered the builders and turned back to her keyboard.

A tinny fanfare rang out from Mia's belt-hooked phone case and she plucked out her little Samsung to read the newly arrived text with a groan.

'Charlie Soames is waiting on the yard and wants to show me a scan. I asked Vicente to deal with him, but Charlie doesn't believe the poor boy understands a word of English. It's only his lisp Vince struggles with – we all do. If it's a damaged sacrioiliac or suspensory we're in trouble.'

Charlie, the equine vet, was part of the ever-changing pack of admirers Mia had trailed throughout her adult life, shy undergraduates now replaced by wolfish hopefuls of all ages who became besotted as soon as they met her. Mia no longer called them 'mates', but she remained apparently unaware of the effect she had on them.

'Thank you, chuck.' Her voice softened to its native Lancashire as she hugged Laney tightly. 'I am so grateful you're here for us. And I know you're busy working today, but please go to the hen night at least. I need you there.'

Silently Laney listed all the reasons why she shouldn't go, but she said, 'Of course.'

Mia hugged her tighter, a lean whip of gratitude and emotion. 'I knew you wouldn't let me down. The fancy-dress theme is "birds of a feather", so all the girls are going wild with ostrich plumes, apart from Abuelita, who appears to be channelling Lesley Joseph.'

Chapter 11

Grateful to be alone, Laney dedicated the rest of her day to fine-tuning the radio commission, a serial dramatisation of a turgid prize-winning novel about the salt trade, hamstrung by the author's intense dislike of dialogue. It had been an uphill struggle finding anything quotable; writing five forty-minute episodes had been torture, but as it was the only decent iron she had in the career fire right now, she had to give it her best shot.

As the sun burned brighter on the writhing silver surface of the Thames, she reworked each scene with increasing frustration, munching biscuits and barely noticing lunchtime come and go; she ignored regular picture texts from Simon, finally turning the phone off. If she bombarded him in this way on a filming day, he'd go ballistic, she thought murderously. Then she paused to look at the river, iridescent and hazy now as a clutch of canoeists slid by, and realised that he probably wouldn't go ballistic at all. Simon was the most laid-back person she knew: nothing bothered him, not even getting booed off stage during a doomed attempt to make it as a stand-up double-act. The main reason they'd given up was because he couldn't bear to see how much the audience rejection hurt her.

She drummed her fingers along the edge of the desk, sucked her lower lip and reread the screen page in front of her, one eye closing critically. It needed more action. The salt book's plot was very heavy on practical detail and creative imagery, but thin on sexual tension and violence, prerequisites for high ratings.

She started hyping up a very dry scene featuring heavyweights arguing on a Liverpool dock by throwing in a brawl, a kind-hearted prostitute and a night of stolen passion. Just as she was debating a three-in-a-bed romp – always popular for previews – she heard a step behind her and her heart skipped at the polite cough that followed. Only Simon could clear his throat in that sexiest of male mating calls, like a roguish fifties film idol with naughtiness permanently on his mind.

'I know I shouldn't interrupt,' came a husky drawl, 'but I brought you something irresistible to distract you, just for a few minutes ... Me.'

Laughing, she turned around. Dressed in a crumpled mauve linen suit that would have made most men look as camp as Quentin Crisp, Simon was holding a huge bunch of gladioli in one hand and a delicious-looking cake from Burley's overpriced deli in the other.

Seeing him never failed to excite her. He was still Withnail and all her teenage heroes rolled into one – Byron, Wilde, James Bond, Rochester and Rossetti – a bundle of contradictions that came together in one long, lean six-foot vision of roguish splendour. He looked like a rock star, dressed like a dandy, thought like a poet and behaved like a naughty schoolboy.

Dwelling upon whores and passion had got her very hot under the collar. Simon had been complaining a lot of late that she only wanted to make babies, not love, but now she felt ravishing and ready to be ravished. She'd always been at her horniest when the sun was high in the sky, not at the end of a long day when bed was ready to hug her to sleep. She could hear the river lapping behind her and feel the cool breeze coming through the open windows, lifting her hair. Her long, wraparound summer dress fell open seductively as she lifted one leg over the arm of her chair, raised her hands to the nape of her neck and threw back her head wantonly.

Simon's eyebrows shot up.

'Mummeeeeeeee!' came an excited screech as feet thundered up the wooden stairs. 'We're going to have a tea parteeee!'

'I picked Hope up from school,' he explained, as Laney hurriedly crossed her legs.

A moment later, her five-year-old daughter burst into the boathouse, one navy sock up and one down, her striped school dress covered with green paint, dark curls on end.

Simon looked sheepish. 'Obviously, I'm the irresistible part of this package, but Hope and cake are my back-up.'

A chunky missile of excitement hurled herself into her mother's arms. 'Me and Daddymon need you to come outside.'

Hope called Simon 'Daddymon' to distinguish him from her birth father, whom she referred to as 'Daddy-o' (although this appalled Oscar, who, Laney suspected, would have preferred his youngest child to address him as 'Mr Benson').

'All my best toys have come. There's cucumber sandwiches, scones and Monster Munch.'

'A picnic.' Laney nuzzled her warm cheek. 'How lovely!'

'Malin's setting it up for us,' Simon told her.

She bristled. 'You brought her along too?' Malin was a platinum-haired twenty-year-old Swede with a body as lean and slim as those of the bronze ladies holding illuminated globes in the Art Deco lamps Simon was addicted to buying for the house.

He gave her a devilish smile. 'She's going to give the dogs a run along the river while we have our feast, then we'll drop her and Hope at the village playground, where they have a play date with another au pair and her charge. They can walk back from there.

We'll go on ahead. I've sent the builders home early so we can have a foreplay date.'

She glowered at him over Hope's dark head, no longer feeling wanton. Simon had orchestrated this to get her back to the house. She didn't want to go back to the house. She hated their house right now.

The Demons' recent purchase was a huge Victorian villa on the opposite bank of the Thames from Wootton, just a few miles downstream in the bustling village of Burley-on-Thames, famed for its two Michelin-starred restaurants, its overpriced shops and the traffic jams on the famous old bridge. Simon had borrowed massively to buy it during the property slump, convinced it was a bargain. Praised by Pevsner, Red Gables was a riot of Gothic high camp that had enjoyed many roles in its long life, from guesthouse to retirement home, hippie commune to recording studio. Most recently it had been a stage school, its rooms filled with eager little hopefuls tap-dancing on the dining-room parquet, singing Lloyd Webber numbers in the turquoise-panelled drawing room and reciting audition speeches in the parlour. Simon loved the irony of the theatrical connection, its grand shabbiness and the fact that there was ample space for his many offspring to have a huge en suite bedroom apiece, which still left half a dozen spare for visiting friends, of which the couple had many.

Laney had allowed herself to be talked into this romantic, impractical house because she had fallen so deeply in love with the garden. With lawns sloping down to the river, a grass tennis court, a croquet lawn and its own private pontoon, it was pure Betjeman, and the walled rose garden was a particular joy. She had spent all her free time during their first weeks identifying the rare species before their petals dropped. It was only when cold weather forced her inside that she saw they had bought a money pit that required rewiring, plumbing and repointing. To cheer themselves up, she and Simon had raised the roof with a few legendary Demonic parties, but now that the roof had come off, she felt as though she was living in a ruin.

Red Gables was falling apart, but because it was historically important they could hardly change a tap without consent, and renovations looked set to take a lifetime. Simon adored it and was committed to transforming it into 'the perfect backdrop for my beautiful family'. With his eye for colour and the interior-design connections he'd made from working in lifestyle television, he had grand plans involving hand-painted wallpaper, lashings of velvet, *trompe l'oeil* murals and a canary-yellow Aga – but in truth they could barely afford the new roof joists. Laney increasingly saw the house as the new, expensive mistress he was forced to pimp. As well as recounting the transformation in his monthly style-magazine column, 'Simon Says', he'd agreed that they and the house would feature in several glossies and was currently negotiating a television special. Red Gables might be costing them a fortune, but he was determined to make it earn its keep.

Embracing country life had been his brainchild, and Laney had worked hard to steer him away from the isolated Exmoor manor houses and Cotswold piles he favoured to the more practical option of the Thames Valley. She knew that, for all his dreams of gathering kindling with his kids in his own woodland, he would be working away most weeks, leaving her to drive the half-hour to the nearest shop for Zip firelighters.

When they had first arrived in Burley, Simon wasted no time launching into his fantasy of village life. He'd insisted on towing his family to church despite both his and Laney's ingrained agnosticism ('Life-after-death insurance, darling'), as well as guesting in the cricket team, judging the fancy dress at the fête, attending the pub's curry night and even joining the local book club. But since this initial burst of enthusiasm, he'd been too wrapped up in earning money to make further attempts at involving them in village life.

From his modest suburban upbringing to his current rank as one of the best-known faces on television, Simon had never compromised in his generosity and was gallingly profligate. Once dubbed 'the Eye Candy Dandy' and more recently 'the Big Dish of the Small Screen', his effortless ability to engage and maintain interest in any given subject, as well as his *outré* good humour, had landed him a television presenting career. Although his popularity had gradually slipped from prime-time network and chat shows to daytime Freeview and panel shows, he was still an enduring household name, the cocky coxcomb on the box. His universal appeal, along with his love for and knowledge of architecture and design, food, wine and travel, had kept him in work for over fifteen years.

Right now, Simon needed all the work he could get. New acquaintances always believed him well-heeled, and it was an illusion he was keen to foster, but he was so impoverished by alimony, school fees and extravagance that he took any job offered to him, earning a fraction of his erstwhile prime-time rate. Laney despaired when she read the bank statements and saw how impossibly beyond their means they lived, her heart aching all the more when she saw how much of his income Simon gave away to charities. It was a well-worn media maxim that Simon would be a gold-plated, copper-bottomed national treasure were his reputation not so tarnished and his attention span so short.

Laney and Simon had first married aged twenty-four in her parents' local church in Kent, with four ravishing bridesmaids, a brace of page boys, two dashing ushers and a mother of the bride in full flood. There were a hundred and fifty friends and family at the wedding breakfast, followed by an all-night party for five hundred. The bride had worn white and hardly remembered a thing about the day. The groom had been charming, irreverent, funny and very drunk. After the honeymoon, they returned to the same squabbling they'd done non-stop in the build-up to the Big Day, when Simon had wanted to slope off to Las Vegas and Laney had wanted to call the whole thing off: she was working such long hours on *Eden Place* that she was exhausted.

Looking back, they still proclaimed those early years fun, only recalling the parties and holidays, the evenings cooking together and long nights making love. Laney had run his career alongside her own, then as now, juggling two diaries and income streams. Her writing provided stability, but she'd always known he was the real talent, with his showmanship and creative flair, just so long as she was there to make the maths add up. Working as a scenic artist on television and film sets after graduating, Simon's larger-than-life personality had caught the eyes and ears of a few industry insiders. That clever mind, combined with style, good looks and wit, was tailor-made for television. Brief appearances on daytime magazine shows had led to big hits like *Room Makeover* and *The House Show*.

Not long after Simon had burst into the limelight in the late nineties, the Demons' marriage had fallen apart, shocking their friends and family, if not the public. At the time, rumours had been rife that Simon was gay and one national newspaper had even named and shamed him as living a lie. He'd done himself no favours with the press by refuting the claims with a loud legal outcry that had been labelled homophobic. He was even more vilified for 'proving' his heterosexual credentials when first-born son Louis arrived six months later, not least because the mother was not his wife but *Room Makeover* co-star Lilia Bartholomew.

Unable to bear the day-to-day agony of his betrayal, Laney had demanded a separation, only to feel the pain quadruple when Simon moved in with Lilia and his son, believing he was doing the right thing. They had divorced without a fight, splitting everything equally, including their hearts. While Laney had thrown herself into her work, Simon had lost direction. He was quoted at the time as saying that he 'hadn't even made wood', referring to the fifth anniversary, but it was often taken out of context even to this day. By then, his reputation was distinctly dishonourable.

With OutRage! baying at his heels and no Laney to help make decisions, his career wobbled as he began a long succession of changing horses midstream, both professionally and privately. The union with Lilia lasted just two years and was followed by a succession of ever more disastrous relationships, with four more children, multiple *Cheers!* interviews and two more divorces. He and Laney remained on speaking terms and she even continued to help out with his career, advising against the more ridiculous elements, however well paid. This irritated successive girlfriends, many of whom she also advised against, however beautiful. Close friends like Leo despaired of Demon and his 'womanising', but in shrewder, confidential moments they put it down to a broken heart. The press were far less forgiving, although his public persona was so gregariously likeable that they could never kill off his career, however hard they tried. When Laney had married Oscar Benson, the paps had doorstepped her ex-husband and been rewarded with a face of total despair.

Last year, his remarriage to his first wife had earned them the media tag 'the Burton and Taylor of lifestyle television'.

This afternoon, Laney felt cast in the role of Martha to his George, sniping and resentful. Work abandoned, she endured the tea party with as much good grace as she could summon for Hope's sake, despite Malin's slender brown legs stretched across the picnic blanket.

'More delicious puke-umber sandwiches, Mummy?'

'Thank you, darling.'

'At school today when Mrs Todd asked about our favourite things I said to the class that I love you more than ice-cream and jelly.'

'That's so lovely. I love you more than ice-cream and jelly too.'

'But I love Gogs most of all.' She held up the shabby home-made bear that godfather Leo had given her at birth and which remained her closest companion to this day. Leo had famously taken up knitting as a bet on the set of one of his biggest romcom hits, and now his creations made small fortunes for charity. Gogs was probably the most valuable thing in the de Montmorency household.

'Good choice.'

'I live in Hope' had been Laney's catchphrase during her short, unhappy marriage to Oscar, grateful at least that he had given her the one gift she'd craved throughout adulthood, a child. The fierceness of the love she'd felt from the first moment that tiny starfish hand clutched hers in the maternity suite had shocked her to the core; it still overwhelmed her at times. She continually lived in Hope. Letting Simon try to share that love was still a sticking point and she unconsciously fought to keep them separate, just as her relationship with his five children existed in prescribed doses. She'd not stopped loving Simon in all the time she'd known him, but they'd discovered unconditional love while they were apart, and that was proving hard to overcome.

Simon had no issue with taking on another man's child: Hope was a part of the woman he had always loved more than any other, and therefore a part of him. Laney was more wary. She found it easier to adopt a self-protective stance in her marriage, and was always quick to suspect any ulterior motive. That Hope adored Daddymon cut little ice in this slow thaw. The Demons still veered between love and hate, hot and cold, heaven and hell.

Returning to Red Gables that afternoon, they didn't make love or babies, but argued instead over the shape of the new balustrades on the staircase, the colour scheme for the third guest bedroom and – inevitably – money. When Malin brought the yawning Hope back from their play date at the village swings, Laney and Simon were still on the landing, yelling at each other about hand-painted wallpaper.

'My page rate barely covers the costs for six square inches of it!' she howled. 'So my skipping work this afternoon has just cost us three blue-tits and a hummingbird.'

'Why is Mummy shouting?'

Laney looked down into the hallway, saw a small dark head and felt guilt knot her heartstrings to her vocal cords. 'Bath and bedtime.' She mustered a big smile and swept downstairs.

*

Once Hope was asleep, with Gogs beneath her cheek, Laney and Simon armed themselves with huge gin and tonics and retreated to opposite ends of the vast music room, which they'd adopted as a joint office and which was currently doubling as a repository for scores of boxes of books. It was one of the few habitable downstairs rooms. Laney knew she shouldn't be drinking when she was trying to conceive but Simon, who thought such health warnings wildly exaggerated, was eager to take the edge off her irritability and spark up her libido with a Bombay Sapphire. While he waded reluctantly through his post and email, Laney crabbily added a swathe of fight scenes and romantic trysts to the salt book dramatisation and fired it off, then got up to mix another brace of drinks.

When she came back, Simon was one-finger typing in reply to an email, eyes squinting from keyboard to screen with every long-winded strike. Laney watched him impassively.

'What's for supper?' he asked, as she set his refill down beside him.

'God knows.' Their feast-and-famine relationship extended beyond the metaphor these days as they alternated between ambrosial banquets and beans on toast, depending on the level at which they were communicating. 'I can look in the freezer.'

'Let's go to the Poussin again,' he suggested. Michelin-starred chef Justin Ox was an old friend from the days when Simon had presented BBC food programmes, and had granted the Demons the huge rolling tab that now rivalled what they owed the builders and the tax man.

'We can't afford it, and it's not fair asking Justin to squeeze us in at short notice two days running when others wait three months for a table.' Laney had no desire to go out and be on show as Mrs Demon. She longed to relax and pamper herself, applying Autumn Glow to her grey hairs before soaking in the bath and carefully eliminating any sign of stubble. But all Red Gables' baths apart from Hope's were currently out of commission and it took a brave heart to shower surrounded by sketches of oneself twenty years younger and three dress sizes smaller. She'd done so with the lights off last time.

Then she remembered Mia's request.

'I have to go out.' She reached down to search his pockets for the car keys. 'It's Iris's hen party. Chloe's organised a bash in Morley. I promised Mia I'd be there.'

'Must you? I thought you disapproved.'

'Mia wants me to have words.'

'That's bloody typical of Mia. It's the poor girl's hen night. Oh, that feels good.'

Still groping for the keys, Laney tried to ignore the warm hand sliding up her arm towards her right breast. She didn't want to go out but she had promised Mia she'd be at the hen party, and the thought of escaping from her irritation with Simon was almost selling it to her.

'If I hurry I'll be in time for the male stripper.' She bypassed the hopeful bulge in his trousers and delved deeper.

'You can't just abandon me with these.' He gestured at his Mac screen, which contained rows of emails from fans via the official Simon de Montmorency website. 'Take this one – "Tell me, Simon, why don't we see more of the ravishing Mrs de Montmorency? Regards, Richard HH." Bloody cheek!'

'Depends which Mrs de M he means,' she said glumly.

'Don't be ridiculous. It's clearly you. I think this Richard was at an after-dinner speech I did recently, the one with all the hooting aristos. If it's him, he owns most of the Borders and said he never misses *QuickWits* if you're on it. He was most put out you weren't there. Can you drop him a charming acknowledgement when you get a moment? You're so much better at answering these things than I am. There are too many lascivious ladies this week as it is, most of them terrifying.' His virtual postbag was inevitably crammed with propositions that began: I've been happily married for nearly thirty years and can't believe I'm writing this to you . . .

'Leave them all to me.' She gave the bulge a loving stroke and her fingers closed around the car keys at last. 'I'll tackle them tomorrow and remind the lascivious ladies that the position's filled.'

'Marvellous. Let's go to bed so I can fill the only lascivious lady I care about. Face it, Mrs Demon, we mix our gins like we mix our sin, so you'll be over the limit to drive anyway.'

For a moment, she was tempted. It would be another baby-making opportunity. Mixing gin and sin suddenly felt far more tempting than mixing with leggy under-twenties. But Mia would never forgive her if she baled.

'I'm fine.' She headed for the door. 'Don't bother staying up.'

'Not much chance of that at my age,' Simon said miserably, tucking his pocket back in his trousers, bulge already subsiding. He returned to his computer screen but glanced back as his wife ground to an abrupt halt in the doorway with a cry of horror. 'Don't tell me the builders have spilled mastic on the parquet again?'

'I've just remembered it's fancy dress.' She turned back imploringly.

A slow smile spread across Simon's face as he stood up, clicking his knuckles. A lifelong enthusiastic party host and guest, he'd assembled a costume store to rival the National Theatre's. It was the only one of his many eccentric collections they'd unpacked since moving in, and it was arranged on long rails in the attics. 'How long have we got?'

'Ten minutes max.' She started towards the stairs.

'Theme?'

'Something to do with animals, I think. Mia did say. "Fur, feather and fin" rings a bell. Shall I text her?'

'No time. I have *just* the thing,' he was already unzipping her dress as they climbed, 'but first let's refresh our minds about the birds and the bees.' His hand slipped beneath her knickers to squeeze a buttock.

'I always thought that sounded like a very unnatural relationship.'

She panted her way around a stair-turn. 'What bird in her right mind would want to shag a bee?'

'It's all about the "sting" – ne*sting* and roo*sting* being primary examples,' he said, as he unclipped her bra. 'Stick around and I'll show you some thru*sting*.'

'I told you we haven't time.' Boobs bouncing as she scaled the narrow back stairs, Laney was feeling far from desirable, secretly resentful that Simon was always horny after a day off work when she was exhausted and currently in a hurry. She knew that she was ovulating and they often had their most fast, furious and wanton sex when they had been scrapping, but her libido was flat-lining.

They battled their way past the plastic sheeting that was currently weatherproofing the second floor. As Simon shouldered the light switch, he looked back at her with his devilish smile, eyes as pale and predatory as a wolf's. 'I warn you, resistance is hopeless.'

The attics smelled of theatre dressing rooms, and Laney was reminded of the many times they had stolen naughty minutes when first together in the college prop store. They'd been insatiable then. Trying to get into the mood, she picked a black-feather ball mask from a nearby hook and put it on, then eased off her dress and struck a burlesque pose. Simon's mouth fell greedily on her naked breasts, gathering first one nipple and then the other against his tongue to coax them into tingling high relief.

Laney closed her eyes and tried to imagine they were back at Old Gate with no responsibilities, just two randy, madly-in-love individuals who'd found out what bliss it was to get naked, slot their bodies together and seek nirvana. But when she opened her eyes, the first thing she looked at was her watch. She glanced guiltily at Simon to make sure he hadn't noticed and her heart burned in her chest, filled with love and regret. She wished her body would burn with lust and longing instead. They *would* make love, she decided. They were the forever family now.

Simon pulled a huge red velvet opera cloak from a rack and threw it across the largest prop hamper so that it resembled an altar, on to which he carefully lowered his wife, deftly sliding off her knickers as he did so before kneeling alongside her, his hand taking her ankle and lifting it over his shoulder. Reaching behind, he drew forwards an ostrich boa that he slowly tied around her wrists, its downy fronds whispering against her skin.

'Does that feel good?' he breathed.

It tickled and she was almost certain a spider had just scuttled out of it across her stomach, but she nodded. She was still wearing her mask and felt ridiculously like Batman, but she couldn't rip it off now that her hands were tied and she could tell it was exciting the hell out of Simon.

'We have to be quick,' she reminded him, as he curled the ends of the boa around her ankle and lifted it even higher before starting to kiss his way along her thigh, his teeth sinking into the soft skin and making her yelp.

'Forget the hen party,' he insisted. 'All you're getting tonight is cock, baby.'

Lifting her chin, she peered sceptically at him, relieved to see the glint of amusement in the grey eyes watching her from between her thighs. They stayed locked on hers as his mouth enclosed her clitoris and his tongue began to work its magic, knowing exactly how to flick soft then hard, to circle and swirl and lap in and out of her until she was ready to tumble off the pleasure ledge.

Laney willed her body to leap into sizzling response, but she was barely getting warmed up when he thrust inside her, his pace relentless from the start, pulling both her legs over his shoulders, angling her back and filling her until she felt muscles she'd forgotten about clench in response. It was far from sensual, and it was only a hair's breadth away from being too rough, but strangely thrilling in its novelty and wantonness, and she fought guilty relief that it would undoubtedly be over quickly. Abandoning herself to it, she let out a long, hedonistic groan, which was enough to make Simon come with such force she felt the rushing flood of heat inside her.

Laney beamed up at him.

He pressed a rueful smile to the little birthmark on her right calf. 'You didn't come.'

'I was thereabouts,' she lied, unpeeling feathers from her sweaty wrists, thinking happily of the pregnancy test she could treat herself to tomorrow. Shooting into orgasm orbit would have been lovely, but she was going to be horribly late as it was, and now she'd need to take a shower. 'What am I wearing?' She sat up, hoping Simon had something flattering and understated.

He was watching her thoughtfully, his face in shadow. Then he turned to his rails and drew forward a costume so large-scale and spectacular it had a wheeled rack all of its own.

'Jesus!' She started to laugh. 'I hope it's flameproof.'

Chapter 12

As her candlelit punt glided along the Thames, Iris was so engrossed in exchanging messages with Dougie that she hardly noticed when the gondolier at the helm lifted his boater and broke into an aria, accompanied by an accordionist in another punt.

Soon afterwards, her hens confiscated her phone, but she still failed to enter into the spirit of the occasion, drinking barely a sip of champagne and eating only a few chocolate buttons from the top of a cupcake.

'I've had no appetite for weeks,' she confessed to Chloe later, when they sat down in the private dining room at Morley-on-Thames Rowing Club.

'I wish you'd told me that before I booked this place at forty quid a head.' Chloe peered at her friend's waif-like frame. 'We could have gone extreme potholing instead.'

'This is perfect,' Iris assured her, looking around the familiar faces as if through a sheet of glass. She sometimes felt that being in love had entombed her in an enchanted casket. It felt safe and secure, and the view was wonderful. Her friends had never looked more ravishing, a magical chorus to her ascension.

The hens, meanwhile, were regarding her with mounting anxiety. Few had seen much of her in the past year, for much of which she had been away filming the fifth Ptolemy Finch movie, followed by three months in the UK wrapped up with Dougie. Now that they could see close up what Mia Devonshire privately described to close friends as her daughter's 'love lobotomy', it was obvious how extreme the change in her was.

Even that evening's fancy-dress theme had failed to ignite Iris's famous sense of fun. After much deliberating, Chloe had come up with 'birds of a feather', resulting in acres of marabou, ostrich and chandelle trim, and plenty of boas. There were also a few comedy penguins, a parrot and a Tweety Pie. Chloe herself was loyally dressed in a hired emu-rider suit, jockey on top and bird from the waist down.

The Iris they knew would have embraced the avian theme with delight, insisting upon the most outrageous, and probably comic, creation of the evening. She'd never been remotely self-conscious, and had the enviable ability to dress down and still look ravishing, in the way that only those born truly beautiful can achieve. She rarely wore make-up or changed out of jeans unless she was in character or on a publicity tour, but when she did pull out all the stops she could silence a room. Tonight her hens had prepared a surprise costume: a ravishing peacock dress with a nipped-in waist that made her look like a Mardi Gras queen. But, far from preening and cooing, she was sprawling in her chair like the dreamy kid at the back of the class, feather-trimmed high heels kicked off below the table as she thought of nothing but her fiancé.

'I've never seen anyone that in love,' one friend murmured.

Chloe narrowed her eyes and wondered if Dougie had drugged her. She seemed to recall that he had once been linked to a cocaine scandal. She adored Iris, but her friend was suddenly a stranger.

Iris had always been the sort of girl who seemed too good to be true – as fragile as spun glass, as affectionate as a kitten and as loyal as a Labrador. Women of all ages treasured her and men guarded her fiercely. She was a terrific friend, and eternally optimistic. The X key of her smartphone was always worn blank because she added so many kisses to messages. She never forgot birthdays or betrayed a secret, had a huge sense of fun, and was up for any dare. Fame hadn't changed her, except that she had more numbers stored and less free time, and shopping in Primark or meeting for a coffee meant getting papped.

Inevitably compared to her mother, with whom she shared the wild snakes of hair and vivid green eyes, she maintained that she was of a completely different species. Mia was old-fashioned, passionate and forthright at home, cool and charming in public; Iris was as imaginative, capricious and outspoken in public as in private. Mia looked after her body with a personal trainer, chef and dresser; Iris lived on chocolate, energy drinks and late nights. Her hair was only the same rich burnt-biscuit colour as her mother's by virtue of the Ptolemy Finch creatives, who'd insisted she dye it darker to contrast with Ptolemy's near-white locks. The only time Iris ever went near a hairdresser was when she was on set, which was why she was currently sporting a root-line tidemark where her natural pale blond was growing through. As well as poor nutrition and lack of sleep, she had no vanity. To remain so beautiful was a triumph of genetics.

Her penchant for old cardigans, checked shirts and boyfriend jeans was a running joke among her friends. She looked like a scruffball, often smelled of horse and had never willingly worn heels in her life, although she was barely five feet four. This delighted five-feet-seven Dougie, who could be chippy about his height, although he was less impressed by her choice of bridesmaids, who were both nearly six feet tall. He'd insisted on no high tiaras, heels

131

or big hair for the ceremony. Not that Iris had any intention of sporting them.

'What's the dress like?' asked a friend now.

'I haven't found one yet,' she admitted. 'I tried bidding for a couple of vintage frocks on eBay, but I was sniped at the last minute. I'll have to go shopping this week. I've got to be able to sit astride a saddle in it.'

'Are you really going to ride up the aisle? Won't the dress get all hitched up?'

'Nothing's getting hitched that day apart from me and Dougie. I guess I should take Scully into the fitting rooms with me but Mum would insist on driving the horsebox, and I definitely don't want her opinion, so I'll chance it. There's always side-saddle.'

Another change her friends had noticed in her was a vehement antipathy towards her mother. To hear Iris speak of bubbly, kind-hearted Mia in such disparaging tones was startling. The two had always adored each other, but their current rift seemed dangerously deep.

She looked up at the old wall clock above two crossed oars, calculating the time in LA. Dougie would be with her father, she realised. They'd arranged to meet for lunch at the studio. Her fingers twitched. She longed to have her phone back to wish him good luck, but the hens had locked it in the rowing club's safe.

Chloe was harrying everybody into their seats, having arranged entertainment between courses. They were already running terribly late.

Each inter-course show was to be preceded by a round of tequila shots, served by bare-chested waiters in leather chaps and shot-glass bandolier belts, with a Cuervo bottle in each hip holster. This was a last-minute addition that several schoolfriend hens had come up with, thinking Chloe's plans very staid.

'Please tell me there's not going to be a kissogram?' griped one of Iris's LA acting cronies, who clearly disapproved of a lowly rowing club and thought Chloe a very pedestrian friend.

'Definitely not.' She checked her watch, not caring what the pecking hens thought as long as tonight made Iris happy. 'A fire-eater after the starter, Bruno Mars lookalike performing "Just the Way You Are" after the mains and a fortune teller after dessert.'

The actress looked alarmed. 'Isn't that a bit hocus-pocus?'

'It was the only thing Iris asked for. You know how much she loves all that stuff.'

'So you've arranged for the tarot pack to be made up entirely of the Lovers card, like in the James Bond movie, yeah?'

'Of course not.' Chloe had no belief in the occult, but cheating was definitely off limits. 'I just Googled local availability and liked the name – Psychic Phoenix. It seemed to fit with the theme. I've done it all by email. It's probably a parrot in a gold Liberace cloak.'

Matters were delayed further by the arrival of Iris's beloved Spanish grandmother Jacinta, whizzing along in a new electric wheelchair with a carer in her wake.

'Dad bought it for her birthday.' Iris watched her fondly. 'She refuses to read the instruction manual. So far she's run over three of Mum's dogs and trashed the best Tabriz rug.'

Lito was sporting a tweed twinset, matched with a pheasant-feather hat. She looked better equipped to shoot birds than tequila.

'Where are the *hombres de cuero*?' she demanded excitedly, speeding up to the dining table and almost disappearing beneath it as she failed to brake in time. All that could be seen of her was a pheasant hat on the place setting.

Chloe pulled her out just as the carer raced up and flicked off the chair's power switch, panting. '*Señora*, we agreed that you must let me steer the chair in here.' She eyed the big open doors leading straight out on to a decked riverside terrace as she pushed down firmly on the brake.

Now Jacinta cast her eyes along the table and took in the hens in all their plumed glory, her dark eyes gleaming. It was no secret that the family matriarch had advised her granddaughter against the marriage, but she was clearly under strict instructions to behave herself. 'Iris's fiancé is in America tonight,' she confessed to Chloe in a rasping Hispanic undertone. 'Leo will take him in hand. *Mas vale tarde que nunca*. Better late than never.' She reached for a glass and raised it at the party organiser. '*A beber y a tragar, que el mundo se va a acabar.*'

'Eat and drink, for tomorrow the world will end,' Chloe translated, knowing it was one of the Devonshires' catchphrases. She only hoped the Psychic Phoenix was a bit more upbeat.

Leo Devonshire regarded his future son-in-law for the first time with mild surprise. He looked younger than his twenty-eight years, and was certainly easy on the eye, with an unexpected appealing charm.

It had been all too easy to demonise Dougie, especially after the many long conversations in which he and Mia had discussed the situation. Yet the fact that the guy had flown to America to see him personally spoke volumes for his upbringing and good intentions. As they sat down together at lunch, his hand still ached from the firmest handshake he'd experienced in years. He guessed all that hilt-gripping from sword-fighting and jousting must give one a palm like a vice. Yet this was no horse-trick hillbilly. Dougie was a class act, a well-mannered young blade in a pale blue suit and discreet signet ring.

'Why is it so important to seek my approval?' he asked. 'You hardly need a father's blessing to get married in this day and age.' He was aware he sounded starchy and formal, battling as always, when meeting a Brit in LA, to ditch the transatlantic idioms, and overdoing it so that he sounded like Jeeves brushing down Bertie Wooster's suit shoulders with a pep talk.

Dougie didn't seem to notice. 'I'm an old-fashioned guy. I respect you enormously, Mr Devonshire.'

'Leo.'

He dipped his head gratefully. 'It means everything to Iris that you approve, Leo. And Iris means absolutely everything to me, so

I simply had to come.' He had a glorious accent: soft, elegant and infused with enough depth to carry weight. It would be superb for voiceovers.

'You've only been together five minutes.'

'Three months.'

'I think she's far too young to marry.'

'She needs you there.'

Leo chewed a nail, longing to bite it off but knowing his make-up artist would slay him. The character of Chancellor might be uptight and obsessive, but he couldn't risk offending the American public by ruining his manicure, just as he could never have succeeded in the US with 'British' teeth or bad hair days, as his many hours of orthodontics and salon treatments testified. He'd been allowed a few creased shirts and stubble in series five, when Chancellor had gone through a tough patch, but that was only because his fictional wife had died, and by series six he was immaculate and manicured once more, with a new love interest lined up.

'I can't get away,' he apologised. 'Perhaps I can write something to be read out?'

'We can arrange a video link.'

'This isn't the Golden Globes. I prefer to keep it more personal.'

'It will be personal. Just close friends. No press.' Dougie kept smiling, a slight twitch creasing the edge of one bright blue eye, which Leo took to be the strain of a long flight.

No wonder Iris was so smitten, he reflected. The younger man's face was extraordinary, all that blue-blood chiselling matched with extraordinary colouring, olive skin and sunburned cheeks that contrasted with eyes the same vivid blue as a Greek sea and hair like bleached sand. He had a vivid scar, still tinged red, through one eyebrow and another, faded to silver, on his chin, and his teeth, despite their whiteness, were chipped and uneven. Yet these imperfections somehow only added to his sex appeal, indicators of his love of danger.

'Why marry so soon after meeting each other?' he asked. 'Why not wait?'

'I'm an Aries. We have no patience.'

Leo's eyes narrowed. He had no truck with astrology. Half of America thought he'd been named after a star sign, which irritated him enormously. His adopted daughter, by contrast, was hugely superstitious. No doubt Aries was highly compatible with her star sign, whatever it was. He struggled to remember his own, although he knew it wasn't Leo.

'I would willingly give my approval for a very long engagement. I see no reason to rush things.'

'I won't hold Iris back in any way – quite the reverse. I'll support her right through university, and then into films again or on to the stage if that's what she wants. She's an amazing actress.'

'She no longer seems interested in any of that.'

'She can make up her own mind.'

'And your aspirations?' Leo asked, unpleasantly aware that he now sounded like Maggie Smith playing a fierce matriarch. He should have been whipping out a pince-nez and peering at a notebook between cutting epigrams. Instead he sneaked a look at his watch, aware that he had less than ten minutes before he was due back on set. He should have been in Make-up already.

'The stunt work's good, and I do a bit of acting,' Dougie was saying. 'I'd like more movie work. Shooting on location reminds me of my military training. The discipline never changes, but the geography, warfare and strategy is never the same twice. And the greatest thing about working with horses is the locations. I guess studio work is more like peace-keeping.'

Leo flashed his famous smile, but the dark eyes stayed guarded. 'I'm all for giving peace a chance.'

'I just love the way you act, especially the offbeat stuff you made in the early days. We've worked with some of the same people – Jane George, the Barron-Taylor brothers, Noel Whitmore, Adam Oakes.'

Leo started at a name he hadn't heard in many years. He remembered Adam all too well from both Old Gate and the work they'd done together after university. 'Is Adam Oakes still acting?'

'He didn't make anything for years after *Sink*. I loved that programme. You were great in it.' The cult nineties series had been a super-slick brow-beetling tableau of horny teenage working-class angst shot prettily on film for Channel Four, but after three series it had been axed under the weight of complaints that it glorified drugs, homosexuality and shoplifting.

Leo was shaking his head. 'I'm amazed you've seen it. I was only in two episodes, and those were never aired to my knowledge.'

'Adam's directing now. He mostly works with the cinematographer Preston Williams. Now *there's* a guy who can drink all night and still have a steady hand in the morning. They've just made a drama about a trotting-horse kept outside a high-rise estate in Swansea. It's based on a true story. The horse was set alight by a gang, and its owner later tried to ride down the culprits like Charlton Heston in *El Cid*.'

Leo said nothing, ignoring his mobile phone – switched to silent – flashing frantically as he was called back to the set. He needed to know if the mention of Adam was merely coincidence or a deliberate threat.

'I did the stunt work,' Dougie went on. 'Iris came and watched us shoot on location in Wales. Adam and Preston remembered you well, and told me some wild stories about your early career. I had no idea you had to make such life-changing sacrifices . . . you *and* Mia.' With a big smile, he laid down the cryptic insinuation like a trump card, leaving Leo in no doubt that the young pretender was seeking leverage. 'What is it they say? "If two ride on a horse, one must ride behind?"'

Leo's dark eyes were bush-baby wide. 'I don't ride much any more.'

'Shame.' Dougie smiled easily. 'Such a good skill to keep up for acting roles. Adam told me he always thought you'd be a big star, and Preston remembered meeting you and Mia when Iris was a baby. He says he recognised the unique talent in you that marks out a Hollywood success – like Cruise, Travolta, DiCaprio.'

'What point are you making?'

'You have loyal friends and a strong family behind you, Leo, and I'm proud to be joining that team. You can trust my discretion.'

'Thank you for the reassurance,' he said tightly, wondering just how much Adam had told Dougie, no doubt disarmed by the long sooty lashes and charming manners. He couldn't risk giving himself away by probing more deeply. Instead he adopted a patriarchal expression. 'I appreciate you travelling here personally to ask for my blessing.'

'I love this town.' The charismatic smile widened. 'Now we're family, it would be great to get a leg-up.' He batted his eyelashes. 'I have friends here in LA, but they're just playing at it. I want to come here and make movies. Iris is only fed up because she's typecast; you know all about that. She needs your support right now – we both do.'

'Iris has never used my success as currency. She even wanted to act under a different name until she was talked out of it.'

'Which is why she's so excited that she'll be Mrs Iris Everett soon, backing up the talented Mr Douglas Everett,' Dougie pointed out.

Leo thought he made Iris sound like the ageing treasurer of a Home Counties operatic society, accompanying her husband on the piano. His Iris was still a golden-haired child, with freckles and knock knees, who loved dressing up as a fairy. They had named her after the Spanish word for rainbow, never imagining the gold-diggers that would one day seek the crock at its end.

'I'd like to help you, Dougie,' he said cautiously, 'but I haven't made a movie in at least four years. I'm out of that scene right now.'

'Your representation isn't. Abe Schultz is still the hottest agent in Hollywood. You two go back years. You're godfather to one of his kids, aren't you?'

Leo could feel the sheer ambition melting off the guy.

'I have to get back on set.' He stood up abruptly, reaching for his cell phone. 'I'll text you Abe's direct line at Creative Artists and copy him into the message so he knows who you are. When d'you fly home?'

'Tomorrow night.'

'There's no way he'll see you before that.'

'That's cool. I'm back here on honeymoon in a week. We'll meet then.'

'Does Iris know you're spending your honeymoon in LA?'

'It's a surprise. She'll love it. We'll bring you some wedding cake.'

Leo regarded him levelly, torn between overwhelming fury that this boy was so manipulative, and euphoria at the thought of seeing Iris. By then she'd be married and, for all Mia's assertions, Leo knew there was nothing he could do to stop that happening.

'I'll make sure Abe knows to look after you.'

Dougie smiled widely as he stood up to shake Leo's hand with another killer grip. 'So can I tell Iris we have your blessing?'

'Tell her I'm knitting her trousseau,' he replied, 'and if you let her down, I'll strangle you with it.'

Chapter 13

'She's making a huge mistake. Can I borrow your lipstick?'

'It's Poutrageous – Mummy has to buy it from the States. We think Iris is only getting married because she wants to get out of going to university. Too much like hard work.'

'Couldn't she just refuse to go? Why the big white wedding?'

'You know Iris. She just *loves* to be the centre of attention. Is that Touche Eclat?'

'Have some. Dougie's seriously lush, mind you.'

'That's why she'll never hold him. I heard that the reason the ceremony's so late in the evening is because he never gets up before lunchtime.'

Listening from the toilet cubicle where she'd been sequestered for five minutes, Iris longed to burst out of the door and confront the pecking hens, but she was still sitting bare-bottomed on the loo with her ankles almost tied together by the Wolford tights her friends had insisted went with the peacock dress. Besides, she'd just sent another instant message to Dougie and had no desire to let her fellow revellers know she'd managed to get her phone back from the safe by chatting up the porter. At last the reply she was waiting for came through.

Paz y bendiciones – she read her father's blessing.

She stifled a whoop as the disloyal hens, still preening at the mirrors, moved on to the wayward reputation of her fiancé.

'Dougie was in Vale of the Wolds Pony Club with Lucy Channing's cousin. She says he was notorious. They called him Ever-Ready Everett.'

'I've heard that he now sleeps with half the field of the Pelham Hunt, and is especially fond of mothers and daughters.'

'You don't suppose he's had a crack at Mia?'

The door creaked as another guest entered the Ladies, and walked into the cubicle beside Iris. From the lack of acknowledgement, it clearly wasn't a close ally of the conspirators. In fact the sudden silence struck Iris as quite odd. She was now almost certain she'd heard two matching gulps from the direction of the mirrors.

There was a lot of scratching and clanking coming from the adjacent cubicle, followed by the sound of the door being wrestled shut. Looking down in alarm, Iris saw a sweep of brightly coloured feather-trimmed wires jabbing beneath the partition, brushing her small, creased peacock tail to one side. Looking up, she saw a plume like a Roman candle poking across from above. Whoever was sporting it was making a lot of grunting noises, accompanied by the sound of Velcro ripping and poppers unsnapping. Then, along with a relieved sigh and the sound of peeing, she heard the familiar click-click of a phone screen being tapped.

There were two secret messengers in the Ladies that night, it seemed.

Guessing Chloe had hired some sort of drag queen for the final entertainment slot before they all moved on to the nightclub, she sent a message back to her father consisting of row upon row of kisses and smiley faces.

Alone at Wootton, Mia pounced on her phone as the latest report came through from Laney, who had arrived hugely late. Her first text had come from the car park ten minutes earlier, to announce that she was trapped in her car. Had Mia any idea how to open a Mercedes sun-roof with the ignition turned off, because she'd shut her headdress in it and now dropped the keys beyond reach?

Now she appeared to have extricated herself from that and entered the building, but her progress was no less fateful.

The hens all think I'm the fortune teller called Psychic Phoenix, Mia read in amazement. Shall I reveal my true self or use this opportunity? Iris not seen me yet, but think disguise quite effective. Chloe no idea it's me. xx

Mia felt a quiver of reckless anticipation.

DO NOT reveal self, she typed back, unable to believe her luck. Tell her terrible fate awaits if she marries Dougie Everett. x

Laney was predictably down-to-earth. Can't do that to her. And what if she does recognise me after all?

You can and she won't. You're a terrific actress. Put on strong accent and mannerism. You are SAVING HER LIFE here – and mine. Xxx

Having stashed her phone back in her bra cup, Laney struggled out of the cubicle, wings clattering, and paused to regard her reflection.

Seven foot of brightly coloured blue, green and gold phoenix stared back with its sinister pterodactyl face covering hers.

She fanned out her long tail and straightened her plumage. Doing as Mia suggested seemed far too brutal, but she was sure she'd think of something, a sort of ambiguous 'Beware the Ides of March' prophecy that might just jolt her goddaughter into wanting to stall for time and get to know her fiancé better before joining him at the altar.

Jacinta was thoroughly enjoying the evening and had to keep remembering to glower disapprovingly whenever Dougie was mentioned, but it was hard because she had met so many charming young women and was having such fun. It beat nights out to musicals with her over-protective daughter-in-law. Although Jacinta adored Mia and had shared a home with her son's wife for sixteen years now, she had to admit it was a relief not to have Mia fussing around her. The hired carer was keeping a discreet distance and now being chatted up by one of the tequila waiters.

'D'you mind me asking how old you are?' a charming young actress friend of Iris wondered.

When Jacinta told her she was seventy-nine, the girl let out a shriek of excitement. 'You look *so* amazing. Your skin's fabulous. Is that down to the Mediterranean diet I've read about? All that olive oil and fresh salad?'

'I hate salad,' Jacinta said. 'My son, he bought me facelift when I reach seventy-five. And trust me, I am not as well as I look. I am in constant and crippling pain ...' Chief among her favourite topics was her own ailments, and now she saw the perfect opportunity to list them to a captive audience.

The girl was soon glazing over as Jacinta moved on from her arthritis, through diabetes to her weak heart and two recent mini-strokes. Her hearing-aid battery packed up somewhere between asthma and glycaemia, but she didn't notice, launching into the details of her recent gum disease.

The girl was incredibly relieved when the arrival of another tequila round signalled a new inter-course show, this time the for- tune teller, who swept into the room so dramatically that her headdress took out a light fitting. 'Well, it sure as hell isn't a trained parrot.' She giggled.

Unable to hear much at all now, Jacinta eyed the new arrival rheumily, inclining her head towards her pretty companion. 'The old parrot doesn't learn to talk, as we say in Spain.' She offered a bag of Werther's. 'Toffee?'

'Look to the SKIES for your FUTURE!' The seven-foot bird waved her wings about in front of a mildly amused Iris. 'Trust the WORD of the Phoenix. The SKY holds the secret of HAPPI- NESS. You may see a CLOUD in the shape of your talisman or a STAR that burns more brightly than the others. You must trust that SIGN and follow it, even if it changes your PLANS.'

'You paid for this shit?' one of the hens hissed at Chloe.

Chloe cleared her throat. 'I was led to believe it would be more of an intimate palmistry and tarot sort of a thing.'

'She sounds like Robert Peston on a bad day.'

'There is a WOMAN close to you who gives WISE advice!' the Phoenix carried on, in an accent that kept jumping from Greece to somewhere in Eastern Europe, then back again. 'You must LISTEN to her. She will say it only ONCE.'

Beneath the mask Laney winced, realising she'd now veered into an *'Allo 'Allo!* impersonation. At this rate, she'd have to resign the post of godmother. 'She may not be in your LIFE much longer. I can also see a MAN. A man you cannot TRUST. A centaur. Avoid him. He will bring RUIN.'

Iris was starting to look mildly irritated.

Laney flapped her wings again, making a few nearby hens duck. She was aware she was losing authority. She had to pull out a trump card.

Squaring her huge feathered shoulders, she tipped her head

143

back so her beak pointed upwards. 'I can see a WORD forming in the SKY. It is above me now. A name . . . it looks foreign. S-U-E-N-O. Sueno?'

'It's a place!' Iris gasped, eyes widening before narrowing suspiciously, and she shot Chloe a sceptical look, sensing a plant, but Chloe was genuinely staggered. The Devonshire family kept Sueño secret: it was the Spanish hacienda buried deep within the Andalucían hills, incorporating farmland that had once belonged to Leo's grandparents. Jacinta had been born there. The tranquillity and calm of Hacienda Sueño had long provided a bolt-hole for the family to escape to, and the press remained unaware of it, as did all but the closest of family friends. Indeed, most of the hens were looking blank.

'That is a SAFE place,' Laney said, accent heading towards Hungary. 'Away from the CENTAUR.' She wondered if it would be too much to add that Durham University was a good bet too. Deciding it was, she cast around for a few fortune-telling stand-bys. 'I see a tall man.'

'That's Dougie.' Iris sighed.

'TALL man,' Laney repeated, flapping her wings. 'Dark and handsome. He has a limp and . . . a scar shaped like an . . . er . . . arrow.'

'Who is he?' Iris was taking more interest.

'He will bring good FORTUNE.' The accent was more Polish builder than Aegean goddess now, but at least she had everybody's attention. 'Do not deny him the chance to fill your heart with the courage of a LION. Remember, look to the SKY! *¡Buenas noches!*'

Electing to quit while she was ahead, she swept out of the room, shedding colourful tail feathers everywhere and popping several balloons with her headdress.

Her dramatic exit was then somewhat hampered by Chloe barring her way while she fumbled in a bag for the envelope containing the Psychic Phoenix's fee for the evening.

'I cannot accept payment!' Laney insisted. Taking money felt deeply dishonest given the lies she'd just spun. 'With messages this CLEAR it is my DUTY to pass on predictions.' She spread her wings wide to make the girl back off.

But Chloe had faced far more frightening fowl in her veterinary placements and calmly tucked the envelope beneath a golden shoulder pad. 'I added in the fifty-pence-per-mile travel expenses from High Wycombe you asked for.'

Able to study her at close range through her mask, Laney was struck by how like her father she was. Her skin was darker than Hope's, closer to Oscar's Jamaican tones, but with extraordinary dark blue eyes and freckles across her cheeks, nose and chin. Like Hope, she had wild bedsprings of dark curls and deliciously plump lips, along with that distinctive cleft chin.

To Laney's ongoing frustration, Chloe had always refused to have anything to do with her half-sister, and Oscar didn't attempt to encourage contact between them, even less so Chloe's embittered mother. Laney, though, had enough insight into Chloe's clever mind and warm heart from the girl's long friendship with Iris to remain certain there was a way forward. Tonight, however, was regrettably not an opportunity to unmask and suggest a family day out to Legoland.

For a moment, as Chloe stared deep into the beak, Laney was convinced she'd been rumbled and felt ice-cold sweat drench her, but Chloe simply smiled and said, 'Thanks. That was the highlight of the night. I might book you for my mother's fiftieth.' Was it Laney's imagination or did she detect the ghost of a wink before Chloe turned away?

The whole event had left Laney drained and desperate for another stiff drink. Wings drooping, sequinned talons scuffing, she trailed back across the rowing club car park.

The driver of the Mini that screeched in through the exit was travelling far too fast to account for a giant multi-coloured bird in her path. Laney only had time to throw up her arms with a swish of six-foot, golden-tipped wings as brakes screeched and rubber squealed. Certain she was roadkill, she shut her eyes in horror.

The car shuddered to a halt just in front of her, engine ticking.

Opening her eyes again, the first thing Laney saw was the metallic advertising sign stuck to its driver's door: PSYCHIC PHOENIX, FORTUNE TELLER EXTRAORDINAIRE.

'We should both have seen this coming,' she muttered weakly.

The driver was cowering in the Mini, disbelieving eyes peering at her.

'Are you OK?' Laney asked kindly, aware that being addressed by a seven-foot mythical bird was unlikely to help anybody suffering from shock and whiplash. 'Shall I call anybody?' She felt around in her costume for the phone she knew was in there.

'I am s-so sorry!' came a muffled yelp from inside the car. 'I know I'm a phoney! I know I took your name in vain. Please spare me the fire!'

Laney tried to take off the mask and headdress to reveal her face and reassure the driver, but it had a lot of complicated ties at the back of the neck that Simon must have knotted tighter than macramé, because the thing stayed put as she thrashed about in the car park clutching her head, wings flapping. The terrified fortune teller selected Reverse and careered back at breakneck speed, executed an amazing handbrake turn and belted out of the car park entry gates.

With a shrug of wings, Laney headed back to the Mercedes and set about folding herself inside. Tail feathers poking out of the door, she fished in her plumage to extract her phone from her bra.

How did it go? Mia's latest text demanded.

So-so, she replied. Let's say I planted a seed, but the wedding bouquet's already in full bloom.

Thank you for trying. xx

Simon had sent several picture texts from home that evening, clearly laying into the winebox as he did so. The most recent one made her yelp. In it, he appeared to have set light to Red Gables' crumbling conservatory. The accompanying message read: My heart is burning for you.

It was a long time since he had thrown a big strop. The last one – staged just after they'd remarried, at a time when the press were being particularly spiteful – had been a drunken tantrum involving smashing his entire Lalique collection, and she'd seen that one coming. This one seemed out of the blue, but she'd been insufferably moody of late and feared she must have pushed him over the edge.

Driving back in a blind panic, she ignored the sat-nav's back route and stuck to the main roads. As she swung too fast around one roundabout, she spotted the familiar white, blue and yellow livery of a Thames Valley Police car appear in her wing mirrors. It flashed its lights for her to pull over.

'Late for a party?' asked the first officer, when she'd cut the engine in a lay-by and handed over her keys. 'Faster to fly.'

'Keep your wings on the steering wheel where we can see them,' said the other as he checked her ID. 'Any relation to that Montmorency bloke off the telly?'

'Wife.' She tried not to think about the 'burning' text or her flame-ridden house.

'Avoiding being recognised, I take it. Do you often drive about dressed as a golden eagle?'

'It's a phoenix, actually. It's not my usual look.'

'Could you step out of the car for a breath test, please, madam?'

She could hear the blood thundering in her ears as she more or less fell out of the car, wrestling with her wings, ready to be breathalysed. Terrified that the gin she'd consumed earlier that evening would take her over the limit, she puffed hard into the tube. The headlines swam before her eyes: LOVELY SIMON DM'S WIFE LETS HIM DOWN AGAIN, their beautiful wreck of a home burning while she racketed around drunkenly behind the wheel.

When she was given the all-clear, she wanted to weep with gratitude. Then they started a long-winded kerbside lecture about speeding, official cautions and automatic set fines. 'I'm *so* sorry I was speeding. It's just that I think my house might be on fire,' she explained, and reached back into the Merc for her phone to show them the evidence.

'Why didn't you say so earlier?' The officers forced her back through the driver's door as though they were jamming a ten-kilo Christmas turkey into a small oven. 'We'll radio for back-up.'

Chapter 14

Simon had shipped several more gins and the best part of two bottles of red wine, so the sight of a large golden bird driving through the Red Gables gate followed by a police patrol car with its blues flashing was deeply disconcerting. Then, panicking that his wife must have had an accident, he wove up the slope of the gardens that swept down to the river. In front of him, Kensington and Chelsea barked furiously, still battling for the stick they had wrestled from the pyre before it was lit.

Down by the river, a huge inferno of pallets and demolished partition walls roared beneath a haze of sparks, its golden glow reflected in the many broken panes in the decrepit conservatory nearby, a mock-Victorian contrivance linked to the main house by a long walkway which had once served as the stage school's dance studio. Photographed from beside the mammoth fire, the whole building would certainly have seemed to be alight. Witnessed in person, however, it was simply a sagging mirror to a jolly waterside pyre.

'Isn't it rather late at night to have a bonfire, sir?' asked one of the uniforms.

'I wanted to welcome my phoenix home in a blaze of glory,' he explained cheerfully, lurching sideways.

Laney finally rustled up, wings bent totally out of shape. Her first thought was for Hope.

'What are you *doing* out here when there's a small child in the house?' she demanded. 'You know how lightly she sleeps. What if she's woken in tears again?' She turned to run inside, but tripped over her sequinned talons and fell into a flowerbed.

'She's fine!' He reeled after her. 'Here, let me help you up. You stay here – that outfit will frighten her to death. I'll go and check on her.' He pitched sideways again and landed in a large peony beside his wife.

While the Demons flailed amid the perennials, one inebriated and the other trapped by her costume, the main door to the house flew open and a slender, determined silhouette appeared in a very short dressing gown and pink Crocs.

'Hope is fast asleep,' announced Malin, casting the police an angry look as she marched across the gravel and stooped to haul Laney upright. She ignored Simon, who seemed quite happy lying down, wrestling with his black dogs and laughing.

'Thank you, Malin.' Laney mustered her dignity. 'Could you possibly fetch me some scissors? I want to cut my head off.'

Simon found this hugely funny.

'Pissed as a newt,' the officers agreed as they drove away. 'Wait till I tell the wife. She thinks the sun shines out of him.'

'Strange pair.'

'Nice house. Must be loaded. The au pair's well fit. Bet he's banging her.'

Chapter 15

Late on the same night, Griff Donne touched down on British soil for the first time in almost a year. He'd not returned since the Sudan kidnapping scandal that had blighted his career, although the British media had cast him more as victim than perpetrator. A huge cry had gone out for interviews, but he had avoided them all, preferring to stay away from his home country and ridicule.

Tanned, clean-shaven and muscular, he was a far cry from the gaunt, bearded figure in the photograph that had lined every newsstand upon his release from captivity. Now he headed to the nearest car hire desk. As he took possession of a set of Volkswagen keys, he asked, 'I don't suppose you know where I could hire a hot-air balloon around here?'

In LA, Dougie was ready to party. Never one to let an opportunity go to waste, he'd spent the afternoon calling all the contacts he had in the city, dropping his future father-in-law's name heavily. 'Yeah, I just had lunch with Leo. Great guy. We want to do some work together ... I think we might get Iris on board too, for the right project, a family thing. She'll be in LA in a week's time.' He found that using the Devonshire name bypassed switchboards and opened doors faster than the FBI on a raid.

Feeling sky high after such a successful day, he headed to the Los Angeles Equestrian Center in Burbank to meet up with an old girlfriend who boarded her horse there and who was now part of a crowd of rather Sloaney expatriate Brits based in Tinseltown, many of whom were Dougie's former partying cronies. Having dumped her somewhat ignominiously for Iris, he was surprised by how eager she was to see him again, but he guessed that was the Devonshire magic.

Having dutifully admired her stringy-looking horse, he was introduced to two more glossy-maned girls in the West Coast horse fraternity, charming them with wild tales of filming alongside Con O'Mara in the Ptolemy series. But it was his engagement to that series' leading actress that was the cause of most interest.

'Is she as highly strung as everybody makes out?'

'Was she fired from *The Raven's Curse* or did she quit?'

'Are you guys going to live in LA?'

'Is she really giving up her career?'

150

Piling into a spotless white Range-Rover, they drove along the Ventura Freeway and into Forest Lawn Drive, a tarmac artery that divided concrete, pylons and wasteland to their right from the unfeasibly lush hills to their left as they cruised past huge mortuaries and green fields studded with memorial plaques.

'Where Hollywood buries its dead,' one of the girls said, crossing herself.

'Now contains more plastic than your average landfill,' drawled Dougie's ex.

They took a narrow bridge across the Los Angeles River into a Warner Brothers parking lot to pick up a make-up artist friend who was working on a sitcom there.

As she climbed in, Dougie's phone rang and he found himself talking to Abe Schultz's assistant, calling to set up a meeting.

'Yeah, of course I can meet Mr Schultz,' he said casually, smirking as jaws dropped around him.

They headed south on Barnham Boulevard to cross over the Hollywood Freeway and pick up Mulholland Drive, climbing into the hills to admire the view across West Hollywood.

Crammed into the back seat between two much more spectacular valley views, Dougie was enjoying himself, especially when they stopped off at a house on Outpost Drive belonging to a young actor he recognised from a couple of recent indie films.

Styled like a little Spanish *casa*, the house was shared by three men, and they clearly liked to party hard and fast. Last night's empty champagne bottles still littered every surface, more were chilling in the fridge and there was a bowl on a glass table in the bathroom filled with ready-rolled joints, bottles of pills, a small bag of coke and several fifty-dollar bills.

'It's a myth that nobody stays up late here,' his ex snorted a line, 'but we Brits are definitely the most fun.' She offered him the rolled banknote.

'I like this town.' Dougie inhaled the second line. He blinked in surprise.

'CK One,' his ex told him. 'The coke's cut with ketamine – gives a real buzz.'

Later, they moved on to West Hollywood to hang out in a bar off Sunset Strip, which was so dark Dougie could hardly make out the new faces that joined them, but he knew they had to be beautiful because the door policy allowed no less. He was feeling seriously spaced out. By the time the group moved on to dance at the notoriously cliquey nightclub Greystone Manor, he was struggling to see straight.

'D'you want to come back with me tonight?' his ex asked as they writhed together on the dance floor to DJ Savi. 'For old times' sake?'

Dougie mumbled something about his best behaviour.

'Afraid Daddy Devonshire will find out and retract your invitation to afternoon tea?'

Dougie, who had been surprised by how nice Leo was – dull, even – and how bad he'd felt hinting at scandalous secrets, now found himself saying, 'He's a thoroughly decent chap.' Christ, he sounded like his father. His head spun.

'What's happened to Wild Man Everett?' she laughed, curling around him. 'Are you becoming a "thoroughly decent chap" now you're marrying a "spiffing girl"? Man, they've castrated you like one of their horses.'

'Milfy keeps stallions,' he muttered hazily.

Dougie was incredibly drunk and stoned. Impending marriage into a celebrity dynasty was a very high-grade aphrodisiac as well as a VIP pass. Since his engagement to Iris, he'd made a concerted effort to be faithful, but today, for all its many highs, had dented his ego. He wasn't too keen to be known as Mr Iris Devonshire. His ex-girlfriend had no doubt as to what a bloody-minded misogynist he was capable of being, which made her refreshingly easy company.

Driving him back up into the Hollywood Hills along the winding, wooded Nichols Canyon Road, she pulled the Range-Rover towards an aloe-skirted driveway where huge stone columns topped with rearing horses guarded a hefty electric gate. 'This is where Daddy Devonshire lives.'

The moon was glinting through a huge lemon tree that stretched out over the high perimeter fence, its branches heavy with fruit. Beyond it, he could just make out the silhouette of a mock-Italian bell-tower. It was nothing to Wootton's baronial splendour, but it still had a lot of Hollywood swagger. He reached for the door handle. 'Let's have a quick snoop.'

She stretched across him and covered his hand.

'Let's not.' She clicked the lock. 'This neighbourhood has regular dog patrols and an armed response team.' She nodded at a CCTV camera, which had turned its long metal head to watch them.

'In that case, I'll just wait for my invitation to tea.' Dougie waved at the camera from behind the Range-Rover's black-tinted windows, knowing he couldn't be identified.

'How very respectable you've become,' she teased, unbuckling his seatbelt before reaching down to unbuckle his jeans belt too. 'Iris must keep you on a very tight rein.'

He did nothing to stop her, but his eyes flashed as he said, 'Only when I have the bit between my teeth.'

'You know what we say in the horse world about giving a horse its head' – she started to unbutton his flies – 'and I'm the one who likes a bit between her teeth, remember.'

She lowered her head to his crotch and he let out a low groan. 'Ah yes, I do remember this.' The frisson of being blown in front of his future father-in-law's swanky LA villa excited Dougie far more than he cared to admit. Ex-lovers didn't count as infidelity, he told himself firmly, and besides, he'd not yet exchanged his marriage vows. This had always been one of his ex's finest skills. Even the extensive cosmetic dentistry, cheek liposuction and chin implant hadn't altered her skilful suck. 'Just don't leave any bite marks.'

'Are you kidding?' She looked up from beneath a curtain of hair. 'These veneers cost thirty thousand dollars.' Her smile was as white as it was wicked and wanton.

Dougie smiled back roguishly. Then his chuckle turned into a strangled yelp of pain.

'The fingernails, however, are ninety-dollar acrylic.' She dug them in as hard as she could, making him howl. 'Try explaining these to your bride on your wedding night. You always were a complete shit, Everett.' Leaning across him, she opened the door. 'Get out!'

Seconds later, abandoned in front of his father-in-law's gateway in the full glare of his CCTV with a dick that felt as though it had just been caught in a waste-disposal unit, Dougie ducked into the shadow of the lemon tree, not spotting the outsized, sharp-spined aloe that caught him viciously on the ankles. The emu camera watched him curiously as he reeled back into the light and hurried away.

It was a long, dark and bow-legged walk back down to West Hollywood, and when he finally saw the tall palm trees lining Hollywood Boulevard, he wanted to hug them. Waiting to hail a cab, he pulled out his phone and read a loving message from Iris saying there'd been a batty psychic at the hen party predicting that a man would come into her life with a scar and a limp. Probably all rubbish.

Now limping quite badly and convinced his scars would never fade without an urgent application of arnica, Dougie texted back, I am the only man in your life, Riz my darling, and don't forget it, flagged down a taxi heading west towards his hotel and asked the driver, 'Is there a twenty-four-hour drugstore around here by any chance?'

Chapter 16

Laney had been a member of the 5 a.m. Club for over a year and longed to surrender her subscription. Each morning, while the rest of the house slept, her eyes would spring open, all her greatest fears combining in a waking nightmare. Right now, she was convinced that bankruptcy was weeks away, Simon was having an affair, the aches and pains she'd ignored warned of some terminal illness and Hope would be left destitute and orphaned.

She knew from experience that her terror would seem groundless by breakfast time, but while it raged out of control, it consumed her. Over the past twelve months she'd tried to break the cycle by getting up to read or work, listening to the radio, taking a bath and popping pills, but nothing seemed to break the spell. She longed for sleep to obliterate the despair. Instead, with the end of her world nigh, she lay awake, heart thundering and tears sliding into her hair.

Ashamed of its hold over her and frightened that she was going mad, she hid the truth from everybody, including Simon. Once his eyes closed he was out for the count and could nap through hurricanes and minor earthquakes, particularly after a night when he'd consumed enough claret to inebriate a table of sommeliers.

This morning, however, he was up before six, fumbling around in the dark as he tried to get dressed quietly, unaware that his wife was gripped by Mrs Demon's demons. Laney buried her wet face in the bedding and breathed as shallowly and evenly as she could. She was desperate not to alert him to her dawn insanity: he had enough on his plate this week, literally as well as figuratively. The car collecting him at six fifteen this morning would drive him to Manchester, where he'd spend the next three days joining an 'all-star' judging panel to film twenty back-to-back episodes of the Food TV network's cooking competition *Beat the Chef*. It was conveyor-belt television, peopled by self-publicists clamouring for their fifteen minutes of fame and fading stars desperate not to lose theirs.

Thinking about this, a fresh wave of anxiety flooded her. As Simon's work got sillier and increasingly poorly paid, Laney's fear for their future grew in equal measure.

At last he dropped a kiss on her shoulder and slipped away. A few minutes later, she could hear him wishing effusive farewells to the dogs and she cried afresh, mortally ashamed that she hadn't been able to see him off with a good-luck hug. Determined to get a grip, she forced herself to think about everything she had to do that day, commission-chasing and bill-paying, household chores, phone calls and emails. When a small silhouette appeared in the doorway, the tears and terror melted away.

Hope trailed into her mother's room with Gogs dangling in one hand, eager to snuggle up. With her daughter's small, solid bulk in her arms and her curls beneath her chin, Laney felt soothed enough to snooze for twenty minutes, knowing her worries had now packed up their tents until the next dawn raid. When she took a shower, Hope came too, one of her favourite pastimes being to encourage her mother to draw smiley faces, hearts and animals in the steam on the cubicle's glass wall.

Hope was the only individual in the world with whom Laney was unselfconsciously naked these days. She wasn't sure how much longer that would last. Recently Hope had given half her dolls Crayola pubes, to 'make them more like Mummy'.

By the time Laney had dressed and handed Hope over to Malin to give her breakfast and get her ready for school, the builders were on site, listening to Radio 1 loudly from the scaffolding, revving up power tools and ogling Malin through the kitchen windows, hoping for tea.

Laney drove to Wootton and set up in the boathouse, worried that Simon hadn't yet picture-texted her that morning. She wrapped her laptop cable around her wrist and chair arm and sent him a photo of it captioned Bondage voyage! xx but it felt forced, and she remembered too late that she'd sent the exact same message when he'd flown to Ireland three weeks earlier, that time accompanied by a picture of her jeans belt and ankles.

As always, she missed him terribly as soon as he was gone, however much he'd irritated her during his all-too-brief return. His legion of female fans would no doubt think her monstrously ungrateful for neglecting him so badly, evidence of which was already making her laptop dongle glow as it relayed message after message from his website.

Dear Simon, I have been happily married for thirty years and can't believe I'm writing this, but I have to tell you that I think you are the nicest and handsomest man on the television and I wish my hubby was more like you. Your wife is such a lucky woman. I have had lots of dreams about you lately, and I really wish I could take her place for a day, especially in the bedroom . . .

Not at 5 a.m. you don't, thought Laney glumly. Her eyes widened as she took in the graphic description of what Sheryl from Bedfordshire would do to Simon at a hotel of his choice (preferably within a twenty-mile radius of Leighton Buzzard). She offered a lot more sexual originality and effort than Simon's wife had managed in recent months. What did Simon think when he read these open offers and compared them to her all-too-often closed legs? she wondered fretfully as she composed a terse reply that thanked Sheryl for taking the time to write.

The entire team here in the de Montmorency website office thoroughly enjoyed reading your ideas, she added.

Bad temper now raging, she reread the email from landowner Richard HH complaining that the public didn't get to see enough of Simon's wife.

The Demons were often approached to appear together on quiz shows and travel specials, while their mantelpiece heaved with invitations to balls, galas and fund raisers, but Laney had control of both the work and social diaries, and high-profile joint gigs seldom made it into the schedule. She used her work and Hope as excuses, pointing out that she ran the show from behind the scenes like all good stage managers; but the truth was more complicated than that. She'd once adored accompanying him out professionally, bursting with pride, people-watching, promenading and posing, happy to share in the joy of his wit and talent. But over the years she'd lost some of her laugh-it-off tolerance to being pushed aside in the stampede to get to her husband; when asked who she was by an impatient journalist at a recent awards ceremony, she'd found herself joking, 'I'm Simon's first, fourth and hopefully last wife.' And the press had got far more body-obsessed since the Demons' first marriage, particularly online. Each time Laney ventured out at Simon's side in the glare of the media, she was torn apart afterwards for her dress sense and weight, along with the predictable mention of Oscar and his famously cruel Twitter dismissal. She was terrified that some of it would filter through to Hope. Laney didn't mind being an embarrassing parent for her outspoken opinions and raucous sense of humour, but no five-year-old deserved to be taunted in the playground because her mother's cellulite had been papped on the annual family holiday and plastered all over *Wow!* magazine.

To cheer herself up, she clicked on her laptop's camera, stuck out her tongue and captured a close-up to send to Richard HH – We hope you enjoy this glimpse of a little more of Mrs de M . . . She realised it looked faintly obscene and was about to delete the attachment, but a scrabbling of claws across the wooden floor distracted her. She carelessly clicked Send as she spun around in her chair.

Two Maltese terriers raced across the boathouse's painted floorboards, closely followed by their mistress, Iris. Dressed in a shapeless grey T-shirt and old riding breeches and with her hair scraped back in a pony tail, Iris was far from the peacock of the evening before, but Laney felt she was all the more beautiful for it, and so vividly like Mia it was uncanny.

'Sorry to disturb.' She had dark smudges beneath her eyes. 'Can I have a word?'

'Sure. I've got a dictionary right here.' The Demon joke dated back at least a decade. Laney lifted the book from the desk beside her and flipped through it to a random page. '"Fanfaronade" – boasting or flaunting behaviour, bluster. Via

French from Spanish *fanfaronada*, from *fanfarrin*, boaster, and Arabic *fanfar*, garrulous.'

'Ha ha.' Iris rolled her green eyes.

Unlike her mother, Iris never dropped in unannounced and Laney guessed the identity of the Psychic Phoenix had been rumbled. She braced herself for the onslaught.

But the girl's pale face was pinched with worry. 'I wish you'd been there last night.'

'Er – ah – yes. Simon was home. Sorry. Couldn't get out. Should have sent apologies.'

'You'd have loved the entertainment.' She wandered over to the french windows and peered up at the cumulus shuffling past like sluggish sheep. 'Just up your street.'

'What a shame.'

'Laney, I need to ask you something and you have to be honest with me.'

'Yes?'

There was a long pause and Iris watched the sky. 'Do you think that cloud looks like a horse or a lion?'

'Like a cloud to me.' Laney squinted at it. 'Was that what you wanted to ask?'

Iris turned back, pretty face drawn. 'It's about my birth father.'

'Oh yes?' Laney stiffened.

'I know it's the elephant in the room, Laney, but I can't keep ignoring it like Mum can.'

'That elephant's the only four-legged creature your mother takes no notice of,' she agreed lightly.

'Somebody told me last night that I must talk to a wise woman before I marry, and you're the wisest one I know, so I thought I'd start here.'

Laney had walked into a trap of her own making, forgetting what it was to be nineteen and wildly superstitious. At that age, she and Mia had taken a lot more notice of their horoscopes than parental advice and severe weather warnings. 'Who told you to do that?'

'There was this freaky psychic at the hen party. A fat transsexual dressed as Big Bird. Everybody thought he was a joke.'

Laney flashed a tight smile. 'Sounds it.'

'He kept banging on about the sky. Then, on the way to the nightclub, I swear I saw a shooting star.'

'Are you sure it wasn't an aeroplane heading into Heathrow?'

'Who do you think my real father is?'

'Iris, I have no idea.' Laney felt her ears burn as they veered towards dangerous territory. She should have seen this coming. What a fool to plant seeds on such fertile ground and not expect to have to fight one's way through the undergrowth afterwards. 'You have to talk to your mother about this.'

'She just gets incredibly upset and says Leo should be enough.' The fact that Leo was not Iris's natural father had never been kept a secret, although the Devonshires had remained deliberately vague on the subject and it was among the topics specifically excluded from interviews. 'You know how it is,' Iris huffed impatiently. 'We can't talk about it while Lito's alive because I'm her only grandchild and knowing we aren't linked by blood will devastate her, la la la.'

That Jacinta had always doggedly believed Iris to be her blood relation was the main sticking point. Some – including Laney – believed the old lady knew full well that Leo wasn't the girl's father, but Jacinta was immensely proud of Iris's beauty, her horsemanship and her acting career, claiming they were all down to the Ormero genes.

Iris, who secretly longed for Ormero genes, had been happy to perpetuate the myth and maintain that Leo was the only father she needed, but lately curiosity about her birthright had grown alongside her sense of independence and Leo's increasing detachment. In the early days, Leo had been a devotedly hands-on father, the family moving between ever larger London flats where he'd always decorated his daughter's bedroom first, filling it with murals of ponies, even making her clothes himself; she had been his little doll just as Mia was his mannequin and muse. He'd been in constant work even then, taking his family with him on location whenever possible or getting home at every opportunity.

When the big American break came, he remained a dedicated home-body, half his life spent flying back and forth. LA had frightened him in those days; he craved high walls and history. In Iris's early teens, when Leo's film career had been at its peak, he'd seemed the coolest dad in the world, a hero to schoolfriends and their mothers alike, even if all the schmaltzy kissing and sex scenes had been monumentally embarrassing. Hacienda Sueño had been bought at around that time and a lavish restoration embarked upon, shortly followed by Wootton, a monument to his fee passing seven figures per movie. He remained her funny, eccentric, hard-working and modest father, who took her to art exhibitions and horse shows and loved painting and knitting. But since he'd taken the part in *Chancellor* and been based almost permanently in LA, they'd seen very little of each other.

Fed up with living in hotels and rented accommodation, Leo had bought the Nichols Canyon house, where he now lived most of the year with his assistant Ivan and an Old English bull terrier called Puff Adder who had his own personal swimming pool and shower. There was no bedroom decorated especially for Iris in the LA house; she always felt unwelcome there, like a child in her father's office knowing that he was tapping his pen on his desk and waiting to make a call.

It was inevitable that she would want to fill the gap widening between them. Shallow, charming Dougie was a lump of landfill, as far as Laney could tell, but there was also the need to know more about her genetic father.

Mia had always told Iris that her pregnancy was unplanned when she was not in a stable relationship. She'd sometimes hinted at a young actor who'd gone out of her life before she discovered she was pregnant and whom she could never trace, but she kept most of the details about their love affair enshrined in her heart, unable to share more than a few nebulous facts about him without getting upset. This abstract concept of a father who in no way rivalled Leo had satisfied Iris until recently. Now she was desperate to know more, and had even started to suspect that the story about the actor was a smokescreen for someone far closer at hand.

Laney chewed her lip. 'I can't interfere, Iris. I know no more than you do.'

It was almost true. Mia had shared so little of Dom with her friends that she had only the vaguest recollection of him and, as far as Laney was aware, there was no certainty that he was Iris's father. It wasn't a subject on which she cared to dwell.

Iris's eyes flashed and Laney thought she was going to broach the conspiracy of silence surrounding her conception. Instead, she threw a curve ball: 'Will you come shopping with me for a wedding dress?'

Laney's jaw dropped. 'It's not really my field of expertise . . . '

'You've been married three times!'

She pulled a face. 'Huge meringue followed by creased linen suit followed by green velvet that made me look like a gourd.'

'An upward curve! And I *loved* the green velvet. Please, Godless?' It was the nickname Iris had given her godmother as a child, not used for many years. At her most charming, she was hard to refuse. When Laney explained that she had to reply to Simon's webmail, she insisted she would help: 'We'll get them out of the way in no time, and then you can help me find something really feminine and dramatic.'

Laney knew Mia would be appalled, and it seemed the ultimate betrayal of their friendship, but refusing to help Iris would simply add to the family conflict, and this way she could at least play peace keeper between mother and daughter. She tried not to think of her to-do list, which would now not get done. 'We have to be back by three – I'm collecting Hope from school today.'

'Oh, Godless, you're saving my life!' Iris hugged her tightly before drawing a chair up alongside her at the computer to hurry her email task along. 'I never get to read my website stuff' – she scrolled through the dozens of messages – 'it's all handled by the PR people and I just get sent a representative few. Holy moly, some of these are a bit fruity, aren't they?'

'The South American ones are the worst,' Laney confessed. 'Thankfully most of them are written in Spanish and the automatic online translators can't cope with all the obscenities.'

'I can help you there,' offered Iris, who spoke near-fluent Spanish. 'The stud grooms at Sueño use the filthiest language. Let me have a look.'

To Laney's chagrin, Iris typed one standard reply in Spanish suggesting that they take a cold shower, preferably using bathroom products from the SdeM At Home signature range available from the website, and sent it to them all.

'Simon prefers them personalised!'

'He should do this himself, then. Hang on, this one's title bar says it's to you. Who's Richard HH?'

'Oh, you can delete that.' She blushed.

'It's unread – just come through: "Could the delightful Mrs de M let that glorious pink thing loose and explain why her husband gets all the best lines? RHH PS Do you have your own email address?"'

'It's a work thing,' she blustered, hoping the photo hadn't given him entirely the wrong impression.

'Great! Mum's always saying you're poised for the big time. Is he a producer? We all know *Dalrymple* was just the beginning.'

'That was Oscar's doing.'

Laney had written the screenplay as an unashamed star vehicle for her second husband, which she had presented to him at around the time she'd discovered she was pregnant. Seeing potential, Oscar had set her the task of drafting a sequel and had gone off to sell the idea, far more excited by embryo script than embryo baby. As executive producer, star and script editor, he was in total control of the *Dalrymple* brand, so by the time it had exceeded all expectations and become a big box-office hit, Laney's name was nowhere near it. The movie netted Oscar many millions of dollars and his character was hailed as the new Mr Bean, resurrecting an acting career that had been dead in the water. By then, his second marriage was over.

To her enduring satisfaction, the only draft of *Dalrymple Two* was still on her hard drive almost eighteen months after their decree absolute, and Oscar had failed to win custody of it despite a ferocious fight, appeals and ongoing litigation. Finding his team of writers incapable of re-creating the brand, he was now increasingly desperate to get hold of it.

Iris was still lingering over Richard HH's email.

'Just leave it.' Laney moved deliberately away. 'I'll look at it later. It'll probably come to nothing – what are you typing?'

'What's your personal email?'

'I can't remember offhand.'

'It'll be on here somewhere.'

A child of the e-generation, Iris located it within three clicks. 'Cool. Sent.' She flipped the laptop shut and nodded towards the door. 'Shop.' She whistled at her little white dogs, which were sprawling on the sunny balcony.

Laney looked at the Malteses dubiously as they panted up. 'They won't be allowed in any shops with us, and it's far too hot to leave them in the car.'

Iris scooped them up and kissed their ruffled necks. 'Sometimes there are benefits to being Iris Devonshire, you know.' She handed one to Laney. 'We'll fanfaronade our way through . . .'

Iris had always been awestruck by Laney and had modelled some of her own mannerisms on her, especially in high-pressure broadcast interviews when laughter was the most powerful currency. Larger than life, hugely funny and often fearless, her godmother was an inspiration. There was something truly dramatic, wild and lovable about Laney. She and Simon never stinted, never compromised and never threw a dull party. Even when divorced, they had always been a double-act in Iris's mind, just as Laney had always been Mia's counterpoint when she tied herself up in knots. Iris regretted the long periods that Laney had been out of Mia's life, often because work and geography kept them apart. The Demons' recent rapprochement and move to Burley had thrilled her, especially having Laney using the boathouse as an office. If anybody could persuade her mother to accept Dougie as a son-in-law, it was Laney.

Nevertheless, Iris braced herself for a lecture as soon as they set out for Central London in the Demons' Merc, and listened patiently while Laney made sweeping statements about the bond between a mother and daughter being so great that any disagreement could be overcome, however passionately opposed they were. But when Laney suggested her mother needed more time to get used to the idea, Iris was indignant: 'We've been together months!'

'That's a far bigger proportion of your life than it is hers,' Laney pointed out tactfully.

'Mum and Dad were even younger than me when they married,' Iris fumed, 'and nobody told them not to do it. They *adored* one another and my grandparents were *overjoyed*,' she repeated family lore.

'I told her not to do it.' Laney negotiated past a lane-hogging white van. She smiled. 'And she was as mad at me as you are – madder, in fact. If Hope decides to marry before she's twenty, remind me not to argue. Mind you, I'll probably be too senile by then to care.' She glanced at the car clock, still totting up how long they had to shop before home time. 'Can you text the congestion-charge lot? The number's stored. We'll go to Selfridges. I know where to park there, at least.'

'Isn't that a bit staid?' Iris had been hoping for a secret little back-street dressmaker with amazing vintage re-creations stashed in cellophane pods. Laney always wore extraordinary clothes.

Laney, who had been outsize for several years and bought most of her clothes from market stalls, had no idea where to shop for someone as perfect and petite as Iris, but she imagined Selfridges to be a safe bet. She parked in a multi-storey, which she deemed cool enough for the dogs with windows left open, and they made the short, hot walk along a sun-bleached pavement before being sucked into air-conditioned splendour. Iris was immediately recognised. Within minutes, a small crowd bearing cameraphones was following her around the store. The management intervened and offered privacy.

'You should have called ahead, Miss Devonshire,' soothed a charming PR, as they were settled in a VIP dressing room with champagne.

'What is it you're looking for today?' A personal shopper had appeared.

Laney was gazing around her in awe. 'My goddaughter wants a w—'

'I want something incredibly pretty for a party,' Iris insisted. 'White. Not too fussy. And I have to be able to ride my horse in it. And I want a big floppy hat, a red wig and dark glasses. Could somebody fetch my dogs, please?' She prodded Laney for her car keys. When they were left alone together, she explained, 'Never give too much away, however much they think they know.'

Two hours and a complimentary light lunch later, they were ushered through a discreet exit to an underground car park where Laney's Merc was waiting, barely recognisable after a full wash and wax, having been valet-parked away from the vulgarity of its NCP space at the same time as the dogs had been collected.

'Welcome to the A list.' Iris laughed as she tossed a clutch of stiff yellow bags on to the back seat. She extracted the wig, hat and dark glasses to plonk on her head. 'Now show me where you *really* shop, Godless.'

Glancing worriedly at the car clock, Laney guessed they had just enough time for Portobello Market. 'OK, but the changing room is a public loo, and you must always haggle on price.'

Disguise in place, Iris wove in and out of the crowds, letting out little shrieks of delight as she took in row upon row of vintage clothes.

'Surely you've been here before?' Laney laughed.

'Never. I went to Camden with Chloe once, but it was all Goth stuff and tattoo parlours and we got a bit scared so we headed to Madame Tussaud's.'

Laney was struck afresh by how young she was. 'You haven't *lived*, kid! Why marry now?'

But Iris was pointing over Laney's shoulder at a rack of clothes deep within a shadowy stall. '*That* is my wedding dress.'

Handed two over-excited dogs just as a picture text arrived from Simon at long last, Laney was too distracted to take much notice of the dress. She thought for a frightening moment that Simon had been attacked and had a huge swelling on his face, then realised his tongue was bulging in one cheek and his expression was at its most debonair. There was no written message with it, but she could guess that he was relying on ironic one-liners and Gaviscon to get him through the day. Noticing the time on her phone, she let out a shriek and hurried towards the stall where Iris was mid-negotiation over something alarmingly red and voluminous.

'Pay the lady!' she ordered.

'But you told me to hag—'

But Laney was already running, with a Maltese under each arm. Iris threw a pile of notes at the trader, grabbed the dress and gave chase.

Laney broke every speed limit as she racketed back along the A41 in time to collect Hope from school, convinced she was a bad mother *and* godmother, failing to bestow any useful advice on Iris while actively encouraging the purchase of a wedding dress that looked as if it had done several seasons in Restoration rep.

Lolling on the passenger seat, unaware of the breakneck speed they were notching up, Iris had her Portobello dress on her lap. 'This is going to look so cool when I ride up on Scully. Dougie will *love* it.'

'What's he wearing? Full cavalier garb?'

'Morning suit, I should think. He's amazingly traditional. I love that about him.'

'Like mother like daughter.' Laney tried to play peacemaker again. 'You and Mia really are so similar.'

It was the wrong thing to say. Iris sulkily chewed at her nails, then picked up Laney's phone, which kept buzzing with text and missed-call alerts.

'If they're picture texts don't open them,' she warned, worried that Simon would be sending suggestive vegetable carvings during a bored break in filming on *Beat the Chef*, as he had last month.

'It's the school, asking where you are. They've been ringing all afternoon. Hope keeps being sick.'

'Christ!'

Thrown back against the seat as the car accelerated, Iris dropped the phone. She delved around for it in the footwell, but her fingers closed around something entirely different.

Laney was too busy weaving in and out of the traffic to notice that her passenger had fallen silent. Pulling aside to let past a police car with its siren blaring, she only realised it was on her tail when its driver leaned out and told her to bloody well get off the road.

It was the same officers who had pulled her over the night before. Laney drew up with a sinking heart.

'House on fire again, is it, madam?'

'I have a sick child. My goddaughter will vouch for me.' Laney glanced at Iris, who appeared to be holding up some sort of fascinator accusingly.

Then she recognised the feathers. Looking down, she saw they were littering the floor of the car.

'I can explain . . .' she started hopelessly.

'You'd better,' said the police officer and Iris in unison.

168

The second officer was gaping at Iris. 'It's Purple! Ptolemy Finch's Purple! It's you, isn't it?'

'My fanfaronade club's here,' she said through gritted teeth, glaring at Laney.

Chapter 17

Laney was cradling Hope in her arms, both dozing on the sofa in front of CBeebies, when her phone rang.

Certain it was Simon, she groped to extract it from beneath a cushion before it went to voicemail, and found herself greeted by a bright Estuary voice. 'Laney! Maz Jones, *Cheers!* magazine. How *are* you?'

'Terrific,' she said groggily. 'Would you mind terribly if I call you back, only—'

'I'll keep it *really* quick. Simon was going to get back to me by six with the details I need to brief Friday's stylist, but his phone's still switched off.'

'The *Beat the Chef* recording must be running over,' she said vaguely, racking her brains to think what Maz could be talking about. Iris's wedding was on Friday evening; Simon's children would be staying with them at Red Gables; he had nothing else in his diary.

'We're *so* grateful to you both for agreeing to do this shoot at the last minute,' Maz was saying chirpily. 'I know Simon's dying to show off the new house. All I need is his chest, waist, inside leg, collar and shoe size, and your dress and shoe size.'

Panic mounting, Laney glanced across to the walls lined with packing cases, the windows darkened by scaffolding, then down at her sweaty little invalid, clutching Gogs tightly and whimpering in her sleep.

Reeling off her husband's vital statistics and optimistically quoting her dress size, she cut the call, then took Hope upstairs, knowing she had to calm down before ringing Simon to demand what the hell he'd agreed to. The little girl barely stirred when she settled her in her painted bed, which Simon had shaped like a fairy-tale carriage complete with lizard footmen, mice horses and a jolly rat coachman.

His phone was still switched off. She sent an irritable text asking him to call. It was typical of him to agree to a photo shoot like this on the same day as an important family occasion; her only consolation was that she'd be able to keep the professional make-up on for the ceremony.

Pausing by the antique mirror on the landing, she groaned in horror. Her face was puffy and hollow-eyed, while grey sprouted from her blond crown like frosted reeds from a golden lake. She *had* to do something about her hair.

Going in search of the box of Autumn Glow, she took a call from Mia.

'Iris would rather you didn't come to the wedding,' her friend said in a tight pip of a voice, trying hard not to cry. 'She knows it was me who put you up to the fortune teller thing, but she's adamant that she doesn't want you to be there now. We've just had a huge row about it.'

With a heavy heart, Laney could hardly blame Iris. 'It's fine. I'll stay away.'

'Simon can still bring the kids, of course,' Mia hurried on. 'How's Hope?'

'The doctor thinks it's just a nasty virus. Malin's got it too – she's taken to her bed with a stash of Dioralyte and a week's supply of glossy magazines.'

'So you're holding the fort alone? Do you need me to come over and help?'

'You have a wedding to organise,' Laney reminded her, smiling at such typically impractical Mia kindness.

'I can't bear it that you won't be there.' Mia let out a nervous sob. 'Iris is convinced I'll leap up when the registrar asks for any just impediment and shout in my best Lancashire accent that I'll not let me daughter marry a cloth-head like that.'

'You wouldn't!'

'It's bloody tempting. Dougie's shameless. This morning he texted me from LA asking who I'd recommend for a private sexual check-up.'

'That's his idea of a joke?'

'I gather the message was meant for his friend Mills, but he has my number in his phone under "Milfy" and sent it to me by mistake.'

'I suppose we should be grateful he's taking his responsibilities seriously,' Laney pointed out.

Despite herself, Mia giggled. 'Mills owns a private members' club – my future son-in-law's so posh and thick he must think that's where he goes to have his member checked.'

Laney swallowed. She'd remembered where she'd heard the name before. Old Etonian Miles 'Mills' Milligan ran the notorious Oh So Club, an über-exclusive private media hangout in deepest Soho where celebrities, business moguls and oligarchs got their kicks. Nicknamed the Citizens' Vice Bureau by those in the know, it was a high-class knocking shop and drug den; Oscar had been a member for years.

'Is Mills a good friend of Dougie?' she asked casually.

'He's his best man – a fitting epithet, given nobody could be worse than this bloody groom.' Mia sounded gloomier than ever again. 'I'm starting to think I'm the only one who sees through Dougie. He's even charmed Leo, although the poor love's so stressed out by work it's hardly surprising his judgement's impaired. Rumour has it half the cast are facing the axe when the final series scripts come through next week.'

'They wouldn't fire the lead actor, surely?'

'Nobody's safe,' Mia said darkly. 'Abe's instructed Leo to be on his best behaviour, and that means no time off, but Iris has convinced herself he'll make it over for the ceremony now that he's given his blessing. Jacinta's airing back-to-back episodes of *Chancellor* at top volume in her annexe for the benefit of some of the Ormero oldies who've come over from Spain for the wedding. Iris and I keep hearing his voice and rushing through the house together, thinking he's back, only to find it's a DVD.' She laughed tearfully. 'It seems only yesterday that she thought Leo really was inside the television.'

Having tracked down the hair dye in a kitchen drawer, Laney donned the rubber gloves provided and doused her head in the pungent mix before studying the ravishing picture of the strawberry blonde on the box, perking up at the thought of her limp, greying mop transforming into such leonine splendour. The instructions told her to leave it on light blond hair for fifty minutes. Her stomach was rumbling. It was hours since her light lunch in Selfridges, and she should be fasting until Friday so that she could squeeze into the size-fourteen samples she'd told Maz would fit, but Simon's fans had sent several boxes of home-made biscuits this week that she was dying to try. Since he'd judged television's *Greatest British Biscuit Baker* competition last year, he'd been deluged with the lightest, crumbliest choc chips, butter crunches and shortbreads presented in delightful gingham-lined baskets. This year, he was judging *The Greatest British Pie Maker* and she anticipated an influx of pastry-encased pork and aspic.

The iced cinnamon thins from Leonie in Glossop were particularly delicious, but they barely touched the sides compared to Thelma from Sidcup's millionaire's shortbread. She'd eaten so much that she was just starting to feel sick when Simon called, still at the studio and sounding tired as he explained that *Cheers!* had demanded an answer straight away: 'Ulrika had to pull out at the last minute and they needed a replacement. I tried calling you, but you weren't answering your phone. They're paying eight grand.'

She had to agree that eight thousand pounds would pay for a lot of paint. She only hoped they could do the photo shoot in the garden, which looked quite presentable compared to the house, the roses rambling and blooming riotously.

'We'll be finished long before the wedding kicks off at Wootton,' Simon reassured her. 'I've told Maz we won't talk about that, although naturally they'll quadruple the fee if we do. Oh, and she wanted to know our sizes so I've just left a message on her voice-mail.'

'What did you say for me?' Laney had just cracked into a box of chocolate macaroons.

'Eighteen.' He seemed terribly proud to know it.

The macaroon stuck in her throat and her eyes bulged. 'You said *what*?'

'Eighteen.' He sounded less certain. 'That's what it says on most of your clothes labels, doesn't it?'

'No!'

'Laney, are you OK?'

'The only eighteen things I have – and there are *very* few – are from Hobbs, whose sizing comes up *very* small,' she insisted. 'I'm a fourteen to sixteen normally. You must phone her back and tell her.'

'Darling, I love, adore and lust after you whatever size you are,' insisted Simon, who knew full well that her size-fourteen clothes almost never left the wardrobe unless she was doing a charity-shop run. 'You are perfection. You're going to look ravishing on Friday and I'll be forced to ravish you in the Wootton shrubbery after the wedding as a result.'

'I'm not going!'

'Oh, darling, don't sulk. You know I love your round edges. I can never get enough of you, so anything extra is joyful. Your body is the perfect Rubenesque landscape of rippling curves.'

'I do *not* ripple!' She grew even angrier. 'And I'm not sulking. The reason I'm not going is because I've been barred.'

When she told him about Iris rumbling her feathery subterfuge, he laughed uproariously. 'Laney darling, you have cheered me up. At least you didn't get us all banned. The kids are so looking forward to it. Kitty's been working on her outfit for weeks. So have I, come to that. I'll have to picture-text you updates throughout.'

'Mobile phones and cameras are also banned,' she said, galled by his lack of solidarity – she'd expected him to refuse to go too on principle.

'I'll take you away for a lovely romantic weekend to make up for it,' he soothed. 'We can get mud-wrapped and massaged in a boutique hotel and make babies together in thousand-thread-count sheets.'

Fingering the last corner of shortbread, Laney felt more deserving of a boot camp with a thousand-calories-a-day food count. 'We really can't afford romantic weekends any more.'

'I know. Even buying flowers for my darling wife is a luxury I'm denied these days.' He sighed. Laney had recently stopped their regular florist delivery and taken to cutting blooms from the garden instead, which Simon thought a poor substitute.

'A romantic break doesn't have to cost us anything,' he said now, then reminded her, with a growl, 'There's always Italy.' He was about to present a television travel diary from Apulia, after which he was flying to Umbria to shoot an advert for a pasta sauce range. He'd been trying hard to persuade Laney to come with him.

'You know that's Oscar's access week.' It was the first formal visit between father and daughter in over a year. 'He's promised he'll see Hope in the UK.'

'He's only saying that because he wants to finger you personally for the *Dalrymple* script,' Simon sneered, the *double entendre* not entirely accidental.

'Hope deserves to know her father.'

'Of course Oscar can't be allowed to abandon her.'

'I need to be here for her that week.' She heard a little wail from the top of the stairs. 'She's just woken up. I must go.'

Hope had thrown up again, all over the bed and Gogs, her small body raging with tears, fever and shakes. By the time Laney had changed the bedding, dosed her with Calpol and stayed with her until she'd fallen asleep again, the fifty-minute hair-dye time had drastically overrun. Racing downstairs to recover her rubber gloves and the aftercare conditioning treatment, she saw to her horror that she'd misread the instructions: she should have left it in for just fifteen minutes.

Autumn Glow had worked its way into every blond and grey follicle on her head like red wine through a pale carpet. However many times she rinsed it, her hair stayed stubbornly flamingo pink. Mia had been right. It was hideous. Pulling the towel from her head after washing it for the fifth time, she howled.

'Think positive, Laney,' she told her prawn-haired reflection firmly. 'Call Maz back. Insist the stylist brings a selection of wigs and hats with the size-*fourteen* clothes selection. And tell her Simon's inside leg is twenty-six.'

Another little wail came from Hope's bedroom. Laney rushed across the landing, forgetting in her haste that her hair was now as luridly pink as the Calpol she was about to administer. Two dark eyes glowed fearfully from the princess carriage.

'Mummy's got candyfloss hair especially to make you feel better!' she said brightly.

'We mustn't eat it, Mummy, because then you'll be bald like Grandpa,' she insisted before drifting off to sleep.

Much later, now wearing a headscarf that made her look like Princess Anne at a hunt meet, Laney delivered chicken soup to Malin before raiding the kitchen cupboards for more comfort food, unearthing another offering from a Simon fan – chocolate-coated Turkish delight – which she munched while firing up her laptop, intent on writing an apologetic email to Iris.

Her personal email inbox was not a place she'd chosen to spend a great deal of time of late and was still full of unanswered messages from Oscar's lawyers demanding to see the *Dalrymple Two* draft and making dark threats about what would happen if she didn't relinquish it. The most recent messages were mostly junk, but the name on the one at the top of the list made her jump: Richard HH.

She opened it with trepidation and was curiously disappointed to find nothing personal there, just one line that read Follow this link . . . Every time Laney's curser hovered over the underlined blue word, a hand appeared as though waiting to push open a secret door. She knew it could be spam or, much worse, a virus – she'd once opened an email purporting to be from a garden centre that had bombarded friends' and colleagues' inboxes with hard-core porn for months. But she couldn't bring herself to ignore Richard HH's link.

She poured herself a large glass of wine, braced herself for a total screen meltdown, and clicked on the blue word.

She found herself on a website with just one page. On it was a ravishing vase of deepest red tea roses in full bloom, so exquisite she felt she should be able to pluck one from the screen and breathe in its scent. It took her a moment to realise that the picture was animated, and she watched in fascination as one petal loosened from its red neighbours to float downwards.

She stared at it for a long time, uncertain what to make of it, occasionally moving the cursor around in the hope of finding another little hand to push a door, but there was nothing. As she did so, another petal floated down.

Richard HH was clearly a romantic IT geek. Hadn't Simon said the chap he'd met loved listening to her on *Quick Wits*? After tonight's hair disaster and cruel husbandly size-eighteen accusations, she was happy to hide behind her radio persona, delighted that her voice excited Borders landowners.

She had to admit she felt gratifyingly bucked up. She clicked back to his message again and quoted Blake in reply: O Rose thou art sick. To her surprise, she found her heart palpitating as she pressed Send and switched off the computer, email to Iris forgotten.

Five minutes later she was guiltily enabling her smartphone's email alert.

As she trailed to bed, the light on her phone flashed with a message. Only my close friends call me Rose, and I can assure you I'm in rude health. Are you a fan of Blakes?

Always had a soft spot for Blake Carrington and *Blake's Seven*, she replied before cleaning her teeth, heart thrumming once more. She could picture him in her mind now, tall and sanguine with a ruddy, laughing face and greying hair – he had to be older – a man whose sharp, oddball humour was largely wasted at home, where he yomped his many thousands of acres with a gun under one arm and spaniel at heel, lost in clever thoughts. Climbing into bed, she read: I was referring to the hotel in Roland Gardens. It's rather lovely.

Her face bloomed with colour and she fought a ridiculous urge to thrust her phone under the covers to hide it, as though Simon was invisibly watching from his empty pillow. Richard HH liked Blakes. London's sexiest hotel had featured as one of Laney's top-ten lottery-win locations ever since Simon had taken part in a photo shoot there when he was first starring in *Room Makeover*. To Laney, this was no longer a safe little fantasy about a ruddy-cheeked Hugh Bonneville type sighing forlornly beneath the family portraits and heraldry near Berwick-upon-Tweed: this was full-blown get-naughty-in-the-afternoon-in-a-four-poster stuff.

I'm overreacting, she told herself firmly; it's probably completely innocent. Nevertheless she priggishly replied: Thanks for the recommendation. I'll check it out over lunch with a friend sometime.

I'll hold you to that, he replied moments later, and signed off Rose.

It took a very long time and a lot of imaginary conversations in Blakes' Chinese Room for Laney to go to sleep. In all of them, she was whip thin in body and razor sharp in mind, keeping tall, peppery-haired men in rapturous gales of laughter.

The next morning when the 5 a.m. Club woke her in its evil

grip, Laney was determined to steal a march on it. Her head wanted to juggle death, debt and deceit. But she had a D-Day solution to throw back at it. Dieting.

If she was slimmer, she would be happier, she told herself. If she carried less fat, she would not leave Hope orphaned and destitute. If she was appealingly trim, Simon wouldn't ever stray again and senior producers would stop looking past her in meetings. She was never going to be the sort of woman who met strange men in London hotels at the drop of a hat – or a rose petal – but if she was a fraction of herself, she'd be able to do it in principle. It was all just maths. Forget fourteen to sixteen; eight and ten were better sums for success. All she needed to do was find a way to divide her size-eighteen stomach in two to make it work.

She got out of bed and trailed along the landing to check on a still-sleeping Hope before clunking downstairs to make tea and switch on her laptop. Last night's biscuit crumbs were all over the keyboard.

As she waited for the kettle to boil, she Googled 'gastric bands', wishing now she'd agreed to Oscar's demand and had it done in LA. When she'd floated the idea past Simon recently, he'd been hugely against it, horrified that she would want to go under the knife.

The cost made her balk, along with the thought of surgery, liquid food and publicly admitting what she'd had done. Oscar's pathological need for privacy and America's indifference might have shielded her, but she was in the full glare of the British tabloids now. The press would get great mileage out of Mrs de Montmorency and her 'lazy' weight loss. She should just bloody well eat less, stop boozing and start exercising.

But Laney, who had yo-yo dieted through most of her teens and twenties, knew the misery of each failed fad. The only time she'd truly been happy with her body was around the time of her first wedding to Simon, when an actress friend had helped her get pills from a private doctor that had totally killed her appetite and given her extraordinary energy. While she was taking them, she'd believed that this was what it was like to be Mia. For the first time in her life, she'd hardly thought about food.

After the wedding Laney had abandoned the pills, which were too expensive to keep buying, and made her forgetful. Succumbing to her own bibulous greed and to Simon's love of her cooking, she'd built up a larger-than-life voluptuousness, which occasionally dropped back with heartbreak, house moves, death and divorce but had never again matched the slenderness of her first wedding day.

Laney settled at the keyboard with her tea to Google 'prescription diet pills'. Who knew they'd be as easy as Ocado groceries to buy? she thought five minutes later, already feeling so much thinner that she reread all Richard HH's emails of the night before, dwelling on 'I'll hold you to that'.

She clicked the link to the roses again, disconcerted to find that more petals had dropped. There seemed to be no way to refresh the page. The flowers, while still beautiful, were wilting in real time.

She replied: I think I'll meet my friend at Blakes in July.

Laney shut the laptop lid, the last of the 5 a.m. Club hysteria finally burning out. She picked up her mug and wandered upstairs to find that Hope was snuggled up in her and Simon's bed, Gogs balanced on top of her head. Slipping in beside her, Laney noticed the light winking on her phone on the bedside table.

What a coincidence, Richard HH had replied. I'm meeting a friend at Blakes in July too. When will you be there?

Chapter 18

Griff cast the ballooning manual aside on his hotel bed and picked up his BlackBerry, checking for an email from Dominic, but there were just three text messages from his sister Ceinlys, insisting he must have Sunday lunch with the family in Wales this coming weekend, on pain of death. She'd always shared his obsessive streak, launching herself headlong into something until she achieved her goal. He replied that he'd see what he could do, but it depended on his ballooning training. Returning to the town where he'd grown up meant facing a lot of ghosts; he preferred to focus on floating over the Chilterns.

It was, he had discovered, impossible to hire a balloon in the UK without a pilot's licence. And getting a pilot's licence could not be achieved on a one-week intensive course, although he'd found the next best thing in qualified instructor Neville, an expert gun for hire when it came to training flights and theory.

Neville had told him that he also had to pass written exams on aviation law, airmanship, navigation and meteorology before finally taking his practical flight tests. Bearded and bright-eyed, Neville boasted that he could get any good student flying solo in less than a month, and a truly gifted student in a fortnight. Griff was determined to be that gifted student.

To be granted a private licence, Neville had explained, he required sixteen hours' flying experience spread over at least six separate flights including night flights, plus he had to attend a landowner-relations course.

'My family come from a terrace with back yards smaller than parking bays,' Griff had grumbled. 'We have no relations who are landowners.'

Now holed up in a Maidenhead hotel, Griff had block-booked Neville for the next fortnight. He'd already clocked up his first two hours' flying and had read the manual twice from cover to cover; he wouldn't be satisfied until he'd memorised it.

He tapped his phone against his nose, wishing Dominic Masters had a mobile, but the only way to call him was to keep hammering the camp's number, which required as much dedication as his sister showed voting for her favourite act on *The X-Factor*, and then, when he finally got through, to make sure it was at an hour when Dominic was guaranteed to be in the bar. According to the rest of the camp staff, he was never in the bar these days. Griff knew he was being fobbed off, but left cheery messages anyway. The alternative was email, again not one of Dominic's strong points but Griff was bombarding the camp's inbox too. His phone bill was already in triple figures.

He had listened to their recorded conversation many times now, and on each occasion he was struck afresh by how it moved him. He felt he was a part of it, a vital sliver of solder running between two connections in a circuit board. Transferred to a flash drive, the Nairobi recording was stashed deep within his backpack, ready to pass on to Mia Devonshire. He just had to figure out how to do it. The Cloud Man was his hero; he needed something special.

Before leaving Kenya, Griff had done enough research into Mia Devonshire and her well-protected life to appreciate that she was not a woman one could simply call up to suggest a chat about a mutual friend over coffee – even supposing one could get past her castle keep of security staff, PAs and agents. And this subject was far too sensitive to entrust to a letter. He'd briefly considered trying to set up a meeting by offering to publicise one of the wildlife conservation charities she supported, but his innate honesty wouldn't allow him to be untruthful. Having looked at the Devonshire Foundation website, he also knew that this year's fund-raising was in aid of a riding project for inner-city children, which hardly fitted with Survival TV.

Impatient, impulsive, dedicated champion of lost hearts, tribes and causes, Griff was not one for Machiavellian networking. He always took action while his blood was up and the weather was favourable. He'd returned to the UK in no doubt that Mia Devonshire deserved to hear the voice of the man she had loved as a student.

Flying in from Kenya, his romantic notions of dropping in on Mia at her Oxfordshire home by hot-air balloon to deliver the voice recording had built into an epic act of heroism, fired up by copious free in-flight cocktails. Now that he was here, Griff knew his ballooning skills had a long way to go, and he owed it to Dominic to tell him he intended to make contact with Mia – if only he could get a message to him.

He sent another email now from his phone, marked for Dominic's urgent attention: It is your choice to take no part in a life being lived again. It is mine to light up that life. Your friend, Griff.

Satisfied, he picked up the ballooning manual and started reading from the beginning once more. He knew he should be Googling the target of his heroic act and working out another strategy, but his phone screen was giving him a headache and he'd left his laptop in the car. Instead, he picked up his Ordnance Survey map and studied the area around Wootton Court, using all the information he had just picked up in the chapter about in-flight navigation to plot likely hazards.

Had he consulted with his celebrity-loving sister before embarking on this particular adventure, he would have been told straight away that there was a very big hazard no map could warn him about. The Devonshires' big house on the banks of the Thames was under intense press scrutiny right now, and any plan to float over it was unwise because it was about to be the venue for one of the most talked-about weddings of the year. But Griff had never been very thorough with his research and had always relied upon others to back him up. He was a team player, a man of action, obsessive about minor details yet happy to leave more comprehensive joined-up planning to others. As long as the wind was in his favour, he was certain everything else would fall into place.

Chapter 19

'I am going to die!' Jacinta announced, the day before her granddaughter's wedding. She scanned the occupants of the capacious Wootton kitchen for reaction, but Mia's eyes remained fixed on the seating plan she'd spread out beneath the bright lights on the island like a patient on a slab, and Iris was gazing dreamily up through the vaulted glass ceiling at a daylight moon as perfectly bleached and curved as a deckchair waiting amid the clouds.

The members of the Ormero family were chattering among themselves at the vast glass table, drinking strong coffee and eating *churros* while Mia's cats treated them as human climbing-frames.

'I die thees summer.' Jacinta drew out the words with her throat-iest Spanish inflection. When nobody took any notice – they were accustomed to her theatrical pronouncements – she rapped her walking stick repeatedly against the table, making the glassware jump. 'I would like my last weeshes known.'

'Can't it wait, Jacinta?' Mia looked up from her seating plan in horror. 'We still haven't worked out what to do with Dougie's many stepmothers and feuding aunts yet – not to mention the seven ex-girlfriends.' The guest list, which had crept to well above the cap of a hundred, contained an alarming number of women once scorned by Everett men.

'They all love him to bits so will be happy to sit anywhere,' Iris insisted, turning to the tiny, white-haired sparrow she adored. 'Lito, are you certain? Is that what the doctors say?'

'I am quite certain, *bonita*.' The old lady drew the ivory handle of her stick to her small chin, dark eyes wide in their creased ham-mocks of crow's feet and face powder. 'I do not want to ruin your day, my little one. But so much family is gathering here, and I cannot let this opportunity pass without making it clear that I must be buried *en España* with my darling Dmitri. I am so looking for-ward to being with him.'

'Oh, Lito.' Iris rushed to hug her, bending down to lay her cheek upon the pure white hair neatly parted at the crown. 'I adore how much you still love him. I know I'll always feel the same about Dougie.'

Iris had been just two when her Russian grandfather had died, his love of cigarettes and vodka getting the better of him with a fatal heart attack before he'd even reached sixty. She'd only known him through her grandmother's eyes. Now those dark eyes were filled with tears at the prospect of seeing him again.

'We will ride together in heaven.' Jacinta looked up at the moon as though her husband was sitting in its deckchair crescent beckoning to her. 'And we will watch our handsome Leo every day, which is more than I can ever do at his home here.'

'There's always Skype.' Across the island, Mia laid down her pencil with an impatient sigh, almost certain her mother-in-law was making a scene now because Leo hadn't returned from the States. If Jacinta was trying to pull a dramatic eleventh-hour stunt to stop Iris marrying then it was surely too late, although she couldn't help admiring her gallantry. The old lady disliked it whenever Iris compared Dougie to her Russian grandfather, clearly thinking the stunt rider entirely inferior.

'I was always the fire to Dmitri's ice,' she was telling Iris. 'When he died, I thought I would be burned alive in the grief. It was my wish that his body was buried in the family plot in Spain. I knew my father would watch over him there and it has kept Ormero blood running hot through our veins. Now I am ready to join them at peace in Sueño.' That her son's success had created the wealth to buy up old Ormero farmland, along with many surrounding *fincas*, and create the Hacienda Sueño where the surviving family members and many of their descendants now lived meant that Jacinta had become a long-distance matriarch. She had lived in England for more than six decades but had always insisted that her heart remained in Spain, where she would eventually be buried alongside her husband.

'Please don't say that, Lito!' Iris pleaded. 'This is a week to celebrate, not mourn.'

Jacinta let out a melancholy sigh. 'I was just seventeen when we married, and like you, Iris, I went against my family's wishes but I have never regretted it, *bonita*. I believe all girls should marry young, when you have the grace and energy to please your husband.'

Mia gaped at her mother-in-law. Surely Jacinta wasn't about to change her mind and bless the match too?

'My only regret,' she was saying, 'is that Dmitri and I had to wait so many years before God granted us our handsome boy.'

'And such a shame that handsome boy can't be here now,' Mia said, pencilling Dougie's warring stepmothers as far apart as she could with a side note to check that the large flower arrangements were strategically placed in the sightlines. Iris had been overjoyed when Leo had texted in the early hours, hinting there was an outside chance he'd be able to get home, but they'd heard no more from him since and Mia strongly suspected that that meant he was back in the studio.

'He'll make it home in time,' Iris insisted hotly. 'He promised he'd try his hardest to be here.'

'He'll meet himself coming back if he does.' Mia sighed, looking up at the wall clock which showed the time in the UK and LA. If Leo managed to get a flight in the next two hours, he might arrive with the first guests . . .

'My Leo, he works so hard.' Jacinta reached up to stroke her granddaughter's cheek with a warm hand, its skin as soft and loose as a kid glove. 'Dmitri wanted many strong sons to look after us when we grew old, but we were not so blessed. I had almost given up hope when my darling Leo was given to us by God. You must start a family straight away.'

'Dougie wants lots of children,' Iris told her happily. 'Horsemen, sportsmen and pretty girls, he says.'

Mia managed to curb any negative comment as she pencilled another Everett stepmother beside Iris's godfather, a notorious drunken groper. This morning she'd promised herself she'd set her unhappiness aside, stay calm and try to make tomorrow a happy day. If Jacinta now wanted to join Leo in offering her approval, that was her right.

Jacinta took Iris's hand in hers and admired the huge ruby engagement ring on the slender finger. 'I will not live long enough to meet my great-grandchildren, *bonita*.'

'You will, Lito!'

She shook her head. 'I shall look down on them from above and hope that they inherit their mother's looks and kind nature.'

Iris had been bubbling with excitement all week, and refused to entertain sad thoughts. Instead, she squeezed the old lady's hand, certain she could tease Lito out of her gloom. Notoriously Gothic, she pronounced global disasters on a daily basis, between her large-scale consumption of soap operas and reality television. 'We won't let you die just yet.'

'God will decide that, *bonita*.'

'Then He will just have to wait.' Iris looked up at the moon and entreated, 'Please let me have my special day.'

There was a curious lull in the huge kitchen and Iris noticed her grandmother and mother gazing up at the glass roof as though they half expected a lightning bolt to rip through it. She anticipated another lecture on the unsuitability of her match, but they remained silent, Mia squinting disapprovingly at a cobweb the housekeeper had missed, Jacinta fingering the cross at her throat as she sent up a silent prayer to the moon's smirk. Somehow their rueful restraint today was almost worse than their outspoken censure of recent weeks.

Iris felt a sudden overwhelming sense of indignation. It was the eve of her wedding day, yet even the family pets were avoiding her eye, the motley pack of cats and dogs lined up on every chair, stool and sofa. It felt like a wake.

'I love Dougie with all my heart and we WILL prove you wrong!' With a stifled sob, Iris fled outside, her two Maltese terriers at her heels like animated fluffy slippers.

Mia braced herself for the loud slam, but Iris closed the door carefully, making Jacinta chuckle. 'She probably thinks I will have a heart attack if she bangs it, but I will not die yet.' She raised her stick to bar Mia's way as she rushed in her wake. 'Leave her be, *muñequita*. She has all her life ahead. I have only my death, and that takes a great deal of preparation. I will need your help.'

Mia eyed her anxiously. 'Please tell me you're only saying this as a last-ditch attempt to make her stop and think about what she's doing?'

Jacinta nodded to her family members on the opposite side of the room, none of whom spoke English, although Iris's recent outburst had left them earwigging frantically and clearly wishing they had a dictionary. 'There is a lot to arrange before I die, and we do not have long.' She tapped the seating plan with the rubber stop of her cane. 'You are very good at arranging things, Mia.'

Registering the glint in her mother-in-law's eye, Mia decided to call her bluff. 'If you want me to arrange your funeral, it will have to wait until after the Wootton Gala, Jacinta. Leo will be here then, and I hope Iris will be back from honeymoon, so we can talk about it all together after the fund raiser.'

'My end must not ruin your special birthday party.' Jacinta peered at the plan on the lava-stone surface of the kitchen island.

'That really has nothing to do with it,' Mia insisted gently. 'The Devonshire Foundation raises huge amounts for charity, and this year's gala is a landmark one, with such a big new project at stake.'

'If you have to postpone it again, it will be my funeral,' Jacinta predicted, with a crackling roar of laughter. Then she pulled her chin back and fixed Mia with a determined look. 'We may live our lives as we wish, *muñequita*, but God decides our fate, as Iris is about to discover.'

Mia reached for her eraser, deciding that Jacinta would have to be relocated from one of the front tables to the rear of the marquee beside her own ancient uncle Roderick, a man with such a strong Lancashire accent and speech impediment that the old lady would be convinced her hearing-aid batteries were flat again and hopefully keep quiet.

*

187

Iris slipped into the stallion barn and greeted her soulmate, Lorca, a hot-headed young Vaquera horse whose coat was the same deep dappled chestnut as sunlight through a smoke tree. 'I'm sorry you won't be a star tomorrow,' she breathed into his neck. 'But you'd never stop at the altar.'

Lorca was '*tres sangres*' or 'three-blood', a potent trinity of Andalucía war horse, racing thoroughbred and fiery Arab. Iris loved the breed, Spain's unofficial equine secret weapon, the lion-hearted fighting horse the Ormero family had once bred better than any other *yeguada* in Spain. Iris had always believed that Dougie would be *tres sangres* if he were a horse.

He'd been strangely edgy since his return from LA, despite a successful lunch with her father, who'd not only given his blessing but also put him in touch with Abe Schultz. Iris guessed that wedding nerves, mixed with the prospect of a career break, were playing on his mind. It made her want to curl lovingly around him, but they'd had time for no more than a few snatched conversations all week. The trip had clearly had a huge effect, and Dougie now seemed set on returning to LA as soon as possible, even talking about living there, although Iris – who knew he would never leave his horses behind – was quietly confident that wouldn't last. They were both prone to sudden obsessions that soon passed. After shooting the most recent Ptolemy Finch movie together, they'd made excited plans to buy a small, romantic Hungarian castle they'd found perched on a hilltop, an idea that had rapidly lost momentum when they realised it had no electricity or drainage, was four hours from the nearest airport and – most importantly for Dougie – had no pasture for horses among its wooded and lake-covered seven hectares.

She moved along the aisle to Escultor, his neck emerging over the half-door, platinum mane so long and curly he looked like he'd had salon extensions. He was to be her consort the following morning and as usual he regarded her with the doe-eyed, soulful sympathy of the Carthusian holy brothers who had bred his ancestors.

To her grandmother's regret, Iris had long-since forsaken the

Catholicism in which she'd been brought up, but now she said a silent prayer into Scully's gleaming neck, wishing that tomorrow would bring luck and life to all who were there.

Her phone sounded with the hunting-horn ringtone she'd assigned to Dougie, making the stallion retreat warily to the back of his stable.

'Darling Mrs Everett!' he hailed her, with that deep, seductive clip. In the background, she could hear shouted conversations and laughter. He was staying at his mate's Soho club for his last night as a single man.

'I take it you're already partying like a bachelor?' she laughed.

'Having a siesta after a long lunch.' He was trying hard to sound sober. 'Just watching a movie then I'll hit the gym. Ready for tomorrow?'

'Sort of. Abuelita has just announced her imminent death.'

'The old lady? Christ. D'you think she'll hold on twenty-four more hours?'

'Yes.'

'Well, that's all right, then. Hey, baby, what are you wearing right now?'

'A frown,' she said coolly. 'Don't call Lito "the old lady", it's disrespectful.'

'You *are* tense!' He whistled. 'I wish I was there to massage your every tight little bump and pip.' His voice dropped to a purr. 'Tomorrow night, Mrs Everett, you will be putty in my hands.'

'And you will be considerably harder in mine.' She tried to get in the sexy swing, but she could definitely hear a female voice behind him saying, 'Douugieeee!'

'Who's that?'

'Just the television,' he said unconvincingly. 'Now, Riz darling, I think you should pack quite a *lot* of clothes for the honeymoon.'

'I have. You still haven't told me where we're going, so I've got something for every occasion. I really struggled to get it all into just one suitcase.'

'Oh, you are the sweetest thing. Please tell me there are no cardigans.'

'Maybe one or two. They're very practical for layer—'

'We'll head straight for Rodeo Drive.'

'So we're definitely honeymooning in LA?' She tried to keep the disappointment from her voice.

'We can visit your father.'

'He'll be here for the wedding,' she said determinedly.

'Even if he is, we can see more of him there. One never gets to talk to anybody for more than a minute at one's wedding, even close family.'

'The same's true of LA. I've been there for months on end, remember, and I never saw him.'

'It's where I need to be for my career, Riz. I have some chums who know the scene. They've offered to help set us up out there.'

'We are just talking about our honeymoon here, right?'

'Why not stay on?' He was slurring his words, clearly quite drunk.

'What about the horses?'

'We'll train and breed there – there are some great barns. You can go to UCLA, do a little bit of acting in the vacations.'

'You know I want a break from that.'

'Life's all an act, baby!'

She was certain she heard a woman laughing in the background. But then Dougie was murmuring sweet nothings and getting horny again, and she let him soothe her back into laughing, flirtatious anticipation as he reminded her just how much he loved her and how well he was going to look after her, a gladiator at her side.

Their wedding would be very intimate and filled with love, she reminded herself. Her closest girlfriends would be arriving soon, a merry band to help her pamper and preen and get her beauty sleep – all except Chloe, who was on her placement. Iris envisaged kind, sensible Chloe in her farm overalls, disapproval on her face.

She mustn't dwell on absent ones, she told herself firmly. Instead she listened to Dougie's husky drawl and let herself float in it, loving every bold, bawdy word. He was her knight in shining armour.

Yet as soon as she rang off, Lito's words were rattling through her head: 'I am going to die this summer.' She hoped her grandmother was wrong – but it worried her that she would be in America over the next few weeks. She didn't want to stay there indefinitely – her mother would go demented for a start: she and Lito always trod a fine line between adoring one another and slipping arsenic in the sun-downers. In recent weeks, they had agreed on just one thing: Iris shouldn't be marrying Dougie Everett.

Scully's head had reappeared over his half door. She pressed her forehead to his long, noble face and let out a low sigh, wishing her father would return. She knew that he was having a horrible time on the show and was typically trying to play it down in his modest way, but she was hurt that he wouldn't stand up to the studio and demand the time off for her wedding. However unjustly, she took it as another painful reminder that he was not her natural father. She knew so little about the man with whom she shared half her genes that her mental image was of Lawrence of Arabia appearing through the mirage, vague and heroic, a distant figure who might one day march into her world and disrupt its cosy order.

Scully let out a deep, throaty whicker, and Iris turned. Her mother had walked into the barn with two mugs of tea, anxious to make peace, the usual crew of dogs trailing in her wake, stretching up to touch noses with curious horses as they passed.

'*Pax?*' She handed Iris a mug of tea before wrapping an arm around her.

Iris clutched the warm mug. '*Pax.*' Then she looked into a pair of eyes as green and unguarded as hers. 'Do you dislike Dougie because he reminds you of my real father?'

Mia said nothing but the mug lurched so violently in her hands that a tsunami of tea slopped over its rim, scalding her fingers.

'I know he seems a bit wild,' Iris went on, 'but his spirit will never be broken,' she straightened Scully's long forelock, 'and that's what makes him so exciting.'

'If you're having second thoughts it's not too late to say,' Mia blurted.

She shrugged off her mother's arm, causing more hot tea to slop on to the concrete below. 'I'm not.'

'I didn't tell anybody about my doubts when I married,' Mia hurried on, 'and I couldn't bear you to suffer the same fate.'

Iris looked at her incredulously. '*You* had second thoughts?'

'Oh, I was on to forty-fifth or -sixth thoughts by the ceremony – and so was Leo.' Mia had swapped mug hands and was shaking her dripping fingers, her rings glittering reminders of that fateful day, much supplemented since then with new settings and solitaires. 'Your father took the vows so seriously – we both did – but for him the Church was beyond question. He still went to Mass every week in those days and to promise something in front of God meant no going back.'

'You got married at Gretna Green, not St Paul's,' Iris pointed out.

'Marriage is a big thing wherever you exchange vows,' Mia said. 'We were young and frightened and we adored each other. My pregnancy was beginning to show and I was ill all the time. We'd gone into it thinking it would be a fun party for our friends and then suddenly realised it was serious.'

'I am not pregnant,' Iris hissed. 'And I'm taking this very seriously.'

Mia stepped closer. 'I've almost lived my life again since that year, and I know how one rash decision can affect that lifetime. I so desperately want you to be happy, my love; I'd do anything for that.'

'I *will* be happy,' Iris insisted, her eyes on Scully, who was stretching his dark muzzle towards his mistress now, nudging at her sleeve, wanting Mia's attention. As her mother reached automatically to stroke his cheek, Iris noticed that her fingers were still red from being scalded, the nails bitten down. By tomorrow evening, they'd have had false ones professionally applied, but today the truth was as vulnerable and exposed as her emotions. 'Was it a rash decision to have me?' she demanded accusingly.

'Never!'

'But my real father didn't want me?'

'No!' Mia started back in alarm, making Scully shy away. 'It wasn't like that at all.'

'What was it like?'

Mia pressed her hands to her lips, speaking through her fingers. 'You were wanted more than anything in the world. You kept my heart beating when it was broken. You were my life and Leo my rock, but I was so very young.'

'Unlike you, I am *not* between a rock and a hard place,' Iris snapped, furious that Mia always deflected the subject. 'I'm marrying the father of my future children, not a man prepared to take over the role at short notice, then switch channels.' She lifted her chin defiantly, hating herself for the resentment pouring out, her perfect day yet again shadowed by doubt and disapproval.

As Mia stepped back, eyes wide with hurt, her phone started to ring. She pulled it out, her face falling when the number on the screen wasn't Leo's.

'Hello? ... Aunt Vee!' Relieved at least to have an excuse to get away from Iris's fury, she hurried out of the stables for better reception. 'No ... it's still going ahead ... Well, I'm sure Uncle Roderick has that wrong ... no, Dougie's a *stunt* man ...'

Iris turned back to Scully. 'Why does nobody think this wedding is a good idea?'

'I think this wedding is a *bloody* good idea,' Mia told Laney on the phone later. 'I've been looking for an excuse to have a drink for ten years. My father dying followed by my mother a year later – nah. Leo refusing to let me adopt children – nah. But now I've finally

193

got it. Thank you, Dougie bloody Everett. Welcome to the family! Cheers!'

It was after midnight. Everybody at Red Gables was asleep apart from Laney, who was curled up on the kitchen sofa with the dogs and a hysterical friend on the line.

Mia had been sober for almost a decade – she and Leo had gone through AA together. Tonight, however, she'd fallen off the wagon.

'How many have you had?' demanded Laney.

'Jusht a glass. I found the caterer's stash. Champagne. Do it in style, I say. Ashley, it'sabit average. Not even vintage.'

'You've had more than one glass to sound like that,' Laney reproached her. The only other occasion on which she remembered Mia slipping off the wagon was not long after completing the twelve stages.

'I had a Xanax firsht,' she admitted. 'Christ, I feel woozy. Make me laugh, Laney. Ineedabloodygood laugh.'

Their usual roles had been reversed. For once Laney was totally sober, partly because she had a photo shoot first thing tomorrow and couldn't risk bloodshot eyes clashing with her pink hair, partly because she was punishing herself for not being pregnant. Today her period had arrived to stamp out any last vestige of hope. She felt suicidal with self-hatred, certain that the drinking had to stop, even if that meant she and Simon wouldn't find much to laugh and flirt about.

The diet pills might not be a good idea where conception was concerned either. They'd arrived from South Korea with no dosage instructions or health warnings, but she'd convinced herself that being slimmer could only increase her chances of a healthy pregnancy. She'd swallowed two earlier that evening and was still pinging off the walls as a result. Simon's children were all staying with them this weekend, so she'd had a baking marathon, churning out biscuits and cakes galore to fuel them and bribe *Cheers!* into thinking of her as a loving wife and mother, not a hyperactive pink-haired malcontent. To her delight she'd had no desire to sample them.

Sleep looked set to be a more major issue – but at least it meant she was fully awake to deal with Mia's wedding-eve drinking crisis.

'I'm coming round,' she insisted now.

'Pleash don't – Irish might see you. She's still awake. All her friends are here.'

'Does she know you've been drinking?'

'No, I'm hiding in the second kitchen. They're still doing hot chocolate and midnight feasts. God, they're *children*, Laney. Children with cars, smartphones and shex lives, but still greener than grass. She's my little b-baby g-girl, Laney. She's t-too young.' She took a deep, shuddering breath, clearly trying to pull herself together. Laney heard the tell-tale gulp of more champagne being knocked back. 'She tried to talk to me about her father again tonight – before her friends arrived. I d-didn't know what to bloody say.'

'I take it the studio didn't let him have the time off?'

'Not *that* father.'

Laney held her breath. 'Which father are we talking about?'

'Her daydream father – the anthology of little fragments she put together after my undergraduate debriefing.'

Laney winced.

'I know I should have been more open with Iris about it all,' Mia went on, 'but I couldn't honestly see the good it would do. She's always had Leo who loves her unequavicob … unequivobac … loves her totally. As far as she's concerned, he's her father and that's it.'

'Don't you think she deserves to know more? You've never really told her anything about Dom.'

There was a muffled sob at the other end of the line. 'He has nothing to do with this! I'm living my life again as though he never existed, remember?' she slurred angrily, years of bottled-up hurt mixing badly with booze and Xanax. 'Iris knows I was selfish and headstrong and made a lot of mistakes. Her conception was far from immaculate, and while it's something I'll never regret, I think she can be shpared the details, don't you?'

Laney thought about The Night That Never Happened and said nothing. As thorns in her side went, it was a miniature rose's compared to current grievances, but it still had the capacity to draw blood if she worried at it.

Mia had started to cry. 'I only ever wanted what's best for Iris. Now I'm going to be a total wreck at her wedding. Can I come and shpend the day with you tomorrow? We can take Hope to Legoland again. The wedding's not until late evening – and you have to come, in disguise.'

'Enough! I'm not taking you to Legoland and I'm not dressing up in disguise again.' Laney adopted brutally pragmatic tactics. 'Tip the rest of that champagne down the sink and take me – that is, the phone with me on it – to the nearest bathroom and we'll sort you out.'

Five minutes later, crashing around her en suite with an electric toothbrush and Laney now on hands-free, Mia was sounding no less spaced out but had stopped slurring and seemed helpfully sleepy.

'I don't know what I'd do without you, Laney,' she said, voice vibrating with the brush. 'I love you, lovely friend.'

'You will be magnificent tomorrow. You are a brilliant mother. And Iris will be happy because this is what she wants. Now get some sleep.'

'You are so fab—' There was a whoosh of tap water. 'Can this please be another night that never happened ... like at college?'

'So you've been thinking about it too?' Laney knew she sounded like she'd swallowed a brick.

'Oh, fuckety fuck!' The brush was switched off. 'Haff's here. I can hear voices. I completely forgot his plane was delayed. Vicente's been waiting for him at the airport since eight.' The Spanish riding coach Juan-Felipe Javiero, known to all as Haff, was an old family friend and one of the wedding house-guests.

'Surely he'll go straight to bed?'

'He's Spanish! He'll expect a meal, wine and conversation until two or three. I can hardly expect the girls to look after him. And I'm in my specs and pyjamas. Can you come round after all?'

'No! Show him some good old-fashioned British hospitality: take him straight to his room and ask him whether he wants one dog or two on his bed.'

'Haff!' Mia forced a smile and tried hard to focus on her late arrival. She gripped the door to steady herself. '¡Es bueno verte! ¿Cómo estás?'

'All the better for seeing you,' growled a voice as predatory as a lynx, and she was enveloped in expensive aftershave as stubbly kisses landed firmly on her cheeks. Renowned for his hot looks, hot blood and hot temper, Haff was a distant cousin of Leo's, a former Olympic medallist and a rare SMD – or straight man in dressage – who regularly escaped to the UK during the Spanish high summer to coach adoring female clients, most of whom he'd also seduced. That he had yet to bed Mia was a cause of much ongoing frustration.

Haff now held her at arm's length, black curls falling into his playful eyes, the scar on his left cheek a deep artificial dimple to his expansive smile. 'You are beautiful as always, Mia. Where is Leo?'

Feeling really quite dizzy now, she was grateful that he was more or less holding her up. 'Still in Los Angeles.'

Haff was one of those rare professional male riders who looked just as good off a horse as on it, with the compact, wide-shouldered body of a professional cyclist and a penchant for the finest linen and cashmere. As always, his handsome, craggy face was tanned the colour of cognac, with more laughter lines than an Almodóvar movie. As fit and flirtatious in his early forties as he had been in his twenties, he possessed the same fiery toughness as the Spanish stallions he rode.

'Let's go straight to bed and I will make love to you,' he suggested, eyes gazing deeply into hers, hands sliding up her arms to her throat and then her face. He'd always been so entirely unapologetic about his desire to seduce her that it had become something of a running joke between them. But now his expression changed as he took in the reddened, half-focused eyes behind their glasses. 'You have been crying?'

'It's nothing.' Mia turned away. No longer supported by him, she drifted dizzily and dramatically left. She was dead on her feet now, the Xanax-and-champagne cocktail having left her almost comatose. 'Would you like a drink?' she offered, drifting in the other direction as she zigzagged to the kitchen. 'Are you hungry?'

'No.' He picked up his suit carrier and followed. 'I will just take you to bed.'

'I'm wildly flattered as always, Haff, but it's a big day tomorrow.' She was starting to cannon off the furniture, her vision blurring. 'And I have a huge amount to orgasm – I mean organise.' She closed her eyes in horror as her muddled, sedated brain started to misfire completely. 'A huge amount to *organise*.' She walked straight into the arm of one of the big gold suede sofas that sat around a marble coffee-table, pitched over it and landed amid a colony of Pierre Frey cushions. When she made no move to get up, Haff realised she'd passed out.

'Which is why, *mi corazón*, I am taking you to bed.' He laughed throatily, laying his suit carrier gently on top of her and picking up both to carry them upstairs.

Having settled Mia in her bed with a small pack of dogs at her feet, a glass of water and some paracetamol on the bedside table, and her alarm clock set for seven, he found his way to his usual guest room. He could hear girls laughing and chattering overhead, the deep throb of the bass beat from the music being played. Below him somebody was watching television.

Plugging in his iPod earphones, he settled back on his bed and switched on to his favourite hip-hop flamenco fusion, Ojos de Brujo. He picked up his phone and started to scroll through the legion of texts that had been arriving all day from English dressage clients who had discovered he was in the UK and wanted to book in for lessons. He sent a blanket reply saying he was attending a family celebration and would be returning to Spain straight afterwards. As many of his clients were also mistresses, juggling them could be complicated and he wanted to devote himself to seducing Mia this summer, when they were combining forces to set up a Javiero Dressage Coaching Centre in the UK. A collaboration between his own charity and the Devonshire Foundation, the dressage schools enabled underprivileged kids to work with horses in high-school movements. Haff already had two similar projects running in Spain, both heavily subsidised, but the euro crisis was threatening them with closure as grants were cut. The Devonshire Foundation's support was invaluable: it had already taken over the lease on a city farm in north London, and this year's Wootton Gala was dedicated to raising funds to equip it as a training centre. The project was closer to Haff's heart than any woman, but Mia's unique blend of nervy intensity and earthiness fascinated him. Having taught her the principles of balance, cadence and rhythm in the saddle, Haff wanted to enjoy the ride for himself.

When Laney crept beneath the duvet beside Simon, it was already growing light outside.

'What have you been up to?' he asked groggily. 'Don't tell me Mia's still having a crisis?'

'She went to bed hours ago. I was just checking the roses.'

He rolled away from her, pulling his pillow over his head. 'You're obsessed with those wretched bushes. They'll look fine for the photo shoot.'

Laney lay awake with her heart racing. She hadn't been checking the roses growing alongside the crumbling bricks of Red Gables' walled garden. She'd been staring at the rich red blooms on her laptop as dawn began to break. They were fading fast, petals now scattered beneath them like blood on a battlefield.

She closed her eyes and tried to calm down, grateful that she'd resisted the temptation to contact Richard HH again: escaping into fantasy was not the answer to her insomnia. Lying shame-faced and restless beside Simon, she tried not to dwell on The Night That Never Happened, knowing her Demon had never remembered it and that they'd overcome many more secrets and betrayals in the two intervening decades. Yet the little thorn in her side felt as though it had nicked an artery.

Three hours later, the *Cheers!* stylist did all he could to prop up insomnia bags with tightening potions and cover-up lotions, disguising the cochineal hair tint with a variety of hats and scarves. Laney, whose heart had sunk as soon as she saw the rail of vast tent dresses being trolleyed into the house, knew she looked more mutton than lamb as a long day of posing and smiling began.

Simon looked as his most Byronic and dandyish, and the house proved surprisingly photogenic, the couple's eccentric furniture hauled around to cover up the worst of the builders' debris and Laney herself ('Stand behind your husband, love – that's it, behind the sofa – and put your arms around his shoulders with your face just peeping out around his'). By late afternoon, Simon's kids had arrived for their weekend visit and there were several big group shots staged around the huge kitchen table, and one with them all draped on the vast ornamental staircase like the Osmonds, with Simon's fabulous white smile beaming from the faces of all five of his children alongside his own. Only Hope stayed well away from the camera's glare, playing with Malin in her nursery, which was out of bounds to *Cheers!*. Laney and Oscar had a codicil to their custody arrangement that strictly forbade Hope's inclusion in any publicity until the age of sixteen.

The Demons put up a united front, albeit a bickering, bitching one.

The comely journalist that Maz Jones had sent along clearly fancied Simon like mad and was desperate to get him on his own, elbowing Laney out of the way with suggestions that she make coffee or check on the kids, but the Demons were harder to halve than an unripe avocado, and just as bitter. While the photographs may have been phonier than a snow scene in June, the interview found Laney and Simon at their waspish, witty best with the ultimate double-act of quotes and counter-quotes to prove just how in tune they were. The journalist visibly wilted as she took shorthand, her flirtatious Simon fantasies crumbling before her eyes. Laney felt extraordinarily alert, energy crackling out of her. She'd barely eaten a thing in two days. If she hadn't just suffered the humiliation of cramming herself into articles from the Rail of Shame, she would have sworn she'd dropped a dress size.

Simon brought her down to earth with a twelve-stone bump. He was telling an elaborate story about a recent trip to the races, at which Laney had worn a hat so outlandish that the winner of the 3.15 had turned tail in fright, when he let slip that she wouldn't be attending that evening's wedding.

'My wife's millinery choices are legend, and one can't blame Iris for refusing to be upstaged. She doesn't want anything to frighten her horse when she rides up the aisle. But all is not lost. I'm smuggling in a camera hidden to stream the action live to Laney here at home.'

In trying to kick him under the garden table to make him shut up, Laney shinned the journalist, who let out a bleat of pain.

'So, you won't be at the Devonshire wedding, Laney?' she asked, rubbing her ankle. 'I thought you were very close to the family?'

'I am, but I have a prior engagement I can't cancel,' Laney said smoothly, narrowing her eyes at Simon, who was swigging more Pimm's and typing into his phone.

'Washing her hair again.' He didn't glance up.

Laney grabbed the Pimm's jug and stomped huffily inside to refill it. On the countertop, her phone was flashing with a new message.

The lovely friend I'm meeting at Blakes in July is being somewhat elusive on dates, alas, Richard HH had emailed. How does it fit in with your plans if I were to reserve a table every day?

Spatting with Simon had made her feel devilish. If he was rudely tweeting to half a million followers during an interview, she had every right to cyber-flirt with one.

I really admire your reserve, she replied, adding, It fits in with my plans very well indeed.

Chapter 20

This was Griff's third flight of the week and Neville was becoming a firm friend. Today's change of wind direction had finally enabled the two to navigate the curling Thames Valley. To Griff's delight, this put the balloon on a direct flight path towards Wootton, which also made for much trickier piloting and meant Neville was able to start teaching his eager student the importance of controlling lift in turbulent air. Despite a perfect ballooning evening breeze, the scorching day had left pockets of hot air, which made it difficult to get adequate lift, particularly with the small envelope of the training balloon. This was the lowest they had flown, reminding Griff of his flights along the Mara River basin with Dominic.

Flying through the densely populated UK was far noisier than the African plains. For the past hour, Griff had heard a cacophony of dogs barking, lambs bleating and occasional drifts of music and laughter between propane blasts. The two-man balloon was not equipped with the whisper burner that Dominic used, and today it was roaring.

'In these conditions, when the burner is in far greater use, one must keep a particularly close eye on fuel level and pyrometer,' Neville explained, blasting the flame for a lengthy spell, which caused the balloon to drift very slightly upward and then veer noticeably left. 'The thermals today are powerful and one's direction can change often, making it essential to monitor compass readings and keep in close contact with the ground crew. You pilot while I radio them.' He relinquished the blast-valve trigger, which Griff took over willingly, loving the challenge of keeping the balloon level. As he was learning, that sensation of gentle, weightless drifting could quickly be replaced by a yo-yo of ascent and descent if one didn't maintain the correct heat level.

Neville appreciated having such a dedicated apprentice, who already had many hours of flying experience. 'We must locate our landing site soon,' he said now, as he came off the radio to his ground team, currently parked in a lay-by further along the river, awaiting instructions. The breeze was dropping and progress had become frustratingly slow.

'Already?' Griff gazed out at the horizon, knowing Wootton could only be a mile or two further on. He'd driven past once or twice now, but the prospect of floating almost directly overhead was too tempting to pass up.

'As you know, a pilot is always looking for sites just in case he needs to make an emergency landing,' Neville lectured, blasting more heat into the envelope. 'That way we can afford to be choosy when it comes to a controlled descent. Today, I want you to make the choice. You'll learn a lot from this.'

Griff smiled to himself. He'd already made up his mind.

Chapter 21

Laney saw the hot-air balloon float past as she worked in the garden, its burners letting out a dragon roar. 'Look, darling – up in the sky!'

'Are Noddy and Tessie Bear in it?' Hope pointed her trowel at it as it drifted downriver towards Wootton. 'Are they going to the wedding?'

Laney wiped the sweat from her brow with her forearm and pulled off her gardening gauntlets, noticing the time on her watch. The evening ceremony was just minutes away. 'I don't think so.' She wandered out of the low evening sunlight towards the wobbly table she'd set up in the shadow of one of the rambling-rose arches and reached for the after-sun spray from the debris of Hope's picnic tea, now dancing with wasps. She started to apply it, wincing as cool liquid met reddened skin. Her sunburn would no doubt clash horribly with her pink hair. Her eye make-up from the photo shoot had long since slid from eyelid to bag.

This evening she knew it would be easy to feel a bit sorry for herself, left out of her goddaughter's wedding like the bad fairy. But in fact she was delighted to be alone with Hope, singing with her, letting her eat as much cake as she liked and not even caring when she pulled the petals off the loveliest Beau Narcisse rose trying to help Mummy with her 'dead-heading'.

There was a reason for Laney's euphoria beyond the pure joy of motherhood and the effects of the little pills from South Korea. She had hugged it to herself all day and had secretly checked at regular intervals on her phone. Richard HH had written another email. She pulled out her phone and looked at it again. I like very long lunches ... preferably ones that carry on through dinner.

Just reading it made her laugh and gather Hope into a giggling, twirling hug. Her moods were swinging on a barometer determined by her inbox. They'd been exchanging messages all evening as the midsummer sun rode high in the sky, and she felt like Titania after sipping Puck's love potion.

Escaping inside from the gathering midges, she plonked Hope in front of the Disney Channel while waiting for her bath to run and opened her laptop to check on the state of her roses. No more petals had dropped.

Laney dabbled with the notion of quoting Shakespeare, something about summer's lease being all too short, but her attention was caught by the television. Hope had her nose almost pressed to the screen, practically inhaling a *Cinderella* spin-off in which the heroine wafted around in a haze of butterflies and bluebirds being assisted by mice in waistcoats. To Laney, that was what Blakes Hotel in July felt like: make-believe, a fairy tale to play along with.

Long lunches v. good, although I must warn you I have a short attention span, she replied.

His response was waiting for her after she'd put Hope to bed. I am very sparky, I can assure you. But do let's get the conversational mores over and done with beforehand. Lovely weather, isn't it? How was your journey? May I say how absolutely ravishing you look?

She danced to the fridge to pour herself a glass of wine. As soon as she got a reply from Richard HH, she started thinking of snappy one-liners to fire back. Lovely, easy, and you may. Your shooting breeks are very dashing.

Thank you, he'd replied already. I like to think they go with my nipple tassels and tricorn hat.

How uncanny that we wore the same thing.

Are you doing anything fun this evening?

Don't long lunches last into the evening?

I meant right now. Are you home alone again?

Spoilsport. She glared irritably at the message. She needed the silly fairy-tale fantasy, not a reality check pointing out that the pumpkin was waiting. 'What's with the dying roses?' she wanted to demand. 'Is that the usual RHH calling card to women you admire on the radio? Have you sent the link to Kirsty Young and Libby Purves as well?'

Instead she typed: According to my best friend, I should be disguising myself as a silver-service waitress and stealing into my goddaughter's wedding to rescue her from an unhappy match, but I rather think I'm going to have a bath. She switched off the computer so that she couldn't be tempted to engage any more. Richard HH was back in his portrait-lined study, sitting beneath two crossed blunderbusses, his feet up on a spaniel, nursing a large Scotch and sending a wilting-rose website link to Sandi Toksvig.

Topping up the lukewarm water left from Hope's bedtime bath to make a deep, bubbly, scented cauldron, Laney sank back in it, deliberately not thinking about him or the wedding she was missing. Instead, she listened to Queen and wondered what she was going to do about the letter she'd had from the DVLA that morning, telling her that she now had nine points on her licence, thanks to her Psychic Phoenix and wedding-dress dashes, and was one Gatso-camera snap away from a ban.

Freddie Mercury provided the answer as 'Fat Bottomed Girls' gave way to bicycle bells.

'On your bike, Laney!' she proclaimed, imagining herself miraculously shedding weight as she pedalled over the Chilterns.

She couldn't help the fantasy rolling back in. By the time she surfaced, she was cycling through South Kensington in soft focus, a fresh-faced vision of slender health, skin glowing in the July sunshine, tea-dress lifted by the breeze to reveal lacy adulteress knickers that her lover would slowly lower in Suite 007 at Blakes Hotel after their long, flirtatious lunch.

Chapter 22

Wootton was putting on a spectacular show. Tens of additional hired hands had been working with head gardener Franco all week to make the lawns and beds as splendid as the fairy-tale parterres and rose walks in the Disney movies Simon's stepdaughter loved. The topiary had been freshly trimmed so that the giant green animals seemed about to spring into life and start dancing around in a cloud of magical dust.

Not that Simon paid them any attention. He'd barely glanced at the marquee erected alongside one wing of the house, complete with mock-Regency columns to match Wootton's architecture, the terraces, water features and forests of greenery from which a long lantern-lit walkway wove into the gardens. Neither had he noticed the silk-trimmed, arabesque pergola at the foot of the long grass avenue that ran from the baize-smooth lawns through the woods to the riverbank, where rows of gold chairs were now set out for guests to watch the nuptials.

It was on one of these that he was sitting now, fingertips tapping distractedly on his iPhone.

'Put that *away*, Dad,' hissed a hugely embarrassed Kitty, just thirteen and very self-conscious in cobalt-blue Vero Moda. 'You're not supposed to have it. Are you tweeting again?'

'I told that security guard it links my pacemaker to the local emergency response team. Why has my browser stopped working?'

'Here.' His son Louis grabbed it and started fiddling. 'You need to reset the protocols.'

'How exactly do I do that?'

'Take the battery out.'

Middle son Teddy now slumped into the empty seat beside his father, having just wandered down from the main house, where he'd enjoyed a long snoop on the pretext of finding a loo. 'Man, this crib is sick. They've got, like, fish in the walls.'

'I designed the interiors,' Simon told him smugly. He batted away a caterpillar that had just fallen from a tree branch on to his lap.

He wished Laney was here and now deeply regretted coming without her, however much the kids were relishing the occasion. It wasn't until he'd arrived that he'd realised just what a big deal this was for Mia and just how seriously she was falling apart over it. He'd only seen her briefly, putting on her perfect-hostess act as guests arrived, but he knew she was held together by a thread. She looked immaculate and betrayed no sign of the wreck that had kept his wife up talking half the night, but he had known her long enough to recognise the haunted look in her eyes.

Her seat on the front row of the wooded auditorium was one of very few still empty as she lingered in the stable yard, helping with last-minute preparations before the bride mounted.

All the other seats were taken up with an enchanting array of guests, most of them of Iris's generation. Simon was surprised to be one of very few over thirty, the majority of whom appeared to be from the Ormero family or Dougie's haw-haw brigade. It was certainly a select guest list and a rather eccentric one. He supposed he should feel privileged.

'Dougie Everett is sooooo buff,' sighed Kitty dreamily as she gazed at the figure slouching against the pergola with a disreputable-looking best man, both smoking cigarettes.

Simon gave him a cursory glance and decided he looked stoned out of his mind, eyes half closed and waistcoat buttoned wrongly. 'Buff as in buffoon,' he muttered under his breath. He knew that if Laney were here, they'd have fun trading sharp rebuffs while they waited for the wedding buffet, but his kids were deliberately avoiding his gaze.

He craned over his shoulder to see if there was any sign of the bride, then picked up his phone again.

Neither Iris nor her mother had managed much sleep the previous night, but while one had the same over-excited frisson she felt when riding a stunt in a movie, the other felt as though she was about to walk on stage without having learned the script.

Iris looked spectacular. The Portobello Road dress was a puff-sleeved, tiny-waisted cavalier extravaganza in deep cream silk and red velvet; it was Faye Dunaway's Wicked Lady with a hint of *Children of the New Forest* and worked brilliantly on horseback, the huge skirt falling over Scully's silver rump, with matching red ribbons and roses braided through his lattice-plaited mane. Her own long curls were pinned loosely at the nape of her neck and, having just forfeited a plumed hat that she felt made her look like Dick Whittington, she was now arguing with her mother about wearing the 'trousseau' that Leo had FedExed from the States that morning.

'He knitted it himself!' Mia insisted.

'He didn't. It's still got the label on it.'

Perhaps naïvely, Iris had believed Leo would come back for her wedding. The dawning understanding that he wouldn't felt like abandonment. He had no need to give her away, she thought wretchedly. He'd done that already.

Mia was hugging the crocheted shawl closely to her chest. It was new-season Ralph Lauren and as easy to pick up in LA as an actor's résumé. He'd probably sent his assistant out for it. With the shawl had been a handwritten card: *Follow your heart, little one, and I will always be with you, because I am in that heart as you are in mine.*

Mia was livid with Leo. They'd spoken so often about this in recent weeks, with Leo adamant that Iris was making a huge mistake, yet he now seemed happy to let it happen from a distance, too busy and distracted to kick up a fuss. Panic was rising ever higher in her chest, like water gushing into a cabin in which she was trapped in a sinking ship, all the time knowing her daughter was about to be dragged under the surface. They'd floated around in an ever diminishing air pocket for weeks. Now she knew she had to take a deep breath and dive down to try to open the jammed door.

'I must tell you something!' she said frantically.

'This really isn't the right time, Mum,' Iris snapped.

Mia dabbed her tears with the Ralph Lauren shawl. 'I really do know how you feel. I wanted to marry your real father just as much when I was your age.'

Staring at her mother in shock, Iris fought to steady the impatient Scully, who was napping to get going and whinnying at the stabled horses in the courtyard around him. Above the clatter of his hoofs on the flagstones, they could hear the string quartet playing in the distance. Then a strange growling sound came from the direction of the river, like a lion roaring. Hearing it, Scully stood stock still, ears pricked intently.

Paying it no heed, Mia rushed on: 'I have *never* stopped loving him, or hoping he would come back to me.'

That strange mock-lion roar came from the woods again, making Scully start back, metal shoes sparking against stone, white flanks swinging around, forcing Mia to leap away.

'Why are you telling me this now?' Iris said, fighting to steady him. Scully was trotting on the spot now, an impatient stone-banging piaffe interspersed with snorts.

'Dougie is *nothing* like your father was. He doesn't even come close.'

'He's about to become your son-in-law.' She shortened her reins, preparing to turn towards the stone archway leading out of the courtyard. 'I'm *not* going to change my mind about this, Mum, and I won't keep Dougie – or the rest of my life – waiting any longer.'

'You deserve so much better than that little twerp!' Mia was too het up to think what she was saying. 'He has no morals whatsoever! He tried to get me into bed the first time you brought him here.'

Iris froze. 'Take that back!'

Too late, Mia realised that desperation had pushed her across an invisible line. As Laney had predicted, telling Iris about Dougie's misdemeanour at Wootton was about the worst thing she could have done, and at this eleventh hour it was maternal suicide. She'd never seen Iris look so incensed – she half expected her to turn Scully's rump towards her, kick him into capriole and propel her into orbit. He was already hammering at the ground like the Anvil Chorus, almost cantering on the spot, head bobbing and foam flying from his mouth. Iris's face was as deathly pale as his coat, apart from two small spots of angry colour that blazed in her cheeks.

'So you want me to marry someone like my real father?' she snarled. 'Someone who walked away and let you raise his child without him, who never cared to know what became of you or me? I don't think so! Where is *he* now, huh?'

Mia let out a sob. 'He's with me all the time, and more so than ever today.'

Scully's hoofs drummed faster on the cobbles, as Iris gasped, 'Are you telling me he really *is* here?'

Midway through blowing her nose, Mia looked up at her in confusion.

Iris was beside herself with excitement, her anger eclipsed by incredulity. 'Is that why Leo won't come back? Would they fight each other? Where is he sitting?'

'He's right here, Iris.' Mia placed both hands over her heart just as Scully lost patience and lunged forwards, taking off across the stable yard for twenty metres before Iris could pull him up. 'He's always been here.' Mia thumped her folded hands against her chest.

But Iris didn't see the gesture as Scully reared. She only heard her mother's words. Staring tearfully at the darting white ears rising up in front of her, she whispered, 'He's *here.*'

Chapter 23

For ten minutes, as the balloon gradually descended, Griff had dismissed all potential landing sites they passed until the Wootton estate came into view. Only the roof of the huge Palladian house was visible among the trees, several hundred square feet of gleaming hipped and ridged lead, edged with intricate balustraded parapets.

'Jesus wept,' he exclaimed. 'That is some spread.'

'Too much woodland,' Neville pointed out, eyeing the fuel gauges worriedly. 'We'll need to get clear of that. Let's not lose any more height. My team will have to try to contact the landowners.'

While Neville got on the radio to discuss the options with his crew, Griff admired the scale and splendour of Wootton in its densely wooded parkland. This would be a trial run, he decided. Then, as soon as he was fully licensed, he could wait for the same weather conditions and return alone.

'We can't land here,' Neville reported, coming off the radio and immediately firing up the burner, which Griff had neglected. 'There's a special request out from the landowner for privacy today. The local airfield should have notified you when you contacted them.'

'Should they?' Griff asked innocently, still gazing at the house, imagining the satisfaction of planting the recordings of Cloud Man in Mia Devonshire's jewellery box before slipping away unnoticed.

'We need to be over a thousand feet.' Neville triggered the burner again, then cursed as the balloon failed to rise, forced down by a strong thermal column that was edging it back towards the river, even lower this time so that the basket was just metres above the treetops.

'They can't stop us making an emergency landing, surely?' Griff studied the fuel gauge and realised it was perilously low. 'What about that field?' He pointed at a swathe of emerald pasture beyond the woodland, dotted with a few old trees but otherwise empty and inviting. 'There're no power cables and it looks as though there's a public lane running along the far side.'

'We have to try to put down safely,' Neville agreed, looking out across the tree canopy. 'We should just make it.'

Shielded in dusky evening shade beneath the trees, the wedding guests were oblivious to the hot-air balloon just beyond the wood, its roaring burners muffled by the leafy canopy as the string quartet and hubbub of conversation filled the glade.

Standing by the pergola at the riverside, which afforded them a clear view upstream, Dougie and his best man Mills watched with interest as it edged along just a few yards above the trees.

'You don't suppose it's a late guest, do you?' Dougie suggested idly.

'Perhaps it's Leo.'

'At least that might hurry Iris along.' He yawned and rolled his head on his neck to loosen stiff muscles. 'Where the bloody hell is she? My father's going to start picking off my stepmothers with a catapult in a minute.'

Disgraced political *roué* Vaughan Everett was not in the best of moods, having found himself sharing a row of seats with three of his four ex-wives, all of whom hated him. Dougie's stepmothers had all accepted their wedding invitations, even though they had no contact with Vaughan or his eldest son. To Dougie, that proved their contemptibility: they had grasped the excuse to dress up and gawp at the Devonshires' pile. His own mother was the only former Mrs Vaughan Everett not there, preferring to stay hidden in her villa in the south of France, from which she'd rarely strayed since a botched facelift three years earlier.

The guests were restless, sensing trouble. When there was a startled, throaty cry from the front row they strained forward excitedly, but Jacinta had nodded off in her wheelchair and woken with such a start that her hat had fallen off. It landed on Iris's Maltese terriers, which were on her lap. They attacked it furiously, then, hearing a roar behind the trees, sprang to the ground and charged into the woods.

The bored guests perked up as Mia made her way to her seat, a blade of tear-streaked tension in beautifully tailored rust silk, her burnished hair pinned neatly beneath a pillbox hat.

'Stop texting, Daddy,' hissed Kitty. 'It's kicking off.'

Far behind them came a trumpeting whinny and Simon craned round once more as Esculter clattered out from beneath the Wootton stable yard's arch, marching on to the grass, high knee action like a can-can dancer. Neck arched and nostrils flaring, he began to jog, performing the classical *passage*, a slow-motion trot, his dark eyes gleaming with touches of white.

'Beautiful!' Dougie breathed rapturously as Iris came into view.

'Looks likely to bolt at any moment,' muttered his best man.

'My bride or the horse?' drawled Dougie, thinking he'd never seen Iris look more ravishing.

Iris was almost as pale as the silver-coated stallion. She rode across the ornate lawns and into the arcade of chestnuts that led to the water's edge. Guests leaned away warily as the stallion bounded past, snorting with every stride, the heat and tension seeming to shimmer off his body. Halfway along the aisle, Iris reined him back and looked around the guests, her green eyes moving from one face to another.

Watching her over his children's heads, his squirming twin daughters on his knees, Simon was surprised to see her so unsmiling. Laney always maintained that the one positive thing from the unfortunate Devonshire crisis was that Iris was so loopily, giddily and happily in love. But today she was as stony-faced and tense as her mother.

Then he raised a quizzical eyebrow as those vivid green eyes counted their way down his row. Finding his face there, Iris stopped and stared. Smiling encouragingly, he gave a discreet thumbs-up, but Iris carried on staring at him.

'Why's she looking at you like that, Dad?' whispered Teddy.

'Have you nicked the ring or something?' chuckled Louis.

'She probably just wants you to put your phone away,' muttered Kitty, hugely embarrassed that her father was holding up the wedding even more as Iris stared at him in that freaky way. Other guests were turning to peer at them now.

Simon's smile was fixed as he tried for a double thumbs-up. On his lap, the twins waved excitedly. And suddenly, breaking into a ravishing smile at last, Iris gave a thumbs-up in return.

At this, Scully let out a deafeningly shrill call and bounded forwards into a crab-like canter. Iris barely shifted in the saddle as she regained control, but it meant that she arrived at the makeshift altar rather more speedily than she'd intended, like an eager Pony Clubber racing for the line at a gymkhana.

While the registrar and the best man jumped nervously backwards into the pergola, Dougie stood his ground as Iris pulled up in a perfect four-square halt in front of him, gazing down with total devotion.

Wootton's head groom Vicente was on hand to take Scully, but just as the young Spaniard stepped forward to reach for the reins, a dark shadow fell across the clearing as the hot-air balloon loomed into view between the trees. It let out a long, roaring blast.

Scully was a brave horse, but he had just been forced to stand in front of the mares' boxes for the best part of half an hour while tearful, fearful Mia – normally his calm champion – talked to the girl on his back, a wait that had revved up his heart and hormones to melting point. Now he'd been ridden to the waterside to face a mythical beast. His nerves couldn't take it. Going swiftly into reverse, he began to turn on his haunches to flee, catching his leg on a flowered archway as he did so and bringing it down. As guests screamed and leapt away, he reared back and practically sat down, trapping the long skirt behind his hind legs so that Iris was dragged backwards from the saddle.

The balloon basket was almost trailing in the river now as its burner fired again and again to try to gain height. When it finally drew in line with the long clearing in the woods it caught an updraught that hoisted it clear of the water and propelled it towards the bank, on a collision course with the pergola. The best man and the registrar jumped out. Then, finding themselves inches from Scully's flailing front legs, they dived in opposite directions.

Vicente and Mia were trying to separate horse and bride before one crushed the other, but the dress was tangled beneath flailing hoofs, yanking Iris with it. Scully was desperate to get away, bellowing with fear. Quick-thinking Iris was ripping at the skirt to escape from it, but just as she'd almost managed to free her legs, the balloon smashed into the pergola and brought it crashing down. Scully reared back, still dragging her with him and cannoning into Vicente, who fell between two rows of recently vacated chairs.

At last Dougie saw fit to make his heroic move as he calmly stepped forward and reached out for a rein. 'Whoa. Stand still! Whoa, old chap.'

He'd handled horses all his life and, for a moment, Scully regarded him with something close to equine relief before his dark eyes bulged with white rims again as he gaped at the huge basket lurching towards the back of Dougie's head.

Iris saw it too as she scrabbled out of her skirts and screamed, 'Let go of the reins and duck!'

The last thing she remembered of her wedding day was Dougie's incredulous expression as he said, 'My darling Iris, don't you know that they teach you out hunting *never* to let go of the—'

Chapter 24

'Can you *believe* Daddy had his phone with him throughout and didn't take a single picture?' Kitty lamented at her stepmother. 'I think he was tweeting non-stop.'

'Deplorable behaviour,' Laney agreed distractedly, opening the oven to check on the crackling and almost searing her eyebrows off as a blast of heat burst out. She had yet to master Red Gables' vast industrial gas range, which had once catered for fifty little wannabe actors and was far too much for their own family needs, but which they couldn't afford to replace. She thought enviously of Mia's custom-sprayed remote-control Aga, which had barely heated a croissant in its life.

Laney was the one who always insisted that the family should gather around a table together for formal weekend lunches, particularly when Simon's children stayed, yet every time she wondered afterwards where her demented grace-saying, shoulder-jogging *Waltons* aspirations had come from. She knew sibling rivalry, fussy eating, furtive texting and sniggering was all they would get. Simon always backed her up nobly with a beautiful table setting, patriarchal joint-carving and much witty if sarcastic repartee, but he and she would still end up sniping at each other, usually after too much wine. Laney was starting to suspect that it might be kinder to send the kids to McDonald's and carry on bickering, eating and drinking without them. Not that she felt remotely hungry, even though the kitchen was filling with the mouth-watering smell of roast pork. The little Korean pills were having an amazing effect, although her concentration had dwindled in direct relation to her appetite.

Today she was doubly distracted. She knew she should be worrying about poor battered Iris, who was still in hospital being patched up, but Kitty's reports of Simon's furtive phone-fiddling at the disaster-struck wedding were getting under her skin, just as they were intended to, and she was also juggling dozens of quick-fire, needy calls from Mia, which ran along the lines of 'She's just gone into X-ray again. Can you call Lito and let her know? I'll cry if I do – I can only talk to you,' and 'Have you seen the *Sunday News*? Bloody Dougie's all over it and not because of what happened yesterday. We mustn't tell Iris yet.' She fretted about the animals too, all the dogs at Wootton that hadn't been walked, and Scully, who was now lame and shaken: 'Charlie Soames just called to say that he might not be sound for the quadrille at the charity gala, but I can't bring myself to think about that when Iris has a crushed leg.'

The phone started ringing again as Laney was trying to make gravy, the chrome splashbacks all around her acting like an unflattering hall of mirrors to reflect her pink hair and matching pink, hot face. Holding the phone to her sweaty ear, she stirred the lumps in the roasting pan with her free hand and used her knees to keep the dogs away.

'That bloody idiot man in the hot-air balloon who tried to kill my daughter' – Mia was breathless with indignation – 'Iris thinks I hired him! Can you *believe* it? And I've only just found out the police released him without charge last night saying it was an accidental landing and he wasn't paparazzi after all. But I'm sure Simon said he recognised him. Is he there? Can you ask him?'

'He's outside with the boys. How's Iris?'

'It seems her leg's not broken after all, thank goodness. She's got a hairline fracture to one ankle and a grade-three MCL tear, whatever that is.'

'One up from grade-two flute, one down from grade-four

piano,' Laney joked, gravy pan spinning as she tried to stir a bubbling black caramel. 'Are they keeping her in much longer?'

'Another night at least – they have to keep an eye on the concussion. I suppose I should go home but—' She gasped as a thought struck her. 'What if Dougie tries to get in here to see her? She's desperate to talk to him. Should I show her the piece in the *Sunday News*?'

'No!' Laney had gleaned enough from their fractured calls to know that Mia's revelation about Dougie had come at precisely the wrong time. Mother–daughter relations were hardly going to be helped by a sordid tabloid exposé.

'I can't *believe* she won't even bloody talk to me. I don't want to go home. Wootton is full of house-guests who don't know what to do with themselves. Lito's having a whale of a time telling everybody that she's going to die and explaining exactly how she wants her funeral conducted.'

'Come to lunch here,' Laney found herself offering.

'How can you possibly think I could eat at a time like this?'

'Nobody apart from Simon will put fork to lips, so you'll be in good company.'

'Oh, God, she's brought dogs,' Simon groaned as he watched Mia park her car.

'How many?'

'I can count at least four but they're not the big drooling buggers.' He threw open the front doors. 'Mia! Poor, poor baby. Welcome! How's Iris?'

'I hope you don't mind me bringing a few of the little ones, but when I popped home to change just now, they were all cooped up.' Mia's voice wobbled, but her tears were rigidly contained for the sake of the Demons' children.

As soon as she was through the door, she abandoned her pack of dogs and scooped up Hope in delight. 'My little chunky monkey! I brought you sweets and presents!' Then she spotted

Simon's twins, just six months older than Hope, and shrieked delightedly, stooping to gather them into her embrace.

Mia's love of children had never diminished in all the years the friends had known one another; if animals were her comforters, small children were her dream catchers.

Holding up a brace of miniature terriers to stop them mauling the Labradors or each other, Simon sidled up to Laney and whispered, 'Is this really wise? She looks terribly wound up. D'you want to take her somewhere quiet to talk instead?'

'You know Mia. She'll just keep putting on the show until she's ready.'

'I thought Leo was coming back,' he muttered. 'What in hell's he up to?'

'No idea.' They exchanged a familiar look. 'Shall we fish?'

He nodded. 'Rods out, darling.'

There was a thundering of feet on the stairs as Simon's older boys staged an appearance for the first time that day amid much blushing, hair-flicking and shrugging, pulling at the hems of their T-shirts and saying a shy hello. Mia was a knock-out to teens as well as tots.

'Wow! You two are looking sooo dishy! Where is ravishing Kitty? There you are!' She beamed upwards as Kitty scuffed shyly downstairs, wearing her best sparkly leggings and lip-gloss to impress. 'That dress yesterday was the one bright spot in an otherwise very black day. Come and give me a *huuuuge* hug.'

With a captive audience for her Keep Calm and Carry On act, Mia wasn't about to let the mask slip. Today the consummate actress was playing children's entertainer, eager to garner approval in the wake of her only child's hostility.

For the next hour Laney seasoned, mashed, tossed, served, cleared and forced a bright smile as the family lunch passed with more conviviality and laughter than any she could remember. Left too long, the meat was as tough as rhino hide and the gravy like heatwave tarmac, but Kitty and the boys didn't complain and

Simon ate his way through three helpings, poured lashings of wine, which only he drank, and complimented everything wildly. Increasingly hyper, Mia ate practically nothing as she chattered and joked, mostly about her upcoming gala. It was as though the previous day was a minor cloud passing through life's sunshine.

'I think I'll go to Spain for a couple of days to escape the media interest,' she told them. 'Haff's lined up some horses for me to see. I want the stallion quadrille to be a real showstopper and all my celebrity wives are signed up in principle, so I need to mount them beautifully.'

At this Simon fought giggles. Trying to keep a straight face, he asked, 'Is Haff that amazing little chap we met at Sueño who looks like Danny Trejo in breeches?'

Mia was affronted. 'Juan-Felipe Javiero has represented Spain in the Olympics three times and was one of the most senior riders in the Fundación Real Escuela Andaluza del Arte Ecuestre. He is an artist on horseback.'

When Simon looked blank, Laney explained, 'That's the Spanish Riding School in Jerez. We went there after the sherry-tasting. You spent the first half of the show singing along with the music, then fell asleep.'

'Ah, yes, I remember. Men in headscarves and funny doughnut hats trotting around in a big sports hall.'

'The hats are called *calañés*,' Mia explained haughtily. 'They are both traditional and practical.'

'Are you going to make your footballers' wives wear them at the gala?' Laney caught Simon's eye.

'Perhaps Leo could knit them.' Simon snorted with laughter. 'We'll flog them in the auction afterwards ... or better still, sell Haffle tickets to win one.'

Mia was looking mutinous so they put on serious faces, and Laney asked, 'What does Leo make of it all?'

'He's all for showcasing what the inner-city dressage school will be teaching talented youngsters,' she said smoothly, bright smile back in place. 'It's great publicity, and we'll donate the horses to the school afterwards.'

'I was talking about the wedding.'

Mia swallowed uncomfortably, the smile wavering. 'He's quietly relieved it didn't go ahead, of course, but terribly worried about Iris. We both are.'

'Will you take her with you to Spain?' asked Simon.

'That's what I wanted, but she says she can't possibly travel yet. She'll be on crutches and need physiotherapy, but she insists I must go.'

The Demons exchanged glances, guessing that Iris had more or less ordered her mother to stay away.

'Who's looking after her while you're gone? Is Leo coming back?' Laney asked hopefully.

'Chloe's arranged to finish her placement early – I think she feels rather guilty for deliberately staying away yesterday. I only wish Leo were showing such contrition.' Her eyes flashed. 'Perhaps if I put him in the auction catalogue as the final lot, he'll demand some time off. He could never resist top billing.'

'Does that make you the final Lot's wife?' Simon topped up his wine.

She looked at him, unblinking. 'I never look back, Demon. You of all people should know that. Let's offer him with no reserve.'

Simon had agreed to conduct the charity auction that year, always a highlight at the Wootton Gala, its catalogue inevitably packed with luxury donated lots, from the best opera tickets to days at the races and lunch at the Plump Poussin.

'I always prefer people with plenty of reserve,' he said carefully, glancing at Laney again, but she was still watching Mia worriedly, sensing the façade starting to crack.

'Perhaps I'll just auction his passport,' Mia rattled on. 'What d'you think, Laney?'

'I'd go for a piece of knitting,' she ventured. 'Safer.' She could see Mia's lip wobbling as the unhappiness started to break through the surface. Simon saw it too and the Demons' invisible fishing rods were put away.

As soon as pudding was cleared, he tactfully ushered the children outside so Laney could gather her friend in her arms.

'I'm sorry I'm being so uptight!' Mia sobbed. 'I'm s-so relieved the wedding didn't happen, but there's nothing I can say to Iris to convince her it wasn't my fault and she's so terribly upset. The only way I can persuade her to come home is to get out of the way. That's why I'm going to Spain.'

Over her shoulder, Laney could see two of the terriers shredding Simon's best shoes, but said nothing. Mia so rarely dropped her mask that she wasn't about to give her the opportunity to pick it up.

'You really didn't have anything to do with what happened yesterday?'

Mia laughed through her tears. 'Oh Laney, if I had, you know no horses would have got hurt and I'd have staged it a lot better. It was such a mess. Now, not only is Iris convinced I hired the balloonist to deliberately land on us all, but she has this crazy idea that Dom was there to witness it ... ' She pulled back and looked up at her guiltily, green eyes searching. 'Laney, I keep meaning to say something to you, but I'm frightened it will hurt you.'

'Anything.' Laney smiled nervously, certain she was going to bring up the night she'd spent with Simon all those years ago. 'I need to hear the truth.'

'That hair colour is absolutely awful.'

Chapter 25

'I came as fast as I could. This had better be good. Three hundred chickens are depending on me.' Chloe blustered into the hospital room and dumped a service-station bag crammed with chocolates and newspapers on to Iris's bed, making her howl. 'Sorry.' She moved it, pushing her dark glasses to the top of her head and peering at her friend. 'You look pretty good.'

Fragile and wild-haired, Iris's golden colouring and mint-green eyes contrasted absurdly well with the toothpaste-blue hospital blankets. But she always looked exquisite, even with dark circles under red-rimmed eyes.

'I've been crying all night.'

'It suits you. Gives your face some colour. Any word from Dougie?'

'About a million texts, but he's stopped now they're giving him an MRI scan. They transferred him to Oxford last night because there was no bed here. He's got one hell of a lump on his head and blurred vision and is claiming partial amnesia, which handily dates back to last weekend. And I know whatever the papers have raked up is dirty, but I can't get past the *Sunday News* pay-wall on my phone and now the battery's run out and I don't have my charger here. Nobody will tell me a bloody thing. They're behaving like I'm a feeble-minded loon in a sanatorium. Mum did her "What's a newspaper?" act. God, I *so* hate her for what she's done.' Her small hands clenched into tight fists.

She was still wearing her engagement ring, Chloe noticed, its ruby enormous, like a fat blood blister. She'd never heard Iris speak of her mother angrily, and she already knew that there was a better target for Iris's fury, but was none the less a wary messenger, bracing herself to duck bullets as she pulled the tabloid from her plastic bag and laid it on the arched frame that was protecting her friend's injured leg like a poly-tunnel. 'It's not great reading.'

Iris picked it up with a cry of horror as she read the headline. 'Oh God, he *paid* someone for sex!'

'She's called Jodie Field.' Chloe had already Googled the situation comprehensively. 'She's a friend of Milligan's – no surprise there. There are lots of injunctions out preventing stories, but the press all know who Jodie is and watch her comings and goings.'

'Coming being what it's all about.' Iris sighed miserably. 'She's a high-class hooker, isn't she?'

'She wouldn't put it like that, but yes.' Chloe was laying into the chocolates she'd brought. 'She calls herself a sex therapist to the stars. If they have a droopy willy or a bit of a fetish they go to see her. It's all over Twitter. Dougie was papped visiting her two nights before the wedding.'

'If she's a friend of Mills then she could be a friend of Dougie's too?' Iris suggested desperately.

Chloe shook her head, munching a comforting truffle. 'He was with her all night, and the "source close to Miss Field" goes into some very specific detail. My guess is that another client got the gossip about Dougie's masochism thing and saw a way of screwing the boy screwing Purple.'

'Could you put that more gently?' Iris closed her reddened eyes and sagged back in the pillows, then snapped one eye open again. 'What "masochism thing"?'

'That's on Twitter too.' Chloe pulled her phone from her pocket. 'You really don't need to fork out two quid on newsprint these days. It's been trending since the early hours. Look.'

Iris read a few of the posts under #Purplewedding and groaned, casting the phone aside. 'It's all made up. God, I need more painkillers. I have to talk to him. This is all my bloody mother's fault!'

'You can't really believe that?'

'Of course I do! Everything was orchestrated and carefully timed, right up to the long delay in letting me ride down to the river, pouring her heart out about Dad, and my real father being there at the wedding. Then she accused Dougie of trying to get off with her. She was improvising because she knew the balloon was going to be a few minutes late. I'll never forgive her.'

'I'm sure you can't control hot-air balloons that strategically,' Chloe said pragmatically. 'Where can I get a coffee round here? I've been up since five.'

'There's a machine somewhere near Cardiology.' Iris rubbed her aching head. 'My mother had a hissy fit when she found the decaff wasn't Fairtrade. She and Dad have been in cahoots over this, believe me. Dad has Hollywood's best stunt coordinators on his side. That balloonist was a total plant.' She pushed the tabloids away.

Chloe pocketed her phone and gathered up the paper, which had fallen open at the horoscopes. She scanned Iris's sign, knowing how much store her friend set by these things. 'Apparently Sagittarians are ready for some me-time.'

'You can say that again.'

Chloe closed the paper and scrunched it under one arm. 'You have to hand it to Psychic Phoenix. She was pretty bats, but she got her prediction right. "Look to the sky," she said.'

'Trust me, she was a part of the conspiracy,' Iris said darkly.

Chloe tried to recall everything the hen-party entertainer had said. 'What did he look like, the balloonist? Don't tell me he was dark and handsome with a limp and an arrow-shaped scar?'

Iris scrunched her eyes shut, trying to remember the features that she'd seen directly above Dougie's beautiful face as the balloon basket had listed forward to crown him. It had only been a split second's glimpse, but it was a face she found hard to forget, shadowy and smoky-eyed, with inky, razored hair, falcon-beak nose and straight dark brows. He'd looked every inch the hit-man. If she saw him again, she'd scream her head off.

She was starting to feel the tell-tale clammy foretaste of a pain spike. 'Can you ask one of the nurses if my analgesia's due while you're out there?'

Griff limped along the hospital corridor with a large bouquet of cornflowers, peonies and lavender as camouflage. He'd smashed a few toes in the emergency landing, his foot trapped against a propane canister when the basket tipped.

While waiting for a space in the hospital car park, he'd put in a call to Neville, who was unforgiving. His balloon was shredded and his piloting reputation on the line. 'I'm the laughing stock of the Chilterns ballooning community, Mr Donne. The police had me detained for almost three hours. Believe me, you'll never get your PPL in this country. You are a liability and a danger.'

Now he had an even tougher call to make, but this one he knew he had to do in person. He'd got to issue a very big, heartfelt apology and try to rescue his reconnaissance mission, most especially correct one disastrous oversight, and he had no time to lose. Visiting hours were almost over. Griff's ability to talk his way through war-torn border patrols, illegal roadblocks and circles of spear-pointing tribesmen had nothing on the reception desk of a large NHS teaching hospital, but he was finally within sight of his quarry. He pushed his way into Room D376.

'Please don't throw me out. My name is Griff. I have to explain how sorry I am.' He lowered the flowers and smiled charmingly.

Hands aloft in an almost evangelical welcome, an elderly man was regarding him in tearful confusion from beneath a metropolis of tubes, vents, drips and bleeping apparatus. 'Griff! Son! Have you come to take me home?'

Plonking the flowers at the foot of the bed and smiling nervously, Griff retreated hastily, backing straight into a figure emerging from the room opposite and causing her to drop the newspaper she was carrying, its pages fanning across the floor.

'Here – sorry – let me.' He gathered it up.

Short and stocky with wild bedsprings hair, she shot him an irritable look and stalked away. 'Keep it.'

Peering into Room D377, Griff saw a haze of streaky rust hair and experienced a chest-kick of relief and trepidation. 'Please don't throw me out. I have to explain how sorry I am.'

Iris looked up at the man framed in the doorway holding a tabloid, its front and back pages now crumpled in a way that made her fiancé look as though he was lying beneath Wayne Rooney.

She would have screamed very loudly indeed, had her painkillers not bottomed out to such a degree that her injured knee was exploding. She reached for her call button but dropped it on its wire. The pain of reaching for it again made her almost pass out.

He was across the room in a flash, despite a pronounced limp. Clearly thinking she wanted to call Security to throw him out, he took it and held it away from her.

'Please don't be angry with me,' he said in a soft Welsh accent, his voice urgent and apologetic. 'I'm learning to fly a balloon and these things are completely random. I will try to make it up to you in any way I can.'

In a cold sweat, Iris eyed him fearfully. She remembered those intense dark eyes only too well, along with the beaked nose and military-short hair. There was a fresh scar on his cheek, a livid gash shaped like an arrow. She gazed at it in amazement.

'I know what happened is tragic for everybody,' he was saying. 'Me included. You see, I lost something when the balloon came down, something *really* important.'

Iris wanted to shout that she had lost something quite important too – the happiest day of her life and her ability to kick him where it hurt right now – but her knee was such torture, she couldn't speak.

He was still holding the scrunched newspaper, she realised, Wayne Rooney's head swallowing Dougie's legs in a perverse Greco-Roman wrestling move.

'Go away and tell my mother to make her own apologies!' she spluttered.

Misunderstanding, he blathered on: 'I will of course apologise to your mother, too, but I can't get close to the house and I must get my flash back. The ground staff say all the balloon-crash debris was cleared away by the crew, but they haven't found the little antelope and neither has Neville, and my laptop was stolen from my car the other night with my life on it, so I need my flash as back-up.'

Iris was battling severe pain and mild delirium, so her concentration was not at its best. As far as she could fathom, the man had been carrying an antelope on the balloon; an antelope called Flash.

God knows what evil plan he and her mother had cooked up between them, using the poor creature to stop her marrying Dougie at the last minute.

Now he had fallen silent and was staring at her in a way that was freaking her out. She could almost swear there were tears in his eyes. 'Why didn't I realise? You're so like him, so incredibly like him.'

With an almighty effort, she sat up and grabbed the alarm cord, wrestling it from his grip and sinking her palm down on it with a cry of relief.

A moment later, a male nurse appeared at the door with a small plastic beaker of pills, closely followed by Chloe with a steaming coffee.

'Make him go away!' Iris howled, pointing at Griff.

'Let me at least leave you my number.' He looked around for a pen.

'No!' she screamed. 'I never want to see you again. Flash is better off without you! We have wild muntjac at Wootton. He can live with them. At least he can have a happy life!'

The man's dark brows knotted together. 'I don't think you've quite understood—'

'*Go* away!'

The male nurse started to steer him from the room, 'Please don't make me call Security, sir.'

With a final look over his shoulder, the man was gone.

'Who was he?' Chloe took the painkillers from the nurse and looked around for the water jug. 'Seriously good-looking.'

Grabbing the coffee cup, Iris tipped its scalding contents into her mouth to chase down the pills. 'According to the Psychic Phoenix, he should be bringing fortune and the courage of a lion.' She lay back, closing her eyes, face glistening with sweat. 'That means bloody Laney was definitely in on this whole plan too. She predicted all this, remember?'

Chloe let out a gasp of amazement as she registered the truth. 'My *stepmother* was the Psychic Phoenix?'

'Ex-stepmother,' Iris corrected. 'Just as she is now my ex-godmother. And yes, Mum put her up to it.'

'You have to admit she was bloody good.'

Iris opened one eye. 'I thought you loathed her too.'

'It was a terrible thing to do,' Chloe agreed tactfully, but it was clear that her opinion of Laney had changed completely.

Chapter 26

Late the following morning, Dougie sauntered into Room D377 wearing a neck brace and carrying a huge, hand-tied bunch of deepest burgundy roses.

Iris wanted to hate him, but the moment she saw his face her heart gave such a determined beat of loyal happiness that she was certain he could hear it echoing around the room. Those dark-lashed blue eyes regarded her sheepishly, his face so handsome and winning, her old-fashioned, brave-hearted knight, who lived by out-dated feudal rules.

'Poor baby.' He made his way stiffly to her side to take her hand. 'How are you?'

'I'll live.' She snatched it away. 'You?'

'Severe whiplash,' he reported in a martyred voice, sitting down uncomfortably.

'Appropriate, given your proclivities,' she hissed.

'Eh?'

'Jodie Field treated you to a Miss Whiplash session, I gather. It's gone more viral than Legionnaires' in air-conditioning.'

He had the grace to look abashed, fiddling with the raffia tie on the flowers. 'It's not what you think.'

'What *is* it, then? Practising for your wedding night, were you?'

'In a manner of speaking, yes' – he mustered an ill-judged

smile – 'that's *exactly* what I was doing. I was so worried, Riz baby. When I was in LA, I was att – that is, I had a bit of an accident to my todger and I wasn't sure how much the damage had affected my . . . performance. It was bloody painful. A friend said there was a very discreet clinic I could go to . . . I had no idea the sort of service Miss Field offered.'

'From what I hear, it's well known. Couldn't you have talked to *me* about this "accident"?'

'I wanted everything to be perfect.'

'Forgive me, but reading a tabloid report on the morning I should have been waking as your wife that claims you were banging a hooker three days ago is hardly perfect.'

'C'mon, Riz. I'm hardly the first boy who saw out his bachelor days like that.'

She gave an enraged howl. 'And what's all this about masochism? Since when have you had whip marks on your dick?'

His eyebrows shot up. 'They weren't whip marks.'

'What were they? Friction burns?'

'They were . . . nail marks.'

'Whose bloody nail marks?'

He didn't answer.

'*Who*, Dougie?'

'It was after I went to see your father. It happened at his place on Nichols Canyon. I don't remember all the details – I was a bit stoned, to be honest.'

Iris let out a terrified bleat. 'Are you saying Leo was involved?'

He opened his mouth, then closed it again, suddenly seeming undecided what to say. In the end he said nothing, which made Iris even more panic-stricken.

Overwrought, she looked down at her shaking hands, her modest French manicure freshly painted for the wedding and already chipped. There, nestling on her left hand, was the huge ruby engagement ring. She started to pull it from her finger, sobs catching in her throat.

Dougie leapt forward. 'Don't do this, Iris!'

It struck him clean between the eyes, ricocheted to the far side of the room and skittered beside a drip stand.

'It's over!' she screamed. 'I never want to see you again!'

'At least give me a chance!'

'You can go to hell! And you can bloody well leave my father alone! No wonder he didn't want to come home. I've heard of scratching one another's backs, but this is a whole new ball game. All you care about is your career.'

Suddenly Dougie's eyes bulged wide. 'Whoa! You have it ALL wrong, Riz!' A red mark was forming where the ring had caught him, like a bindi. 'I can explain—'

'GET OUT GET OUT GET *OUT*!'

This time, the nurses did have to call Security.

Chapter 27

Iris dreaded going back to Wootton when she was discharged from hospital, and dabbled with the idea of taking up Chloe's invitation to convalesce at her mum's high-tech home high in the Chilterns, a converted windmill known locally as the Obelisk, but she couldn't face Chloe's mother's nosy bossiness, and she wanted to see Lito and the horses.

As it transpired, she found Wootton's wrought-iron gates, high walls and wooded acres a sanctuary. With Mia away, the place was extraordinarily peaceful. All the guests had left bar two aged Spanish cousins, happy to sit on a sunny terrace with Jacinta and talk about her life and her proposed death, which was the only subject on which she currently cared to dwell. She hardly mentioned the wedding. There was no evidence left of the interrupted ceremony, the marquee and walkways cleared away, the chestnut avenue freshly harrowed, mown and rolled to remove any signs of the basket's crash landing.

Only Iris and Scully bore physical scars, she with the ugly blue braces on her knee and ankle, and he with an elegant green stable bandage wrapped around a puffy lower leg. Charlie Soames had called every day to check it personally. 'He says it ees just a strain,' Vicente told her.

'Can you take a look?' Iris asked Chloe when she popped in for her daily visit, weighed down with chocolates as usual. Chloe had no objection: Wootton's fairy-tale courtyard of mare boxes and stallion stalls was always heaven and she relished an opportunity to diagnose.

She asked Vicente to trot Scully out, then totally forgot which leg she was looking at as she admired the Spaniard's taut-breeched bottom. Face flaming, she located a swollen hind leg and examined it for heat and sensitivity.

'Probably nothing more than a strain, but I'd get it scanned if you're really worried. Could be his check ligament,' she hazarded cautiously. She let the stallion's leg back down, straightened and hastily flattened her wild halo of hair as she found herself nose-to-nose with Vicente at Scully's head. He was seriously dishy, Chloe realised faintly, his handsome face both haughty and kind in the unique way of Spanish men.

His dark eyes deepened with worry. 'Then it ees his old injury.'

'Let's get the Lightning Man in,' Iris suggested.

'He's not still alive, is he?' Chloe laughed.

The Lightning Man was a local legend: octogenarian ex-jockey Sandy Cox claimed he had developed an incredible healing touch with horses after being struck by lightning. He'd had some astonishing results with Wootton stock and Mia had once been a big fan, but Charlie had talked her out of it as mumbo-jumbo.

'We could get him over while Mum's in Spain.'

Vicente sucked his lip, clearly reluctant to do anything without Mia's say-so.

Chloe, who saw men like Sandy as no better than the Psychic Phoenix, and considerably less entertaining, shot the groom a sympathetic look. 'I'd keep him on the bute and box rest, and hose the leg daily, and I bet he'll be right in a week. How long's Mia away?'

'Hopefully for ever.'

Chloe wasn't used to such bitterness from Iris. 'You don't mean that.'

'Hmph.' Iris moved across the flagged yard with a clatter of crutches to say hello to head-bobbing Lorca. 'She's buying lots of horses.'

'That's exciting.'

'It's a waste of money if she thinks it'll make those stupid bitches in her quadrille ride any better. They're only in it because they're married to rich or famous men. Most of them have got such huge fake boobs they'll knock themselves out in the first sitting trot.'

Iris had come back from hospital in a very bad mood indeed, Chloe decided. She was crying a lot, which was understandable, but the waspish comments were new and worrying.

'The horses are going to be part of the specialist dressage centre for underprivileged kids, helping teach them all the high-school stuff,' Iris was saying, her pretty face focused as she concentrated on the bigger picture. 'Haff's found a yard just outside the City. It's his baby. He's only here three or four times a year, but he's bringing a couple of young guys over from Spain to run it. Mum's the trustee and the Devonshire Foundation's putting up the dosh. The gala's raising funds for that this year.'

Chloe was impressed, but Iris clearly thought it was doomed to failure if Mia was steering it. 'Mum should stick to battered pets and endangered species. It's what she really understands. She gets bored easily with kids, regardless of their privilege. Thank God she only had me.'

'Your mother loves children!'

'It's her tragedy that I've grown up.'

233

Chloe saw no point in arguing any more so she suggested they join Lito and her cousins on the terrace, where they were drinking *vino de mesa* made from the family's own vines. They spoke in Spanish, so she understood very little, but she was relieved to see the expression soften on Iris's face until eventually she nodded off, strong painkillers and an overload of emotion wiping her out.

For several days Iris hid at Wootton, crying a great deal. When venturing out of her rooms, she spent a lot of time with Lito, and with Chloe when she visited, resisting her friend's attempts to get her further than the Wootton boundaries, even if it was just uphill across the fields on a quad bike to have lunch at the Obelisk. 'Your mother is an amazing person, Chloe, but she's so overwhelmingly into positive thinking. I really can't face her right now.'

'I get your point.' Chloe sighed. 'I can't face her right now either. Why d'you think I'm spending all my time here?' She'd brought a pile of textbooks with her to go through that day. 'I get no peace at home. Mum has so little to occupy her mind, she keeps trying to interest me in ladies' lunches and pampering sessions. Now my placement's over, she wants us to go on holiday to a shamanic-drumming detox retreat in Vermont before a shopping blitz in New York. I told her I have a perfect retreat, including retail therapy, here with you.'

'Retail therapy?'

'I stop off at the petrol station for chocolate every time I drive here.' Chloe pulled a Crunchie wrapper from beneath the books on her lap. She was putting on weight away from the gruelling placements. 'My ruddy metabolism is slower than a croc's heart rate,' she complained now. 'God, I must exercise.'

'We were going to ride all over Europe,' Iris remembered sadly. 'You can ride Lorca here, if you like. He's bored stiff.'

'No thanks.' Chloe returned to her textbook. 'I like a steady Eddie, whether four-legged or two-. I don't share your taste in hotheaded horses or men. How many messages today?'

Iris looked at her phone. 'Eight.'

Dougie was making unabashed attempts to woo his fiancée back. Local florists were doing a roaring trade in bouquets, as was the nearby old people's home, which benefited when Iris refused to have them in the house. He also left long, rambling voicemail messages. He now seemed to be blaming the entire battle-scarred-manhood thing on a drunken encounter with an aloe bush in Nichols Canyon.

'He's a fantasist,' Chloe insisted coolly, studying a chapter on small-mammal castration. 'Who dick-whips an aloe vera? I know he's a public schoolboy, and most of the ones I know will get the heirloom out on the flimsiest excuse to bat a bread roll around at a rugby dinner, but not vegetation on a public highway. Besides, aloe is a natural antiseptic.'

'I don't want to know,' Iris insisted. She'd said nothing to her father, who was still working fifteen-hour shifts. The studio had been forced to reshoot an episode on what was supposed to be his day off, so he barely had time to eat, sleep and learn each new script. He sent regular jokey messages to cheer her up and she sent back rows of kisses.

Meanwhile, Dougie's texts and emails were ever more pleading and drunken, his measures increasingly desperate. He had even allowed 'friends' to talk to the press, which won him no sympathy from Iris or others. Protestations of his utter despair were splashed all over the tabloids today, along with papped photographs of him looking artfully sad. Commentators shared the universal sense of relief that Purple was single again. Rumour rumbled that the entire engagement had been a publicity stunt, and social networks were still trending on the story.

This irritated Iris enormously. 'I hate the wall of Chinese whispers. Why keep the wedding totally private if this was a publicity stunt? There were no press there and only a few close friends.'

Those close friends were the only network that she was interested in, and her phone screen took a constant barrage of tapping activity as she kept up a daily dialogue with her inner circle, who knew how much this was hurting her.

She refused to answer Dougie's messages and ignored all calls and texts from her mother.

'Why should I talk to her? She and bloody Laney ruined everything for me.'

'Some would say you had a lucky escape,' Chloe said, frustrated by Iris's anger, which she felt should be directed entirely at Dougie. 'Go to university like you planned, fill that clever mind, empty your heavy heart, shag a few Law students. Works for me.' She knew that 'shag a few' was a gross misrepresentation of her one-night stand with drunk Josh, who hadn't even remembered her name afterwards.

But Iris remained unimpressed. 'Didn't work for my mother. She got pregnant in her first year, remember.'

'We have better contraception now.' Chloe watched her friend's set profile, well aware that she was dwelling on the circumstances of her conception again. 'And better DNA tests.'

'What if my birth father really *was* at the wedding?' she whispered. Her eyes suddenly stretched as wide as saucers. 'God, you don't think he's Vaughan Everett, do you?'

'Euch!' Both girls shared a horrified look.

'Can't be.' Chloe shuddered. 'Your mother would have pulled more than that balloon stunt to stop the wedding if he was.'

'Laney knows the truth, but she won't tell.' Iris sighed. 'She and Mum have always kept each other's secrets.'

'Like us.'

'Not telling anybody that you once laughed so much that you wet yourself in the back of our car is hardly on a scale with this.'

For two days, Iris had avoided going anywhere near the boathouse or being seen from it. She knew Laney was there each day, and from her bedroom window she could sometimes see the light on late at night as her godmother put in her usual crazy work hours, slotted around childcare and Simon's schedule. Laney had taken to cycling to Wootton along the riverbank from Burley, crossing the bridge at Hocking Lock and wobbling through the water meadows on her purple mountain bike, trusty laptop in the basket.

Spending so much time with Chloe should have made it easy to demonise her godmother, but Chloe had been surprisingly reluctant to ridicule Laney of late, and Iris felt mildly ashamed about her simmering resentment, aware that she should tackle the impasse. It was her best opportunity to find out the truth about the scuppered wedding and, more importantly, grill Laney again on what she knew about her birth father.

When the opportunity presented itself, however, she flunked it. Three days after she'd come out of hospital, Iris was hobbling through the vegetable garden on her crutches, intent on pulling some carrots to take to Scully and Lorca, when her Maltese terriers let out a flurry of excited barks and she saw the Demons' black Labradors bounding up. Now she could hear Laney's voice, Simon's drawl and Hope's chatter beyond the wall. They were heading to the house, no doubt to check on her at Mia's behest.

Chloe had headed to the Cotswolds to meet up with a university friend at a game fair so Iris was on her own that morning and feeling at her most antisocial. She hopped as fast as she could towards the potting shed behind the runner-bean frames.

This was one of Franco's secret lairs, filled with the smell of black tobacco smoke and compost. Wootton's elderly plantsman was a distant relative of Leo's and ferociously proud of his work, most especially his precious topiary. Answering only to Mia – whom he adored – he was not averse to chasing any other member of the household off a newly seeded lawn or away from a sprayed bed with a sharp-pronged rake. At this time of year, with everything in full bloom and the big gala coming up, he was at his most insufferable.

The potting shed was immaculately tidy, its benches groaning with trays of seedlings and the shelves with plant pots arranged in height order.

Peering through the dusty window to see if she could spot the Demons through the beans, Iris noticed a little antelope carving sitting on the sill.

She picked it up and studied it. There was a tiny clip on its back where it had clearly once hung from something – a necklace perhaps? But it looked too big. It had a seam in the middle like a secret box. She tugged at the ends and let out a squeak of surprise when it came apart to reveal a USB connector, the last thing she'd expected from a little wooden ornament in a dusty potting shed.

'You break it!' hissed an accusing voice, making her drop it in alarm.

Franco was shorter than Iris and just as slight, but his body had the gnarled decrepitude of an ancient vine compared to her sapling straightness. He wheezed like a leaking tyre as he bent over to retrieve the two pieces of the flash drive, eyebrows shooting up as he spotted the high-tech wizardry inside. 'It is spy bug?' He held it at arm's length.

'You don't know what it is?'

'I find by river the day of … that is, after …' He avoided her gaze.

'When the balloon came down?' Suddenly she remembered her bizarre conversation in hospital with the dark-eyed balloonist who claimed he'd lost an antelope called Flash.

Franco was creasing his deeply lined brow. 'I thought was just lucky charm,' he confessed. 'You know what it is?'

'A secret weapon.' Iris reclaimed it, propping herself up against a bench to relieve her weight-bearing leg as she slotted the drive back together. 'Can I take it?'

He nodded. 'I no want spy bug.' Then he jerked his head towards the garden. 'People look for you. They walk over my herbs. Señora de Montmorency with the pink hair, she is one of them. I tell them go away.'

'Thank you, Franco.' She surprised him with a ravishing smile, her first in many days. 'You did the right thing.'

*

Back in the house, Iris slotted the flash drive into her computer, but its files were password-protected and no amount of random guess-work would yield access. She didn't even know the balloonist's name, she realised, remembering the intensity with which he had looked at her. He'd said his life was on the little flash drive. Now his life was in her hands, but she had no idea who he was. Pulling it from the slot, she threaded it through one of the tassels of her Fossil bag to secure it there. It would just have to serve as a lucky charm after all. When her mother got home, she might interrogate her about the hired wedding crasher, but for now she was more interested in getting Dougie off her back.

She still couldn't shake the memory of him saying that an inci-dent at her father's house had led him to Jodie Field. She knew she should face the truth and speak with Leo, but it was well past mid-night in LA and, even with his punishing schedule, he would be in bed at this hour. She sent him a text asking him to call when he had time, then limped to the stables to see the horses and take photographs of them to text him, which she knew he would love. Just as she was trying to get Scully to pose with a carrot in his mouth, like Groucho Marx with his cigar, a message came through from Dougie.

Flying to LAX, she read. Call me when you're ready to talk.

She wandered back to the house, jumpy now, seeking reassur-ance. Tracked by her Maltese terriers, she went to her parents' rooms, conjoined by their huge shared dressing space. Most of the wardrobes were packed to capacity; Leo in particular hated throwing anything out. From previous forages, Iris knew there were vintage designer treats behind almost every door. She also knew that there were secrets in the highest cupboards, which was where she went now, her little white dogs watching her curiously from the peacock-green silk button-back chair in one corner as she balanced on a stool and reached down a stash of boxes marked OLD GATE.

Chapter 28

Mia arrived back from Spain looking magnificent, her burnished mane sun-streaked, skin golden and foxglove-freckled, the dark bags erased from beneath sparkling green eyes. Recharged, empowered and de-stressed, she was ready to organise the biggest and best charity gala ever for the Devonshire Foundation.

Her unremittingly positive frame of mind had taken a great deal of self-control and she was hurt that Iris had replied to none of her many calls or texts, but she hoped that they would be able to talk now that her daughter had had more time to realise what a lucky escape she'd had.

She was mortified, therefore, to be greeted by tight-lipped disapproval at home.

'Dad doesn't work crazy hours just so you can buy pretty horses for footballers' wives to pose about on at a garden party!' Iris railed when Mia showed off the photographs of her new stallions on her iPad, hopeful that they could bond over their mutual love of Spanish horses.

'They're for the Javiero Dressage Coaching Centre,' she explained, but Iris remained unforgiving.

'Inner-city kids don't need fifty-thousand-euro Carthusian stallions!'

At least her daughter was talking to her again, Mia comforted herself, albeit in a shouty way, but Iris flatly refused to be drawn on the subject of Dougie and the wedding: 'It still hurts too much. You know what you did.'

Powering noisily into the kitchen on her electric wheelchair to hijack the uncomfortable reunion, Jacinta was no less furious with her daughter-in-law: 'You abandon us all alone here after that terrible day!'

'I've been away less than a week.' Mia felt all her positivity drop-ping away. 'Iris wanted me out of the way. Besides, you've had half the Ormero family here – Sueño was deserted when I was there.'

'You are needed here.' Jacinta narrowed her eyes. 'You must organise everything.'

'I know.' She perked up. 'I've called a gala committee meeting for this—'

'Not the gala. My funeral. You are being very selfish, Mia, very selfish.'

Desperate for reassurance, Mia rushed to the boathouse, where Laney was working, but her friend pulled no punches. 'Your family really want your support right now, Mia, not just your charitable causes. Iris is in a terrible state.'

'She needs a project to take her mind off things,' Mia insisted, desperate to throw herself into action, always her first line of defence.

'That tactic doesn't work for everyone,' Laney said, more kindly.

But, secretly delighted that her daughter was going to be at home for the foreseeable future, Mia was determined to get her involved in the gala and hoped it would help them find their way back to the closeness she so desperately missed. Iris had always loved the gala, and having originally agreed to star alongside Dougie's stunt display team in this one, it seemed vital that she had something else to do to take her mind off him.

She called a lunch meeting for the committee, to which she invited both Iris and Laney who, to Mia's amazement, arrived on a bicycle, with large sweat patches under her arms, her hair now faded to an almost normal strawberry blond.

'Have you been given another driving ban?' she asked.

'Not quite. I'm cycling to get fit and thus enhance my chances of conception. Simon calls it menstrual cycling. Don't you think I've lost weight?'

'You definitely look different,' Mia said tactfully. Laney was wearing unflattering sports gear with none of her trademark floaty dresses, chunky jewellery and flip-flops. 'Iris has gone out with

Chloe to watch an old Pony Club friend play polo near Windsor. She knows how much I wanted her to be here.'

Aware that Iris was spoiling for a fight with them both, Laney was secretly relieved. Still without an appetite and fed up with being virtuous, especially as Simon was now away doing his awards ceremony, she broke her pledge to drink nothing all month and succumbed to the heavenly Meursault that Mia had put out to complement a spread of exotic salads. Although the Devonshires no longer drank, they kept an impressively stocked cellar to treat their guests.

The gala committee were a rather pious lot, mostly designer-suited trophy wives on a perpetual diet, so by the time they got to the meeting proper, Laney had consumed most of the bottle and was feeling gloriously feisty and jolly, brushing away concerns about health and safety, car-parking and auction versus prize raffle, quite forgetting that she'd only been invited there to talk about the cabaret, which she did with great gusto when asked, although she was far too squiffy to remember most of her ideas.

'It's all going to be Spanish-themed, of course,' she said airily. 'Lots of castanets and cally-knees hats – you know, with the funny headscarves.'

'*Calañés*,' corrected Mia, with a fixed smile.

'Those too. I plan to base it loosely around the plays of Lorca.'
'You *what*?'

'I thought I'd start with *Blood, Sweat and Tears Wedding*. Always an ice breaker. Then *The House of Bananarama* will get everyone dancing.'

Mia rolled her eyes. 'Moving on to Any Other Business ...'

They were waving off the last of the committee when Chloe Benson's neat little Fiat 500 pulled in through the gates, One Direction pounding from the stereo. Clearly in a hurry, Chloe pulled the car up under a topiary lovebird and didn't get out as Iris clambered uncomfortably from the passenger door, blowing kisses. Like Laney, she'd enjoyed rather a lot of wine that lunchtime, along with some much-needed flirtation, and it had put her in rebellious mood. Tossing her long hair, she flounced inside as best she could, given she was slightly squiffy and balanced on crutches.

'Can I have a word?' Mia asked quietly as she passed.

'Laney has a dictionary. Ask her. You could both start with "total bitches".'

'That's two words,' Laney muttered, earning herself a filthy look as Iris clanked off, crutches squeaking on the marble floor and Maltese terrier claws skittering in her wake.

Mia rushed after her, dragging a reluctant Laney with her, tracking Iris down in the oak-panelled study where she'd limped to the sun-drenched window seat littered with papers. 'Please don't be like this, Iris. We must talk.'

'You ruined my wedding!' Iris swung back accusingly.

'You can't blame me for Dougie sleazing around with a call-girl.'

'Not that! And Jodie Field isn't a call-girl.'

'Actually he did ask your advice on that front,' Laney reminded Mia.

'He *what*?' Iris gasped.

'Sorry – not important.' Laney started to back into the hall. 'I think I'd better go. I'm collecting Hope from school in half an hour and I'm on a bicycle, so I must—'

'You're just as bad!' Iris howled, limping after her. 'In fact, you're worse! At least Mum has the excuse that she's my flesh and blood and has used me as compensation for twenty years because my real father didn't care enough to stick around and my adopted father won't share her bed—'

'Iris, please stop this!' Mia gave chase, but Iris ignored her, stalking Laney across the marble, crutches squeaking like tortured mice.

'But you're just an interfering cow, aren't you, Laney? You're so desperate for Mum's freebies you'll do anything she tells you, including keeping quiet about the fact your husband might be my father!'

'Iris, no!' Mia's voice was hoarse with tears.

Almost at the door, Laney froze before turning slowly back to face them as the pent-up anger poured out of Iris at last.

'I've known for ages!' she screamed. 'I'm sure everybody knows! Just like they know Leo Devonshire is gay.'

'I-I-I should have talked to you about this years ago. Oh, God,' Mia stuttered.

'I *knew* years ago, Mum. I've processed it. I figured it out long before he based himself in LA so much. And I knew Ivan was his partner as soon as I met him. They love each other.'

Edging towards the door, heart racing so fast she thought she'd faint without fresh air, Laney was trying to keep as quiet as possible, but she kept bumping into things. Almost within grasp of the handle, she sent an ornate floor vase of walking sticks flying.

'Wait!' Iris limped up to her and Laney realised she was carrying a book she'd picked up in the study. 'We haven't talked about Simon.'

'There's nothing to talk about!' Mia snorted with laughter, then stopped because Laney was staring at her.

Laney was fighting an urge to run. She sensed the moment had arrived to face the Demons' demons. It was now or never, she told herself.

'You and Simon spent a night together, Mia,' she reminded her in a shaking voice. 'Three weeks later, you told me you were pregnant.'

Mia's mouth fell open in horror. 'And you told Iris this?' she squeaked, barely able to believe the betrayal.

'Don't worry – Laney's kept the conspiracy of silence. I found your old diaries, Mum.' Iris held up the book. 'You didn't write much, but there was a rare entry for one night in March that reads "Dominic didn't show. Spent night with Simon. OMG, Laney must never find out what happened."'

'How *dare* you read my diaries?' Mia stormed.

'Laney must not find out *what*?' demanded Laney.

Mia backed away, holding up her hands. 'That night was a long time ago. I am not going to talk about it!'

'Fine!' Iris howled, banging a crutch on the floor. 'Good old family secrets! Whatever Leo did to Dougie in LA last week that left him barely able to walk had better stay in the dressing-room closet too.'

'*What?*' Mia and Laney both chorused in shock.

'I am not going to talk about it!' Iris mimicked her mother. 'I'm going to Spain with Chloe tomorrow!'

Laney backed further towards the door, tripping over walking sticks. 'I'm going to collect my daughter now.'

'And I am going to die this summer!' came a deep voice from the inner hallway, followed by a mosquito whirr of electric-wheelchair batteries as Jacinta powered in. 'So weel you please stop this arguing. What are you talking about that's making chew so angry?'

They all stared at her in silence, Leo's beloved little madonna who thought that her granddaughter was her one remaining descendant with Ormero blood and must never know that her only son lived with his gay lover and their very spoiled dog in a treetop house with more knitting needles than crucifixes.

Mia rallied first, ever the consummate actress. 'Iris says she is going to Spain, Jacinta. Isn't that lovely?'

'I know, *muñequita*. I ask her to take my final wishes to the family so that they can prepare for the funeral. I have written a letter to Father Miguel stating what I would like to happen when they welcome my body home.'

'Oh, Lito, must you be so macabre?'

'There is not much time and you are busy, Mia, so I weel do this my way.' Her eyes glittered. 'Iris has a broken heart that must be kept busy.'

'Just what I was saying!' Mia's mask slotted into place. 'What about the Wootton Gala? Will you be back in time?'

'I'm not sure.' Iris shrugged non-committally. 'I might go

straight to LA when my leg's a bit better. See Dad. Ask him about the old college days, that sybaritic foursome I've read about,' she hugged the diary closer, 'the Demons and Devonshires sharing everything.'

Mia's eyes flashed as she glanced warily at her friend, then her mother-in-law. 'Leo's coming here for the gala. It's my birthday, remember? You must be home for that.'

'Oh, yes – the big four-oh.' Iris's eyes were swimming with angry tears. 'Maybe you can hire your hot-air balloon pilot again.'

'I loved being forty!' Jacinta exclaimed. 'It was when I had my little boy. I think you should have more babies, Mia. That would make Leo happy.'

Unable to listen to any more, Laney sloped from the house and rushed to gather her bicycle to wobble back to Burley. Her heart was thumping unpleasantly in her chest and she was almost faint with fear. It was the first time she and Mia had mentioned that awful night at college in more than twenty years. She had never since confronted Simon about The Night That Never Happened, however angry, drunk or vindictive she had been. During their long on-off relationship, he'd had two other wives and countless lovers, and fathered many children, and yet that one night with Mia had always been on an entirely different scale of hurt, and what might have come of it rattled her to the core. She would never be ready for that conversation.

Still squiffy and also puffed out, she arrived at the school gates ten minutes early, thus encountering the most eager of the gossipy mums, who recoiled politely from the sweaty sports gear, pinkish hair and wine fumes.

Plucking her phone self-importantly from her basket, Laney opened a picture text from Simon showing off the mother of all hotel suites in Edinburgh. She closed the message without replying, and spotted a new email from Richard HH. They had been exchanging messages all week now, mostly teasing and irreverent, occasionally surreal and sometimes creeping towards flirtatious.

This one was no exception: I expect your undivided attention tonight, darling L. You can tell me a saucy anecdote.

She'd made the mistake of mentioning that Simon would be away, wowing the catering industry with the speech she'd written full of naughty anecdotes, most of which were entirely fictitious. Feeling disloyal, she replied, No, and pocketed her phone as the gates opened for home time.

As always, having Hope to herself was a delight, throwing balls for the dogs in the garden followed by a rampaging game of hide-and-seek, plant-watering and then a long snuggle on the kitchen sofa watching *The Clangers*, which Daddymon had recently persuaded his stepdaughter was the height of cool.

But many hours later, after bath, bedtime stories and a lot of rooibos tea to get rid of her post-lunchtime hangover, Laney settled at her laptop under the pretext of doing some edits to Simon's Christmas book, but really to check if Richard had replied.

Her face went clammily cold as she read a new message from Oscar's lawyers, filled with even darker threats about what would happen to her if she did not surrender the *Dalrymple Two* script, which they claimed was her ex-husband's intellectual property. This was the first email that specifically mentioned court action and listed the terms under which she would be sued and the likely costs, which ran into hundreds of thousands of dollars.

Instead of replying to it, she wrote another message to Richard HH, desperate for distraction, trying to joke about her day, but her hands were shaking so much it came out as deranged rambling about her fear of Oscar and his legal team. She even typed her name wrong, signing off 'Lane7', which made her feel like a supermarket aisle.

She gloomily visited the dying roses before heading to Google to try to fathom America's copyright laws.

The speed of his reply lifted her spirits: Are you OK?

Do you know anything about intellectual copyright?

I know people who do. Why?

It wasn't exactly a flirty exchange, but as Laney outlined her long wrangle with Oscar over the *Dalrymple* script, it was a tremendous relief to lay it all out on a page, for her own clarity of mind as much as anything else. She never felt able to talk to Simon about it, however willing he was to listen, because it involved Oscar and he inevitably got terribly wound up. This required a cool head.

Bored landowner Richard HH, sitting beneath his blunder-busses in his oak-panelled study, had an admirably cool head: I don't want you to worry about this a moment longer, darling creature. Leave it with me and I'll see what I can find out. Meanwhile, change the file name on your computer to something obscure if you haven't already and protect it with a mind-boggler of a password, and make a great many back-up copies externally including emailing one to me for safe keeping.

Ha ha. How do I know I can trust you? Digging through desk drawers while she waited for a reply, Laney found a collection of novelty flash drives given to Simon as corporate freebies or sent to him by fans. Ignoring the ones shaped like hearts, naked women and suggestive fruit, she found a cute-looking black Labrador from an animal charity and copied the *Dalrymple* script on to it.

'My guard dog.' She kissed its plastic head as she slotted it back together. Her inbox already contained a new message: I give you my word. It is no less honourable than my heart, but less reckless. You are in danger of possessing both.

That night, Laney fell asleep almost the moment her head touched the pillow for the first time in over a fortnight. Buried deep beneath the covers with the Labradors bookending her and a cat on her feet, she had the strangest sense of being looked after. But when she woke at five as usual, panic attack raging, she was immensely relieved that she hadn't sent a copy of the script to Richard HH.

Chapter 29

Andalucía in July was as punishingly hot as the bonnet of a racing car smouldering off the Jerez circuit in an endurance test. Even the breeze-cooled slopes of the hills near Arcos de la Frontera offered no respite from the relentless heat, the scorched earth thrumming and crackling drily to the accompaniment of crickets as greenery shrivelled, heat hazes shimmered and sherry vines ripened.

Standing proud amid cork forests and rolling hills on its own plateau midway between Jerez and Arcos, Hacienda Sueño was shouldered by two hundred hectares of pasture and alfalfa fields. Once legendary for breeding fighting bulls and training the Vaquera stallions that shared the rings with them, the estate now served the tamer purpose of breeding pure Andalucían horses for Doma Clásica. Horse-breeding was a macho business in this part of Spain, and Sueño had testosterone, blood and sweat mixed into its rough mortar.

The hacienda was a fierce white in the barren landscape. Lying at the end of a mile of cactus-fringed drive, beyond gates and grilles, its low whitewashed buildings were linked around two rectangular courtyards. The larger was accessed through a bell-towered archway with a large kennel to each side and the stud brand silhouetted above it in wrought iron. At this courtyard's centre was a circular well; Lito remembered seeing her father holding the stable lads over it by their ankles when they had upset him. Although terracotta-roofed staff accommodation, workshops and garages took up its longest flanks, this courtyard was dominated by the crenellated gable ends of two vast stallion barns on the eastern side, which housed twenty valuable Pura Raza Española, almost all bearing the Sueño brand. The horses that lived inside these temperature-regulated havens wanted for nothing and were tended by a small army. Beyond the buildings there were indoor and outdoor arenas, then the far more artisan enclosures and barns for the mares. At a stud like Sueño, mares were never broken to ride, but kept in large farmed groups like cattle, their manes and tails shaven so that the breeding quality of bone and muscle could be assessed at a glance, and their age instantly determined by the length of hair left on their docks.

'It's a bit bloody sexist, don't you think?' grumbled Chloe. It was years since she'd visited Sueño, the hacienda reinvented in that time from tumbledown farm stud with two stallions to full-blown *yeguada* with artificial-insemination unit and embryo-transfer programme. The breeding side fascinated her, but it was a male-dominated business.

'Totally sexist,' Iris agreed, 'but if I had to choose between standing in a barn with a load of oversexed men for twenty-three hours a day or hanging out with my girlfriends in the sun, I know which I'd choose.'

Not that the girls could hang out in the flame-throwing sun. It was too hot to sit by the pool that sizzled with glittering cobalt perfection in a white-wall enclosure among the citrus trees in the meticulously irrigated garden. Instead, they passed the first few days of their stay in the air-conditioned stallion barns or watching the horses work in the huge, airy, vaulted indoor school. Stud manager Chus and his son Alejo, who rode up to eight horses a day, were artists in the saddle, and the girls were happy to sit in the gallery reliving their Pony Club heyday.

Between times, they sat in the shade of the arched cloisters that ran the length of the smaller courtyard, reading and talking, scrapping and laughing. Chloe had brought her textbooks, which sat like a cooling-tower on a buckling old table beside her laptop; Iris had an electronic reader jam-packed with novels that she raced through with addictive speed, giggling often and crying occasionally. Iris still cried a lot, Chloe noticed, but it was more predictable now, cued by a sad movie or song. She was clearly trying her hardest to battle the bad temper, being by nature kind and upbeat. The change of scene was definitely helping take her mind off the cancelled wedding.

They had the main *cortijo* to themselves. The hacienda's principal house wrapped itself around a private inner courtyard shaded with cork and olive trees. It had been restored from almost total collapse, Leo sparing no expense in reintroducing traditional materials and craftsmanship so that it was dense with marble and terracotta, traditional heavy Spanish doors, wooden ceilings, wrought-iron chandeliers and window grilles, Moorish-influenced mosaic and fretwork. Intended for occupation by a large extended family, the formal salon was the size of a hotel foyer, the dining room could easily seat twenty, and the double-height library-cum-study was big enough to house a full-sized bronze statue of two Andalucían stallions rearing in the centre of its tiled floor. Intimidated by the scale and the over-zealous air-conditioning, Iris and Chloe confined themselves to the big modern kitchen and its adjacent small sitting room, which was crammed with trophies, many dating back to the Ormeros' bullfighting days.

Chus and his wife Marta, who lived in the house that linked the two courtyards, insisted they must join the communal Sueño lunch each day in the cool of the open-sided dining room, with its vine-framed terrace overlooking the well, a three-hour marathon of meat, wine and cigarette smoke, the staff on their best behaviour while the pretty daughter of the house was visiting. The younger grooms were particularly star-struck to find Purple at their table.

Embarrassed by such formality and eager to put everyone at their ease, Iris inflicted her rusty Spanish on them, delighting everybody with her eccentric vocabulary, much of it gleaned from Lito and therefore hopelessly old-fashioned. The lively lunchtime conversation was almost all dominated by football and horses, and even though Chloe spoke barely a smattering of Spanish she found the camaraderie uplifting, for all its obvious machismo.

Chloe couldn't help but notice how the men gaped at Iris while their eyes brushed past herself like fingers flitting painlessly through a candle. Legendary flirt Haff was away teaching, but his deputy rider Alejo was just as smouldering of eye, and clearly smitten with Iris. Broad-shouldered and narrow-hipped, thighs bulging in tight olive-green breeches like pickled cucumbers, he had a cheekily handsome, full-lipped face like Velázquez's Bacchus, and the cocky self-assurance of a man who knew few could equal him in the saddle. His good looks reminded Chloe of Vicente, head groom at Wootton.

'How soon are you going to ride?' he asked Iris in Spanish on the second day.

'Not this week' – she pointed to her strapped leg – 'but Chloe will ride if you have something steady.'

'We have no lazy horses here,' Alejo said unenthusiastically.

Chloe, who had picked up on her name, could guess the score. 'Actually, I have lots of work to—'

'I'm sure you can find her something nicely mannered,' Iris insisted, still in Spanish. 'We called her Benson Hedges in Pony Club because she'd jump anything, even five feet of birch.'

Hearing 'Benson Hedges', Chloe snapped, 'Actually I got that nickname because of my hair,' reaching up to flatten the bedsprings. 'Somebody said it looked like a hedge.'

'Nonsense. You were the best rider there.'

Chloe noticed Alejo's eyes narrowing, but he shrugged and said no more. Like all men, he would do anything Iris wanted. Old-fashioned rebellious heroes couldn't resist her, and Sueño was full of wannabe El Cids, all of whom were delighted to have a pretty Jimena Díaz in their midst.

The only person apparently dismayed to have the girls there was Nieve, the *cortijo*'s rotund, mono-browed housekeeper, who spent each day meticulously cleaning every inch of the main house, tutting furiously when she found stray flip-flops and unmade beds. She also rigidly controlled the air-conditioning, keeping the house Arctic at all times.

In the evenings, while Iris, in two jumpers, hobbled around the state-of-the-art kitchen making tapas, Chloe would head through the stone arches to the sitting area to do battle with a plasma television the size of a snooker table. All the dwellings at the hacienda shared the same satellite feed and, as with everything at Sueño, it appeared to be pointing towards Mars and not Venus. After several evenings of badly dubbed action movies, Spanish sports channels that seemed to show nothing but football and cycling, quiz shows involving hyperbolic audiences and hostesses in bikinis, they finally struck lucky with National Geographic.

Settling down with bowls of *patatas bravas*, tortilla and Manchego cheese, they admired footage of silver-backed gorillas at play.

'I never knew you could cook.' Chloe piled in, her diet under serious threat.

'Only tapas. Dad taught me.' Iris watched a baby gorilla swinging from its mother's back. 'He and Mum used to host dinner parties of ten or twenty when I was little that lasted all night. But that was before he quit drinking and started to watch his cholesterol. Now he just works, and she has horses and charidee.'

'Living in different time zones must rather put the kibosh on entertaining,' Chloe ventured. 'I don't understand why your mum doesn't spend more time in LA.'

'She wants to be close to Simon. Isn't it obvious?'

Chloe said nothing, wary of crossing Iris on the subject of Simon de Montmorency, which her friend hadn't let go since leaving England. In many ways it made sense that somebody as entertaining, quickfire, capricious and fertile as Demon should be Iris's father, yet Chloe didn't buy it, however neatly it added up. In her unique way, meanwhile, Iris had added *uno y uno* to make ku*dos*, now believing she had not one but two famous and talented fathers.

'I always knew there was history there,' she went on. 'And I *like* Simon. OK, so he can be a bit of a lightweight and he still dresses like an eighties pop star, but I'm genuinely happy if he's my natural father, and we all know he's the cleverest bugger on telly, despite those crappy daytime shows he does. He's one of Mum and Dad's best friends, so it's all quite cosy. You and I will both be Hope's sort-of sisters, and we can all be one happy fucked-up family.'

'I like being an only child,' Chloe said quickly, looking away as Iris's eyes tried to catch hers in a moment of unspoken apology, knowing full well the magnitude of Jane Benson's jealousy over her husband's second marriage, the rages and paranoia that had dominated her only daughter's teenage years, making it incredibly difficult for Chloe to accept Hope or Laney as a part of the family equation.

'OK.' Iris held up her hands. 'But you know I've always wanted brothers and sisters, and what hurts more than anything is that I might have five half-siblings. Why didn't he and Mum *tell* me?'

'Simon probably has no idea.' Chloe admired a gorilla beating his chest on screen.

'Oh. My. God. You're right. What should I do?'

'You need to speak to your mother,' Chloe said matter-of-factly, a mantra she'd repeated regularly since they'd arrived.

'I miss her,' Iris admitted in a small voice. 'When I texted her today to send kisses to the dogs and Lorca, I added one for her.'

'Did she reply?'

But Iris wasn't listening. She was gazing at the television with her mouth open. 'It's him!'

'Who?' Chloe looked at the huge screen, where a handsome young man was hiding in the bushes talking to a hand-held camera about approaching gorilla poachers.

'Balloon Man!'

Chloe shook her head. 'That's the guy from *Undercover Safari*. You know.'

'No, I don't.'

'Griff ... um ... '

'Rhys-Jones?'

'Ha ha. No. He's ex-SAS or something. Half the vet undergrads are in love with him. Griff Donne! That's his name. They pulled the show after he got kidnapped in Sudan. He nearly died. I heard he was writing a book.'

Iris stared at the screen. Griff Donne was looking stubbly and sweaty in the rainforest, a far cry from his formal apology in her hospital room. 'That's definitely the man from the balloon.'

Chloe squinted thoughtfully as Griff went deeper into the rainforest, still talking to camera as gun-toting poachers closed in. The documentary was at least three years old, but Iris was right: at the time of his release he'd been stick thin, and the man she'd seen in the hospital had been built like Hugh Jackman, but he was definitely the same person.

'Must have fallen on hard times to take freelance ballooning jobs for desperate mothers of brides.' Iris was glaring at the television.

'Perhaps he's still paying off the ransom? Or it could have been a publicity stunt.'

Iris got up to fetch her handbag and untie the little antelope. 'He dropped this when the balloon crash-landed, but I can't read anything on it.'

Dark eyebrows shooting up, Chloe held out her palm and Iris surrendered it. 'Don't corrupt it whatever you do. I haven't forgotten Campgate.'

Always a technical whiz-kid, Chloe had mastered file-merging, video-embedding, tweeting and blogging while Iris was still trying to crack iTunes. But her IT skills could be just as destructive, as she had proved when Iris's private photos of several friends' naked horsebox frolics at Pony Club Camp had appeared all over Chloe's Facebook page.

'That was a long time ago,' Chloe insisted. 'I've moved on to trolling egomaniac slebs on Twitter now. Mostly my dad.'

While she was busy code-cracking the flash drive, Iris watched Griff Donne and his team tracking the armed Congolese bushmeat poachers with no weapons or back-up. He looked like a typically tough military musclehead, she decided, programmed to think like a survival textbook and with the emotional intelligence of a spark plug. Dougie – who had been thrown out of the cavalry for reasons Iris had never quite got to the bottom of – claimed the armed forces had lost their time-honoured heroes and were now full of domesticated mercenaries, trained to live with the enemy and kill in cold blood. As far as Iris was concerned, Griff Donne summed that up. Thinking of Dougie meant that tears inevitably sprang to her eyes, and she brushed them away angrily. Griff Donne had wrecked their day and her future happiness.

'*Oooo*-K.' Chloe had deciphered the password with the aid of a downloaded app. 'We have lots of JPEGs, some Word docs, music and video clips, I think. Let's look at the pics . . . '

Iris dragged her eyes from the television where Griff was doing his final piece to camera, still sweaty and stubbly and now with a lot of mud and dirt on his ripped T-shirt as he told viewers that they had managed to send the poachers on a wild-goose chase.

On the computer screen there was a mosaic of thumbnails. 'These are mostly scans,' Chloe explained, 'passport pages, personal insurance, birth certificate, that sort of thing.'

'So his life really *is* on that thing. When's his birthday? I bet he's an Aries.'

'April the twenty-second.'

'Just Taurus, but that figures. Full of bullshit.' She turned off the television and shuffled closer to peer over Chloe's shoulder and check the year he was born, realising that he was about a year younger than Dougie.

Chloe clicked on another file and the screen now filled with tiled photographs of hot-air balloons. 'Here we go.'

'That's not the Thames Valley.'

'Africa, I think – there's zebra and kudu.' She clicked through the photos, many of a balloon inflating and then on to more taken from the air. Similarly, most of the videos featured shaky phone footage of wildlife from above, accompanied by sound effects of air

256

rushing, a gas burner blasting and a man talking, but it wasn't Griff's Welsh accent. This man had a distinctive deep timbre with an accent that was part African plain, part Brian Blessed playing Heathcliff, although it was impossible to make out exactly what was being said above the roaring. 'He should have this back,' said Chloe, rolling her cursor over Word document previews now. 'There's a lot of research notes here about Kenya and conservation.'

'I'm not going to lose any sleep over it,' Iris said coolly, although a small part of her felt bad for snooping.

When Chloe started to click through to the MPEGs, they braced themselves for some bad-taste thrash metal, but instead they heard the distinctive voice again, this time overridden in parts by background chatter and music, but far more audible. Its owner was talking about the miners' strike.

'Who *is* that?' Chloe cranked up the sound.

'He's got to be a politician or something.'

The voice was magical, threaded with passion and laughter, animated and hypnotic. Listening to it for just a few minutes, Iris found herself caring passionately about what happened to Dinfield Colliery, its workforce and the kid who'd bunked off school to line up beside his father on the picket line. But when that soundbite ended abruptly and the media player jumped to the next file, the story had changed and the man was talking about something much more personal.

Sitting side by side as they listened, both girls' jaws slowly dropped as the man described how he had walked away from a life wrecked overnight. The description of the physical struggles he had endured as he made his way across Europe and the Middle East was throat-clenching, the prejudice and cruelty he'd encountered beyond understanding. Yet he told his story without self-pity or melodrama. Whoever he was, he deserved to be heard.

'I agree Griff Donne needs this back,' Iris said shakily. 'Do you think he's still alive, that man?'

'There are no more sound files.' Chloe clicked back to the scanned documents. 'I have an email address for Griff.'

'Tell him to come here and collect his antelope.'

'We're in the middle of Spain, Iris. Wouldn't it be easier to post it?'

'He can come in person.' Iris's eyes glittered. 'He owes me an explanation, for a start.' She clicked the television on again, where an earnest man in glasses was now talking about the mathematical statistics surrounding comet collisions.

Flicking to the dubbed action-movie channel, they saw a young Brad Pitt sitting in the back of a Thunderbird convertible talking to Susan Sarandon and Geena Davis in a dubbed voice so deep he sounded like a Spanish Barry White. Iris watched it for a few moments, smile widening. 'Hey, I have an idea …'

Chloe regarded her nervously. She knew that expression too well.

Chapter 30

Dougie had to work hard to persuade Leo to meet him again. It took almost a week of texts and calls, plus the intervention of agent Abe Schultz, before he acquiesced and allowed the young man to visit him on set in San Fernando Valley. This time there was no cosy chat over lunch in the star's trailer. Instead he was taken to a small meeting room beside one of the production team's busy open-plan offices running along the back of the film stage. Dougie had an unpleasant feeling that a legal team was hiding in a cupboard, ready to listen in.

Anybody hiding in a cupboard would have developed serious cramp in the half-hour that passed before Dougie heard a female voice call: 'Mr Devonshire, your visitor is waiting just through here. Can I bring you coffee?'

Nobody had offered Dougie a coffee. By now he'd transformed the pages of an abandoned notepad into origami horses and was staging a small stampede on the table. The hubbub in the production offices increased tenfold as the door opened and Leo came in. 'I'm sorry I'm late.' Even though he was eyeing Dougie with grave suspicion, he couldn't help but be mannerly, holding out his hand.

Dougie stood up to shake it. 'Is it always this busy out there?'

'They're finalising the new scripts that go out today. It's the penultimate episode. Even the cast doesn't know how the series is going to end yet.' He sat down. 'As I recall, the last time we met I said I'd strangle you if you let Iris down.'

'I'm here to offer you my throat,' Dougie said with quiet sincerity.

'What a shame I left my garrotte in my dressing room.'

Beneath the studio make-up, Leo looked exhausted. Dougie had overheard enough chatter in the office while he was waiting to gather that they had been shooting a courtroom scene since seven that morning. Now one of the extras in the jury had just been taken sick and it looked as though they would have to do the whole thing again for continuity.

'I am not about to get involved in my daughter's romantic life,' Leo steepled his fingers beneath his chin, 'although I won't pretend I'm not relieved the wedding didn't go ahead. I gather the British gutter press ran some pretty sordid stuff about you last week.'

Dougie nodded. 'It was mostly true.'

Leo admired his honesty, if not his morals. He'd barely exchanged more than a few bolstering texts with Iris since the wedding disaster, and had no idea how she felt about Dougie right now, although Mia reported that she'd given him his engagement ring back and was now sulking in Spain with Chloe, only communicating with her mother to ask after the dogs. He was relieved she'd gone to Sueño, and only wished he was there with her.

'I love her.' Dougie's voice caught. 'I'm miserable without her. I want her back.'

Leo regarded him for a long time. Dougie's handsome features were etched with tension, bruised smudges beneath the blue eyes, chin unshaven and hair uncombed. If anything it just made him better-looking. Anglophile Abe Schultz already adored the boy on the basis of one meeting and was only too happy to help him out, regardless of his bad publicity in the UK. It was purely down to Abe that Leo had agreed to see Dougie today. The agent loved nothing more than a big gamble, and had seen exactly what Leo had on that first encounter: charm and ambition matched with the unique charisma that set him apart. With his photogenic looks and high-end stunt training, Dougie could be very hot property indeed. Abe had been looking to sign talent with old-fashioned action-hero credentials for a long time, and it was in his interests to smooth over Dougie Everett's problematic personal life and start putting him in front of casting agents as soon as possible. Earlier today, he had ecstatically reported to Leo that the boy really could act.

Was he acting now? Leo wondered. If so, he'd happily forfeit his own place on set for the next few hours to the younger man. Let Dougie stand in the spotlight and feel the slow burn of career fail-ure as layers of skin were pared away with each age-defying chemical peel, each soul-destroying critical review, each shame-making fake interview, each income-slashing reduced billing. Leo had been horrified when Iris followed him into the industry, even more so when her decision to bow out of the public spotlight for academia had been redirected by Dougie Everett and his stam-peding stunts. Now he was determined to horse-whip this handsome youth out of his daughter's life once and for all.

Despite the pain on the young man's face, Dougie's appearance alone in LA on what should have been his honeymoon didn't smack of a broken heart. He clearly wasn't averse to a little implied blackmail as well as hefty doses of nepotism, as Leo already knew.

For the first time, he noticed the paper horses on the table, an exquisitely folded little white cavalry charging towards him. Picking one up, he admired the symmetry. 'I gather Abe's taken you in hand this week.'

'He's been great, wants to set me up with meetings and auditions, but I didn't fly here for that.' His blue eyes still seemed genuinely tortured.

Leo set the horse down, this time facing the others. 'You won't find Iris's forgiveness in LA, but you will find stardom, I guarantee that.'

'You really think so?'

Leo let out a weary sigh, turning another horse around. 'I'm afraid I do. Only lightweight objects make it to the top of the acting industry these days . . . like any polluted pond.' He flashed his charming, clever smile, glancing inconspicuously at his watch.

Dougie flashed his winning smile back. 'Success here means nothing without Iris.'

Leo calculated the degree to which Dougie's success would be enhanced by marriage to Iris and knew precisely why he was here today.

'When those tabloid stories came out, I explained everything so badly,' Dougie was saying, playing the wronged crusader to perfection. 'I know I should have told her the truth straight up, but I was just too bloody embarrassed and, to be frank, it's a hell of a blur. Now I have to prove to her what really happened. That's why I'm here. You are the only one who can help me, Leo.'

'I very much doubt that,' Leo snapped.

'I just need your driveway CCTV footage.'

Leo blinked in surprise. 'Why on earth would you want that?'

Dougie explained that an ex-girlfriend had attacked him outside Leo's gates on Nichols Canyon using nail-bar acrylics as weapons. 'I was drugged. It was pretty much date rape. I had no idea which way was up. It'll all be on camera.'

Caught between horror and laughter, Leo tipped his head back and ran his hands through his hair. 'Jesus, you must have balls of steel coming here to ask me for this.'

'I'd obviously rather forget the whole thing happened, but that rather presupposes I remembered it, and I can't remember a thing.' He looked up at Leo through his dark lashes, eyes as tender and blue as fresh bruises. 'I know I owe Iris an apology and a frank explanation, and that's why I'm here. I have to see what I did. That's on your CCTV.'

Leo let out a sardonic laugh. 'Given the veiled threats you made during your last visit, I think I have every right to threaten to broadcast that footage across the internet unless you leave my daughter alone, don't you?'

'Absolutely,' Dougie said smoothly. 'Just as I have every right to go to the police and get hold of the footage that way.'

Suddenly realising where the little bastard was going with this, Leo felt sick.

'My ex-girlfriend assaulted me in front of your property,' Dougie went on, 'and you are sitting on valuable surveillance evidence. I'm sure you'll agree it's not the sort of publicity any of us needs right now and the only justice I care about is getting Iris back. But I will take it further if I have to. It was a vicious attack deliberately staged in your driveway because I was marrying your daughter. My ex's father's a High Court judge, so between her father and mine we could rock the establishment a bit.'

Realising he was chewing his nails, Leo balled his fists to stop himself. It certainly wasn't the sort of public-interest story the network behind *Chancellor* would look kindly on. They liked their stars squeaky clean, and young actors falling out of cars with mauled private parts in their stars' driveways was not a ratings winner. Dougie Everett now had a double stranglehold on his reputation – first the connection with Leo's distant past through Adam Oakes, and now this.

'Leave it with me,' he said flatly. 'If it's still on disk, I'll get that night's footage copied and sent around to you. Where are you staying?'

'Le Montrose. Honeymoon suite.'

*

When the electric gates at the entrance to Hacienda Sueño's long, opuntia-lined drive swung open to reveal the fortress shimmering in the distance, Griff took his foot off the brake and laughed. He should have Ennio Morricone playing on the stereo, he realised, not some trashy local pop channel. It was gloriously *The Good, the Bad and the Ugly*.

He'd been in Wales when Chloe Benson's email had arrived to say that his little carved antelope had been located and was waiting in Spain. His desire to leave the UK had been so great that he had hardly questioned the demand that he collect it in person. His London agent was trying to wrestle him out of his Survival TV contract, keen to tie up a six-figure book deal for his inside story of the kidnap, which he couldn't tell unless the channel's stranglehold was lifted; he was also dangling the carrot of a BBC special. But Griff remained convinced that Dominic Masters's extraordinary story would salvage his career. Without his laptop and back-up disk, he had nothing substantial with which to pitch the Cloud Man idea or proof of his life and work, nor could he guarantee Dominic's cooperation. He was eager to get back to Kenya, but he had yet to gain his balloon licence and his money had run out.

Visiting his family in Wales had reminded him just how much he needed to get his income back on track. He had been paying his sister's mortgage for three years, along with his parents' rent. He knew they would find a way of coping if he had to stop, but pride wouldn't let him admit that the money was no longer available. He'd never saved a bean. Any extension on his overdraft required proof of forthcoming income streams, and that river had long since run dry. He had to keep his agent on side.

More than anything, he felt it was his duty to get a message to Mia Devonshire that Dominic Masters was alive and well, without upsetting any more people. As ever, Griff's hot-headed enthusiasm had got him into a corner: she was hardly going to welcome a personal visit, given he'd ruined her daughter's wedding. That daughter, he was sure, was Cloud Man's child.

Now he'd been offered the luckiest of all breaks. He just had to play it incredibly carefully, which never came easily.

The old hacienda complex glared at him on the horizon, squat and bug-eyed, its windows shuttered as he drove down the mile-long drive skirted by cacti, nature's barbed wire. He could see an archway flanked by two stone kennels where huge mastiffs panted on chains. Beneath a bell-tower a gleaming black metal hieroglyph was riveted to the wall in the shape of a cross above a closed eye.

Driving through the archway, he looked around for somewhere shady to park. A face appeared at the car's window.

'¡*Alo!*' came from a toothy smile. 'I park car in shade for chew, ¿*si?*'

'Thanks.' He stepped out, almost floored by the dry heat that scalded his skin, fooled by an hour's air-conditioned drive from the airport into thinking it was cool outside. The light was blinding, bouncing off the white walls all around him.

As the young man drove towards a stretch of open-fronted bays fronded with bougainvillaea, an older character shuffled out from a heavily studded door and started to pull the iron gates shut beneath the archway.

'Mr Donne!' came a throaty purr as a slim figure appeared through the bright light, a wild mane of sun-bleached hair glimmering.

Griff perked up. This was no longer spaghetti western; this was Bond.

Then he clocked the pronounced limp and bright blue strapping as Iris clattered up to him like an angry hammer drill. She looked tired, her sunburned nose peeling. 'You've missed lunch. Everybody's having a siesta. Come inside – it's impossibly hot out here.'

'My plane was delayed,' he explained as he followed her through a shady stone passageway and into a leafy courtyard dancing with butterflies.

Limping at speed, Iris led him beneath a long, cloistered walkway dotted with tables that all appeared to be covered with veterinary tomes and into a house so dark and cool it was like walking into a crypt.

'We can't figure out the air-conditioning,' she explained. 'Only Nieve, the housekeeper, knows how to work it and she insists this is an ambient temperature. We think she's trying to freeze us out. Coffee?'

Griff nodded, his teeth chattering. He couldn't stop staring at her. He'd seen all the Ptolemy movies and was a huge fan. Purple's cool logic infuriated him slightly, although her beauty, fighting skills and armoured bikinis had entranced him. He knew the woman in front of him was capable of a great deal of emotion, as witnessed in hospital, but today she was speaking in the same modulated way as her most famous screen character.

'Thank you for coming.' She was gazing at him unblinkingly, that cool Purple death-stare. 'You will be aware that you are not somebody I am particularly keen to be reacquainted with.'

'I quite understand. I am just very grateful that you contacted me about the antel—'

'But as you *are* here,' she cut in, 'you can give me a full and frank explanation of the way you and my mother conspired to ruin my wedding. She and I need to talk, so it would help to know a few facts.'

'I beg your pardon?'

The death-stare darkened. 'Was Leo involved as well? And what about Laney de Montmorency? Mum always gets her to do her dirty work.'

'Laney de who?'

She lifted her chin high and he was struck again by how like Dominic she was, the extraordinary bone structure, the wide-set eyes and small, straight nose. 'I hope they paid you well, Mr Donne, because you're about to pay it back big-time.'

Griff gaped at her. She might be channelling Purple, but she was back on the James Bond script. He pulled himself together. 'Where's my antelope?'

'In the *cortijo* safe.'

'Can I have it back please?'

There were goose bumps all over her arms too, he noticed. It really was seriously cold.

Then he heard a step behind him and spun around to see a second girl framed in the doorway, sultry and menacing. He vaguely recognised her, curvy and broad-shouldered with a dark halo of hair and ferociously clever eyes. She certainly wasn't Spanish. Her teeth were chattering too. 'We heard the man in the voice recordings, the one who lost his arm.'

He began to sweat, despite the cold. 'You've accessed the files?'

'Is he still alive?' demanded Chloe.

'I can't talk about it,' he hedged, wondering how much they had heard and read. If he blew Dominic's cover totally, he would never forgive himself. The man didn't want to be found, and now Griff had lobbed home-made MPEGs into the garden of his long-lost family for mass broadcast. 'I *must* have that flash drive back.'

'Of course you can,' Iris said, in her Purple voice, 'as soon as you tell us what we want to know.'

Chloe held up his car keys. 'These are going in the safe with the flash drive until you do.' She held up a bundle of familiar items in her other hand. 'We also have your passport, wallet and phone. You're going nowhere until you talk.'

He blinked in disbelief, waiting for them to shriek, '*Joke!*' but they said nothing, both giving him death-stares now. He looked from one to the other, the stout, wild-haired wallet snatcher and the exquisite Purple, whose green eyes were as sharp and intense as freshly cut limes. She really was extraordinarily beautiful. And unless he was very much mistaken, she had just invited him to stay in a way that refused to take no for an answer.

Suddenly Griff burst out laughing, earning himself even more furious looks. If there was one thing he'd always been good at, it was the long siege. And even from the most cursory glance, it was obvious that Hacienda Sueño was a seriously nice crib – once one got past the cacti and the mastiffs.

He smiled widely. 'In that case, I'm all yours. Where am I sleeping?'

'*Whaa-at?*' Iris dropped the Purple act with two syllables and three octaves in the one word.

'I'm in no great hurry to get back and I need that research,' he assured them easily. 'Now, would you like me to sort out the air-conditioning?'

Chapter 31

Laney had been working at the boathouse since dawn, trying to get together the final chapters of Simon's Christmas book and travel memoirs, knowing that the delivery payments would inject much-needed cash into the house fund. As well as the sleeplessness, deadened appetite and short attention span that had resulted from popping her Korean pills, she was finding herself increasingly tearful. At first it had been alarming, but she'd grown accustomed to it, like occasional hiccups, and indeed barely noticed the intermittent sobbing when she was alone.

Mia had found her weeping over eggnog recipes when she'd popped in after her morning ride, eager to go through the cabaret ideas. 'Whatever's the matter?' She'd rushed forward to wrap her arms around her.

'I hate eggnog!' she wailed.

'Me too – ugh.' Mia rubbed her shoulders kindly. 'Mind you, the memory of your double-chocolate martinis is enough to make me want to drink again. Write down the recipe then come up to the house to help me plan the staging for the gala.'

Laney knew she should insist on working, but her sinuses were so blocked from all the spontaneous weeping that she needed fresh air to clear them, plus she'd promised Mia she would write her cabaret and was guiltily aware she'd barely made a start. If she saw the setting, she might get some inspiration, she decided, blowing her nose noisily.

'It's worse than when Iris is here listening to Lady Gaga,' Mia grumbled as she led Laney past the windows of the granny annexe where a deafening dirge was playing. 'Jacinta's choosing music for her funeral. Rodrigo's *Concierto de Aranjuez*,' she identified as they walked around the corner of the house to the wide lawns. 'I thought the stage could go there, up against the water terraces.' Realising she'd lost her companion, she swung back.

Laney had stopped in her tracks, weeping desolately again. 'Is Jacinta really dying?'

'Laney, chuck, of course not.' Mia raced back to hug her. 'Both Leo and I have spoken with her doctor, who agrees she's only doing this to get attention. She *could* have another stroke, but maybe not for years. She's as strong as an ox, honest. I'd no idea you were so fond of her.'

Mopping her eyes, Laney mustered a smile. 'I'm fine! This is hay fever.'

Mia was nonplussed. She'd never known Laney suffer from hay fever. She eyed her cautiously as she asked, 'How are the comedy sketches coming on?'

'Well, I don't think *The House of Bananarama* is going to get Leo on the first flight home' – her plans to incorporate all the greatest hits of the iconic girl band into one of her Lorca-themed skits were still in embryo – 'although I know he was a big Siobhan Fahey fan at college.'

'He loved Shakespeare's Sister,' Mia remembered fondly.

'Is he still filming around the clock?'

'He's fine.' Mia clearly didn't want to talk about it. Not talking about things was a refined skill these days. Any mention of Iris outing Leo as gay and Simon as her most likely birth father was as firmly off-limits as it had been for two decades. All she wanted to talk about was the gala, her smartphone permanently in hand while an ever-expanding leather document case full of notes lived under one arm like an oversized clutch bag.

She fished it out now. 'We'll have to start casting the cabaret this week,' she said. 'You'll go through the performers list again today, won't you, and match some names to roles? Damn, I must have left the print-out in the house.'

'You've already emailed it to me,' Laney pointed out, having read the list of the high-profile wives of actors, singers, comedians and other celebrities with almost as much excitement and fear as she'd read Richard HH's most recent communications.

'Good. Most of them will need their arms twisting again, but I can take care of that. I've already got Sylva, Kerri and Gabby confirmed in my quadrille.' All three were former glamour models, the first now married to an ageing rock star while the other two were famously loyal to their badly behaved Premiership husbands. All three were keen riders.

'The new horses arrive in two days' time,' Mia went on eagerly. 'My quadrille ladies don't have much time to practise, although they've seen the choreography and had costume fittings.'

'Something supportive, I hope,' Laney muttered, trying not to imagine all that silicone bouncing around on high-stepping Spanish horses. Simon would be in ecstasy.

'They'll get lots of support from Haff,' said Mia, misunderstanding. 'He'll stay here for intensive rehearsals until the event.'

They listened to strains of the fourth movement of Mahler's *Symphony No. 5* echoing loudly from Jacinta's annexe. Laney felt tears spout as soon as she heard its haunting sadness. Music was an instant trigger for her at the moment, her emotions running as high as her pill-popped central nervous system.

Thankfully, Mia was walking too far ahead to notice this time, still talking about Haff. 'I was going to put him in the guest suite as usual, but that's directly above Jacinta's rooms and I'm worried he might not get much peace with all the funeral dirges.' She marched out on to the lawn, small heels spearing the shorn grass, followed by her pack of dogs. 'He wants us to perform the quadrille right here in the garden for dramatic effect, but Kerri and Gabby are frightened of leaving the fenced sand-school, so getting them half-passing along the poplar walk is a tall order. Do you think there's enough space here to create an arena with white boards?' She spun on the green expanse *Sound of Music*-style, arms wide. 'It's on a bit of a slope, but that shouldn't matter. We can use it for the other ridden displays. There's a brilliant local milliner, Bibi something, who's agreed to let us have a fashion show of her hats with the models on horseback, although the committee's being stupidly stuffy about health and safety – we'll need riding helmets underneath, which will look ridiculous. Mind you, the hats are already so silly it may make no difference. God, what's her name? Bibi—'

'Bibi Cavendish.' Laney stared at a peacock strutting towards them. It had been a Bibi Cavendish hat that she'd worn to the races with Simon when she'd frightened the horses. Tears sprang to her eyes again – she must have looked ridiculous.

Mia was halfway across the lawn now, surrounded by adoring dogs as she carried on her excited Maria von Trapp spin. 'Haff's persuaded the Portuguese Equestrian Dance Company lot who are doing a UK tour this summer to ride with him here, and Dougie was going to get his disreputable mob to stage a jousting demo, but of course that's all gone out of the window, and I was never keen on the idea. It's far too brutal. Maybe I can get a falconer.' She stopped spinning and laughed as she realised her dogs were circling her in confusion. 'Or even those ladies who dance with border collies. What do you think?'

Laney mopped her eyes, hugely embarrassed that tears were falling like rain now, not helped by the beautiful music still pouring loudly from the house. Bloody Jacinta had replaced Mahler with Albinoni: she'd be starring in her funeral sooner than she imagined if she didn't play a few jollier tracks soon, Laney thought murderously.

'Oh, your poor hay fever.' Mia had caught sight of her streaming eyes. 'Let's go somewhere nice for lunch.'

'I haven't time,' said Laney, frantically trying to smile. 'I've got a crisis meeting with the builders at midday.'

'Don't tell me Simon's changed the design again?'

'Something like that.' Fred and his team were threatening to move on to another job because they still hadn't received the hugely overdue interim payment. Laney knew that if Simon was around he'd quickly charm them into staying on, but he was filming in Italy so it was down to her. Given her current propensity for crying non-stop and forgetting which day it was, she feared it would be an embarrassing scene.

She'd planned to focus the afternoon around Hope, but now she'd have to try to squeeze another few hours' work in somewhere. Oscar's access week started tomorrow, and arguments raged because he'd wanted to take Hope out of school early and fly her to LA, which Laney insisted would disorientate a five-year-old who hadn't seen her father in three months, even if Laney travelled with them, which she couldn't afford and Oscar wouldn't countenance. Now a compromise had been struck and Oscar had agreed to rent a serviced apartment in London, which meant that Hope could carry on at school that week and spend longer with her father during the summer holidays, when he would take her to the States.

The thought of Hope being away for so long brought the waterworks to a peak. She hurried blindly towards her bicycle.

Mia followed. 'Laney, are you OK?'

'Fine!' Laney squeaked. She reached for her helmet.

'I can't believe you're still belting about on this thing.' Mia tapped at a dusty tyre with the toe of her shoe. 'You're certainly looking a lot trimmer.'

'You think so?'

'All that pedal-pushing's having an amazing effect. The weight's positively falling off you.'

The tears dried faster than dew in a heatwave and Laney almost floated above Wootton's balustraded roof like a helium balloon. To date, the only person who'd said anything was Hope, complaining that she couldn't get comfortable snuggling her head into her mother as they curled up in front of CBeebies: 'Mummy, I miss your fat tummy.'

'Let's do lunch tomorrow, then,' Mia suggested. 'After you've dropped Hope off with Oscar. I'm worried about you, Laney.'

'I'm fine, and I've got a *Quick Wits* recording then.' She swung her leg over the saddle. 'I tried to get out of it but it's in some provincial theatre in the middle of nowhere and the producer freaked at the thought of getting a stand-in. I figure at least it'll take my mind off things.'

'Perhaps I could come along too,' Mia suggested, 'for moral support?'

Laney knew her cachet among her fellow panellists would rocket if she had Mia in tow. 'If you're sure?'

Mia glanced behind her to an open window through which Barber's *Adagio* was now flooding. 'Absolutely. It'll be requiems all the way tomorrow – that or Wagner – and both will finish me off. You always cheer me up when you're performing. We'll get there early and buy you some new clothes that fit. I always love shopping in the provinces.'

'I have absolutely no money.'

'My treat.' Mia kissed her goodbye. 'A little thank-you for all the time you're putting in for the gala when I know you're stressed out and worked hard enough as it is. That sexy Holden babe from Old Gate is looking way too good to cover up in baggy layers.'

Laney cycled home on such a high that nothing seemed beyond her. Fred would be putty in her hands; Hope would enjoy her week with her father; Simon's Christmas book would be a huge best-seller; her comedy sketches would be worthy of any celebrity wife's stage time; and she would fit into size-twelve jeans again before the week was out.

Instead she found that the builders had already packed up their equipment and left Red Gables, and Oscar's assistant had left a voicemail to say that he was sending a nanny to collect Hope tomorrow and fly her to the States as originally planned. The message was unapologetically up-front about the reason: 'Mr Benson cleared his diary on the understanding that you were willing to discuss the *Dalrymple Two* script during his visit to the UK, but as your most recent email makes it categorically clear you will not, he prefers to entertain his daughter under the terms of the custodial agreement, which state that access should be granted in his primary residence.'

Laney went straight online to try to get herself on the same flight, but it was fully booked, as were all direct flights tomorrow. The earliest one she could get on would cost her over a thousand pounds, and by then Hope would be beyond her reach on the twenty-eighth floor of Century Towers in Oscar's stark, Modernist apartment. Heart racing, she called Simon in Italy, but his phone was switched off, meaning he was either out of signal range or filming, or both. She then called her mother and cried a lot, but had to agree that there was nothing she could do about this and the most important thing was to be brave for Hope.

Even so, when she came off the phone she felt nothing but overwhelming red-mist anger. Oscar was naturally not answering any one of his six lines, although it was admittedly just after five in the morning Pacific Central Time and he was a man who had never belonged to the 5 a.m. Club. There was only one person she knew guaranteed to be getting up at that hour on weekdays to clamber into the car that the studio sent to collect him. She called Leo on his cell phone.

'Yeah?' The voice was groggy.

'Darling, it's Laney. I know it's early, but I need your help. Oscar insists Hope comes to him this week and I can't be there.' Her voice shook. 'If you have *any* free time perhaps you could go and see her or invite them to your place – you are her godfather and you know Oscar thinks your marvell—'

'Hang on,' the groggy voice cut in. 'I'll get Leo for you. He's in the tub. It's Elaine, did you say?'

'Laney,' she corrected, almost too surprised to speak. Through waves of stress and pill befuddlement, she recalled Iris shouting that her father had a live-in lover. She felt prickles, ashamed that she knew something he still kept secret even from his best friends.

She heard a door being opened, muffled conversation, then water splashing before Leo came on the line, full of kindness and practical help. 'Of course I'll see her. I know how worried you must be. I have Thursday and Friday off this week—' He broke off as the other voice, sounding far more lucid, muttered something in the background. 'Sorry, Laney – just my assistant reminding me of stuff we're doing, but it's *nothing that can't be changed.*' The sarcasm was clearly intended for whoever was in the same room. 'Leave it with me to sort something out, darling. I'll call you as soon as I do.'

'I love you.' She laughed with relief. 'When are you coming back? We miss you desperately.'

But he'd already rung off.

She went up to Hope's room to plan what to pack for her, but the anger bubbled up furiously again and she found herself throwing small T-shirts at the framed picture on the chest of drawers in which Oscar looked cuddly and paternal, his typecast character and a far cry from the obsessive-compulsive control freak he was in real life.

Back downstairs, she tried and failed to calm down with a mug of tea before venting her spleen with a long, furious email full of expletives to Oscar, which she knew was hugely ill-advised, but made her feel a lot better.

Realising he'd missed her call, Simon had sent a picture text from Apulia's San Leucio Basilica in Canosa di Puglia, where the temple's remaining columns jutted up, undeniably phallic. It read: Thinking of you makes what's inside my trousers like this xxx. A second text was cued up: Thinking of her does not. The photo was of an ancient Italian fan with few remaining teeth holding out an autograph book on which he had clearly written, *To Eufemia. You sexpot! My wife must never know about us. Love and kisses, Simon de Montmorency xxx.* He had the flashiest signature, a big looping calligraphy with the S and Y swirling extravagantly, practised over many evenings in his early twenties when fame had first beckoned. Back then, Laney had teased him for his superficiality, but it had served him well and his autographs now sold for surprisingly good money on eBay, much to his delight. Laney only wished she had a few spare to sell now.

The messages were clearly intended to reassure her that he was behaving, as best he could after what appeared to be a very boozy lunch, judging from the number of wineglasses on the table behind poor, gurning Eufemia. Simon's behaviour – and humour – always got very silly after daytime drinking. If she told him about Oscar flying Hope to LA right now, she knew she'd cry non-stop and he'd only try to joke her out of it, which would madden her. She'd let him sober up with this afternoon's shooting session first. They could talk after Hope went to bed that evening. Instead of calling, she took a photograph of Kensington and Chelsea asleep on the blue velvet sofa, from which their master had strictly banned them, and texted Behaving badly.

Desperate for a cheering distraction, she returned to her computer and clicked on Richard HH's latest message. They'd exchanged several in the past week, all deliberately light-hearted and innocent on her part, but showing off her humour. She treated each communication as a tiny break when she was working or a cheering comforter when she was not.

My darling L (he'd become increasingly informal, and she secretly loved it although she told him off), your last message made me laugh uproariously and look forward to our *very* long lunch all the more. You must send me excerpts from the book you are writing; it sounds riotous fun to read, although you seem to work far too many hours, darling creature. Is a wife who ghosts for her husband a haunted spouse? That makes you a serial offender, oh ghostly one.

He'd spoken with a media lawyer friend on her behalf, he explained, who had assured him the *Dalrymple Two* script was her property. I hope this message reassures you that – while you have everything to fear from my dishonourable intentions holding you to this favour – you have nothing to fear from Oscar Benson and his threats. RHH x

Dear RHH, she replied, I am *so* grateful for your help. You are terribly grown-up. Oscar is being insufferably childish right now, as is Simon for that matter. She always sounded like a Noël Coward heroine when she wrote to him. Somehow she imagined them talking like Celia Johnson and Trevor Howard in *Brief Encounter*, all clipped speech and impassioned adverbs. If I'm a wretched haunted spouse, I do need exorcising, and I fear exercising my imagination doesn't count.

The house phone was ringing. Frightened that it might be Oscar on the rampage, she let the machine pick it up, still typing: Thank you so much for speaking with your friend. I will of course return this favour . . .

'*Bellissima* Laney! *Amore mio!*' It was Simon, hamming up his bad Italian so that he sounded like a nasal and slightly slurred Casanova. '*Amo solo te. Sei la mia rosa! Vita mia, luce mia, anima mia . . .*'

Laney tensed. She had no idea what he was saying, but there were far too many *mias* for her liking. She had a strong suspicion he was reading from a crib sheet somebody else had given him, somebody with a throaty female giggle, judging from the background noise. It wasn't his most romantic gesture.

' . . . *che cosa desidera?*' he finished, then blew a long, squeaky kiss before hanging up.

She crossed her arms guiltily in front of her, contemplating her unsent message. Then, deciding that low-level flirting hardly constituted any sort of infidelity, especially since the man had merely been offering legal advice, she added: I look forward to our lunch, but would definitely like to hear more about your dishonourable intentions first. Must I dress accordingly? LdM

Her face flamed for ten minutes after sending it, convinced she'd made a total fool of herself. He must have read her message straight away because his reply came through almost as quickly as he could have typed it: My darling L. I would be happy to help you exorcise husbands past and present. I am also happy to help you exercise – I always think working up a sweat together is so much more fun, don't you? I insist you dress for my dishonourable intentions. You've put in a request for me to sport my shooting breeks, after all, and so it's only fair for me to point out that I have a hopelessly old-fashioned penchant for stockings and suspenders ...

Reading this, Laney felt a sudden muscular clench in her solar plexus, so totally unexpected that she thought she might need the loo. Then she realised what it was. A tiny but distinct spasm of desire, over stockings and suspenders of all things. She *hated* stockings and suspenders. Yet the idea of wearing them to meet Richard HH for lunch in Blakes was thrilling. There was the spasm again, just at the thought of it, not because of the stockings – she usually got chafed thighs and they always fell down – but because the idea of meeting him was so naughty and forbidden it made her feel incredibly, wantonly powerful. She would do absolutely nothing about it, she told herself firmly, but even taking it this far had made her feel ten times more desirable than she had before. There must be something hugely beneficial in that, surely?

Then Laney buried her head in her hands and groaned. Her young daughter was flying across the Atlantic tomorrow and she was flirting adulterously with a stranger over the internet. She was a monster.

She flipped down the computer lid and went back upstairs to get Hope's things together.

Later, with huge dark glasses covering her reddened eyes, she braved the gossiping mothers at the school gates and collected her most precious creation, who was covered with green ink and chattering happily about painting a giant frog for next week's school fête lily-pad hoop-la. Knowing that Hope would now miss the fête – which Simon had agreed to open – Laney felt choked with anger at Oscar again. She was determined to have a shamefully indulgent mother-and-daughter afternoon, starting with swinging and sliding in the village playground, then the naughtiest nursery junk food for tea, the schmaltziest Disney movie, the foamiest bath and the longest bedtime story. At some point she would have to break the news that Hope was going on an aeroplane tomorrow with a nice lady who was a bit like Mary Poppins and that a few hours (and a lot of movies) later her father would be waiting to welcome her for a week's holiday in the city where she'd been born.

Hope took it surprisingly well. In fact, she was so excited that it took Laney hours to settle her. She felt ashamed to find herself wishing for at least a few inconsolable tears and an assurance that she would be missed. The only disconcerting moment came when, drifting off to sleep at last, Hope murmured, 'I'm going to fly with Mary Poppins to see Daddymon tomorrow.'

'Not Daddy*mon*, darling.' Laney reached for the photograph of Oscar. 'Daddy-*o*. You're staying with Daddy-*o*.' She held up Oscar's benign, smiling face with its hamster cheeks and basset-hound eyes.

But Hope was already asleep.

Simon was dining out with the crew when Laney phoned. He carried the phone outside, but the signal was too bad to speak. She tried to tell him about Oscar's change of plan, but by the time he'd bellowed, 'What?' for the third time and they'd been cut off twice, she decided to send him a text instead: Oscar insists Hope goes to LA tomorrow.

She put on Fleetwood Mac, then read the rest of Richard HH's most recent message telling her of his penchant for stockings and suspenders. The words that had made her feel so rapacious earlier now just made her feel foolish, particularly when she read on. I think you deserve a very long, gentle but firm dressing-down, darling L, from buttons and zips to clasps and clips. I am adroit at undressing women, although your big, headstrong heart has always been naked, and is as brave and brazen as mine. I'm always here for you. RHH x

She had three missed calls from Simon, who had now texted back. Be strong. Love you, love you, love you. xxx PS I'm always here for you.

As Stevie Nicks sang of sweet little lies, Laney braced herself for the tearful explosion, but found her artificially controlled mood had swung again and cauterised her non-stop weeping. She gathered the remainder of her Korean pill stash and marched to the loo, determined to flush them away and embrace normal behaviour, even if that meant Snickers between meals and biscuit crumbs in bed when Simon was away. She'd just have a quick wee first.

It was then that she found she could pull down her jeans without undoing the flies. Without warning, tears flowed down her cheeks again, this time accompanied by total euphoria. She hid the pills back in her knicker drawer and lay awake until dawn, happiness slowly dissipating as she counted down the minutes until she had to wave goodbye to Hope.

Chapter 32

Mia was determined to cheer up Laney, whose strange, tearful behaviour she worried might be her fault. Since Iris had found her university diary and read out the entry for The Night That Never Happened, Laney had gone off the rails. Mia knew that her friend had a lot on her plate with mutinous builders, multiple deadlines and Simon never at home, but this recent change in her normally sanguine, cynical demeanour was extreme.

Laney was once again sporting huge dark glasses when Mia picked her up, tears edging out beneath them as she snivelled for the first ten minutes of the journey, unable to say more than, 'H-h-hope's g-g-g-one!'

'There is always hope,' Mia reassured her distractedly as she groped in the glove box for fresh tissues, momentarily forgetting that Laney's daughter was flying to LA today.

'No, *Hope*!' she spluttered. 'She was p-p-picked up first thing this morning.'

'You poor darling. I'm sure she'll be incredibly well looked after.' Mia reached across to squeeze Laney's shoulders and the car veered across three lanes of the M4, but neither woman noticed as Laney explained how painful it had been to wave goodbye.

'The hired n-nanny, Sonia, was actually really l-lovely and kept hugging me and assuring me it would be all right. Hope was as happy as anything and can't wait to fly in a plane.'

'But she's like that at school, isn't she?' Mia reminded her. 'Then she leaps into your arms at home time like she'll never let go.'

'It's seven days until home time, not seven hours,' Laney said forlornly, staring anxiously at her phone. 'Sonia's promised to text as soon as they're boarding and then again when they touch down. I don't trust Oscar to call at all. Did Leo tell you he's agreed to visit them? Thank goodness for the godfather.' She put on her best Vito Corleone accent, trying hard to be upbeat.

'We didn't speak last night,' Mia admitted.

'I thought he always called you during his lunch break?'

'Well, he's been skipping lunch a lot lately,' she said brightly. 'Where are we going again?'

Laney checked on her phone. 'The Corn Exchange, Newminster-on-Avon.'

'Can you put the postcode into the sat-nav? We'll hit the high street first. I'm taking you shopping, chuck. I hope you're ready for skin-tight leopard-print Lycra because it is *ready* for you.' That was a line from Laney and Simon's ill-fated stand-up routine almost twenty years ago.

Remembering the truly dreadful leopard-print leggings she'd forced Simon to wear as her stand-up partner, Laney was gripped with such inexplicable giggles she couldn't speak, and appalled when they turned into sobs.

Mia thrust another tissue under her nose, the car drifting across lanes again. 'This isn't like you, Laney chuck. Something's badly wrong.'

She lifted her shades to mop her eyes, which she knew were hollow from lack of sleep. 'It's just been a difficult week.'

'That old diary Iris found . . . It was rubbish, honestly. There's nothing to tell.'

'You wrote that there was something I must never know.'

'It was just a general comment. You know I don't remember a thing about it. I was so drunk. We both were. It never happened.'

Laney eyed her sceptically, debating whether to have it out at long last, but Mia was veering between motorway lanes again and she needed to stay alive long enough to make this recording to earn some money: Fred the builder had been leaving irate messages.

'You're right. It never happened.' She turned her face away to blurrily read new phone messages while trying hard not to sniff too audibly. Simon had texted a photograph of the ravishing Melendugno peninsula, its sea as turquoise as a Ulysses butterfly, the rocks as bleached as cabbage whites. Better than Stratford-on-Avon was all he had managed to add. Realising she must forgive his dreadful geography and be grateful he'd remembered that it was her radio-gig day, she replied, Hope Llandudno still sunny.

Even though she knew she shouldn't, she looked through the last message from Richard HH, which she'd saved to her phone so that she could savour it for the few days Simon was away. She hoped it would get her in the mood for *Quick Wits* to know that at least one listener would devour today's recording with a partisan ear when it aired, but it just made her feel more vulnerable and foolish: Your big, headstrong heart has always been naked, she read. Mia was right: she needed to go shopping. Naked was not a good look.

Newminster-on-Avon had a pretty Georgian high street lined with chain stores and a pedestrian precinct containing endless discount sports shops, empty pavement cafés, a lacklustre busker and an antiquated department store called Boyle & Blunt.

'Sounds like a pair of highwaymen,' said Mia, trotting up the steps.

'Or a very dodgy singing duo put together for Children in Need.' Laney, who had refused to take off her dark glasses despite the overcast day, groped for the huge bronze door handle shaped like a B and they swung inside.

They loved the high kitsch and antiquated eccentricity of Boyle & Blunt, which held a treasure trove of musty departments interlinked by narrow wooden staircases and garishly carpeted walkways. Hardly touched since the fifties, it boasted original wooden shelving, ancient rotating clothing displays and elderly staff in polyester uniforms crackling with static. The prices were a fraction of those found in the Henley and Marlow boutiques, and there were discount rails everywhere. Arms filled with potential bargains, Mia and Laney hit the changing rooms, reappearing in the aisle at regular intervals to compare outfits amid much hilarity as they discovered why so much of the shop's stock was discounted: the Boyle & Blunt fashion buyer was clearly trying to disguise the citizens of Newminster as inanimate objects.

'I give you ... prêt-à-Portaloo!' Laney leapt out in a bright blue maxidress that made her look like a vast plastic lavatory cubicle.

'Deckchair!' Mia appeared beside her in a striped linen shift.

Moments later they were posing side by side in matching shiny fake-leather trouser suits that were already making them stream with sweat.

'Bin bag?' Mia suggested.

'Landfill.' Laney studied her own reflection critically, resigned to the fact that she inevitably came off far worse in the comedy fashion show.

'Dralon sofa!'

'Knitted loo-roll cover!'

'Two-man tent!'

Anybody trying on clothes in adjacent cubicles must have thought a bizarre game of word-association was going on.

Feeling guilty that Mia was trying so hard to cheer her up and failing so dismally, Laney checked her phone obsessively as she trailed Mia to the lingerie section, but there was still nothing from Hope's temporary nanny. The underwear department was more Hogwarts than La Senza, and it was soon clear that the average Boyle & Blunt customer favoured supportive flesh-tone ranges, with names like Lady Gertrude and Madame de Monde. There was, however, a surprising treasure trove in the bargain baskets filled with heavily discounted stock still left over from Christmas. Matching wisps of colourful lace were piled high, tangas and G-strings, balcony bras, basques, camis and suspender belts, all originally intended to coax the ambitious Newminster-on-Avon husband into parting with his cash; and many had done so, only to have their gifts returned unworn straight after Christmas.

Fishing through the luscious lucky dip and pulling out a glorious suspender belt in orange and green pinstripe, Laney tried to put herself into a more positive frame of mind by contemplating Richard HH's love of stockings, but she just felt frumpy and guilty.

'Try it on!' Mia urged.

'I think I'm more of a Lady Gertrude girdle girl, these days. Simon is drawn to flesh tone . . . or perhaps it's just flesh generally. He loves old-fashioned underwired racks.'

'This is for *you*, not your husband.' Mia pulled out everything that might fit her friend. 'You've forgotten what it's like to know you've got something naughty on underneath. If beauty comes from the inside, shaking your booty comes from the undies.'

'I'd rather go commando than wear a pinstripe suspender belt.'

Hearing a text alert, she grabbed her phone from her bag and read that Hope was boarding her flight. I will take every care of her, the nanny Sonia assured her, no tears at all so far. Laney burst into such loud floods of tears that the crackly polyester assistants gathered to offer tissues and ask if there'd been a death in the family.

'Let's play it safe and go to Marks & Sparks,' Mia said gently. 'You can't go wrong with Per Una.'

Dark glasses back in place, Laney trailed in her wake, muttering, 'By my green candle!'

'That's Pa Ubu. Have you forgotten everything from university?'

'I remember everything,' Laney said pointedly. 'You're the one who's chosen to forget things, Mia.'

Mia refused to take the bait. 'I haven't forgotten the first time we went shopping together and you blew an entire term's living allowance on a Vivienne Westwood corset top. I thought you were so cool.'

'I still have it,' she said proudly. 'It's investment dressing. My assets are far too big to fit into it these days, of course, but Hope might want it as classic vintage when she's older.' Her voice wobbled at the thought of Hope taking off over Heathrow right now.

Five minutes later, Mia had her trapped in a changing room as she and an assistant fed in the latest range. 'This shopping trip is all about *you* – Per Una means "one woman",' she insisted erroneously.

'Yeah, and this one woman ain't Twiggy – I need a bigger size,' came the voice from within. 'Fourteen is a still bit – ugh, ruddy zip – ambitious.'

'Keep trying,' Mia insisted. 'You'll be pleasantly surprised, I promise.'

Marks & Spencer on a busy Saturday morning in Newminster-on-Avon wasn't exactly *Pretty Woman* on Rodeo Drive, but Mia was a determined soul and Laney's mood veered dangerously close to happiness when she found that her friend was right. Having bought clothes without trying them on for years, she'd outsized herself by a hefty degree. Her love of eccentric, heavily embroidered tailoring, flamboyant frills and boho smocks had padded her up like an over-upholstered chaise longue covered with throws. Now Mia insisted she must pull off the flounce and stretch simple ticking across her padding to show off her shape. But it was quite a stretch.

'I told you to stop bringing me size fourteen,' she grumbled.

'You *are* a size fourteen. Well, very nearly. Clothes are supposed to be fitted, not totally loose.'

'Are they? *This* fitted?' She stepped out.

'Wow!' Mia and the assistant both looked delighted at the sight of her tightly tailored curves in a short-sleeved navy-blue dress that Laney personally thought looked more suited to making a maiden speech in the Commons than cycling to and from the boathouse to write comedy sketches and after-dinner speeches. But there was no denying that it flattered her newly trim figure.

As her friend selected half a dozen pieces, it dawned on her that they made up a perfect capsule wardrobe for a charity fund-raising celebrity's consort. She could guess exactly what Mia was up to. Next she'd be lured into a salon to have her roots darkened or whatever new fad was supposed to defy encroaching middle age. Then it would be toxic injections – Mia's own forehead hadn't moved in over five years. For the sake of her charity gala and her reputation, she clearly wanted to turn Laney into a Stepford wife. Mia was always generous to a fault and refusing such kindness would be terribly hurtful – but it made Laney feel curiously as though she'd been cast in her first acting role for twenty years.

'Sam Cam's always wearing M&S,' Mia said breezily as she paid with her card, insisting that Laney keep the blue dress on.

'I've always been more of a fan of Shirley Williams as a casual-separates trendsetter.'

'Don't be ungrateful. It's perfect credit-crunch wear.'

'I might need a few ab crunches to sit down in any of it. I'd better not eat for a week.'

'Well, I'm starving.' Mia looked at her watch. 'Have we got time for that lunch?'

Laney had to be at the theatre in ten minutes for the pre-recording brief and knew that any sandwiches laid out in the dressing rooms would have been wolfed ages ago, along with the wine, crisps and biscuits. The *Quick Wits* panellists were always insatiable, especially her favourite camp comedy writer and co-glutton Michael Moy, with whom she had something of an unofficial double-act. He and Laney usually fought for every last crumb. Right now she had no appetite whatsoever, but Mia was already steering her towards the food hall. 'You *must* eat, Laney. I know you're losing weight and that's terrific, but you'll faint without something substantial inside you at least once a day.'

'I used to say that to Simon.' Laney sighed wistfully. The last time they'd tried to have sex, just before he left for Italy, they'd both been tired and had almost given up halfway through, only carrying on because she was close to ovulating. It was hardly the stuff of rampant sirens.

While Mia gathered her healthy-option whole-food, organic and Fairtrade lunch selections without breaking her stride, Laney dithered, finding so much choice bewildering. Ten days ago she'd have happily eaten the lot. Now even a salad looked unappetising and she felt a sweaty, clammy-handed panic at the thought of making a decision. She picked up a bottle of water and set it down again, selecting half a bottle of champagne instead.

'Don't you want a sandwich to go with that, Laney?' asked Mia, moving aside as a small, determined figure burrowed her way to a hummus wrap. Hearing the name, the little figure looked up sharply, studying Laney's face intently.

Laney tried to ignore her, hoping she'd go away. But the woman, who had small, pale-lashed eyes and grey hair gathered tuftily into two clips so that she looked like a koala, was beaming with recognition now.

'You're married to that lovely man off the telly, aren't you?' she demanded.

'That's right,' Laney said through gritted teeth.

'He's such a nice man, your husband.'

'I'll be sure to tell him you said that, thank you.'

'Is he really friends with Leo Devonshire?'

'He really is. We both are.'

'You're so lucky. I've seen all his films. He's fantastic.'

Standing anonymously beside Laney, Mia smirked. Despite appearing in acres of news coverage with her famous husband, she was a pro at avoiding public recognition. Today, sporting casual jeans and a skinny-fit white Joseph shirt, her wild hair worn loose beneath a baseball cap, she was nothing like the carefully styled, designer-clad vision who stood proudly at Leo's side on photo stages the world over, always with her hair up and her famously shapely legs on show. Laney might eschew most public outings with Simon these days, yet she cut such a distinctive figure that she was inevitably pounced upon by one of her husband's eager fans every time she tried to nip into Tesco or the bank.

'I'm here in Newminster recording *Quick Wits* for the radio,' she was telling the woman. 'Perhaps you've heard of it?'

'Is Simon in it?'

'No, just me. It's hosted by the lovely Michael Moy, with guest panellists pitching their wits on a series of unusual—'

'I never miss Simon on *Dinner Party Planners*. Now he *is* witty. You're a very lucky woman, you know, Lorraine, very lucky indeed.'

Thanks to South Korea's pharmaceutical exports, Laney's swinging moods were no longer under her control. Just as she could succumb to tears, laughter or forgetfulness in a split second, so her temper had shortened to a hair trigger.

'How do you know I'm lucky?' she snarled.

The woman edged back along the chiller cabinet, cannoning into Mia.

'I read his column every week,' she bristled back. 'It's so warm-hearted and funny.'

'*I* write that!'

Uttering apologies to the woman, Mia hastily steered the spitting Laney to the tills, hissing, 'What's *wrong* with you?'

'It happens all the time and I hate it.'

'It's part of the job, Laney.'

'Well, I'm on annual leave.' She thrust a twenty-pound note at the cashier and stalked tearfully towards the nearest exit, not waiting for her change, which Mia grabbed.

By the time they reached the stage door, Laney's mood barometer had swung again, this time towards jittery abstraction. The pre-recording meeting was just getting under way in the green room. Introducing Mia to her fellow panellists, she laid into her champagne as they all looked through the notes outlining that week's themes. Laney felt her face redden as she saw this show was to focus on infidelity.

Michael Moy pulled his chair closer and said in an undertone, 'You're looking mighty foxy, Lady Demon. Have you been researching today's show?'

'No!' She swallowed a frothing mouthful of champagne that rushed up her nose.

'Would you like to?' he purred in an undertone, always eager to play-flirt with his favourite panellist. 'I'm at a loose end later.'

'I don't think your loose end and mine are mutually compatible, darling.'

'But our loose morals are.' He winked. 'Tell me who he is. No married woman looks as good as you do without an admirer.'

She laughed, already bucked up. 'There *is* a listener who writes wonderfully suggestive emails,' her mind flitted back to RHH's recent messages, 'although he could be my daughter's headmaster for all I know.'

He stole a sip of her champagne. 'In that case, we must flirt outrageously on air today, to make him jealous and flush him out.'

Running on nervous energy and a shot of alcohol on an empty stomach, Laney needed nothing more than that to guarantee another high. Dressed as a Tory dominatrix, mood swings and sharp wit as her weapons, she took on a new persona that was straight back to her early script-writing heyday, when a stand-up career had still felt like an achievable goal. Between them, she and Michael stole the recorded hour. They'd always made a good double-act, but today they were unstoppable, egging one another on to the most risqué limits of the broadcaster's moral boundaries, reducing her fellow panellists to weeping, giggling wrecks, which would keep the sound editors busy all night ensuring that a clean version of the show could go out the following evening. It was Laney at her most charmingly cut-throat. The producers were beside themselves: 'Fi Glover's having another baby in November. We should bring you in to talk about some maternity cover.'

Having watched in total astonishment from the audience, Mia couldn't tell if her friend was a comedy genius or simply going mad. It had been years since Mia had seen Laney perform in public, and she'd been as brilliantly, side-achingly funny as ever, but the machine-gun speed with which she'd fired out her wit had been unnatural. She'd also flirted outrageously with Michael Moy who, Mia was pretty sure, was gay, but none the less proved a worrying foil for her friend's erratic behaviour. Feeling protective, she made her way to the stage door.

A tall man in his late twenties, with long, unkempt hair the colour of conkers curling over the collar of his scuffed leather jacket, was loping along beside her. Mia recognised him from the audience because his deliciously infectious laugh had drawn her ears as often as his handsome face had drawn her eye.

As they both waited to be buzzed in, he turned to shake her hand. 'Kit Lucas.' He had an unmistakably sunny California drawl to match his big, toothy smile and eyes as hazel gold as a sunset over West Hollywood. 'I came to meet Mrs Benson – I mean de Montgomery.' He flashed that big smile again, eyes crinkling. Then he tilted his head. 'Hey, don't I know you?'

A lot better than you know Mrs Laney de Montmorency, thought Mia speculatively as they were let in.

Laney was surrounded by her fellow panellists in the green room, holding court. Somebody had produced a bottle of prosecco and they were all toasting the show out of plastic cups.

'My gorgeous friend Mia!' She bounded forwards, blue dress riding up. It was definitely a size too small, Mia realised guiltily. But at least all the cycling had tanned Laney's legs to the colour of amontillado sherry and her blue eyes sparkled as brightly as her smile. She looked radiant, if mildly pissed. 'Mia should be on this show – she's much funnier than me,' she was saying now. 'We thought about doing a stand-up act together once, but we both wanted to do the straight man so we quit.' She threw her head back and laughed, showing a lot of white teeth as her middle-aged male chorus of commentators, columnists and comedians guffawed along lustily.

For a moment Mia eyed her friend grumpily. Laney was acting so wilfully. She needed her to snap out of it. Turning to the American, who was now furtively trying to read something on a folded piece of paper in his jacket pocket, she beckoned him forwards. 'Laney, this is Kit Lucas. He's *dying* to meet the famously witty Ms Benson de Montgomery.'

'Really?' Laney's smile wavered as Kit hastily dropped his crib sheet back in his pocket and proffered a tanned hand.

'Ms Benson de Mont-mmmm! You look sensational. Hi! I've heard *so* much about you! I love your work. I've seen all your shows.'

He clearly hadn't. Knowing how short Laney's fuse had become of late, Mia waited for her to cut him down to size.

But, still on a massive high from the show, Laney was disappointingly gracious. 'What's brought you here, Kit?'

'I'm from Screen Pro Creatives Incorporated. We wrote to you about a film script you have that we want to develop?'

As Laney took this in with raised eyebrows, Mia could almost see her friend's already inflated ego rising over her.

'What script would that be?'

'You didn't get the letter?'

'I get a lot of letters.' She shrugged. 'If they look like bills, I don't open them. Most letters I get look like bills.'

'Then we need to talk confidentially, Mrs Benson Montgomery.' Kit was mesmerising her with that easy smile, iced-bourbon eyes twinkling. 'You are one talented lady, and the agency wants that talent. Man, am I looking forward to working closely alongside you. I'm going to start by buying you dinner tonight.'

He might be lousy at memorising names, Mia reflected, but he was right up there with the best at smouldering. She suddenly realised she was jealous. As Laney's lovely wide smile widened yet further, she knew she longed for a career that meant her talent was rewarded with laughter and applause, and Hollywood agencies sending handsome strangers to woo her. But to Mia's astonishment, Laney let out her throaty laugh, then tutted. 'My dear Mr Lucas, you do realise you've got the wrong former Mrs Benson?'

'You mean there's more than one?'

Mia watched in total amazement as her friend shimmied up to the dishy Yank, fished in his inside pocket and pulled out his crib sheet. 'This piece of paper is utter rubbish. I'd expect more of Screen Pro Creatives' research team. The Mrs Benson you're looking for is Oscar's *first* wife. Let me write down her address ...'

Mia's mouth opened wide as Laney held up an arm and flicked her fingers, into which a pen was obediently thrust. Twirling Kit round to use his back as a leaning board, she ripped off a corner of the paper and wrote down Jane's address.

'Laney, what are you doing?' she gasped.

'Keep out of this, Mia,' she hissed as she spun him back and smiled up at him. 'Tell her she'll win an Oscar and she'll be all yours.'

'Thank you so much.' The smile flashed again as he read the address. 'The Obelisk. Sounds cool.'

Laney hooked her arm through Mia's to tow her from the theatre, muttering in an undertone: 'I think we should go back and buy that underwear after all.'

'What are you playing at, Laney?' she demanded, as soon as they were outside. 'You've gone bats today.'

'He's Oscar's scout.' She was hurrying along the pavement towards Boyle & Blunt. 'The moment Hope's gone, that goof turns up. It's so obviously a ploy. He's after the *Dalrymple* script. Oscar has no subtlety whatsoever. I hate it that he always takes me for such a fool.'

'Maybe that's because you always play the fool.'

'The reason Oscar's a lousy comic these days is because he takes himself far too seriously.' Laney crossed the road without looking and was almost flattened by a pensioner on a mobility scooter. 'But he still hires good comedians.'

'Isn't sending Kit to the first Mrs Benson a bit cruel?' asked Mia, who knew Oscar's domineering first wife through their daughters' long friendship.

'You're right.' Laney paused guiltily. 'The poor boy will be eaten alive.'

Chapter 33

Mia drove along the M40 in sulky silence. She had had such high expectations of the day – bolstering Laney's ego with a girlie shopping spree, having a chance to unwind and talk away from Wootton – but instead she had been overwhelmed by her friend's hyperbole. Laney was a much more grounded person at home or working in the boathouse; she was obviously upset that Hope had left for the States and no doubt missed Simon's support right now, plus she was convinced of Oscar's plot, but that was no excuse for her to behave so selfishly and erratically, crying one minute and flying off the handle the next, then buying almost everything in Boyle & Blunt's lingerie bargain buckets without trying it on.

Oblivious to the disapproval radiating beside her, Laney carried on in wisecracking mode for almost half an hour, describing Simon's juvenile picture texts from Italy, then complaining about Oscar and his dishy-but-dumb henchman. 'All he cares about is the bloody *Dalrymple* sequel. How could he send that badly briefed idiot and think I'd fall for it? He's obviously a hired stud. I suppose I should be grateful – it's one of the only things Oscar's ever bought me.' She laughed bitterly. 'He's one of the cleverest men I've ever known, but he has no scruples whatsoever. I half expect to receive a ransom note in a day or two, saying he's keeping Hope in LA until I surrender the script.' That triggered hysterical tears, which took two motorway junctions and half a packet of tissues to get under control.

'I bet he hardly sets any time aside for her.' She blew her nose. 'I'm so grateful Leo's going to make time to see them. It was lovely to hear his voice again.' She fiddled with the air vent in front of her. 'He was in the bath when I called. I think Ivan answered the phone.'

Mia was in the motorway fast lane. 'Oh, yes?'

The air vent was now stuck open, blasting Laney's hair upright. 'He sounds very nice,' she shouted over the din. 'Is he our sort of age?'

Mia knew Laney was fishing, but she didn't trust her friend's mood.

'Bit younger.' She cut the ventilation fans and turned on the stereo so they were blasted instead by Annie Lennox singing 'Walking on Broken Glass'. Laney pulled out her phone and started typing a long message as they climbed up the Chiltern Gap.

Mia pulled off at the Stokenchurch junction and drove south, dropping down into the wooded flanks of the hills. The sun was dancing through the tree canopy so they drove alternately into blinding light and tunnelled darkness. 'Can you slow down? I keep mistyping,' complained Laney, thumb flicking around on her phone.

Mia put her foot down and racketed out on to the Skirmett road.

'Shit! Now I've pressed Send early. I only managed to get as far as the "I've just bought very sexy stock" instead of "stockings". He'll probably think I've been out buying hunting attire – or sheep.'

'I'm sure Simon will find both just as appealing.'

'The message wasn't for Simon.'

Mia slammed on the brakes, ignoring the beep of protest from behind as a furious Jag almost rear-ended her Range-Rover. 'Who then?'

'I think we're causing a traffic jam,' Laney pointed out helpfully, as the Jag tried to edge past them, only to come face to face with a Transit van which now added to the beeping.

Teeth clenched, Mia drove on as far as the next village and stopped in the pub car park.

'Oh, good. I need a drink.' Laney released her seatbelt.

'I don't,' Mia hissed, killing the engine. 'And it's closed until six. Please don't tell me you're already sending messages about your stockings to Kit Lucas?'

'My seduction Kit.' She laughed, then straightened her face when she saw Mia's expression. 'It was a man called Richard, if you must know.'

'I must. *Who* is Richard?'

'He's a big fan of my radio appearances,' she said with satisfaction. 'I've never met him.'

'Yet you send him messages about your stockings?'

'My stock,' she corrected. 'He could think I've been buying Oxo.'

'Tell. Me. *Everything*,' Mia insisted.

Ten minutes later, while Laney gazed at her imploringly, Mia rested her forehead on the steering wheel and closed her eyes. 'You are *so* wrong, Laney. This is so dangerous. Just because you don't trust Simon, you can't start flirting with strangers on the internet. He could be a pervert.'

'Breeks and nipple tassels aside, he's always struck me as gloriously sane. And he really cheers me up. Look at me – I'm losing weight, I'm performing at my best in front of a live audience.'

'You're crying a lot.'

'Hormones.' She waved a hand. 'I'll hold it together.'

'Are you going to meet him?'

'Of course not. I'm far too much of a coward, even with your lovely Pa Ubu makeover.'

'Per Una.'

'Simon's always away. You know how women throw themselves at him, and he's a terrible flirt, especially when drunk, which he is quite a lot these days. I wish I could be a perfect celebrity wife like you, but I'm not. Even without the constant cash crisis, I'm just not good at oiling the machine. I want to be the engine driver. I always have.'

'But you are! You absolutely hold Simon's career together. It would fall apart without you – and it did fall apart without you for a long time. His career was so dead he'd signed up to go in the jungle just before you came back, remember?'

'At least I could have kept a close eye on him there. There are cameras everywhere. Right now he calls the shots – or texts them.' She looked at her phone, but there were no new messages.

'He always wants you to go along with him,' Mia reminded her.

'I can't leave Hope.' Laney rubbed the phone screen to remove specks of dust. 'You must know what that's like. You went through it with Iris.'

'I'd love to have those days with her all over again,' she admitted. 'They passed so quickly. Now she just hates me.'

'She'll come round. You two adore one another.' Laney leapt

gratefully on the change of subject. 'Is Dougie really history, d'you think?'

'Iris would probably take him back in a breath, but she'd have to climb over my dead body to do so.'

'If she loves him that much, is he really so bad? I know he called you Milfy and sucked up to the dogs, plus got a bit drunk early on and tried to get off with you, but most men do, and he is charming.' For all his swagger, Dougie had struck Laney as very dashing.

'He's been trying to blackmail Leo.'

Laney's jaw dropped.

'Dougie knows Adam Oakes,' Mia explained. Clearly Laney didn't recognise the name, so she added, 'Have-it-away *Howard's Way* Adam from Old Gate. The one Simon punched.'

Laney's blue eyes narrowed. 'We're supposed to have forgotten that night, aren't we?'

Mia ignored the dig. 'Adam and Leo slept together at college. It was just before our wedding. It was a student fumble really, but Adam was pretty besotted and tried to talk Leo out of marrying me. Then they worked together on a television series called *Sink* and it got quite nasty, with Adam turning up at the house at all hours – I could cope, but Lito was living with us by then and Leo was terrified she'd find out. He was in bits.'

Laney had to blink a lot to take this in. Have-it-away Adam, the Casanova of Old Gate, and Leo Devonshire, the heartthrob of the Brit Pack, were ex-lovers.

'Dougie worked with Adam and his boyfriend recently,' Mia went on. 'Given that Dougie could probably charm Colonel Sanders into telling him the secret recipe, it's easy to imagine Adam boasting about his conquests to him after a few Southern Comforts on location. I'm only amazed the story hasn't emerged sooner, but I think Adam was genuinely very fond of Leo, so maybe it would have stayed hidden if that little bastard hadn't batted his eyelashes at him.'

'What's Dougie going to do with the information?'

'The funny thing is, Leo doesn't think he'll do anything. He seems to think Dougie's heart is set on Iris and that he only hinted at what he knew to reassure him it would stay *en famille*. As he points out, he's far more likely to get outed by his own studio. The producers are already threatening not to renew his contract unless the latest rumours are dealt with, and they have nothing to do with a college fling twenty years ago.' Mia watched an elderly couple cross the pub car park en route to a footpath, a white-muzzled retriever panting at heel. 'Laney, Ivan is much more than a PA. He's Leo's lover. They've been together over a year.'

'Ah.' Laney didn't react with the shock Mia had anticipated.

'You *knew*?'

'I was there when Iris shouted about it, remember?' she pointed out. 'And we've always sort of known he was in denial.'

'Oh God. Then I must have learned to live in denial too. I've lived my life again, like Dom's card said, but in denial, and now I have no Leo and no Iris.'

'Don't be ridiculous. He's not about to divorce you, is he? His whole career is based around being the sexiest heterosexual metrosexual on the planet. You can work your way through this.'

Mia pulled a handkerchief from her cuff to blow her nose. 'He knows the network will never let him come out while he's under contract to do *Chancellor* – and he would never do it while Lito's alive anyway – but he and Ivan are a big thing. They adore each other. It's sweet.' Tears welled. 'Ivan calls me his stepwife.'

'Christ.'

She started to sob. 'And they want to have a b-baby!'

'Shit.' Laney clambered across the central console to hug her. 'Oh darling, darling Mia. You deserve true love more than anybody.'

'I have been tempted, lots of times, but my heart was totally lost when Dom went. Leo is my rock. I can talk to him about anything.'

'But surely you've had affairs? You have all those adoring admirers.' She had never been allowed to cross this territory before and she was terrified of being gunned down, but Mia laughed tearfully.

'When you hide behind very high walls, the only way to play away is to keep it incredibly close to home, and much as I love Franco leaving flowers on the kitchen windowsill, I'm no Lady Chatterley quivering in the potting shed. Spanish men are incredibly persistent, but sweetly old-fashioned. Haff's been trying to get me into bed for at least two years now. He's even proposed more than once.'

'Are you tempted to Haff and to hold or just Haff it away?' Laney asked idly. Then she remembered how radiant Mia had looked returning from her recent trip to Andalucía. 'You've slept with him already!'

'No!' Mia shook her head furiously. 'He tried exceptionally hard to seduce me in Spain last week,' she admitted. 'It was quite funny really and it's the closest I've ever got. But I can't talk to him in the same way I can talk to Leo, and we really haven't got much in common apart from the fact he's an amazing horseman.'

'I'll be utterly discreet if you Haff an affair,' Laney said excitely.

'Oh, Laney, I can't!'

'Why not? Leo is *living* with somebody. Have sex with the horseman – you might not want to be bride to his groom, but you can still roll in the hay. Surely Leo wouldn't resent you Haffing a little fun.'

'Just lay off the Haff jokes,' she snapped. 'It might be hard to believe, but I'm genuinely happy being Leo's wife. I know he and Ivan have talked about making a more formal commitment, but it's not a big thing for them. Not like having a baby.' Her face crumpled. 'They are really, really broody.'

'Don't tell me they want you to be gestational carrier?'

'I'm far too old for them to consider me a suitable surrogate and, besides, I could never give a baby away. I'd love another child, but that chance has gone. The statistics are so terrible over forty.'

Laney looked stricken. 'Christ, Mia, we're only thirty-nine. Are you telling me I should knock off the folic acid and make Simon glove up in case we conceive something statistically terrible?'

'Sorry – that's unforgivable of me.' She blew her nose again. 'I know you're trying for a baby and it will be gorgeous. I'm being defeatist. I just feel I'm losing Leo as a friend over this. He's so guilty and stressed all the time, and so terrified the story will get leaked. The last thing I want to do is compromise his privacy with a love affair of my own. He's given me the most amazing lifestyle and been an incredible father to Iris, and I won't jeopardise that. I can't believe you're willing to throw up everything you have with Simon for a random stranger on the internet.'

'C'mon, Mia, lighten up! All I'm doing is *thinking* about it. It's cheering me up no end, and it'll do the same for you. Look how happy you were when you came back from Spain, despite all the shit going on. That was because you felt gorgeous and desirable from Haff trying to get into your pants. It's empowering. Imagine how you'd feel if he was taking you to bed and making you ping off the walls with orgasms left, right and centre – and sometimes all three simultaneously.'

Mia's face flooded red, like blackcurrant cordial through water.

'I bet Haff's great in bed,' Laney went on, 'all that showmanship and rhythm.' She clambered back into her seat, inadvertently knocking the gearshift out of Park and kneeling on the electric brake. On the dashboard, her phone was flashing with a message.

Keep stocking up, darling L, and I will think of a hundred wonderful ways to lower your investments when we finally meet ... this month? x

Mia was right: she really was in danger. This time when she read his words, her heart lurched, her entire body jolted *and* her groin tightened.

It was only when she looked up that she realised the car had rolled across the car park and pranged a van emblazoned with

NUTTY BAR STARS LTD, boasting the finest bespoke pub snacks in the Home Counties.

'Oh hell.' Mia leapt out as a bald man jumped down from the van, spilling *Daily Mirror* pages.

'Taking life with a pinch of salt since 1991,' Laney read below the van's logo. She took a picture and texted it to Simon: Just like us.

She was about to get out when Mia's phone rang beside her. She picked it up happily. 'Hi, Haff! How're you doing?'

'You are not Mia.' He had the richest Hispanic voice, all *vino tinto* and Ducados smoke.

'She's a bit busy.' Mia was apologising to the Nutty Bar Stars man as they examined the smashed wing of his van. 'I'm her friend, Laney. We haven't met, but I've admired your *calañés* at close range. Can I take a message?'

'Tell Mia I am in England,' he announced importantly. 'I will come to Wootton in one week.'

Gripped by a rash Cupid's urge, she dropped her voice conspiratorially. 'Of course I'll tell her, but it might have to wait. I'm afraid Mia's just had a car accident. I think she's in shock.'

'*¡Caray!* She is hurt?'

Outside, Mia was exchanging insurance details with the van driver, who was looking positively skittish and pink-cheeked under her captivating, apologetic charm. Laney could hear him saying that it probably wasn't worth the excess of making a claim. 'Not badly hurt,' she told Haff, 'but I don't think I should leave her alone, although I have got work to do this evening . . . '

'I will come to visit her.' He rang off.

Already feeling guilty for meddling, Laney closed her eyes, waiting for the dizzying mood flips to settle down again, but her heart was thrumming absurdly fast and her fingers itched to pick up her own phone.

Dearest RHH, she typed an email very quickly before Mia could come back and catch her, I look forward to asset-stripping. xx

*

'There's nothing wrong with me,' Mia laughed when Haff turned up unannounced at Wootton bearing flowers and a DVD of his Olympic glory, insisting he would devote the evening to taking care of her. 'But the gala committee are all here, so it's great you're free. You would not *believe* all the health-and-safety directives we have to wade through tonight, plus I've been thinking it would be lovely to put together a PowerPoint presentation about the Javiero Dressage Coaching Centre to show on the day. Maybe you can take charge of that? We can put it forward for discussion this evening.'

Haff smiled weakly and spent the ensuing three hours sitting at a table between two local Devonshire Foundation stalwarts obsessed with the dangers of loose horses, flies and dung.

'Have you heard about the hard-hats fiasco, Juan?' one demanded, pronouncing his name 'Gene'. When he looked blank, she consulted her notes. 'The message has come back from the event insurers that safety helmets *must* be worn by all professional models, which doesn't help the fashion show.'

'Eh?'

'The milliner Bibi Cavendish is donating some of her amazing creations for a fashion show,' Mia explained. 'I want the models to be on horses, but we can hardly put designer hats on top of crash helmets.'

'Hire performance riders. They have their own insurance. There are many pretty girls who ride in circuses and movies that can model hats.' He glanced at his watch, knowing he had a long drive back to Essex, where he was teaching from seven thirty the following morning.

'On the case!' One of the stalwarts made a note.

'I'm *so* glad you came,' Mia enthused when Haff apologetically took his leave before they could move on to Hygiene Facilities, Lavatories and First Aid. 'That tip about hiring riders not models was inspired.' She saw him to the door and kissed him on each tanned cheek. 'You're a total love.'

Taking her face in his hands, Haff kissed her far more robustly, his lips cool, soft and expert against hers. 'I come back in one week and we will make that total love.'

Mia laughed as the running joke completed another lap of its flirtatious marathon, but as she closed the door behind him, she knew that talking to Laney today had made her uncomfortably aware that she couldn't keep running for ever.

Chapter 34

Dust danced in the light pouring through the high windows of the indoor school. Caught in one of these sparkling illuminated columns as though Scottie was about to beam her up, Chloe laughed in amazement, the horse beneath her trotting on the spot as the man standing alongside them tapped his long whip lightly on its rump.

'Is easy, no?' Alejo chuckled, taken with his new pupil and her gratifying delight. Making clicking noises with his tongue, he moved the horse forward so that the trot became an elevated *passage* and Chloe sat quietly on top, a supportive shock-absorber of concentration and calm.

Alejo was impressed by the girl's dedication and lightness of touch. She had none of Iris's beauty, but she was easy to teach, knowledgeable about the horses and even-tempered. '*¡Muy bueno!* Feel good?'

'Very,' Chloe panted, gazing down at him adoringly. '*¡Muy bueno!*'

Chloe was enjoying riding so much that confidence was bursting from every cell of her body. As soon as she'd swung into the saddle this week, she found everything looked far lovelier from horseback. Alejo's big sexist ego had become masterful expertise and Iris's tearful tetchiness was beautifully poetic. Even after she dismounted, the glow stayed with her: the hacienda was the most romantic place she had ever been and even her veterinary textbooks read like Cervantes. Most of all, she loved the Sueño horses, big-hearted, balletic and beautiful. She was so happy right now she wasn't even bothered that Marta's amazing cooking had added another Dunlop to her midriff, and the hot wind, sun and dust had made her hair more unmanageable than ever. It certainly didn't seem to bother Alejo, whose hard, sexy eyes appraised her with increasing interest.

'*¡Muy bueno!* Feel him come up between your legs! Higher, higher – *¡si!*'

Alejo had a way of making his instructions sound highly suggestive, a trick he'd lifted from the maestro Haff, just as he used the great man's horses to teach and to flatter his riders. For the past three mornings he'd given Chloe lessons on one of the *yeguada*'s older stallions, Uranio, a chunky dappled grey with an ugly coffin head, the huge, muscular neck of a T'ang sculpture and a thin, wispy tail that flicked from side to side like a maharaja's chowrie. With the kind, steady disposition of a police horse, Uranio had been Haff's most reliable performing partner in the Escuadra Real in Jerez for over a decade and he could piaffe in his sleep.

'Oh. My. God. This feels amazing!' Chloe whooped.

Watching from the small gallery, Iris scowled and scratched the hot skin beneath her knee brace. Chloe clearly had a mammoth crush on Alejo – hardly surprising, given that he kept instructing her to 'do exactly as I do', of which loving himself was the mainstay. Chloe now talked about Alejo non-stop, which frustrated Iris because it stopped her talking about Dougie non-stop.

The morning lessons, which had started with Iris chatting along too, calling encouragement and generally feeling part of the fun, already felt like exclusive dates as the normally cynical Chloe fell deeper beneath Alejo's finger-clicking, whip-tapping spell. Iris needed the unromantic pragmatist who repeatedly told her Dougie was too hot to handle and made her want to lock her heart in the deep-freeze, but her friend was melting in the Spanish heat.

Picking up her walking stick, she hopped outside into the searing morning sunlight. She'd abandoned the crutches now and was trying to put increasing weight on her leg each day, determined to get back into the saddle before their return. If nothing else, it would enable her to ride over Griff Donne at speed.

The sun was punishing today. Just limping across the main courtyard, Iris felt as if her eyes were treading water in the sweat pouring off her brow. She could smell amazing aromas coming from the stud manager's house as Marta slow-cooked her trademark *cocido*, the spicy ham and chicken stew Iris adored.

She knew Nieve and her small army of village girls would be staking out every corner of the icily air-conditioned *cortijo* with mops and brushes, making it impossible to find a quiet corner to cool off. She could hear languid splashes from the azure pool as Griff executed speedy lengths with the effortless ease of a seal. He could swim for hours and had already turned walnut brown from two days at the poolside.

He seemed completely untroubled that he was effectively being held prisoner, and Iris was beginning to wonder just who was trapped here. He seemed to be having a great holiday, lazing in the sun and eating Marta's amazing food. Convivial, courteous and fascinated by everything that went on, he'd already charmed everybody working at the hacienda. They all pronounced his name 'Grief', and he was certainly causing Iris a lot of that.

It had seemed a funny idea to 'kidnap' the man who had crashlanded on her wedding and demand to know more about his co-conspirators, not to mention the amazing voice recordings he'd left on the flash drive. But he was giving away nothing – and he was now taking too much advantage of her hospitality, Iris felt. She also had a sneaking suspicion that he was still working for her mother, so it suited him perfectly to stay and spy on her; she'd played right into his hands. She knew the simplest solution would be to tell him to leave, but rather like the air-conditioning, the house safe was a complex piece of over-engineered gadgetry: having secured his car keys, wallet and passport inside it with the flash drive, the girls now couldn't open it. So Griff remained at Sueño and Iris spent every spare minute trying to crack the safe's codes.

Meanwhile Griff had slotted into the Sueño routine as easily as a key in a lock, especially at the lunch table. In the past three days, his seemingly unending interest in everyone and everything at the hacienda had revealed more about Chus, Alejo, Marta and the rest of Sueño's inhabitants than Iris had ever known, from Civil War family tragedy to romantic secrets hidden in the sherry vines. His Spanish wasn't great, but he had a way of drinking in answers as though he understood and valued every word, and those listening in learned things about their friends and workmates that would deepen alliances and affections.

Unlike the rest of the adoring Sueño crew, Iris determinedly deflected his constant interviews and those earnest, questioning dark eyes. Having perched on studio sofas across the world enduring cross-examinations while promoting each of the Ptolemy movies, Iris had no desire to open up about herself to a media-savvy stranger, especially a man who might still be in her mother's employ. Nor did she laugh at his jokes, which came often and were upbeat and quirky. She preferred her humour black and ribald, like Dougie's.

She missed Dougie wretchedly, craving his determination and strength. The urge to contact him was a constant ache, but she'd received no more messages since he'd flown to LA and she'd vowed to stay strong and hide in this hot, dusty cauldron until the tears stopped.

She was desperate to swim – last night was the first time she'd risked it, late in the evening when the sun had slipped behind the hills and the cicadas had been singing at their loudest. She'd escaped from the action movie Griff and Chloe were half watching and wandered outside, finding herself by the pool almost without thinking. There she had pulled off her dress, slipped off her leg braces and slid into the soupy water with a satisfying whoosh of weightless ease. Now she craved the support of the water again and its glorious cool.

Limping through the dappled shade of the olives to the covered seating area, Iris located her e-reader, but she'd only got three pages into her favourite Georgette Heyer when the battery died. At the same time, Nieve came out with a large rug from the salon, draped it over several chair-backs and started bashing it with a long-handled implement shaped like a pretzel, sending up clouds of dust.

Iris stalked across to the pool, not caring that the freeloading seal was there.

Griff was floating on his back on an inflatable in the shallow end, wearing dark glasses and lime-green trunks that made him look browner than ever, droplets glimmering on his abdomen like diamante studs on an oiled leather saddle. His ID necklace trailed in the water like a leash from a surfboard. She wished somebody would grab it and tow him out to sea.

'Hello, lovely,' he called, in that laughter-laced Welsh voice. 'Are you joining me?'

Ignoring him, she clattered into the little poolhouse. Several spare swimming costumes waited there for guests, and she was certain one of her mother's would fit. Mia always bought super-flattering designer bikinis and one-pieces guaranteed to make one look ultra gym-fit. Iris's own bikini, abandoned on her bathroom floor the previous night, was a saggy knitted thing she'd bought from a beachside trader in Ibiza.

Annoyingly, none of the spare swimsuits appeared to have been bought with her mother's impeccable taste. The cups on all the bikinis seemed big enough to house her buttocks rather than her breasts. She opted for a bead-trimmed purple tankini, and only realised after pulling it on that it was maternity wear, with a ruched, expandable front that proclaimed BABY ON BOARD. At least it would give Griff something to think about, she decided, dragging on the baggy, beaded bottoms.

Griff watched her from his Lilo as she limped out. Her pale freckled legs, which had been smothered in factor-50 all week, still displayed faint tidemarks where the support braces had covered her skin. She hobbled to the pool and sat on the edge, lowering her legs beneath the cool blue surface. The water felt freezing compared to the previous evening, the contrast between water and air temperature being so much greater in the late morning. Bracing herself, she slipped in and let out a yelp of shock.

'You get used to it.' Griff laughed. 'Feels warm as a bath to me now.'

She started to swim, weak leg miskicking as she splashed around inelegantly, swallowing water. The bikini bottoms felt even baggier under water, billowing out like a jellyfish skirt and forcing her to swim with corkscrew kicks as she clenched her buttocks to hold them up.

'Such a great place you have here.' Griff bobbed in the rip-tides as she thrashed out a few lengths. 'I saw the photographs of how it used to look. It's an amazing restoration.'

'Glad you like it.'

'It's just a shame they used mahogany for all the hand-carved doors. The deforestation along the Amazon has to be seen to be believed.'

'Feel free to leave through a hand-carved door at any time.'

'I will, as soon as you give me my flash drive and my car keys.'

Given his technical brilliance, Iris suspected he could get them out of the safe himself in no time, but he was showing no inclination to do so and she was too proud to ask.

'Does your mother ever come here?'

'Of course. She was here last week, buying horses.' She was forced to tread water briefly to fish down and haul her bottoms up, inadvertently giving herself a wedgie, which at least kept them in place.

'I'm just a bit surprised, given all the bullfighting history.'

'That was in the past.' She swam on.

307

'But it's still going on around here, isn't it?'

'If you want to go to a *corrida*, I'm sure Chus can arrange something. Just count me out.' She plunged past him, making his Lilo spin like a coracle.

'Do I take it you're as passionate about animals as your mother?'

Trying to think up a witty retort involving scapegoats, male chauvinist pigs and animal husbandry, she misjudged her turn at the shallow end, her hand grasping nothing but water as she reached for the tiled side. She splashed around bad-temperedly, then set off for the deep end again.

'You should both come to Africa,' Griff was saying as she motored past. 'The conservation work going on out there is amazing. Are you sure you should be doing this much fast swimming with torn ligaments?'

Her leg was really aching now and she was worried she'd overdone it, but it was easier to avoid the constant questioning if she kept doing lengths.

But when she turned again to launch herself back through the deep end, a searing pain ripped through her injured leg as if a machete had sliced off her kneecap. Her body curled in a reactive, self-protective spasm and her head sank beneath the surface. Eyes wide with terror, she could see the bottom of Griff's Lilo and his hairy legs dangling down. This was immediately replaced by a cloud of bubbles as he plunged in to save her.

When he hauled her up the steps and laid her down, the heat of the sun-baked stone tiles made her feel as though she was on a red-hot griddle, but she'd swallowed so much water that when she tried to scream she just made a slurpy, throaty noise.

Griff quickly put her in the recovery position and checked her breathing, his dark-eyed face closing in on hers. Lungs still full of water, she spluttered, gasped and managed to croak, 'Don't even think about mouth-to-mouth!'

'I wasn't.' He smiled. 'You are definitely alive and breathing.'

The pain skewered her leg afresh, so violent she almost passed out, eyes clenching shut.

She was aware of Griff's shadow moving away and bright sun flashing red through her eyelids. Then she felt his hands on the soft hollow between the tops of her thighs and her hipbone and let out an outraged squawk.

'Your pants had fallen down,' he explained, pulling them up before turning his head to examine her knee. As he did so, the identity tags dangling from his neck clanked against her beaded tankini bottoms.

Mortified, Iris listened to the sound as she tried to blot out the pain. Clink clink, like a wind chime. She could feel Griff's body heat and smell the chlorine from his skin. He ran a hand along her flinching, pain-seared leg.

'Is it easing at all?'

'A little,' she said, tears scalding her eyes, although whether from pain or the humiliation of having flashed in front of her enemy house-guest, she couldn't tell. The stabbing sensation was receding, sawmill blades shrinking to jabbing razors.

'I think it might just be cramp.' He kept a warm hand over the drum-tight thigh muscle just above her kneecap to ease the spasm.

As Griff kept a reassuring pressure on her leg, Iris gritted her teeth and counted out the pain, listening to the percussion of ID tag against bead to focus away from the blood rushing through her head. Clink clank. The cicadas were singing. Creak, creak, creak. She could hear something else too: a familiar no-nonsense female voice alongside a far deeper, languid Spanish burr.

'Chus he keel me if he know I sweem not ride.'

'It's just too bloody hot to do anything else, Alejo.'

'I love the way you say my name . . . Alley Jo, like American DJ.'

Chloe and Sueño's head rider were heading their way. Iris tried to struggle upright, knocking Griff off balance. But his ID tags had caught in the beading of her tankini bottoms and, as he fell away, they shot down her legs again.

'No!' She made a grab for them, accidentally catching his tags so that he was pitched headlong into her crotch with a garrotted gulp.

'This pool is so lovely,' Chloe's voice was immediately behind the Moorish arched door in the wall now, 'and so sexy, I always think—'

The door opened. Iris's eyes met her friend's. Chloe and Alejo froze as they saw Griff's face buried in her writhing groin.

'I think we should have coffee.' Chloe went into rapid reverse, ejecting Alejo so fast that he disappeared into a laurel hedge, spur rowels spinning.

By the time Griff's tags were released from Iris's bottoms, he was helpless with laughter, but Iris was too furious to speak. The cramp in her leg had passed, but she was aflame with rage and mortification. She hated Griff Donne, especially when he said, 'Your Brazilian's getting a bit overgrown, by the way. I guess that's the opposite of Amazonian deforestation.'

'It's French,' she hissed. 'And I haven't had it done since the week of my wedding, the one you ruined. Just as you have ruined *my life*!'

'Steady on.' He tried to help her as she clung to the bougainvillaea trailing from the wall to pull herself upright, purple and pink petals shedding in her hands. She elbowed him away, determined not to cry.

'I love Dougie and you wrecked everything!'

'How many times must I repeat this? It. Was. An. Accident.'

'I *know* my mother was behind it.'

He started to laugh again. 'In a very roundabout way you could be right, in which case – even though I've never met or corresponded with your mother – we've both collaborated to do you one hell of a favour.'

'How can you possibly say that?'

'Look at you.' He threw out his arms as she clawed herself upright with the aid of the trellis and turned to face him. 'You're a child, Iris. A sweet, tantrum-throwing, sulking child with your big, princessy wedding plans.'

She tugged up her tankini bottoms, which had started to slip again, and looked around for something to throw at him.

'Face it, little one,' he went on, 'you are far too immature to get married.'

'Take that back!'

'Why? It's the truth.'

'You just made a very big error of judgement.'

'I don't think so.'

Unable to find something to throw at him, Iris elected to throw herself. Howling, she executed her best rugby tackle and tried to push him into the pool, but it was like hurling her weight against one of the stone lions in Trafalgar Square. She turned away, defeated, and limped towards the poolhouse without another word.

'See you at lunch!' he called, loping towards the house.

Having persuaded Chloe that they should take their coffee in her room to keep out of Nieve's eagle eye, Alejo proceeded to kiss her in a way she imagined was ascribed to Latin lovers in the erotic books her mother devoured on her Kindle while pretending to work her way through the Booker shortlist. It was certainly passionate, if also stubbly, sweaty and rather like being ravished by an amorous sink plunger. Every time she thought she'd got the hang of it and was matching his pressure and angle, he'd de-suction and reattach somewhere else: her lips, shoulder, cheeks, neck and forehead were repeatedly sucked and anointed.

Over-excited by the sight of Iris and Griff at the poolside, amazed at the softness of Chloe's caramel skin and the delicious curves beneath her baggy polo shirt, Alejo was fast-tracking their first kiss, hurrying Chloe out of her comfort zone.

All sorts of exciting things were happening to her body, little happy twitches and vibrations and warm, buzzing sensations, but she couldn't stop her mind whirring and analysing, trying to make sense of what was happening and rejecting it as faintly ridiculous. She was also starting to panic that her lack of experience would put him off.

'You are a virgin?' he asked, between stabbing his tongue into her mouth at different angles as though chasing the last traces of dessert in a plastic pot.

'Not totally,' she gulped, hoping he wouldn't want any more detail on her drunken university one-night stand with Josh the law student, which had lasted less than two minutes. Alejo was bound to be a far more accomplished lover, if only she could let herself go enough to enjoy the ride.

Taking a break to put some music on in the hope that it would loosen her inhibitions, Chloe caught sight of Griff en route to the house from the pool. She wished she and Alejo shared some of the white-hot heat she'd just seen at the poolside. Iris always had men falling at her feet, eager to pleasure her. If she hadn't been so wrapped up in her desire to get back to kissing Alejo and finding that heat for herself, Chloe might have stopped to think more about the implications of what she'd just witnessed, but right now it showed she had an awful lot to learn in that department. That was where Alejo came in.

Rihanna's voice was grinding its way raunchily into the room and Chloe looked at her prospective Latin lover in nervous antici-pation.

But his handsome face was scowling as he narrowed his eyes. 'How can you listen to this crap? I fetch good music. Don't go away. *Quédate allí.*' He daubed her face with a few more wet, stub-bly kisses and stroked her backside before disappearing through the door with a wink and a click of his tongue, the same thing he did with his horses.

Extremely nervous now, Chloe worried that Alejo might have gone to fetch condoms as well as music. She wasn't sure she was ready for a full seduction yet. And then she worried that perhaps he hadn't *got* condoms – weren't they against Catholic beliefs? –

and that she should really be a liberated woman and have some on hand just in case. The only place she knew to find them was the safe, where she and Iris had crammed all Griff's stuff, giggling furiously when a Durex foil fell out of his wallet.

Chewing her thumbnail, she decided the condom could wait. She couldn't risk being out of the room when Alejo came back. Instead, she'd pop into her bathroom to clean her teeth and have a flannel wash, knowing she must pong from riding. Alejo was probably doing just the same thing in his rooms, she thought. Ten minutes later, thinking he might be having a full-blown shower, she nipped back and gave herself a more thorough wash, eyeing the door anxiously in case he burst back in to find her with a flannel thrust down her breeches. Then, realising these would leave creases on her thighs and bum, she dragged them off, threw on a spotty summer dress and squirted so much deodorant over herself that the room filled with white mist and she had to flap the doors like mad to dispel it.

It was only after half an hour, when Griff called along the corridor to say lunch was ready, that she realised Alejo wasn't coming back.

Having been sidetracked by his father shouting at him to help with a grain delivery, Alejo had quite forgotten about Chloe waiting to hear his music choice. But he flirted his way easily back into her affections over lunch, and found her gratitude rather charming.

'We listen to music together after lunch, yes?' he suggested, dark brows flying suggestively high.

'Oh, yes please.' She looked like she was going to cry with relief.

'Where is pretty Iris?'

'She has a bit of a headache.' She didn't dare look at Griff.

'Women, they always say that!' Alejo's bad joke was rewarded with lots of ribald laughter around the table, not least from Chloe.

'I never get headaches,' she said, too quickly, earning a hot look and a wink from the young Spaniard, which flustered her to the extent that she lost all coordination with her knife and fork, sending a blob of bean stew shooting across the table.

Watching her, Griff could already guess at the dynamic. This confident, no-nonsense girl was incredibly inexperienced with men and, as notches on bedposts went, Alejo probably wasn't far above self-pleasure. Griff had observed the flirtation blossom and suspected that, for all his posturing, cocky Alejo was no more experienced romantically than Chloe: living and working in the male-dominated hacienda provided few opportunities for romance, although his role model was clearly globe-trotting, womanising Haff.

Like a dog sensing an approaching thunderstorm, Griff had always possessed a sixth sense for impending heartbreak. Quietly pondering the situation, he spun out the long meal with questions in his broken Spanish. His great skill had always been to fit into a new tribe quickly and seamlessly, whether in the least explored corner of the world or at a friend's family home. His secret was to ask the questions they loved to answer, not the awkward ones that made them feel threatened and wary, to respect their customs and timescale, to accept their generosity with grace and never refuse their food. He ate everything on his plate as always.

But today he couldn't shake an overwhelming urge to influence events. Watching Iris's clever friend become ever more pliant and self-effacing with the handsome and arrogant Alejo made him uncomfortable. His old-fashioned code of conduct meant he had to step in.

After the dessert – '*flan*', Marta called it, but Griff knew it as crème caramel – he asked Chloe to walk with him to the cross hidden in the alfalfa, which he'd heard marked the spot where one Ormero forefather claimed to have seen the Virgin Mary in a vision that told him to build his house on the land.

'Isn't it a bit hot?' she said, looking longingly at Alejo, who gave her another wink. 'I was going to have a siesta.'

'Mad dogs and Englishmen – and Welshmen,' he insisted,

hooking an arm through hers. 'I need to tell you something very important.'

Guessing he was going to reveal the secrets behind the balloon crash and the contents of the antelope flash drive, Chloe acquiesced. She shot Alejo an apologetic look as they headed off into the blistering afternoon heat and was gratified by his furiously lowered brows and jealous *toro* snort. This was her small revenge for his failure to come back to her room before lunch, she told herself.

But as soon as they were out of earshot, Griff began a totally misguided lecture that infuriated Chloe: 'Don't waste your time on men like Alejo, lovely. Trust me, he will not make love to you, he will simply seek out an entry point and look for a quick exit afterwards. I know men like him. I was one once.'

'Who do you think you are – my father?' she huffed. 'If it hasn't escaped your attention, we're both consenting adults.'

'Think of it as big-brotherly advice. Alejo's like one of the stallions here when a mare in season is led past him: full of noisy, attention-seeking action, but as soon as she goes out of sight he forgets about it.'

Her face flamed. 'How *dare* you?'

'If you want him to give you more respect, you must show him just that spirit,' he ploughed on, undeterred. 'You are clearly a very feisty girl. Tell him to—'

'Fuck off!'

'Well, that's a start, but I was thinking more along the lines of insisting that he takes you out on a few dates first.' He beamed at her eagerly. 'You'll have a lot more fun going to bed with a cockled beefcake like that if you build up the suspense and call the shots.'

Chloe had heard enough. 'What makes you think you know it all? You've spent so long living with primitive tribes you're starting to behave like you're in one. Alejo has nothing on you. You're a total hypocrite! Look at you and Iris this morning!'

'That wasn't what it—'

'She's incredibly vulnerable right now and you took total advantage.' Guilt that she'd neglected her melancholy friend in recent days compounded her indignation. 'She's the one you should be talking to now, not me, starting with an apology. I can't believe I told her yesterday that she'd misjudged you. She was right when she said you're a pompous bastard and a freeloading sleazeball.'

Griff winced. 'Not my biggest fan.'

As they reached the cross where the madonna had given her real-estate advice, Chloe turned the tables on Griff with a lecture of her own: 'Iris is incredibly beautiful and seems so strong and wilful, but she has some really big hang-ups; it's not just the Dougie thing that's turning her life upside-down right now. There's a lot of crap going on to do with her family, and she's not speaking to her mother; they're usually very close, so it's really screwing her up.'

'What about her father?'

'I can't talk about it, but she's really not in a good place.' Chloe was already worried she'd said too much.

'I think this is a very good place.' Griff was looking around at the blue-topped horizon, where fields baked to the colour of biscuits shimmered in the heat. He still had a trace of the arrow-shaped scar on his forehead from the balloon crash, Chloe noticed.

'What happened to Iris's wedding *was* purely an accident, wasn't it?'

'Absolutely.' He hung his head. 'I appreciate that it was unforgivably clumsy of me. Although I gather she was going to marry a total prat.'

Chloe reluctantly conceded the point.

Thinking he was forgiven, Griff was smiling at her now as he went on: 'Stopping beautiful women wasting their time with total prats is my speciality.'

Realising he was referring to Alejo again, Chloe's anger boiled over. 'Do you include yourself in that category?'

'As they say, it takes one to know one.' He laughed. 'And you're right, I should apologise to Iris, although not for what happened this afternoon. That was a life-or-death situation. You'll find out soon enough.'

Thinking that he was referring to her sexual naïvety again, Chloe found she couldn't shake the image of his face pressed between her friend's thighs. 'You egotistical bastard! You might think sex is the answer, but going down on somebody that unhappy doesn't bring them up for long. Half the reason Iris is so confused is because men have been trying to get her into bed since before she reached puberty. When she got famous, they wanted some of her celebrity status and money as well as her body. The only truly genuine man in her life is Leo, and he's never around any more. Dougie was a total shit, yes, but that's no excuse for you to come here and fuck with her head. You should have left her alone.'

'There was no time to worry about what was going on in her head, trust me.'

Before she had time to think, Chloe's hand flew up and slapped his face, sending him flying into the alfalfa. She was much stronger than Iris, with a right hook like Calzaghe.

Running back to the hacienda as fast as she could in the punishing heat, Chloe was now pouring with so much sweat that she squelched. When she rounded the corner to the first courtyard, Alejo was lounging coolly on a quad bike parked beneath the archway, smoking a cigarette.

He tossed it aside and stood up as she panted into the shade, his dark eyes suspicious. 'I was about to come find you.' Then he took in her anguished face and his expression changed to fury. 'What Grief do to you? I keel him if he hurt you!'

'He did nothing! We were talking about Iris.' Aware that she was revoltingly sticky, she tried to shuffle past him, but he barred her way, reaching up to cup her sweat-slicked face.

'Everybody have siesta now,' he said in a soft voice. 'You want to spend time with me?'

'I need a shower, and then I really must talk to Iris.'

'I play you my favourite music while you shower,' he insisted, 'and Iris can wait a little bit, no?' He brushed her damp lips with his thumb. 'We must take up where we left off.'

That was what he said at the start of each riding lesson. The fizzing and twitching had started up in Chloe's lower abdomen again, a pulse ticking excitedly between her legs. If he even fancies me sweaty, he has to be pretty keen, she thought, realising that Griff's pompous lecture had done her a favour after all. Alejo was jealous that she'd gone off for a walk with him. She'd tackle Iris later. First, she wanted to be kissed again.

'Of course,' she agreed, although secretly she had decided they would start all over again, and this time she was going to be in charge. She headed for the safe: she'd make sure she had that condom to hand this time.

Walking back into the cool of the *cortijo*, Griff headed straight to the boiler room to turn down the air-conditioning. Then he cut back out through the cloistered walkway towards the sleeping wing. Iris had a room on the first floor with a balcony overlooking the alfalfa fields towards Arcos de la Frontera. Griff had been given a huge guest suite at the end of the long lower corridor below, with its own small terrace shaded beneath a vine-covered pergola. He hesitated at the bottom of the stairs. He knew he owed her that apology. She was brattish and silly, but she had been through a traumatic time and he'd contributed heavily to it. What Chloe had told him weighed on his conscience. That Iris could be so childish was hardly her fault: it was obvious her mother had cosseted her appallingly, whereas her adopted father had gradually withdrawn his indulgence as the china doll became flesh.

Now Griff thought about Dominic Masters's traumatic journey through life and his ferocious independence. He raked his hands through his hair, his own childish idiocy plain for him to see. He had no right to play God and try to pass on the message that Dominic was alive. His romantic idealism had been in overdrive again.

He could hear male laughter drifting from Chloe's bedroom to the left of the stairs, the sort of throaty, sensual sound that punctuated kisses, all accompanied by some loud Spanish pop music. Griff touched his cheek, still stinging from her power slap, guessing his advice had been idiotically misguided there, too. Chloe was right. He belonged in the bush; it was time to go back.

Still at the foot of the stairs, he hesitated, wondering how to make his peace with the two girls, particularly Iris, to whom he'd been so judgemental. He certainly wasn't the entertaining kidnap victim they'd hoped, and the secrets on the USB drive would now stay with him until he'd made it back to Kenya to speak with Cloud Man. Realising there was a very simple way to remedy the situation, he headed back through the house and the huge salon to the cavernous library where the safe lived behind a shelf of fake book spines.

It took him less than ten minutes to navigate the electronic wizardry and open the door. Mia's birthday was the obvious code, and he'd done enough research to know when that was. Thinking about her made him all the more determined to see Dominic again before she turned forty and his prophecy reached its unofficial deadline. It wasn't long now, the point at which she'd have lived her life again since loving him.

Inside the safe there were half a dozen fat rolls of euros, some official-looking papers held together with elastic bands, several jewellery boxes and – rather alarmingly – a small handgun. His car keys, wallet, passport and flash drive weren't there.

Irritated that his simple exit plan had been foiled, he started cramming the contents back into the safe. A sheaf of photographs fell from the tied papers. They were of a girl on a horse, and for a moment he thought it was Iris, her beauty was so extraordinary. Then he saw a toddler sitting on the pommel in front of her and realised that this was Mia with her daughter, taken many years ago here in Spain. He studied the young Iris closely, white-blond ringlets clouding round her face, the ultimate Miss Pears. She had been exquisite even then.

Other photographs were of various Ormeros posed in bull-fighting gear, plus a couple standing on two plumed horses, waving at the camera, which he assumed must be the grandparents Iris had spoken of who had performed in a circus. At the bottom of the pile was another of Iris, now grown-up and perching on the edge of a low, curved wall that he recognised as the well in the main Sueño courtyard. Blond ringlets now transformed into snaking dark corkscrews, she was cuddling a scruffy dog on her lap, her face so infused with laughter that he couldn't help smiling. She was ravishing when she laughed. It occurred to him that she hadn't laughed once since he'd been there.

Carefully tucking the photographs into the pile of papers and locking them back into the safe, he decided his missing property could wait until he had made Iris Devonshire laugh just once.

A squeak of rubber against tiles made him turn and he found Iris watching him from the doorway.

'I had the same idea, but you'll never get into it. Somebody must have changed the codes. I've asked everyone here and even texted my dad in LA, but nobody knows it. I guess we'll have to blow it open so you can leave.'

A moral dilemma raged in Griff's conscience as he debated whether to crack open the safe again or crack his best jokes instead, but Iris clearly wasn't in a laughing mood, and before he could make up his mind, she'd turned away to limp towards the kitchen, grumbling, 'I take it you were planning to make a getaway?'

'I was thinking about it.' He followed her.

She pulled a lump of Manchego from the fridge and took it across to the breadboard to match with hunks of salt-bread. 'You owe me an apology and an explanation first.'

Making her laugh was going to be hard, Griff saw, familiar irritation beginning to mount. She was hardly a barrel of fun.

But he couldn't forget the joyful, breathtaking face in the photograph, or, if he was truthful, shake the image of her swimming earlier.

He had registered the familiar punch of lust when he admired her body in the pool, but he had dismissed it as no more than he felt for any pretty girl. In the same way, he'd watched her mouth move as she ate and talked at the Sueño table in recent days, and the seductive sweep of that amazing hair from one shoulder to the other. He knew his reflexes well enough to recognise physical desire. He resented the way his body could settle itself so wantonly upon another's when his head was not at all connected. Her brattish attention-seeking was infuriating. Clearly Iris felt no physical or emotional interest in him, and winding her up had been surprisingly satisfying, but making her laugh was not going to be so easy.

'I'm sorry. I'm a beast.' He got through the formalities.

'Is that it?' She turned to look at him, breadknife in hand, green eyes glittering. 'Your apology and explanation?'

He eyed the knife warily. 'Would you like me to say it again, only kneeling?'

Her mouth twitched in amusement. 'No need. I can wait for you to do better.'

Perhaps he should cut his losses after all, Griff wondered, trying not to notice the delicious way her bottom wiggled as she cut bread.

'Would you like one?' She held up a sandwich so enormous it looked like a whole loaf.

Griff was completely full after lunch, but his chapel-going Welsh mother would have disapproved if he had refused to break bread when offered, so he nodded. 'Thank you.'

The second one she made was even bigger. As they moved outside to the shaded cloisters to eat them, Griff hung back and squished his down hard on the plate with the palm of his hand. Even so, it almost dislocated his jaw and was so dry and dense that table-talk was impossible. Not that conversation would have been easy with the Spanish pop music throbbing in Chloe's room. Getting a good comedy routine on the go was impossible.

Amazingly, Iris ate her doorstep in no time and settled down with her newly charged e-reader to devour some more Georgette Heyer, plugging in her iPod and bobbing her head as she read, suspicious green eyes swivelling towards him from time to time, clearly waiting for a signal that a better explanation and apology were coming.

Discreetly feeding chunks of sandwich to the pride of feral cats that always threaded around the courtyard table legs at the sight of food, Griff studied a stray veterinary textbook, shamefully aware that the pangs of lust would not go away.

'I am truly sorry,' he breathed, knowing that whatever she was listening to on her iPod meant she couldn't hear him. 'I should never have come here. I should leave, but I'm not sure I can now. You are utterly breathtaking.'

When he glanced up, the green eyes were watching him closely. Then they returned to the e-reader.

Chloe had figured out the secret to good kissing: rhythm. The Spanish pop music's beat was making her body come alive under Alejo's roving hands and using it as a metronome meant she finally fell into synch with his delicious, delving tongue. Together they moved lips, tilted faces and changed sides. Kissing reached whole new heights. All the sucking and pecking she'd failed to match up to earlier now became desperate, thrilling hunger for Alejo's hands on her face, her arms, her waist and her breasts.

But although he kissed – fantastically as she'd now found out – and his fingers moved greedily around her body above her clothes, he made no move to get inside them or it.

Eager to go further, Chloe lay back on the bed, pulling her with him and whispering, 'I have a condom.'

Pulling back, he muttered, 'I cannot.'

'Why not? We both want to.'

'I want to very much,' he looked down at her, eyes black with desire, 'but my church will not allow it.' His hands were still moving up her legs, warm thumbs caressing the soft skin of her thighs.

Chloe covered them with hers to bring them to a halt. 'In my body, it's an entry requirement.'

He looked confused. 'My father, he bring us all up as good Catholics. His rules go in this place. I must wait until I marry.'

About to snap that no glove meant no love, whatever Chus dictated, she looked into his handsome, troubled face and realised he meant the whole shooting match – sex before marriage was a no-no for the stud manager's family at Hacienda Sueño. Alejo was saving himself for his future wife.

'Please do not make me leave, Chloe.' He kissed her lips so lightly and skilfully she thought she'd faint with longing. 'You are so beautiful. I love to make out with you so much. I just cannot make love to you.'

'What *can* you do?'

He shrugged. 'Touch you . . . kiss you.'

'Anywhere?'

A slow smile spread across his face. 'I guess anywhere, yes. Nobody has said otherwise.'

'And I can touch you anywhere?' His body was like Hacienda Sueño, she decided, a wide-shouldered fortress protecting a beating heart of kind horsemanship and family values.

'I think so . . . but not my ears. I have very tickly ears.'

Naturally, Chloe reached straight for his ears, and he collapsed into giggles on top of her, an enticing weight of writhing muscle and forbidden manhood, growing large and hard against her belly. Her hand burrowed to explore it demurely through layers of denim and Calvin Klein, almost sending him into orbit.

'Can I touch you here?' she checked, fingers stretching wide to assess its impressive scope.

His breathing intensified and he let out a groan. 'Touching me there is *so* good.' He started kissing her again, those hungry rhythmic kisses that made her lips dance in time, just as her body now leapt in response beneath his.

Propping herself on one elbow, she tilted her head back to look into his face, his dark eyes flooded with lust. 'I want you to touch me too,' she ventured cautiously, reaching for his hand.

His eyebrows shot up, as did her heart rate when his fingers found their way to her nipple, which pipped with pleasure, sending a lovely fizzing depth charge to her groin. She couldn't wait to steer his hand in its wake.

As his lips followed his hand to her breast, he looked up at her through his lashes and checked: 'You are sure about this, Chloe?'

'Totally sure,' she insisted. If he went too far, she already knew she had the perfect self-defence move. She just had to tickle his ears.

Chapter 35

The three stallions that clattered down the ramp of the vast articulated horse transporter into the Wootton yard were swaddled in padding and robes, like boxers ready for a fight. By breakfast time they had all been shampooed and groomed with lavish care and filled with best meadow hay by Vicente, and were squealing temperamentally at one another as they started to work out the pecking order with all the other stallions. No longer tucked up and tense from the journey, they were ready to be admired, and Mia was dying to show them off.

Having phoned her way around lots of dressage chums to extend an open invitation to pop by, along with the WAGs who were riding in her quadrille and the charity committee who were working so hard to raise the funds for the school, Mia summoned Laney from the boathouse, where she'd been writing since dawn as usual.

'You must come and see them – they are *absolutely* beautiful.' Mia sighed. 'I keep rushing out to see them to convince myself I'm not dreaming. I was even in the barn at two this morning with my mobile, videoing their arrival so I could email it to Iris.'

She didn't add that Iris had just sent a rather starchy message back saying she'd rather her mother videoed Lorca and Scully, whom she was missing like mad, along with the dogs. In fact, nobody seemed very interested in Mia's new horses. Charlie Soames had spent far more time looking adoringly at her than at them when he'd popped in to check them over before his morning calls, and Jacinta's first reaction upon seeing the little jet-black stallion, Balthasor, was to go into an excited reverie about how lovely it would be to have four matching ebony horses pulling her coffin in the funeral cortège.

'I must get back to the house and call Spain to arrange it.' She turned her chair with a clattering whirr, making all the horses start back in their stalls. Setting off along the barn aisle at speed, she slammed on the brakes and reversed with a shrieking whine, the horses now pressed against their back walls.

'You weel ask Haff? He know the best horses in España.'

'He's coming here today. You can ask him in person.'

'¡Estupendo!'

Mia looked at her watch anxiously, hoping Laney would hurry up: she needed to talk to her before Haff arrived.

He'd been peppering her phone with little texts all week as he moved around the UK coaching and doing lectures, all his missives very civilised and practical, but disconcerting in the light of Laney's recent talk of love affairs and letting the imagination free to go there. Mia's imagination had gone there far too often lately, especially in the news blackout from LA. When Mia called Leo, he seemed to be forever tied up in contract meetings and long confabs with Abe. Haff, by contrast, was ever-ready and admiring.

Since her car confessional with Laney, Mia had been increasingly jumpy about his stay at Wootton to coach the quadrille. Using the excuse of Jacinta's loud funeral music booming out night and day, she'd already told the staff that he could stay in the Folly instead of the far grander guest suite in the house. She wanted fresh air and a lot of prickly shrubbery between her and the Spaniard.

'The Folly' had been the euphemism coined in the original estate agent's brochure for Wootton's rather OTT summerhouse, a nickname that had stuck. Hidden behind an arched gap in a thick yew hedge in the furthest corner of the gardens, where formal lawns gave way to woodland, it was a turreted outhouse that had been variously used as a Wendy house, party room and teenage annexe; Iris had lived in it for several months during one of her more rebellious phases, but had found it spooky, spidery and bitterly cold in winter. At this time of year, however, sunlight streamed in and it was filled with the scent of the lavender planted so thickly around its base it seemed to float in it like a boat in a purple sea. At just a short walk along the sheltered honeysuckle bower to the stableyard, with its own shower room and television, Mia felt justified in putting her guest there. She'd make sure nobody told him it was allegedly haunted.

She would have preferred to put him in the boathouse, which was even further away and out of sight beyond the formal hedging and a lot of trees, but she could hardly boot out Laney, even if her ardent recommendations to start an affair with Haff were to blame for Mia having such disturbingly erotic dreams about him.

'Great horses.' Laney panted up on her bicycle, barely putting on the brakes as she peered into the dark barn before carrying on towards the house, calling over her shoulder, 'I've only time for a *really* quick coffee. Script deadline today.'

Mia gave chase. 'Have you heard from Hope?'

'Every night as promised. Sonia the nanny is a superstar. I wish I could afford to hire her. Malin's spent all of her week off sunbathing topless in the garden. Thank God Simon's away. Mind you, it has its plus points – Fred came round to demand his money again, clocked her, and all his men were back on site the next day. I think it's easier for him to issue threats at close range. I have to make today's deadline or the scaffolding goes.' She jumped off her bike and dived into the house.

Seriously out of breath now, Mia followed. 'Remind me, when is Leo seeing Hope?'

'Today – well, this evening our time. It's his day off, isn't it? Are you two OK? Is he still stressed out about the new series?'

'No, it's all good,' Mia said easily, although she no longer knew Leo's day-to-day schedule, his once-clockwork calls having become all too sporadic and brief of late. But he had texted her late last night to say that he had to talk to her about something very impor-tant and could he Skype at his usual time today? 'I'm just so busy with the gala preps that I keep missing him, and Haff's arriving today so it'll be all go from now on.' Her eyes flashed.

'That's what you want to talk to me about?' Laney, who was punching her requirements into the coffee maker with switchboard-operator speed, turned back to face her.

'That's what I need to talk to you about,' Mia agreed, although in truth she wanted to talk to Laney about everything that was keeping her awake at night, from Leo's silence to Iris's Spanish exile and Jacinta's death threats, but her friend was so volatile right now that she only shared the most immediate dilemma.

On the surface Laney seemed more breathless and distracted than ever, but her advice was still the hard-hitting, from-the-heart, partisan stuff Mia needed.

'Of *course* it's OK – it's just fantasy,' she insisted when Mia asked whether she was right to banish Haff to the garden during his stay. 'Putting him beyond climbing roses, ornamental thistles and carp pools gives a buffer zone, and it becomes even more romantic to imagine him battling his way through them to get to you after lights-out.'

'I'm not sure I'm ready for that.'

Laney keyed in the coffee-machine code for Mia's Fairtrade decaff. 'If you weren't, you'd have put him even further away.'

'You're using the boathouse.'

'I was thinking of a Premier Inn.' Laney looked up as car wheels crunched on gravel. Leaving the coffee machine hissing, she wandered to the window.

On the gravel carriage turn in front of the house, a man stepped from a gleaming white Audi Sportback into the shadows cast from the topiary. Wearing a midnight-blue polo shirt and white jeans that set off his mahogany skin and black hair to perfection, he was instantly mobbed by a small Spanish army of fans from the estate team, who were soon raining hugs and kisses upon him.

'Gosh, he's a bit sexy.' Laney whistled. Then she let out a gasp of recognition. 'Oh. My. Life. *That's* Haff?' The Spanish dressage rider was not at all as she remembered. The little man on horseback in the funny beret she'd seen in Jerez had been like a Mediterranean Lester Piggott; this muscular, well-dressed stud was pure Spanish *caballero*.

Hearing a nervous intake of breath beside her, she glanced sideways to see Mia had gone very pink, her green eyes gleaming like those of a dog sensing walk time.

Suddenly Laney felt a cold sweat encase her, and for once it had nothing to do with the little Korean pills that made her ever more jittery, sleepless and unpredictable. This was cold, hard recognition. Mia was a lot closer to a love affair than she'd imagined. This was no abstract concept like Richard HH, with his clever, bold messages and his dying roses: Laney could switch all that off with one button. Mia had Haff staying within sleepwalking distance of her big, lonely bed, and she clearly couldn't switch off her new-found desire.

She had already raced outside, sliding to a halt in front of Haff, delighting him by throwing her arms around him and raining kisses on his cheeks.

'Juan-Felipe Javiero, meet Laney de Montmorency.' She waved a hand over her shoulder to where Laney was sidling down the steps.

'We've spoken on the phone.' She held out her hand.

He kissed it, then pressed his lips to her cheeks in a cloud of expensive aftershave, his voice a gravelly Spanish purr: 'En*chant*ing to meet you, Laney.'

Cycling back to the boathouse afterwards, Laney reflected that it was the first time she'd exchanged kisses with a man who had not once stopped looking into another woman's eyes.

In an attempt to even up her cycling tan, Laney had taken to setting up her laptop on the small table she'd moved out on to the boathouse's balcony. It was very cramped and she had to keep shifting around to stay in the sun, but her tactics were paying off as the skin on her upper body deepened to a tawny gold to match her legs. Wearing a bikini top was starting to ease away the T-shirt tidemarks, although the more idle traffic that puttered, rowed and powered along the Thames wasn't always appreciative of her Rubenesque curves. One old fart in a small cruiser was particularly disapproving: a whiskery regimental type, wearing a blazer and peaked cap, he cruised past at the same time every day, pipe rammed into clenched teeth beneath his bristling moustache. And every day he called, 'For goodness' sake, put it away, madam!'

Today, Laney flicked him the finger and carried on working, ignoring her phone buzzing with texts, which were bound to be silly photos from Simon or, worse still, badly disguised romantic overtures from Kit Lucas under the pretext of discussing script development. For all his affable stupidity, it hadn't taken him long to understand that she'd sent him to see the wrong Mrs Benson, and now he was back on her case, laughing off her British sense of humour at playing the wrong-ex-wife prank and deluging her with texts and calls asking to talk confidentially about the work Screen Pro Creatives knew she had to offer. He was an appalling actor, but Oscar had always hired cheap talent, to make himself look better by comparison.

When she'd told Simon about it, he'd thought the whole thing hilarious. 'Surely Oscar knows that no man with an IQ lower than his pulse rate will ever seduce you into doing anything. He was married to you, after all. Wait until I tell the crew.' He'd now relocated from Apulia to Umbria, where he'd be filming the pasta sauce commercial, which Laney had only just discovered featured half a dozen leggy models racing across a sunflower field to try to divest her husband of clothes and fusilli tossed in delicious pesto. She was sure the original outline had featured comedy mamas and lusty old ladies, who seemed more in keeping with Simon's usual fan-base.

'Apparently the client's had a last-minute confidence crisis and changed the brief,' he explained. 'They think fat housewives and old biddies aren't "aspirational" enough so they asked for glamour models. You should see them – they're all La Cicciolina clones and are frankly terrifying.'

'I'm surprised the client didn't swap *you* for somebody more aspirational,' she said jealously. She'd hoped news of Oscar's hired Lothario might make him jealous, but he was far too self-obsessed.

'Perhaps the Italian glamour models have been hired by Jamie Oliver on a secret mission to seduce me into revealing the recipes out of the Christmas book,' he mused excitedly.

Today's picture texts were all of the La Cicciolina lookalikes: This one is after my gluhwein, and You have no idea what this one would be willing to do for the secret behind my moist Stollen.

Working was the only way she could keep her mind off her husband's seductive sunflower coterie, and stop worrying endlessly about Hope, with whom she'd spoken daily in LA, short jolly conversations that made her cry afterwards because she wanted her home so much. While she was hidden in the boathouse, Kit Lucas was easy to avoid, and she hoped he'd simply go away.

Much harder to ignore was Richard HH. They were exchanging emails daily now, sometimes several in one session, which was horribly addictive. To Laney, it was like having a packet of biscuits open in a cupboard or half a bottle of wine in the fridge in her pre-Korean-pill days. The rapid-fire jokes and increasingly hot flirtation gave her far greater highs than any sugar rush or boozy session; each email was a high to savour and revisit. In her most recent message, she'd jokingly mentioned Kit Lucas and his transparent mission to woo a controversial film script from her. His reaction was unexpected, the usual teasing joviality replaced with genuine concern: He has no right to do this to you, darling L. Send him straight back to your ex-husband with a message that this is harassment and that you will expose his tactics to the media if he persists. I have close contacts who can help persuade Mr Lucas to leave the country very swiftly if you wish. RHH x

Laney now had alarming images of shotgun-toting gamekeepers in tweeds arriving from the Borders to march Kit Lucas on to a transatlantic flight.

Shifting her chair around so that she was facing the sun again, she tilted her Mac screen forwards to reduce the glare and ignored a shout coming from the river, knowing it was the allotted hour for her whiskery heckler to make his return journey.

'Hey, Mrs Benson Montgomery!' came a sunny American drawl. 'Laney!'

'What the . . . ?' She looked up to see Kit Lucas standing in a small rowing boat that was wobbling precariously. Titian tresses falling into his amber eyes, sea-green shirt unbuttoned to reveal a chest as golden as a carp, and pale grey jeans hugging his snake hips, he looked ridiculously staged, like a young Kevin Bacon playing it dumb in a teen flick. 'Any chance of a cup of coffee?'

'No.'

'C'mon! I rowed all the way from Morley.'

'That's less than a mile upstream – even the current's on your side . . . or it was.' She watched impassively as he started to drift away to the left. The little boat wobbled all the more as he hurriedly sat down to retrieve the oars.

'You have to watch the undertow there – it's really strong,' she said helpfully as he suddenly picked up speed, disappearing behind a weeping willow. 'And watch out for the—'

There was a loud splash.

'—overhanging branches,' she finished, standing up and looking for her wrap so that she could head down to the bank and check he wasn't drowning or frightening the ducks. As she did so, her whiskery boating nemesis puttered into view.

'Madam, for goodness' sake, put them away!'

Poking out her tongue, Laney pulled up her bikini top and flashed at him just as Kit Lucas burst up from the water directly in front of the boathouse. With a yelp, she fumbled with the bootlace straps to cover herself, her ears ringing so loudly with embarrassment that at least she couldn't make out the barracking coming from the little river cruiser.

Much closer to hand, Kit's goofy smile was positively blinding.

Slicking his hair back from his handsome forehead, he looked up at her through long, golden eyelashes. 'If a coffee's out of the question, I don't suppose you have a towel? And before you send me back to the first Mrs Benson, I know her towels are fluffy. She had me trapped in her hot tub for hours, trying to persuade me to take up Tantric meditation. I also now know you definitely wrote *Dalrymple.*'

She burst out laughing.

The sunny smile sprang wider. 'I admit my talents might not lie in reading my research notes, but I have at least figured out which Mrs Benson is which. Now can I please borrow a towel?'

Chapter 36

'You have to push off now, Kit. I have work to do.' The memory of flashing her boobs was repeating on Laney, making her blush all over. It was humiliating enough that her ex-husband was paying this bad-acting American to flatter her, without flashing at him. She now needed to eject him so that she could have a wee, a scream and a foot-stamp, in that order.

Having dried himself as best he could with a hand towel, Kit was now draped hunkily against the tiny kitchenette peninsula, dark red tresses flopping into his languid eyes as he attempted to get into role. 'You have such a strong dialogue voice, Laney. It sings. The original *Dalrymple* deserved an Academy Award. Its sequel will have best screenplay written all over it.'

'As you have Oscar written all over you,' she said. 'The door is just there.'

He sidestepped her neatly, draping himself against a wall instead and knocking one of Leo's paintings askew. 'You seem very uptight.'

'What happens when the past, the present and the future walk into a bar?'

His handsome face tilted in anticipation, straight brows creased in an actorly show of interest.

'It's tense,' she said in a monotone. She really needed a wee now, but she wanted to get rid of him first, partly because she didn't trust him and mainly because she knew every noise from the small cubicle off the main living area was amplified into the boathouse.

After a long delay, he laughed uproariously, showing those spectacular teeth.

'Time to go,' she said firmly.

'Sure. I'll make the coffee first.' He crossed to the kitchen again.

With a howl of frustration, Laney dived into the loo.

When she emerged, he was predictably tapping away on her computer, so absorbed in his task that he hadn't apparently heard the thundering rattle and asthmatic wheeze of pipes that always accompanied the loo flushing. He was a truly useless criminal.

Laney crept right up behind him and checked the screen. He had got as far as her work-in-progress documents file, but now that she had disguised *Dalrymple Two* as 'Romantic Novel First Draft' and changed the eponymous protagonist's name to Gaylord, he hadn't even got close. Instead, he was reading her salt radio script.

She silently lowered her mouth to his ear. 'GET OUT!' she shouted. He let out a satisfying yelp.

He was quick to recover, standing up and adopting his screen-writing-collaborator tone as he gestured towards the laptop. 'This is seriously good.'

'Get out.'

'The sex scene on the docks is in*spired*.'

Arms wide, she herded him towards the door. '*Out*.'

'I think my craft might have gone after I capsized . . .'

'I tied it up. It's still waiting for you.'

'Wow! You so float my boat.'

'Out!' She jettisoned him from the door and closed it, then hurried to retrieve her Mac from the balcony table before closing the french windows and drawing the curtains.

Turning up the volume of her iDock, she found Nine Inch Nails' 'Closer' was playing as she checked her emails, anticipating the heart-leap. There it was. She adored his reliability.

My darling L. Please tell me he's stopped bothering you? If not, would you like me to come and rescue you? Love the idea of your little writing boathouse. Enticingly watery . . . I could snorkel past anytime. RHH x

How long can you hold your breath? she typed before going in search of her diet pills. Her appetite was showing dangerous signs of returning and her Korean reserves were dwindling.

I defy you to hold yours longer, gorgeous girl, he had replied when she returned. The music was still pounding around her as she settled to read on. I have been holding my breath since the very first reply you sent to me, when that delicious pink tongue of yours poked from my phone screen. I can't tell you the naughty things I have since imagined that tongue doing. RHH x

Finding her tongue now hyperactive in her mouth, Laney typed, I am holding my breath too. The American came to call at my boathouse this evening and is still outside. She cocked her head and listened to Kit crashing around in the willows, trying to retrieve his boat and talking to himself in the loud, jokey way that hopes it is being overheard. He is very eager to trade skin for script; it's such a crazy world. His journey was totally wasted. I can't stop my skin tingling because of you. I get so horny ten times an hour I have to turn a circle. I'm like a marionette right now. I stop breathing when I think about you . . .

She reached for her cup of tea, finger hovering over the Delete button, trying hard to think about breeks and blunderbusses and receding hairlines.

She wrote on: I look for your messages like an addict looks for a fix. You are wonderful. I am still holding my breath.

BREATHE! xx was all he replied.

Mia's welcome supper for Haff was greatly hampered by the presence of Jacinta, who grilled him endlessly in Spanish about black Escalera stallions and hearses, then moved on to coffin designs. The Ormero and Javiero families went back a long way, and Haff had enormous respect for the old lady. She'd been a magnificent rider in her day and great childhood friends with his late mother, the two women remaining close even after Jacinta had shocked the family by running away to be a circus performer with her Russian.

Although he listened respectfully, nodding in all the right places, his dark eyes trailed continually towards Mia, a crinkle of a smile touching their tanned corners and a gleam deepening those black pupils.

For the first time in two weeks, Mia was quite grateful to Jacinta for her morbid obsession with her passing. She'd originally intended to talk to Haff in depth about the quadrille choreography and her concern that the riders weren't up to his high standards – not least herself. But she was all over the place tonight, as jumpy as a cat on a carpet charged with static electricity, and didn't trust herself to make sense. Watching the deep-red glow of Rioja being lifted to Haff's wide, sensual lips, she longed for the numbing confidence of alcohol in her blood, but knew she mustn't slip again. Leo relied on her to keep their shared vow not to drink, and even at this distance she couldn't let him down, her twin soul. By the time they'd joined AA five years ago, his drinking had got so out of control that he had barely functioned as a human being, although as an actor he had never failed.

When Lito and Haff moved on to brandy and started discussing funeral readings, she excused herself with an apologetic smile and goodnight kisses.

'The night is still a child,' Haff complained.

'You both default to Spanish social time. I am on English anti-social time, I'm afraid.' She faked a yawn. 'Besides which, this family's date lines all need calling. My daughter wants to be texted with photographs of her dogs and my husband has a play date in Los Angeles that he has promised to share. I hope you find the Folly comfortable, Haff. There's a torch by the back door if you need it.'

'Is OK. I can see through the dark.' Those eyes creased again and Mia had the distinct impression he could see straight through her clothes as well. It left her so ridiculously knock-kneed that when she walked out of the room she could feel her ankles swinging out, like Eric Morecambe exiting after a song.

In her bedroom, still rattled, she sent a hasty text to Iris saying dags okky then took a shower and rubbed a vat of moisturiser on her face before settling down with her iPad to Skype Leo.

But when she dialled, he wasn't there. She waited, refreshing the page, redialling, checking all her settings. She texted him from her phone to say she was ready and waited again. Hearing nothing, she called all his numbers from her mobile, receiving no answer at each. Nor was there any answer from Ivan's cell phone.

Finally, just past midnight, she received a text: My darling Mia, I am so sorry. Forgive me. L

Sorry for forgetting to Skype me, or something worse? she wondered fretfully, but when she texted him to ask, there was no reply.

Laney was still in the boathouse, still online and exchanging ever longer and more intimate emails with RHH, when the alarm on her phone went off, making her jump as though her conscience had crept up behind her and shouted, 'BOO!'

Realising to her horror that it was almost midnight and her allotted hour to speak to Hope, she went to fetch a glass of water. She felt wide awake, but dizzy and disorientated, her whole body thrumming as though somebody had attached a Sodastream to her heart and it was carbonating her blood. The palpitations were getting worse the longer she took the pills. She had to get a grip on herself. Tonight's LA call was special.

Leo should be with Hope and had promised to share the conversation. She'd intended to be at home, the dogs poised to snuffle into the receiver, which Hope loved – they were still at Malin's mercy, she registered wretchedly, and would no doubt be book-ending the hall runner outside the au pair's bedroom door, listening to the faint throb of MTV.

She would have to tell terrible lies and say that she was still working, head throbbing with guilt at her recent adulterous emailing binge. The Sodastream in her chest was pumping out bubbles non-stop now, her heart racing like a mill-wheel in a tsunami. A searing neuralgia pinched at her temples and behind her eyes, and her eyelids started to twitch. For a terrifying moment, she thought she was having a stroke.

By the time her mobile lit up with an international call, she could barely see straight.

'Hello, Mummy!' came Hope's bright voice.

'My gorgeous girl!' She tried not to sob too obviously, gripping the kitchenette surface with her free hand. 'Have you had a lovely time with Daddy-o and Leo?'

'We went to the zoo today. Who's Leo?'

'Your godfather, honeybunch. We all used to have picnics together in Griffin Park when you were a baby. Didn't you and Daddy-o meet Leo today?'

'Daddy-o goes to work every day. He's really boring.'

'Is he there now?'

'He said he has lots of meat to eat until after my bedtime.' There was a mumble in the background and she corrected herself: 'Lots of meetings. Lions eat lots of meat, we saw them at the zoo. Sonia took me there. My favourite animal was the seal because it's really funny and does tricks and likes being tickled like Daddymon.'

'He is quite seal-like,' she agreed, feeling choked as she thought about Simon, the double-barrelled kick of missing him and betraying him winding her for a moment.

'I miss Daddymon.'

'I miss him too,' Laney said, snapping the lid closed on her computer and the latest unfinished email to RHH. 'Now, tell me more about the zoo . . . What other animals reminded you of people you know?'

'There was a tapir. It was really funny, like you.'

'A tapir?'

'Yes. And a lemur that looked like Granny Holden with her dark glasses on.'

'A *tapir*?' Laney cranked the laptop open again to Google one. Sure enough, an image of a seriously ugly South American mammal came up, looking like a cross between a Moomin and a warthog.

'Tapirs are my favourite. Sonia bought me a cuddly one. It's my best ever toy – apart from Gogs. I love you to the moon and back, Mummy.'

Laney cheered up. 'I love you three times round Saturn,' she said, playing their favourite guess-how-much-I-love-you game. In anthropomorphic terms, she decided, tapirs rocked.

Chapter 37

When Dougie settled down in his LA hotel suite to review the footage from Leo Devonshire's CCTV cameras, it made for depressing viewing. On the plus side, he'd clearly been a lot more stoned than he'd thought, making the spiked-drink date-rape line pretty convincing. He could hardly stand up, stumbling around beside the Range-Rover for almost thirty seconds before tripping into the aloe off-screen. On the other hand, the sight of him cross-eyed and lurching around her father's driveway entrance with his wedding tackle hanging out was unlikely to endear him to Iris, or make it easier for her to forgive him now that that wedding tackle had been handled by a pro.

If he was brutally, objectively honest, the footage made him look as though he was reeling around desperate to pee, not hopping about in agony having been savagely attacked by a vengeful ex. Infuriatingly, a branch of lemon tree was obscuring the camera lens in one corner, making the car's number plate impossible to read. As evidence for prosecution it was pretty much inadmissible.

He threw the disk on top of the pile of DVDs on his hotel bureau, then carefully picked it up again. It would be about the dumbest thing he was capable of doing to muddle it up with the acting showreels that Abe Schultz had been sending out to casting directors all week in glossy boxes emblazoned with his photograph, copies of which he took along to any meetings. He knew he was highly capable of being dumb, for which he seldom spared regret or apology. Dougie had blazed through life thus far with a healthy awareness of his faults: headstrong overindulgence and supreme thoughtlessness, both long-standing Everett traits that had served the family well from Crusades to credit crunch. His father was fond of saying, 'It's not just who you know that counts, it's what you know about those people.'

But Dougie was from the branch of the family that preferred action to politicking, and sharing the fact that he knew about his future father-in-law's gay college affair was not something he was proud of. Leo Devonshire was kind in a way that Dougie found almost incomprehensible. He would have made a glorious dynastic ally, just as Iris would make a heavenly wife. But this knight had pillaged the kingdom very ignominiously, demanding favours before the wedding feast was even laid upon the court's round table.

He'd tried to make contact with Leo again this week to make peace, but the actor's PA was being obstreperous, telling him that Leo was far too busy to take any calls. Abe had also hinted at emergency meetings to do with contracts for the next *Chancellor* series and had been forced to abandon Dougie that day, so he guessed Leo was indeed up to his neck in work. From what little he'd seen of life on a big-budget network drama, a career in acting was no easy ride once the star billing on movies ran dry. Dougie, who had always lived to ride, felt his heels kick an imaginary horse's sides as he sat in his air-conditioned room far from his familiar herd.

He tapped the CCTV disk against his lips before reaching for a pen and scratching the shiny side to make it unreadable. It was not his get-out-of-jail-free card.

This, he realised, was one of those occasions when an apology on a grand scale was required. Iris had never been able to resist big, romantic gestures, and he was certain he could win over both parents too if he staged it right. He already knew the time and place; he just had to figure out the stunt. His team would be at his disposal: they'd had a booking for that day which had now fallen through.

He called his business partner, Rupe, a killingly posh and gratifyingly dim ex-polo professional, who was currently running the stunt team in the UK single-handedly. But when Dougie explained that he'd need their best trick horses on the twentieth of July, there was a lot of horsy laughter and sniggering as he was told they'd just taken another booking that day for all eight Friesians and a stunt rider in full medieval armour.

'Modelling job,' his partner told him, still honking and snorting happily. 'I'm just calling around some old girlfriends to get the totty lined up.'

'We're providing the models?'

'Yah. Something to do with health and safety. The lady's getting back to me to confirm tomorrow – if I've got the girls, the job's ours.'

'When she does, tell her you've remembered you have a prior booking,' he snapped.

'No way, José! The models are practically going to be in the buff, Dougs. I've assured her of my personal assistance throughout, yah?'

Dougie ground his teeth. He'd been far too distracted by his love life and his Hollywood dreams of late, taking his eye off the business, which Rupe now considered his baby.

'I'll match whatever she's paying and give you a week off.'

'Basically it's for charity, yah?' he said stubbornly. 'They're only paying costs, but it's for a rally great cause with loads of slebs so we'll get lots of press, mate. A riding school for thick kids or something. Sounds like my old al jihadder.' He snorted with laughter again.

'I think you mean alma mater,' Dougie corrected wearily, wishing Rupe had an intellect to match his horse sense. But suddenly his own mind went high-goal as he asked, 'Where exactly is this celebrity event being held?'

'Somewhere near Henley, I think. Hang on, I wrote it down somewhere. Wootton Court. Sounds a bit familiar.'

'It should do. You were there for a wedding a couple of weeks ago.'

'Bloody hell.'

'What's the woman's name?' Surely Mia wouldn't go within a million miles of his stunt team for her fund raiser now. She'd been very grateful for his offer of a jousting display when she'd thought he was going to be a part of the family, but he'd assumed that alliance was off.

'No idea. Sounded ancient. Said she was on the committee – she mentioned somebody called Bibi Cavendish?'

Dougie smiled widely, sensing a glorious cock-up. 'Of *course* you must take the booking. It's in a terrific cause, after all. She wants a knight in full armour, you say?'

'I'm taking this one, Dougie,' he bleated. 'If it comes through, it's my gig. You're hardly going to be welcome there.'

'Impossible to give almost-naked girls a leg-up, or swap phone numbers in full armour . . .' he mused idly, eyebrows shooting up as he found himself on a website showcasing some truly awful hats. 'And a knight with a full-face helmet is hardly going to be recognised.'

'Will you be back in the UK in time?'

'I'll swim the Atlantic if I have to. In full armour.'

Chapter 38

Haff covered his eyes with his hands as tabloid favourite Sylva Rafferty bounced around him in the arena on a stocky little bay stallion called Quito, who was visibly wincing as her petite rear end landed in the small of his back. She weighed next to nothing, but her enormous silicone breasts continually pitched her off balance so that her hands tugged at his soft mouth and her legs flapped at his sides.

'*¡Vaya cruz!*' Haff moaned in an undertone to Mia. '*Berzas, bufas, peras, brevas – ¡ay di mi!*'

The great trainer was not impressed with the riding skills of the horse-mad WAGs whom Mia had recruited for her dressage quadrille. They had admittedly got off to a poor start when poor little Kerri Hughes, first up that morning, had promptly fallen off the exuberant Balthasor. She was currently hiding in the house in floods of tears, supported by best friend Gabby, who now flatly refused to ride at all. Meanwhile Haff watched despairingly as Sylva, the sex-kitten third wife of rock legend Pete, kicked a highly trained sensitive Spanish horse around the arena as if he were a gymkhana pony, her huge chest bouncing.

'Her *lolas*, they are simply too big. She cannot ride for toffee.'

Sylva panted past shouting, 'I heard that!'

'That's a bit unfair. They're a new pair, after all,' Mia said, knowing how hard it was to bond with a horse – Sylva was sitting on Quito for the first time. The little Bratislavan former glamour model and armour-plated self-publicist was the best of Mia's quadrille riders by far and she couldn't risk losing her, particularly as her husband was orchestrating the music, something guaranteed to be a crowd puller.

'Why she get them made bigger I no understand,' said Haff, misunderstanding, and admiring Mia's small, pert breasts in a fitted polo shirt.

Thankfully Sylva was made of tough stuff and was already trotting around them in tight circles, ready to issue a challenge in her Slovak purr. 'Now, Mr Haff, you provide the toffee and I'll ride for it ...'

Haff swallowed nervously and suggested they try some basic lateral work.

Heaving a sigh of relief, Mia hurried to the house to talk Kerri and Gabby into staying on. The girls were sitting at the kitchen island, texting and messaging like wildfire on jewelled smartphones while conducting an animated conversation about hair extensions.

'Oh, there you are, Mi,' said Gabby in her languid Dagenham monotone. 'Me and Ker, we don't fink this is for us.'

Gabby Santos da Costa was a long, thin whip of blonde ambition whose young fame and subsequent marriage to the highest-paid Premiership striker had been won on the harsh battlefield of manufactured girl bands. As such, she was a Maine Coon of catfights and a very tough negotiator.

'I'm *so* sorry Haff was a bit abrupt,' Mia soothed, 'but he's honestly the best trainer.'

'Oh, he's all right – football coaches are far worse.' Gabby was tapping another message into her crystal-encrusted phone. "'S not that, Mi. I've just heard Hailey Laycock's dropped out of *Celebrity Dinner Party Planners* and they've offered me the gig. It's a full week's filming, so no-can-do on the gala. Soz.' She turned her trout pout down at the corners.

Mia counted to ten. It was one of the shows Simon presented. 'You can't do this to us. Call them and say no! Think of the charity.'

'This is, like, a *big* career break for me, Mi.' Gabby raised a Scouse brow as she clawed at her phone screen, replying to a message while she spoke. 'I see *Loose Women* calling.'

Mia turned to Kerri in desperation. 'You can still ride with us, can't you?'

Unlike her friend, Kerri was utterly in awe of Mia. Petite, dark-skinned and curvily burlesque, she'd blinked her way into the limelight through a television reality show and seemed endearingly grateful for her luck and her marriage to a Rottweiler-faced England goalie. But that morning's fall had shaken her. She thrust out a saline-plumped lower lip. 'I don't want to do it if Gabby's not.'

Mia knew she had to be Machiavellian. Excusing herself politely, she dashed back outside to call Laney and insist that she contact the daytime cooking show's producers and put a stop to Gabby appearing on it.

'I really haven't got that much influence,' Laney apologised. 'If she wants to be a small-screen star then you'll have to make her think your quadrille's going to get her on prime time as surely as donning ostrich-trimmed Lycra, topping up her spray tan and jiving with Anton du Beke.'

'But that would be lying.'

'The secret of building castles in the air is good foundations,' Laney insisted. 'Tell them there's something going on at the gala that's very hush-hush but involves *lots* of cameras and celebs ... Let them imagine the rest. Simon gets back from Italy today so I'll make sure he's in on the ruse – he can start a Twitter rumour. By the time those girls realise they've got the wrong end of the remote control it'll be too late to pull out.'

'You. Are. Brilliant!' Mia whooped.

Before she rang off, Laney demanded: 'What's going on with Leo, by the way? He stood Hope up at the zoo yesterday.'

Mia gripped her phone tighter. 'Yes – sorry about that. He's really tied up right now.' She had switched into auto-protect mode, but her voice shook as she fought not to break down and weep out her fears, terrified that last night's 'Forgive me' text meant he was breaking down big-time.

Lacking sleep, missing Hope like mad and het up because Simon was coming back, Laney was not at her most intuitive or sympathetic. 'Well, tell him I'm so pissed off I've thrown his thimble collection into the Thames. I must go. I'm cooking Simon a welcome-home feast and the pan under the Christmas pudding's boiled dry.'

'Christmas pudding?' Mia gazed up the cloudless July sky.

But Laney had already hung up.

Talking Gabby and Kerri around took half an hour of heavy hints, impassioned pleading, flattery and a great many costume compromises, fraying Mia's patience to shreds, especially when Jacinta burst into the room, electric wheelchair at full pelt, crying, 'I must have bagpiper at my funeral. Do you know one?'

When Mia made it back out to the stables, Quito was drying off under the heat lamps and Sylva had Haff pinned up against the saddle racks in the tack room, telling him his teaching technique needed refining. 'You are too dry, I think, like your Spanish soil. If you want me to ride for toffee, Mr Haff, I must feel sweet and sticky . . .'

'Mia!' he burst out gratefully. 'We weel rearrange choreography. We make everything much simpler and cut it down to five minutes.' Shooting Silva a wary look, he guided her towards the battered old table in the centre of the room where his notes and diagrams were laid out. 'The music will need to be shortened too.'

'I'll get Pete to change it,' Sylva purred easily, winking at Mia before wandering back outside to call her husband. A moment later they could hear her saying, 'Yes, baby, I agree she should have asked Carl Hester to be in charge of it ...'

'Please tell me this isn't going to be a total disaster,' Mia groaned, pressing the balls of her palms to her forehead to try to stop the migraine that was descending fast.

Haff put a warm arm around her, growling in her ear, 'Tonight, I take you to the Companhia de Dança Equestre Portuguesa, which perform in park here in your capital. Then you will see what quadrille should be.'

Our very long lunch is getting longer, darling L; a lifetime would not fit in all we must say and do when we meet. You light up my days and keep me awake at night. RHH x

Laney quickly deleted the message, aware that Simon could walk through the door at any moment. The Labradors had been patrolling the hallway all afternoon, letting out squeaky yawns of anticipation, tails thudding the furniture as canine instinct told them their master's return was imminent. Guilty instinct meanwhile told Laney to eradicate all evidence of Richard HH's messages from her phone and laptop and welcome Simon home from Italy with a fanfare of love, certain that taking a rare day off work to play domestic Demoness would put her life and marriage in a better perspective.

She hadn't cooked a proper meal for ages, her desire for food eclipsed by lust and Korean appetite suppressants. Today she'd deliberately not taken her diet pill and had embarked upon preparing Simon's favourite comfort food, not pausing to wonder if it was wise to serve such a hearty British meal on one of the hottest days of the year.

Chopping onions, her mind flew to Richard HH. In the past twenty-four hours their communications had crossed an invisible line, and he was no longer somebody she could drop from her contacts at whim. She'd already confessed too many truths about her fears and desires. Right now, he was more of a confidant than Mia or any of her other friends, and more of an intimate than her husband. She longed to have been brave enough to reply to his message to say that they had to stop communicating, but the thought of it made real tears thread through the onion ones and drip on to the wooden board.

When Simon came in through the door to find his wife weeping quietly over a mountain of onions, he gathered her straight into his arms. 'I can smell how upset you are,' he laughed, his eyes watering too as he kissed her before dropping down on his haunches to hug the ecstatic dogs. 'Ken! Chels! Come to Daddy!'

Laney mopped her eyes with the backs of her hands, grateful for the onion camouflage. The palpitations in her chest had returned and her stomach was churning as she gripped the worktop to breathe deeply and waited for a now-familiar dizzy head-rush to pass.

'I was going to offer to take you to the Poussin tonight, but this is a rare treat.' Simon was eyeing the surfaces, which were covered with abandoned mixing bowls and chopping boards, raisins littered everywhere like rat droppings, butter pats melting into spilled flour and split sugar bags leaking like slow egg timers. 'What are we celebrating?'

'Lots of things.' Laney straightened up, her head clearing. 'You coming home, of course. Plus I've finished drafting *Demon's Festive Treats* as well as the travel guide, so you just need to look through the manuscripts to add your witty asides. Then we can deliver them and get paid.' And we're celebrating my decision to stop emailing Richard HH, she added silently and immediately felt sick again, not helped by Simon lifting the lid on the pot bubbling beside her so that the kitchen filled with the rich, boozy smell of plum pudding.

'You are quite brilliant, darling.' He peered into the steamer, feigning enthusiasm. 'Do I deduce that we're sampling a recipe from *Festive Treats*?'

'I knew it was a mistake.'

Simon turned to protest that he loved Christmas pud, but then he saw Laney's face. It was waxy, her eyes glazed and one lid thrumming with an involuntary spasm. She seemed to be struggling for breath.

'Oh Christ, you're ill!' He dropped the lid and rushed to her. 'Sit down. Let me fetch you some water.'

'Just a bit queasy.' She let him steer her on to a kitchen chair, put her head on her knees and fought to breathe normally.

'Darling, you've been pushing yourself too hard.' He crouched in front of her, holding her hands.

'I'm fine. Honestly.'

'You don't think you're overdoing the diet-and-exercise regime a bit? You know I loved you the way you were.'

'I'm *fine*.'

'You're disappearing before my very eyes,' he said uneasily. 'I keep telling you I want to see more of you, yet every time I come home there's less.'

'Haven't you heard less is the new more?' she joked, deciding the black linen shift Mia had bought her in Newminster had been a mistake: it was far too funereal and made her look washed out. 'I've been cycling a lot.'

'I thought you saw the gynaecologist about that?'

'Bicycling, Simon.' She sat up, rubbing her clammy face to bring back some circulation.

Simon eyed her. She still looked horribly grey and both lower eyelids were running with tiny tremors now. 'It could be an overactive thyroid,' he suggested. 'Cherry, the make-up artist on *Beat the Chef*, has one she's always banging on about. Apparently she thought she was going through peri-menopause, but it was hyperthyroidism all along. Middle-aged women are particularly susceptible, according to her GP. We should get you checked out.'

'I'm *not* middle aged!' Laney snapped. 'I'm thirty-nine and my reproductive system is still a lyre of sweet melodies.'

Simon gripped her hands again, his handsome face lighting up.

'Oh, God, darling, I'm a fool. You said there are lots of reasons to celebrate – could this mean . . . ?'

'I'm *not* pregnant.' It came out more sharply than she'd intended. Seeing his eyes darken with regret, she tried to make light of it but her joke sounded like an insult. 'The lyre obviously needs tuning better.' The word seemed to hang in the air with its phonetic namesake . . . Liar . . . liar.

Simon looked away and made a fuss of the dogs, who'd rushed round the house to find welcome-home gifts, a sock from Chelsea and one of Hope's cuddly beanie toys from Kensington. Laney choked up even more.

'I have cooking to do!' she said brightly, eager to get the homely welcome back on track. 'I hope you're hungry. It's broccoli and Stilton soup to start. I thought we'd eat in the dining room for once. Malin's out, so we have the place to ourselves. You can lay the table now, and me later.'

Despite being exhausted from two days' filming in the scorching Umbrian heat during which he had eaten his own body weight in pasta, Simon cracked open the Barolo he'd brought back and attacked Laney's enormous, unseasonal meal with gusto, guzzling the deliciously rich soup followed by a plate piled with bangers, mash and cabbage swimming in onion gravy.

'God, this tastes so British! You are spectacular, darling.' He beamed across the table, checking the latest on Hope's visit and whether Oscar was behaving, sharing her concern about Leo's uncharacteristic withdrawal, laughing at the prospect of Mia trying to dodge Haff's carnal intentions, less amused by Kit Lucas and his hapless boating mission, then asking after her work and for village news. All the time, Laney was aware that he was watching her closely. Demon was very good at hiding his fears behind quips, laughter and flippancy, but she knew him well enough to recognise that she was under intense scrutiny. Tonight, rather than talking about his trip with florid anecdotes and character vignettes as he usually did after being away, he kept the focus entirely on her.

Gamely trying to keep up the pretence of normality, she talked, drank and soldiered through her food despite her non-existent appetite and a raging stitch in her chest, keen to show him that she was eating as well as ever. But her secrets kept rising in her throat to gag her – diet pills, internet flirtation, retail therapy. She felt like a child who had binged on every sweet in her Christmas stocking then stolen her siblings' and was now trying to force down turkey with all the trimmings.

'You've been spending too long at the boathouse, forgetting to eat.' His pale grey eyes gazed into hers and she was forced to look away, guilt griddling her ribs. Her eyelids were rattling with spasms again and she rubbed them, forgetting she'd applied make-up to wow Simon. She found herself longing to be back at the boathouse now, exchanging emails with Richard, to whom she could confess everything, from her penchant for bottom-slapping to her paranoia that Simon was going to stray.

When she brought out the steaming plum pudding finale and set light to it, the licking flames reminded her of the fire that ignited inside her with every message from RHH. He was thinking about her now too, she was certain. He felt the same way as she did. They'd never met, yet her fantasies revolved around him ever faster, making her giddy with lust. His presence burned merrily in her heart and groin right now.

She looked up at Simon again and felt great ripples of lust rising through her. All the thrilling little horny twinges and spasms of recent days had acted like early tremors to an earthquake, which was now taking hold.

'Laney, are you feeling OK?' He was watching her warily across the table.

Barely able to breathe for lust, let alone speak, she licked her lips and nodded.

He was across the table like a shot, pushing aside the untouched Christmas pudding, which fell to the floor, to the Labradors' delight. He clambered on to her lap, long legs straddling her, and drew her up into a kiss that seemed to turn her eager body inside-out.

Laney had almost forgotten what it felt like to have desire course through her like this. She always had a Pavlovian response to Simon and found his touch thrilling, although that thrill sometimes took quite a bit of stoking these days, especially after too much wine. Lately love-making had revolved around red circles on calendars and blue lines on test sticks. Tonight, however, she was in a whole new league of sensual response. Eyelids thrumming, heart palpitating, skin scorching and ears deafened by the rush of blood, she wanted him inside her with such blind hunger that his shirt buttons flew off and ricocheted from the walls as she fought her way into his clothes.

'Steady on!' He laughed as he found his way far more gently up her shift dress, his long, warm fingers slipping beneath her knickers and easing them over her hips.

'These are rather racy.' He admired the Boyle & Blunt bargains, but she was now too rapacious to speak.

With the colourful lace tanga still swinging from one ankle like a hoop-la, she wriggled her legs out from beneath him so that they rested on his thighs and locked on target, now so wet with lust that she sucked him straight up inside her to the hilt.

'Wow,' he gasped, as he balanced in a half-plié, her thighs weighing down on his. He tried to shift her further back on the chair.

Not noticing, Laney groaned in amazement as her body seemed to take over with near-supernatural possession, internal muscles she'd forgotten she had drawing him in and out of her in long, rippling shockwaves of pleasure.

'Got a ... spot of ... cramp,' Simon gasped.

Laney felt the orgasm coming with such sudden power she had no volume control and the groan turned into a long, ecstatic wail, totally drowning out Kensington and Chelsea's baritone barking as they lumbered away towards the front door.

While Simon let out his own bark of consternation, Laney

hollered and laughed, her entire body jerking and shuddering with a Frankenstein weirdness that absolutely thrilled her.

'Hi there.' Simon held up a polite hand as Malin belted through the dining hall with her new boyfriend en route to her room, both positively scarlet as they looked straight ahead. Laney didn't notice their presence and Simon had the worrying sense that she hadn't really noticed his either.

Chapter 39

Haff's idea of a London 'park' was sweeping parkland in front of a privately owned stately pile near Amersham, so Gothic and grandiose it made Wootton seem like an artisan doll's house. This evening's show was the British debut of the avant-garde riding troupe Companhia de Dança Equestre Portuguesa, known for their outrageous choreography and extraordinary horsemanship, combining classical dressage with contemporary dance and *son et lumière*. It had been sold out for weeks, but Haff's VIP passes guaranteed them front-row seats with complimentary drinks, cushions and even a soft fleece blanket to go over their knees. The other guests were immaculate, and Mia felt embarrassed to be deliberately dressed down in her usual disguise of jeans, shirt and hat, this time a black leather trilby worn low over her nose. Haff looked sensational in black jeans and a flame-red cashmere sweater that suited his colouring absurdly. Mia noticed he drew hungry looks from women all around them but hardly seemed to register it.

'The company director is an old friend of mine,' he told her. 'You meet him later.'

It was obvious from the start why Haff wanted Mia to see the show: it blew all her preconceptions of a pretty quadrille in flamenco dresses into orbit. This was pure theatre, with animal power.

Within minutes every hair on her body was standing up, like a tiny antenna downloading data.

The horses were Lusitanos, close cousins of her beloved Andalucíans. She'd always thought them meaner and coarser, but these doe-eyed visions danced as though suspended on invisible wires, obedience and exuberance combining as they burst in and out of the coloured light, some at liberty, others ridden by girls in extraordinary costumes, seemingly fused to their mounts like ravishing centaurs, long hair interwoven with manes and tails, diaphanous skirts trailing threads and ribbons that laced around the dancing legs. Mia wondered what the gala committee's health-and-safety stalwarts would make of it.

The horsemanship took her breath away, the riders so skilful and light-handed, the horses totally focused on the body wrapped around theirs, the ultimate fusion of training and discipline as they seemed to dance in the ever-changing lights, four-legged fireworks that burst from darkness in *croupade*, *ballotade* and *capriole*, the most difficult of classical training movements. She found herself thinking how much Iris would adore it, feeling a stab of regret that they were still only exchanging texts.

Mia was so transfixed that, forgetting she might be recognised, she pulled off her hat to see better, turning to Haff in amazement when a particularly spectacular *coup de théâtre* left her breathless. She was genuinely baffled when she realised the performers were taking their final bows, glancing at her watch in disbelief, unable to believe two hours had passed and it was over.

'Come and meet the performers.' Haff laughed as she let out a shriek of excitement, then picked up her bag, hooking it over one muscular shoulder, so virile that even a coral-pink Chloe Paraty couldn't detract from his bristling machismo.

A three-quarter moon hung in the sky, almost kissed by Venus. It was incredibly warm, the fleece blankets still neatly folded beneath the seats they had vacated, spare cardigans and jackets crammed through bag straps or tied around waists.

The stately pile's stables had long ago been converted into office suites, so the troupe had set up a temporary encampment behind a high bank of yews, well accustomed to creating a home from home on tour. The two horseboxes had been parked end to end with makeshift wooden stalls fixed to running rails on their sides and awnings pulled overhead to create neat lines of partitions in which horses were being washed down, rugged up and settled for the night. Fanning out in a semi-circle around them were caravans and tents, all creating a cosy Portuguese *campismo* by a thoroughly British ha-ha. At the centre of this, trestle tables had been set up in a gazebo, where some of the team were laying into huge trays of salad, risotto, roast-cod dumplings, cold meats and cheeses. Mia hadn't eaten all day and her mouth watered at the smell of piri-piri chicken cooking on a portable barbecue.

Haff introduced her to the principal rider and company director Uxío and his dancer wife Rute, both wiry and diminutive.

'Uxío and I competed against one another many times,' Haff told Mia, 'in love as well as grand prix.' From the wistful look she saw Rute giving him, Mia guessed he had won more than once. As the old friends caught up in a curious mixture of Spanish, Portuguese and English, she tried to imagine Leo's parents living this life, when Jacinta had been as fit and sinewy as Rute, travelling and setting up by day, balancing on a horse as it cantered around a big-top by night. As more figures drifted into the gazebo to fill their plates and talk about that evening's show, she was reminded of being on set with Leo – he'd made so many movies on location, in a travelling band of brothers who'd worked, played, laughed, wept and slept together. In abandoning acting, she'd missed out on such camaraderie, and on nights like tonight she craved it. Suddenly she found herself wanting to run away to join the circus.

For the first time, she understood why Iris had fallen for Dougie. He was a circus performer in his way, the dashing stunt man who travelled with his horses to ride daring, breathtaking tricks, his devotion to his animals and dedication to their training marking him out beyond mere entertainers: he was the ultimate nomad player. Her heart burst with shame that she had never seen it before, had never tried to understand the attraction, however inadequate she thought Dougie was as a fiancé. Iris had loved him and Mia had poured scorn. She longed more than ever to make amends.

Uxío opened a bottle of Douro and took her along the stable lines to meet the horses, soon trying to sell her a Lusitano stallion, his sales pitch backed up heartily by Haff: 'He has the best Veiga blood lines in Portugal. We get you very good price.'

Mia was tempted to buy the horse for Iris, but she had made mistakes like that once too often. Instead, just as she had politely refused the wine, Mia gently deflected the salesmanship, laughing as Haff tried ever harder to coax her into striking a bargain, by turns cajoling, flirtatious and charming. 'We are *giving* him away, Mia!' Haff loved horse-trading, revelling in the bravado of double bluffs and stand-offs, then the aggressive thrill of deal-striking. In the years she'd known him, he'd alternated between trying to sell her horses and attempting to seduce her with the same bold enthusiasm, and seemingly never took offence from rejection, always happy to try to strike a fresh deal on the next occasion.

Tonight she was too tired and hungry to want to look gift horses or seductive Spaniards in the mouth, let alone run her hands down their legs and sit astride them. But it came as no surprise, driving back to Wootton in Haff's car, when he reached across and placed a tanned hand on her thigh. Having been fantasising about bacon sandwiches, Mia batted it affectionately away and debated asking him to stop off at an all-night garage so that she could buy some snacks.

She was still trying to make up her mind when she realised Haff had pulled off the main road and they were bumping along an unmade track.

'What are you doing?'

'I have picnic.'

'It's eleven o'clock.'

'I am on Spanish time, remember? And you are hungry.'

Her stomach let out a disloyal growl as they arrived on the banks of the river, which glinted in the moonlight like a shot-silk scarf abandoned by Mother Nature as she trailed downstream to bed. Mia peered out into the darkness and saw they were on a track in a large field dotted with huge oaks, a rickety mooring ahead of them.

'This is private land. It belongs to a client.' Jumping out of the car, Haff went around to the boot and pulled out a hamper, portable stove and checked blanket, like an eager fisherman about to set up for an all-night session.

Mia stayed in the passenger seat wondering what to do. She was seriously hungry, but she longed to be at home in her pyjamas, raiding her lovely larder fridge and with Haff safely installed in the Folly. It was obvious that his moonlit riverside picnic was part of an elaborate piece of foreplay.

The blanket was already spread out close to the riverbank, surrounded by glimmering hurricane lamps. The little stove puttered and a pot sizzled on top, filled with tiny pieces of chorizo popping and hissing. The smell was sensational, forcing her to get out and investigate, although she adopted a defensive stance, keeping her arms crossed in front of her and her legs apart, like a gangland rapper.

From the basket, Haff pulled out bowls and a huge Thermos flask.

'Gazpacho. My mother's recipe.' He patted the blanket beside him.

'I'll eat here, thanks.' She perched stubbornly on the car bonnet, realising too late that it was scorching. She edged around to find a cooler spot.

'As you wish.' He laughed, handing the soup up to her along with a spoon before sitting down to eat his, muscular legs spread in front of him, elbows resting on his knees and bowl cupped in one hand as he stared out to the river.

Mia slurped the cold, spicy soup hungrily. It was deliciously fresh and hugely garlicky. 'So a client owns this, you say?'

'Yes.'

'Did you seduce her on a picnic blanket here?'

'No.' He glanced at her over his shoulder, dark eyes glittering. 'We were standing by a tree as I recall.'

She laughed, a nervous reflex.

'You should let me make love to you, Mia. It is all for pleasure. Your body will open like an exotic flower.'

Mia laughed even more. The thought of opening like a flower might be corny as hell, but it was disturbing in its simplicity. She suddenly found her head filled with images of orchid heads popping out of buds with their drooping, dewy lips parted. The garlic in the gazpacho was making her very hot, for all its cucumber cool.

'Why is it funny that I want to give you physical pleasure?' He smiled slowly.

'You're just such a dinosaur, expecting me to fall for all that opening-flower stuff.'

'I say nothing that isn't true.'

She spooned up the last of the soup.

'How long is it since you shared your bed with a man, Mia?' he asked.

'None of your business,' she said primly. It wasn't the first time he'd asked, and her reply never changed.

The chorizo was messy to eat, perching on the bonnet, with the big hunks of crusty *pan de sal*. Soon she had deep-red oil slicks on her shirt and was feeling hotter than ever, the spices pounding through her blood. At least it was too dark to see the stains, she thought with relief, until Haff offered her a big bottle of Evian.

'I'm not thirsty, thanks.'

'This is to clean your shirt.'

'Oh – right. Thanks.'

As she reached to take it, he held on to it. 'Would you like me to do it?'

'I can manage.' She wrestled it away.

Smiling, he turned to watch the black river in front of them, a watery thoroughfare of nocturnal activity, water rats and voles plopping in and out, a barn owl staging fly-bys as she staked out the banks for good hunting spots, craneflies and moths buzzing up to the flickering lamps.

Mia doused the front of her shirt with water that was gloriously cool against her hot skin. She cupped handfuls to rub around the back of her neck and, realising she was furiously thirsty after all, had a long series of glugs to quench the effects of the salty food.

Still staring at the river, Haff had started to sing one of the traditional old flamenco songs he loved, the deep masculine voice so well suited to the yearning, sensual rasp of the words. He was the only man she'd ever met with a voice as deep as Dom's.

She had almost lived her life again and never forsaken Dom. She had by turns loved and loathed his memory, turning it around in thoughts and in dreams, occasionally in fantasies, always with an ache of regret that still felt like physical pain. She sometimes wondered whether a love affair would lay the ghost to rest and liberate her, but she'd taken her marriage vows to Leo seriously and had always put her family's needs first.

If she was Laney, she knew she would never have waited around like this, however much she adored Leo. A full-blooded sensualist like Laney craved physical pleasure, which was why she ate and drank too much as well as seeking sexual thrills, even if that meant courting danger. She and Simon were at it all the time, as far as Mia could tell, and trying hard for a baby.

Mia knew Iris had always longed for a brother or sister, and her throat ached when she thought of how much she would have loved to have more children. She no longer abused her body in any way, eating only the best food, exercising religiously. And yet it would never host another life, never fill the emptiness left by Iris growing up.

She looked down at Haff's black hair, curled like giant springs, his shoulders wide as a yoke. He was still singing, elbows loose on his knees, a glass of wine in one hand. For all his philandering, he would marry eventually, a young Spanish girl to bear him lots of little Haffs while he bred his beloved horses. And he would probably be a terribly good husband, faithful and strong, practical and old-fashioned.

For a brief, crazy moment, she wondered whether life with Haff might not be happier: she'd be living and working with the horses she adored in a country she had always loved. But even as she thought it, she knew it would never happen. Haff merely wanted to make love, not a life together, and her greatest weakness had always been that she loved for life, unconditionally. She wasn't sure she could have sex without triggering something she couldn't control.

She took another cool mouthful of water, feeling it escape from her lips and run down her neck on to her chest, heating fast as it snaked between her breasts.

Haff turned to smile at her again, the dim flickers of the hurricane lamps lighting up the livid scar on his cheek. 'You want me to take you home now?'

When she didn't answer, he turned to watch the barn owl swoop past. A marsh frog was calling noisily from the reeds.

He knew exactly what effect he was having on her right now, she was certain, but this time he made no move.

Mia felt every nerve ending jump and fizz. Perhaps Haff could give her love. He could give her a child. Just thinking about it made her body jolt with such force she expected it to light up, illuminating the riverbank. By making love, they might just make life. Laney was right: she wasn't too old. If it was almost time to live her life again, this was the only way she would survive the pain of passing that deadline.

Not pausing to think it through any further, she unbuttoned her sticky shirt. As it landed in the long grass with a swish, Haff turned again, his handsome, battered face moonlit and smiling as she faced him in a peach lace bra, water still glistening on her chest.

'My beautiful Mia.' He stood up in one smooth, languid movement and took her in his arms, warm hands caressing her back as his hands slipped up to the nape of her neck, drawing her into a kiss that seemed to be the only thing holding her up, her body suddenly weightless. A furiously lustful pulse thudded in her ears, chest and groin, so fast and loud it seemed to be making music. Then she realised that what she could hear was her phone ringing in her pocket, pumping out Ravel's *Bolero*.

'Don't answer it.' His lips moved to her throat, waking sensations beneath soft skin that been asleep longer than Briar Rose.

'I must.' She pulled away reluctantly. 'It might be an emergency.'

It was Leo. 'Thank God you picked up.' He let out a strange wail of a laugh. 'I just walked out.'

For a moment, she thought he meant he'd walked out on Ivan. 'Why? What's happened?'

'The network issued an ultimatum, saying I had to quit living with a man or quit the show. So I quit.'

Still uncertain, she hesitated to ask, 'Quit which?' He was doing the wailing laugh again and sounded close to hysteria. Instead she said, 'I'm proud of you.'

'Oh, Mia, I need you so badly right now, I can't tell you.'

She stole a look at Haff, who had turned away to light a cigarette, the muscles on his shoulders bunching like cobblestones through his polo shirt as he hunched over to strike the flint wheel.

'Abe is up in arms,' Leo went on. 'He says I'll never work on prime time again. It will probably finish me off financially, but we'll find a way through – we can sell one of the properties.'

Mia watched Haff wander to the edge of the river, smoke pluming from his Marlboro.

'I spent most of yesterday in emergency meetings,' Leo rattled on. 'Abe wasn't letting me out of his sight.'

That would explain the broken zoo date, thought Mia.

'He did everything in his power to try to persuade me not to quit,' Leo went on, his soft voice shaking with emotion. 'Today, I quit.'

Mia was now almost certain the walking out had been on *Chancellor*, but just to make sure, she asked, 'How does Ivan feel about it?'

'He's right behind me. The show's giving me forty-eight hours to think about it, but I'm not going to change my mind on this one, whatever Abe says. They can hardly sue for breach of contract, given it's up for renewal.'

'What are you going to do?'

'There's the thing. I really want to take time out to work on the Lorca biopic I've always planned to make, maybe do some travelling, take some theatre work, enjoy being a father again—'

She opened her mouth to ask whether that meant enjoying being a father to Iris or to his new baby with Ivan, then stopped herself, aware that he was too overwrought to take her jealousy right now.

'—but Abe has just come up with a radical plan that he thinks will still save my reputation and career, and we're going to need your help. It means facing a lot of public interest.'

She felt a bolt of relief run through her. 'Are you coming out?'

'No, but you are.'

'I'm sorry?'

'You're coming out to LA.'

Mia found she couldn't speak. She was incredibly cold, standing in a field wearing just a bra on her top half. Her teeth were chattering. But she was rooted to the spot, unable to move.

'You have to fly here as soon as you can,' Leo was saying. 'Abe's assistant will arrange it all.'

'Why?' she croaked, jumping as she felt a warm hand on her back – Haff was wrapping the picnic blanket around her shoulders, warm and weighty.

'I have absolutely no regrets about this decision, but I can't risk Mamá finding out anything that will hurt her. She's so fragile. Abe thinks the media will be on side if you come here and we put up a united front, especially if you do what you do best.'

'What do I do best?' Haff had taken their plates and glasses to the riverbank to wash them.

'Act.' He cleared his throat uncomfortably. 'You're a better actor than I will ever be, we all know that. Abe thinks if you come here and look ... well ... frail, the cynics will back off.'

'You want me to pretend I'm ill?'

'No! Just ... ambiguously pasty.'

'Is Abe laying on a make-up artist for the "pasty" look?'

'The American press love you – so do the Brits, come to that. They love *us*. We need to be Leomia right now.'

'With a hint of terminal illness?'

'I'll have to cite personal reasons for leaving the show.'

'And woe betide you if your mother or the public discover the truth,' she howled, suddenly outraged. 'What about Iris? What do we tell her?'

Thinking about her brave, affectionate child whose heart was already so bruised, Mia shivered even more at the prospect of breaking into Sueño's spell with something like this. It would hurt her terribly if it was handled wrongly, and their relationship was already on hot coals.

'Tell her the truth if you must.' Leo sighed, suddenly sounding terribly tired. 'Just get here soon, Mia. I need you.'

She wanted to scream that she had her own life here in England, the gala, friends, her animals, the love affair she'd just been about to embark upon, but she knew that was entirely selfish and would hardly register with him right now. She'd not heard him so agitated and needy since he was drinking heavily, her friend of a lifetime who shared parenthood with her, who had sacrificed so much to give his family an extraordinary life, and provided his wife with every material pleasure she could wish for.

Haff was packing the plates back into the basket, gathering up the stove and blowing out all but one of the hurricane lamps.

There was silence on the other end of the phone and Mia wondered whether Leo had hung up on her. Then she heard him crying.

'Of course I'll come,' she said quietly.

Still wrapped in the picnic blanket, Mia couldn't stop her teeth chattering all the way home. She kept picking up her phone, wanting to text Leo with reassurances, yet too angry with him to do so, and Iris to warn her of what might be about to happen, but she didn't know how to go about it in case she blew a hole in her daughter's fragile shell. Iris needed the peace and protection of Sueño. In the end she told her that Leo had decided not to renew his contract with *Chancellor* so she was flying to LA and would call her from there.

More than anyone, she longed to speak to Laney, but she was far too unpredictable just now to trust. In any case, if she spoke to her friend, she knew she would cry, and if there was one thing she was utterly determined not to do, it was that. When Haff tuned in to a radio station playing sad rock ballads she thrust out her hand and switched it to Radio 4.

They listened to *Brain of Britain* for the last twenty minutes of the journey. To her amazement, Mia got seven questions right. Haff smoked a cigarette out of the window, ran over a lot of cat's eyes and complained about the colonial stupidity of driving on the left.

He was not the most sympathetic man in a crisis. Back at Wootton, he rushed to the passenger door and announced his intention to carry her into the house and make love to her all night. 'I weel make you forget all the sadness,' he rasped in his oak-aged Spanish accent, angling for his grip like a forklift. 'I will open you up like a—'

'Flower, I know.' She burrowed past him, discarding the picnic blanket and fleeing inside to her room, pursued by an ecstatic pack of dogs, calling over her shoulder, 'This flower is artificial. It will never open.'

By the time she'd cleaned her teeth, Abe Schultz's assistant had already emailed details of her LA flights to her phone.

At last she texted Laney, asking her to keep an eye on Haff and the WAGs, and most especially Jacinta.

It was almost one in the morning, but the reply was immediate. I'm here whatever you need. I love you. We all love you. Leo loves you. Don't forget that. It's you me and Mia. L xxx

Mia gave way to a dam-burst of relief and wept. 'I love you too.'

Chapter 40

By coincidence, Mia's flight to LA took off within an hour of Hope's plane landing back at Heathrow, although Laney saw nothing of her friend, who had slipped discreetly through first-class check-in unrecognised.

The Demons were the cause of much fascination on the arrivals concourse, but for once, Laney was far too excited to care. When Hope finally burst out of the gate carrying a huge stuffed tapir, she let out such a yodelling shriek of joy that Terminal Three almost launched a security alert.

'Play it down, Laney darling,' Simon muttered, through a big smile, 'we're on camera, remember?' They were being discreetly snapped and videoed on dozens of mobile phones as the public around them recognised Simon. It was always the same scenario in a crowded place: some people asked him to pose with them or thrust the phone lens into his face; others were furtive, like undercover reporters, gliding past with handbags at strange angles then rushing behind a pillar to review their footage.

Laney usually got wound up by the intrusion, but today she wouldn't have noticed if Mario Testino was waving his Nikon at her, her attention entirely focused on her daughter.

While mother and child whirled around together, Simon took Hope's luggage from Sonia.

'Simon! Can I have a snap of you with your lovely wife?' asked an excited voice. Someone from the crowd sidled forward with an iPhone to take a picture of Demon and the young American nanny. Normally Laney would have been fuming, but she didn't bat an eyelid, watching indulgently as Hope did a flying leap into her stepfather's arms. 'Daddymon! Look at my tapir!'

Laney behaved even more uncharacteristically the following day when the *Daily Mail* ran a papped photograph of her at Heathrow looking drawn and gaunt with the line *Laney de Montmorency Dramatic Weight Loss* followed by unflattering insinuations, ranging from a gastric band to the Demons' marriage being in crisis, which meant Simon was trolled non-stop on Twitter. But Laney thought the piece marvellous, unable to see beyond its headline.

'Dramatic weight loss!' she repeated happily to herself, all her best intentions of binning her little blue power pills abandoned. She badly needed the energy now, with Simon and Hope back home and a pile of overdue script work that she'd put off while concentrating on book deadlines.

But her artificially enhanced highs came with ever deeper, headpounding lows, and she was scrapping with Simon more than ever. He reacted badly to a house and diary in chaos, not understanding why his wife's usually brilliant multi-tasking had gone to pot, with post unopened and calls unreturned, clothes unwashed and food uncooked. The contrast between glamour models in Umbria and red bills at Red Gables clearly fuelled his resentment.

'This place is a bloody mess,' he grumbled as he fell over discarded toys.

'Well, tidy it up,' Laney snapped.

'What are you working on that's so important?'

'A radio adaptation of *Madame Bovary*.' Flaubert's classic about an unhappy marriage wasn't putting her in the best wifely frame of mind, but Simon was being even more selfish than usual, expecting to feast, party and canoodle while his dry-cleaning was collected and his travel arrangements confirmed for the week ahead. She just wanted to be alone in the boathouse with her own work and Richard HH's messages.

Laney had broken her promise to herself and written to him again. She had kept it deliberately light-hearted and chatty to make clear to him that their correspondence was always going to be more *84 Charing Cross Road* than *Fifty Shades of Grey*, but he read straight between her lines: I know you too well. I'm here for you. Talk to me, darling Laney. RHH x

While Madame Bovary had yet to uncap her Mont Blanc to pen an illicit love letter, Laney's internet romance was yet again filling her home screen with truths while her home life felt increasingly like a lie.

Chapter 41

Griff was showing no sign that he was tiring of his idyllic Andalucían custody, and was even threatening to make himself invaluable as a practical asset. Although he swam for hours each day, he was incapable of standing still for long. Already a firm favourite with the hacienda staff, his offer to help around the farm had been cheerfully accepted. In recent days he'd been seen mending fences, heaving water containers, helping to jump-start the ancient temperamental Matbro teleporter that shifted bales, herding mares from the quad bike and even getting up at six one morning to help with the mucking out so that one of the grooms could go to a family celebration in Puerto Real. The adoring staff called the Welshman *el dragón sonriente*, the smiling dragon. Marta cooked up ever more mouth-watering lunchtime feasts in his honour, while Nieve had relinquished control of the air-conditioning and let Griff set it at whatever level he wanted.

Working on the yard or in the fields all day, Griff saw little of the girls, who spent the hottest hours reading and talking; he had no need to be in the house as long as he could plunge into the pool to cool off.

Iris was grateful that he kept his distance and was proving useful around the hacienda. For all his boundless energy and work ethic, he was infuriatingly laid-back and played everything down so much that it was easy to forget he was effectively still being held prisoner. She had spent a frustrating amount of time failing to crack her way into the safe to liberate his car keys so that he could leave, and had given up for now. He still owed her an explanation, after all. On the previous two evenings, he'd politely asked to use the *cortijo*'s elderly computer to check his emails, but otherwise took no interest in life outside Sueño and seemed entirely unbothered about leaving.

Iris couldn't resist giving him the odd prod. 'Don't you want to get back to your Cloud Man?' she asked, on his second night at the computer.

Fixing her with his intense gaze, he told her that he was waiting for more information to come to light; and she had a curious feeling he wasn't talking about the files locked in the safe. He often fixed her with that intent stare when they were in the same room, the child psychologist watching the toddler. At other times he went into a strange sort of stand-up routine that she didn't get at all, although Chloe found it hilarious when she was around to witness it. Most evenings, Iris avoided being in the same room as him, which made for a lonely existence now that Chloe spent so much of her free time with Alejo.

Chloe's riding was going from strength to strength. Having graduated from sturdy Uranio, she was now allowed to ride several of the yard's highly trained stallions, trying out Doma Vaquera as well as Clásica, relishing the swift balletic twists and turns of the highly trained bullfighting horse. The same could not be said of her sexual adventures. After an encouraging start, she and Alejo were making slow progress, and his taste in music remained a small sticking point.

To jaunty Spanish pop, they spent hours each day making out but not making love, unable to graduate from one to the other. However excited they became, however hot and horny and moany-groany close to abandoning themselves, Alejo remained stubbornly pious.

He was what her university friends called an above-stairs man, happy to plunder everything from the waist up, but reluctant to burrow lower. While Chloe's boobs got regular, lengthy fondlings and every inch of her upper torso had been stroked and kissed to reduce her to a squirming, wanton wreck, the eager and excitable contents of her knickers went unexplored.

'It does not feel right to touch you there,' he explained.

'You don't want to?'

'I want to, but I cannot.'

He was less demure about being touched himself, although he still imposed limits. Through the jeans or breeches was fine – she'd stroked and caressed her way around the magnificent bulge beneath the cloth layers and fly buttons, feeling it swell and strain to be with her, yet she was banned from releasing it. The moment she started to ease his zip over its expanding glory, he covered her hand with his. It was like having a birthday present she still wasn't allowed to unwrap a week later.

Chloe was a patient girl, but lust was getting the better of her. She writhed with frustration by day and night, and knew that Alejo did too.

This evening, as the Spanish equivalent of the Osmonds harmonised cheerily and they lay side by side in her bed kissing frantically, she knew she had to say something.

'Alejo, I respect your Catholic beliefs totally, but this is driving me crazy.' She propped herself on one elbow. 'I want you so badly.'

'And I want you,' he agreed, his eyes dark with desire as he gazed up at her. 'We will find a way, trust me.' He reached up to stroke her hair, but she ducked away, aware that a week of writhing on pillows and riding in the dusty heat had left it impenetrable. He could spend as long as he liked exploring her boobs, but her hair was out of bounds, which she felt was far more understandable than his reluctance to release the trouser snake.

'You are funny girl.' Alejo smiled, placing a loving hand on her breast, which he lifted to marvel at its weight, his thumb tracing the tight, excited nipple.

Chloe caught her breath, trying to ignore the Iberian boy band crooning happily to an accompaniment of what appeared to be ukuleles. They would find a way, she agreed silently.

'I'm going to ride today,' Iris announced the following morning, as she blew on a mug of milky coffee. She was utterly fed up of being invalided out of the one pastime guaranteed to make a stay at Sueño worthwhile. She remembered her grandmother once saying that the dry Andalucían heat and dust, which were currently turning Chloe's hair into a matted bramble tiara, became the embrace of an angel on the back of a horse.

'Your leg's not strong enough yet, surely?' Chloe regarded her worriedly, concern combining with reluctance to have her cosy equine *pas de deux* with Alejo turned into a threesome. 'I thought the doctor in Jerez said to keep resting it.'

'She said I was doing fine,' Iris said breezily. The specialist had in fact advised caution, insisting that she keep using both crutches instead of the stick she'd been substituting, and warning her off any strenuous activity until she'd had her follow-up appointment in the UK, but Iris felt that riding hardly counted. 'I've been swimming every day and it's feeling great. I'll take one of the horses around the alfalfa fields.'

'Chloe's right, lovely,' came a soft Welsh reproach. 'You're far too weak to ride.'

Iris watched Griff munching his way through his tenth *churro*, the deep-fried, sugary dough fingers that Marta made fresh each day. 'I've ridden all my life. I did all my own stunts. I think I know my limits.'

'At least take some company.' Griff smiled at her, teeth white against his tanned face. 'I'll come if you like.'

'That's a good idea,' Chloe enthused, eager to avoid herself and Alejo being roped into it.

They were eating breakfast beneath the covered walkway in the small courtyard, the sun peering over the far wall where the geckos were darting out of the crevices to take up the best sunbathing positions, like competitive Germans on a pool deck.

'I'd rather be alone,' Iris said archly. 'And I'd hate to drag you away from your yard work.'

'I didn't know you could ride,' Chloe said to Griff, fighting to reclip the wild halo of hair that made her increasingly self-conscious.

'Anything. Horses, camels, elephants – four legs make the best off-roaders in some terrains.'

'Did you really see the Nadaam in Mongolia?' asked Chloe, cursing as the clip broke and her hair sprang back up.

'I really did. Here.' He handed her a spare plastic butterfly claw from the table, which Iris recognised crossly as her own, discarded last night.

'Thanks. Is it true that children as young as three ride in it?'

Iris rolled her eyes and feigned an overwhelming interest in the emerging geckos while Griff described travelling and riding with the Bedouin to watch the legendary thousand-strong long-distance horse race. Although she always found his stories as fascinating as everybody else did, there was something about the nonchalant way he spoke of his adventures that irritated her: the way he played them down so much, whether it be a Saharan camel trek past illegal uranium mines with Tuareg nomads or tiger-spotting deep in the Indian rainforest on a caravan of elephants. Chloe claimed this was modesty, but Iris thought it the opposite and found him infuriatingly arrogant, a typical military muscleman. She'd heard enough to know that he'd been a rising star in the Royal Navy, entering Officer Training straight from Cambridge University, then joining the élite Special Boat Service, taking part in highly secretive and dangerous so-called 'black ops'. During one such mission in Nigeria, a cave had collapsed, leaving him lucky to be alive, with forty stitches in his head and a lot of smashed bones. As part of his long recuperation, the navy had secured him a place on a trip along the Dong Nai River to search for the last surviving Vietnamese rhinoceros. It had been filmed for National Geographic, which was when Griff Donne had been talent-spotted as a television natural at twenty-five.

Brave, diplomatic, hugely practical and well read, he was the perfect escort if one's plane crashed in unmapped territory. His affable, personable demeanour made him a terrific ambassador, despite the misjudged trek into Sudan that had led to his team's kidnap. Iris personally thought him irresponsible and juvenile, a ridiculous Dan Dare figure in a modern world. He was also incredibly stubborn, refusing to take a hint, so when she headed to the stables after breakfast, she found him marking her all the way.

'I said I'd rather be on my own.'

'Fine. I thought I'd ride today too, that's all. Chus has offered me the pick of the yard.'

'Shame there are no elephants or camels,' she snapped pettily, 'but I'm sure Uranio will be happy to step into the breach.' Now that Alejo had upgraded Chloe to one of the yard's flashier, younger horses, safe, steady Uranio was available and Iris had been planning to take him out herself, but Griff probably wasn't much of a rider and would need the safest horse on the yard.

'I'll need something bigger,' he insisted, eyeing up the lines of heads looking eagerly over doors along the aisle of the stallions' barn.

'Nonsense. Uranio is a true old war horse,' she insisted, adding without thinking, 'He could take a soldier in full armour.' Then she caught her breath, a punch of pain in her throat as she thought of Dougie.

Griff registered the flinch but said nothing, watching as she instructed the groom to fetch tack for the little dappled stalwart and for Lamiaco, the pure white stallion that no one was allowed to ride apart from the yard manager and his son. 'Mico', as he was known, was the horse that Chus took to the big *ferias*. His speciality was the Spanish walk, an exaggerated, high-stepping procession pace that he would perform on the crowded streets at the big horse fairs while Chus, in traditional costume, rode him one-handed and doffed his hat to the ladies.

From his time at Sueño, Griff knew that Mico was Chus's pride and joy and a very valuable horse. He was certain the burly stud manager would not have allowed Iris to ride him in her current state, but he'd set out early that morning with a lorry full of mares that he was delivering back to a stud near Córdoba and would be away all day. Taking full advantage of his father's absence, Alejo had disappeared with Chloe and was not around to consult on the matter. Iris was the daughter of the hacienda's absent owner and a very persuasive soul. The young groom muttered that the horse had not been ridden for at least two weeks, but she insisted she'd ridden the stallion several times on her last visit; although he was hot, she also knew he was very brave and very well trained, and most importantly would make Griff feel very small, plodding alongside on Uranio.

Griff would have been happy to ride a donkey if it meant ensuring that Iris returned safely, but one look at the huge, eye-rolling Mico and his stamping foot made him elect to take the ride himself. Iris was consequently livid when she returned from popping to the loo to find the Welshman already mounted and piaffing on a pure white cloud of Andalucían power. 'How do I stop him doing this?' he laughed. As if in answer, the horse sprang into an animated trot. Delighted to be out of his stable at last, he bounced

372

away beneath the high Moorish arch that led out to the pasture, hollering to the mares there.

Trotting behind him on Uranio, Iris felt like a milk float chasing a Mercedes, the stocky little horse's legs whirring along the dry stony ground ten times for every huge, floaty stride of Mico's. She finally caught up with Griff on the pasture track and told him crossly to bring the horse back to walk. Her knee was already hurting like hell from the jolting percussion of being back in the saddle. Even though she was a far better rider than Griff, she knew there was no way she'd have been able to sit Mico's huge vertical movement without total agony.

Pain drilling, she snapped, 'Please stop jogging.'

He eyed her impractical shorts and singlet. 'Mico mistook the dress code. Aren't Pony Clubbers supposed to wear jods and ties?'

'As long as we carry a hoof-pick we're fine,' she said through gritted teeth. She slipped a foot from the stirrup and stretched out her aching leg to ease it. 'Slow down.'

'I *am* trying,' he told her as Mico high-stepped with huge, extravagant trot strides. Griff was bouncing around all over the place. The horse was wearing a traditional bullfighting bridle with a severe, long-shanked *vaquera* bit that, in his inexperienced hands, was jabbing painfully at the stallion's soft mouth.

'Loosen your contact,' she huffed.

Doing as he was told, Griff managed to settle the hot-headed horse back to a high-stepping jog. Eyes rolling, Mico snatched at the bit and started to crab sideways, banging Griff around all the more, but at least he was going a lot more slowly.

'You should have let me ride him,' she told him off, discreetly easing her foot out of the stirrup to stretch her throbbing leg as Uranio dropped back to a walk.

'Not with that knee.'

'I've been swimming every day to strengthen it.'

'I know. I've been watching. You have a kick so screwy, I'm amazed you don't spin around five times a length. You should take your physio seriously and cut out dangerous stuff like this. You're not ready. Do you want to be lame for life?'

'Don't be ridiculous!'

'Don't take silly risks, then.'

'You take them all the time.'

'It's my job.'

'Ha!' She glared at him as he zigzagged on the wild-eyed stallion. 'So you're finally admitting my mother's paying you to keep an eye on me?'

'Trust me, nobody's paying me to do this.' The horse was pirouetting beneath him now, plunging up and down like a mechanical rodeo bull. 'If you get back in one piece, that will be my reward. If I do, it'll be a miracle.'

Looking across at him, Iris fumed at the insinuation that she was a weak female in need of noble gestures. She'd assumed he had wanted to ride Mico to show off and try to be macho like the other men at Sueño, but now she saw that he was being an old-fashioned gentleman, taking the more difficult horse to spare her the discomfort and danger. He certainly rode more like a country pastor than a *caballero*, heels down and chin up, hands high as a begging dog's paws.

Slipping her foot back into the stirrup, she eyed the long, straight avenue ahead where the track climbed up through the alfalfa to the vines that flanked the steepening hill. She knew Mico was an out-and-out showman's horse with barely any forward gears.

'Race you to the top!'

Little Uranio was no sprinter, but as he trundled into his workmanlike canter and then, ears flattening, revved up to a gallop, he left Mico far behind.

Eyes bulging, the flashy white stallion launched into a paddling trot as though he was under water, still going sideways. Then he discovered his long-lost canter gear and propelled Griff on to his neck as he sprang forwards, part rocking horse, part sewing machine and very slow.

Streaking ahead, Iris looked over her shoulder to reassure herself that he was safe, and kicked on as the alfalfa gave way to the vines, delighting in the sensation of speed and horse before finally pulling up at the brow of the hill, happy to have made her point.

Looking back again, she saw that Griff and Mico had now got into a surprising rhythm and were looking almost stylish. The big horse's mane was flying like foam against a true blue sky and Griff, standing in the stirrups to spare his rump, was tanned as deeply as any Spaniard *caballero*, his shoulders as wide and his smile even wider.

Perhaps he can ride, she conceded grudgingly as Uranio dropped his head low and puffed beneath her, exhausted by his victory.

Then she watched in horror as Mico seemed to crumple, those high-stepping front legs folding under him and his body crashing after it, propelling Griff straight over his head and into the hard, dusty track as fast as a boulder from a trebuchet.

With a scream of horror, she threw herself out of the saddle and limped down to them.

Mico was already on his feet, looking surprised and slightly embarrassed. Griff was still in the dust, deadly still.

Dropping down beside him, she pressed her face close to his to check his breathing.

'Don't even *think* about giving me mouth-to-mouth.' He opened one eye.

'I wasn't.' She smiled with relief. 'Don't go away. I'll fetch help.'

'Can I touch you here?'

'*Sí.*'

'Here?'

'*Sí.*'

Chloe was almost there and she knew it. Alejo's resolve was weakening. He was her *si-sí* man all the way. She was just a few zip teeth and some jaunty silk boxers away from unleashing the beast.

'*¡Auxilio! Accidente!*' The youngest groom burst into the room.

'Great,' she muttered as Alejo rolled away like a commando, frantically doing up his flies and running for the door.

Griff tried not to cry out too much as Iris drove him towards Jerez at high speed. It wasn't just that he was in agony: she was the worst driver he'd ever shared a car with. In his quest to take a camera into the most impenetrable and dangerous corners of the world to capture its people and wildlife, he had been driven by rebel fighters, bandits and one drug smuggler, but Iris, piloting a Seat from Arcos to Jerez, ranked very high on his terrifying chauffeur list as she drifted around, seemingly oblivious to all other traffic.

'The ambulances here would charge you a fortune,' she said, cutting a corner too fast and ending up on the opposite carriageway facing a huge juggernaut that flashed its lights and beeped as she steered to safety at the last moment. 'Like Chlo said, it's probably a dislocated shoulder, so no need to panic. Good job the doctor said I'm fit to drive now, as long – whoops!' She almost totalled a team of cyclists coming the other way as she overtook a tractor on a blind bend. 'As long as it's automatic. These Seats are very punchy, aren't they? I might get one.'

'Hang on, this is *my* bloody hire car we're in!' He'd finally recognised it.

'The car hire company dropped in replacement keys yesterday,' she admitted. 'You were busy swimming so I signed for them. I forgot.'

'You didn't think to mention it? I thought you were desperate to be rid of me.'

'You've got quite easy to ignore.' She wrinkled her nose. 'I hardly remember you're around most days.'

'What's wrong with *your* car?'

'Chloe won't let me drive the Fiat. It's not an automatic, and I haven't passed my test.'

Swinging around, he let out a cry of pain and shock. 'You *what*?'

'I've had loads of lessons and passed my theory, but I was always away filming, and when I finally took the practical test, a driver waiting in the lane beside me at a roundabout recognised me as Purple and drove straight into me.'

'Literally star-struck, then,' he muttered as she slammed on the brakes just before she rear-ended a camper van.

'It was hardly my fault, but they had to fail me. I'm very good.'

Her phone rang and he watched, appalled, as she fumbled to answer it. 'You can't take that call without hands-free!'

'What are they going to do? Take my licence away?'

'At least let me answer the call.'

'Can't.' She looked at the screen and almost veered into another oncoming lorry, its horn sirening behind them. 'It's Mum.'

Eyeing the road warily as it widened into a dual carriageway, he took the phone and shut it firmly in the glove compartment.

When Griff returned to the waiting area in Jerez General Hospital, his broken collarbone reset and firmly strapped, Iris had reclaimed her phone and was punching a text message into it, looking pale. For once, she left off the trail of kisses when she pressed Send.

'Everything OK?'

'I can't get through to anyone in LA,' she muttered, pocketing the phone angrily.

'Is it a work thing?'

'Not exactly.' She regarded him suspiciously, still clearly believing he had insider knowledge. 'Let's get back to Sueño.'

This time when her phone rang while Iris was driving at breakneck speed, Griff's left arm was far too tightly strapped to his side to stop her answering it. 'Chloe!'

Griff listened to one side of the conversation, at least reassured that Mico was doing fine even if his own well-being was once again in peril.

'Just an overreach, you think?' she was saying. 'Oh, that's great . . . No, all fine. Broken collarbone, but nothing serious . . . '

Wincing, Griff twisted in his seat and reached out with his good arm to take the wheel and steer them back into the slow lane before she mounted the central reservation.

'. . . coming back now, yes . . . Oh, right. But I thought you'd been at it all week? Really? That's *so* sweet. I thought Alejo would be straight in there. Well, if you think having the house to yourselves will really make a difference . . . ' She glanced up as they passed a blue exit sign. 'For you, darling, anything. Have fun.'

Tossing the phone into Griff's lap, Iris slammed on the brakes and checked her mirrors before reversing towards the slip road she'd just overshot.

'What are you *doing*?' he yelped as horns beeped furiously.

'Let's go to Ronda for lunch,' she said, as they made it to the lip of the exit. 'It's very beautiful.'

'I'm from Wales,' he reminded her weakly. 'I doubt it's a patch on its namesake.'

Half an hour later, his eyelids were struggling to stay up as the monotony of the road and the painkiller injection kicked in. 'Are we going to Wales after all?' he mumbled.

'It's a bit further than I thought.' She peered at a passing road sign and reached down to turn on the stereo. It was still tuned to the local pop station Griff had been listening to when he drove from the airport a week earlier, planning to pick up his flash drive and head on to Africa. They were playing Eva Cassidy's version of 'Somewhere Over the Rainbow'. Griff finally closed his eyes.

Chapter 42

When Griff awoke to an elbow in the ribs, he conceded that Ronda indeed rivalled its Welsh namesake, perched atop a great rocky precipice, its famous Puente Nuevo bridge spanning the deep El Tajo gorge like a giant cathedral entrance.

As well as vastly underestimating how long it would take to get there, Iris had taken the wrong turn near El Bosque and they were far too late for lunch. The town was having its afternoon siesta in the broiling heat, only the hardiest tourists out and about.

Iris led the way to a little tapas bar called La Cuadrilla, located off an alley deep in the old town. It was almost deserted, one waitress listlessly wiping tables and flamenco music playing tinnily from the loudspeakers on the walls. Settling in a window seat, they drank sweetened iced lemonade while Iris scanned the close-written blackboard, translating everything and making recommendations: 'The Serrano ham here is fabulous, and you must try *boquerones fritos* – that's deep-fried anchovies, but they'll make your taste buds explode, as will the *pincho moruno* ...'

Watching her order in rapid Spanish, still woozy from industrial-strength painkillers, Griff realised his eyes had slid involuntarily down to her small, pert breasts, the light behind her casting them as perfect silhouettes in her cotton T-shirt, the nipples at two o'clock. A sharp, involuntary draw of lust pulled at his belly.

He forced himself to look away, certain that any desire he felt was from seeing her on the big screen in moulded-silver bikini armour, kick-boxing a CGI hydra or standing moodily alongside Ptolemy, the two exuding a sexual energy that was never discharged. Almost every man he knew fancied Purple: she was the ultimate hard-to-get fantasy figure, pointy ears aside.

Their little table was soon crammed with plates of salty Serrano ham, marinated pork tenderloin, spicy stuffed pimentos, fat Sevilian olives and an obscenely large bowl of *patatas bravas* drenched in salt and vinegar.

Iris plundered it all at speed. 'God, I love tapas, don't you?' she moaned happily, then eyed him quizzically as he made much slower, one-armed progress, still groggy. 'Are you secretly craving laverbread?'

'Welsh as slate, me.' He smiled.

'Ironic, given you sleep under canvas as often as a roof,' she pointed out. 'What are you working on next?'

He selected an olive. 'I need to go back to Kenya.'

'Is that where the man on the voice recordings is?'

'That's right.' He had no intention of talking about Cloud Man, so quickly changed the subject. 'Who do you need to contact in LA?'

'Just family. What about yours? Are they still all in Wales?' She looked around for a napkin to wipe her hands and, not finding one, licked the *mojo* sauce from her fingers instead.

Nodding, Griff stared at her, suddenly finding the olive incredibly difficult to swallow, furious with himself for his inability to keep his eyes from her body. Eventually he said, 'You probably wouldn't understand a word my da says. He has a very strong accent.'

'Which bit are you from?' She picked out another chip and sucked the salt from it as she gazed out of the window at a stray dog.

'A little town in Gwent where everyone knows everyone,' Griff muttered. 'It's very insular. I couldn't wait to get out. Tadcu – that's my grandfather – insisted Da and my uncles spoke only Welsh at home when they were growing up. He only allowed a television in the house after S4C started broadcasting, and even then he kept it in a locked cabinet so they couldn't watch British profanities.'

'Do you speak Welsh too?'

'The first time I spoke it was at his funeral twelve years ago. I got my da to translate something I'd written, but I wasn't allowed to say *hunanladdiad*. It's a word nobody uses in our family.'

'What does it mean?'

Debating whether to tell her, he watched her pretty face, so familiar from the Ptolemy movies. He much preferred her with the prosthetic pointy ears, he decided. They made her seem like she might actually listen to answers instead of tilting her exquisite head and adopting the correct expression.

'It means "suicide".'

380

'You grandfather killed himself?'

'My da always says that Thatcher killed him; but she didn't kick away the chair.'

Her green eyes stretched wide, tears already forming in perfectly framed close-up, and Griff felt as though he'd just shot a kitten after mistaking it for a wildcat. 'Why did he do it?'

'He became very depressed when the colliery closed,' he said flatly. 'He'd been a miner all his life, the head of a big family, a local "character" – he sang bass in the choir. Not that I ever knew him like that. He was never in work during my lifetime and only left the house to go to church, walk the dog or buy a paper. When I was thirteen, he hanged himself. I found him when I came home from school.' He looked away, ashamed now for trying to inflict his pain on her.

But she took him totally by surprise, arms as light as wings closing around him, careful not to hurt his shoulder as she pressed the gentlest kiss into his hair. 'It must have been the most awful thing for you all to go through. You were so young. I can't imagine what it must have felt like.'

He tried not to breathe in the scent of her skin, so close to him, intoxicatingly warm, the tiny moles on her throat close enough for him to kiss. She was still wearing the dusty vest and tattered old denim shorts from riding, he noticed. It struck him now as far sexier than an armoured bikini.

'I might not have spoken Welsh, but I knew *dianc* means "escape".' He watched her sit down and tuck her spilling hair in a neat twist beneath one shoulder strap, as he'd seen her do many times when tackling food at Sueño.

'And you *dianc*-ed?' She reached for a pimento.

He laughed at the made-up word. 'I was already determined to leave, and Tadcu's death drove me on. Dad wanted me to be a boxer, but I was a bright kid and I knew the best way out was to get good enough grades for a university place.'

'I had you all wrong.' Her eyes were apologetic. 'I thought you were a rugby-playing meathead who went to Cambridge on a military ticket and got his kicks playing out some modern-day Hemingway fantasy.'

'Sums me up perfectly. You must help me redraft my CV.'

Worried she'd offended him, she went on, 'Acting out every sci-fi geek's fantasy on screen is a far less noble profession.'

'How old were you when you got the part?'

'Thirteen,' she mumbled, making the connection with downcast eyes, 'fourteen when the movie came out. I used to spend mornings fighting the forces of evil with a flaming sword and afternoons writing essays about the rise of Communism in the twentieth century.'

'Strange childhood.'

'It was already strange before the Purple thing happened.' She pulled a free chair across to prop her bad leg on. 'But it was good strange. I can hardly complain. Thousands of girls dream of having my sort of luck, and Purple was kind of useful to hide behind through adolescence. She has a lot more guts than me. She'd follow poachers into the Congolese jungle armed with nothing but a microphone boom too.'

'Actually, I was pretty scared that day.'

'And when you were kidnapped?'

'Seriously scared.'

'So why d'you keep doing it?'

'Because I'm too bloody nosy. I have to find out what's behind the myths and secrets and guns and bravura, and then I get too angry not to tell people when I do find out. I'm really not this intrepid, chest-beating idiot in safari shorts with a crocodile tooth hanging round his neck the media want me to be. I'd be dead long ago if I were.'

'What are you then?'

'An "anthropologist" is the technical term, but I prefer "observer". The more I've been in these situations, the more I see the fear in everyone. We all have it. Harnessing it is the secret. Once you learn to use it, there's no shame in admitting to its existence, and it might just give you the advantage over others that enables you to survive.'

She smiled. 'A good actor would say much the same thing. You have to acknowledge it to overcome and disguise it. That's why you have the chest-beating-idiot act.'

'I do not do that!'

'You just don't realise you do it. My mother's the same with the Princess Grace of Monaco number, as you've probably noticed, or on a bad day Princess Diana on *Panorama*.'

'I've never met your mother,' he reminded her.

'Yeah, yeah.' She rolled her eyes disbelievingly, stretching forwards to check her phone, causing the chair she was resting her leg on to tilt so he had to grab it with his free hand. 'She's flying to LA today, as you also no doubt know. I'm *so* mad at her. She promised she'd look after my dogs personally, and now she's leaving them with Nacho, who treats them all with the sensitivity of a hunt kennel-man.'

He tipped the chair upright very carefully so as not to jolt her knee, disappointed that she was behaving like a brat again. 'Hunt hounds are among the happiest creatures I've ever met.'

'Just goes to show how much you know.' She typed a message into her phone with lightning-fast fingers, finishing with a flurry of Xs. 'My mother's stallion still isn't sound after the balloon crash. I've told Vicente the groom to get the Lightning Man in while Mum's away. He has magic hands.'

'Why is she going to LA?'

She kept fiddling with her phone, clearly uncomfortable. 'Probably an awards ceremony. They always wheel her out when Dad's up for a bit of silverware – it helps with the PR.'

'Marriage not good?'

'Put it this way: *I* always wanted to marry for love. What's the Welsh word for it?'

'*Cariad.*'

'How funny. Dougie has a horse called that. She's a cow, actually – she'd flatten anybody for a Polo – but you can shoot bows and arrows from her back so she earns her keep.' She angrily blinked away an emerging tear. 'I miss the stunt horses so much. Harvey's my favourite, the old hunter – Dougie worships him. He's so clever he can wash himself off with the hosepipe clenched in his teeth.'

Still holding the chair, he could now see up the frayed shorts to the hollow at the top of her thigh and an enticing flash of pink knickers. He looked quickly away. 'Dougie's passionate about fox-hunting, isn't he?'

She swept her hair away from one shoulder. 'The Pelham want to give him a mastership – get a bit of Otis Ferry glamour into the pink-coat PR – but he thinks it will tie him down. His father was MFH with the Wolds for years. The Everetts take their hunting *very* seriously.'

'And you?'

'Not my scene.' She swept her hair the other way, a move guaranteed to bring a heel down sharply on his libido's kick-start. 'I prefer dressage.'

'So, let me get this right,' he watched her mouth as she ate another olive, oil glistening on her lips, 'you don't much like hunting and you don't want to carry on acting, both of which are Dougie's great passions – a man who doesn't want to be tied down. Just what *do* you two have in common?'

'Sex.' She lifted her chin angrily. 'And we love travel and horses and . . . What exactly are you looking at?'

He'd been gazing at the flash of pink knickers again. He looked up sharply and winced as his collarbone twinged. 'Sex, horses and travel. How very *Don Quixote*.'

'Not a lot of sex in Cervantes.' She straightened her shorts. 'I studied it for Spanish A level. Some think Dulcinea's a figment of Don Quixote's imagination.'

'Romantic love's a figment of anyone's imagination.'

'You are *such* a cynic!'

'All those girls who dream of being you; they just want to kiss Con O'Mara and—'

'Actually Ptolemy and Purple can never kiss because he'd forfeit his immortality.'

'It's all daydream, isn't it? Like you and your handsome cavalier. Now he *is* a chest-beating idiot – in breeches.'

'How dare you? I love Dougie!'

'He's a total bastard from what I can tell.'

'That's just what my mother's told you.'

He laughed. 'What do I have to do to convince you that I'm not in cahoots with your mother? I saw that tabloid exclusive. It was carpeting the corridor outside your hospital room. I know how much it must have hurt you. And I know you're hiding here in Spain to try to get your head round it.'

'So why are you being so nasty to me about it? Haven't you done enough damage?'

He was brought up short, asking himself the same question. He already knew the answer, but was far too ashamed to admit it. He was vile about Dougie Everett because he was jealous of him. Iris had worshipped Dougie, who had swept her off her feet in the most old-fashioned, romantic way possible – in a suit of armour with a noble charger beneath him – and who still seemed to own her heart. Griff now longed to step into the breach, not just into her bed but into her clever head and kind heart, but he had made the worst of all starts.

'I'm sorry,' he said, with feeling. 'I had no right to say those things.'

'It's nothing that's not been said before.' She chewed her lower lip hard, gazing across at him. 'The thing is, I could probably forgive him the indiscretion before the wedding. He pointed out himself that he wouldn't be the first bridegroom to have a final fling, and at least she was a pro. He's old-fashioned, red-blooded, blue-blooded and bloody-minded. That's what I love about him, whatever anybody else thinks. But something happened in LA just before the wedding that he won't talk to me about. I only know it was really bad.'

'Is that why your mother's flying there?'

'Maybe.' The idea was clearly new to her.

He watched that angelic face, now caught in a shaft of sunlight that fell at an acute angle through the window, turning her green eyes cat-like as the pupils contracted.

'The Buniko people of Papua New Guinea revere the acuchea tree,' he told her, leaning forward so their faces were close together. 'God only knows why, because it's no more than a poisonous little shrub, but the fact it's deciduous makes it very rare over there. They have a saying: "The truth rises like acuchea sap." You see, if that tree is cut down when it's dormant, it can be carved into sacred objects or burned in ceremonies without poisonous fumes, but if the sap has risen, it will kill the tribe.

'Just like romantic love, tribal myths rely a huge amount upon make-believe – a shared fantasy can make a whole community revere a poisonous little tree. The wisest of the Buniko have probably suspected for years it's a useless piece of vegetation that holds them to ransom, but they're far too frightened to admit it. Now, I think Dougie's a useless piece of vegetation too, and I think part of you knows that, but you don't want to lose your religion just yet. You don't want to know the truth either, because that truth is rising sap, and you won't be able to cut down the tree once it's flowing.'

'I think I'll wait for the sap to rise, thanks all the same.' The vivid green eyes regarded him through the sunlight, unblinking, suddenly so Purple-fierce she could have been wearing an armoured bikini. Griff felt an involuntary and inappropriate spark of lust strike against a petrol splash of anger.

Good intentions abandoned, his red-dragon temper let loose its flames. 'Face it, Iris, if Dougie Everett really cared about you, he'd be over here right now trying to win you back. Instead he's out in LA, furthering his career and covering up whatever sexual transgression he committed out there last time. When are you going to *wake up?*'

Her foot landed back on the floor with a clunk as she stood up and reached for her crutches. 'I am wide awake, more's the pity. If I was asleep there'd be an outside chance you're just a nightmare!'

'Almost marrying that idiot was your nightmare, not this. You just have to wake up and see what you've been wasting your heart-ache on.'

'I want to go back to Sueño,' she said in a small voice, making him feel as though he'd just resuscitated the kitten only to put the gun to its head again. Just as shamefully, the wave of compassion hitting him failed to quash the continuing desire, and he had to battle not to lunge across the table, scattering the last of the olives, to kiss her and apologise. Only his sling and his shame stopped him.

Walking wounded, they headed back to the car in silence, Iris's crutches clanking angrily against the paving.

'I'll drive,' he insisted when they arrived at the hired Seat, now scorching in direct sunlight.

'You can't steer properly with that sling on.' She opened the driver's door and posted her crutches through to the rear seat before she clambered in, gasping as her bare skin encountered hot seats.

'You can't steer properly without one,' he muttered, crossing himself and climbing in too, reluctant to fight an injured woman for control of the wheel, particularly one he now wanted to kiss. Physical contact was certainly not a good idea.

As soon as the engine started the radio burst into life with Marvin Gaye's 'Let's Get It On'. Griff closed his eyes and decided to pretend to be asleep, a technique that had always proved incredibly effective in dangerous territory.

When Iris's phone rang, he kept his eyes tightly closed and braced hard, sensing death might be imminent as she yelled into it, 'I'm driving, Mum, I'll call you back . . . I know I haven't passed yet. It's cool. I have an experienced licence holder in the car instructing me.'

Griff was forced to hide a smile.

He wasn't smiling two minutes later when she parked in a lay-by and stepped outside to return the call, standing close enough for him to pick up most of what she was saying, her voice climbing scales: 'It's not *fair* to make you do this. He's not thinking straight . . . No, that wasn't sarcasm, Mum. This is all Abe's idea, I guarantee – he just wants to preserve his ten per cent in prime-time network TV . . . Of course I won't say anything, not even to Chlo . . . Yes, I promise. If anybody asks me whether you're terminally ill, I say, "No comment," but it'll stick in my throat.'

Hastily feigning sleep again as she got back in, Griff let a small moral war rage in his head as the car got under way again, but he knew he had to say something: 'Iris, I apologise, but I couldn't help overhearing what you just said to your mother.'

She carried on bobbing her head, eyes fixed on the road, a white spaghetti thread trailing from each ear, and Griff realised she'd put on her iPod so as not to disturb him with the radio. He also noticed that they were driving on the wrong side of the road again.

Slumping back in his seat, he closed his eyes tightly.

Chapter 43

When Iris and Griff got back, Chloe was reading her veterinary books in the shade of the olives, a glass of wine on the go and a strained expression on her face. By trying to hide the fact she'd been crying with huge dark glasses and covering her matted hair with a hat, she inadvertently looked like an undercover spy furtively awaiting an assignation. She asked politely after Griff's collarbone, but her eyes were already pleading for a quiet word with Iris over the rims of her shades. Chloe normally avoided girlie chats like the plague, but today she badly needed help, mustering a wobbly, grateful smile when Griff announced he was going into the house to send an email.

'Why aren't you watching Alejo ride?' Iris settled beside her friend. 'Have you had an argument? I thought today's siesta was Seduction Central?'

'All he does is kiss.' Chloe groaned, covering her face with her hands and talking in a muffled voice. 'It's like being fourteen. He wants to kiss and listen to music. He says he's a good Catholic boy. I don't *want* a good Catholic boy.'

Iris was secretly rather impressed that a swaggering show-off like Alejo had such old-fashioned principles.

'I want a wild sexual awakening,' she complained, looking up at Iris over her fingertips. 'I am frankly *bored* of kissing, and I can only listen to so much Lagarto Amarillo before I feel my knickers freezing over. I need Rihanna or Katy Perry.'

'So take the initiative, in music and love-making.'

Chloe covered her face again. 'I did. I've never been so embarrassed in my life. Oh God, it was awful. You see, this afternoon, I decided I had to take it to another level, so I put my hands down his breeches.'

'And?'

'And he *proposed*!'

Iris stared at her, struggling to take this in. 'He asked you to marry him, right?'

'It was ... *so* humi*li*ating!'

Iris hopped across to hug her. 'What did you say?'

'"No", of course – we don't love each other. He loves football, action movies, fast cars and terrible music. He never reads books or goes to the theatre. All we've got in common is horses and the fact we want to shag each other's eyes out. He doesn't have to *marry* me to do that. It's such a mess.'

'Does this mean it's over?' Iris asked, trying to keep the hopeful note from her voice as she envisaged getting her friend back and having a few adventures together.

But Chloe looked crestfallen at the thought that her holiday romance was over. 'There must be a way through this.' She pulled away and adjusted her hat. 'He's the sexiest man I've ever met. I'd be happy to stick to kissing to plucky Spanish music all siesta if he'll just forgive me. Do you think we can ask Griff to have a word with him?'

'Griff?'

'Alejo idol-worships him. They all do. If Griff can convince him that I won't put my hand down his pants again and that he doesn't need to marry me, we might get back to how we were. What d'you think?'

'I wouldn't ask Griff to give romantic advice to anybody. He's a wherever-I-lay-my-hat man, remember.'

'I just want Alejo to lay his hat in my room again. He doesn't have to lay me.'

'On your head be it,' Iris muttered.

'It can't be any worse than this.' Chloe sighed, lifting off the hat to reveal the matted doughnut that her hair had now moulded itself into. 'It looks like a *calañés*.'

'I think it's sexy.' Iris tilted her head. 'You look like a forties forces sweetheart. But we can try to tame it with a conditioning treatment if you like,' she offered cautiously, knowing Chloe was paranoid about letting anyone touch her hair. 'I've got a vat of Kerastase with me.'

Chloe crammed the hat back on her head. 'Only if you ask Griff to have a word with Alejo for me. I'd be too embarrassed.'

'C'mon, Chloe, you're never embarrassed by anything. You can work out which sex a baby chick is and castrate horses and stick your hand up cows' bottoms.'

'Not all at the same time. And I'm not good with men, you know I'm not. Remember, I'm the woman who wasted four years of celibate teenage life on that crush on Henry at Pony Club before he announced at my eighteenth birthday party that he'd decided to have gender reassignment. *Please*, Iris.'

'I never knew Henry became Henrietta!'

'I think he's only halfway there.'

'Henriet?'

It was the silliest of jokes, but it somehow hit the spot perfectly to dissipate the day's tensions and they started to laugh. Soon they were too helpless with giggles to speak. Tears running, they gasped for air, tried to straighten their faces, looked at one another and dissolved again.

When Griff wandered back out into the courtyard, he stopped in his tracks, realising that Iris was laughing, that elusive sight captured in the photograph he had found in the safe. She was utterly beautiful when she laughed.

'What's the joke?' he asked, eager to know the trigger he'd failed to locate.

She was laughing almost too much to speak. 'Chloe fancied . . . boy called Henry . . . Pony Club . . . having a sex change . . . halfway there . . . Henriet . . . get it?' She doubled over again.

Griff smiled weakly.

Pulling herself together first, Chloe gave him an apologetic look, then nudged her friend.

Iris bit her lip as she remembered what Chloe wanted. Straightening up with the aid of her crutches, she gave her a reassuring smile and Chloe melted away, muttering something about finding conditioner.

Iris took a few deep breaths to make sure the giggles had finally stopped, then stepped in front of Griff as he made to follow Chloe into the main house. 'Alejo will be riding now, won't he?'

'I guess so.'

'I need you to talk to him man to man.'

He looked surprised. Then, raising an eyebrow in Sean-Connery-as-Bond fashion, he said, 'Actually, I'd be talking man to horseman.' He watched her face expectantly.

'OK, if you want to be pedantic about it.' Iris frowned.

He let out a frustrated sigh. 'What do I need to talk to him about?'

He was tired, she thought. Those big dark eyes, usually so bright and alert, were hooded, and he was avoiding looking directly at her. She shuffled into his line of vision and said, 'Chloe.'

'Christ, has he done something bad to her?'

Clearing her throat, she was about to explain about the misguided breeches grope. But even as she thought it through, she felt her face burn in sympathetic horror for her poor friend's mortification and knew she couldn't possibly betray that confidence.

'Whatever he's done, I'll find out and I'll put it right,' he fumed, dark eyes alert again, glowing with kindness and valour. 'I'll get the answers. Trust me, I won't let it rest until he's told the truth.'

This is what he does, she remembered. All that laid-back *laissez faire* isn't an arrogant front at all. He's naturally modest, but when he feels passionate about something, he lights up and won't give in. 'He's done nothing wrong,' she assured him. 'He's proposed to her.'

The dark eyes widened.

'She said no,' she rushed on. 'And she's pretty sure he only asked because he really wants to sleep with her but he's too frightened of his dad and the local God Squad to do that without getting engaged, and she's not up for that at all, so we need you to gauge his feelings. Not deep feelings or anything,' she added brightly. 'Just sexual, really.'

His eyebrows knitted together. 'You want me to go across the playground and ask my friend if he fancies your friend?'

Put like that, it made her feel hugely silly. She opened her mouth to protest that it wasn't her idea, and shut it again: that would be babyish too.

He was looking at her expectantly now, but she found she couldn't say anything at all, because as she gazed back helplessly, she was no longer seeing weary arrogance in his eyes. As well as the kindness still lingering and a glint of impatience, she saw amusement, intelligence and even an edge of fear. Beyond that, she saw something that made her stomach fill with butterflies. She saw the answer to the question she was making him ask Alejo. He wanted to sleep with her.

At last she dragged her eyes away, and he shifted his arm uncomfortably in his sling. 'OK, tell me what to say.'

'I don't know. Tell him Chloe worships his body but isn't ready to marry him just yet. Why not tell him that story you made up about the weird tribe in Papua New Guinea and their tree, and ask if his sap's rising? You might have to edit out the bits about the poison.'

He laughed. 'You know I made it up?'

'I still liked it.'

'I'm sorry I came over far too heavy about your fiancé. I know it's none of my business what you—'

Her fingers closed over his mouth. 'Ex-fiancé.'

She could feel his lips lift into a smile, his breath soft and warm on the skin around her nails. Gazing into his eyes, she was certain she could see fear edge further into them as amusement retreated behind the forest of lowered lashes. Was it the fear he'd talked about over tapas, she wondered, the sort that made for deeper understanding of human nature?

'And I am *incredibly* grateful you said it,' she assured him, removing her hand from his mouth to kiss her fingers before pressing them lightly back again. As she did so, his lips grew firmer against her fingertips and, seeing the answer in his eyes, the butterflies performed synchronised loop-the-loops in her belly. She quickly pulled her hand back to her side.

'Now get a six-pack,' she instructed.

His eyebrows shot up and he reached down to pull up his T-shirt. 'I kind of already have one, if you hadn't noticed.'

'Stop! I don't need to see it!' The butterflies dived up and down together in a Mexican wave. 'I was talking about beer,' she explained quickly. 'Get a six-pack of Estrella to take to Alejo. He likes beer. It might help loosen him up.'

*

393

While Griff headed reluctantly off to speak with Alejo in the stud manager's house, Iris concentrated on cheering up Chloe, starting by attempting to tame the doughnut with a bottle of conditioner and a wide-toothed comb in front of the huge television on which the movie channel was having a chick-flick night. Dressed in joggers and an ancient T-shirt, Chloe settled down with a pot of calendula cream, which she started to blob on to her upper lip, nose and forehead – the sun had punished them with darker freckles and dry skin.

To Iris's embarrassment, the first chick flick starred her father being charming and self-deprecatingly gorgeous as he wooed Julia Roberts around Rome. It was one of Chloe's favourite movies because it also starred an adorable dachshund called Luigi; in fact, there had been eight dachshund artists, according to Leo, but she wasn't about to spoil Chloe's fun by telling her so. Her friend totally bought the canine plotline; it was the humans she was less convinced by.

'Anybody who believes two people can fall in love like that' – she clicked her fingers – 'is just silly.' They watched as Leo and Julia gazed into one another's eyes upon first meeting as a background track of Take That's biggest ever ballad made clear they had lift-off.

Iris said nothing, trying not to think about her own butterfly lift-off on the terrace with Griff earlier. It must have been lust, not love, she decided.

'I adore this film,' Chloe went on, 'but if your father dropped my dog in the Trevi Fountain, I'd thump him, not accept his proposal of marriage after ninety minutes of comedy near-misses around Rome's prettiest tourist spots.'

'It's just a romantic fantasy, like *Don Quixote*,' she pointed out, again finding her mind drifting towards Griff. 'We all know it's never like that and most men would take advantage when they got stuck in the lift in Hotel Locarno with a beautiful woman, but it's lovely to daydream.'

Chloe huffed, 'Alejo would just propose to her.'

By the second movie, which was also one of her father's big hits, Iris was starting to realise that this was in fact a Leo Devonshire chick-flick night. It was another of Chloe's favourites, this time featuring Leo pursuing Sandra Bullock around the rodeo circuit, largely on horseback, the joke being that he was a charming self-deprecating British aristocrat. Iris always found it strange watching her father in films, although this one had better lines than the last and he'd ridden almost all of his own stunts, which she loved to watch.

'If they ever make a sequel, Dougie could ride in it,' Chloe said idly, making Iris inadvertently dig the comb so hard into her head that she howled. 'Sorry – just testing the water.'

'It's still too hot.' Iris reached for the conditioning treatment and scraped the remainder on to her friend's head.

'Go steady or I'll never wash it out.'

'It's incredibly matted.'

Ultra-sensitive on the subject of her hair, Chloe got even huffier. 'I so hate it. I'm going to get it straightened again next term. It was cute when I was a kid – even I loved it then – but hamster cheeks and chubby wrists were cute then too.'

'Like Hope's.'

Chloe's shoulders shot up towards her ears.

'Sorry,' Iris rubbed her back gently, 'just testing the water.'

To Iris's surprise, she made a valiant attempt to stay with the subject for once. 'It's lukewarm. And the hamster-cheek-chubby-wrist thing really *is* a good look when you're five.'

'She's a sweet kid, Chloe.'

'So you keep saying.' Chloe picked at the frayed end of her joggers' tie cord.

'I always wanted a little sister to dress up and pamper.'

They watched Leo sitting on a wild-eyed rodeo horse and being counted down until the gates opened. 'You're so lucky having Leo as a dad.' Chloe sighed. 'Mine's a nightmare.'

'Oscar's got two fabulous kids, so he must be doing something right,' Iris said, refusing to be deflected.

'Mum would be terribly hurt if I saw anything of her.'

Iris had long guessed as much, and she knew it had taken a lot for Chloe to say so. 'I'm sure she'd get used to the idea,' she said gently.

Chloe shook her head, scattering blobs of conditioner. 'She's still so hurt about Dad leaving us. She always made Laney out to be such a gold digger, saying she only got pregnant for alimony.'

'I'm not my godmother's biggest fan, but that's so not her, and I really don't think she got anything personally from your father when they divorced.'

'I've started to work that out. Dad's such a mean sod. His time and affection are even harder to get hold of than his money – and worth a lot less.' She watched the screen as Leo whispered in the horse's ear before they released the chute. 'You're so lucky.'

'I used to think so.' Iris watched him curl the buck rein tighter around his hand. 'When I was Hope's age I idolised him. I suppose she idolises Simon in the same way. Ironic.'

'When I was five, I just wanted a dog,' Chloe muttered as Sandra Bullock chewed her nails fretfully in the crowd.

Iris hugged her friend from behind. 'When I think about Simon maybe being my father, I get so excited at the thought of having brothers and sisters. You're so lucky, Chlo. You have no idea how jealous I am. It breaks my heart that you do nothing about it.'

'Keep combing,' Chloe muttered. But as Leo's horse sprang from its stall and started flipping itself inside-out around the ring with him on board, she said in a small voice, 'I think I would like to get to know Hope.'

Iris was so elated she didn't notice Chloe's earring get caught in the comb and fly across the room, hitting a bullfighting trophy. 'Will you come for a picnic or something when we're back? You, me and Hope?'

On screen, Leo was lying motionless in the dirt as Sandra battled her way through the crowd and sprang over the barriers.

'I'll think about it,' Chloe said. 'Stop jabbing at me like that and we'll have some wine.' She got up so fast that the comb stayed trapped in her hair as she stalked through to the kitchen, pausing briefly to watch one of Leo's trademark clinches, twenty seconds of stomach-tightening romantic celluloid that had received over a million hits on YouTube.

In the kitchen, she spotted the replacement hire-car keys abandoned on the work surface. 'Don't you think we should give Griff his stuff back now so that he can leave?'

'We can't get into the safe,' Iris pointed out.

'I got it out days ago. It's all in my room.'

'Why didn't you say?'

Chloe looked shifty. 'I wanted to listen to those voice tapes again.' She pulled the cork. 'I think I know who it is.' She eyed Iris cagily, Afro comb still poking from her slimy, matted hair, calendula-cream moustache on her upper lip. 'I'm not sure you're going to like it.'

Iris swallowed uncomfortably. The truth was like poisonous sap in a tree, she remembered, suddenly uncertain she wanted to know Griff's secrets. She didn't want him to leave Sueño on one of his far-flung missions. She wanted him to stay and recover, not fly off into danger. He was injured.

Footsteps and male laughter drifted through from the open doors to the covered terrace and courtyard.

Holding the wine bottle, Chloe let out an alarmed bleat and reached up to tug the comb from her hair and wipe the cream from her lip, in such a blind panic that red wine cascaded over her head. 'Shit – do something, Iris!'

But Iris proved useless by getting such terrible giggles that she was doubled up by the time Griff burst eagerly through the door with Alejo at his heels, carrying several Estrella bottles. 'Look who's come to watch a – oh!'

Afro comb now dangling over one ear, calendula cream on her nose, joggers hanging from her saddlebags to reveal her biggest knickers and red wine dripping off her head and shoulders, Chloe was no Julia Roberts in a romantic birdcage lift or Sandra Bullock in a cute Stetson and tight chaps.

The Estrella crashed to the floor.

Chloe screamed and fled towards the bedrooms.

Alejo muttered several Spanish expletives and turned to stalk back across the moonlit courtyard towards his father's house.

Griff, meanwhile, was across to Iris like a shot, where she was still bent double, tears pouring down her face.

'Iris, are you all right?' He helped her to a sofa. 'What happened? Is it food poisoning?' Then he studied her more closely. 'You're laughing.'

It took Iris ages to recover her breath, although the laughter was eclipsed by horror on Chloe's behalf as she struggled up, brushing past him in search of her crutches and finally managing to splutter, 'What'd you bring him here for?'

He handed the crutches to her. 'I thought that's what you wanted.'

'Not tonight!' She started clattering after Chloe. 'She needed a pampering night to build up her confidence. Do you know *nothing* about women?'

'Clearly not.' Griff began to follow Alejo, then decided against it. The boy was an arrogant sod.

Heading into the library, he started up the computer and checked his messages again. He'd sent a barrage of emails to Dominic at Mara River Camp in recent days. He knew Cloud Man was a lousy correspondent, but the email address was a general one and, from experience, he would have expected an acknowledgement by now, especially as he'd asked for messages to be passed on in person that he had news of Mia. Frustration had made him act rashly, and as soon as he'd got back from Ronda today he'd chanced his luck, sending an urgent message that simply read: Some lives are too short to live again. Griff would never reveal what he'd overheard Iris saying to her mother, but hoped this was enough to elicit a reaction.

At last a message had come back: Cloud Man has left for England, the camp's manager had written. A good drinking buddy of Griff's during his stay, he had added in a PS: Ngara says the trip is costing him an arm but not a leg. He says you will understand the English joke.

Griff realised that Dominic had bought his ticket with the money given to him for a prosthetic arm.

'What did he say?'

He swung around to find Iris standing in the archway that led to the bedroom wing. For a foolish moment, he thought she meant Cloud Man, but she was talking about Alejo.

He minimised the screen. 'To be brutally honest, I really don't think it's going anywhere.'

She clanked her way across the room on her crutches. 'So he *is* a good Catholic boy?'

Griff watched as she stopped just a couple of feet away, pausing by one of the pillars. She was still in the dusty vest and shorts, streaked hair tumbling over her face, and he struggled again with overwhelming and unsolicited urges to lay eyes on those tiny pink knickers once again. 'He's done this before. He's not going to marry her.'

'Well, that'll be a relief to her – not the previous history, obviously, but the prospect of being eyed up for life at Sueño cooking stew all day was a worry.'

'He's not such an innocent as he makes out.' Griff edited his tale, having heard a great deal more from Alejo's personal guide to seduction than he cared to repeat. 'I got him wrong,' he admitted. 'I thought he was trapped here, but it turns out he's setting the spring mechanism. He always proposes to girls he wants to sleep with, apparently. That way he doesn't have to . . . ' He cleared his throat.

'Have to what?'

'Use a condom.'

'Jesus.' Iris banged her head gently against the pillar a couple of times. 'Is that it?'

'In a nutshell.' He knew he could have phrased it better as soon as he said it.

Her eyes gleamed and Griff's heart lifted, knowing laughter was there, but the timing was all wrong. She blinked hard, beautiful face serious. 'What an idiot. Please don't tell Chloe this.'

Seeing a shadow move, he glanced through the archway that led to the bedrooms. 'Where is she?'

'In the shower.' Iris clanked past him towards the kitchen.

'Don't you think it would be kinder if she knew the truth?'

'No! We'll tell her he's a good Catholic boy. I'm having some wine.'

Having slipped back into the shadows of the bedroom corridor, Chloe wrapped her arms around herself, trying to stop the anger burning through her belly and chest.

She'd been planning to fetch her phone so that she could send Alejo an apologetic text before her shower, but now she was fighting an urge to race across the courtyard, track him down and impale him with the Afro comb. She could hear Griff still talking, his voice raised as he called through to the kitchen where Iris was fetching wine.

In a distant corner of the house, the huge plasma television was still mumbling away to itself, showing romantic comedies to an empty room. There was nothing particularly romantic or comic about the way she was feeling now.

'Chloe's my oldest friend and a million times smarter than me.' Iris came clanking back into the room beyond the arch. 'But she sees everything too academically, as though sex is an exam module she has to sit.'

Chloe snarled silently to herself. Iris had no idea what she was talking about; her university of life was destined to be an ivory tower that dashing princes regularly scaled to woo her.

As if to prove her point, she heard Griff say, 'I can think of worse things to revise for.' There was an unmistakably seductive tone in his voice.

Chloe knew she should stop eavesdropping, but somehow her feet were glued to the spot as she heard lovely, outspoken Griff falling into the pit into which so many others had fallen before. It must be incredibly crowded in there.

'As long as one never gets caught cheating,' Iris sounded amused, her kittenish little laugh preceding a teasing flirtation, 'especially with the invigilator.'

'Surely sex toys don't count?'

The throaty laugh exploded into irrepressible, hiccuping, child-like joy.

Listening in wonder, Chloe almost jumped through her skin as she felt a warm hand on her back and a voice whispered in her ear: 'You are spying on them?'

Pulses instantly on high alert in every corner of her anatomy, Chloe whipped the comb from her hair and spun around to face Alejo, contemplating the softest spot to bury the tines.

'I cannot stop thinking about you,' he breathed, his dark eyes lifting to meet hers, brimful of lust. 'You excite me so much. Do you have an answer for me?'

Looking into his handsome face, Chloe realised she had a lot to learn from this experience, not least that it was time to move on. Later tonight she planned a swift exit. But first, she had an entry requirement she wanted to set straight.

She kissed Alejo all the way along the corridor, cannoning off walls, into her room. They were seriously good at kissing now. His body leapt eagerly against hers, the forbidden fruits ripe for plucking. Tipping back on to her bed together, they needed no Spanish pop or Rihanna, their hips inching closer together, slotting perfectly, ready to make their own rhythm at last.

'You know what I want, baby?' He looked up at her, black-eyed with lust.

Reaching down, Chloe plucked at last. Every zip tooth sighed with relief as she let Alejo spring out to say hello. He groaned ecstatically as her fingers closed around him, drew battle lines from shaft to tip then circled, spanning and cupping. He was as magnificent as she'd hoped and she felt a delicious spasm of expectation run through her.

Reaching to her bedside cupboard, Chloe drew out the condom and dropped it on his chest, smiling down at him. 'Will you marry me?'

He looked up at her for a long time, not wanting her hand to stop rotating and stroking. Then he started to laugh, lifting the condom from his chest and holding it up between his first two fingers like a cigarette. 'For you, I make an exception. I hope this is not a short engagement.'

'That's rather up to you.' She started kissing him again, reaching out to take her unconventional engagement ring.

Without the covering fire of Spanish pop, it was perfectly obvious what Chloe and Alejo were up to, the bedroom being close enough to the reception rooms for sound to travel. Griff's brows lowered disapprovingly when he heard the tell-tale moans, but Iris knew her friend well enough to hope she was calling the shots. Tonight, she felt similarly empowered, giddy with new-found attraction.

'Is your sap rising?' she teased Griff, now swinging from her crutches, the Rioja making her incredibly flirty.

'You want the truth?'

'Yes. I can feel your truth rising.'

Griff was not playing. 'Hear that thumping noise?'

'What thumping noise?'

'It's the sound of you on the rebound, leaping into bed with me.'

She looked at his kind, lively face, with its expressively arching brows, unable to believe she'd thought it so frightening at first. Dougie's icy blue eyes and cruelly curling mouth were far colder, his drawling voice so distant that it always seemed to be echoing in the back of his head, whereas Griff talked so directly and passionately, his eyes always locked on hers with such interest and compassion and – most recently – down-dirty horniness. He was doing it again now. How could they not kiss? The butterflies in her stomach were all mating like crazy; it was a positive orgy in there.

She walked towards him as seductively as was possible on two crutches. 'I am *not* on the rebound.'

'This afternoon you were proclaiming undying love for Dougie Everett.'

'Then I woke up.'

'All the more reason not to sleep with somebody else immediately.'

With a snort of frustration she clanked back to the kitchen for more wine. 'Don't tell me, you have a girlfriend.'

He crossed the room to the arches that led to the trophy sitting room where the television was now showing *Daddy Long Legs*, in which Leo was being charming and self-deprecatingly gorgeous as he found himself looking after a newborn baby chimp while coincidentally falling for one-time Hollywood über-babe Minty Drover, playing a zoo-keeper.

Watching for a moment, Griff found himself laughing as Leo made a fumbling attempt to seduce the simmering Minty. 'He's very good.'

'That was the first film he made in the States.' Iris shuffled alongside him to hand him a glass of wine. 'He never wanted to act. He always told me he planned to be a theatrical designer, envisaging big, arty parties and lavish meals for his friends between celebrated first nights. Ironic that Demon was the one who ended up doing more of that.'

'Who is Demon?'

'Simon de Montmorency – he's the inspiration behind all these characters.' She nodded at the screen, where Leo was running through New York in pyjama bottoms with his hair on end, looking raffish and adorable. 'Dad's spent his career cashing in on impersonating one of our closest family friends, while Simon swags beautiful houses, hosts parties and lives an Epicurean life on the small screen. It's like they swapped.' Iris limped into the room to pick up the remote control and switch it off, the sudden silence ringing in their ears.

'Simon and his wife Laney were at college with my parents.' She ran her tongue over her upper teeth. 'I'm pretty certain he's my real father.'

'What makes you think that?'

'I read one of Mum's old diaries that made it clear they'd slept together just before she found out she was pregnant. Then, before I came here, Simon's wife Laney – she's my godmother – said as much. There was a huge row. That's why I left.' She limped back across to him, eyes glittering. 'Coming here wasn't really to do with Dougie. Hear that noise?' She cocked her head.

He cocked his head too, playing along warily, dark eyes not leaving her face.

'It's the sound of a clear conscience.'

Griff was staring at her intently, his dark gaze searching hers as he said: 'Are you sure you're not mistaken about your real father?'

'When Mum was doing a big last-minute number on me at the wedding, she cried a lot and told me my father was there. Well, Simon *was* there, plus all his kids. Mum hardly invited anybody from her own circle, yet she invited him. It makes so much sense. She's always fed me this story about an actor she was in love with, but it's so flaky, you can tell it's made up, just like she says there were lots of boyfriends around that time. It's the one bit of acting she can't make convincing.'

'How so?'

'Leo's a great performer, but it's my mother who puts on an Oscar-worthy performance almost every day of her life, without ever getting any applause.' She hobbled back to the kitchen island to fetch her own wine. 'Everyone apart from my grandmother knows Leo's gay, although we all pretend not to for her sake. She's convinced herself that I'm her natural granddaughter and nobody has the heart to tell her otherwise, especially Mum, who's cared for her since my grandfather died. It's a huge sacrifice, but that's my mother all over. She always puts others before herself, human or animal. She married Leo to have a father for me. Even though she was pregnant with Simon's child, she kept quiet because her best friend was in love with him. And she sacrificed all her career dreams and ambitions for me, devoted her life to raising me. I have none of her strength.

'When I was offered the Ptolemy films, I desperately wanted to be a successful actress so I could achieve what she never got the opportunity to do. That's why I took on the part of Purple. Dad – Leo – was dead against it. He knew I'd hate it and he was right. I guess I saw Dougie as an escape hatch, but it turned out he just saw me as a door to the star dressing room.'

'I thought you had a place at university?'

'That's what I really want to do: I long to learn more. But I'm not super-academic like Chloe. I'm frightened of letting them all down.'

'Face the fear, remember.' He smiled.

Iris faced it, looking him straight in the eyes and almost melting with the warm, dark signal that came back. It was happening again, the butterflies flying in formations.

Not waiting for doubt to creep in, she hopped towards him on her crutches until she drew close, then let them fall away, reaching up to put her arms around his neck. 'Does this frighten you?'

'It is quite scary, yes.' He looked unfazed.

'Are you going to run away like Alejo?'

'Depends if you put your hand down my trousers.'

'Would you propose if I did?'

'You could try me,' he joked, but his face was serious. 'Iris, I should have told you something when I first got here. Something about the—'

Stretching up on her one working tiptoe, Iris kissed him full on the mouth to shut him up. It felt incredibly good, the butterflies all high-fiving their wings together. Eventually, running out of breath, they pulled apart. 'Better stop the sap rising.' She leaned her forehead against his.

He said nothing, the sap rising with too many truths, the message in his eyes absolutely clear. He wanted to take her to bed.

'Hear that thumping noise?' she whispered. 'It's just my heart.'

'Is it going quite fast?' His lips moved close to hers again. 'I can't hear it for the sound of mine.'

'Very fast,' she breathed. 'Very hard.'

He kissed her this time, his mouth searching now, tongue sliding alongside hers. She curled around him, the butterflies thoroughly out of control, escaping into her chest and down into her groin.

Stealing across the library to retrieve her phone, Chloe froze when she heard Iris asking about a thumping noise, terrified that the patter of her fast feet had betrayed her presence, but as she peered anxiously along the salon into the kitchen, she could see them kissing again.

She was pleased they were getting together: she liked Griff, for all his do-gooder bluster, and Iris deserved someone to break Dougie's spell. Griff was funny and genuine and strong and clearly adored her. She only hoped they didn't get so carried away they needed a condom, because the only one in the house had just been put to glorious service, an exception to Alejo's rule that she hoped would save his girlfriends from unwanted engagements as well as pregnancies in future.

Chloe had no intention of being part of that future long-term, but she was already vacillating over her plan to leave so soon. Alejo looked so charming asleep on her bed. and the room was so peaceful without his music. A trip to the local *farmacia* for earplugs and *preservativos* could take their fledgling fornication into a whole new realm.

But then, as her hand closed around the phone, she noticed the computer still switched on. Griff hadn't signed out of his email account.

Reading the message on screen, she pressed her hand to her mouth to stop herself letting out a squeak of recognition. She'd been right. And that meant she would be leaving tonight after all.

Iris's butterflies had joined together to create one big butterfly now, flapping its delicate wings inside her body and seeming to lift her right off the ground. Kissing Griff was like flying. She could feel his body tensing as he let out a low groan between kisses. Then, as he pulled away, she saw his face was white with pain and realised to her horror that she'd been dangling off his broken collarbone.

'Oh, God! Sorry! Did that really hurt?'

'Didn't feel a thing, but this would definitely be against doctor's recommendations.' He laughed, eyes dancing once more. 'As someone trained in emergency battlefield medicine and survival techniques, I must warn you that we will not pass first base until I'm satisfied that our injuries are stabilised, and that includes your broken heart.'

'Can I have a date for that?'

'I never give deadlines.'

'No, I mean a date – dinner maybe, or the theatre. I'm asking you out.'

He smiled, hearing his own advice played back to him. 'And when you're passed fit, I'll accept. But only when you're ready. Not before.'

'I warn you, I'll expect to sleep with you on the first date.'

'Sure . . . I think I can live with that.'

Back on her one tiptoe, she kissed him very lightly on the mouth. 'You'll have to tell me the moment I'm fit enough.'

'Hear that thumping noise?' He pressed his forehead to hers and they gazed at one another through their lashes. 'It's me counting the seconds.'

They both looked around as they heard heavy soles clunking along the back hallway that led past the storerooms to the stable courtyard, and Alejo appeared, looking furious. 'Chloe, she has gone where?'

'She's in her room. We thought you were in there too.'

'No, I tell you she has gone. I ask where. She take her car just now and wave at me as she drive past. Then I discover she has taken all my breeches which are hanging on Mamá's line and draw big love hearts on bottom. *And* she still have my iPod Shuffle.'

They rushed to Chloe's room, to find a note on the desk addressed to Iris, alongside Griff's passport and wallet, his phone and Alejo's iPod.

Maybe it is just a romantic fantasy, but I am going to deliver the antelope to Mia before Cloud Man lands. I think that is where it belongs. If she shoots the messenger, I'm happy to take the bullet. C xx

PS Tell Alejo he was very engaging. Lo extraño.

PPS I've wiped his music collection, for the sake of all womankind.

'What does she mean, "deliver the antelope to Mia before Cloud Man lands"?' Iris turned to Griff in confusion, butterflies stilled with sharp pins of fear.

He ran his hands through his hair. 'Iris, I need to tell you the truth.'

Clutching his iPod, Alejo reversed out of the room. 'Trust me, Grief my friend, that never works. Women, they hate that shit.'

Chapter 44

Jacinta was secretly delighted that her daughter-in-law had left her with Haff for company while visiting Leo in LA. He spoke so charmingly of all the things she loved – Spain, horses, the Ormero family, the Church, and death. Unlike most of the Wootton incumbents, he kindly indulged her morbid obsession, currently centring on tombstones. In turn, she lectured him on the subject of marriage.

'You must take a wife soon,' she told him sternly. 'You will be an old father like my Dmitri. Marry a young wife. The Benson girl is very sturdy so will breed good children, and training to be a vet, which would be very useful.'

'Benson, you say?' He looked blank.

'Not a Catholic family,' she sighed, 'but you cannot have everything. Mia was not of our faith, but has always followed her vows to Leo and to God.'

Haff promised courteously he would give taking a wife a lot of thought. Jacinta knew he was soft on Mia. She was old and frail, but her mind was sharp. It was good that Leo and Mia were making this time to be together. Her son worked far too hard and, much as she loved her daughter-in-law and knew that she stayed in England to look after her and the family, it was not a good thing for a couple to be apart so much. She also hoped Mia would talk to him seriously about his mother's death when she saw him in LA, and suspected that this was largely what the trip was about. She told Haff as much over breakfast together, cinnamon-dusted French-toast *torrijas* made to her own recipe.

'My Leo cannot bear to face up to reality, but he must accept that he will lose me soon. I have told him this many times, but he will not listen. I trust Mia to bring him home this time. More *café con leche*? When are you rehearsing the quadrille? I will watch.'

'*Lo siento mucho.*' He dipped his head apologetically. 'Not today.'

What Jacinta hadn't accounted for was Haff's several English mistresses, all of whom had been feeling neglected while he devoted so much of his time in the UK to his inner-city dressage school, the fund-raising gala and the divine Mrs Devonshire, who was patron to it all. He had a very full schedule trying to satisfy them while she was away.

'I must go to Midsex to teach.' He looked at his watch, standing up.

'Middlesex,' she corrected.

Haff kissed her on both cheeks.

Jacinta looked at him forlornly. 'What about the quadrille?' She had been thoroughly enjoying the sight of the pretty girls on their stallions this week, which reminded her of her circus days.

'Escultor is still not totally sound, and the new bay stallion Quito has a bad back. Vicente says there is a man coming here to treat the horses – the man who was struck by a thunderbolt and has magic hands.'

Jacinta crossed herself and decided to catch up on daytime television instead.

She had just settled down with Lorraine Kelly and a celebrity chef when Laney de Montmorency paid her daily visit, sweeping in to thrust some drooping begonias she'd grabbed from her garden into a vase and check her vital signs.

'Jacinta! How're you doing?'

Jacinta was not entirely happy with Mia's overbearing friend stopping by every day en route to the boathouse to check she was still alive, but at least she never stayed long and was an invaluable source of celebrity gossip.

'That man's an absolute bastard,' Laney observed now, as she watched the chef sharing a joke with Lorraine about haggis. 'Has four kids under five, all with different women, and struggles to remember their names – rather like my husband,' she added brightly. 'And he had an affair with Aneka Fenner last year.' She had named showbiz's best known yummy mummy, hostess of *Britain's Got Cakes*.

'Your husband did?' Jacinta asked in shock.

'The chef. Have you chosen a tombstone yet?'

'It is a decision that cannot be rushed. I have time.'

'How much exactly?'

Jacinta shuddered at the impertinence. 'It will be this summer.'

'That soon?' Her blue eyes filled with compassion. 'Oh, Lito, that's such a waste. You're still the beating heart of this family. Life – and death – is so *bloody* unfair. Can they do nothing? Surely there's some sort of treatment available.'

'My doctor says I am beyond repair.'

'Have you asked for a second opinion? I can search the internet for you if you like, make some calls.'

Jacinta was touched by her kindness, although, looking at Laney's pallid face and pinched eyes, she thought she might be in greater need of a medical opinion for herself. 'If you must, but you find no miracle cure. The only thing in my body that is not falling apart is *mis dientes*.' She drew back her lips to show off perfect little cream teeth. 'I can eat toffees whenever I like.'

'You rebel.' Laney smiled. 'Can you write down exactly what it is you're suffering from, so I get my facts right?'

Jacinta's inventory of ailments took almost half an hour and one full side of A4. As she wrote, she said, 'The man is coming today who cures the horses. The Lightning Man, I think they call him. Maybe I'll ask him to cure me?' She cackled.

'You must!' Laney insisted.

'God will not approve.'

'Of course He will.' Laney gave her a wise look as she took the piece of paper. 'After all, He struck him by lightning in the first place. What have you got to lose?'

'Mia would be very angry.'

'She'll be a lot angrier if you peg it in the middle of her gala.'

Laney cursed herself for her short temper as she cycled to the boathouse. She had no right to wind up Jacinta, whom she always found great value. But she was having a bad week. Her palpitations were now so bad that she felt as though the Sodastream plumbed into her heart was alternating with a spin-dryer and a pneumatic drill. She knew she should cut down on the pills, but she was almost into a size twelve again.

That week, with cash arriving in the bank from the Christmas book delivery and Simon's recent television work, the builders had started work on Red Gables full-time again. To celebrate, Simon had hosted an impromptu garden party yesterday, mostly cronies from television and advertising, only a few of whom Laney had previously met, plus some more familiar faces from London she hadn't spoken to for ages. But at the last minute she'd discovered that the party clashed with a birthday celebration for one of Hope's friends. After Laney had spent three hours at a soft-play centre, enduring conversations that always started 'Such a shame your husband's not here', she and Hope returned to find Simon and his guests as drunk as students, lurching around the lawn missing air kisses and saying, 'Marvellous house' a lot as they looked blearily at the scaffolding.

Laney had made an effort to dress up in a floaty white tunic dress that hid her still-thick middle while showing off her tan and her cycling-toned legs, with lots of chunky jewellery that made her feel like the old Laney. Simon had certainly fallen on her with enormous pride, spilling large amounts of red wine down her front as he drunkenly towed her and Hope around new acquaintances.

The fact that she'd been wearing a dress that wouldn't have zipped up a month earlier had made her feel completely different about her body. She liked it again at long last. She liked dressing it and touching it and pampering it. And men looked at her differently, with the hard-eyed sexual stare she'd forgotten existed. For the first time since having Hope, she wanted to fill herself with something other than just more babies. But if she'd thought losing weight would settle anything, she'd been wrong – her work–life balance still tipped the scales one way, no matter how much she weighed. Being thinner, however, did cheer her up enormously.

Cycling to the boathouse now, despite the pressure washer going in her chest where her heart should have been, she felt victorious. That morning, when she'd found her size-twelve jeans zipping up again – just – she'd finally understood how her parents had felt when their golf handicaps went down. And when she'd stopped in Burley for headache pills, the Indian pharmacist had shyly told her she looked magnificent. The *Daily Mail*'s side panel of shame was taking an active interest in her now, this morning running a much more flattering photo of her arriving at her own house party accompanied by headlines screaming LANEY SHOWING OFF DEMON WEIGHT LOSS!

The one least impressed was Simon, who had responded to all the Twitter speculation about their marriage with characteristic sangfroid, tweeting that his wife was leaving him a pound at a time. Privately, he pleaded with her to eat more because she was making herself ill, advice she ignored. At least she was feeling horny all the time – her rapacious appetite for sex exhausted him too much to complain about her domestic neglect.

At her desk, she found messages from her two admirers, both now courting her mercilessly, both with highly suspect agendas.

Kit – always more full-on because he had a very clear agenda – had rowed downriver again, leaving chocolates and a bottle of champagne: *Share these later . . . ?* He had been trying Milk Tray Man tactics all week.

Richard HH's ongoing offer remained far more tempting: My darling L, he wrote, July is racing by. Let me buy you that lunch. Just to talk and meet, no more than that . . .

Laney finally felt slim enough to do it, and keyed up enough to want it more than anything. But she wasn't sure her heart would hold out.

'Hey, Laney! You're here at last! You got my gifts?'

Groaning, she looked up to see Kit drifting downstream fast in his boat. 'Go away!'

'I just wanna . . . Holy smoke, this thing's going a bit fast . . . just gotta get the oars and . . . Jesus!' He disappeared from sight, calling, 'I'll be right back!'

Laney closed the french windows and returned to her desk to read the rest of Richard's message, face flaming as her overactive heart flew alongside her racing eyes, devouring his words and kindness. She always read his messages ridiculously fast at first, then reread them again and again, savouring every phrase, every thought, and that incredible strength. She'd been pouring out her worries about her marriage in recent days, deeply hidden among the jokes about Seduction Kit and bawdy stories, but unmistakable whispers of truth. His insight never failed to astonish and touch her. He'd been married several times himself, he'd explained with typical candour, and had made terrible mistakes he deeply regretted. He was terrified of getting it wrong again and hamstrung by inhibition as a result. Maybe she felt the same? Or maybe she didn't love Simon in the way she once had? He obviously drinks too much, he wrote, as well as taking you for granted and possessing the emotional depth of Tigger.

The only time Laney got irritated with RHH was when he was unpleasant about Simon, which she knew was hypocritical, but it pricked too hard at her guilty conscience.

On cue, her phone lit up with a picture text showing Fred the builder disapprovingly holding up two wine bottles he'd found on the scaffolding: He says it's looking like Chianti-town round here, Simon had written. I told him we're Riesling to the challenge. Que Syrah Syrah. Are you responding to all my sexy emails, oh wonderful wife?

Glancing across at her horribly underwritten *Madame Bovary* script, then back to the phone, Laney knew she was measuring out her marriage in picture texts and misconceptions. She had no desire to face the lascivious ladies from his website today, although she knew the inbox was at capacity again.

Book the table as soon as you like, she typed to Richard HH. I'll be there.

'Hey!' came a muffled cry through the french windows. 'I'm back! Nearly went over the weir, man! Have you put that champagne on *iiiiiii* – egh!' There was a loud splash, followed by the sound of an alarmed duck taking flight.

With a deep sigh, Laney stomped to the windows. The boat was floating upside-down five yards into the river, bubbles rising near by, the duck quacking away. There was no sign of Kit.

'Bugger.' Kicking off her shoes, Laney raced down the steps to the wooden jetty, already pulling her dress over her head ready to dive in. A puttering engine was making its way steadily along the far side of the river.

'By all that is sacred, madam, put it away!'

Grabbing the life ring, she jumped into the water.

It was a long time since the Lightning Man had been to Wootton, and the stable staff had changed many times since. Only the old gardener Franco remembered the sensation that ex-jump jockey Sandy Cox had created when laying his hands on horses and 'curing' them of every kind of ailment, from old ligament injuries to sweet-itch.

He was clipping the topiary when the buzzer went on the front gates. Knowing that only the old lady was in the house and took for ever to get to the intercom, if she heard it at all over her blaring television, he went to open them. A small black hatchback drove in, its airport car hire ID number still swinging from the rear-view mirror like an oversized air freshener.

Franco would have liked to point out that tradesmen visiting the stables should use the back gates, but he faltered as the tall, handsome man with a shock of white-blond hair stepped out; he looked far too big to have been a jockey and wasn't at all as Franco remembered. But as he stepped forward to redirect him, the man turned to look up at the house, handsome face now a livid mask of burned skin.

Before Franco could stop him, he strode up the steps two at a time and pulled on the bell. A cacophony of barking dogs greeted the noise.

The housekeeper was off that day so, after a long pause, the mosquito whine of Jacinta's wheelchair was heard, along with more barking and scrabbling paws.

At last one of the two doors beneath the columned portico opened and a grey head poked out. '¿*Cómo puerdo ayudarte?* What d'you want?' she demanded nervously.

'I apologise for the intrusion.' His voice was hypnotically deep. 'I had to come here.'

'I know who you are,' she interrupted, holding a hand up to Franco, who was starting up the steps, secateurs aloft, to intercept.

'You do?' He stooped to the yapping, barging pack of dogs, stroking ears and scratching necks.

Jacinta, who despaired of Mia ever controlling her unruly pack, watched in amazement as they settled into an adoring, obedient line.

'You'd better come in.' She buzzed into reverse. As he passed her, she saw the vivid scars and crossed herself.

She whizzed after him. He was standing in the centre of the huge entrance hall now, looking up to the domed skylight – a hot-air balloon was crossing the blue sky above the house. Almost all of the dogs were sitting beside him, looking up too.

Iris had babbled on about this man many times, his amazing healing powers – he just laid a hand on an injured horse to cure it – although Mia had become cynical of late: her veterinary friend had talked her out of such unproven nonsense. He certainly looked a breed apart, despite the scruffy old beige cords and the denim shirt, the scarred face, the hair so blond it could have been spun from light. He possessed a very still, almost unearthly, presence that seemed to fill the hallway. His quiet smile, when he turned it on her, burst through his scars like an armistice on a battlefield. His deep blue eyes were bright as pilot lights and equally incendiary. She had the distinct feeling that they could ignite an inferno capable of razing a city when he was angry.

'I am Señora Devonshire,' she said grandly. 'My daughter-in-law has spoken of you in the past, although I'm afraid she no longer has any interest in what you do.'

His eyes bored into hers and she fingered the Reverse button, but he said nothing so she carried on: 'She is away in America with her husband at present. There is not much time. I thought this summer will be the end, but maybe I am wrong.'

'Maybe you are, *señora*.' The deep voice was so hypnotic that it was no wonder horses keeled over in a blissful stupor, she decided.

'Through here.' She revved past him into the huge kitchen, its table scattered with the paperwork and post that had spilled into chaos just twenty-four hours since Mia's departure. It included Jacinta's brochures of tombs and cenotaphs.

'Has somebody passed away?'

'I am planning ahead for my own funeral,' she said proudly.

'You are very well organised.'

'I like to think so.' She beamed at him, buzzing closer. 'You came close to death once, I heard?'

He looked at her curiously. 'I did.'

'I think I will have only one chance at it.'

'It's more important to remember that we have only one chance at life,' he said, and she noticed how he angled his head when he spoke so that his scars were hidden, clearly a practised move. He would have been such a handsome man without them, she thought sadly.

'You are a brave man, I think.'

'Instinct takes over,' he said quietly. 'It's not always the right thing to do, but it generally aids survival.'

'They were saying much the same thing on *Jeremy Kyle* this morning about teenage pregnancy.' Jacinta drove across the kitchen to the far surface to eye the coffee maker, which she still couldn't work, no matter how often the staff explained it. She had decided he was rather fascinating company. 'This makes twenty different types of coffee, I'm told. My daughter-in-law is addicted to coffee, but without caffeine. It's like being addicted to cigarettes without nicotine or wine without alcohol, don't you think? What is the pleasure in a pretend sin?'

His deep voice was barely more than a breath. 'When is she back?'

Jacinta turned up her hearing aid. 'You want your coffee black, did you say?' She peered at the machine hopelessly and pressed a few buttons, which made it bleep furiously. 'You may need to help me.'

When he made no move, she abandoned the idea, reversing into the island and triggering the soft-open recycling drawers. She turned the chair to face him again, increasingly bad-tempered. He might have healing hands, but they weren't very helpful ones.

'When does Mia come back from America?' he asked again, his deep voice now echoing through her head like a film voiceover.

'It is open-ended.' She turned the hearing aid down before returning to her wheelchair controls as she tried to navigate past the island once more. 'She is organising the gala here, of course, but she has people handling everything, so she can stay as long as he needs her to.' She cannoned into a couple of corner units. 'Her marriage is more important. She and Leo know they must make time together. They are still very much in love.'

He was being singularly unhelpful, she thought, just staring at her in that strange, still way. At last she got past the unit and whizzed across the room, pointing up to the photographs on the wall. 'They are so beautiful, yes? It takes a beautiful couple to make a beautiful child. I think maybe they try for another baby.'

He looked at the framed photographs on the wall featuring the family, many of Iris from infancy to adulthood.

'We are so proud of Iris. So like her father. She is in España at the moment. She loves our mother country. She has much Ormero blood in her veins. You see her movies?'

'I don't have a television.'

'No television! Are you crazy? It is God's way to show us the world. Come with me.' She accelerated through a huge, oak-framed conservatory towards a door leading to a separate wing. 'Come, come! You are just in time for *Loose Women*. They will bring my lunch in a minute. You must join me and tell me what it is like to face death. Then you will lay hands on me.'

Twenty seconds later, she crashed into a huge Murano-glass horse's head, upended a potted fig and buzzed back to the kitchen. 'Why you not come with me?'

Surrounded by a transfixed chorus of dogs, he was still staring at the pictures, studying Mia and Leo on red carpets and awards rostra, with friends and family and on horseback in Spain, riding the two matching buckskin stallions that Jacinta's father had given them as a wedding present. The handsome side of his face was torn with emotion. 'I think I should leave.'

'Do not heal the horses before you heal me!' she pleaded, accelerating towards him at full pelt. 'You cannot deny an old lady. Leo will give his heart for more time with his *mamá*, even if it's just a week or two . . .' Her dark eyes were imploring as the wheelchair screeched to a halt, sending the dogs scuttling away and pinning him against the wall. 'I am ready, may God forgive me. Lay your hands on me.'

'*Señora*, I have only one hand.' He held up his right arm.

Jacinta gasped, noticing for the first time that the sleeve was knotted below the elbow.

'Then lay it on me twice.' She braced herself for a thunderbolt as a warm hand tentatively touched her forehead.

When nothing happened, she opened first one eye and then the other, before heaving a disappointed sigh. 'I told Laney as much. *Nada*. It was worth trying, I suppose. I am going to watch *Loose Women*. You can show yourself out. You know where you are going, don't you?'

He nodded. 'I know exactly where I'm going, *señora*.'

Having kept a close and wary eye on the house, Franco looked up from clipping the beak of one of his yew lovebirds when the door opened and the blond man emerged, stalking back to his car with a small pack of the Devonshires' dogs panting at his heels. He had to push them away to stop them jumping in with him.

419

Franco hurried to press the gate button as the engine started, calling the dogs back, relieved that the visitor was leaving. He disliked anything occult. While the car waited for the gates to open, one of Iris's little Maltese terriers spotted a pigeon strutting across the road and shot out through them.

The little Fiat that came careering around the corner and into Wootton's wide entrance had spotted that the gates were opening, accelerated to catch them and was now travelling far too fast. Its driver had hardly slept since setting out from Spain more than twenty-four hours earlier and was rattling with caffeine overload. While she saw the loose dog straight away and swerved to avoid it, she didn't spot an oncoming car or register the need to take her foot off the accelerator until her windscreen was a sea of black car, topiary and Franco's screaming face. A pair of secateurs skittered off her bonnet and there was a terrific crunch. Then she saw nothing but white as her airbag deployed.

On the opposite side of the two entangled radiator grilles, Dominic got out, fighting a horrible sense of déjà vu. His car had taken far less of a hammering than the Fiat that had slammed into it. To his relief, the old gardener had dived into a topiary squirrel to safety in the nick of time.

In the little Fiat, the girl's breathing was shallow and her skin clammily cold.

'Are you OK?' he asked. 'What's your name?'

She groaned, eyes shut, too overwrought to speak.

'She is injured?' the gardener panted, having extracted himself from the yew.

'Just shock, I think.' He loosened the scarf around her neck.

'Feeling ... dizzy.' She tilted her head back and looked up through her sun-roof, then closed her eyes again.

'She is friend of Iris,' Franco explained. 'Her name is Chloe.'

Dominic sent him to fetch help and call for an ambulance, then checked her pulse, which was quite strong but extraordinarily fast.

'Think I'm going to be sick.'

Having counted at least eight coffee containers, three Red Bull cans and several bags of sweets, Dominic wasn't surprised. He leaned past the airbag into the car, helped her out and carried her to the steps, where he carefully sat her down.

'Take deep breaths,' he told her.'Your blood pressure has dropped because you've had a shock, but you'll soon start to feel better.'

She tried to lie back, but he settled her with her head between her knees in case she vomited.

At the top of the steps, the door flew open and Jacinta buzzed grumpily out beneath the portico, shouting in Spanish, 'Franco! The dogs are all over the road! Our neighbours have called to complain!' She spotted Dominic. 'Haven't you gone to the stables yet? What is Chloe doing there?' Then she saw the cars and crossed herself. '¡Válgame Dios!' She glanced up at the sky. 'I knew I should never have asked a man you'd struck down to help me. Forgive me!'

Chloe let out a groan and Dominic checked her pulse again, which was slowing to something approaching normality. 'You're doing great, Chloe. You should start to feel more human soon.'

'I know that voice.' She lifted her head and blinked a few times, rubbing her clammy face in her hands.

He kept his scarred cheek turned away as her dark eyes slid across to him, still blinking rapidly.

'He is the Lightning Man!' Jacinta called from the portico. 'It's all rubbish, trust me. Don't let him lay a hand on you. You're better off with a shot of brandy de Jerez.'

Still looking at Dominic, Chloe shook her head. 'You're not the Lightning Man.'

'I'm not,' he agreed.

There was a clamour of voices and running feet as Franco reappeared with Vicente from the stables, trailed by a small, stooped character of indeterminate age wearing a cowboy hat and a Johnny Cash T-shirt.

While the two Spaniards started shouting at Dominic in their mother tongue, the stooped character sidled up to Chloe, who was still staring at the blond man, her brow creased.

'You OK, missy?' he asked in an accent that was part Texas affectation, part Oxfordshire burr.

'Of course she's not,' snapped Dominic, taking no notice of Franco pointing at him and shouting, '¡Estafador!' and 'Impostor!' repeatedly, while Vicente called the police from his mobile. 'She's had a bloody bad shock.'

At the top of the steps, Jacinta was squawking, 'I knew he was an impostor!'

'*I* am the Lightning Man.' The little man in the Stetson pressed a gnarled little hand to the top of Chloe's head, letting out a 'Euch' as he did so.

'I couldn't get all the conditioner out when I last washed it,' she mumbled, still staring at Dominic in amazement. Then she gave a gasp of recognition, her eyes brightening. 'You're Cloud Man! You told Griff Donne about leaving everything behind. You left Mia behind. But you're here. Oh my God, you're here!'

'You really know who I am?' He moved closer, and as he did so, Chloe finally saw the scars, so brutal and vivid, one lashless eyelid almost fused shut.

She nodded, unable to speak for horrified compassion.

'I have to get out of here,' he breathed.

'I think that's done the trick.' The Lightning Man removed his hand from Chloe's head and wiped it on the back of his jeans. 'You should feel a lot better now, missy.'

Chloe let out a scream as, lunging forwards, Franco and Vicente took hold of Dominic and hauled him off the step.

'I have called the police,' Vicente told him as they wrestled him towards his car like a pair of over-excited Miami cops. 'They weel take impersonating somebody else to gain an old lady's trust and trespassing on Mr and Mrs Devonshire's property very seriously.' Slamming him against the side of the car, they pinned his one arm behind his back to hold him there.

'I didn't impersonate anybody,' he muttered. 'She invited me in.'

'Stop it!' Chloe leapt up. 'Leave him alone!'

Racing towards them, she kicked Franco in the shins, making him squeal and let go.

'*¡Jesús, María y José!*' cried Jacinta. 'Look at her! She has already recovered from the accident! It's a miracle!' She watched in wonder as Chloe laid into Vicente to make him release Dominic.

Now standing beside Jacinta, admiring his handiwork at a safe distance, the Lightning Man looked smug. 'They never fail.' He held up his hands. 'These are miracle workers.'

'You don't know what he's been through!' Chloe was howling at Vicente. 'Let him go or I'll bite you!'

A moment later, Vicente howled as her teeth sank into his arm.

Now free, Dominic ducked away, eyeing the open gates.

'Your car's hardly dented,' Chloe insisted, ever-practical, however extreme the circumstances. She turned to fight off Franco, executing a perfect karate kick that rendered the little Spaniard tearfully speechless. Then she spotted Vicente coming back at Cloud Man and jumped on his back. 'Go!' she shouted at him. 'Good luck!'

Leaping into his car and starting the engine, he clicked the gearshift to Reverse and stamped on the accelerator, pulling away from the little Fiat with a clatter of snapping bodywork as the crushed bumpers detached. Gravel spitting and engine revving, he reversed in a perfect arc around the carriage sweep and out through the gates.

Letting Vicente go, Chloe dusted him down and apologised, as he blushed deeply. 'You are amazing girl, Chloe. I always think that. Crazy beautiful girl.'

'Are you a good Catholic boy?' she asked breathlessly, then smiled at the bafflement on his handsome face. 'Buy me a drink sometime and maybe we'll find out.'

Franco was less forgiving, hissing through a newly broken tooth as he lumbered up, eyes still watering. 'Why you do that?' he demanded furiously. 'You know heem?'

'He's Cloud Man,' Chloe explained, glancing up at the steps where the bowed little ex-jockey stood chatting to Jacinta. 'Arch-rival of the Lightning Man.'

'You kidding us, right?' Vicente looked as excited as a boy with a new comic-strip hero.

She smiled enigmatically. 'Who d'you think really made me feel better?'

At the top of the steps, the legendary local healer had removed his Stetson respectfully before bowing to shake Jacinta's liver-spotted hand. 'Delighted to make your acquaintance, ma'am.'

'Would you like to come inside for a coffee?' she offered. 'I have a machine that makes twenty different varieties. You may have to lay your hands on it to make it work.' She beamed at him. 'And I would like you to lay your hands on me, *señor*.'

'It would be my pleasure, ma'am.'

Chloe began to walk towards her mangled car, which Franco and Vicente were trying to push out of the way of the electric gates so that they could close again, then she let out a cry of horror: she had no way of contacting Cloud Man. She knew from all the texts she'd been getting in the past day that a furious Griff and Iris were on her tail, only prevented from flying in ahead of her by a Spanish air-traffic controllers' strike. She had really screwed up this time.

Retrieving her phone from the car as Vicente ushered ten dogs through the gates, she pressed a rarely used speed-dial: 'Mummy, I'm at Wootton. I've had a bit of a prang. Can you come here and fetch me?'

Chapter 45

'We must stop meeting like this.' Kit grinned up at Laney from beneath the pink towel that was draped over his head.

'Stop falling in the bloody river, then. And stop hassling me. You won't get the script off me.'

'But your writing is *so* genius.' He was laying into the chocolates he'd delivered earlier.

She laughed drily. 'We both know it's *Dalrymple* you're after.'

'I find you fascinating. You are so sexily British, all that passive aggression and simmering tension, and such a sharp mind. You're clearly molten lava underneath. Man, you turn me on.'

'Oh God, I knew I should have let you drown.'

'You sound just like—' He stopped, thinking.

She spun back to face him, smiling victoriously. 'Oscar?'

'I was going to say Dame Maggie in *Downton*. Man, I *loved* that series. I see a script from you working along very similar lines, if we vibe it up with your humour and set it in the future instead of the past.'

'Spare me.' She removed a lump of pond weed from her ear before rubbing it with her own towel, far bigger and fluffier than the one she'd given him. The boathouse had a shower and even a little washer-dryer that she could run her wet, sludgy clothes through, but she certainly wasn't about to jump to it while Kit was prowling around unmarked.

'OK, here's the deal,' she said. 'You can tell Oscar that I want this to stop. He knows I'm not prepared to sell him the *Dalrymple Two* script at the price he's offering and I am *not* about to let him steal it in some seduction fantasy with you as bait. Frankly, even if you were a better actor I wouldn't be interested. I'm a happily married woman.' Face burning at her hypocrisy, she rushed on, 'Which is something I could never boast during my time as Mrs Oscar Benson.'

'You tell him,' drawled a voice from the door.

She swung around to see Simon, with Hope's lunchbox. 'I brought you cucumber sandwiches, darling. Would you like me to throw out the pond life?'

'Yes, please.'

'Hey, chill out, I'm going.' Kit held up his hands and sauntered damply through the french windows. But any plan to slip gallantly away through the reeds was hampered because his boat was still bobbing upside-down by the jetty. He needed help to turn it the right way up. While he and Laney sloshed around, heaving it over and bailing it out, Simon started on the champagne and issued helpful instructions from the balcony, reluctant to get his white Incotex chinos wet. With a bright pink Savile Row shirt and very dark glasses to hide his bloodshot eyes, he was a peculiar fusion of wronged husband and hungover dandy.

'I have half a mind to call you out to a duel!' he shouted when Kit finally wobbled off. 'If I see you here again, I will!'

Laney squelched back inside and froze as she saw Simon studying her computer screen over his dark glasses. 'I thought you were looking at my emails. What's this? "I have a lover! I have a lover!"'

Looking over his shoulder, she was flooded with relief to see that it was her *Madame Bovary* radio script, not a Richard HH message.

'I have to finish the rewrites on that scene,' her heart was palpitating more than ever after the near-miss, 'and I'm hugely behind. The lascivious ladies will have to wait.'

'Along with the object of their lascivious desires.' He tipped his chin lower, regarding her over the tortoiseshell rims of his shades, pale grey eyes weary, the laughter lines of the irrepressible joker deeply furrowed. 'I'll leave you to it, darling. Only popped by to play sandwich boy and throw out interlopers. Talking of which, there was a terrific ding-dong going on at the big house when I passed the front gates. I had to come in the back way. Is Mia auditioning kick-boxers for this gala?'

'She's in LA, remember? Jacinta said something about the Lightning Man coming. He's pretty unorthodox, by all accounts.'

'Well, lightning may not strike twice, but Oscar's girl was knocking seven bells out of somebody on the drive.'

'Runs in the family. Her father likes to throw extremely low punches.'

Chapter 46

In South Yorkshire, Alison Stubbs poured her brother another cup of tea, trying to stop her hands shaking. She had not looked him in the face since opening the door an hour earlier. 'You'll have to go before our Adele comes round. She's bringing the baby.'

'Of course.'

'Let me break the news slowly. I clean forgot I said I'd sit for her this evening. Your call knocked me for six. I still can't believe it's really you sat here.'

Dominic kept quiet about the fact that it had taken him equally by surprise. His Wootton experience had taught him that dropping in unannounced was not a good tactic, so he'd bought a mobile phone from a service station. It had taken him almost an hour to figure out how to call Directory Enquiries and then, to his alarm, the service had put him straight through to the only Stubbs listed in Dinfield, so that seconds later he'd found himself speaking to his big sister for the first time in twenty years. Now he was sitting in her kitchen.

He'd tried to explain about his disfigurement on the telephone, but it never prepared people for the shock of seeing him, more so somebody who had known and loved the young Dominic Masters. This was far tougher than he could have imagined, his sister veering between joy, compassion and anger.

'I couldn't believe it when I heard your voice.' She stirred sugar into her tea with a frantic rattle. 'You sound just the same.'

'Look a bit different.'

'Happen we all do.' Still she wouldn't look at him. 'Except Mia, maybe. She's not changed a jot. Have you seen her?'

He shook his head. 'She's in LA.'

'Of course. It's in today's paper.' Alison reached for the *Daily News*, which was lying on the table. Leafing through to a celebrity gossip page, she thrust it at him. In a Hollywood news column, unsubstantiated rumours appeared in little speech bubbles. One of them had the headline LEOMIA UNITED. 'It claims he quit the show he was in because Mia's ill,' she explained. 'There's been no official announcement, but it's what everybody's saying. It sounds serious, poor duck.'

Dominic closed his eyes, remembering Griff's message coming through to say that some lives were too short to live again. That day Dominic's balloon had almost been shot down by poachers and he'd interpreted the words to mean his own life. At that moment he had known with absolute certainty that, if he was likely to die any day soon, he must see Mia first. But now he realised the full horror of his misunderstanding: 'You mean it could be terminal?'

'Life's terminal, cock.' Alison snatched the newspaper back, anger welling. 'Why not ask her yourself? That way, she'll at least know you're alive. Dad was never granted that privilege, but you still owe that poor girl an explanation.'

'I wrote to her before I left England. A birthday card.'

She drew in a sharp breath of recognition. 'Mia got in a right state over that, but the family all reckoned it was a hoax on account of the fact it wasn't your handwriting. She'll be made up when she hears from you.'

Dominic kept his eyes scrunched shut. The photographs he'd seen in the Wootton kitchen had spoken for themselves, capturing a close marriage that he had no right to disrupt. The Devonshires had a daughter who would be devastated. Now he'd learned that Leo had just sacrificed a huge role to care for Mia. 'I'll not turn her life upside-down again, Al. I'll fly back to Kenya tomorrow.'

'You. Will. Not!'

'You sound just like Mum used to.' He smiled sadly.

Her round face was set with anger as she stared at the newspaper story. 'I remember how devastated that girl was after you disappeared. It broke her heart. Dad used to invite her here for tea on his birthday every year. It was going to be your birthday, but he said every four years wasn't enough. She always managed to make it, no matter what was going on in her life, never let him down. She never forced herself neither – I think she was embarrassed sometimes, she felt she had no place here when you'd turned down her proposal, but—'

'I didn't turn her down!'

She ignored the outburst. 'Dad worshipped her. It was a way of keeping you alive for both of them. After he died, I found letters she'd written to him that he kept in a biscuit tin. They were really beautiful.'

'Can I see them?'

'I'm not sure I've still got them. They were with Dad's private things. I was going to send them back to her, but we fell out over the funeral and I've not seen her since. It was Dad she came to see. He didn't have a lot in his life. She knew how much she meant to him.'

'Why did you fall out?'

'She wanted to pay for the funeral, but I told her we weren't bloody paupers. You know how proud Dad was. He had a funeral plan with the Co-op. It was a good send-off. Shame you missed it.' She couldn't keep the edge of bitterness from her voice. 'He died not knowing you were alive. What you did to us, it's so bloody cruel. We'd have looked after you. I looked after our dad for over a decade.'

'I didn't want to burden you more.'

'How can you say that? You think coping all this time not knowing what happened to you wasn't a burden? You walked out on us the night our Adele was born. *I* nearly died that night, *she* nearly died that night. But you were the one that didn't care about us enough to let us know you were still alive.'

Dominic stared at her, but he wasn't seeing her any more. He was back in the hospital ward, his dreams as shattered as his body, determined to spare his family the pain of his blighted life. 'You know what I was like as a kid,' he said quietly, 'what a nasty little sod I was, how everyone thought I was past helping. I was in that much trouble all the time, Dad told me more than once he wished I'd never been born.'

'But you turned it around. You found your acting. You made something of yourself.'

'The accident killed that lifeline. Look at me, Al.'

Alison forced her eyes up at last, the same vivid petrol blue, now cushioned by creases that spoke of hard work and laughter. He saw the pain and fear in them as they were faced with the brutal legacy of his accident.

'I knew there would be no more roles I could play, not the ones I wanted,' he said, 'including that of husband to the most beautiful girl alive. I thought I had no future. Better Mia lived her life without me. Better you all did. Like Dad said, better I'd never been born.'

'You bloody idiot,' she said, the blue eyes filling with tears as she reached out to cup his face. 'We love you. No accident could burn that love away. And I don't know what made you change your mind and come back, but I'm so grateful you did.'

He thought briefly about Griff, so young and impulsive, yet wise. As he did so, he knew he could no more return to Kenya to be Cloud Man just yet than he could play Hamlet at the National Theatre. 'Someone keeps reminding me that you only get one life.'

'Well, I'm glad you're back in this one.' Alison tucked his hair behind his ears, just as she had when he was a boy. 'Get this cut – you always grow it too long.' The mantel clock struck the hour. 'Adele will be in any minute.' Her blue eyes were apologetic. 'Give me time to talk to her and the rest of the family about this. When can you come again?'

'Not for a while.' He set aside his mug and picked up his mobile, eyeing it warily. 'We'll speak on the phone soon.'

'We will.' She hugged him tightly. 'Now I've got your number and I know where you work, you'll not get away this time, even if I have to come out to Africa to find you.'

'I could take you on safari,' he offered, knowing he would be ten times more relaxed in the Mara than in Dinfield.

'If I win the Lotto, maybe.' She chuckled, leading him to the door. Then she paused to eye him over her shoulder as she reached for the latch. 'You will contact Mia, won't you? Write to her at least?'

'I'm not much of a one for writing these days.'

'You were always writing each other letters when you were—' She stopped herself, glancing at the space where his right arm should have been and blushing crimson.

As Dominic stepped out on to the pavement, Alison ordered him to wait and shot back inside. He looked along the terrace of houses, almost identical to the one where they'd grown up. There were a lot more cars parked outside, and satellite dishes had been breeding on walls, but nothing much else had changed. Spotting several curtains twitching, he turned his scarred profile away from view, knowing his visit would be the subject of much speculation.

Reappearing now, she thrust an old Jacob's Cream Crackers tin at him. 'I just remembered I'd put it in the sideboard with my wedding photos. Read them. You'll see that Mia never stopped loving you.'

The house on Nichols Canyon was decorated so similarly to Wootton that it always threw Mia to be there, recognising the same fabrics and ornaments, the French cushions and the Murano-glass horse's head identical to the one at home. Leo had flown Simon out especially to do it, around the same time that Laney's marriage to Oscar had hit rock-bottom. They all knew it had been a deliberate move on Leo's part, playing Cupid to reunite the Demons at last, carefully engineering it so that Simon could enact the heroic 'rescue' that had brought Laney and Hope to the UK.

Both LA house and UK mansion formed mirror-image 1920s

theatre sets for Leo's backstage life. Even the dog bed in which Puff Adder the Old English bull terrier slept was styled like an Art Deco settee, complete with fur throws and marabou-trimmed cushions with his masters' faces captured in needlepoint.

Although Mia lived among identical stage props, she never really noticed them until she was in LA, spotting the duplicates and the duplicity.

Ivan Pollack fitted in so perfectly with the twenties theme that he could have been added by Simon as a finishing touch. But he was no cool-eyed, languid blond youth born to drape himself over a chaise longue, tennis racquet in hand, and look peevish. Short, muscular and deep-voiced, Ivan might still be in his late twenties, but he was just a moustache and a pipe away from patriarchy, with outrageously bushy eyebrows and hairy legs, and a penchant for teaming cable-knit sweaters with white Bermuda shorts. A well-read foodie with a quirky sense of humour and a super-organised mind, he balanced Leo's workaholic LA life with a quiet strength Mia envied, her own distracted agitation exacerbated because she'd forgotten to pack her Xanax.

Thrown together, like relatives in a hospital waiting room, while Leo's career was resuscitated in long meetings with Abe and the *Chancellor* team, Mia was grateful for Ivan's solid, upbeat charm. She'd hardly seen Leo, nor had an opportunity to speak candidly about his situation. And for all that Ivan accepted she was his lover's wife, here in Nichols Canyon he marked her like a loyal guard-dog warning a guest not to wander too close to his master's chair.

Today they were sharing lunch on the wooden veranda that ran around the house on the canyon side and was level with the tree-tops, waiting for Leo to return from meeting his lawyers. That evening Leomia were due to attend a launch party for British fashion-label offshoot Stellar. Under instructions to say little and look frail, Mia was dreading it. So, Ivan informed her with the gentle one-upmanship of two-man pillow talk, was Leo.

'I've told him Abe's idea sucks, but you know how loyal he is,' he fretted. 'They go back a long way. Leo's so stressed about it he can't stop knitting baby clothes. I have to wrestle the needles off him at night, but even so I wake up at three or four and hear click, click, click. It's maddening.'

'At this rate, your child will have more cable-knit jumpers than you,' she joked, earning herself a wary look from beneath the thick brows.

'You disapprove of us wanting a baby together?'

'I think it would be better if your relationship was public knowledge, for the child's sake as well as both of yours.'

'This is Hollywood. Things don't work that way.'

'Have you found a surrogate yet?'

'We have a shortlist. We're looking for the best genetic match.' He was watching her face closely.

'The opti-mum?'

He laughed, but his eyes were serious. 'This means a lot to Leo.'

'But you would rather he came out first, wouldn't you?'

'I just want him to be happy,' he said firmly. 'Right now, he's happiest planning our baby. We're both so looking forward to being parents. Leo will make a great father.'

'He *is* a great father.'

'I'm talking biological father.'

'We're a non-bio family.' She forced herself to smile despite a sharp, jealous stitch in her side.

His brows knitted into a furry caterpillar. 'You mustn't feel threatened by this, Mia. We're all family. You're my stepwife, remember, honey?'

Mia knew Ivan meant well, but right now the Sylvanian Families solidarity didn't help Leo. They all knew his public position was tenuous and Abe's solution absurd. She could still remember the British media backlash when Simon had sought to prove his heterosexual credentials early on in his career. She pushed her plate away, grateful that losing her appetite with all the recent stress meant she'd dropped a few pounds and would look fittingly gaunt for that evening's Leomia outing.

'We have Iris to think about,' she said gently. 'She's been through a lot lately.'

'How is she?' Ivan's brows lifted over his dark eyes like canal lock gates opening.

'Licking her wounds in Spain. She's not happy about this trip.'

'You heard Dougie Everett's still here in LA? Now Leo's connected him with Abe, doors are opening fast.'

'Leo's way too nice for his own good.'

'We both agree on that. I've not met Dougie, but I hear he's seriously cute-assed and is making twenty-league strides towards stardom already – he's following the footsteps along the Hollywood Walk of Fame like Cinderella's ugly sisters power-walking to the palace.'

'He must think that if he becomes a big star, Iris will love him all the more. But he doesn't know her at all. She always prefers underdogs.' Mia cupped her chin in her hands.

'Leo says exactly the same.' Ivan grinned. 'Maybe it's no bad thing Abe loves the guy and thinks he'll be huge. In fact he already *is* huge. Have you seen the video footage yet?'

She shook her head.

Ivan dropped his fork with a clatter and stood up. 'You've missed a treat. Come see. I'll make you a copy – you have to have this for the family album.'

Both high-tech freaks, Ivan and Leo had linked up the huge main television with all the computer hard drives in the house. Within seconds Mia was watching footage of her daughter's fiancé just days before the wedding, wobbling about in grainy black-and-white night vision, semi-erect, his eyes glowing like those of a fox in lamplight.

'Hung like a bison, huh?' Ivan sighed.

She tried not to look, but it was impossible to ignore something of that significance. 'What is he *doing*?'

'You can ask him tonight,' Ivan suggested cheerily.

'I'm sorry?'

'Everett's attending the Stellar party too. It's Abe's idea, to get a bit of a buzz going.'

Her jaw dropped. Then she growled, 'There'll be one hell of a bloody buzz when I clobber the little sod.'

Ivan tutted with amusement. 'Uncle Abe will *not* sanction that, lady. He's convinced having Dougie at the same party as Leomia will take the press eye off the *Chancellor* rumours. Didn't Leo say?'

'Leo and I have barely had time to speak about anything,' she reminded him.

'Right now, yours is not a speaking part, honey,' Ivan assured her. 'Just remember to smile bravely and look ill.'

Dominic rarely flew on commercial airlines, and when he did he tried to book a starboard window seat, where the scarred side of his face would be largely hidden, knowing that others around him found it unsettling and occasionally even offensive. But flying standby to LAX, he was among the last to be checked in and found himself on the aisle, his burns clearly on show to all who passed. While some prurient passengers developed amazingly weak bladders as an excuse to gawp at regular intervals, others avoided him.

Trying to blot out the cabin around him, Dominic read some of Mia's letters to his father, which he'd been forced to store in a clear plastic bag when the Jacob's box was construed as a suspicious package upon boarding.

The final letter she'd sent was the most upsetting. She and Leo had been in LA with their daughter Iris, who was promoting her first movie, and Mia had been unable to get back to visit Dinfield on his birthday, which had clearly troubled her, doubly so because it had been a leap year, reminding her constantly of Dom. She wrote openly of how much she still missed him, and how talking to his father made such a difference to her life: *You are the only one who understands how much I loved him. Sometimes I want to shout it from*

every red carpet and stage here in LA:'I loved Dominic Masters! I am
so lucky to have known that!' He would have hated it here. Maybe it is
best that he was lost to acting because this town would have stolen his
soul. She went on to promise that she would visit him as soon as she
got back to the UK, but Dominic knew from Alison that his father
had died before that happened.

Aware that he was starting to cry, he put the letter down and
focused on the screen in the headrest in front of him.

Among the movies on show was the most recent in the Ptolemy
Finch series. He watched the first twenty minutes without earphones, convinced he would hate it. Then, sucked into the action,
he pulled on the headset and got totally lost in the remaining hour
and a half, unaware that he was holding the hand of the woman
next to him until the titles rolled. She turned to him afterwards, her
face loaded with compassion. 'Were you injured in Afghanistan?'
she asked.

'Nottinghamshire,' he said flatly, returning to the letters.

The cameras focused, flashbulbs strobed, questions were fired and
all was showbusiness as usual, but the Devonshires knew as soon
as they arrived that the fashion-house launch party was not good
PR. Old rumours about Leo's sexuality were too ingrained now. As
Leomia had lived apart for most of the past year, the sight of them
walking arm-in-arm along a red carpet was clearly a sham, and
Twitter was buzzing with it before they even made it past the coat
check.

'Abe's idea of damage limitation stinks,' Mia hissed furiously as
they lined up to kiss the designers. Her attempts to talk to Leo on
the way to the venue had been scuppered by constant incoming
calls on his cell phone, and she was popping with stress, relying
upon her acting mask to see her through, but it was slipping as fast
as the thick Pan Stik that made her look as though she was auditioning to play a corpse.

She forced her face into a rictus smile as a camera blinded her with its flash, her lips barely moving as she breathed at Leo, 'I think you should come out.'

'Let's not talk about this here, Mia.' He spoke without moving his smiling mouth as they posed together for another photographer. Impossibly handsome in a dark suit, he was the clichéd debonair British hero.

'This is the first chance we've had to speak alone together, Leo.' She matched his ventriloquist act.

'There are fifty cameras pointing at us!'

She ignored his warning, struggling with her Ms and Bs as she kept up the big white smile. 'Trust me, a small baby won't care if you're straight or gay as long as it's happy.'

His smile didn't falter. 'Not while my mother's alive. It would kill her.'

'According to Lito, that's happening this summer whether we like it or not. I've told you enough times.'

They broke off the ventriloquism double-act briefly to kiss the designers, who cooed over Mia's hair and exchanged witty lines with Leo before they were conveyor-belted on towards trays of drink, their stiff-jawed conversation resuming.

'Mamá always says she's dying.' Leo collected a pomegranate spritzer. 'When she did it last year and I totally screwed the series shooting schedule to get back, she made me watch three days of daytime chat shows before announcing she felt much better.'

'She needs to see you,' Mia whispered.

'What do the doctors say?'

'That it's only a matter of time before she has another stroke.'

They had made it into the party proper now, rictus smiles springing firmly back into place as they took in roving reporters and fashion PRs hovering near by, eager to forge introductions and create photo opportunities.

Leo ignored them all and steered Mia to the quietest corner. 'We'll fly her here for a second opinion. Our medics are much better.'

'Lito won't agree to that.'

'She has no choice— Hi!' He acknowledged an acting acquaintance who patted his shoulder as he passed.

Mia waited until the man was out of earshot. 'She has every right to do as she wishes, Leo. She's been making plans all summer – the music, the coffin, the horses. She's completely serious. She seems to be ready to go. She keeps saying she's looking forward to it.'

Leo was looking at her intently now and she knew she had his undivided attention at last, the false smile having faded, the sincerity back in his big, dark eyes.

'You really mean she really might be . . . ' he swallowed, '*dying?*' The last word came out with involuntary force, making those around them turn round. '*This summer?*' He gazed at her, bushbaby eyes filling with tears, the tensions of the past few days threatening to bubble over.

Mia took his hand and led him as far back from the hubbub as she could. 'It's a possibility.'

'And here was me thinking this week couldn't get any worse.'

Reaching out to take his other hand in hers, she kept her voice deliberately low and calm. 'There's an element of hyperbole in it, but she may genuinely be putting in the final performance of her life. Can we go somewhere quieter and talk?'

'Of course.' He gripped her hands, his own shaking. 'We'll go home.'

She shook her head, unable to face Ivan and his group hugs right now. 'Somewhere else. Just you and me.'

'Leomia is public property. It's never just you and me.'

'Don't be such a drama queen. We'll go for a McDonald's Drive-thru and park up on the hill. Nobody will have a clue. Can you call for the car to come back?'

The Devonshires exited the launch hand-in-hand through the back entrance at exactly the same moment that Dougie Everett's car arrived at the front amid flashbulbs in overdrive. It couldn't have been timed better, and the young Brit got just the publicity his agent had been dreaming of as he stepped from the limo and Leomia's tail lights disappeared over the horizon.

Faced with a salvo of lens shutters whirring, Dougie stopped to stare if not to pose, unaccustomed to the intensity of interest. Abe had offered him one of his pretty assistants as an adviser that night but he'd refused, keen to be seen out alone while he was trying to win Iris back.

The blinding lights dimmed once the paps realised that, despite the film-star looks, Dougie was still a nobody, and he lined up to meet the designers feeling out of his depth, wishing he had Iris at his side. An ambitious British reporter for a cable television show, who had done her research better than most, was quick to pounce on him.

'It's Dougie Everett, yes? You know the Devonshires really well, don't you? Can you comment on the latest rumours about Mia's health?'

'She's an amazing woman,' he said carefully, wishing he'd taken up Abe's offer.

'It's been said here that she's not looking too well tonight.'

'She's probably sick of the sight of me,' he joked, and saw immediately that his quip had misfired.

'What's the situation between you and Iris right now?'

'She's in Spain,' he said flatly.

'So was it *hasta luego* or *hasta siempre* after the wedding was called off?'

'I'm afraid my Spanish is execrable,' he flashed his big smile, 'but I can say one joke.'

'Can you share it with the viewers?' She thrust the microphone closer.

'*Hay tres clases de personas: las que saben contar y las que no.*'

'What does that mean?'

'There are three types of people: those who know how to count, and those who don't.' He'd learned it by rote for his wedding speech, to appeal to the Spanish relatives. 'As I'm in the latter category, right now I'm counting myself very lucky ...'

Sitting on a bench high in the hills looking back down across Los Angeles, Mia and Leo made raspberry noises with their straws as they sucked up large full-fat Cokes to chase down two Big Macs and a shared bag of mini-doughnuts.

'See how much fun it is to pig out occasionally?' Mia gasped for air, cheeks aching. 'That caffeine hit is better than Class A.'

Surfing on an equally powerful sugar rush, Leo laughed, pulling her up and towing her out of sight of the car so that the driver couldn't see him gather her into his arms.

'There's nothing to be ashamed of in hugging your wife.' She let out a squeak, almost winded by the tightness of his grip.

'I don't want him to overhear.' He pressed his forehead against her shoulder and burst into loud, racking tears, the overwhelming stress of recent weeks exploding out of him with minimal warning. Leo knew he was being totally selfish, clinging to his oldest friend and muse for comfort when he'd got them both into this situation, but he was grateful that Mia let him sob until he was played out.

'You can't go back to *Chancellor*,' she said, when he eventually pulled away. 'It's destroying you.'

'I need time out to think it through.' He stared up at the sky with reddened eyes, watching as an aeroplane pretended to be a shooting star amid the real constellations. 'We'll get flights tomorrow and I'll come back to Wootton with you for a few days. See Mamá.'

'She'd like that more than anything in the world.' Threading arms together, they wandered back to their bench to sit down again. Mia explained everything that Jacinta had said about her ongoing ill-health, leaving Leo in no doubt that he must tell Abe he was flying home.

'He can hardly complain I'm not behaving like a family man.'

He pulled a napkin from the fast-food bag to blow his nose. 'And he knows I can't miss the Wootton Gala.'

'You remembered about that?'

'Of course! I haven't forgotten it's your birthday either. Life begins at—'

'Don't say it,' she warned. 'When we were in our twenties, we made a list of forty things we planned to do before the big four-oh, remember, and I've done less than a quarter of them.'

'You still have a week.'

'Three days.'

'That soon? Aren't you normally going demented with stress over it by now?'

'I've had other things to worry about.' She patted his leg. 'Actually, it's been quite a relief *not* thinking about it. Apparently Haff's shouting at the WAGs, one of my committee has arranged a mounted fashion show without actually organising any clothes, and Laney seems to be going with a Lorca-meets-Bananarama theme for her sketches.'

'Sounds just like Laney. Is she still having this internet affair?'

'Hotting up all the bloody time.' Snuggling closer on their bench, they shared the last of the French fries and chattered on, immensely grateful for the marriage of true minds that made it so easy to talk for hours whether at home, on Skype or on a bench overlooking the City of Angels.

'Have you ever considered an eye patch?' the taxi driver asked cheerily as he drove Dominic north along the San Diego Freeway.

'Why would I when I can see ten per cent out of this eye?'

'You're a ten-percenter? Hey, why didn't you say you're an agent?' he whooped, reaching into the glove box for a computer disk and handing it over his shoulder. 'Here, have my latest script. Where'd you say you were headed, man?'

'Nichols Canyon.' He pulled out one of the letters his sister had given him and read out the house number.

'Leomia's place?' The driver whistled. 'I heard his lady's in town on the radio round-up just now. She's looking real ill, they say. Poor guy must be in pieces. They're such a great couple. Excuse me.' He took a call on his headset.

Dominic looked down at the signature on the letter, the bold hand he remembered from the letters he'd received half a lifespan ago, before he'd gone away thinking she would be better off without him. He would never forgive himself for his arrogance now that he knew how much she'd suffered without him.

There was no number on the letterhead and he tapped his phone against his knee in frustration, aware that he had no way of warning her.

As the taxi driver chatted into his Bluetooth earpiece, they turned right on to Santa Monica Boulevard and he stared out at the palm trees and office blocks, as far from his life in the Mara as the winding dual carriageways and leafy Oxfordshire lanes that led to Mia's big white house in England. Their lives had led them in opposite directions, but he couldn't resist the magnetic force that was pulling him towards her now.

Turn around, turn around, turn around, a voice in his head shouted as they drove along La Cienega towards Sunset. His heart was so huge in his chest that the J. Arthur Rank gong and striker might have been crammed in there, hammering in the start of a movie.

When Mia and Leo arrived back at the Nichols Canyon house at close to midnight with red eyes, salty fingers and McCafé moustaches, Ivan was hyperbolic, livid that they had stayed out late and pop-eyed with fear. Ivan rarely got upset, but when he did it was nuclear, the humorous stoic igniting into full scream queen.

'We had a weirdo here! A real frickin' weirdo!' He fell into Leo's arms. 'Why do people think they can hang around your gates just because you're fucking famous? They go on one guided Holly-wood Homes of the Stars tour and think they can terrorise us.'

Mia went to make tea, which was stupidly twee and British but she couldn't think what else to do. Leo often had trouble from over-zealous fans, which was one of the reasons he always equipped his properties with such high security.

'It's all on the closed circuit,' Ivan was saying in the next room, his deep voice shaking. 'He leaned on the buzzer for ages. I was all over the panic button, but you know what the cops are like. They can't do anything unless it's an intruder.'

'Did you phone the private response service?'

'Yeah. The security guys moved him on. They took him way downtown, so he won't be back tonight. Jeez, he was freaky – like something out of a horror movie. That face will haunt me.'

'All the more reason to go to the UK for a bit,' Leo said. 'It'll take the heat off things here, and I need to be at Wootton this week.'

'You can't leave me here with creeps like that around! What happened to "I can't face the charity gala without you, Van"?'

Mia wavered in the kitchen entrance, mugs rattling in her fingers. She'd never witnessed Ivan like this, although she knew from Iris that he could throw major tantrums. In many ways it made sense. Leo needed that practical stoicism on a day-to-day basis, but he thrived on drama and neediness, and there was no doubt that Ivan was genuinely rattled.

'We're going to Wootton *together*,' Leo was saying. 'You're coming too.'

'What about Puff Adder?'

'We'll get a sitter.'

'He's never been left here without us!'

'I have to see my mother, Ivan. And I want you to meet her before – before—' Unable to finish, he looked away. From the doorway, Mia saw the utter desolation in his face.

Ivan's low voice shook. 'What will you introduce me as? Your PA?'

'That's right. She's an old lady. She's dying.'

Ivan's lips turned into a furious, tight M as his cheeks inflated like a bullfrog's. 'I have been through a *deep* shock tonight. I cannot

443

handle this right now. You cannot comprehend *what I saw* just now.'

'Whoever he is, he's gone,' Leo reassured him, with another hug, and this time Ivan broke down on his shoulder, sobbing quietly. 'Come to England, Van. It's beautiful. You'll like it. I can't bear to be there without you.'

With a throaty sob, Ivan kissed him so lovingly that Mia was winded.

When they pulled apart, Leo pressed his forehead apologetically to Ivan's eagle-wingspan chest. 'I'm sorry we left you to deal with a gate stalker alone, Van. I know they freak you out.'

'Actually, he wasn't after you. He said he was looking for Mia while she's in town.'

Mia jumped in surprise. The mugs rattled again. 'Me?'

'You.' Ivan's bushy eyebrows closed together over his big brown eyes like a Greek letter pi. 'He left a note. The cops didn't even want to see it. Here.' He fished a piece of paper from his pocket to hand to her.

As soon as Mia saw the writing, she knew it was the same as the birthday card she'd received almost twenty years earlier. Her legs gave way under her and she landed ingloriously in Puff Adder's sofabed, which the bull terrier took in very bad part, launching an attack on her arm before snatching the note.

'No!' Mia tried to grab it back and the dog snarled at her furiously, turning to shred it.

While Leo rushed forward to help Mia, Ivan dashed sideways to comfort Puff Adder, who had already reduced the note to scraps.

'What did it say?' Leo demanded. But Mia, who hadn't even finished reading it, was too upset to speak.

Watching jealously as Leo enfolded his sobbing wife in his arms, Ivan cradled Puff Adder. 'It said something like "It's taken me twenty years to admit I was wrong, and I am sorry. I do exist and I will love you until the day I die, no matter how many lives we live,"' he told them. 'It was signed "D".'

Chapter 47

Laney found arranging childcare for an adulterous liaison all too horribly practical and real, like pre-booking a black cab as a get-away car from a bank robbery.

Richard HH had told her he was in London on Friday and, having said yes to lunch, she'd now spent all week embellishing an over-complex lie to enable her to go, spinning the tale that she had to rehearse the gala cabaret with a few of the performers in the West End just before the event. Her guilt was assuaged by the fact that Simon was behaving just as suspiciously, always on his phone writing furtive texts, and getting uncharacteristically irate when she'd forgotten to write a meeting with his publishers into his diary that week, which she suspected clashed with an illicit liaison of his own.

The thought of meeting Richard HH immunised her from the all-too familiar pain, keeping her fantasy world alight. But on Thursday evening, as she battled to finish *Madame Bovary*'s second episode, she received a message that read: Darling Laney, bloody meeting's now run across lunchtime ... Her cry of disappointment was cut short as she read on: so have booked us for afternoon tea instead. Please note, I always take afternoon tea very late (a family tradition). Table reserved from 8 p.m., under 'HH' x PS I am an old-fashioned rogue, but promise to behave if you do.

She was furious with him for moving the goalposts faster than a wonky Subbuteo table, yet at the same time she was white hot with excitement at the thought of all the wicked, wanton potential that came with dinner. But now she'd have to ensure Malin was available to babysit – she was already minding Hope this evening, to enable Laney to work.

Pacing across the floorboards between her desk and the little kitchen area, she started a dozen replies calling the whole thing off, then changed her mind and erased them. It was early evening and she had at least another hour's work to do on the Flaubert, but her mind was totally scattered, stress levels peaking. She read her horoscope online, which gloomily predicted that Geminis were in for a stormy patch, but softened the blow by pointing out that all gardens needed rain for the biggest blooms to grow. Navigating her way back on to the website that Richard HH had first linked her to, she found to her horror that the roses were desiccated to almost nothing, just a few dry petals clinging to the heads. Surely there had to be a Reset button?

She started clicking her mouse frantically on it, at first so engrossed that she thought the rapping she could hear was her finger tapping on the device. Then she realised somebody was knocking on the boathouse door.

Kit Lucas was holding a bulging delicatessen bag and a huge bunch of sunflowers, a seductive vision on the wooden deck, all big white smile and long auburn lashes, loose shirt rippling in the breeze. With the late-evening sun streaming through the weeping willows behind him, framing him in a golden halo, he could have been brought to life from the teen annuals she'd drooled over as a girl. But right now she failed to appreciate the vision of splendour in front of her, her mind full of RHH, dead roses and Flaubert. Besides, sunflowers still had unfortunate connotations of Simon larking around in an Umbrian field pursued by busty blondes.

'Hey, Laney.' The lazy smile widened as he thrust the bouquet into her arms. 'I figured I should apologise.'

'How extraordinary. I didn't hear you fall in.'

'This river has some crazy currents going on, so I tied up the boat behind the willows.' He pointed upstream. 'I've been practising. I'm getting pretty good at rowing.'

'Not catching crabs any more?'

He flashed the big smile again and held up the deli bag. 'I've never had crabs, but I'm very partial to abalone. The lady at the deli assured me *moules de bouchot* are pretty close. Can I cook you dinner?'

'No.'

His face fell.

She crossed her arms determinedly in front of her chest. 'You're bloody persistent, I'll give you that, but you won't get the screenplay.'

'I know, and I've told Oscar that.'

'So you *admit* you're working for him!'

'Not any more. I resigned. Now he knows my cover's blown—'

'Your cover was always blown, Kit.' She sighed. 'You were like a man wearing a fig leaf in an air tunnel.'

'You don't understand. He's prepared to play dirty. He said to do whatever it takes,' he went on urgently, 'so I told him to take a hike. You saved me from drowning, Laney. I could never do what he plans now.'

'What's that? Tying me to a chair with gaffer tape and forcing me to hand it over?'

'Kinda.' He pulled an apologetic face.

She laughed incredulously. 'There are laws against that. I know he's a control freak, but I think I'm pretty safe.'

'He's getting desperate.' Kit looked genuinely worried. 'He's had a team of script writers working on this for months and none of them can get the *Dalrymple* vibe. The backers are threatening to pull out.'

'He can easily afford to pay me what it's worth,' Laney huffed.

She knew Oscar loved to play the big-bucks big-shot with flash cars and houses, hiding behind his dark glasses and sharp suits, yet he boxed very clever with his cash and had accumulated a significant fortune through some very shrewd investments in films. Brought up by his single mother, a night cleaner at Gatwick Airport, he'd come a long way from his days doing stand-up on piers and in clubs, but he still managed his finances with the same penny-pinching care that had enabled him to buy his first house at twenty-one and dodge taxes for most of his life.

For *Dalrymple Two*, Laney had asked half a million dollars, which was still modest, given its eight-figure budget. She didn't expect to get that much, but the twenty-thousand-dollar offer on the table from her ex-husband was a huge insult. More than anything, she wanted a screen credit, her name having been omitted from the first film entirely.

In her heart, Laney knew that even twenty thousand would help stem the Demons' ongoing financial crisis, but she glared stubbornly out at the river, wishing that her moustached nemesis would chug by. She could do with somebody to hurl insults at right now, and Kit was being far too nice.

Still blocking the doorway, she eyed him shrewdly. 'Surely Oscar won't pay you now?'

'I'll get by.' On came the big beaming smile again. 'His ex-wife's seriously hot on me.'

'I am not!'

'The other ex-wife. She offered to take me to a shamanic retreat in Vermont that clears the body and mind.'

'The latter being already fairly empty in your case,' muttered Laney.

'I'd like to fill your body tonight,' Kit said huskily, then held up his deli bag again.

'Thanks for the offer, but I'm working,' she said firmly, stepping inside and starting to close the door.

'Hey, aren't you afraid of what Oscar plans to do?'

'He's hardly going to do anything this evening.' She peered around the door. 'Is he?'

'I think so.'

Looking at his face, Laney saw he was serious. Letting the door swing open, she felt for her bag and phone. 'Surely he can't have hired anybody qualified in gaffer-taping women to chairs in that time. Evil criminals take a while to make contact with – you can hardly look them up in the Yellow Pages.' Yet even as she said this, her already palpitating heart was forced into even more startling velocity. She now envisaged men in balaclavas bursting into Red Gables and holding Malin at gunpoint, demanding to know where the computers were kept while Hope slept upstairs. Simon was still in London, recording the finals of the *Greatest British Pie Maker* cook-off, on which he was a guest judge. Her pulse was as fast as hummingbird wings, her head hopelessly light and empty. She had to get home to protect her daughter. She raced towards the door.

Kit stood in her way. 'Oscar said he has someone who owes him a favour from the old days. Someone called the Big Dipper.'

'Oh, God, he would have a name like a fairground attraction.' Her ex had befriended a lot of lowlife when working the clubs, priding himself on his gangland connections. 'Don't tell me the Big Dipper likes to drown people?'

'I think he's tall with a stoop.' Kit watched her grasp for the doorframe and miss, staggering backwards, clutching her head. 'Laney, are you OK?'

'Fine – just a . . . bit . . . breathless. Oh, bother.' Her vision blinkered as she felt her legs give way. But instead of the floor coming up to meet her, two hands caught her as Kit made the save faster than a quarterback on a tricky catch.

Battling to stay conscious, Laney heard him grunt with effort and she mumbled, 'Please don't try to carry me. I weigh a ton.'

'Lightest ton I've ever hauled.' He lifted her across to the purple sofa.

'I must get back to Hope.' She fought to stand up.

'You stay there until your breathing settles,' Kit ordered, checking her pulse. 'Jesus, you're seriously hypertensive. Are you taking anything for that?'

'I'm on tablets,' she muttered, thinking guiltily about her diet pills. She tried to stand up again, battling the grey mist. 'Please let go. I must get home to my daughter.'

'She'll be quite safe. The Big Dipper's coming to the boathouse.'

'In that case I'm definitely going to spend the rest of the evening at home.' She closed her eyes, trying hard to breathe normally and quieten the buzzing in her head. 'Let me get this right,' she puffed: 'you're here to woo me with food and sweet nothings to apologise for the fact that some giant henchman with a stoop is about to creep in and attack me?' She wished she felt strong enough to leap up and empty his deli bag over his head.

She could hear Kit talking, but it was a while before she could take in that he was suggesting they hatch a plan.

' . . . so we plant a fake *Dalrymple Two* file here, but you write a load of shit on it instead of the real deal.'

Eyes still closed, she managed a faint laugh. 'Never a truer word, given my output right now.'

'We have time,' he went on eagerly. 'I told Oscar you work here all night and generally take a nap between ten and midnight. His guy will come then.'

She peered at him groggily. 'You set this up?'

He looked very pleased with himself. 'I figured it'll get him off your back.'

She rubbed her face. 'Oscar's far too smart for that. As soon as this Big Dipstick sends him the file, he'll speed-read the whole thing on his phone in an hour.'

'Not if we put it on CD-ROM. Even the best henchmen don't carry a disk reader with them. Besides, you'll have made your point. I'd love to see his face.'

Even with her heart fizzing and banging in her chest like bottles of pop in an overturned lorry, she had to admit it was a cheering image. 'That's almost clever.'

He ducked his head modestly. 'I am almost clever. I'm almost a good seafood cook too, so I'll be your mussel man while you're the brains.' He went to retrieve his abandoned groceries. 'I never double-cross someone on an empty stomach.'

She watched him warily, wondering if this was an elaborate trick.

But there was something so likeably quixotic about Kit, and he was such a bad actor, he had to be telling the truth. Wandering unsteadily to the desk, she retrieved her phone and texted Malin to tell her to double-lock all the doors and put the chain on the broken back door, adding cheerily: Nothing to worry about – just trying to stop the dogs wandering again!

Pressing Send, she gazed at her Mac. She'd already worked five solid hours without a break that afternoon, her eyes throbbing from screen glare. She guessed she could cut and paste some of *Madame Bovary*'s dialogue to create a realistic-looking screenplay in less than an hour, changing all the names to those of *Dalrymple* characters, then add a polite postscript reminding Oscar of the asking price for the genuine material.

Her phone vibrated. Malin had texted back, promising to be extra secure, adding that her new boyfriend was there.

As Laney's replying row of smiley faces winged its way to Red Gables, Simon texted a photograph of himself, looking debonair in a red velvet suit: I'll have a finger in every pie tonight, but I'd rather have three in my darling wife . . .

He'd clearly been laying into the green-room wine at the cook-off. Hands shaking, she started to compose a reply, telling him about Oscar's bizarre plan, then deleted it: she couldn't lay that on him just minutes before the show was recorded in live time. Instead she wished him luck and told him not to get any more pie-eyed and to be nice as pie to everyone, adding a long row of kisses that even her goddaughter would have been proud of.

'You have vermouth – cool!' Kit called from the kitchen, making her jump – she'd forgotten he was there, her brain like wool. 'I'll add it to the cooking liquor. I hope you like garlic.'

'I chew it daily and dab it on my pulse points,' she muttered, not wanting him to think that she was after anything more than protection tonight. She had no appetite, the thought of seafood turning her stomach, but at least cooking was keeping him busy. She'd done much the same thing the night Simon had come back from Italy,

451

she remembered, guilt and fear mounting with every minute that passed.

She tried to imagine explaining to Simon later that she'd shared a cosy supper with Oscar's hired stud while laying a trap for his hired henchman. That famously sardonic unflappability might crack – and if the roles were reversed she would certainly want to kill him, although when she thought about it, this was true of much of her behaviour recently. If Simon found out about her late, late lunch with Richard HH, he would be shaken, stirred and almost certainly licensed to kill.

She fought mounting panic again, remembering Simon bringing the vermouth to the boathouse in the first place. Dressed in a white tuxedo, he'd arrived late one afternoon not long after she'd started to use it as an office, bearing bottles, cherries and his favourite Art Deco cocktail shaker, insisting he must make her Manhattans. They'd made tipsy, clumsy love on the purple sofa and against her desk, when he'd inadvertently wiped her unsaved work by leaning on her keyboard during the throes of passion. After the flaming row that followed, he'd tweeted to his followers that Mrs Demon was contemplating divorcing him for his Manhattan data transfer, causing a rush of female followers to declare their willingness to replace her.

She mustn't think about Simon, she reminded herself. She had a trap to set for the Big Dipper. They'd laugh about it afterwards. Alternatively, she'd briefly make the headlines as the drowned wife of celebrity foodie and design guru Simon de Montmorency, found mysteriously floating in the Thames surrounded by CD-ROMs.

Blinking hard to focus on the screen, she started to create a fake script, typing film directions around her latest radio play so badly that the words came out as gobbledegook. Oscar would never be fooled.

'How's it going?' Kit was looking over her shoulder at the screen, sucking his fingers. 'Food in five, yeah?'

She got back to work, turning *Madame Bovary* into the dummy *Dalrymple Two*, pasting in sections from early drafts of the original

Dalrymple, which she'd emailed to herself while writing and still had because she never got around to tidying up her inbox. Flying high in there were all Richard HH's most recent messages, which she knew she must delete or hide. But just seeing them gave her reassurance, a rock to cling to in an increasingly stormy life. The prospect of meeting him tomorrow evening made tonight's events seem all the more surreal.

Without thinking, she sent him a message: Simon away, and Seduction Kit here offering his services and seafood as we await the Big Dipper. Will tell all tomorrow. Thinking about that keeping me going . . .

Kit served the mussels swimming in a thick cream sauce that billowed aniseed vermouth fumes. He opened a bottle of Californian Chardonnay as rich and oaky as Marmite. Perching on a rickety stool, Laney fought waves of nausea.

'Here's the plan.' He started to brief her as he pulled fat yellow flesh from the shells. 'We leave the doors open. You pretend to be asleep when the guy arrives. I'll hide out of sight. If it goes wrong, I'm here to protect you.'

Laney jumped as Simon's ringtone burst from her phone. He'd be calling for a pre-pie-judging 'Good luck', which she was far too wound up to manage. Diverting the call to voicemail, she asked, 'Why would it go wrong?'

'Trust me, it won't. Eat up.'

She battled her way through half the bowl, then developed such chronic, bilious indigestion she had to go out on to the balcony for gulps of fresh air.

Her phone was lighting up with Simon's ringtone again. She diverted it once more.

Tonight's full moon had already risen in the dusky sky and was a snowman's head sitting on top of the willows on the opposite bank. She hoped he'd help fight off Oscar's henchman.

Then she heard a boat engine in the distance, making its way downstream, the low growl of a bow-rider.

Kit stepped out on the balcony behind her and listened too.

'Surely that's not *him*.' She gripped the rails tighter. 'It's not yet nine.'

'Better get ready just in case.' He took her hand and pulled her back inside.

While Laney flapped about, hands shaking crazily as she copied her fake script on to a CD and labelled it very obviously 'Dalrymple Two', Kit threw their half-eaten meal into the sink, killed the lights and hid behind the kitchen peninsula.

Laney draped herself on the sofa, gasping for air like a landed fish.

The boat puttered straight past.

Laughing, Kit emerged. 'Man, we have to do something about your breathing. Nobody hyperventilates like that when they're asleep.' He cocked his head, 'Oh, hell.'

The boat engine was back, a deep throaty wash as it reversed into the boathouse lagoon. He crept across the room to peer through the windows. 'It's him. Jesus, he's tall.'

'Isn't he being a bit obvious?' Laney gasped. 'Surely he could switch off the engine and float in like any self-respecting thief.'

'Maybe Oscar wants him to be up-front and negotiate,' Kit whispered encouragingly, then let out a disappointed sigh. 'Maybe not. He's putting on a mask.'

'Balaclava?'

'Mickey Mouse.'

'Fitting. Oh Jesus.' Laney shakily adopted her position on the sofa, shallow breaths now remarkably similar to those she'd been taught to do when panting between her final labour contractions. Then she let out a screech as Kit picked her up in a fireman's lift and carried her behind the peninsula.

'What are you doing?' she whispered frantically as he laid her on the floor and crouched over her so they were both hidden from the big windows. They could hear footsteps on the jetty below now.

'He'll never believe you're asleep over there,' he breathed. 'You sound like you've just run a marathon.' The big smile beamed down at her. 'But he *will* believe you're making love. Oh, yes, baby. Oh, yesss!' he cried out. 'Oh, Laney, you are *good*.'

Laney's eyes stretched wide with alarm.

'Oh – oh – *oh*.' Kit panted in time with her. 'Don't stop, Laney baby. Don't stop!'

The footsteps were coming up the balcony steps.

Powerless to do anything but pant, Laney blinked in terror as she heard the french windows creak wider.

'Oh, baby, baby, baby,' Kit groaned throatily, eyes not leaving hers now. 'You are beautiful. So goddamn beautiful. Don't stop.'

The sound of rushing blood in her ears was far too loud for her to pick up on much that was going on beyond the peninsula, but she was almost certain she heard a low grunt as a high forehead hit an overhead beam horribly close by.

Without warning, Kit bestowed on her a long, noisy kiss. Clamping her mouth tightly shut, Laney could see his amused golden eyes, one of which winked as their sound effects became those of breathless lip suction before he pulled away so she could pant again. 'I am never going to forget tonight! You are sensational. Where did you learn these things?'

Laney failed to see the funny side, moonlight spilling through the windows on her little writing room as an enormous, stooped shadow moved about in search of bons mots. Surely he'd seen the disk by now. She'd left it almost at the top of the pile.

'Yes, Laney! Oh, yes, yes, yes!'

Kit had clearly missed his métier in porn voiceovers. He really sounded terribly convincing and, with six foot of glorious stud muffin hovering over her, she wasn't entirely sure her loud hyper-ventilation was purely pep pills and panic. There was something strangely exciting about the situation, but she guessed that could be down to oxygen starvation.

When he went in for another kiss, she threw in an authentic

gasp, deciding she might as well get in some practice before tomorrow night.

It was the cue Kit needed to go all out on the method acting, eyes fixed on hers. His hands threaded through her hair and, kisses growing deeper and more urgent, his weight shifted on to her so that she was suddenly aware of muscular thighs to either side of hers and an extremely large bulge between. Perhaps it wasn't just the voiceovers he'd missed as his porn calling, she thought weakly, struggling to break away although her lower body was arching towards his in an involuntarily carnal way.

There was a loud clank from beyond the peninsula. Not missing a beat, Kit covered her mouth with his hand to stop her shrieking as he called, 'Oh, baby, you have what it takes!'

Releasing her mouth, he plunged back into the kiss with even more enthusiasm and Laney felt another seismic tremor run through her pelvis in response. Mortified by her wantonness, she turned her head to one side. Kit's lips traced her earlobe, breathing, 'I want you so much.'

Was he still acting? she wondered, as his mouth slipped lower, breath hot on her skin, tracing her neck and collarbone. Closing her eyes, she indulged in a brief, shameful fantasy that he was Richard HH who had rushed in to make a heroic rescue. Suddenly the seismic tremor was threatening to become a full-blown, earth-moving quake. As Kit started unbuttoning her dress, his mouth finding its way to the lift of one breast and on towards its dark areola, she felt such a sexual charge that she expected her knickers to light up like a red bulb on a schoolboy's circuit-board, illuminating the little kitchenette with disco flashes.

At that moment, her phone started to ring 'Honky Tonk Women' from the peninsula. Beyond that, she heard the roar of a boat engine starting outside.

The spell broken, Laney wriggled away. Kit tried to hang on to her. 'We don't have to stop,' he pleaded.

'We so do.' Still panting and fumbling to button her dress, she stood up to find her phone and saw the state of her desk. 'He's taken the whole bloody computer!' she cried in horror. 'Oh, God, no. How could we be so stupid?' She raced towards the doors. 'He's not taking my income away. My whole working life's on that thing. Come back, you bastard!'

Kit overtook her in a flash, leaping down the steps three at a time as the little boat pulled away. At the wheel, still wearing a Mickey Mouse mask, the Big Dipper turned in surprise as the young American ran along the jetty and made a flying leap, landing in the water with his hands gripping the side of the boat, making it rock wildly before hauling himself on board and making a grab for the laptop resting on a bench seat.

Laney raced on to the jetty in time to see him disappear as the Dipper opened the throttle and the boat raced off into the darkness.

'Hello? Laney? Hello?'

She looked down. The phone was in her hand, its face lit up with a picture of Mia on her stallion. 'Y-yes?' She held it shakily to her ear.

'I'm at LAX. I'm coming home! I can't tell you how relieved I am. I have *so* much to tell you. The most awful wonderful weird thing has happened. God, it's been so stressful. I have to see you as soon as I—' The call was cut off.

As Mia's photograph disappeared, to be replaced with a screen-saver of Hope poking out her tongue, Laney was shaking so much that the loose boards beneath her feet on the jetty were rattling. Her messages icon was flashing. Richard HH demanded, What's happening? Are you OK? V worried. x

She clutched the phone to her chest and wondered what Oscar would do when he opened her computer in LA and found all the outrageously personal messages they'd exchanged. He would almost certainly forward them to Simon, as well as every scurrilous online gossip site he could find. She had a sudden horrific vision of the Burley Hornet running them as a serialisation. She clung to a thread of hope that Oscar wouldn't be interested enough to read them – although, given how deeply she'd buried *Dalrymple Two* behind passwords and fake names, he'd have to read more or less everything on her hard drive to find it.

She could hear something splashing in the river, far louder than the usual wildfowl. Stretching out from her post again, she saw Kit rounding the corner, swimming one-armed. As he encountered the undertow, he disappeared briefly under the surface before bobbing up again.

'I got it!' he announced victoriously, lifting her laptop on to the jetty and then clambering up after it. 'You don't have to say, "My hero!" but feel free to do so if you want.'

'My hero!' She picked up the Mac and hugged it gratefully before realising water was pouring from its keyboard and ports. On closer inspection, it had a smashed screen and pond weed embedded in its sodden keyboard. Still, she forced a smile, knowing Kit had been utterly heroic to spare it from Oscar's scrutiny, even if her work had been drowned.

He was dripping water everywhere, his teeth chattering.

'You must be freezing.' She steered him back towards the boathouse. 'Come back in and have a shower.'

'Will you join me?' he asked hopefully.

'I have to reply to an email,' she said.

'You'll need water wings and a propeller to send anything from that baby now,' he pointed out as she carried her dripping Mac inside.

'I can use my phone.'

While Kit was singing 'Holding Out For a Hero' in the little wetroom, Laney examined her laptop and tried not to cry. It was clearly way beyond repair. She supposed it was highly ironic and served her right that the only thing on it that she'd backed up recently was *Dalrymple*. She'd always been hopeless at making copies of anything else.

All her *Madame Bovary* scripts had been lost, along with many photographs and all her private messages, including the precious, funny, honest and seductive emails from Richard HH. It was certainly one way of hiding the evidence, she thought wretchedly, wishing she'd saved their correspondence on her phone, the thumb-dabbing pulse to her touch-typing main artery.

She settled down with it now, cursing how hard it was to type a heartfelt message on a tiny touch-screen. But she battled on, not caring how long it took or how many mistakes she made as she shared her thoughts and her heart with Richard, telling him what had happened. It alarmed her that she needed to talk to him so badly now, yet the prospect of meeting him in person was paralysing her with fear. She found herself suggesting that they should try to speak on the phone first. I'd so love to hear your voice reassuring me it'll be OK; not sure I can meet you without talking first, she finished, adding her number and a row of kisses.

As she pressed Send she heard a car pull up outside, then feet pounding up the boathouse staircase from the water meadow side. It was well after midnight, and she couldn't take another Big Dipper intrusion. Anger mounting, she picked up the sopping laptop, ready to hurl it at the big goof.

To her astonishment, it was Simon, still dressed in his red velvet suit, which matched his wild red-rimmed eyes. 'Working late, darling?' He spotted the laptop dripping in her hands. 'Not going too well, I see.'

'You're supposed to be staying up in London tonight,' she squeaked, putting it down.

'Change of plan.' He headed straight for the three-quarters-full Chardonnay bottle like a homing missile, then hunted around for a glass. 'I thought I'd come home early in case I could catch you and young Kit *in flagrante delicto.*' He cast his gaze around the debris of moules in the sink as he filled a tumbler that spilled over its brim. 'Instead I think I may be *in vino veritas.*'

Laney's eyes automatically darted to the bathroom door, but the shower had fallen silent and she prayed Kit had heard what was going on and would have the sense to stay in there.

'Kit was here, yes. He helped me fight off an intruder.' She felt her face colour as she grabbed her bag and busied herself throwing her notepads and pens into it. 'Oscar sent a heavy here to steal the *Dalrymple* script.'

'Gosh, how many gentleman callers you've had, Mrs Demon,' he sniped, then gazed at the laptop again. 'Did you wash this in a misguided attempt to clean up your act?'

'It fell in the river. I'll explain everything on the way home.' She was desperate to get him outside again, but he'd plonked himself down on the purple sofa now, cradling the wine in one hand. His face was ashen.

'Laney, there's something I've got to tell you. Something I've been doing that I'm deeply ashamed of.' As he spoke, his phone let out a persistent message alert in his pocket and he fished it out to silence it, then hesitated as he studied the screen, colour flooding into his cheeks.

Watching him, Laney's own blood ran cold. It was a message from a mistress. She knew his face too well to believe it could be anything else. Her heart burst like a firework. We're both at it. The Taylor and Burton of the small screen strike again.

The bathroom door opened. 'Hey, Laney, that's some shower!' Wearing nothing but two towels, Kit was a vision of ripped Californian splendour.

'Oh, hell.' Of course he hadn't had the sense to stay put. He was a man who thought moules marinière was a crime-fighting essential. And he was wearing both towels on his head.

'Hello again.' Simon regarded him over his wineglass, his voice steely. 'I'm afraid that, as an Englishman, I'm duty bound to kill you first and ask my wife questions afterwards.'

'I can explain!' bleated Laney.

Simon stood up, pale grey eyes deadly. 'Shut up, darling. I always think a crime of passion should have minimal dialogue and a lot of blood.'

'Holy shit!' Kit raced for the french windows.

'Good idea – drowning's much less messy.' Simon followed as a loud splash came from outside.

Laney panted on to the balcony in time to see Kit swimming away from the jetty. Crossing between the two tall willows as he headed out of the lagoon, he suddenly disappeared under water.

Simon had stomped down to the river and was lighting a cigarette with shaking hands.

When thirty seconds had passed without Kit coming back up to the surface, Laney started to panic, running down to join him. 'What if the current's got him this time?'

'I am *not* ruining this suit by jumping in there.' Simon glared at the rising bubbles and the towels now floating on the surface.

Laney had kicked off her shoes, and was wrestling her dress over her head when Kit bobbed up near by, bursting for breath, smiling winningly as he eyed Simon in trepidation.

'I got a bit tangled with the weed down there.' He grimaced. 'I'll be outta here as soon as I've caught my breath. Nothing happened with your wife, sir, trust me.'

'He's telling the truth!' Laney was struggling to pull her dress down again, its skirt rucked up under her armpits, making it hard to put up a dignified argument.

'Forget it – I'm not going to drown him, just my sorrows.' Simon flicked his cigarette into the river beside the American. 'It's not you I want to pick a fight with, Kit, it's my own conscience.' Not looking at Laney, he turned back towards the boathouse. 'Let's go home.'

Laney was about to hurry after him when Kit called her back with an urgent whisper.

'You gotta help me,' he told her, teeth still chattering, staying low in the water. 'I have absolutely no clothes.'

'I'll leave the boathouse open,' she promised wearily. 'Just stay out here until we're gone.'

Inside, Simon was polishing off the wine straight from the bottle and reading the message on his phone, which he pocketed when she came in, his mood even harder to decipher, cool sarcasm switching to guilty compassion. 'You look worn out. Let's get you home to bed.'

'Nothing happened between me and Kit.' She waded straight in, not caring if the Californian had to shiver out there all night as long as she could explain herself to Simon. 'He was just trying to help. You will not *believe* what Oscar set up tonight.'

'Tell me later.' He drained the wine and reeled to the door. 'I want to get out of here.'

Grabbing her bag, she followed him out to the car, which was parked almost entirely in a lilac bush.

'I'll drive.' She grabbed the keys from him. He was obviously plastered. 'I can't believe you weren't stopped and breathalysed coming here.'

'Tonight, I've eaten pork pie; veal, ham and egg pie; game pie; and chicken pie.' He clambered into the passenger seat beside her. 'I've eulogised over steak and kidney pie, shepherd's pie, cottage pie, fish pie and stargazey pie, even homity bloody pie – I told them I hadn't fought my way to the top of the food chain to eat vegetarian food, but it kept coming, from asparagus with a flaky pastry to goat's cheese and red pepper with short-crust.' He turned to her as she started the engine, eyes glittering in the half-dark. 'I came back here to eat humble pie, but now I find my appetite's completely gone.'

'What exactly is your point?'

'I have enough carbohydrate in my system to soak up a vat of wine. I am perfectly safe to drive.' He closed his eyes and almost instantly fell asleep.

Starting the engine, Laney suspected she had enough amphetamines in her system to cause an accident, but was too desperate to get home to worry. She drove incredibly carefully, her chin practically resting on the steering wheel as she focused on the windscreen. When her phone rang in her bag, she almost swerved off the road.

Simon woke with a start, groped for his own phone and then realised it was hers.

'Who on earth would call at this hour?' He fished it out of her bag. 'Unknown number.'

'Don't answer it!' she wailed too late, as he pressed it to his ear. She was certain it had to be Richard HH. Who else would call after midnight? She'd just emailed him her telephone number, after all, telling him Simon was in London tonight.

'Hello? . . . Yes, it's Simon . . . No, still up . . . Don't worry about it . . . Of course I will. You too, darling.' He rang off. 'That was Mia. She's on an aeroplane and sounding rather stressed. Says she forgot to tell you that she gets back mid-morning tomorrow and has to talk to you straight away. Rather screws up your London rehearsals.'

'Actually, that's more of a teatime thing,' she muttered.

He tapped her phone against his knuckles, then said lightly, 'How wonderfully Thora Hird. Will you take sponge fingers along?'

'It might even be a bit later than that,' she said.

He was tapping the phone so hard now that the battery fell out, but he said no more.

Laney knew she should be brave and ask him what he'd been doing that he was so ashamed of, but her nerves were shot to pieces. It had to be bad, and she couldn't risk falling apart before tomorrow evening. If Simon was having an affair, she was perfectly justified in having one secretive dinner date.

When they arrived at Red Gables, the Labradors howled and scrabbled ecstatically in the kitchen, but the house was impenetrable, Malin having double-locked everything as instructed. The little windows of the turret room in which she slept were now in darkness.

'We'll have to break in,' Simon decided. 'That top kitchen window is open.'

'You'll never fit through it.'

'Not me – you. You're so slim these days, you'll easily slip through.'

Malin's new boyfriend's second encounter with the Demons was not a great deal easier than his first. Sent downstairs by the nervous au pair, who had heard strange noises and was now following him, holding up one of Simon's Art Deco bronze ladies as a weapon, he threw on the lights and burst into the kitchen to find Laney dangling through a window while being heaved by Simon from behind.

'Hi!' she said brightly, then spotted Malin peering out from around his arm. 'Can you possibly babysit tomorrow evening?'

Chapter 48

Iris had always imagined that great love affairs started with firework moments in dramatic settings. That had certainly been the case with Dougie: the first time she'd seen him, one misty morning on location on the forest-fringed Baltic coast, her heart had exploded; six months later, when he had stood at the top of the steps at a Leicester Square première, given her an emerald necklace and kissed her, her body had seemed to float high above the West End.

With Griff the moments came thick and fast, like firecrackers, but they had no sense of time or place, detonating at random twenty-four hours a day. Every eye-meet was a Technicolor explosion of freefall happiness, every touch a spark. Every thought of him made her heart feel like a Catherine wheel, and she was suddenly so tactile that she stroked every inanimate object she passed. When packing to leave Sueño in pursuit of Chloe and the flash drive, she'd kissed each pair of unworn riding socks as she stuffed them into her rucksack, hugged her sundresses and pressed her polo shirts to her cheek, seeing at last that she'd merely been showboating in the shallows with Dougie. She and Griff needed no romantic backdrops or big love scenes: they couldn't stop talking, laughing, kissing and gazing at one another wherever they were, so that even La Parra Airport felt as romantic as a moonlit gondola sliding beneath the Bridge of Sighs.

A dispute among Spanish air-traffic controllers afforded them their first dinner date – a burger at the terminal – and they even slept together afterwards, snoozing on the departure-lounge seats, waiting for the strikers to resume work. Iris had never felt more comfortable or alive in someone else's company. They knew they could have returned to Sueño to wait it out, but the hire car had been returned and they were at the stage of mutual infatuation where delays were welcome, however urgent their cause, because time killed together felt like love in suspended animation. Mostly they talked, delighted to share secrets, laughter and high-grade flirtation, however dreary the environment. By the time the air-traffic controllers agreed to negotiate a new deal, she and Griff had shared childhood experiences, favourite movies, first crushes, landmark moments, career highs, hopes and ambitions, pet hates and greatest phobias.

Sitting together in the coffee bar nursing espressos and jumping with shocks every time their fingers touched, Griff finally told her the full story behind Cloud Man and his extraordinary interview: 'When he had his accident, he decided to make a new life to spare those in the old one the sacrifice of looking after him, but he's the ultimate survivor. He's a bloody hero, Iris. I've never met anyone like him. As soon as I heard his story, I knew I had to let Mia know he was still alive.'

'But surely if he'd wanted my mother to know he would have contacted her himself?'

'He did. Almost twenty years ago he told her to live her life again as though he had never existed. That's like pointing at the elephant in the room and saying, "Forget you ever saw that." It doesn't work. But he's very black and white. When he makes a decision, he stands by it, and he genuinely thought she would be better off without him.' He ran his hands through his hair, rolling his eyes in wonder at the Captain Oates sacrifice he admired but still couldn't fathom. 'For two decades, he's blocked out the past totally. He knows nothing about Mia's life now. Celebrity culture means nothing to him. If he's in England again, it's bound to come as a shock.'

'Meanwhile Mum's not even there,' Iris sighed, 'and Chloe is one step ahead of us with the flash drive.'

'Thing is, Dominic doesn't know I recorded our conversation.'

'Shit. And you're afraid Chloe will mess things up for him?'

He shook his head, dark eyes turbulent. 'I think I've already done that pretty comprehensively, but I'm worried she won't make it any easier.' He glanced at the departures screen, which still read DELAYED beside all flights. 'That's why we have to get back there.'

She stared into her coffee cup, watching a little raft of foam float from one side to the other. 'Griff, you think Dominic Masters is my real father, don't you?'

He reached to take her hand, almost melting the tabletop as the shockwaves rattled between them. 'There's a very high probability. And I'm pretty sure Chloe thinks so too.'

When she lifted her face to look at him, his dark eyes flooded with relief to see that she was smiling. 'She's always been way cleverer than me. When I told her I thought Simon was my birth father, she said the only genes we had in common were Levi Strauss.'

'Where *are* you, Laney? I *need* you! I've just found a naked American asleep in my bloody boathouse. My mother-in-law claims to have been cured by a miracle healer. The gala's tomorrow, it's total bloody chaos here and *DOM WAS IN LA!*'

Laney say bolt upright, phone clamped to her ear. '"Dom" as in Dominic Masters?'

'Yes! At least I think so . . .'

'Bloody hell!' She held up her hand apologetically to Simon as he padded into the bedroom bearing two cups of tea, the daily papers under one arm. 'I'm coming straight round. Give me twenty minutes. Are you sure it was him?'

Simon's heart sank. When he'd stolen out just five minutes earlier, she'd been fast asleep, beautifully peaceful for once, and disturbingly fragile now that she had lost so much weight. But she was on the phone and had Hope tucked alongside her in bed, playing with the lace trim on her mother's camisole as she chattered loudly to herself about wanting a pony, demonstrating the glitter-sprinkling and ribbon-bestowing involved in horsecare with her little hands.

'Will you buy me a pony, Daddymon?' She trotted to the end of the bed and whinnied at him.

'Of course I will, precious one. As soon as you buy me a Ferrari.'

As Simon settled the mugs on the bedside tables, Fred appeared at the window, tapping like a persistent pheasant and saying in a muffled voice, 'Your cheque bounced.'

Simon stalked over and threw up the sash. 'Unlike you, if I push you off that scaffolding. Can't you see my wife's in bed?'

Fred's mouth disappeared into a shocked thin line as Simon slammed the sash down.

He knew he had been behaving wholly out of character this week, walking off set with barely a kiss on the cheek to the winner as soon as Britain's best pie was announced, tweeting increasingly bitter tirades about the slightest irritation, and now snarling at his long-suffering builder. His famous sangfroid was showing hot-blooded battle scars.

'I have to go to Wootton to see Mia.' Laney was out of bed now, wrapped in just a sheet.

Aware that Fred was still wandering the scaffolding, Simon hurriedly yanked at the old shutters, which were over-painted and stiff, still awaiting restoration. They were plunged into darkness, making Hope shriek excitedly. 'Let's all be sleeping ponies!' she suggested happily.

'Makes a change from flogging a dead horse, I guess.' Laney

clicked on the light, having slipped on some insanely flimsy underwear that Simon didn't recognise and, in other circumstances,
would have thoroughly enjoyed, even with the snorts and whickers
she was exchanging with a giggling Hope.

'I'm catching the London train at ten,' he complained as Laney
tottered around getting dressed. 'We *must* talk before I go.'

Pulling on clothes at random, Laney was extremely eager to
avoid talking, only too aware that last night's incidents in the boathouse had yet to be discussed, along with Simon's furtive phone
messaging. She hadn't forgotten him saying he had something to
confess, but she refused to let the evening ahead be ruined by any
more high drama or last-minute changes. She'd put in too much
work and invested too much heart to let RHH down. Simon
coming home last night had thrown her, but she knew that he had
to be in London for an editorial meeting late morning, followed by
lunch with the team publishing his Christmas treats book, after
which he was due in the Lightbulb Television offices all afternoon,
undoubtedly followed by drinks in Soho House. By then she would
be on her way to another part of London to meet RHH. She just
had to see Mia first and then she was planning to pamper herself
for hours.

'Brrr.' She made a pony snort and hopped into an old pair of
shorts, looking over her shoulder at Simon. 'There's no time to talk.
Mia's in a terrible state. I have to be there.'

For a moment guilt clawed her as she realised what a shabby
friend she'd become, just as she was a shabby wife, using every
opportunity to her advantage. But her need to meet Richard was
overwhelming now. Self-justification coursed through her as she
reminded herself that Mia could be just as selfish at times, and
Simon was undoubtedly behaving far worse than she was. She had
no intention of sleeping with RHH; she just wanted to know him
at last, the man to whom she had told so many secrets, confessed
so many fantasies and trusted so implicitly. Tonight was their
night.

'Mia thinks she saw Dominic Masters in LA,' she told Simon, eager to keep off the subject of 'talking', 'but you know what she's like – when he first disappeared, she saw him everywhere. Do you remember when she was convinced he worked on the wet-fish counter at Tesco but it turned out to be a Ukrainian called Olaf?'

'Not really.' He rubbed his stubble-dusted face and yawned, hangover clearly raking at his temples. Stepping closer and glancing at Hope, he lowered his voice urgently: 'Laney, I *really* have to talk to you in pri—'

'I'll take Hope with me to Wootton.' She dragged a comb through her hair. 'You don't need the car, do you? You can get a cab to the station. Whee-he-he!' She let out a whinny. Then, misreading his bleak expression, she held up her hands. 'OK, *you* take the car and I'll cycle. You're back here later, aren't you? Only I have no idea how long these rehearsals will drag on, and I'm not sure if Malin will be up for babysitting terribly late.'

He was watching her carefully, his face guarded. 'How late do you think you'll be back?'

'Hard to tell.' Laney hid her face in her T-shirt drawer. 'If it goes on ages, I might be best to crash in London at a hotel or with one of the old gang.'

'I'll see what I can do,' he said in a frozen voice.

Chloe had done nothing with Griff's flash drive since she'd returned from Spain; the little carved antelope was still clipped to her duffel bag, from which she'd virtuously dug out her academic tomes to read at home while listening to Adele and hiding from her mother, who wanted to take her on a meditation retreat. Chloe didn't want to meditate, but she did need time to think. So far, she'd deflected all Iris's frantic texts demanding to know where she was and begging her not to give the Cloud Man voice recordings to Mia, but her plans were changing. Now that she'd met the man behind the words, she was convinced he should have his voice back.

Today she was trawling search engines for clues about the legendary safari balloonist; she was certain he had to be out there, and she longed to track him down before Iris and Griff came back to steamroller her into playing it all their way.

Chloe was one of the best Googlers around, with online detective skills worthy of her own private agency. Dominic Masters was among the toughest nuts she'd yet had to crack, but by midmorning she'd made the theatrical connection, and an hour later she'd located a married sister in Dinfield, whom she called straight away. Uncertain if Dominic had been in contact with any family since returning, she tactfully explained that she was from RADA's alumni association, trying to trace a Mr Dominic Masters. 'Of course, duck.' Alison Stubbs didn't think to question the hours of detective work that had gone into tracking her down as she obligingly passed on a mobile-phone number.

Before Chloe could call it, a pop-up box on her laptop told her that her father was ringing her Skype address from LA.

'Hey, Chlo.' His voice, gravelly as always with its affected Cockney edge, sounded even more bad-tempered than usual. 'Has a red-haired kid turned up today asking your mother to clear his mind?'

'Not that I've seen.'

'If he does, tell him I'm going to have him killed. What are you up to, gel?'

'Not a lot.' She fed Dominic Masters's number into her phone as she spoke, wondering if a text would be the best way to start. Then she dropped her mobile on to her keyboard in shock as her father's voice came out of the speakers in fits and starts of data lag.

'What did you just say?'

'I said I think it's about time you got to know your sister,' he repeated. 'Little Hope.'

'I know her name.'

'She's a great kid. I want my girls to get to know each other. I've squared it with your mother.'

Chloe leaned hard on her phone and keyboard as she took in the enormity of this statement. 'Mum's OK about it?'

'Sure. She agrees it's time to put her differences with Laney aside for the sake of what's important.'

For a moment, Chloe's heart sang, but then her eyes narrowed. She knew him too well. 'And what's important to you is a certain film script, isn't it?'

He didn't deny it. 'You're a smart kid, Chlo. A chip off the old block.'

'No.'

'You name it, I'll treat you. I heard you might need a new car ...?'

'My car's fine. It's at the garage having its dents straightened. I am *not* stealing the—'

'I'm not asking you to *steal* it ... just take a look around. I heard the computer it was on has been destroyed, but if there's another copy, my daughters will have a better future.'

She was about to tell him to get lost, but her attention was caught by a photograph on screen of the Mara River Camp tourist balloon flying over the annual river migration, a spectacular ribbon of wildebeest unfurling across the dusk-shadowed valley. 'I'll look, on one condition.'

'Name it!'

'You are the only man I know who can pull the strings to get what I need fast, although pulling ropes might be a more accurate description ...'

It was only when she ended the Skype call five minutes later that Chloe picked up her mobile to call Dominic Masters and realised it was already on an open line to the number she'd fed in for him. She must have pressed the Call button when she'd leaned on it earlier.

Wincing with mortification, she cautiously picked up the handset and held it to her cheek. 'Er ... hello, Mr Masters?'

'Hello.' The voice was magical, as deep and dusty as a gold mine. 'It's Dominic.'

'I take it you heard that?'

'Have we' – he broke off as a Tannoy loudly announced a final call to board a flight – 'met?'

'Briefly. Are you about to fly somewhere?'

His laugh was even more amazing than his voice, a deep rumble of disarming openness. 'From what I just heard, it sounds as though I might be ... '

Earlier that morning, Spanish air-traffic controllers had gone back to work, so Iris and Griff were now driving from Stansted to Wootton in a hire car. Feeling increasingly apprehensive at the prospect of taking Griff home, Iris fell silent. Her recent memories of Wootton were still of Dougie and rushing headlong up the aisle. They had been planning to come back from honeymoon so that he could take part in a ridden stunt display at tomorrow's gala. He'd started sending texts again, clearly thinking he was still in with a chance. She wished she could have stayed in Spain. Having Griff beside her was like a protective force-field, its span so wide that an army of Dougies couldn't ride through it, but what they had was still so new and magical that she was reluctant to expose it to the full battering of life in the Devonshire spotlight or introduce him to her family so soon after her broken engagement.

She looked at him now, so compassionate, clever and honest, and she knew that she had never felt anything of this intensity in her life. During her mother's many tearful tirades and lectures in the build-up to the disastrous wedding, Mia had insisted that when Iris found a lifetime's love she would feel completely different. Now that she had and did, she was frightened of losing it. She wanted to wrap what they had in tissue paper and lock it in a jewelled box. The butterflies went on a rampage at the thought of having Griff alone in the dark, but that led her to another dilemma: where they were going to sleep. She knew of old that the house would be at capacity during gala week. Unwashed and weary, the first thing they'd both want to do was shower away the travelling grime and scrape off its stubble, but the intimacy of sharing her little bathroom seemed too much.

She stole another glance at him. He had the most perfect profile of any man she knew, his brow straight and noble, jaw angular, eyes so dark and focused. How could I ever have thought it a frightening face? she wondered dreamily, and decided that perhaps she could share her loofah straight away after all.

He was looking back at her now, smiling with amusement. 'OK?'

She blushed, not wanting to admit to thinking about the sleeping arrangements. 'This gala tomorrow, it's a very big thing for Mum,' she warned him. 'She's always horribly uptight. And it's her birthday. Maybe we should wait, and talk to her afterwards.' She yawned pointedly, snuggling back in her seat. 'And sleep together.'

'I think we should definitely sleep together.' He smiled widely.

Iris realised she might have made a mistake. 'I said "sleep on it", didn't I?'

'You said "sleep together".'

'Well, I *meant* sleep on it.' She turned her flaming face to the window. Then, fireworks exploding and butterflies dancing, she added, 'Together.'

When they arrived at Wootton, the front gates were wide open and two tradesmen were peering at the circuit board of the electric mechanism. Griff braked hard as a woman on a bicycle skidded through ahead of them.

'It's Godless,' Iris groaned, watching Laney pedal up to the house with Hope strapped into a rear-mounted seat, holding air reins and pretending her mother was a pony. 'No doubt called to open her arms and provide soggy shoulders for my mother.'

Mia was out of the door like a shot. 'Laney! Thank God!' She fell on her friend and sobbed while Laney struggled to hold the bike upright with Hope still strapped on to it. 'It's all such a mess!'

Griff had parked the car beneath a topiary cockerel and was walking around to open the passenger door for Iris when he saw the bicycle, with its child seat, pitching towards the gravel. With split-second reflexes, he dived across the drive to catch it with his good arm while Laney soothed her sobbing friend.

When Iris finally struggled out of the car and on to her crutches, she was besieged by ecstatic dogs. At the front of the pack, the two Maltese scrabbled up her legs, dark eyes huge, pressing their chins to her shins and yelping joyfully.

'Hi, Mum,' she said, trying to shuffle through them all to the bicycle love-in.

Blind with tears, Mia stumbled forwards, treading on both Maltese as she flung her arms around her. 'My little girl is home!'

Iris pulled away awkwardly. 'This is Griff Donne.'

It was not quite the dream scenario she'd envisaged for the introduction.

Mustering a gracious smile, Mia turned to him, confusion crossing her face. 'Have we met?'

'Very briefly.' He was trapped on the wrong side of the bicycle that he was still holding, his other arm in a sling, and could neither shake the hand being offered nor kiss the wet cheek.

A dental-drill whine from the top of the steps made them all look up as a throaty voice called, 'Iris! ¡Bonita!'

Jacinta had accelerated out of the front doors at such high velocity that her chair almost whizzed straight over the top step. Braking in the nick of time, she teetered on the edge, gazing down at her granddaughter with huge, limpid eyes. 'The Lightning Man has cured me, Iris. I am cured!'

'Oh, Lito!' Iris hobbled across the gravel then threw down her crutches so she could hurry up the steps to embrace her grandmother and push her chair back from the brink.

'It's getting very biblical round here,' muttered Laney, as Mia collapsed tearfully into her arms again, babbling incoherently about her life not existing without Dom.

Meanwhile Jacinta told her granddaughter, 'Your father, he is so happy!'

'He's here?' Iris gasped.

'Yes! At long last your *papá* is here!'

'I want to see him.'

'He's taking a nap for his jet lag.' She patted her granddaughter's arm. 'His assistant person is still awake. He is a very strange fellow. When I ask if he is married, he tell me he is married to his work, then he look very sad. Maybe we will find him a nice English girl while he is here, eh? Have a toffee.' She offered a bag of her favourite tooth-pullers.

On the gravel, Laney was trying to get close enough to Hope to unbuckle her from the bicycle seat, but Mia was still clinging to her. 'I have to talk to you!' she pleaded.

Griff was keen to relinquish his role as animated bicycle stand and join Iris on the porch as she listened to Jacinta, who was demonstrating her miracle cure, arms outstretched. 'The Lightning Man, he lie both his hands on me like this.' She placed her hands on her grey head as though she were dancing to 'Agadoo'. 'And I feel like new. When Cloud Man do it, I feel nothing at all, but of course he only have one hand.'

'Did you say "Cloud Man"?' gasped Iris.

'Arch-rival of the Lightning Man, they say. Such a terrifying face, like the devil burned from sulphur. Young Chloe Benson helped chase him away. She was *muy valiente*. I tell Haff he must ask her out to dinner. Such a shame she is so plain.'

Griff almost dropped the bicycle as he caught Iris's eye.

'When was this, Lito?' she demanded.

'Three, four days ago.'

'So Dominic was here,' Griff breathed without thinking.

Mia let out a strangled sob, clutching Laney closer. 'He's been here too! God forgive me, I missed him here *and* in LA.'

'I hope he's collecting air miles,' Laney muttered distractedly, trying to get to Hope.

'When was he in LA?' Griff demanded.

But Mia was crying too much to answer. A small blue hatchback drove in through the open gates with a cheery toot of the horn, and she buried her face in her friend's shoulder. 'Oh, G-God, all these g-gala people. I simply can't cope with anybody else right now. P-please let's go somewhere quiet. I have to talk to you.'

Laney swayed, the bicycle leaning over dramatically. 'I have Hope with me,' she looked horribly torn, 'and I have to go to London later.'

Iris rushed down the steps. 'We'll look after Hope,' she reassured her, starting to unbuckle the seat straps, to Hope's obvious relief. The little girl was looking distinctly green; motion sickness had eclipsed pony fantasies. 'Griff's fabulous with kids, aren't you?'

'Absolutely.' Griff beamed at Laney, clutching the bike to his side as its small, rein-clutching rider was liberated. 'Iris promised to introduce me to all the horses here, Hope. What do you think? Would you like to come too?'

While Hope whooped with delight, eager to embrace all things equine, Laney looked edgy and protective. 'She can be funny with strangers.'

'Griff isn't a stranger, Godless,' Iris insisted, watching her own mother's face for reaction. 'He's family now.'

But Mia's eyes remained hollow with misery. She was too caught up in her own drama to take in what Iris had said. With a bolt of recognition, Iris understood how much her mother had suffered in losing Dominic.

From the porch above, Jacinta hailed the small, stocky man who was stepping from the little hatchback. 'Here is the *genio* who will enable me to show an elegant turn of foot at the gala!'

Pulling herself together, Iris looked from the man to her grandmother. 'That isn't the Lightning Man!'

'No, *bonita*. This is my chiropodist, Mr Singh.'

Apart from poor Lorca, who kicked at his box door furiously, all the Wootton stallions were out on the upper lawns, where Haff was putting his WAGs through their paces, music blaring from the temporary speakers. He was riding the now-sound Scully in place of Mia, who was too upset to rehearse.

Back on her crutches, Iris clanked into the stallion barn and introduced Hope to her irascible horse, showing her how to feed him a mint from a flat, outstretched palm, which made the little girl shriek with giggles.

Fed up with being neglected, Lorca pulled faces and attention-sought shamelessly, nipping, eye-rolling and pawing with his front hoofs.

'I'll ride you all the time now, my darling, I promise,' Iris told him, and Lorca eyed Griff triumphantly, making the Welshman smile as he acknowledged that his biggest rival had four legs and a brain smaller than a matchbox.

Emerging from the tack room, Vicente greeted them with a shy smile, and suggested Hope might like to meet the new foals in the nursery barn.

'We have to find Chloe,' Griff murmured quietly to Iris, as they headed across the courtyard and along a covered walkway to an open-sided barn. 'She obviously saw Cloud Man when he was here.'

While Hope watched, entranced, as the foals came up to her on spindly, big-kneed legs, their fluffy baby coats like half-blown dandelion clocks, Iris tried her friend's number again, but it went straight to voicemail as usual. 'Chlo, I really need to talk to you. I'm at Wootton with Griff. We're – er – looking after Hope for a bit. Can you call when you get this?'

Leaving the foals to enjoy their lunch, they went along to watch the quadrille rehearsals, Hope cantering ahead, bucking skittishly and occasionally shying at clumps of daisies.

'The gala committee *has* been busy.' Iris whistled.

The two interlinked marquees were at least three times the size that the modest wedding one had been, with even more terraces, stages, fountains and foliage, like a small-scale Alhambra. The main stage in front of the water cascades was tented to match its grand neighbours, with a full-scale lighting rig and sound system, with which the engineers were still fiddling.

'Amazing fountain.' Griff gazed at the steps of water that dropped away from view as far as the eye could see.

'Dad had it modelled on one at Chatsworth House that he and Kate Winslet shared a clinch in for a costume drama – I forget which, although I remember he said she was a seriously good kisser.' Iris was admiring the horses practising on the uniformly striped lawn beyond the marquee: a white-boarded dressage arena had been laid out, stretching as far as the tall yew hedge, ivy frothing from Greek urns balanced on top of the letter marker cones. A steep row of seating rostra was still being erected along its far side.

The three new stallions were spectacular, dappled grey, black and bay, along with Scully, pure white and a class apart. His rider was also a class apart from the others, barely moving in the saddle as he encouraged the horse to dance for fun.

Bright red in the face from their efforts, huge chests bouncing, the WAG riders were battling to keep time and control. Great swathes of stripy blond hair extensions scraped back into pony tails, dark sweat rings on their pastel T-shirts, make-up sliding off, they were a far cry from the cucumber-cool, pouting clothes-horses the public usually saw. But they were making an incredibly good job of it, Iris saw, their horses dancing in time to the grinding, pulsing beat from the speakers.

Thundering across one diagonal, Sylva Rafferty was only just in time to cross in front of the diminutive Kerri Hughes, who was riding across the opposing one while texting on her jewelled iPhone.

'How many times, Kerri? Halt at text!' Haff bellowed as he flew in their wake in an extended trot so smooth he might have been on rails. Spotting his favourite client's daughter, he told his riders to stretch their horses and take five before riding over to the boards, dark eyes glowing. 'They look good, huh? You like the music?'

Throbbing through the speakers, a familiar rock riff had been cut through with Spanish guitar music to create an amazingly sensual, rhythmic soundtrack. It was only marred by the roaring water cascade and shrieking feedback from the main stage as the engineers tested radio mikes.

'Pete Rafferty mixed it especially in his studio,' Haff went on, dropping the reins and patting Scully's baroque arched neck, now granite grey with sweat. 'Is amazing, no? The man is a *legend*. He come here tomorrow and I shake his hand.' He looked positively skittish. Then his face hardened: the rock legend's comely wife was sneakily practising piaffe in the far corner, spurs jabbing into little Quito's sides. 'Let him rest! He needs a break! *¡Ave María purísima!*' Scrunching up his weather-creased face against the sunlight, he spotted Kerri making a call while her stallion stuffed his face with one of the potted urn arrangements. He tutted despairingly. 'Tomorrow they wear the frilly flamenco dresses with no pockets so they cannot carry their phones – it will be fine.' He sighed, turning Scully into the arena to confiscate Kerri's iPhone before they tried the canter pirouettes.

While Haff was bawling out Kerri, Gabby Santos da Costa thundered up on Balthasor, who had spotted a potential source of Polos. 'Iris!' She hauled on the curb rein, only just stopping him in time to avoid jumping the white boards. 'Great to meet you at last. I loved you as Purple! I just *know* we're going to be best mates.'

Iris smiled awkwardly, feeding the stallion a mint and loosening his curb chain. She had no idea who Gabby was and had no desire to appear rude, but she liked her current best mate, even though she wasn't answering her calls. She quickly checked her phone: still nothing from Chloe.

Gabby was beaming at Griff, who had now hoisted Hope to his hip, where she was pretending to ride, using a lot more leg than Haff's quadrille ladies. 'It's Dougie, isn't it?'

'This is Griff Donne,' Iris said tetchily.

'Who?' She tilted her head to admire Hope, who was feeding Balthasor a mint under Iris's guidance. 'Is this your little girl?'

Iris didn't hear Griff's answer because her phone sprang into life with Chloe's photograph beaming from the front.

'At last! You OK, Chlo? I've been worried sick.'

'Never better.' She sounded unusually chipper. 'I'm at home. Mum's just left for a meditation retreat with her new toy-boy. Would you like to come for lunch?'

Iris watched the little figure hanging from Griff's side, now scratching Balthasor's raised upper lip with shrieks of delight. 'We'd love to, but we've got Hope with us.'

'Great! Bring her.'

She missed a beat. 'Are you sure?'

'Absolutely!'

Not pausing to wonder why Chloe hadn't sounded her usual sardonic self, Iris rang off, hopelessly excited, whispering to Griff, 'You wait until you see the Obelisk – it's the weirdest house ever.'

'Are you sure it's OK to take Hope there without her mum's permission?' he asked quietly, but was distracted by Iris running her fingers up the side of his face and threading them through his hair, making every other hair on his body spring to attention.

'Trust me, Godless wants nothing more than for Hope and Chloe to get to know each other,' she insisted, already texting her godmother to let her know where they were going. 'Mum will bang on for hours. Poor Laney should charge analyst fees.' She looked up sharply as a voice called her name.

A tanned, moustached figure was picking his way across the lawn towards them. Dressed in a petrol-blue cable-knit tank top and matching shorts with incredibly white trainers, he looked like he'd just wandered off the cover of a seventies knitting pattern.

'Oh shit, it's Ivan,' Iris muttered. 'Dad's secret boyfriend. He is *seriously* LA.'

'Iris baby! How are ya?' Ivan beamed. 'I bet this brings back memories, huh?' He gestured at the marquees.

'Well, the gala does happen every year, Ivan,' she said kindly.

'I mean the wedding. Poor you. Sounds quite a show – Ivan

Pollack.' He thrust out a hand towards Griff. 'Were you there? Bad day, good outcome, huh?'

Griff's knuckles were crushed in a grip that would have reduced a Corvette to a Dinky car. 'I dropped in briefly. Griff Donne. This is Hope.'

The little girl shook Ivan's hand with a vigour to rival his, adding an elaborate series of fist-punches and high-fives. 'I'm five years old,' she said brightly, 'and I have two daddies.'

Ivan's face lit up. 'Hey, that's cool!' He gave Griff a warm smile. 'You and I must talk later.'

'My Daddy-o has a fat tummy like you,' Hope told him warmly.

'Sounds a great guy,' Ivan said, with a stiff smile, then stepped back in alarm as a stallion snorted past. He watched the WAGs in open astonishment. 'Leo keeps telling me I must learn to ride English-style. It looks pretty . . . bouncy.'

'This is Spanish Doma Clásica,' Iris told him. 'It's very passionate and beautiful – and bouncy, like my mother.'

'I wasn't aware she has Spanish blood?'

'Dressage is in the horse's blood and the rider's sweat and tears.'

Kerri Hughes rode past, struggling to maintain shoulder-in, eyeliner streaming down the sides of her nose, armpit sweat rings now meeting in the middle over her enhanced cleavage like a Chanel logo.

'I think I'll stick to ball sports.' Ivan shuddered.

'Oh, they've all got balls,' Iris assured him. 'They're *caballo entero*. It says "macho" on their passports.'

Both Ivan and Griff watched the horses with new-found respect.

'Is Dad awake yet?' Iris asked hopefully. 'We're going to a friend's for lunch and I'd really like Griff to meet him first.'

He shook his head. 'The lag's just wiped him out. He's exhausted. You know he worked six eighty-hour weeks in a row this last series?'

Iris hugged herself. 'How do we make him stop?'

A hairy arm wrapped itself around her and Ivan said in a low, shaking voice, 'I think he just has. Now we've just gotta figure out how to get him started again.'

Chapter 49

Leo awoke from the best sleep he'd had in weeks. He didn't even need to soothe himself with his knitting. Stretching out in his bed, he listened to the sounds drifting through the open windows. Normally Wootton was a haven of peace, but on the day before the annual gala workmen yelled, lawnmowers whirred and delivery vans roared along the drive. He rather liked the reassuring hubbub of activity. It was peculiarly British, from the strains of Radio 2 jingles to the chatter of magpies.

He pulled on his running gear and went to find Ivan, who was sitting with Jacinta on the terrace, both admiring the new landscape of marquees, sound stage and seating. Ivan was looking very tight-jawed and hollow-cheeked, Leo thought anxiously, then realised he was just trying to work his way through one of his mother's notoriously chewy toffees.

'*¡Leo, mi cariño!*' Jacinta threw open her arms and tilted her face up to be kissed. 'I just tell your assistant Ivor that you and Mia should have another baby. It is never too late. As you know, your father and I were in our fourth decades when we were blessed with you. God, he rewards patience.'

Leo caught Ivan's eye apologetically, then did a double-take as he noticed an amused sparkle beneath the thick, curving brows. 'He sure does,' he said through teeth glued together with toffee.

'Iris is back,' Jacinta told him happily. 'She has gone out to lunch with a friend, but she cannot wait to see her *papá* when she returns. She looks happy again. Sun-kissed!'

'She has a new man.' Ivan stood up.

'Already?'

'Maybe impatience is rewarded too,' Ivan suggested kindly, stretching his hamstrings and taking a deep breath of English country air. 'Let's run.'

'I'm sorry,' Leo said, as soon as they were out of earshot, pounding along the track that led around the back of the walled garden towards open fields. 'Mamá's's obsessed with *los bebés*.'

'So are we. See how much we have in common?' They were running along the avenue of limes, which arched over them now. 'This place is beautiful, just like you promised. But your mom is right. It needs more kids. It's a family home, and I can see why you said from the start that you want to keep it in the family. Mia would be perfect to carry our child.'

Leo spun around so that he was running backwards, unable to stop smiling. 'You really mean that? You know that's what I want, but you always—'

'I changed my mind. It might not say macho on my passport, but I've still got the balls to admit when I'm wrong.'

When Mia and Laney got to the boathouse, they found that Kit had left it spotless, with a vase of wild flowers on the desk and a note, which Mia swept aside as she opened up the laptop, not noticing that it was sitting in a small puddle. 'I have so much to tell you. First, we need to use your computer – oh!' A small frog leapt out, making her jump back in alarm.

'It drowned.' Laney stooped to retrieve the note.

Mia sobbed and laughed as she placed a little white plastic Pegasus beside the useless computer with a shaking hand and tugged away his jewelled wings to reveal a USB flash drive. 'It's the Nichols Canyon CCTV footage. I've been too frightened to look at it until I had you with me, and now your computer's broken so we have nothing to watch it on.'

Pocketing Kit's note without bothering to read it, Laney wrapped an arm around Mia's narrow shoulders and steered her towards a stool. She'd dropped a stack of weight she could ill afford to lose. 'What exactly happened?'

Perching on a stool, Mia explained about the visitor to the LA house and Ivan having him hauled away from the gates by Security, all captured for posterity on camera and saved for her on disk alongside Dougie's ignoble visit.

'Christ, Leo's security cameras capture more high drama than *Corrie*,' Laney gasped afterwards, wondering if it would be wrong to offer to nip home for Simon's laptop so they could see it after all, but Mia was crying again so she decided it was best not to.

'The awful thing is, it's a relief that I can't watch it.' She buried her face in her hands. 'I don't want to. I don't need to see it to know it was Dom.'

'How can you know it was him if you don't look?' asked Laney, pragmatically.

'The note he left was in the same handwriting as the birthday card he sent after he disappeared.'

Laney cast her mind back to the note Mia had received soon after marrying Leo. 'We agreed that was a crank.'

'Everyone else agreed. I knew it was him. Who else would quote Ned's Atomic Dustbin?'

Laney had to concede she had a point, but she remained cynical. 'Are you sure it's not some crackpot? After all, the birthday card wasn't in Dom's writing. It looked like a kid's handwriting. Lito said the man who came here was so terrifying that Chloe Benson had to fight him off.' An awful thought occurred to her. 'What if it *is* Dom and he's gone mad?'

Mia burst into noisier sobs and Laney hugged her automatically, trying not to look at the wall clock and panic. 'Just let's get through the next forty-eight hours, eh? You've worked so hard on the gala, and the show must go on, remember? Talking of which, I have to be up in London later and really must—'

'You think I give a monkey's about the bloody gala when Dom's out there somewhere?' Mia howled.

'Mia, I know that what Leo's been going through has put a lot of stress on you, but imagining that Dom is back isn't going to help anybody, least of all you. You've done this before, remember.' Laney plucked her vibrating phone from her pocket to read an incoming message.

Mia stared, appalled, at her usually soft, easygoing friend, looking so rattled and hollow-eyed, the sympathy carved away from her face, those clever blue eyes pinched with tiredness and her temper apparently shortening every day. Glaring at her phone screen now, Laney barely glanced at the picture text from Simon before deleting it.

'Laney, are you ill?' she asked fearfully.

Laney slammed the phone on the table. 'Just because I'm suggesting we should focus on the gala does not mean I'm ill!'

Mia recoiled, disorientated by her moods, which lashed one way and then the other like an angry horse's tail. 'Why are you going to London?'

'I'm meeting RHH for dinner.' Laney had never been able to lie to Mia.

'You can't!'

'Why not? What's wrong with meeting an internet friend for a perfectly innocent meal together? Simon swans around flirting with Italian glamour models and exchanging steamy emails with half of South America.'

'Does he know you're meeting RHH?'

'Of course not!' she snapped, picking up her phone again and turning it around in her hand.

'And *that's* what's wrong about it.'

Laney glared at her self-righteously, determined not to let the guilt fairy in. 'Ours is a marriage of true minds and false alibis – and Simon has the track record to prove it. Anyway, who are you to be my moral arbiter? Simon slept with you behind my back, after all.'

Mia recoiled in shock. 'That was a long, long time ago.'

'The Night That Never Happened. What was it you said in your diary? "Laney must never know"?'

Mia's green eyes shot up to the ceiling, feigning fascination with a fly that was buzzing around. 'It was all a stupid mistake.'

'Sleeping with your best friend's boyfriend usually is.'

'We didn't sleep together! Not in that sense. We talked, cried quite a lot and then passed out in the same room. It was all bloody undignified, if you must know.'

'Simon cried?' Laney was astonished. Over the years she'd imagined all sorts of furtive goings-on as R.E.M. boomed out, but weeping wasn't one of them.

'The girl he loved had just accused him of being gay. He was in bits and he was *very* drunk. He thought he had something to prove, so he made me swear not to tell you what a blubbering idiot he was. I couldn't stop the waterworks either. I thought my world had ended because Dom hadn't come to see the play.'

'But you told me you were going to have a one-night stand with Adam Oakes that night.'

'I was so upset about Dom I couldn't think straight. I had this crazy idea that I needed an insurance policy. I'd just that night found out I was pregnant.'

Laney stayed very still. 'You mean you already knew?'

'Iris is Dom's baby, Laney. I'd never slept with anybody else in my life.'

'Did he know about it? Was that why he disappeared?'

She shook her head violently. 'He never knew, but he must have already felt trapped. That's the only way I can explain it. I didn't know I was pregnant when I proposed on his birthday – it was just a stupid spur-of-the-moment thing. I'd always known I wanted to marry Dom – I'd have married him the day I met him. That never changed in the four years we were together. I couldn't imagine life without him. But however much I knew he loved me back – and I *knew* he loved me – I was always the follower, always the chaser, never certain he wouldn't just keep walking if I fell back.

'When he wouldn't give me an answer, I guessed I'd already fallen too far behind. It felt like my world was ending. I kept trying to convince myself that would change when I saw him again, but he didn't turn up to the last night of the Lorca play, and I knew then that I had my answer. I was so angry with myself for trying to rush things. That same night I discovered I was pregnant, and I panicked. I knew Dom would want to stand by the baby when he found out – all that Yorkshire moral fibre meant he had to do the right thing, and his father would force him to if not. But he was on the cusp of such great things and I wasn't supposed to be a part of that any more. I couldn't have trapped him, forced him to turn his back on his ambitions and spend his life playing the reluctant husband and father.'

'So you needed to line up somebody else fast to put in the frame?' Laney muttered. 'And when the Adam plan fell through, Simon was a willing accomplice.'

'It wasn't like that!'

Laney's phone was pinging with more incoming messages, but she ignored it, pushing it furiously away. 'You spent a night with my boyfriend and let everyone believe he might have fathered your child as an *insurance policy*?'

'C'mon, nobody thinks Simon could be Iris's father.'

'Iris seemed pretty convinced that day she found your college diary.'

'She's always resisted the idea of a father who disappeared before she was born, but she never seriously believed it could be Demon. Please don't let this have jeopardised your marriage, Laney. He honestly didn't do a thing. He loved you then and he loves you now.'

'I should like to point out that he's become a father several times over since we met – at least once while we were together. *That* jeopardised our marriage.'

'You know he regrets that more than anything. He's changed so much. You are his bedrock, Laney. He worships you. You two getting back together was so wonderful and so right. You can't throw that away now.'

'All we do is work and fight.' Laney sighed. 'I'm so tired and stressed all the time that I'm horrible to him. When we remarried, Hope came with me, but now I can't even give Simon faith or charity.'

'Simon always wanted you back, Laney. He only asked for you, not your babies.'

Laney winced, her rawest nerve prodded with a hot scalpel. 'At least nobody could accuse me of trying to trap him into marriage by getting pregnant.'

Registering the hit, Mia pinched the bridge of her nose, collecting her thoughts. 'When Dom disappeared, I was beside myself with unhappiness. I thought about getting rid of the baby, but the idea of killing the life we'd created together was unbearable, even if he wouldn't share her. Leo's always been Iris's father. Everybody accepted that.'

'Does Leo know she's Dom's?'

'I don't think it matters to him,' she said. 'When he proposed, I thought he was just being kind, but he was completely serious. He wrote letters and poetry, read up on pregnancy and childbirth, cried his eyes out telling me he wanted to do it and convinced me we could make it work, that we could look after each other and a baby, a holy trinity protecting each other. I needed Leo and his homespun pleasures, just as he needed me. And in a funny way it *has* worked, for many years. Iris had a tremendous childhood. She's been the most important part of my life. I don't regret it.'

Thinking about the shamefully Disneyesque daydreams that she'd let herself indulge in recently, including raising Hope in idyllic isolation on the Borders with an old-fashioned, breek-wearing father figure, Laney finally understood a little of what Mia had done.

'I've always worried that I trapped him,' Mia said, 'that he's been duty-bound to look after me. I'm sure Ivan thinks that.'

'Rubbish!' Laney leapt to her friend's defence. 'You've been a fantastic wife, a far better one than I've been to Simon. Look at the way you've supported him, always put him first, created a stable family home with Lito and Iris at its heart, his three generations of beautiful, witty, incredibly strong women – it's the dream support team for most men I've ever known. And unless you've acted your socks off, you've never even been unfaithful. You've hidden behind your high walls, safeguarded from falling in love again.'

She let out a tearful laugh. 'How could I fall in love when I never fell out of it?'

'Believe me, it's possible,' Laney said without thinking, glancing at her phone with its message light flashing.

Mia gaped at her. 'Please tell me you're not talking about your internet man. You've never even met him.'

Laney shifted awkwardly, scalpel grinding through the nerve endings now. 'So what's Leo going to do now his mother's had a miracle cure?'

Mia looked out to the river, where a mother duck was cruising proudly into the boathouse lagoon with her offspring outriders. 'We both know she hasn't been cured, Laney, but at least she's stopped trying to control the dispatch date.'

'The list of ailments she gave me was pretty comprehensive.'

'As she herself says *very* often, it's a miracle she's still on the planet. But she's got a lot of fight and she has her boy home. I think she'll keep Leo suffering the agonies of closet living a little longer.'

'Surely he has to tell her the truth.'

'Well, he can hardly introduce her to a new grandchild without some sort of explanation, especially when it starts calling Ivan "Daddy" too. He's got to talk to Iris as well. We both have.' She picked up the little jewelled Pegasus standing between them. 'Whether Dom's on this thing or not, I am going to tell my daughter that I've never stopped loving her real father. She deserves to know absolutely everything about him.'

Laney reached out and squeezed her hands. 'Good for you.'

'And you need to cancel that dinner date and talk to Simon before it's too late.'

Laney snatched her hands away so fast that the winged horse skittered across the room. 'I have no reason not to meet RHH,' she said, but she knew that wasn't true. He was much more than just her secret displacement activity now, and Laney was prepared to cross the invisible line between fantasy and reality.

'Please, Laney! You'll regret this.'

Laney leapt up, grabbing her phone. 'If you'll excuse me, I have to get back to Hope. I've left her far too long as it is.' She stalked out.

'Don't go, Laney!'

Her feet hammered away.

Mia groaned, rubbing the back of her neck as she went in search of the dropped flash drive. She looked up hopefully as footsteps came bounding up the outside stairs, but it was Leo, wearing such dark glasses it was amazing he could see where he was going.

'There you are, baby!'

'Did you just see Laney?' Mia asked.

'No.' He yawned and kissed her cheek. 'I've missed this place. I loved painting here. Knitting's great for defusing stress, but it doesn't touch this.' He peered at his work on the walls. 'I was rather good, wasn't I? This landscape's better than Abe's Monet.' He pushed his glasses up on to his head and peered closer. 'Maybe not.' He stooped to pick up the Pegasus flash drive as his foot knocked against it. 'Hey, I recognise this. Disney gave a load away in a competition when we were promoting *Myth*. One had real diamonds. I don't think it was ever found.'

'Keep it,' Mia muttered. 'I don't want it any more.'

The amused expression on his handsome face turned to concern. 'You've been crying, darling.' He rushed to hug her.

'Girl talk with Laney,' she explained, stepping back and cupping his face in her hands. 'How are you feeling?'

'Great. Really great, in fact. Ivan and I have been talking too.'

'Yes?'

'Mia, we'd like you to carry our baby.'

Standing on the mooring beneath the belly of the boathouse, leaning against one of the stilts, Laney was too busy typing a message to Richard HH to notice the murmuring of conversation above. After many false starts and attempts at false jollity, she ended up simply saying, I am coming tonight, which at least had excitingly sexual connotations that cheered her up.

He replied straight away. If you're sure. RHH x

It wasn't quite as flirtatious or saucy as she'd expected – 'I'll make sure you come, darling Laney' or 'Let's come together' was more his usual line – but she reminded herself that he was in meetings all day, and anyway, their dinner was going to be a perfectly respectable affair, not the sordid one Mia predicted. She was merely meeting a fan of her radio show with whom she'd struck up an amusing acquaintance.

Denial in place, she hurried back towards the house, taking the woodland path as a shortcut. As she did so, she glanced at a text she'd just spotted from Iris and then reread its contents in such disbelief that she walked straight into an overhanging tree branch.

'Hope!' she shrieked, setting off at a sprint this time.

Chapter 50

The Obelisk had been Oscar Benson's fantasy Bond-baddie headquarters made reality, complete with high-tech electronics that he'd abandoned with no instruction manuals when signing the house over to his first wife in the divorce settlement. The famous windmill with which it shared its plot was visible for miles around, but its ultra-modern neighbour was cleverly concealed in a dip alongside a stretch of woodland. Two huge concrete posts topped with intimidating camera poles guarded the gates to the public road, which swung open when Griff's hire car approached. Only accessible through the deep fir woods, the long drive was a gleaming black river of tarmac along which Oscar had once driven his sports cars at high speed, awarding himself points for each squirrel and rabbit he took out. It was like going from day to night as the car plunged into the densely planted pine, the canopy overhead blotting out the light and making Griff think of Tolkien's grim Mirkwood.

'It's more of a fortress than Sueño,' he muttered. Closer to the house, there were more barriers and gates. Griff peered at a flat screen built into yet another concrete gatepost. 'What's that?'

'Fingerprint reader,' Iris explained, leaning across him to touch it. As she did so, the familiar charge of excitement ran between their bodies and her mouth couldn't resist brushing against his. Once their lips touched, she was helpless to pull away, and the kiss deepened.

'Child on board,' a sing-song voice reminded them from the back seat. 'And Gogs.'

Hope peered around her battered bear, giggling furiously as Iris blushed and wriggled back into the passenger seat, the studded metal gates swinging open.

Griff whistled. 'That's definitely statement architecture.'

Part garage forecourt, part Gherkin, the Obelisk was a long, flat rectangle propped up on concrete legs with a huge phallic glass dome balanced on one end. It was exceptionally ugly. To its left was the hangar-like garage complex that had once housed Oscar's large collection of totally impractical and undrivable cars in temperature-controlled and hermetically sealed splendour. A swimming pool and gym complex lay beyond that, consisting of metal trusses connected by gleaming glass flies' eyes.

With a loud purr, a panel opened in the Obelisk's phallic dome and Chloe stepped on to the roof of the garage forecourt, waving at them. 'I'll come down!'

'How?' Griff was peering at the structure in confusion. 'There are no stairs.'

'There's a lift,' Iris explained.

Moments later, Chloe appeared from a door hidden in one of the concrete legs and walked forward to welcome them, regarding Hope with anxious excitement, taking in the untameable Benson hair and broad-backed solidity, along with the same heart-shaped mouth as her own. When Hope beamed up at her and whinnied, scraping her foot against the dry earth like a pony, it was the perfect introduction: Chloe had always felt more confident around animals than humans.

Holding her breath, Iris watched as her friend reached out an uncertain hand and touched the little girl's head, a broad smile stretching across her face as she ruffled the wonderful bedspring hair before dropping down to be on the same level, vet to miniature pony.

'Hello, Hope. I met you a couple of times when you were very little. I'm Chloe. We have the same daddy.'

'I have two daddies.' Hope trotted out her favourite line.

'You call our daddy "Daddy-o", don't you?'

'He likes cars and has a fat tummy. I like ponies,' she added brightly.

'Me too.' Chloe smiled, taking her hand. 'Do you want to see my house?'

When they all reached the door in the pillar, it opened, revealing the lift. 'It's only designed for two,' Chloe said. 'You'll have to wait until it comes back down.'

'What happens in a power cut?' Griff laughed.

'There are floating stone steps at the back leading up to the Zen roof garden,' Iris explained, as Chloe and Hope stepped into the lift. 'They're treacherous – Oscar was always falling off them into the reed beds. I think he sued the architect.' She looked from her crutches to his sling. 'Best wait for the lift.'

'Is Oscar really as much of a monster as he's always made out?' Griff asked in an undertone once the lift doors had closed.

'He's bloody strange. I always used to think that was where Chloe got the more suspect aspects of her personality, but given what her mother's like, I think the question should be where she got any nice characteristics from.' She gripped his hand when the lift returned and they stepped in.

Confined in the small space, they looked at one another for the briefest moment before their mouths took on lives of their own, rushing together in an urgent seal of lips, tongues and breath, hands running across shoulders, up throats and through hair. When the doors opened, they burst apart reluctantly.

'Why can't this house be fifty storeys high?' Griff breathed.

'Oscar probably wanted it to be,' Iris was trying to control her wobbly legs enough to walk in a straight line, 'but the local council could only take so many backhanders before fingerprints showed up.'

Griff stopped short: he had walked out of a lift with most men's fantasy woman into a small boy's fantasy house. He preferred the lift with Iris, but this was some compensation.

Little girls were less impressed, and Chloe was showing Hope around the space-age house at full throttle, well aware that the pony element was distinctly lacking, a design flaw that had somewhat blighted her own childhood. 'It's all controlled by computers and is totally eco-friendly, sustainable, et cetera, which was the only way Daddy-o got the planning – ironic given he's such a petrolhead.' She wasn't quite up to speed with talking to a five-year-old yet.

Hope looked puzzled. 'What's a petrolhead?'

'Well, we're pony-mad, so I suppose you could call us hoof-heads. Daddy-o is car-mad, so he's a petrolhead.'

'I heard Mummy call Daddymon a dickhead last week,' Hope said. 'Does that mean he likes—'

'Puddings!' Iris rushed forward. 'Especially Spotted Dick.'

Griff was admiring the kitchen, which had glossy black-marble-panelled walls and one huge minimalist island that appeared to be a solid slab of wood the length of a cricket wicket without any evidence of an unsightly appliance or sink. Abandoned ingloriously on top of it, like a drunkard on an empty dance floor, was Chloe's tatty university rucksack, spilling textbooks and notepads.

'Help yourselves to drinks,' called Chloe as she led Hope through to the huge reception room, in which a grand piano was laden with framed pictures of her clearing huge fences on small, solid ponies.

'What would you like?' Iris asked Griff as she leaned on the island, turning to find his mouth against hers.

'You.'

Oh, the bliss of kissing him. Any minute now she'd be spread-eagled on the glossy wood top, dragging him with her. But, remembering Hope was within earshot, she pulled breathlessly away.

Flustered, she reached beneath the surface and pressed a button, which suddenly caused a section of the wood to slide away and reveal a huge professional hob. 'Damn, that's not it. I'm looking for the fridge.' She closed it again. Then she turned sharply as she heard Chloe saying to Hope, 'Daddy-o was in a film called *Dalrymple*. Have you heard of it?'

'Are there ponies in it?'

'No, but it's very funny. Your mummy wrote some of it.'

'All of it,' Iris corrected cheerily, having had the full story from her mother when Oscar was threatening his ex-wife with lawsuits to get his hands on the sequel. She raised her eyebrows questioningly at Chloe over Hope's head, but her friend's kind gaze darted away.

'Would you like to see the cinema room? We can watch a bit of *Dalrymple* if you like.'

'Yes please! Is there popcorn?'

'Absolutely. There's a machine in there. Let's get drinks first.'

Chloe led Hope back towards the kitchen and pressed a button that made one of the shiny black walls slide back to reveal a vast fridge entirely made up of wine racks and bottle holders with an ice-maker the size of a small tumble-dryer in the middle. Chloe lifted a flap in the door, which contained a stash of Innocent smoothies. She plucked out two.

'What's going on, Chloe?' Iris whispered as she passed.

'I'm just getting to know my little sister,' Chloe whispered back, but those clever, honest eyes stayed lowered as she hurried away, explaining to Hope that the cinema room they were about to enter had twenty speakers and heated massage seats.

Iris watched her worriedly. Chloe was fundamentally honest and a lousy actress, which made it very hard for her to cover up. She definitely had a hidden agenda, and Iris doubted it had anything to do with Cloud Man.

Griff had wandered away to admire the view from the glass walls that ran the full length of the rectangle on stilts. 'This place is amazing.'

On a long, narrow table set up at one end there were piles of old architect's plans and structural engineer's drawings. Beside these was an OS map covered with pen marks and computer print-outs of weather charts. When Griff picked them up to study them closely, he noticed a hand-held weather monitor lying beneath. 'I think these are flight predictions. Is Chloe's mother a hot-air balloonist?'

'Not to my knowledge. Oscar used to fly a helicopter, I think. Oh, hell.' From the window, she'd spotted a figure charging out of the woods on a bicycle, bouncing over the hard mud ruts like an extreme-sport fanatic. 'It's Godless. I'd better go down and intercept.'

While Iris rushed for the lift, Griff watched as Laney leapt off her bicycle and squared up to the huge modern house, taking a step back when she failed to find a front door. Clearly unaware that there was an automated way up, she rushed around the house just as the lift doors opened and Iris stepped out, finding nothing more than a bicycle. Griff tapped helpfully on the window to attract her attention, but it was triple-soundproofed reflective glass and she could neither see nor hear him. His attention was now distracted by a map he knew well that was sitting on the table beneath him, one he had studied many times when first back in England learning to fly balloons. It was the close-scale map of Wootton.

Outside, Laney had started climbing up the floating steps with what little strength she had left after cycling from Wootton. Fuelled by a mother's protective fury, she avoided falling into the reed beds and hauled herself on to the gravelled roof terrace. Battling vertigo as she ran between the Zen boulders into the glass egg, she then faced a terrifying suspended spiral perspex staircase with no hand-rail that led down into the main body of the house. Oscar took sadistic pleasure in designing terrifyingly un-child-friendly houses, she thought angrily, going down it on her bottom.

'Where is my daughter?' She thundered into the main room, cornering Griff by the table, her blue eyes wild.

He held up a map for self-protection like a shield. 'Chloe said something about a cinema room?' He gestured vaguely in the direction Chloe had headed and then, seeing Laney storm off like Boudicca into battle, dashed in her wake.

Reappearing from the lift to find the house's main reception area empty, Iris listened for sounds of Laney issuing recriminations for random babysitting, but heard nothing in the soundproofed stillness. Guiltily aware that she'd brought Hope here without her godmother's permission, she set off in search. Then, passing through the kitchen, she spotted Chloe's old rucksack on the huge wooden island with the antelope flash drive hanging from it.

Iris stalled uncertainly. It was technically Griff's property. They needed some leverage to get Chloe to tell them what she was up to. Surely it wouldn't be wrong to take it back.

But as she stretched across the surface to try to grab it, grasp-ing the edge of the wooden slab for stability, she touched several pressure pads and the whole thing started to move beneath her, hatches opening to reveal bins and waste disposals, a hot-water spout popping up, a vast television dropping down and a V-shaped breakfast bar springing out on two sides with her on top.

'At least let her finish watching the film!' Chloe's voice drifted through from another room.

Still lying on top of the expanded kitchen, Iris reached under the surface to press a few more buttons in the hope of reversing the process, but the windows around her suddenly turned opaque, tiny spotlights glimmering up from the floor and rap music streaming from hidden speakers as 2Pac announced he wasn't a killer but not to push it.

'This is all wrong.' Laney's breathless, hysterical tones came closer. 'There are formal, prearranged ways of doing these things. This poor child flew all the way to LA just a few days ago and hardly saw her father. I can't have her hurt again. I would happily invite you to come for visits and outings to get to know Hope, Chloe, but you must see this is totally unacceptable. I had no idea she was here.'

Starting to panic, Iris leaned over the edge of the worktop and looked down at the row of buttons, spotting a red one, which had to be an override. Punching it with relief, she found everything folding back up.

'I want to finish watching the film! I love Daddy-o pulling funny faces and making farty noises,' came an indignant little voice as Hope pulled away from her overwrought mother to race back to the cinema, dodging past Chloe who was trying to pacify Laney.

'I'm so sorry we jumped the gun, I really am, but I do want to get to know Hope. She's lovely. Please both stay a bit longer. I was going to make lunch. Stay for lunch!'

'I'm on a diet!' snapped Laney. 'I'm still trying to lose those fifty pounds.' It was a direct reference to the infamous Twitter quote, retweeted by Chloe, in which Oscar had dumped his second wife.

Chloe hung her head. 'Me too. I inherited Dad's heavy-handed approach. It's never bothered him, but I can't sweat it off in the gym no matter how hard I try.'

Laney turned to look at her in surprise. 'I won't tell you what your father's been putting me through recently, but it hasn't been easy,' she said quietly. 'It's not fair on you to say more. Believe me, I'd love you and Hope to be close. I'm sorry I overreacted. We'll set up another lunch.'

Following behind them like a UN peacekeeper, reluctant to intervene, Griff caught Iris's eye and his brows shot up as he saw her lying on the island gripping its sides like a nervous surfer.

Laney didn't appear to notice anything amiss. 'There you are, Iris. I think you owe me an explanation, don't you?' She clutched the island as though she was going to faint.

Iris had never seen her godmother look so ill. She seemed to have shrunk back into her skin in just a few weeks, her clothes hanging off her, her skin grey and her blue eyes staring. Certain there had to be something terribly wrong, she clambered down to put her arms around her, the little antelope dongle still digging into her palm.

'What is it, Godless?'

'Just having a bad day.' Laney smiled fiercely. 'I'll be fine as soon as I've found a babysitter for tonight. Did you say you were free? Malin's let me down and I have to go to London.' Her eyes were desperate hollows.

Iris glanced at Griff, felt her butterflies stage a collective fly-past, and shook her head apologetically. She had the flash drive now: she and Griff could debrief in every sense. 'We're needed at Wootton. We've been travelling for two days. Besides, I haven't seen Dad yet, and I'm worried about Mum.'

'Of course.' Laney rubbed her sweating face with shaking fingers. 'Go home and talk to your mother. Trust me, she's in a confessional mood.'

'I can babysit,' Chloe offered dispassionately. When Laney stared at her in disbelief, she shrugged with a half-smile. 'I have to be at Heathrow first thing tomorrow, but I'm free until then.'

Laney burst into tears and hugged her. 'You are *so* lovely!'

'Get off my hair,' growled Chloe, but she looked rather chuffed.

Chapter 51

Sitting on the Wootton terrace alone after lunch, Leo was knitting furiously, wool ball leaping like an electrocuted guinea pig to his right, a swathe of ribbed white fabric growing ever longer over his knees.

'Funeral shroud?' ventured Ivan, carrying out a tray of coffee. 'Because it looks like it's no longer needed.'

In the glasshouse that ran the length of the walled garden, Jacinta was taking Griff for a guided tour of the grape vines that Franco had lovingly transplanted from Sueño. The sound of her wheelchair crashing into potting benches reached them across the lawns, along with gales of laughter. The Welshman had proved an immediate hit, his natural curiosity appealing to Jacinta, who had wasted no time in listing her many newly cured ailments, then launched into long tales of her childhood on the hacienda while they admired the reminders of her beloved Spain that now filled the Wootton gardens.

'It was going to be a cot blanket, but a white flag could come in just as handy round here.'

'I take it Mia said no.' Ivan sighed, grateful for the opportunity to speak alone again. Leo had been very subdued over lunch, at which his wife and daughter had not been present.

'Not exactly.' He looked out across the tops of the Alhambra of marquees to the curve of wood-fringed hill in the distance where Mia was walking with Iris, two specks at this distance, a pack of dogs swarming around them. 'She said the gift of life is the greatest thing you can offer somebody you love.'

'What does that mean?' The jet lag had hit Ivan at last and he was struggling to keep his eyes open, great yawns tugging at his jaws.

'I'm not sure.' Leo set aside his knitting. 'But you need the gift of sleep, Van.' He glanced at the glasshouse in which Jacinta appeared to be singing folk songs, delighted to have such a receptive audience. 'Mamá will go for her nap soon. Forget coffee. Let's have a siesta too.'

There were now so many visitors and tradesmen at Wootton that there was barely a space left to park and nowhere on the estate guaranteed to offer any privacy apart from the furthest corner of the meadowland. That was where Iris and Mia were walking, the dogs racing around them as they waded through the sward being grown for hay-making, so high it tickled the backs of their knees. Reaching the shadow of the beech woods that marked the end of Wootton land, they turned to look down towards the river.

Mia, who hadn't stopped talking and crying since they'd set off, was now out of breath and eyeing her daughter with trepidation, arms wrapped tightly around herself, feeling chilly despite the impossibly muggy day, a storm lying dark and threatening on the horizon.

'It felt as though my world ended when Dom disappeared. It was only the thought of you that kept me going. The first time I saw your face I couldn't stop crying with happiness. You had the same expression of utter determination as he did. I never stopped believing that he was alive, even though I was no longer a part of that life.'

'And now he's back.'

'*If* it's him. Laney says I'm just imagining it.'

'I'm sure it is, Mum. I've heard the recordings. Here. You must listen to them too.' She pressed the little wooden antelope into her mother's hands. 'It's all on here. They call him Cloud Man in Kenya; Griff says what he does in the Mara is extraordinary. He takes on poachers. He sounds the most incredibly brave man.'

'He was.' Mia held the antelope up to her chest.

'*Is.*'

501

Mia stared at the river for a long time, watching the storm draw closer. 'I've lived my life again as though he never existed. It's what he wanted.'

'Is that why you never talked to me about him?' Iris was appalled. 'You did as he asked even though it meant keeping the full story from me?'

She shook her head. 'Forgive me. Talking about him just broke my heart. It still does. I thought telling you I had lots of boyfriends at college would make it easier to cope with the way he'd gone and the hurt it left behind. I didn't want you to inherit that. Perhaps he was right: better that he hadn't existed.'

'Then I wouldn't exist.'

'No!' Sobbing now, Mia wrapped her arms around her daughter. 'You made life worth living! Protecting you has been the most important thing in my world. Dom would never have done what he did if he'd known about you.'

'He thought you were going to graduate from Old Gate to become the greatest actress of your generation.' Iris pulled back, covering her mother's hand, which was gripping the antelope. 'It's all on here. The accident left him so badly disfigured, he thought he'd hold you back and burden you. He thought he was setting you free.'

Mia closed her eyes, knuckles whitening as she gripped the flash drive tighter.

'He says he always regretted writing to you.' Still holding her mother's hand, Iris started to tug her in the direction of the house. 'Come and listen to the recordings. I so want you to hear them.'

Mia stood her ground, eyes still shut. She looked as though she was praying. Letting go, Iris stepped back and watched her worriedly. 'Have you stopped loving him?'

'Never.'

'I think we should go to Kenya,' she said. 'Let's go and find him.'

Mia opened her eyes, as deep green as the beechwood canopy behind her. 'I'd be a stranger.'

'We know he wants to find you. He was here and in LA.'

'Because of this!' Mia held up the antelope, suddenly furious, her own storm breaking long before the one that was moving across the river. 'He had no desire to be found until this happened. And I will *not* listen to it. I can't bear to hear his beautiful voice again when I know he never wanted me to.'

Lifting her arm behind her head, she hurled the antelope into the woods, stepping back with the force of her throw so that she crashed into Iris. They watched in dismay as half a dozen dogs leapt up in eager pursuit, racing one another to retrieve it.

'You can't just throw the past away,' Iris insisted hotly. 'Dom exists. He wants to see you.'

'Forgive me, Iris,' Mia said, stumbling away. 'I can't let myself believe it just yet. I have to be strong for Leo. Laney's right: we have to get through the next twenty-four hours somehow.'

Iris set off in pursuit. 'Why live anything resembling a real life when we all can act one so skilfully?' Putting an arm around her mother as they walked towards Wootton, she whistled the dogs back, gazing at the beautiful old house. 'Your gilded cage awaits.'

'Leo and I had nothing when we married, you know that. We had each other and you and that was all we needed. We've always been the best of friends. I love him very much. He's the kindest man I know.'

'I love him too, but he's got Ivan now. It's not fair to make us keep covering for him.'

Stopping, Mia turned to her daughter. 'Iris, there's something else I must tell you. Leo has asked me to have his baby.'

Iris stared at her, wide-eyed and open-mouthed. It was as though the last half-hour had never happened: her eyes glowed with hope, still a little girl desperate to believe in fairy-tale twists. 'He wants us to be a family again?'

'I would be a surrogate mother so that he and Ivan can have a child. You know how much they want a family together.'

The fairy-tale twist went one turn too far, tightening Iris's heart-strings to breaking point. 'What do *you* want?'

'I want what's best,' Mia said carefully. 'Leo's been so kind to me.'

'Oh, Mum.' Iris hugged her. 'You don't have to pay him back. You don't have to buy your freedom. You just have to take it.'

'I'm frightened of living my life again. I've made so many mistakes.'

'I don't think you have a choice.' Iris leaned back and looked into the kind green eyes. 'You turn forty tomorrow. Haven't you heard? Life begins at forty.'

Mia smiled, resting her forehead against her daughter's so their noses touched. 'If anybody gives me the bumps I'll need resuscitating.'

'If Leo gives you a bump, we all bloody will.'

They collapsed with giggles, so overwhelmed by relief that they could hug and joke together again that they had to kneel down on the grass.

Wiping her eyes, Mia spotted Griff making his way towards them from the bottom of the meadow. 'Your handsome friend must think I'm terribly unwelcoming. I'll make up for it over supper, I promise. Ivan's offered to cook.'

'Would you mind if we just crashed out?' Iris said, turning away to hide the blush stealing through her cheeks. Seeing Griff in the distance now, her heart released a thousand new butterflies with wingspans as wide as her smile. 'We're both dead on our feet from travelling.' Hers felt readier to run and skip through a meadow than ever before.

'Of course, chuck.' Mia helped her up and kissed her cheek. 'It's always chaos the night before the gala, as you know – there's the fashion-show hats to pick up and Haff still hasn't done his presentation about the inner-city dressage schools. You two have a rest. There'll be time enough tomorrow. We will make it a good day, won't we?'

Iris nodded, eyes shining. 'We will. You have my word. I'll make damned sure of it.'

Her certainty reminded Mia so vividly of Dom that she felt light-headed, and it was a moment before she realised what Iris had called over her shoulder as she bounded away down the hill. 'I thought I'd put Griff in the Folly, if that's OK?'

'Haff's in there,' Mia called back, but Iris was already out of earshot, racing through the wild flowers in a very Laura Ingalls Wilder way. About to shout louder, Mia was distracted by one of her youngest rescue dogs returning from the woods covered with leaf mulch, proudly bearing the antelope flash drive in its mouth to drop at her feet. Starting after Iris, she hurled it away again, only to find it brought back. For two hundred yards, she played a reluctant game of fetch with her dogs, tripping over them, until she veered left to the riverbank and hurled the antelope into the reeds with a satisfying plop and a quack from an outraged duck.

By the time Mia walked back to the house, her mind was full of Dom again and she had forgotten about the double-booked Folly.

Haff was an impeccably neat house-guest. Years of travelling among a large band of exhibition riders in cramped horsebox living accommodation had lent him a military minimalism and order to which he still adhered as he travelled around Europe, competing and training clients. He always kept his suitcase beneath the bed, his towels folded on the rail, his clean breeches and shorts put away in a drawer. The only sign of his occupation at the Folly was a small washbag hanging from the back of the bathroom door and a pair of silk pyjama bottoms beneath the pillow on the bed, behind wispy muslin drapery, in a corner of the eccentric summerhouse.

Iris and Griff noticed neither as they burst through the door, kissing frantically, already pulling their clothes off.

'Jesus ... I ... want you ... so badly,' Griff moaned, liberating her from her shirt.

'I want... you ... too.' Iris dragged his T-shirt over his head. 'I've wanted to ... kiss here ... for so long.'

'We should ... have done this in Spain.'

'We can.'

'Oh please don't stop ...'

'Come up here.' She took his hand and led him across the room to where steps led up a little circular turret at the back of the Folly to a room, most of which was filled with a waist-high platform that housed a circular sunken bath in its centre. Surrounded by *trompe-l'oeil* panels featuring Moorish arches and paintings of white villages on hills sweeping down to the sea, the effect was pure Grenada. Griff expected Albéniz to start strumming out of hidden speakers. The only light came via a small mirrored ceiling dome, reflecting in the stormy afternoon sunlight that filtered in to cage them in rainbows. It was wildly over-the-top, but also incredibly sexy, especially when Iris turned a dial so that a huge ceiling rose pumped out a jet of steaming water, clouding through the spectrums to multiply them. They seemed to be kissing amid holographs.

Discarding the last of their clothes, they stooped into the mosaic pool, water flattening their hair to their heads and slipping between their eager mouths as they explored lips and skin, tongues tasting and fingers roaming in delighted wonder.

'You have ... the most beautiful ... body.' Griff dropped his head to kiss one small, pert nipple and the other until they hardened into perfect pink rosehips, then watched the water stream over them.

Iris perched on the edge of the sunken bath and reached behind her to where a mother-of-pearl tray contained luxury shower gels and bath oils. Selecting a bottle of Jo Malone Wild Fig & Cassis Body Wash, she popped open the top and Griff held his breath as he waited for her to decant it over her gorgeous body for him to rub into every corner until it lathered and slithered.

Instead, she aimed it at his chest and fired a long squirt, her green eyes glittering with excitement.

Bellowing in mock outrage, he selected a bottle of Pomegranate Noir for retaliation.

When they finally slotted together, breathless, hearts racing, laughter fading, they were the slipperiest of sweet-smelling lovers. Supported on the bath's rim, one leg pulled up, Iris bit her lip at the mounting pleasure peaks as she admired Griff sliding in and out of her. Then she looked into those dark eyes, unwavering in their bravery and honesty. They fitted together so perfectly. She felt each butterfly in her belly take off in delight before landing softly on her heart and folding out its wings to bask.

When Haff hurried into the Folly, he was far too preoccupied to notice a trail of steam floating down from the bathroom. Carrying a laptop that he'd just borrowed from Mia, with a big pile of notes about the Javiero Dressage Coaching Centre that he was supposed to transpose into a speech and slide show for the fund raiser the following day, he threw them all on to the table and checked his watch, stifling a yawn. He'd been working non-stop since daybreak, even skipping lunch so that he could drive to west Berkshire to rehearse with his friends from the Portuguese Equestrian Dance Company, who were performing a special display with him tomorrow. Skipping lunch was unheard-of for a Spaniard like Haff, skipping his siesta even less so. His service-station prawn sandwich was gurgling in his belly. Plugging in his iPod to listen to hip-hop flamenco, he clambered up on to the Folly's sleeping platform and lay back to power-nap.

'That's odd – I don't remember a computer being here.' Iris paused to look at the little Vaio on the table, rubbing a towel through her hair.

'I don't remember this room being here.' Griff took in the chandelier, open fire, squashy leather sofa and huge flat-screen television. 'This is some summerhouse.'

'It's supposed to be haunted by a devastatingly handsome Restoration dandy.' She leafed through the notes about the Devonshire Foundation, always amazed by the sums of money, which ran into many millions, that her parents' trust had raised for different causes over the years. Mia played down her work so much, but it had taken extraordinary commitment.

'You made that up!' Griff was laughing.

Iris loved the way the muscles on his chest moved, like a golden sea ruffled by the wind. 'It is haunted, honestly. The yew circle where this folly is built used to be a sword-fighting arena. Apparently some poor young nobleman bled to death having defended a lady's honour in a duel, and now wanders around white-faced at night, sometimes riding a black horse. I had a huge crush on him when I went through a Gothic phase after reading the *Twilight* series. I was always hanging around, hoping I'd bump into him.'

'Then I hope he steers clear tonight. He doesn't want another duel. I bet he was always ogling you through the ectoplasm.'

'It was a very one-sided relationship,' she confessed sadly. 'I used to drape myself on that sofa, imagining he would come and do delicious things with his cold fingers all over me.'

He eyed the sofa, eyebrows lifting pleasurably. 'You'd think he'd warm his hands first.' He blew slowly on his own.

Her eyes trailed along the length of his irresistible tanned torso to the red towel wrapped around his narrow hips and her smile widened as she saw the unmistakable bulge distorting its fluffy midst. 'It did get *very* cold in the middle of winter. I used to lie on the sofa in front of the fire wearing three pairs of tights, dreaming of ghost love.' She wove her way towards him.

'You needed somebody real to keep you warm.' He caught the corner of her towel and tugged it so that it came away.

'It got very, very cold. Imagine this in blue.' She held up her hands and glanced down at her naked body, so recently soaped, loved and filled but already craving more.

'Now my thoughts are very, very blue.' He took her hands and pulled her over the back of the sofa.

*

508

On the sleeping platform, Haff opened one eye and peered through the muslin, certain he'd just heard voices over the boom of his iPod, but he could see nothing. The computer was waiting there menacingly, paperwork fanned out beside it. His hopes of seducing Mia had been fading fast since her return from LA with her husband. Leisurely fantasies based around taking her to bed were no longer a siesta treat, and the prawn sandwich had clearly been slightly off: his belly was now clenching painfully. He needed fresh air. Heaving a sigh, he shuffled tracks to some soothing Rodríguez, clambered down and collected the paperwork to carry outside on to the raised decking at the front of the summerhouse, pausing to look across at the storm rumbling darkly on the horizon.

The blood was pounding through Iris's ears far too loudly for her to hear anything, apart from her crashing heart and fast breathing. The leather sofa was a nightmare to make love on. They kept shooting the seat cushions off it and landing on the hard-springed webbing base.

'Come to bed.' She slithered off Griff and held out her hand, then shrieked with laughter as he slid his arm around her and lifted her up to carry her across the room, kissing her all the way. Neither of them noticed that the computer had now disappeared, although they did detect that the bed smelled faintly of horse.

Chapter 52

Laney spent most of the short train journey from Maidenhead to Paddington locked in the loo, alternately crying off her make-up and reapplying it. Convinced that she was travelling without a ticket, the guard pounced on her when the train stopped at Ealing Broadway.

'This is a first-class ticket, madam,' he pointed out. 'You have your own loo to cry in.'

That made Laney want to weep more. She was ashamed of the rash, self-indulgent sod-it moment that had led her to press the touch-screen's 'VIPs only' rectangle on the ticket machine, thinking, Tonight is all about *me*! This is my fantasy. I deserve first class! With contrary speed, she'd very nearly not got on the train at all, tempted to rush home and change into ancient joggers to veg in front of *Brief Encounter*.

As soon as she arrived in Paddington she had to spend just thirty pence and twenty seconds in the ladies' loo to realise that her ten outfit changes before setting out that night had led to the wrong decision. The pretty flowered shift she'd originally bought for Iris's wedding, and which Simon had found so sexy, now swamped her like a chintz lampshade on a nightlight. The Boyle & Blunt bargain undies and stockings felt hot and itchy. Her hair, statically charged by too much nervous combing and the threatening storm, lay limply against her head at the front with a shark-fin kink at the back.

She was already running late, but she found herself racing across the concourse towards Monsoon. The staff were about to lock up and regarded her with alarm as she elbowed her way in, shark fin riding high.

'I know exactly what I want!' she insisted, diving through and grabbing the first dress she found. It was a fraction of the cost of the designer number she was wearing and gave off electric shocks all the way to the till, but she needed a new skin tonight.

'You do know this is a twelve?' the cashier asked kindly.

'Yes.'

'Would you like a gift receipt?'

Laney had to spend another thirty pence to discover that a twelve was still too tight, but it did up with a lot of tugging. The blues and turquoises brought out her eyes; a streak of red and a plunge neck added panache. In the long mirror, she had strange new hollows and curves, her face so much older than it had been when it was plump, pink and smiling.

'I don't smile any more,' she told her reflection, as travellers gave her a wide berth and the lavatory assistant loitered near by, fingering her two-way radio.

She reapplied her make-up with shaking hands, reminding herself that this was all about fantasy, those 5 a.m. Club moments when she had focused upon Richard HH whisking her up to his baronial Borders estate where she could indulge Hope in an idyllic childhood of tickling trout, climbing trees and riding ponies. She would be the sort of mother who did the school run and cooked high tea, read bedtime stories every night, and shared life with a self-confessed old-fashioned rogue who was also erudite, open, decisive and in control.

Before that came flirtation and seduction, she thought with a shiver, determined to summon her mojo as she exchanged a knowing look with her reflection and added another layer of lip-gloss, painting back the old Laney. Richard HH would whisk her up to his hotel room to be tickled, climbed and ridden, to exchange bedtime fantasies and be thrillingly controlling and decisive.

She studied her finished face. While a long way from the sort of well-preserved perfection Mia achieved, she looked far more as she'd hoped to, lips breaking into that rare smile, eyes ready to laugh and flirt instead of cry.

She hurried back up to the main concourse and headed automatically towards the tube before having another sod-it moment and about-turning towards the taxi ranks. It was just ten minutes to Blakes in a cab; she was late; she deserved it.

The smell of cigarette smoke hit her the moment she stepped out into the muggy air in the sunken taxi pass. She was so vividly reminded of sharing a last Camel Light with Simon before they'd gone to get on the milk train back to Old Gate College after night-clubbing that she pressed her fingers to her lips.

Queuing, she forced her mind back to the fantasy that now kept the dawn panic at bay, the long-range daydreams involving an idyllic life miles from Red Gables' tarpaulins and scaffolding, with a pretty writing room overlooking Richard HH's sleepy parkland and vast lake, watching him stalk around in his breeks with his shotgun or set up his easel to capture the waterfowl in gouache. She closed her eyes indulgently as her fantasy RHH looked up at her. To her horror, he now resembled Prince Charles.

Laney tried to rid herself of the image, scrunching her eyes more tightly shut to conjure a pepper-haired, breeks-wearing gentleman. As she did, something unexpected hijacked her fantasy. Climbing up the wisteria on the east-facing Georgian façade towards her writing-room window, rose clenched between his teeth, grey eyes like liquid platinum with the scorching heat of his love, came Simon.

'Cross over, please!'

Eyes snapping open, Laney found she'd reached the front of the queue and the taxi controller in his yellow tabard was trying to wave her to the little pedestrian island to take up position by a designated cab spot.

'I'll just go to the back of the queue again if that's all right.' She smiled apologetically, turning tail.

Last in line once more, she tried to rev up Richard HH at his easel, but HRH was still *in situ*, dabbing Hooker's green on his rough rag paper to capture some mallards, and Simon was making dramatic progress up the wisteria.

'Would you like *this* cab, missus, or are you going to the back of the queue again?'

'I'll go to the back again, thanks.'

Why was the queue so short after eight o'clock? Laney lamented, looking down the line and calculating that her husband would barely have scaled three more rungs of trellis by the time she reached the front again. When they arrived together in London, Simon always insisted on bounding up the steps to Praed Street to hail one, but she was of an altogether lazier disposition. He'd always tried to motivate her into his self-assured, idiosyncratic mindset, but she was a naturally cheery, cautious cynic. They were by turns optimist and pessimist, idealist and pragmatist, protagonist and victim. But he had always been her hero. In fantasies nobody else ever climbed up her wisteria.

No longer aware where she was going, she wandered back into the main station, listening to the echoing announcement listing all the stops to Penzance. For a ludicrous moment, Cornwall was the most tempting destination she could think of. But then her head filled with images of holidays there when she was first married, hours in bed pursuing silly running jokes and spinning daydreams between love-making, eating and beach-combing. Nowadays holidays were rare, high-stress feats of juggling four families' calendars. Even time off at home felt like a rushed coffee break with a workmate, hiding one's silent dread of impending redundancy.

The departures board offered her the opportunity to return home in twenty minutes. The taxi rank still offered her Richard HH in ten minutes. She tried to blot out a sudden mental image of Prince Charles nursing a gin sling at Blakes and pulling at his cuffs with an impatient grimace, one side of his mouth curling up in bemused disappointment.

Simon was her wisteria climber extraordinaire, she realised with a noisy sob. He'd saved her from Oscar. His rescue may have come months too late to liberate her from the day-to-day torture of living with a total egotist – the Bensons had been mid-divorce by the time Simon landed in LA – but he had gathered her into his arms and told her she was his one true love and that he was taking her home.

She fumbled in her handbag for her phone.

Dear Richard, she typed as she walked towards Platform 4, bumping into other passengers in her haste. I am the worst of all people because I bore my heart to you but not my soul. I bore myself sometimes.

She crammed her ticket into the barrier slot and shot through the gates, still typing.

I have a very fickle heart, but I'm a constant soul. I've only ever had one soulmate and that is my husband. I love him.

Blind with tears, she fell over a luggage trolley.

It is better that we never meet. Forgive me. L x

The diners in Blakes had been feeling rather sorry for the handsome man sitting alone at a table for two, looking at his watch and checking his phone in the conspicuously poised and mannered way that belied increasing vexation. He was a compelling figure, and immediately recognisable to many, beautifully dressed, the high-cheekboned face immaculately composed, but his extraordinary eyes dark with unease. He looked like a nobleman about to meet his fate on the guillotine, and many romantic female hearts around the dining room went out to him.

He quite lost their sympathy, however, when he let out a holler and pocketed his still-glowing phone, leaping from his chair and thundering out of the dining room at such speed that he upturned his table and cannoned off waiters. Throwing money at the maître d's desk as he passed, he was already shouting, 'Taxi!' long before he made it outside.

Laney was planning to take full advantage of the first-class loos on her return leg, heading towards the cubicle as soon as she boarded, intent on plundering First Great Western's toilet tissue to cry into.

'Madam, surely you must know that you cannot go in there while the train is stationary!' a voice barked from behind a *Telegraph*.

She froze, turning slowly to study the pinstripe trousers and very shiny shoes. When he lowered the paper briefly to turn a page, she saw the familiar white moustache and jutting chin of her Thames-cruiser nemesis. He was travelling on the 20.26 Paddington-to-Newbury train.

Retreating to a seat at the opposite end of the carriage, she reread her sent message to Richard HH, feeling as if she'd climbed a cliff face only to fall over a precipice. Yet with the fall came an overwhelming sense of relief. As soon as she was back at Red Gables, she was going to flush her Korean diet pills down the loo, along with her folic acid and chaste-tree berry, red clover and Siberian ginseng. Laney de Montmorency was going to stop rattling and start rolling back the years to find her *joie de vivre*.

Doors were slamming, the train engines revving as they prepared to depart. She mopped another leaking tear and gazed out of the window, watching a late passenger running along the platform to catch the train before it moved off. That distinctive lope was immediately recognisable, with the slight limp he publicly ascribed to a heroic rugby accident at school but was in fact the result of falling off a wall by his local Croydon chip shop when drunk as a teenager.

Making it through the first door just in time, he wove through the carriage as the train moved off.

'Simon.'

'Gosh – hi – wow.' He was flustered, no witty one-liner at the ready. His hair was wild and windswept from running, one side of his shirt collar was up, and there were florid streaks on each cheek.

'What a coincidence,' she stammered. 'I thought you'd have gone home hours ago.'

'Got a bit waylaid.' He sank into the seat opposite her, still breathless from running, his pale grey eyes searching her face. He seemed shell shocked.

Those dark-lashed eyes were so infused with pupil they were pure silver linings. Knowing how close she had come to betraying him, she couldn't bear to look at them, turning to stare out of the window instead as west London slid by, her throat so full of sackcloth and ashes that she could hardly speak. 'I almost did a terrible thing, Simon, a terrible, terrible thing.'

He moved to the seat beside hers, arms enfolding her, pulling her into the crook of his chin. 'Sssh, I know. I know, baby. But you didn't do it. And I love you.'

She stared at his shirt buttons, heart hammering. 'You know?'

He swallowed, pressing his lips to the top of her head. 'I almost did a terrible thing too.'

She pulled back and was blown away by the intensity of that pale, heartfelt gaze. The train was heading straight into the storm now, the lights flickering as lightning crackled and rain flicked on the windows.

'Could we both stop behaving badly for a bit, do you think?' she whispered.

Cupping her face in his hands, he pressed a kiss to her lips. 'You and I will always behave badly,' he breathed. 'We just have to do it together. A very wise man wrote to me not long ago suggesting that he would like to see a lot more of my wife, and I couldn't agree more.'

'Oh, God,' she whispered, closing her eyes as shame engulfed her.

'Actually, he wasn't that wise,' he muttered; 'he was a bloody fool. I can't tell you how much I've grown to hate him and how jealous I was that you opened your heart to him whenever I opened my inbox. I enjoyed receiving his emails far more than my own.'

She opened her eyes again. 'It was you!'

'Forgive me.' His eyes were tortured. 'You were hiding so much of yourself away, it was the only way I could find of reaching you.'

'Was it some sort of fidelity test?' Her voice shook with mounting anger. 'A honey trap?'

'God, no! That first message was a pathetic ruse to persuade you to take more of a part in my public life. I invented RHH to try to coax you out of hiding. I thought he might succeed where I'd failed. When I have you with me it makes such a difference, and I know it's hard with Hope to think about, but you've more or less stopped coming to anything I do. I've felt so selfishly neglected and shut out.'

'It's not just Hope, it's my work.' Laney looked away guiltily, thinking of her over-sensitive reaction to all the vicious internet jibes about her weight, the *Daily Mail* side panel of shame, the Burley Hornet and the lascivious ladies constantly insinuating that her duty to her husband was to be desirable and her failure to be so could lead to imminent replacement.

'I know how hard you work.' His pale eyes sought hers again. 'And I know how many extra hours you have to put in behind the scenes to make my life run smoothly, how much you have to juggle and compromise, and how unhappy that makes you. Richard HH was supposed to cheer you up and help me out. Instead I created a monster.'

'I tried to make him go away.'

'I know. But you made me laugh too much to let go. You were so sweet and honest in your replies and I was so shabby spinning you along. I felt terrible. Suggesting lunch was my get-out strategy. I thought you'd never agree and that would be an end to it.'

'But I did.' She groaned, anger turning to shame as she remembered her flirtatious replies. 'It was the dying flowers. I thought it was an omen, saying time was running out, like the petals dropping in Hope's *Beauty and the Beast* video.' She flushed at the memory of her hyped-up fear that her prime was withering away.

'What dying flowers?' He was nonplussed.

'One of the first messages you sent contained a link to a page with a vase of damask roses. Each time I checked back, there were fewer petals.'

'I just thought they were some pretty flowers. I had no idea the bloody things were dying. You know how rubbish I am on the internet.'

'For a man incapable of managing his website inbox, you're remarkably good at mastering email on your phone.'

He reached up to stroke her cheek with his long artistic fingers. 'Richard HH was right when he said I'm a thoughtless bastard who takes you for granted. He's always been my guilty conscience as well as my guilty secret. His words are mine, my thoughts, my advice and my fantasies.'

'Oh, God, I wrote porny scenes for you!'

'I thoroughly enjoyed them, although the thought that you might want to do them with somebody else made me jealous as hell.'

'He never had a face,' she said quickly, 'just tweed breeks and nipple tassels and a sense of humour that made me adore him.'

'I kept thinking you'd guess it was me. But it got completely out of hand. I wanted to hear from you all the time. They've been the best conversations we've had in years.'

'I felt like I'd known him all my life. I trusted him.'

'He felt the same way, even when you were with that idiot play-boy Oscar sent. Although I – I mean he – was bloody jealous.'

'I felt in love.'

'He loves you too.' He kissed her very slowly and thoroughly, thunder rolling around them.

'I wanted to have an affair with my own husband!' she gasped in amazement.

'You still can.' He started to kiss her again.

She laughed. 'Is it too late to go back to Blakes?'

'Far too late. You'll be naked by Slough.' He let out a growl of delight as his hand crept up under her skirt and discovered the stockings.

As she kissed him back with increasing abandon, a throat was cleared noisily beside them. 'For goodness' sake! I shouldn't need to remind you that a first-class carriage is *not* the place for frottage.'

They pulled apart in surprise as Moustache Man marched past en route to the buffet.

Simon was looking at Laney again, eyes shining. 'My wife deserves first-class frottage.' Exchanging a long, naughty look, the Demons collapsed into silent laughter.

Wiping tears from his eyes, Simon pulled her in under his arm.

'What were you going to do if I'd turned up in the restaurant?' she asked.

'Buy you dinner, probably.' He tucked her hair behind her ears. 'I'm a terrible comfort eater, as you know.'

518

'Me too.'

'Not recently. I've been seeing far too little of you in every sense. You look utterly beautiful, but please don't lose any more weight. I keep thinking you're going to slip through my fingers.'

Head hanging, she told him about the diet pills. 'I'm going to flush them down the loo.'

'Too right you are.' He was appalled. 'It's so bloody dangerous taking things like that! You've always had a beautiful body. No wonder you bit my head off every time I suggested you were over-doing the cycling lately. God, I'm an idiot. I thought it was all Bradley Wiggins's fault. I was going to start letting down your tyres.'

'The pills have made me feel deathly,' she admitted, staring down at her hands. 'I know I have to do it the right way or not at all. But I love the cycling. Perhaps I'll even start horse-riding again with Mia. I've never dared try because I was too fat.'

'You were not too fat!' he protested. 'And you've always ridden me beautifully.'

She stared at her hands. 'I think we should stop trying for a baby, Simon.'

Covering her hands gently with his, he said nothing.

'We'll still make love a lot, and laugh a lot and talk a lot and comfort-eat a lot.'

He pressed his lips to her ear, whispering, 'I want what you want.' Then he pulled his chin back in sudden recognition. 'Actually, I spoke with somebody today who would very much like to watch us do all those things on a pretty much daily basis – at least, they didn't mention making love, but the rest were manda-tory.'

She sagged back in her seat with a sigh. 'Don't tell me Malin wants her boyfriend to move in?'

Tutting, he reached across and turned her face towards his so their noses brushed and they went cross-eyed, an intimate grimace they'd shared since their first ever kiss. 'Lightbulb TV are pulling the plug on *Dinner Party Planners*.'

'Oh, hell.' That meant a huge cut in their income. They would definitely have to sell the house now.

'But they're about to make a pilot for a live daytime cookery magazine show they're describing as *Good Housekeeping* meets *This Morning*. They had lined up that ghastly bankrupt sleb chef with the hair transplant as presenter, but he's dropped out because his super-injunction is getting a bit too much Twitter interest again.' He cleared his throat and studied his nails.

'What have you been up to, Simon?'

'It's a great-sounding show. The host challenges couples to out-cook one another, profiles new chefs and reviews recipes, tests products, goes out and about researching great British food – I'll insist on a no-pie clause in my contract.'

'So they want you to do it?'

'Just the pilot for now, but it's a start. They've even got a new title – *The Demon Cooks*.' He didn't quite meet her eye. 'There is just one catch . . .'

She gazed at him in sudden alarm, panic rising, wondering if 'cooks' was a verb or a noun. She was happy on radio, but television was her nemesis. 'I will not be Fanny to your Johnnie.'

'Actually, it's the house they want me to do a double-act with.'

'They want Red Gables?' She laughed. 'It's only got half a roof.'

'But it has one hell of a kitchen. The exec producer was at the party the other day and fell in love with the place. Now they want to film the pilot there. If this takes off, the place really will pay for itself and school fees on top, and you and I won't have to work such crazy hours. We'll both be working from home.'

She thought about her submerged laptop full of creative ideas, all destined to be discounted or ditched, now flood-damaged stock in every sense. Maybe she wouldn't have to sell *Dalrymple Two* to Oscar for a fraction of its value after all. Having a husband cooking at home was a great idea. It was one of the things she'd missed most as their mutual work diaries filled up. Now it could *be* work.

'Let's do the pilot,' she agreed, 'but if it leads to anything, we can't let any cameras in the house during weekends or school holidays, and they can't show Hope on screen.'

He kissed her victoriously. 'They'll show a lot of hope, but none of our children.' He lifted up his phone, finger quickfire on the screen.

Laney watched him suspiciously. 'What are you doing?'

'Tweeting,' he said matter-of-factly, not looking up.

'About us?'

'I'm proud of you.'

'I do *not* want to be tweeted about,' she huffed. 'Shouted about, sung about, eulogised about, fine. Tweeted about, no. I deserve more than a hundred and forty characters. It's demeaning.'

'You know I'm a slave to my timeline these days.'

'Exactly. Even the pharmacist in Burley reads your tweets about me. I'd rather have a sonnet.'

'"She's funny and warm and sexy and canny,"' he read aloud as he typed. '"I'll always be a Johnnie to her Fanny." Genius! I'll have to do the other twelve lines in – oi!'

She snatched the phone away just as Moustache Man came back from the buffet, shooting them a disapproving look as he staggered past with a hot sausage roll and a miniature bottle of Bordeaux. Then he did a double-take as he recognised Laney.

Her inner naughty schoolgirl took over. 'My *fanny*?' she gasped at Simon, rolling her eyes and holding the phone away. 'How very dare you?'

He took his cue. 'Well, you did say you didn't want to get pregnant, darling.' He gave her a devilish look and she felt love burst from her chest as he went on, 'So we must have a johnny . . . '

Unaware of Moustache Man's glowering presence, he launched into another kiss, hand delving beneath her dress again and hitching it up to reveal her stockings.

Please say it, Laney prayed, as she kissed him back with all her heart.

'By all things sacred, madam—' was all she heard before her own and Simon's laughter deafened her to any more.

'We'll never stop behaving badly,' she agreed with glee. 'I just hope to God they have a bleep delay on *Demon Cooks*.' She was still holding his phone and Simon watched as she started tapping the screen.

'What are you doing? I have nothing to hide, I promise.'

'I know,' she muttered, 'which is why I'm deleting your Twitter account. Our private life isn't a status update any more, Simon.' She threw the phone back on the table. 'Your feed is no longer for public consumption. Tonight you're off air.' Curling her arms around his neck, she lifted her mouth to his.

'I can hardly breathe already.' His lips landed against hers and the Demons kissed all the way from Hayes to Maidenhead, blissfully unaware than at least half the carriage was tweeting feverishly about them.

Chapter 53

Dougie had missed his horses enormously while in LA. Having flown into Heathrow as the sun set, he drove straight to the yard from the airport, visiting each in their stables, pulling ears, scratching necks, checking legs and coats, talking all the while with the low, reassuring tone he reserved only for his most trusted friends. More than one ex-girlfriend had pointed out that he was much kinder to horses than women, which had always irritated him enormously, although he secretly conceded that he understood them far better. And after this enforced separation, he knew categorically that he couldn't survive without them. He had already lined up a barn for them in LA as soon as he could square it with Rupe and raise the money to fly them out. He was equally unsure that he could survive much longer in La-La Land without Iris.

He knew he had to win her back. She was just the same as him, endlessly chasing rainbow-ends. Dougie missed her positivity and drive, the way she forged her own path, not caring what others thought. He had envisaged them as the new Hollywood Brit power couple, the Leomia of their generation, but whereas being with Iris opened doors, on his own Dougie found himself at endless castings where he was asked to open his shirt before he opened his mouth.

Yesterday he'd been offered his first film role – admittedly a modest one, as second sidekick to a muscle-man action star, but the film had a major league budget, and Abe saw it as a huge personal career achievement to place an unknown actor so lucratively. As far as Dougie could tell from the script, his part involved running in and out of rooms shooting a variety of weapons, shouting, 'Motherfucker!' and jumping sideways when things exploded. He now just wanted to stay in England and ride his horses until he'd earned their passage to Tinseltown.

Grabbing a head collar, he went to see the herds out in the fields in the gathering dusk, his Friesian black pearls moving towards him like shadows, so gentle, passive and affectionate, so unlike anything in LA. He saved the longest reunion for Harvey, the herd alpha and his team's senior stunt horse, a white moon that parted the black clouds in the field when he recognised his master and charged up. Dougie's most loyal servant and ally, Harvey was increasingly short-sighted and hard of hearing these days, as long-toothed as he was long-suffering but with a heart still as bold as a colt's. Dougie would ride him in the Wootton Gala, in full armour. Now semi-retired, Harvey enjoyed a few days' hunting over the winter and only came out to perform tricks on special occasions, most of his days spent languishing in the fields. When he knew he was on call, like now, he lifted himself up from a leg-resting, slump-backed sixteen-two lawnmower to well over seventeen hands of neck-arching, skittish battle-charger.

Clipping the head collar on him, Dougie led him back towards the yard for a bath, laughing as the old horse plunged and danced beside him, making sure the black pearls knew the white diamond was first in line again.

'Going into battle tomorrow, old fellow,' he said, patting his neck, which glowed salmon pink in the last rays of the evening sun.

Dougie had spent much of his transatlantic flight writing the speech that he was planning to make the following day. It was short, but impassioned and hugely heroic, with no motherfuckers or explosions whatsoever. He saw himself as the masked Desdichado riding into the tournament to conquer all and claim Lady Rowena as queen before unmasking himself to reveal that he had been heroic Ivanhoe all along. He was convinced Iris would be won over. He just had the slight problem of making sure he wasn't recognised before taking his cue.

The working-lights illuminated the rented yard as if it were a sports stadium, and Rupe was whistling along flatly to Coldplay on the radio as he loaded the horses' display tack into the lorry's lockers, heavily embellished Portuguese bridles and the Australian stock saddles they used because they were almost impossible to fall off. 'I hope the nudie models can ride through a storm,' he drawled, listening to the thunder circling.

'Why exactly are they naked?'

'The hat designer thinks her bonnets will look better that way – apparently she's *very* particular. Mummy wore one of hers to Ascot once. It looked like a dinner plate over her face. She couldn't see a thing and ended up walking into the Gents behind Sir Henry Cecil. The good news is the hat designer won't be there tomorrow.' He cocked his head cheerily, like a gun dog listening for shots.

'And the bad news?' Dougie demanded, knowing Rupe's stupidity of old.

He cocked his head the other way, hearing the shots without changing his cheery expression. 'Bit of a cock-up on the models front.'

'I thought they were polo-playing, stunt-riding ex-girlfriends of yours?'

'Yah, well, thing is, almost all my ex-girlfriends hate me,' Rupe explained affably, 'so they said no, basically.'

'You do *have* models lined up?'

'Oh, yah – all under control. Mummy sorted it. Apparently her local hunt did a calendar last year to raise money and some of the female mounted followers took their kit off to pose behind wheelbarrows and so forth. They were all frightfully game for this. They've signed disclaimers saying they're happy without hard hats, and we've promised to cover nipples and—' He whistled and pointed to his groin. 'A very nice lady called Cynthia has sent me the itinerary.' Rupe checked his iPhone. 'We're part of the afternoon entertainment and must be there no later than midday. There's a charity auction and some speeches over lunch, then the fashion show straight afterwards. You'll be in full armour and lead out the girls, do a few circuits while they play some computer-voiceover thingy on a big screen. Then it's back to the box and we head off with a fat cheque.'

Leaning back against Harvey, cigarette dangling between his lips, Dougie smirked. He had no intention of leaving Wootton in a horsebox. He intended to stay and reclaim his rightful place in Iris's bed. To achieve that, he would get to try out his speaking part. He patted the speech folded in his pocket and reached back to scratch Harvey, who disapproved enormously of smoking and gave him such a sharp nudge with his nose from behind that the cigarette flew from his mouth. The horse took two steps forward to extinguish it under one metal shoe.

Standing on the ramp, Rupe looked up as thunder rolled in the far distance, but the sky remained uniform navy blue. 'Weather's drawing in.'

Dougie could see the stars starting to gleam. It was too early in the year for Orion the hunter, but he recognised Pegasus as he looked east towards Wootton.

'Don't forget my suit of armour,' he called to Rupe as he led Harvey into the wash-box.

*

Mia's thoughts wouldn't stop whirring, jumping between Dom, Leo and the gala with dizzying velocity. Her need for order and certainty was being assaulted from all sides. Mostly she thought about Dom; his face was in her mind's eye all the time, his voice in her ears, his hands on her body. She knew he'd been badly injured, that he must have changed beyond recognition, and more than just physically: his role in life was no longer speaking others' words but inspiring lives and fighting injustice, the entertainer and political fighter rolled into one. In her head, he was still her Dom and always would be. Now that he was back in her mind and hijacking her heart, she couldn't let him go. She hugged him to her like a cloak of dreams, protecting her from the stress of a hundred different demands on the night before the gala.

The only way she could cope was to act her way through it, adopting a character of calm serenity, blending Portia's sharp mind and Rosalind's charm as she tackled the constant texts and calls with lightning speed. Her committee had most of it in hand, and anything they didn't, she'd decided it was too late to change.

'Bibi Cavendish is still insisting her hats cannot be shown with another designer's clothes and she won't release them until we agree,' fretted the stalwart in charge of the fashion show.

'I'll get someone to pick up some pashminas in Morley first thing,' she soothed.

'The computer guys are still here and want to have a dry run through the PowerPoint presentations on the big screen.'

'They're not written yet. Tell them it'll be fine.'

Wootton was full of people, but none whom Mia longed to have around her. These all needed charming, supporting, thanking and feeding. Ivan's promised supper had yet to materialise as he slept off his jet lag. Leaving Jacinta happily revving around with a takeaway menu taking orders, Mia ran upstairs to find Leo, the magical cloak clutched ever tighter around her tense shoulders as she remembered Dom's straight-talking integrity and that he was never afraid to make a difficult decision. But thinking about him meant the tears started again, so that by the time she'd reached the first stair-turn she was out of character and back to herself.

Mia and Leo had always slept in separate rooms, connected by a shared dressing room the size of a double garage, scene of much shared hilarity and long, happy styling sessions. Marching through it, she hammered on his door.

'Forgive me, Leo, but I won't have your baby and I think you should come out!' she cried tearfully.

There was a long pause and eventually Leo stepped from his room, blinking anxiously, one side of his face creased from sleep. 'OK, so I'm out now.'

'I meant come out of the closet.'

'I rather think I've just stepped into it.' He indicated the walls of cupboards, playing for time. But he was watching her nervously, eyes like saucers: his most loyal ally was finally making a stand.

'It's crazy to sacrifice your personal happiness for a career you've started to hate,' she implored. 'Your mother *will* survive the shock. You should do it tomorrow.'

'What? In front of everybody at the gala?' He turned pale, leaning against a tallboy.

Mia reached out to touch his kind face, still ludicrously handsome despite sleep-creases and stubble. 'You keep asking me what I want for my fortieth birthday,' she said gently. 'Well, this is it. I want you to come out. Not in front of everybody. Just those you love. And I *love* you, Leo.'

There was a sob from behind the door to Leo's bedroom and Ivan appeared, tears streaming down his face into his moustache. 'Oh, Mia! You have *no idea* what you saying that has just done to me. I am *in bits.*'

Guilt coursed through her. 'I'm so sorry I can't agree to carry a baby for you both.' She stroked his huge, shaking shoulder as Leo embraced him. 'I need to start another life, but not that one.'

'That's not why I'm crying!' he howled. 'That was Leo's idea. He thought it might make you happy. I always said you were too old, plus you obviously pass on the curly-hair gene. It's what you said about the birthday gift. That is just the sweetest thing I ever heard. Come here, Mia baby. I love my stepwife.' A muscular arm shot out and he drew her into a group hug.

On the decking outside the Folly, Haff was studying the sky fretfully as the gathering stormclouds covered the last red streaks of sunset, like black ashes over embers. Short of a typhoon, he was determined his WAGs would perform the quadrille, although he rather hoped the clouds would open just as his public address was about to start so that everybody rushed home without listening to it. He found public speaking, especially in English, nerve-racking. He was feeling increasingly ill, although he couldn't tell if it was nerves or the prawn sandwich.

In the past two hours, he had studied the sky a great deal more than his laptop, and now the battery was running flat as the storm approached. He had prepared video and photograph footage to accompany the short presentation Mia had asked him to make about the Javiero Dressage Coaching Centre, and was now worried that it was about to vanish without being backed up.

The Folly was in near-darkness. He picked up the laptop, stepped into his yard mules and headed to the main house to ask for help.

'Fuck, I just saw the ghost.' Griff blinked hard, still half awake.

'Are you sure?' Iris propped herself up on one shoulder, drawing the muslin aside. She peered out into the darkness. 'I can't see anything.'

'A white face came floating through here, I swear. I couldn't see a body.'

'I don't think he's a head-only ghost. At least, I hope not. What a waste when I had all those fantasies about his cold fingers.'

'Are you not at all scared?' he whispered, as though the ghost would jump out and shout, 'Boo!' if he spoke louder.

'Nope.' She turned to look at him in the half-light. 'You mean to say the man who's faced cannibals and poachers and kidnappers is frightened of ghosts?'

They jumped at a crack of thunder.

'Are you frightened of storms, too?' she breathed in his ear, making all the little hairs stand up, along with another part of his anatomy.

'Of course not,' he insisted, and started at a flash of lightning.

'You know what they say about storms?' She sat up beside him and slid one leg across until she was astride his hips. 'You just have to ride them out.'

When Haff hurried in through the back entrance to Wootton, the first person he encountered was Leo Devonshire, looking troubled as he talked on his cell phone.

'No, Abe, I am *not* going to change my mind. The answer is still no. Tell them I'm not going back and that's final. They can do what they like.' He rang off and smiled apologetically at the little Spaniard. '*¿Está todo bien, Haff?*'

'I need back-up,' he said urgently.

'Why? Have we got intruders?'

'Computer. I must save file.' He nodded outside as lightning lit the windows.

'Oh – right.' Leo remembered the Pegasus flash drive in his pocket, unaware that it held his own driveway's old CCTV footage. 'I don't think this is needed any more. You take the wing off, see?'

'*Gracias.*' Haff slotted it into the port and started clicking to save as thunder clattered overhead and the lights dimmed.

'There's a huge Chinese meal being laid out in the dining room,' Leo said. 'I hope you'll join us.'

Haff's stomach was still doing battle with the prawn sandwich and let out a gurgle of dissent. 'I never eat the night before a big competition. Is the same with tomorrow. I ride better when hungry, yes?'

Leo nodded. 'I don't blame you. I feel much the same way about acting.' A smile broke across his face, as unexpected as the lightning outside. 'In which case, tonight I'm going to stuff my face!' He patted Haff affectionately on the shoulder and wandered back towards the hubbub in his house.

Stomach churning, Haff hurried back to the Folly, the laptop still glowing in his hands. As he clambered up the steps, the first big drops of rain started to fall.

He raced inside, eager to make it to the loo. As he did so, there was a terrified scream.

A light was switched on and then they were plunged into darkness as a power cut wiped out Wootton's electricity supply.

'I'll get the cold-fingered bastard!' shouted a deep voice.

Terrified, Haff fled, racing across the lawns towards the safety of the stable yard.

Chapter 54

When Hope had shown her new babysitter around Red Gables earlier that evening she'd reminded Chloe vividly of her younger self, trotting from room to room in the big, chaotic house, explaining her parents' ambitious plans and reducing Chloe to tears of laughter more than once with her own ideas of how to enhance the space: 'Daddymon wants oat panelling and packet floors, and Mummy and me want a Disney Princess ballroom with furniture that talks and lots of sandal ears.'

'You mean chandeliers?'

Most of the rooms in the extraordinary house were still uninhabitable. On the ground floor, the Demons appeared to live in the huge kitchen and one bombsite of a makeshift office. Chloe was hardly surprised Laney escaped to the boathouse so often.

'Mummy's computitator got dropped in the river yesterday,'

Hope had explained sadly. 'She said she lost all her work, but the dog saved *Dalrymple*.'

Chloe had stared at her in shock, then turned to look at Kensington and Chelsea, who'd panted up at her. 'What dog?'

But Hope didn't know and was much keener to talk about ponies. Once she'd settled her in bed, Chloe wandered around the kitchen and office, glancing half-heartedly at the piles of papers and clutter in case anything doggy jumped out, but she had no real enthusiasm for the task. She felt like a common thief. She knew that she had struck a deal with her father, and he would be proud that she had got into Red Gables already with an opportunity to snoop, but she suspected that his story about Laney taking the film script without his permission was not the whole picture. Iris certainly didn't seem to think so. Now she'd had a look, she could stop, she told herself. That was all she'd promised to do.

The storm was breaking at last, thunder seeming to shake the house around her, the sky lighting up outside. Standing in the Demons' kitchen, she found herself plunged into darkness.

With no idea of the geography of the room, she walked straight into the big peninsula, almost winding herself. She felt along the shelves and drawers for a torch, fingers cautious in case she encountered glasses or sharp knives. In a drawer full of napkin rings, her hand closed around what felt like a small model animal.

The lights came on.

Chloe was holding a black plastic dog. She already knew that if she pulled at each end it would come apart to reveal a flash drive. She wanted to stuff it back into the drawer, but she could imagine her father's face wreathed with pride, his bear hug, his undivided attention on her for the first time in months and his open acknowledgement as he collected his Best Comedy Oscar that he owed it 'all to my clever daughter, Chlo, a chip off the old block'. And she remembered the terms of their deal. She couldn't back out. She needed his help too badly.

She'd just plugged the back end of the dog into her tablet's USB drive and was clicking her way through to its contents to copy them when Hope appeared, woken by the thunder. 'I'm frightened. What are you looking at? Can I stay?'

She hurriedly crammed the tablet into her duffel bag and held out an arm. 'Would you like some hot chocolate?'

'Are you going to have a gin and tonic? Mummy always has a gin and tonic when I have hot chocolate. She says it's what grown-ups do.'

'I think I'll have a hot chocolate too.'

'Are you not grown-up yet then?'

'I don't feel very grown-up right now,' she admitted.

Five minutes later they were cuddled up together on the kitchen sofa with the dogs when Laney and Simon stumbled in, far earlier than Chloe had expected, sopping wet and kissing like teenagers. Simon tried to hide his frustration when he realised the babysitter had not only failed to get their child to sleep, but also needed driving home.

'Where's Malin?'

'Self-defence class,' Laney said, rushing across to kiss Hope. 'I'll take you straight up to bed, my darling.' She threw her arms round her sleepy daughter while Simon let out a deep sigh, clearly having hoped such a statement would be directed at him.

He was as charming as ever, driving Chloe back to the Obelisk, asking her about university and her placements, telling her how marvellous it was to see her at Red Gables at last. 'I think it's absolutely wonderful that you're getting to know Hope,' he said, as they chased the storm. 'Laney's so thrilled. It's broken her heart that you two haven't been close.'

'She's a nice kid.'

'So's her big sister. I hope we see a lot more of you. We're just coming through a bit of a tough patch.' He cleared his throat. 'This is a real icing-on-the-cake thing for Laney, you and Hope making friends. She works so hard and she gets very few breaks. I'm tremendously proud of her.'

Suddenly Chloe saw that tears were streaming down his cheeks. She pretended not to have noticed, uncertain what to do. 'Mind that tree,' she pointed out helpfully as they started to weave around on the Obelisk's long drive.

'Sorry.' Simon laughed, mopping his face with his cuffs. 'It's the Russian ancestry.' He fell back on the old de Montmorency myth as standby, a family tree which Chloe knew was as artifical as a plastic fir hung with baubles at Christmas, but which the public still adored, herself included. 'We all cry. You only have to watch Chekhov, Chloe – in fact, I recommend you do. *Three Sisters* is a real nail-biter.'

Chloe thought guiltily about the dog's bottom still plugged into the tablet. She reached inside her duffel bag and her fingers closed around it, but she couldn't bring herself to hand it back, terrified that if she confessed to stealing, the Demons might stop her seeing Hope again.

Instead she leapt from the car with a gruff farewell as soon as they reached the Obelisk, running through the pelting rain. Then, waiting for the lift, she looked back at the tail lights of the Demons' car: if a man cried because he was so proud of her, she knew she would have found true love.

She summoned Skype on her tablet as soon as she was inside. It was lunchtime in LA and he was online on his cell phone.

'Dad, I've found it.'

'Already? You star! The car's yours.'

'I said I didn't want a new car. You already gave me what I want.' She looked out of the huge windows to the garage hangar where a large, high-sided white trailer was now parked, its contents protected from the elements by tarpaulins and bungees. The weather could ruin everything, she thought, looking down at the maps on the table in front of her. 'But I do need something else.'

'New teeth? Boob job? Name it.'

'I want credit where credit's due, Dad.'

*

'Wow.' Griff fell back against the pillows.

'Wow,' Iris agreed breathlessly.

Exhausted, they lay side by side, sweat cooling on their chests, hearts slowing towards normal.

'Poor old Ptolemy, missing out on that,' chuckled Griff. 'I'd take mortality any time.' It was intended as a joke, referring to the cruel twist in the Ptolemy Finch movies whereby the boy hero risked losing his immortality if he kissed his comely sidekick, but to Iris it was a reminder of everything she longed to forget.

She lay in silence staring at the ceiling before turning her back to him.

'What is it?'

'You did *not* just sleep with Purple, Griff. You slept with me.'

'I know, Iris.' He wrapped his arms around her, kissing her shoulder. 'I'm sorry. It was supposed to be funny.'

'Well, it wasn't.'

There was another long pause.

'You know it's not Purple I'm falling in love with,' he said quietly.

Her heart thundered far louder than the passing storm, lightning flashing in her head. Love. He felt it too, and he was brave enough to say it out loud, her lion-hearted Griff. As she turned to kiss him, her phone rang on the bedside table.

'Leave it.' He kissed her deeper.

'It might be Chloe.' She wriggled away to snatch it up before it cut out.

'I love you with all my heart, Riz.' It was Dougie's languid voice. 'I can't bear how bad life feels without you. I'll do anything to have you back. Please don't forget that.'

She hung up and switched off her phone.

'Was it Chloe?' Griff asked, lifting his head.

'Voicemail service,' she said quickly.

As Griff enfolded her in a muscular arm, she curled tightly into him, loving how protected she felt, yet riddled with confusion.

Chapter 55

On the morning of the gala, Haff was woken just after seven by a phone call from Mia in tears. 'Where are you?' she sobbed.

'Good question.' He looked around blearily, then remembered he'd ended up in the Wootton horsebox after some confusion involving a man chasing him from the Folly insisting he was a ghost.

'I need you!' Mia was sobbing.

Haff sat up in bed and groaned. Typical! The beautiful Mrs Devonshire had finally come to the boil when he had spent the night alternating between a back-breakingly uncomfortable mattress and sitting on a chemical loo. His body ached so much, he could barely move. 'Ssh, *cariña*.' He wondered if he was capable of standing up. 'I am not far away.'

'We've lost two quadrille riders!'

He made it up on the third attempt, then sat down in shock as he took in what she was saying. 'There has been an accident?'

'Kerri Hughes has just phoned me. The *Daily News* is running a story today accusing her husband of having an affair with Gabby Santos da Costa. All hell's broken loose her end. There are paparazzi everywhere.'

'So? They can still ride. I stand on podium for team bronze between two warring mistresses and it was all good.'

'Of course they can't ride, Haff! It's a disaster. We'll have to pull it and you can do a longer ridden display or something.'

'It will go ahead as planned. Leave it with me.' He hurried outside, grunting and groaning as he tracked down Vicente, who was in the stallion barn mixing breakfast feeds. 'You and I will ride the quadrille, *mi amigo*.' He explained the crisis. 'We will take the places of Kerri and Gabby. We both know the routine. Nobody will spot the difference.'

Vicente looked doubtful, glancing down at his chest and then across at Haff's, but he nodded. 'You are the boss.'

He phoned Mia straight back to announce that the problem was solved. '¡Feliz cumpleaños!'

Mia laughed. 'That has indeed made my birthday much happier already. You are magnificent, Haff. And I'm sure you'll look very dashing in a fiesta dress.'

He shuddered. 'I am red-blooded Mediterranean. We're not like your British men who like to dress up as ladies at every opportunity. I will phone around for *campero* costume.'

'Don't get much camper than a frilly dress, chuck,' Mia teased, then agreed to phone Sylva Rafferty and get her to Wootton quickly so that the new line-up could rehearse together before the guests started arriving.

Haff stretched his stiff legs by taking his presentation notes and the slide show to the marquee where the computer geeks were setting up, then marched to the Folly to have a much-needed shower and pick up his breeches and boots.

He went straight to the bathroom, failing to notice the couple asleep behind the muslin on the sleeping platform.

'You're not going to believe this,' Griff yawned, 'but the ghost is having a shower now. Listen. He's moaning in pain.'

'That's a Spanish flamenco song,' Iris corrected, sitting up groggily. She'd fallen asleep with her phone beneath her cheek and it had switched itself back on. It was flashing with a text message.

I love you with all my heart, Riz. xxx

She deleted it. There was another text, this time from her mother, demanding to know where she was and asking if she or her new friend could pick up some hats urgently that morning, then call in at the Burley deli for twenty croissants, and eggs for the *torrijas* that Jacinta insisted were cooked in Leo's honour. However many crises raged around her, Mia Devonshire was in full-throttle, multi-tasking gala-hostess mode. Two last-min subs needed for quadrille, she had added as a PS. Can you two vacate the Folly so that one of them can fetch his breeches?

Then she spotted the silk pyjamas poking out from beneath the pillow. 'Oh, fuck.' She turned to Griff, horrified. 'The ghost is a house-guest.'

The previous night's storm had left the gardens at Wootton sparkling, as though they had been pressure-washed and glossed especially for the gala.

Overnight, discreet signs had sprung up guiding guests along the back lane to the rear entrance, where a security team was already in place, ensuring that nobody entered without an invitation or a pass.

Returning from Henley in the Devonshires' huge off-roader, which had all the fashion-show hats and accessories piled in the back, Griff was forced to phone Iris for a pass. A few minutes later, she limped up with a luminous pink wrist tag and climbed in beside him. 'Apparently we have to wear one of these *at all times*.' She strapped it around his broad wrist. 'Sylva Rafferty's handbag dog had already eaten both hers and the Rock Godfather's and puked them up in a potted bay, but I don't suppose anybody's going to throw *them* out for not showing their ID.'

Griff ignored a parking steward, who was shrugging on a luminous tabard and waving at him to a field, and drove to the arrivals bay by the stable yard instead. To their left Pete Rafferty's helicopter was sitting in one of the paddocks like a huge, shiny black insect, the first of several destined to land that day.

'He is a total Ptolemy Finch freak.' Iris groaned. 'I was so relieved you called. I couldn't get away.'

The ageing rocker's fury that he'd been asked to pilot his wife from the Cotswolds to Wootton early for an emergency rehearsal had been soothed by meeting Iris. A huge fan, he'd been entranced to find himself guided round the Wootton gardens by Purple herself.

'I was trying to text Chloe,' Iris fretted, 'but he kept grabbing my hand and telling me he wants to write a new album based on the books. I ended up sending texts to half my address book asking them to call me urgently. My phone hasn't stopped ringing. The only one who hasn't called back is Chloe. I think she's up to something.'

'She's probably still asleep.' Griff yawned, wishing he himself was. A night of non-stop sex had left him woolly-headed and sluggish. But even with his senses dimmed, he was aware that Iris was unusually jumpy and excitable, and he had a suspicion it was to do with last night's late phone call.

He followed behind as she jumped from the car to meet the quadrille riders returning from their run-through. She patted her mother's horse and fed him mints from her pocket, then apologised, blushing, to Haff for taking over the Folly and thinking he was a ghost. 'You and Vicente are so brilliant, stepping in at the last minute to ride. Are you really going to wear dresses?'

Griff longed for his own heroic mission as an opportunity to prove himself to the Devonshires as the rightful pretender to Iris's heart. So far they'd treated him with polite indifference, clearly thinking he was Iris's summer distraction while she recovered from the Dougie heartbreak. But his blood was up and he was determined to make his mark.

Incredibly fresh, Scully was dancing on the spot and snatching at his bit, and Mia was struggling to make him stand still enough for her to jump down. She was wearing the pendant Iris had given her for her birthday, Griff noticed, its green opal glinting in the sunlight. He stepped forward to hold the horse.

'Many happy returns!' he said as Mia ran up a stirrup. He leaned in to kiss her but found himself puckering up into thin air when she walked around to do the stirrup on the other side. He repeated the congratulations.

'Oh, sorry, Griff, I thought you were talking to the horse.' She smiled vaguely, then gasped. 'Actually, I'm glad you're here. Something dreadful's about to happen unless we avert it. I need your help.'

'Anything!' Griff beamed at her heroically.

'I've just seen the caterer's vans arriving. Could you rush up there, apologise and explain that they can't have access to the kitchen yet? Lito's supervising a special welcome-home breakfast for Leo. I think you have the eggs?'

'Oh . . . right.' He sighed as she led the horse away.

Jacinta was presiding over her special cinnamon *torrijas,* which Leo and Ivan were battling through gamely in the Wootton kitchen, sunlight flooding through the high glass roof, cats perched on every surface and stool while dogs drooled underfoot.

Ivan, who missed Puff Adder, fed them constant titbits and ate far too much himself. The old lady terrified him.

'I love a man with a good appetite,' Jacinta said in her deep Jerez rasp. 'Your wife, she is a good cook?'

'I'm not married.'

'You are old for a bachelor, like Juan-Felipe the horse trainer.' She tutted. 'I say to him last week, "You must take a wife soon."'

'I hear other men's wives are more Haff's line,' muttered Leo, who had hardly eaten anything.

'God will put him right,' she said darkly. 'Chloe Benson is a good match for a man. Maybe you weel like her, Ivan? Like you, she is fond of food.'

Ivan flashed a nervous smile and put down his fifth *torrija.*

Beside him, Leo cleared his throat. 'Maybe we can have a talk later, Mamá, just you and me. I can take you for a drive after the gala.'

'Why would I want that? You are terrible driver. You should be taking your wife out to a lovely restaurant. She has work so hard for today, poor *muñequita,* and it is her birthday. You must make her feel special tonight. Have you bought her jewellery? Dmitri always gave me necklaces. He called me his "*lebedi*" because I have such a beautiful neck – *lebedi* it is "swan" in Russian,' she told Ivan.

'I know,' he snapped. '*Lebedinoe ozero* is Leo's favourite ballet.'

'Of course.' Jacinta beamed at him. 'Leo's father took me to the cinema in Jerez to see Fonteyn and Nureyev dance *Swan Lake* on one of our first nights out together. Dmitri was such a romantic man, like my Leo with his Mia.'

Leo took her hand. 'I really need to talk to you about the present Mia has asked me to give her for her birthday, Mamá. That's why we must speak later. I have something very important to tell you.'

'As you wish,' she conceded reluctantly, then patted his knee. 'It is good to have you home where you belong. You make me very happy. It will be a good day; a very good day.'

Arriving at Wootton in a car crammed with children, the Demons were straight into action. While Simon loped into the house with a thoroughly over-excited Kitty and his toe-scuffing sons to hail old friend Leo and talk charity-auction tactics while wolfing Lito's left-over *torrijas*, Laney took Hope and the twins in search of Mia, who was overseeing floral displays being placed on the dressage lawns.

'I hope Laney can calm her down,' Leo confided to Simon. 'She's clearly decided life begins at forty by being reborn as a whirling dervish.'

'You know what they say – if you don't live for something, you'll die for nothing.'

'Thank you for that cheering thought.'

'Pleasure.' Simon finished another *torrija* before wiping his mouth with a napkin. 'Where's Ivan?'

'Upstairs, taking a shower and hiding from Mamá, who has half the single girls of Berkshire lined up to mark his dance card.' Leo rolled his eyes affectionately. Then he chewed a fingernail. Demon was one of the few people he totally trusted. 'Mine is just a marked card.'

Simon knew immediately what he meant. His career as the thinking mum's favourite romcom hero was over. 'Is Lorca about to be shot down on the road to Amarillo?'

Leo smiled. 'Actually, Lorca was assassinated on the road to Alfacar but, yes, that's the situation.'

'Need a bulletproof vest?'

'Just covering fire.'

Mia was far from the glamorous gala hostess as she stood on the lawn in grubby breeches and a faded polo shirt, still sweaty from riding through the quadrille routine, now consulting with Franco about the quickest way to replace the storm-damaged petunias in the Greek urns.

Laney thought she looked more beautiful than ever, but everything seemed wonderful to Laney today. After a night of rumbustious love-making with her husband, she was bandy-legged and non-stop smiley.

'Happy birthday!' She presented Mia with a large sparkly box.

'It's a clock!' Hope said helpfully, jumping up and down.

'With the hands back to front,' said one of the twins.

'And the numbers,' added the other.

Mia ripped it open and laughed. Inside was a reverse-face clock engraved with YOU AND MIA.

'Because it's time to put the past behind us,' Laney explained, hugging her.

'Are you and Simon really OK now?' Mia whispered shakily.

'Better than OK,' Laney assured her. 'The Demons have faced up to their demons and are determined to have a marriage made in heaven. Cue angelic music.'

Thrusting a home-made card between them, Hope led a raucous rendition of 'Happy Birthday' accompanied by the twins.

As the three girls raced off to pick grass for the horses, Laney confessed to Mia in a whisper, 'When the twins' mother dropped them off this morning, we didn't hear the bell and she had to throw pebbles at the windows. Apparently, Hope lifted the cat flap and told her Mummy and Daddymon were busy making babies, which was sweet but entirely untrue.' Mia's amazement was written all over her face. 'We've decided we need to make more time together, not children.' She glanced across at Hope and the twins. 'How are things with Iris?'

'Better – much, much better.' She let out a laugh of relief, green eyes glowing. 'I have my little girl back. I just have to get used to the fact that she's a grown-up. She wants me to go to Kenya to find Dom when we've got through today,' she confessed, her voice faltering. 'But I'm not sure I *can* get through today. I've told Leo he has to come out.'

'Shit.' Laney had noticed the huge dark circles beneath her eyes and the tics pulling at their corners.

'I can't act it out any more, Laney. When I was riding Scully just now, I almost turned him towards the hills and rode for my life to get away. It's such an unfair thing to ask Leo to do, but I don't know how else we're ever going to live the lives we want to.'

Laney had never seen Mia so close to cracking up. It reminded her of the state she'd been in when Dom had disappeared. She was staring at the clock now, eyes full of tears.

'I know I can't turn back time, but I have to find him, Laney. It's all I can think about. I won't sleep until I do. I'm going to let everybody down today, I just know it,' she sobbed, 'the foundation, Haff, and most of all poor Leo. How can I be a party hostess when the only person I want to talk to right now hasn't been invited?'

'Leave today with me and Simon,' Laney said firmly. 'We'll make sure the gala runs without a hitch. All you have to do is be a silent star.'

Hope and the twins were now pretending to be the Three Billy Goats Gruff, trotting across one of Wootton's little ornamental bridges to get to the greener grass.

'I've been a silent star too long,' Mia said. 'That's half the problem.'

One of the twins raced breathlessly up to her and pleaded, 'Will you be the troll, Mia?'

'Mia's a bit busy right now, darling.' Laney gently guided her away. 'I'm a brilliant troll.'

Suddenly Mia turned to Laney, eyes sparkling. 'Do you remember how frustrated I got at college that I was only ever cast as innocent heroines who inevitably die in a white nightie in the last act? I never once got to play a baddie.'

'And I was the exact opposite,' Laney remembered, 'destined to murder and double-cross. Simon always says I was demonised. Does that mean you were victimised?'

Mia shook her head animatedly. 'I'm no victim, Laney, and I'm no silent star either. I always wanted the best speaking part. I *can* act. It's just time to switch roles, and this is my half-hour call.' She hugged the clock to her chest. 'I *am* going to play the troll.'

Behind her, three little billy goats in party dresses cheered, then fell into surprised silence as Mia hurried in the opposite direction.

Fishing her phone from her bag to text Simon, Laney adopted her best troll shamble to terrorise Hope and the twins. As she lumbered up to the bridge, she was too busy typing to realise that the girls had trotted off to be the Three Little Pigs in a gazebo.

'*Who's* that tippy-tapping over my bridge?' she roared, straightening up.

Legendary rock star Pete Rafferty almost fell into the stream with fright.

Laney, who had once been a massive fan of his band, Mask, stood open-mouthed with shock. After what seemed like a full minute, she managed to hold out her hand and splutter, 'Laney de Montmorency. Friend of Leo and Mia. Scourge of billy goats.'

'You build bridges?' he asked, shaking it.

'It was a career change from burning boats,' she said faintly.

As Pete puffed at an asthma inhaler, Laney took a call from Simon on her mobile. 'Have you seen Mia yet?' he demanded. 'Is she holding together OK? Not behaving too oddly?'

'I'm deputising that task,' Laney said brightly, smiling at Pete. 'She's just told me she can't turn back time and she wants to be a baddie.'

'The philosophy with which I've always lived life!' Pete cackled as he admired the ornamental fretwork. 'This bridge is pretty cool. Wouldn't mind one for my gaff. How much do you charge?'

Chapter 56

At eleven o'clock, as cars began to sweep into the back entrance, two flamenco guitarists took to the stage in Wootton's garden, fingers dancing across the strings. Suddenly a sense of dry Spanish air had infused a lush, sweet-scented English country garden. The catering staff swaggered a little more as they circulated with champagne and Midori sangría, the guests flicked their chins a little higher to pose for *Cheers!* magazine, the men strutted and the women turned with a stamp of their feet. The huge numbers of dogs that Mia always insisted were welcome at her celebrations were under constant threat of being mown down by Jacinta who, thoroughly over-excited by the number of famous faces around her, whizzed about in her chair like a loose bumper car, autograph book aloft.

'For my granddaughter!' she explained to everybody she stopped for a signature. 'She's called Jacinta . . . Shall I spell it for you?'

Wearing a red and yellow cotton sweater to honour the Spanish theme, Ivan marked Leo jealously with his eyes as he played the debonair host. With his wife busy preparing for the quadrille – the first of the day's scheduled entertainments – the remaining half of Leomia had teamed up with a tall, dashing man in a flamboyant red linen suit to welcome guests with great charm and bonhomie.

'Who is that man with Leo?' Ivan pounced on Iris as she passed by. 'He looks kind of familiar.'

Iris, who had not forgiven him for his part in pitching the baby idea to Mia, regarded him coolly as she pocketed the phone on which she was still trying to summon Chloe. 'Simon de Montmorency, an old family friend. He always works a party like a chat-show host making a studio entrance. He chose your bedlinen.'

'Of course! The designer. Has he had work done since he was in LA? He looks great.'

'He remarried his first wife.'

'I must get the number of their vicar.'

Iris laughed, thawing a little. 'Simon's conducting the charity auction later. He and Dad were best man at each other's weddings.'

'Leo never talks about him,' Ivan said airily, to make himself feel better.

'Simon talks about himself far too much for anybody else to need to,' she reassured him kindly. A full-scale Leomia production at Wootton must be painful for him to endure, with his lover's twenty-year marriage on display for a rare open day. The flamenco dancers, horses and celebrity wives were all sideshows, but Leomia was the headline double-act the guests had really come to see. Leo was struggling to compensate for his absent wife. As yet more well-heeled and well-known arrivals fell on their popular, dark-eyed host, they asked after Mia constantly.

'She's with the other man in her life,' he explained good-naturedly each time. 'Her stallion, Escultor.'

'Makes her sound like Catherine the Great,' sniped Ivan.

'Better to be Great than Terrible,' muttered Iris, losing sympathy again fast.

'*Touché.*' He smiled, big eyebrows opening like pinball levers as he put an arm around her, voice now low: 'Hey, Iris, I'm full of piss and vinegar, as we say in the States. Mia's doing sweat and tears while the horse does the blood. You've gotta cut back on the venom, honey.'

'Have some champagne.' Iris plucked two flutes from a passing waiter. 'Bodily fluids are so last year.'

As they clinked glasses and called a truce, Iris spotted Griff making his way across the lawns from the stable yard. He was wearing a pale blue shirt that brought out the depth of his tan and made him look more Spanish than the guitarists strumming on stage. He beamed when he spotted her through the crowd.

Ivan saw him too and perked up considerably. With his easy charm and boundless fascination in others, Griff had already gained his trust.

'I took a few bottles of champagne down to the stables,' he told them both now. 'Not sure that was wise.'

Iris's eyes widened in alarm. 'Mum's not drinking, is she?'

'No, but Sylva Rafferty's already cracking open the second bottle and is trying to persuade Haff and Vicente to wear fiesta dresses in the quadrille. Apparently their emergency *traje corto* haven't turned up yet and they're on in five minutes.'

'Haff will never agree.'

'I don't think he has much choice. Sylva said she'd donate a thousand pounds to the charity if he does it. They were starting to strip him when I left. He seemed to be quite enjoying that bit.'

'He's got the hips to get away with ruffles,' Ivan said coolly, 'but that face is pure Jackie Stallone.'

Griff laughed. 'Shall we grab good seats? I'd love to talk to you more about that trip you and Leo made to Easter Island, Ivan. It's somewhere I've always wanted to go.'

Pressing her lips to his shoulder, Iris loved him for his instinctive kindness. As they made their way to the seating with the rest of the crowd, her phone beeped with a message from Chloe: Not sure I'll make it. All up in the air here. C

'I'll just reply to this and join you there.' She jumped back as her grandmother sped past, hot on the tail of a gaggle of soap stars.

What's happening? Iris demanded, then groaned as her screen flashed up that the network was busy. Looking up, she saw that almost every guest was carrying a smartphone in one hand, thumbs sliding back and forth.

The quadrille was practically almost hoof-perfect, an extravagant and expressive start to the entertainment as the horses danced in the heat haze and fiesta ruffles tossed, the gala's Iberian theme drumming and strumming life into a lazy, sun-soaked day, although its hostess was in a daze. Mia seemed hardly aware she was there. Scully took charge, knowing the routine – and was so relieved to find his mistress on his back that he swept around the arena in graceful half-passes and extensions as though on gliders, sitting perfectly on his hocks to pirouette like a rocking horse, then springing forwards to *passage*, polished hoofs landing in perfect time to the beat of the music.

Sylva Rafferty might have been the weakest rider of the four now the warring WAGs had dropped out, but she was a knock-out to look at, and in turn almost knocked out her expensive white smile as her magnificent silicone breasts bounced up and down in sitting trot, shooting hot looks at Vicente each time she passed him, thoroughly excited by the effect of the make-up she'd applied to his handsome face, as were their audience. Wootton's head groom rode sublimely and looked startlingly like Penélope Cruz.

But by far the most spectacular combination was Haff on Quito, his showman's panache carrying the modest little horse so that they outclassed the others by a mile. He was so mesmerisingly graceful that nobody watching thought to question the broad shoulders straining the seams of the polka-dot dress, and not one person laughed, even though he was also sporting a hideous Bibi Cavendish hat to hide his short hair, a rectangular astro-turf busby dotted with silk gerberas and butterflies.

The crowd cheered so heartily afterwards that Sylva, Vicente and Mia's three horses all belted spookily out of the arena, leaving Haff to take such an extravagant bow that his makeshift mantilla fell off. To the crowd's delight, Quito got down on one knee so that his rider could pick it up and flourish it like a *córdoba*.

While the guitarists reappeared on stage to accompany two erotically charged, foot-stamping flamenco dancers and a throaty, melancholic singer, Haff trotted back to the stable yard to do a quick change into some white breeches and a black T-shirt that showed off his narrow hips and big chest to manly perfection. Then he rode back in on Scully, accompanied by two of his friends from the Portuguese Equestrian Dance Company with their golden Lusitanos to demonstrate high-school movements, including the spectacular capriole.

'I must go and congratulate Mum,' Iris told Griff, hurrying away from the seating and between the marquees, where she was again almost mown down by her grandmother.

'Gary Barlow is here!' Jacinta gasped, beside herself with excitement. 'You must introduce me, *bonita*.'

'I don't know him, Lito.'

'No matter. I will introduce myself. This is *such* a fun party. Your mother is so clever. I am certain Leo will never want to go back to America. So many friends here, such love.' She revved off, crying, '*¡A beber y a tragar, que el mundo se va a acabar!*'

Seeing Leo and Ivan exchanging a long, private look nearby, Iris wasn't so sure she wanted to eat and drink as though the world was going to end. She hoped it was just the beginning.

She snatched her phone as it beeped, thinking it was Chloe again, but the message made her heart lurch uncomfortably. Be in the front row for the fashion show. ILY. D x

'Hey,' a languid voice whispered in her ear and she spun round into Griff's lips for a delicious moment. 'You OK?' he asked.

'Fine!' She pocketed her phone.

'The auction's about to start,' he told her, reaching up to loosen the hair she'd hooked behind one ear so that it fell sexily across her eyes. 'I've been asked to be a topless porter in dicky-bow and cuffs.'

'Great!' She hooked her hair back again. 'I look forward to seeing that. Just got to rescue somebody from Lito first.'

Her grandmother had now cornered an attractive blonde by the water terrace. Iris recognised the smoky-voiced singer-songwriter Trudy Dew, who had composed her grandmother's favourite West End musical, *Air!*, which the old lady had been taken to see no fewer than twenty times last year. Jacinta was now demanding that she turn her life story into another hit musical. 'Leesten to this Spanish guitar, Trudy,' she entreated. 'Can you not hear it calling to you? My life is passion, bullfighting, circus, horses, love. What do you think?'

'I think it sounds amazing.' Trudy politely searched in her bag for a card to hand over.

By the time Iris had hopped over to them on her crutches, a lofty, dark figure had rolled up to retrieve his famous wife, with a blond baby papoosed to his chest and a toddler in hand, suggesting they all go through to lunch because the auction was getting under way soon.

Lito turned to Iris. 'I think I will go inside for a little rest, *bonita*. It is too hot out here and my hearing-aid battery needs changing.' She tapped at it in frustration. 'I ask Leo to change it earlier, but I think he only pretended. He is worried I weel bid on everything in the auction. Maybe you can get somebody to bring me some gaz-pacho.'

Iris's Maltese terriers jumped up on to Jacinta's lap to get away from the guests' marauding dogs, and she chuckled. 'I will look after your babies. They like to watch *Jeremy Kyle USA*.'

Iris limped alongside her as she headed across the lawns to the house.

'You must come and fetch me when the cabaret is starting,' Jacinta told her as she buzzed up the ramp into her annexe. 'I want to see Laney's revue. She is terrible *zorra*, but she always makes me laugh. This is a day for laughter.'

Iris lingered in the annexe, fussing around changing batteries, opening windows and arranging a table beside her grandmother with a cool drink, the remote control and her favourite toffees, before finally saying, 'Lito, can I ask you something?'

'*¿Qué?*'

She already had the television at top volume, which didn't make it easy.

'Do you think it's possible to fall out of love with one person and into love with another, or do you think the two get horribly muddled?'

The old lady smiled and tutted. 'If you think you love two people at the same time, choose the second. If you really loved the first, you would not have fallen for the second.'

'Is that an old Spanish saying?'

'No, *bonita*. I think it was Johnny Depp. I always admire that boy. Very like your father, I think. In fact, I will give your father that advice when he talks to me later. It might make it easier for him to tell me what he has to.'

Iris eyed her anxiously.

Jacinta held up a hand and let out a deep sigh. 'I know what he is, *bonita*. I have always known, just as I know that you are not his. But you *are* mine. You are in here.' She thumped her chest with a clenched fist and then coughed, eyes watering, signalling for her drink. When she'd recovered, she carried on: 'I am an old lady and I am allowed to say I do not like what Leo has chosen, even if I must accept it because I love him. God knows what he is and He has given Leo a very good family and great love, which is clemency. But I do worry about your mother. She has been his angel. What will she do if he forsakes her?'

Iris wrapped her arms around her, pressing her cheek to the smoothly parted white hair. 'I think it's the kindest thing he can do *for* her sake,' she said.

Leaving Jacinta sipping gazpacho in front of a wife screaming at her husband to quit hosting bondage orgies in their basement, she slipped upstairs and found her mother changing into an exquisite silk dress the colour of verdigris, which brought out her extraordinary jade eyes, the streaked bronze depth of her hair and the glow of her skin. Standing beside her and watching their reflections in the mirror, Iris recognised that she had inherited her mother's features, but she'd never possessed the unearthly dryad quality that Mia always radiated, as though she was going to fade into a will-o'-the-wisp and disappear magically into an oak tree at any moment. Just as Mia had once played fragile victims and died in the final act with spell-binding brilliance each night, Iris had been typecast at a similarly young age as an action heroine who could fight her way out of any corner while cracking one-liners and taking no prisoners. She'd only dyed in the make-up trailer.

'Dominic's hair's blond, isn't it?' she asked quietly. 'Like mine?'

Mia nodded. 'Almost white, rather like Ptolemy Finch. I loved your blond hair.'

'When they started colouring it for the movies it seemed easier to stick with it. I've been thinking about letting it go blond again.'

'Like Dom's.' Mia's eyes were luminous as emeralds in the mirror. 'Will you forgive me if I behave terribly oddly today?'

Iris pressed her lips to her mother's head. 'I would expect nothing less. You've been behaving oddly for years. Now I'm finally beginning to understand why. Lito says that if you love two people at the same time you must choose the second because you can't have loved the first.'

'Her Spanish sayings are nonsense sometimes.'

'Actually it's Johnny Depp,' she muttered, rushing on. 'But you've only ever been in love with one man. That's just amazing.'

Pressing her hands to her face, Mia took a deep breath through her fingers. 'This is the first day of the rest of my life.'

'Is that one of Ivan's motivational lines?'

'No, it's a bumper sticker Laney had on her Mini Cooper at university.' She wandered across to her dressing table to add more blusher and reapply her lipstick, the will-o'-the-wisp made flesh. 'We always joked that Laney's driving felt like the last day of our lives. Nothing's changed there.' She rolled her glossy lips together and examined her reflection for flaws. 'Iris, I'm going to set Leo free today.'

For a moment Iris didn't register what her mother had said. Then she stood up in horror.

'No!' She moved closer, staring at the face in the mirror. 'You can't out him. I mean, OK, so Lito already knows, but you can't expose him to—'

'Lito knows?'

'She says she's always known. She says I'm still her family even though we don't share blood.' Remembering what she'd said to Ivan, she added proudly: 'Being an Ormero is about sweat and tears.'

Mia burst out laughing, reaching for her hand. 'You can say that again. And I'm not going to say anything to embarrass Leo, I promise you. I love him deeply, which is a great deal easier than being *in* love with somebody, as you know.' Those gentle green eyes searched hers. 'Don't rush into anything with Griff, will you?'

'I love him! I want to spend the rest of my—'

'Take your time, Iris,' Mia said firmly. 'Have the time of your life.'

Chapter 57

Simon was a born salesman, a gavel-twirling flatterer who could convince a crowd it wanted something enough to part with three times its value, drive two competitive bidders into arch-rivalry and persuade a reluctant hand to thrust itself evangelically upwards. Ably assisted by Leo, who acted modestly as head porter in a shabby brown covert coat with the best asides and one-liners of the day, he elicited vast sums of money to add to the coffers. As auction-room assistants, Griff and one of the burly Spanish estate hands had agreed to roam around the crowd holding up lots and eliciting higher bids, bare-chested and beguiling. Only just out of his sling, Griff's shoulder ached as he carried around a huge bronze of a dressage horse donated by a local sculptor, fixed smile in place, aware that his hopes of being heroic were falling short of his usual standards.

Out of the corner of his eye, he caught Iris hurrying out of the marquee, yet again looking at her telephone, but could do nothing as bidding for the bronze heated up, already in four figures.

Sorry so late, Chloe had texted. Thought a friend was dropping me off, but he's had to fly and I'm waiting for a taxi. Can you make sure no horses are around?

This is Wootton; there are horses everywhere, you dolt, Iris had replied, glancing at her watch. The mounted fashion show is on in 15 mins.

Stall it. Be with you in ten. C x

Iris hurried towards the stables.

By the time Haff was prepared to take the podium in the marquee for his speech about the Javiero Coaching Centre, the sum raised towards the inner-city dressage school had already broken Wootton Gala records.

The Spaniard was introduced by Mia. Her voice was clear and true, each word resonating with emotion, First, she thanked the guests for coming and for their generous support, then she talked about Haff and the work he did. 'In a moment, Juan-Felipe will tell you a little bit more about the amazing project that today is helping to fund, but first I want to take this opportunity to thank somebody without whom none of this would be possible.' She looked across at Leo. 'Somebody without whose charity work many lives would not have been worth living, and whose own life is going to change completely today ... '

Unaware that her mother was going off script, Iris had limped down to the stable yard to find the amateur models wavering between panic attacks and revolt, claiming they hadn't been told they were expected to ride naked. Intimidated by the size of the glossy black Friesian horses that they were to ride – they were nothing like the wiry hedge-hopping hunters they were used to – they were equally horrified by the sight of Bibi Cavendish's millinery creations, lined up like giant liquorice allsorts on the fence-posts alongside the main yard. One of Mia's committee stalwarts was shouting at them to think of the good cause while Vicente helped a tall man hold horses ready to mount.

Waving a hat in each hand, which made the horses start back in alarm, the committee stalwart was starting to panic: 'You *all* knew about the nudity! It's in your contracts. Underprivileged children will suffer if you do not do this!' She leapt on Iris with relief as she approached. 'Iris, quick! Help me leg these girls up!'

'We were told nothing would show,' said a mottle-faced girl who whipped in for the Pelham Hunt and appeared to be the ringleader in the revolt. She held up a piece of crumpled elastic. 'What's this?'

'A modesty G-string,' explained the stalwart, and added winningly, 'I also have pashminas ... '

'Does Mum know about this?' Iris asked, seeing a way to stall for time. 'It's a family event. Half the celebrity yummy mummies of the Home Counties are here with their children.' Then she almost fell over as a friendly black nose prodded her from behind with a familiar whicker. To her horror, she recognised one of Dougie's Friesian stallions.

She glanced at the horses gathered on the yard and identified each one as from her ex-fiancé's stunt team. The tall, blushing man in charge of them was Dougie's business partner, Rupe.

'Hi, Iris.' He managed an awkward wave.

'Is Dougie here?' she asked bluntly.

'Um . . . yah, no, hah.' Blushing even more furiously, he gave one of the models such an exuberant leg-up that she was kneeling on the saddle.

'Where is he?' Iris growled. Had Chloe demanded that the show be stalled because she'd known Dougie was around?

'Definitely not here!' he spluttered, fingers crossed behind his back as he turned to entreat the other models to follow their friend into the saddle. 'See how fine she looks, ladies?' The girl did indeed look ravishing, a bronzed slip of hard hunting muscle on a magnificent war horse, plumed organza hat and feathery scarf transforming her into a fairy princess.

The stalwart was holding up her pashminas, like an eager stall-holder at a souk.

Soon draped in a great many designer scarves, carefully arranged to cover nipples, the models agreed to mount, and the stalwart ran around with tit tape to ensure a modicum of modesty was preserved. Affable Rupe, trying to avoid touching anything controversial as he helped the girls mount, was now grabbing them by the ankles and throwing them up over the horses' backs like dead stags.

Iris was still trying to think up a reason to insist they all wait when she noticed something glint in the shadows under the overhang of the stable roof. Limping closer, she saw that a horse was waiting in a stable wearing full medieval barding, metal armour protecting his chest and quarters and a segmented shell arching over his neck. A metal champron covered his face, but Iris would have known that whicker anywhere. Hurrying closer, she saw tufts of grey mane poking out above his face armour and his lower lip drooping beneath. With a series of loud clanks, he turned to look at her with eyes as kind as those of an equine Claire Rayner.

'Harv!' She rushed over to hug him, pressing her lips to the soft muzzle and breathing in his kindness. Only Dougie ever rode Harvey.

How dare he come and hijack the gala? Heart hammering, blood boiling in her veins, she limped through the yard arch and around the back of the stallion barn to the huge HGV horsebox parked there. A knight in full armour was sitting on the ramp, visor tipped up as he smoked a cigarette.

'Hi, Dougie.'

The visor snapped down.

'I know it's you in there.'

He said nothing. Smoke was pluming from the slits around the mouth and eyes in a very ghostly fashion.

'You'd better take the cigarette out.'

Starting to cough, he snapped up the visor, Marlboro ejected at speed.

Watering like mad, the bluest eyes gazed at her, thick sooty lashes blinking furiously.

'I knew it was you!' she snarled.

He looked extremely fed up. 'You're not supposed to recognise me until I ride up and declare my honour. I've written a speech.'

'Now I know why you called me last night.'

'I meant every word.'

'There's no point. It's over.'

'Don't say that! We're so good together. I need you, Iris. You're my rainbow without which there's no sun. I'm so lonely without you. I love you.'

Iris looked at him, so handsome and chivalric, and her anger evaporated, heart filling with sadness as she remembered the fun they'd had undressing with a can of WD-40 and a pair of pliers. 'I've met somebody else, Dougie.'

His blue eyes stared at her for a long time, then he turned away, pulling off his helmet, blond hair spilling out like a golden sea. It had grown since the wedding and fell over his collar now. Streaked by the sun and matched with a deep Californian tan, it made him unspeakably handsome. 'Fast work,' he said eventually.

'Griff's very special.'

'I was very special last month.'

'You can't predict these things,' she muttered, thinking about her conversation with Jacinta and knowing that falling out of love with one person and into love with another was not as simple as jumping from cloud to cloud. There was a transition period where the love for both tore one's heart in two. She knew what she felt for Griff was far more intense and true than anything she'd shared with Dougie, but it didn't stop part of her heart going out to him for what they had lost.

'What sort of name is Griff anyway?' Dougie sneered.

'My name,' came a deep Welsh voice. There was a step on the ramp beside Iris and she turned to find Griff standing behind her, stripped to the waist, six-pack shimmering. For a shocked moment, she thought he'd ripped off his shirt purely to flex his muscles in some pseudo-gorilla display – his tanned chest was oiled, she saw with alarm – but then she took in the bow-tie, wing collar and white cuffs, and remembered he'd agreed to be a porter for the charity auction. Her heart swelled with pride, yet thudded too as she prayed Dougie and Griff would be civil to each other.

But Griff seemed hardly to have noticed the knight in shining armour sitting on the ramp. 'You should come and listen to what your mother's saying, Iris.' He put a protective arm around her. 'It's pretty momentous.'

'Oh God.' Iris turned and hurried back towards the house.

'Wait! I don't give up that easily, you know! I deserve an explanation!' Dougie demanded, but by the time he'd struggled upright from the ramp in the cumbersome armour and clanged around the side of the box, they had both disappeared. Hugely bad-tempered, he clanked over to the stable yard to mount.

The committee stalwart had now tit-taped enough pashminas to her models to restock Tie Rack in every major London railway station. The hunting ladies were red-faced and far too hot. Rupe hastily led out Harvey, who picked his way eagerly across the cobbles, grey ears pricked together over his champron.

Dougie accepted a leg-up from his partner and turned Harvey towards the sumptuous Wootton gardens. 'Wish me luck, Rupe. I've just found a dragon that needs slaying.'

'After twenty incredibly happy years together, Leo and I are going to separate,' Mia told the stunned crowd. 'We are the very best of friends and will remain so. He is the very best of fathers, and will remain so. The Devonshire Foundation will continue to make money for good causes, and Leo and I will work closely together to ensure that that happens. We are a very good team.' She looked across the room at him and saw those bush-baby eyes utterly transfixed by her, fear and relief ebbing and flowing across his handsome face.

'This is my decision. As the old cliché goes, life is not a dress rehearsal.' She held out her hand and beckoned him to join her. 'I am for ever in his debt and I love him more than I can say. I know we could have hidden behind press statements and dark glasses to announce this, but we've lived our entire married life in the public eye and we will no doubt live unmarried life in it too.'

Joining her on stage, Leo put his arms around her, muttering, 'You always were a bloody exhibitionist.' Which broke the tension in the atmosphere: the crowd realised, to their amazement, that they were allowed to laugh.

The Devonshires were a magical double-act, even when improvising the end of their marriage. On stage now, they held hands and gave their audience the very best of Leomia, a private performance that nobody would ever forget, astonished to witness one of the most joyful, eccentric and civilised splits imaginable.

Watching, with Hope on her knee, Laney was trying not to snort as she cried into Simon's comforting shoulder. Arm around his wife with the twins on his knees, he had tears running down his cheeks too. 'He's right. She always was a bloody exhibitionist. She's waited in the wings twenty years to have the last line.'

'She's taking the baddie role for once – that's what she meant by being a troll,' she whispered, barely able to speak for the choking lump in her throat. 'She's letting him go. She's coming out of the dark . . . ' She shut up: Gloria Estefan was singing in her head.

In the entrance to the marquee, Iris stood clutching a pillar for support as she watched her parents on stage, trying to take it all in and battling not to let them both down by bursting into tears. She knew it was the right thing: they lived almost totally separate lives now and it had been waiting to happen for many years, but that didn't make it any less emotional. At her side, Griff's dark eyes checked her reaction: he was aware that she was close to cracking. Others were watching her too, fascinated by the real-life soap opera going on all around them. Iris found illogical laughter bubbling up with the tears and battled to suppress it. She only wished Mia hadn't chosen to do it in front of an audience, but that was typical of her mother. She was looking incredibly calm now, even joking with Leo as they introduced Haff again: 'We both hope he'll have no surprise announcements, apart from the wonderful news about a Javiero Dressage Coaching Centre coming to London soon . . . '

Then Iris saw Ivan standing alone in his garish sweater, undoubtedly knitted by Leo. Part shielded by an ivy-wrapped column, he was holding one of Mia's terriers, his face buried in its neck. Iris felt overwhelmed with emotion for him too. Their relationship had always been spiky but, as Jacinta was fond of saying, the prickliest pears bear the sweetest fruit, and Ivan and Iris were a very prickly pair.

Gently detaching herself from Griff, she made her way over to Ivan and put her arms around him.

'That was an amazing thing to do,' he said in a choked squeak.

'Mum's always preferred giving to receiving.'

'It's the gift of a lifetime.' With a sob, he hugged her back as a small, panic-stricken dog wriggled out from between them and trotted off to greet its mistress, who was coming off stage.

Standing in front of the microphone now, Haff – who had been dreading his speech like a multiple tooth extraction without anaesthetic – was tongue-tied. The audience bubbled and boiled in front of him, whispering, chuntering and exchanging glances, none of them quite certain how to take in what Mia had just said.

Haff cleared his throat loudly to get their attention. 'Hello, I am Juan-Felipe Javiero. I teach dressage. I play video,' he croaked faster than a Benidorm DJ introducing a techno beat, nodding at the technical team, who had a computer linked to the big screen and were running the slide show he had saved to the Pegasus flash drive.

A grainy piece of CCTV footage flickered into view, the over-bright wing of a Range-Rover just visible. Out of it spilled an undeniably handsome but extremely pained-looking figure clutching his crotch. As the car sped away, he turned to face the camera, eyes glowing unnaturally silver like those of a wolf.

'That's Dougie Everett!' gasped a voice in the crowd.

Iris's jaw dropped. Then her throat burned on Dougie's behalf as tittering filled the tent. 'Switch that off!' She turned desperately for help, noticing that Griff was glaring through the open sides of the marquee at something glinting in the sunlight as it moved through the yew arch.

'And here he comes in person, ladies and gentlemen,' he muttered under his breath.

As the technical team quickly killed the video, music blared out of the loudspeakers, heralding the start of the fashion show, and the guests in the marquees emerged into the sunshine, grateful for distraction as a knight in shining armour trotted into the dressage arena, leading a troupe of near-naked girls wearing ridiculous hats.

Unaware that he had just featured on screen, Dougie rode tall and proud, a lance clutched to his side bearing a pennant adorned with Bibi Cavendish's company logo.

Her throat now apparently filled with hot coals, Iris ran out too.

Griff bounded after her. 'Don't worry. I'll get rid of him for you.'

'I don't need protecting,' she insisted, stumbling and hopping to the white boards as the knight clanked up the centre line.

On the nearby stage, the technical team were trying to connect up the PowerPoint file to the big screen that showed close-ups of each hat on sale, along with adverts for the companies donating scarves, jewellery and watches, but the little Pegasus flash drive overrode the media player. As another grainy CCTV tape flickered into action, Leo looked up from a tearful hug with Mia and Ivan to see a tall figure moving into shot, his white-blond hair gleaming like a halo.

'Get it off!' he bellowed, as Mia let out a cry of anguish and ran towards the screen.

The picture disappeared, to be replaced moments later by a twirling image of a hat shaped like a duck. Mia fell to her knees. Like two dark wings folding around her, Leo and Ivan gathered her up and held her close.

'I'll never forgive myself for sending him away,' Ivan told her, riddled with remorse. 'You will see him again, I promise.'

In the arena, Rupe's hunting ladies were gaining confidence as their immaculately trained horses marched sedately out in line, curving black ears pricked together to create Moorish arches over rivers of curling jet forelock, obediently following the glinting silver armour and glimmering white rump of their leading rider and horse, who were delighting the crowd now. Dougie lowered the tip of his lance to the ground and pirouetted around it in a courtly dance, then brought it back to his chest with a flourish and marched on, the models still following sedately.

Watching him, Iris felt compassion and anger staging a battle in her chest. 'That's how a Doma Vaquera *caballero* rides around his *garrocha* pole. *I* taught him that trick.'

Griff took her hand and squeezed it. 'He's an absolute shit pulling this stunt on you.'

'He's a stunt rider,' she said quietly. 'It's what he does.'

'Then he's riding for a very big fall,' he growled.

But Iris's battle-torn heart was bursting at the seams with divided loyalty. She knew she cherished the man whose fingers were now threaded through hers like a dovetail joint, even if he was dressed like a male stripper on Ladies' Night, but maybe her knight in shining armour deserved forgiveness.

As he rode past, clanking like pans in a dishwasher, the knight nodded at her and Iris felt the stitching on her heart give way further. A month ago, if she'd had a handkerchief handy, she'd have thrust it at him eagerly. She'd let him wear her colours too quickly.

'Iris!'

She turned to see Chloe pushing her way through the spectators, puffed out from running. Dressed in old jeans with grass stains on the knees and a polo shirt covered with mud, she stood out from the dressy designer crowd, who parted in surprise as she charged up.

'I said to keep the horses under cover!'

'You have no idea what's been going on here!' Iris fell on her gratefully, whispering, 'Mum and Dad have just split up in front of hundreds of guests and *Cheers!* magazine, and Dougie's in that suit of armour, but you know about that. Why didn't you warn me? It's all such a mess, Chlo.'

'Where's your mother now?' Chloe panted, studying the horizon anxiously over her friend's shoulder.

'Still in the marquee, I think. She's with Leo and Ivan. I'm sure she's fine. Laney's there too.'

'We have to get these horses put away,' Chloe said urgently, stepping back as the knight trotted past again, riding so close to the boards that he could almost have reached down to pluck Iris into the saddle. 'Hang on, did you just say that's *Dougie*?'

'One and the same,' muttered Griff, watching the knight retreat with narrowed eyes and eyeing his armour for weak points.

'We mustn't reveal him to the crowd,' Iris hissed. 'The most awful thing happened a minute ago ...' Her voice trailed away as she realised Chloe was staring at the sky, not listening to a word.

'Oh, bloody hell,' gasped Griff, eyes now glued to the horizon too.

Iris turned slowly, squinting into the sun.

Beyond the distant beech woods, a great yellow dome was rising up like a second dawn.

'It's a hot-air balloon,' he breathed.

'No fooling you,' Chloe muttered nervously, trying to work out which direction the balloon was moving.

A teardrop of sunshine blown by the wind, it burst up over the black woods. Still too far away for its burner to be heard, the glowing envelope was definitely growing larger as it floated steadily towards them.

'Tell me that's just a random balloon passing by.' Iris turned back to Chloe.

'Nobody flies at this time of day unless they know exactly what they're doing,' Griff told them. 'It's far too hot. The thermals are deadly.'

Iris's voice shook as she ventured, 'A cloud man might ...'

But Griff shook his head decisively. 'He'd never fly this close to so many hazards. There's the crowd, the cars and the tents, not to mention the horses.'

'I didn't tell him about the gala,' Chloe admitted in a small voice.

Chapter 58

The balloon was now fully visible, floating steadily towards them from the woods and over Wootton land, flying very low, its shadow falling across the water meadows towards the river. The crowd pointed excitedly, thinking it part of the entertainment.

Chloe had run to the back of the arena, where the committee stalwart was waiting with emergency tit tape. 'You must get them back to the stables!' she begged, but the woman pointed to the big screen where hats were twirling. 'There's still three hats to go.'

At first the jaunty music being piped across the upper lawns and the temporary arena around which the models were trotting drowned the sound of the burner, but as the balloon drew closer and hung beyond the yew hedges just a few hundred yards from the stable yard, its burners broke through the Spanish melodies, great dragon roars rending the air as flames licked up into the canopy.

Dougie's stunt horses were highly trained and well acquainted with gunshots, fires, swinging swords and lances, roaring machinery and even swooping aeroplanes, but hot-air balloons were new on them. They liked the comforting clank of armour or jangle of chain mail. They were being ridden by experienced horsewomen used to the random high jinks of the hunting field, but that didn't involve wearing modesty G-strings which wouldn't cover anything more than a Brazilian at rising trot. As the hunting ladies looked up and screamed, the horses took flight.

Running on to the grass, Chloe yelled at the riders for order like a desperate Pony Club instructor. 'Just pull the reins!'

But then she froze as a terrified redhead bore down on her from one side, duck hat over her eyes, green plumes, scarves and tit tape shedding like Icarus's feathers. From the other came charging a vision in a buckled purple felt capotain. Covering her head with her arms and crouching for self-protection, Chloe screamed. Strong hands plucked her away and Vicente hauled her behind the yews.

'Thank you!' she gasped, secretly thrilled to find herself in the handsome Spaniard's arms.

His dark eyes flashed. 'I might dress like a woman, but I always behave like a man.'

'I had no idea,' Chloe breathed, having missed the quadrille. She found the idea of swapping clothes rather exciting, but had no time to dwell on it as the balloon let out another roar of its burners and a loose horse charged by. Leaving Vicente to run after it, she hurried to find Iris, who was still staring at the balloon, totally shell shocked.

'You'd better fetch your mother.'

'It's him, isn't it?' Iris strained her eyes to pick out a figure in the basket, but it was still too high to see anybody inside. 'Cloud Man?'

Chloe nodded. 'He so nearly didn't agree to do it. He only flew in this morning and he said no as soon as I explained what I had in mind.'

'How did you talk him round?'

'I didn't. I thought it was all over, that he wouldn't do it. Then I saw the balloon going up. That's why I had to get a taxi. You must warn Mia.'

'What exactly is he going to do?' Iris started towards the marquee.

'I have no idea.' She stepped back as a horse charged past. 'I get the feeling nobody tells Dominic Masters what to do.' The balloon let out another great roar, as though in approval, and another hunting lady fell off as her mount reared, then careered across the lawns.

Beyond the yews, the armoured knight had reined to a halt and pulled up his visor to survey the chaotic stampede around him, his own horse unbothered by the mêlée or the big fabric ball floating overhead. To the crowd's delight, the knight now snapped his visor back down and nudged his grey campaigner into full flight. Together, they started to round up the runaway models, drawing alongside and pulling the horses to a halt.

Glancing over her shoulder as she reached the entrance to the marquee, Iris smiled with relief as she watched Dougie take control, so brave and chivalrous as he delivered horses to Rupe and Vicente before cantering after a particularly over-excited young Friesian that was bolting towards the water terraces with a screaming brunette hanging around its neck.

She turned back to the tent and saw her mother huddled in one corner with Leo, Ivan and the Demons.

As she took a deep breath and stepped beneath the canvas, she missed Griff's heroic entrance behind her, but a great many other women in the crowd watched with excitement as he strode into the arena to join the rescue party, tanned chest gleaming like polished oak, resembling a kinky James Bond as he stopped to straighten his bow-tie and tug at his collar, his Special Forces training lending him combat and survival skills unrivalled in a crisis. Then he looked up in shock as a pair of horses thundered towards him two

565

abreast, one as black as the other was grey and metal-clad, its rider's silverwork glinting as he leaned down to grab at the first horse's reins. Griff dived sideways just in time to avoid being mown down.

All the time the balloon loomed larger, a great yellow sun rising and setting within just a few short minutes, now coming down to land in the hay meadow.

As soon as her parents saw her, Iris found herself sandwiched in a hug between them, disappearing into a reassuring, scented confusion of warm arms and kisses breathed into her hair. Heavy cotton knitwear near her left cheek made her suspect Ivan was in on the act.

'I think you should come outside,' Iris said when she broke free, cutting short her mother's emotional explanations about her public announcement.

Mia shook her head sharply. 'I know all this thunder has ruined the fashion show but, forgive me, darling, I need a few more minutes to gather my wits.'

Another great roar split the air outside, and Iris was sure she could see it glow beyond the canvas wall of the marquee.

'It's not thunder, Mum. It's Dominic.'

Mia's face froze.

Rushing to look out of the entrance, Laney let out an astonished squawk.

'Does he travel by stormcloud, like Zeus?' asked Simon, following her.

'It's a hot-air balloon!' Hope shrilled as her siblings crowded round.

Mia hadn't moved, her whole body shaking. 'He's here?'

Iris nodded, tears in her eyes, as she saw the most extraordinary expression cross her mother's face, one she'd never seen before. She was incandescent with excitement, her green eyes as bright as foxfire. It made her look incredibly young.

'He's getting awfully close to that oak tree,' Laney called from the entrance.

Leo put his arms around Mia. 'What do you want to do?'

Her eyes brightened even more, foxfire to phosphorus, a smile bursting across her face.

'Looks like he's landing,' Simon announced.

Mia reached out to take her daughter's hand, her own shaking so much that her wedding ring rattled against the opal one she always wore on her middle finger. 'Are you ready to meet him?'

Iris took the hand, kissed it and pressed it to her cheek, two pairs of matching green eyes so close their lashes almost tangled. 'It's your moment. Let's not overwhelm him. I'll follow in a bit. He's come a long way to find you, remember.'

Mia hugged her tightly.

'He might be rather overwhelmed already,' Laney announced, as she watched the balloon float gracefully down into the field beyond the yews until it was hovering just above the emerald grass, like a giant croquet ball.

Holding both Leo's and Ivan's hands, Mia led the way to greet it, walking serenely past charging horses and weeping women in shredded hats and very little else, as though they weren't even there. Leo gaped in amazement while Ivan let out a nervous bleat and held her hand very tight.

Behind them, Laney gripped Simon, who had Hope on his shoulders, her five stepchildren surging close as they trooped in Mia's wake, along with most of the gala guests. 'I don't like this one bit,' she muttered. 'We never trusted Dominic with her at college so why should we start now? He's about to kidnap my incredibly stressed-out best friend in a balloon and we have no idea—'

'It's been twenty years and, like Iris says, he's just come halfway around the world,' Simon pointed out. 'Let's give him the benefit of the doubt.'

By the water terraces in the garden, Dougie had managed to catch the last of the runaway Friesians, which was being led away by Rupe, the furious hunting lady back on *terra firma* and ripping off her hat as she shrieked, 'I should be threatening to sue!' She tugged her pashmina down to try to cover her bottom.

Loping up with a tablecloth for her to wrap around herself, Griff went to retrieve the hat, which had rolled towards the lip of the first water terrace. When he straightened up, he found he was standing in the shadow of the metal-armoured grey horse and his shiny silver rider, eclipsing the sun like an evil Valkyrie. He stepped back in alarm as Dougie drew his sword.

'I ... chew ... Riz ... phone,' came the muffled voice from behind the visor.

'What?'

Dougie pushed up the visor. 'I said, I want you to leave Iris alone.'

'Never!' Not stopping to think, Griff looked around for something to use as a weapon, and pulled up a wooden post with an arrow sign nailed to the top – it had been hammered into the ground to direct guests through the gardens. Swinging back, he brandished it at Dougie. discovering too late that TOILETS was written on the arrow.

'What are you *doing*?' cried a voice, and they both turned to see Iris, who had been limping behind her mother towards the field where the balloon was landing but had diverted towards them, crutches swinging. 'Stop it!'

Close to, the balloon was as tall as a church, towering over the huge oaks that dotted the hayfield. Butane still roared from the burners to keep it inflated as it rested on the ground, and its pilot stayed in the basket, his face half turned away. Even from the track that led to the field gate, Mia could see the white-blond glint of his hair.

Letting go of Leo and Ivan's hands, she started to run. Pushing through the gate, she set out across the field as fast as a track sprinter.

She could see his eyes now, as intensely blue as she remembered, as luminous with fear and hope as her own. Her heart felt as though it was bursting out of her chest and racing on in front, sprouting wings, powering ahead to beat alongside his where it had always belonged.

Her brain was equally unruly, making her legs go still faster, exceeding any speed she'd ever run, outsprinting the lapwings and skylarks that lifted from the long grass around her, refusing to tell her pounding feet to slow down as she approached the basket. As she did so she started to laugh, infused with such overwhelming joy that she felt as though she could take one last, huge stride and jump over the whole balloon – basket, canopy and all.

And Dom was laughing too, the deep, delicious sound she'd never forgotten, had heard in her dreams so many times, trying to hold it in her head as long as she could after waking. Right now, she felt more awake than she had for years as, laughing and crying, she arrived at the basket, moving far too fast to stop, her eyes not leaving his. Utterly trusting, she jumped.

With equal faith, Dom reached out at exactly the right moment to pull her in so that they crashed back against the far side.

At first, they just stared at one another. Smiles rising and falling like waves, they stared. Mia couldn't stop grinning. He was Dom. She saw the scars, the lines, the weather-warmed skin and the wisdom-infused flecks in the bluest of all eyes, but he was Dom. He was everything she had kept alive. He'd never once left her heart.

'You took your bloody time,' she managed to gasp between gulps of air, unaware that her accent had reverted to nineteen-year-old Mia Wilde's broad Lancashire.

'Forgive me.' His voice remained the sweetest, peatiest sanctuary for ears. 'I made the biggest mistake of my life leaving you behind.'

'Different lifetime.' Her eyes were lost in his, travelling with him again. This time it was the shortest of journeys as two pairs of lips that hadn't met in twenty years crossed the inches that lay between them in less than a breath.

Reaching for the burner as they kissed, Dominic pumped a high flame into the silken cathedral dome above them until the basket lifted off the ground. 'Where do you want to go?'

'I don't suppose you've got enough fuel to make it to Thurle-stone Moor?'

'About five miles north at best.' He pumped in more heat, the envelope struggling to get lift in the hot summer air.

'Wait! Before we do this, there's something I must tell you.'

He eyed her warily. 'We have a lot of things to say.'

'This is too important to wait.'

Standing with her family among the small crowd of guests that had gathered on the field, Laney watched the balloon lift from the long grass and fall back again with mounting concern. 'Are they arguing?'

'I think it's called talking – easy mistake to make. We've been muddling up the two for years.' Simon tried to stop Hope grabbing his dark glasses as she rode on his shoulders, using his ears as reins.

Hope let out an excited whinny as she spotted Chloe nearby, also watching the balloon anxiously. Turning, Chloe smiled and made her way over, whinnying back and blushing to her roots as she passed Gary Barlow.

The balloon was providing surprising entertainment as it hopped up and down. Most of the gala guests assumed that the flight was a birthday gift for Mia, cheering as it lifted off, then groaning as it settled back on the ground. Chloe knew that keeping it inflated at all took supreme skill – the hire team had only allowed Dominic to pilot it because he had more experience than all of them put together – and she was terribly worried that it wouldn't take off again. But she was suddenly too preoccupied by another guilty truth to dwell on it.

'Chloe!' Laney gathered her into her brood with a tight hug. 'Thank you so much for last night. You were our saviour.' She glanced at Simon with a secret smile.

Chloe remembered the theft of the *Dalrymple* script with shame. 'Actually, there's something I must—'

'Meet the Demonics first – Kitty's dying to get to know you, and so are the boys, and the twins are just as excited.'

The introductions to Simon's children made Chloe feel as though she was about to lift off like the balloon, her world inflated by a family eager to pull her on board. But all the time, her conscience burned.

She stepped beside Laney, out of the others' earshot, to watch the balloon bounce another few metres, coming alarmingly close to the biggest oak.

'I stole something from you last night!' she blurted in a frightened whisper.

'You did?' Laney's kind blue eyes were distracted but forgiving. 'I stole things all the time when I was a babysitter – mostly videos and books, as I recall. It's a rite of passage. I'm sure it was nothing too awful.'

'The *Dalrymple* script. I found the back-up drive.'

Laney went very still. 'Oh.'

'I did it for Dad. He really wants it.'

'I know.' She sighed, clearly trying very hard not to scream. 'And you love him. That's what daughters do before they break the moral code. I expect no less from Hope one day.'

'I did tell him he had to pay you for it.'

'That's something.' Laney nodded. 'We could use twenty grand right now.'

Chloe wasn't listening as she blustered on. 'I didn't know how much to ask, so I suggested a million.'

Laney stepped back, cannoning into Simon, blue eyes hugely amused. 'How loud did Oscar laugh?'

'He's sending it electronically. It should be in your account by Monday.'

Laney's eyes were filling with tears as fast as her cheeks filled with a smile. Her phone sang out with a text. Chloe's buzzed at precisely the same time. They ignored them.

'And you'll be credited as original script writer,' Chloe explained earnestly. 'Iris told me you never got a credit for the first *Dalrymple*.'

Almost too choked to speak, Laney reached out to hug her. 'Welcome to the family.'

Chloe guessed being hugged by Laney non-stop was one of the trade-offs for being a part of the Demon clan. It wasn't such a bad deal. Her own mother only ever hugged trees.

Breaking apart, they checked their phones and let out identical cries. They looked at one another in immediate recognition, then across to the lurching balloon.

'I'll fetch her,' Chloe said quickly. 'You text back. Do not let the balloon crash into the tree.'

Despite his many faults, Dougie was an honourable man when it came to engaging in battle. He knew it was unfair to pick a fight from horseback while wearing full body armour and brandishing a sword if his opponent was dressed as a Chippendale and armed only with a twig, so he nobly dismounted and laid down his weapon. What he hadn't taken into account was that Special Forces-trained Griff fought very dirtily indeed and that the first thing he would do would be to push his metal-clad opponent into the long water terrace.

When Chloe ran breathlessly into the garden and finally spotted Iris, all she could see was her friend waving her crutches around as she stood on the grass lip overlooking the cascading waterfall, apparently shouting at nothing. A horse in full armour was dozing behind her, resting one hind leg on a hoof-edge. It wasn't until she got closer that Chloe saw two men fighting on the terraces below: a knight in very wet armour struggling to stand up while a bare-chested Griff battered him with a loo sign.

'I love her!'

'I love her too!'

'Will you two just stop it?' wailed Iris.

As Chloe hurried up to her, there was a loud splash. Dougie had grabbed hold of Griff's leg and dragged him down, both men toppling on to the next level of water terrace between two ornamental stone fish that spouted water over them.

'She's mine now!'

'She's marrying me!'

Iris banged her crutches down angrily. 'I don't belong to anybody and I'm not marrying anybody! I'm nineteen. I want to have the time of my life.'

Ignoring her, they wrestled past the fish and thrashed around amid clumps of water lilies.

'I give up.' Iris closed her eyes in despair. 'Please tell me Mum's happy?'

'You have to come!' Chloe pleaded. 'She wants you to meet Dom. They're about to take off.'

'He's taking her *away*?'

'Not far,' she said reassuringly. 'I've only hired the balloon for the day and there's not enough fuel, but I think they want to be alone for a bit.'

Iris fished in her pocket for a tissue and blew her nose. 'I don't want to watch. I can see him later.'

Recognising a brave front crumbling, Chloe took her into her arms. As Iris exploded into grateful sobs on her shoulder, Chloe registered that she was learning fast from Laney. 'The trouble is, your mother won't go without you two seeing each other.'

'She's told him about me already?' Iris lifted her head.

'You're the most important thing in her life.'

She let out a sob of a laugh, her green eyes shining like polished jade.

'You are so dead!' came a bellow below them, as Dougie stood up, water lilies poking from his pauldrons, and launched himself on top of Griff, who rolled out of the way.

Throwing down her crutches, Iris turned to the big steel-plated horse napping behind her and grabbed Harvey's reins. He awoke with a grunt and a clatter. 'Quick, give me a leg-up and get up here with me.'

'What about them?' Chloe looked across as a spectrum-infused spray of water shot up amid grunts and groans.

'They'll probably keep going until Dougie rusts or they both drown' – Iris settled in the saddle – 'but you'd better bring that sword just in case.'

Chloe picked it up and scrabbled into the saddle behind Iris handing it forward to her. 'What are we going to do with it? Threaten Cloud Man with it if he tries to take your mother away?'

'Of course not.' She urged Harvey into his jousting charge and they raced across the lawn and on through the gap in the yews. She called over her shoulder, 'We'll threaten him with it if he *doesn't*.'

'I'm not sure you need to,' gasped Chloe as they clattered through an open gate and galloped up the pasture field. 'They're taking off! Look!'

'Get this bugger back down, Dom!'

'We have to clear the tree first.'

'How long will that take?'

'Long enough.' Blue eyes met green. On roared the burner, up went the balloon and they kissed throughout.

They heard the barking dogs first: a ragtag pack of Woolton rescue terriers racing ahead of a galloping horse that was making a noise like a scrap-metal van negotiating potholes.

'Mum!'

Mia let out a cry of joy as a girl charged through the field below on an armoured horse, standing up in her stirrups, sword held aloft in a white-knuckled hand as she acknowledged the balloon.

'I've fathered Joan of Arc,' breathed Dom, letting go of the burner in shock so that the balloon lost height early, their basket catching the side of the oak canopy with noisy crashes, throwing them together as they landed. Then they took off, landed and took off again.

'I can't hold her on the ground.' He wrestled with the burners to battle the low thermals that were throwing them around. 'We have to take off or stay put.'

Iris was galloping alongside now. 'Take off! Just be sure to come back to blow out your birthday-cake candles!'

'Iris, this is Dom!'

She raised her sword, letting out a yelp as she saw she was about to gallop into a tree and swerved away.

He had raised his one arm, but grabbed the burner now. Gas flaming at maximum, the balloon lurched into the air. Soon the gala guests were specks on the ground, while Dom and Mia were kissing again.

Far below, Laney kept waving, tears of joy streaming down her face.

'Tenner says they'll land in the river,' Simon predicted.

'Well, that's some housekeeping to look forward to, at least.' Laney wiped away her tears and beamed up at them. 'Along with the million Oscar's paying for *Dalrymple*.'

His mouth hung so wide open she had to stand on tiptoe after kissing his bottom lip to reach the top one and kiss that too.

'Now I suppose we'd better get this cabaret under way.' She turned back towards the gala. '*The House of Bananarama* is cued to go and we can't keep Robert de Niro waiting much longer.'

'De Niro's here?' Simon rushed after her, hardly able to believe the day was happening.

'Of course not, but Sara Dallin promised to look in if she had time, and Keren Woodward sent a lovely note. I heard nothing from Siobhan Fahey, but Leo probably put her off him for life, sending that fan letter covered with black-lipstick kisses in the eighties . . . '

As her voice faded, and the crowd began wandering back towards the garden, Iris rested the heavy sword against her shoulder and looked up at the disappearing basket bearing her parents away, the burner licking up into the envelope like a Chinese lantern.

Sitting behind her in the saddle, Chloe watched too.

'I wish you'd told me what you'd planned,' Iris grumbled.

'You'd have tried to stop me,' she pointed out logically.

Iris ran a hand along Harvey's metal-plated neck. 'Was taking Godless's film script part of the plan?'

Chloe cleared her throat uncomfortably. '*Spem successus alit.*'

'Success produces hope,' Iris translated, looking down as Leo appeared at Harvey's head, scratching his muzzle, then squinting up at the girls through the sunlight, his eyes heavily fringed by the longest lashes in the business.

'I don't know how to thank you both for this,' Leo said. 'Mia's had the most extraordinary birthday party. We all have. Ivan's calling it our rebirth-day party.'

Iris laughed at the LA-ism. 'It was all down to Chloe.'

'We should be thanking Laney,' Chloe muttered humbly.

'We will,' Leo promised. 'We have a little surprise lined up for her and Simon after the cabaret. It was your mother's idea, Iris. She was up half the night looking for it.'

'I'll go and fetch Lito.' Iris picked up the reins. 'She wanted to see the cabaret, although I'm not sure how to explain where Mum's got to.' She gnawed at her lip.

'Just tell her she's out enjoying some air.' Leo smiled.

As Iris turned Harvey in the direction of the yard, Chloe still behind her, they looked across to Wootton. From this high corner of the field, they could see over the top of the yews and into the garden, where Griff and Dougie were still slogging it out on the water terraces, the latter's armour glittering brightly. Now at the lowest level, they were chasing each other round the huge circular fountain, watched by the returning crowd, who clearly thought it was another part of the entertainment.

'I really hope they stop soon.' Iris sighed.

'What will you do if Griff loses?' Chloe asked.

She scratched Harvey's withers. 'He's already won. I love him. My brave knight's been defeated, but I really think Dougie needs to do this, for the sake of his next girlfriend if nothing else.'

'Why?' Chloe watched as Dougie pulled off the arm of his armour and hit Griff over the head with it. 'It's Neanderthal!'

Iris let out a deep sigh. 'He always told me he wouldn't go down without a fight.'

Clever as she was, Chloe took a moment to catch on. Then they shrieked with laughter and trotted towards the house.

The girls rode along the shady track between the kitchen-garden walls and the tall beech hedge so that Iris could limp into the house through the conservatory while Chloe rode the horse back to his teammates in their box. Having abandoned her crutches earlier, Iris hopped gingerly up the steps and claimed one of the many walking sticks that still sat in the big urn just inside the doors, dating from the recent past when Jacinta had used her electric chair less and taken short, shuffling walks around the garden. She then made her way along the corridor to the annexe.

Jacinta's wing was cool and peaceful, far from the noise of the party. In the sitting room *Channel Four Racing* was blaring loudly, the runners going down to the post for a five-furlong dash. Lito's chair was parked ridiculously close to the screen as always, Iris's little Maltese tucked either side of her like fluffy bolsters.

'Don't tell me – you're on the grey.' Iris sat beside her and took her hand. Then she realised the little dogs on her grandmother's lap were quivering all over, pressing their muzzles desperately under her arms as though trying to lift them.

'I knew somebody would come,' Jacinta whispered, turning her head, her soft smile strangely lopsided as she closed her big, dark eyes. Her voice was terribly slurred as she said, 'I'm so glad it was you, *bonita*.'

Iris recognised the signs of a massive stroke, one side of the familiar face collapsing from its high cheekbone. She knew she should get help, but instinct kept her rooted to the spot, unable to let go of the old lady's hand.

The deep, rattling breaths lasted a very little time, hardly long enough to say a prayer, bestow a kiss or pass on an endearment. On the screen, the runners were still streaking towards the finishing post when Jacinta closed her eyes and stopped breathing.

Iris sat frozen in sadness, her hand gripping tighter, the fingers beneath hers still so warm and soft. As she pressed the hand to her cheek and said goodbye, her grandmother let out a loud bellow of delight.

'I win!' she spluttered, her voice still slurred as she turned back towards the screen to check the results. 'Franco put a bet on for me. He shaid I musht back the *caballo* called Devonshire Life.'

She turned back to her granddaughter victoriously. 'Now can you help me get thish toffee out of my teeth, *bonita*? It ish driving me crazy.'

Chapter 59

Chloe found Dougie and Griff by the water terraces, two bare-chested and exhausted victims of the battlefield, the former lying flat in the grass, pieces of battered armour cast around him, while the other was slumped at the edge of the water, his sodden wing collar and cuffs twisted and blood-soaked, eyebrow split, right arm braced across his left shoulder where his recently broken collarbone had suffered a serious relapse. Having fought until they dropped, the two men now had barely the energy to lift their eyelids, their anger spent.

'Here.' She thrust the sword she was now carrying at Dougie.

'Are you suggesting I fall on it, or are you going to touch my shoulders and tell me to arise?'

'It's time to go home, Dougie. Your horses are all loaded up and Rupe's revving the engine.'

'I have to speak to Iris.' He sat up, grimacing: peeling his battered body off the grass was more painful than ripping away a plaster.

'She doesn't want to talk to you right now,' Chloe insisted. Her tone was so resolute that it brooked no argument.

Dougie scrabbled upright and started to gather his armour. 'This is not the end of it,' he told Griff.

'I'm going nowhere,' the Welshman hissed. 'I'm a guest here.'

'Actually you're coming to A and E with me to have that clavicle X-rayed,' Chloe told him.

'I am not!'

She crouched beside him, her dark eyes capable of inducing terror in all men. 'You can see her later.'

From the marquee to their right came screams of laughter as the final sketch of the riotous cabaret rendered its audience oxygen-starved, then thunderous applause exploded.

They could hear Ivan joining the performers on stage and offering effusive thanks as he coordinated the huge bouquets of flowers being given out as the clapping and foot-stamping finally died down. 'Leo and Mia apologise that they cannot be here to do this,' he said shyly into the microphone.

Holding all his armour, Dougie hesitated, his blue eyes wide. 'Is Iris really OK?'

'Never better.' Chloe held out her hand to help Griff up, then chivvied both men towards the stable yard.

As their shadows led the way through the yews, they could hear Ivan carrying on: 'They asked me to offer a special gift of thanks to Simon and Laney de Montmorency, who have been so generous with their time and talent today' – he paused as a roar of cheering applause took over – 'and who are very kindly going to act as your hosts for the remainder of this afternoon. This is from both the Devonshires to both the Demons with heartfelt thanks.'

Chloe paused as she heard Laney gasp and Simon hoot with laughter before they introduced Pete Rafferty to play everyone out.

'What do you suppose they gave them?' Griff cocked his head.

'Life membership to the Leomia fan club?' suggested Dougie.

Griff let out a bark of laughter. 'That's low.'

'Must be offering a discount today.'

'Even lower.'

'Good job Iris is so grounded.'

'Maybe she'll see it as a good thing.'

'It needed to happen.'

'Her real father's the ultimate survivor.'

'Good man?'

'Total bloody hero, boyo.'

'I'd like to meet him.'

'We could all learn a lot from him.'

'That's a sign of a man.'

'Great epitaph.'

'Great life plan.'

'Are you really that posh, or is it put on?'

'It's roughed *off*. Are you really that Welsh?'

Trudging beside them both, Chloe threw up her arms. 'Do you two want to get a room?'

She spoke too soon as Griff pushed Dougie into a thorn hedge and he lunged back to hook a metal-clad leg around the Welsh-man's ankles and tip him into some stinging nettles.

Sighing, Chloe hooked them out and marshalled them on.

'It's an old-fashioned cooking timer.' Simon was not wholly impressed. 'It's not even new – there are marks on it. Just because it's shaped like devil's horns. I don't really get it.'

Laney turned it over. 'Look.'

'It's vintage Alessi.'

'Not that – the inscription.'

Written on the base was TURN THIS ALL THE WAY ONCE A DAY AND UNWIND TOGETHER.

'So?'

'We gave it to them when they got married. It was all we could afford. You inscribed that with the dentist's drill you'd bought to carve candles to sell at craft fairs.'

'So I did.' He admired it, dove-grey eyes looking at her over its horns as it began to tick. 'Does this mean we're starting over?'

'I think you'll find it means we're eating our words, Demon.' She kissed him. 'The best times are yet to come.'

In Wootton's walled kitchen garden, the Devonshires lost all sense of time as they sat together in the afternoon sun.

Jacinta had nodded off, snoring reedily, her mouth hanging open now that it was no longer glued together by toffee. Iris's terriers were still on her lap, curled beneath her hands like two chicks under heat lamps.

Leo watched her indulgently, his own lap crammed with small dogs, his fingers laced through his daughter's. 'You won't regret it,' he told Iris for the hundredth time. 'I am *so* proud of you.'

'I'm taking up my place at university, Dad, not climbing Kilimanjaro.'

'It's what you should be doing: acting your age, not your socks off or your heart out.'

'I am not going to give Griff up,' she said. 'Our love will last for ever.'

'And Dougie?'

'Will you keep an eye on him in LA? I don't want him getting into any more trouble.'

'You're too loyal, Iris. Just like your mother.'

'I loved him so passionately once. That means a lot. I'm starting to understand that you don't always get a choice about who you fall in – and out of – love with, but respecting its power is everything.'

'Frankie Goes to Hollywood said much the same thing – and Jennifer Rush.'

'Are they therapists you see in LA?'

581

He laughed, eyes huge with affection. 'Only Mia would get that joke.'

'You do still love Mum, don't you?'

'Very much.' He pressed her hand to his face. 'Ivan's always accepted that, and I love him so much for it.'

They both watched Ivan and Griff ambling behind the sweet-pea canes, talking animatedly about the likelihood of growing wild primroses in California. 'Lito says that if you're in love with two people—'

'Johnny Depp is a great actor,' Leo interrupted, 'but, trust me, think twice before you take advice from an actor. Especially about how and when to live your life.'

Epilogue

The little balloon floated high over the Masai Mara, so utterly silent that its occupants were able to hear the hoofbeats below.

'The river crossing will be any day now,' Dom told Mia, as always keeping the scarred side of his face turned away when airborne, although it meant looking directly into the sun, his vivid blue eyes creased, hair spun palest gold in the light. 'This will be the last outing for the horses until after it happens.'

'I can't wait.' She shivered excitedly. 'Neither can they.'

They looked down over the basket rim. Far below, two figures cantered on horseback through the tufted brush landscape back towards the camp, hurrying to return before the lengthening evening sun brought out the first big predators.

'Our daughter.' He chuckled, then reached for the burner lever to blast more heat into the balloon envelope to steady their descent. 'Our clever, beautiful girl.'

Smiling, Mia tilted her face into the sun and waited for the roaring propane to stop. Then she said, 'You'll have to start getting used to the idea eventually. It's been two years.'

'I've waited her lifetime to make an honest woman of her mother.' He stretched out his right arm and she curled beneath its foreshortened span, fusing to his hard, muscular side.

'It never does to marry too young.' She laughed as Iris stood up in her stirrups and waved at them, whooping, before racing her dark-haired companion along the riverbank. 'We agreed I'm going to ask you on your twelfth birthday.'

'Not sure I can wait that long.' He turned his mouth to her ear, dropping his voice to that deep engine throb. 'I'm a Yorkshireman, remember. We like to do the proposing.'

'If you like your wives barefoot and pregnant, I'm your dream woman.' She smiled fondly down at her bump, discarded Merrells and swollen ankles before snuggling closer in to his side. 'When we get back to England, I'll have another go at Leo about the divorce. He keeps saying we'll do it after he's finished the Lorca biopic, but that could take years to produce, particularly with Laney writing the script.'

'We can wait until my twelfth birthday. We've waited a lifetime already.'

'Life's only just begun,' she agreed, as he blasted more hot air into the balloon and they kissed again, heartbeats thundering in their ears long after the burner had fallen silent.